S0-CPQ-443

THE
Astounding
SCIENCE FICTION
ANTHOLOGY

SELECTED AND WITH AN INTRODUCTION BY
JOHN W. CAMPBELL, JR.

STORIES BY:

ISAAC ASIMOV, L. SPRAGUE DE CAMP,
LESTER DEL REY, DOLTON EDWARDS, H. B. FYFE,
ROBERT HEINLEIN, MURRAY LEINSTER, KRIS NEVILLE,
LAWRENCE O'DONNELL, LEWIS PADGETT, JOHN PIERCE,
H. BEAM PIPER, WILLIAM T. POWERS,
ERIC FRANK RUSSELL, JAMES H. SCHMITZ,
T. L. SHERRED, CLIFFORD D. SIMAK, THEODORE STURGEON,
WILLIAM TENN, A. E. VAN VOGT and JACK WILLIAMSON

SIMON AND SCHUSTER, NEW YORK

ALL RIGHTS RESERVED
INCLUDING THE RIGHTS OF REPRODUCTION
IN WHOLE OR IN PART IN ANY FORM
COPYRIGHT, 1940, 1941, 1943, 1944, 1945, 1946, 1947, 1948,
1949, 1950, 1951, BY STREET & SMITH PUBLICATIONS, INC.
INTRODUCTION, COPYRIGHT, 1952, BY JOHN W. CAMPBELL, JR.

All stories in this volume originally appeared in Street & Smith's *Astounding Science Fiction* magazine and are reprinted by permission of Street & Smith and the respective authors.

MANUFACTURED IN THE UNITED STATES OF AMERICA

To Peg,

who knows why science fiction developed

TABLE OF CONTENTS

INTRODUCTION

No extensive development of a literary form, the work of many keen and highly trained minds, can take place without some powerful social force behind it. Normally, such a development starts uncertainly, in a loose, uncertain and self-conscious manner; only with passing years and interacting development does it begin to find itself, and its agents of expression—the authors. In any general history of literature, the critical analysts who study the field from the vantage point of half a century or more overlook the straggling, groping, uncertain beginnings, and pick up their thread of discussion only after the field is well developed, sure of itself and its own general nature.

In the development of an individual, as a child there is relatively little certainty. It is hard to determine from the nature of the child what he will become as an adult. He himself feels that, someday, he will become something important and useful; during childhood he is uncertain, probing various directions, seeking self-knowledge by greater knowledge of the world around him.

So with any field of literature. It becomes somewhat understandable only when it reaches adolescence; it becomes a powerful force, with clear meaning, only when it reaches early maturity.

Before it acquires the fine, smooth polish of the mature adult, however, the deep, strong forces that brought it into being are more visible. The adolescent is somewhat gawky; his bones and muscles are sometimes painfully evident. His sincerity of effort and belief is clearer at that time than when, later on, he has acquired somewhat greater polish of delivery.

We are, today, at the point of early maturity of science fiction, a totally new form of general literature, a form that is the legitimate child of the forces that have made our world today. It has, in the past decade, passed through its period of adolescence from the childhood form of self-con-

scious and rambunctious play to a sincere self-searching. The decade from 1941 to 1951 is probably the most significant; the stories in this volume show some of that growth. They have been arranged in chronological order; truthfully, the understanding of science fiction would have been improved had I included some of the stories of 1930, 1935, and the earlier years. But the primary purpose of this volume is to present fascinating and exciting ideas in story form—and those other, earlier stories tended to be very weak in actual story value.

So—here is a sample of science fiction in its period of most rapid growth. And the purpose of this introduction is to explain, in some measure, why it is not a Topsy creation that "jest growed." It's as inevitable an outgrowth of our time as is the vacuum tube and the rocket plane.

Our present civilization actually started during the Renaissance, with the rise of the craftsman. It shifted, during the Industrial Revolution, and has now undergone a change as great as either of those earlier two, into the Technological Era. The Renaissance was, in a large sense, the outgrowth of a great concept: that men could make things they wanted. The craftsman worked the materials nature provided to create beauty and utility beyond their natural forms. The bowl could not merely be a container, but, by application of human art and craft, could become a Cellini masterpiece. Cloth could be not only warm, it could be beautiful and warm. Simultaneously, the study of natural law began—for only by understanding nature could the craftsman make the most of it. Leonardo da Vinci, typical of the greatest minds of his time, was a great artist, and equally a great craftsman-scientist. This was the period when Man learned to make things by controlling nature and natural law.

Where the Greeks had sought to understand natural law—and died of pestilence because they would not apply those laws to the construction of a sewer system—the Romans had developed techniques of getting Nature under control without understanding her. The Renaissance began the period of both understanding and using nature.

The Industrial Revolution brought a second stage of development. Before that time, men made things by understanding natural law; in the Industrial Revolution, natural law was harnessed to make things. Steam engines drove lathes; natural law was turned against the problem of getting what Man wanted. The machine replaced the craftsman.

Man solves most of his problems of life by traditional means; there are precedents for handling this situation or that. The problems of daily life are immensely complex; a routine makes it easier on the mind, relieving it of the problem of continual thinking out of repeated problems.

In a completely stable society, where the work descends from father to son to grandson without notable change, the patterns of life become well worked out, simple, understandable, and each man can settle comfortably into a groove he, and all his neighbors, can understand. There can be a great measure of happiness, because ninety per cent of the problems of life are solved by simple custom and tradition.

By the time the Renaissance philosophy had been at work for a couple of centuries, most of the people of Europe lived in such comfortable, well-rounded grooves. There was little friction in life, and a great deal of simple contentment.

And the literature was as conventional and simple as the life, and, in general, as pleasantly gentle. Of course, in such a period, the truly great minds that see far and feel strongly are violently discontented. Such minds demand change, advancement, not placidity. A Shakespeare is not going to be a calm, contented, satisfied man in any period; such a mind is the core of change, the drive that forces change in any period.

Then the Industrial Revolution started. Immediately, the effects of that change were to make nonsense of all the smoothly worn social conventions. An immense social force was at work, and the old grooves wouldn't hold it. New grooves had to be cut, grooves that lay athwart all the old patterns, gouging men out of their safe, known patterns. Tradition . . . custom . . . precedent . . . all were smashed by the tremendous power of the new philosophy. The unhappiness it brought with it made the Machine the very symbol of the Devil. Because now, instead of solving ninety per cent of life's problems by tradition, one had to solve them by taking thought.

The fury of that storm gradually wore itself out as new traditions came into being. The grandson of the craftsman settled down to being the machine-tender, knowing his machine and his place, and his routine. It was comfortable again.

The literature of the time, naturally, reflected much of the turmoil and misery. But by 1890, it had all settled down again to a gentle glow of understandable, peaceful living. . . .

. . . and the Technological Revolution started.

The Machine, in the Industrial Revolution, did mechanically what the craftsman had done before. The technological revolution brought the organization, the concept of pooled mental resources that forced immensely complex, interacting mechanisms to produce that which never before existed. The original craftsman learned to understand and shape nature; the Industrial Revolution brought the machine that shaped nature. The Technological Revolution has brought the methods of creating new things that do not exist in nature: plastics and automobiles; and the ancient fire that warmed the caveman and powered the steam engine is replaced by that unnatural and supernal fire, atomic energy.

Since 1900, the conventions have been shattered time and again, year after year. No conventional routine built up today can be expected to endure long; some new technique will eliminate its meaning. The most skilled buggy-whip maker is jobless; the washwoman—whose job had endured from before the dawn of history to this century—is gone. The robot washer today does everything the washwoman of old did except talk to the housewife.

Don't think of the robot as a tin man, either; a robot is a quasi-intelligent organization of functional parts. The modern oil-steam furnace is a first-class robot, replacing the old-time furnace man.

The convention of 1900 as to how a boy courted a girl involved the surrey with the fringe on top; in 1920 it included the tin lizzie and the flickers. In 1940 it was the jallopy, jitterbug and the talkies. Today it's back to the living room—well darkened, and with the TV set on low.

The strongest, oldest, firmest foundations of custom and precedent are shaken, torn out, and a new one has to be painfully constructed—but never quite gets established before a new change forces it out.

There is only one precedent, one rule, in the Technological Era: "There must be a better way to do this damn job. . . ."

For those minds that dislike thinking, and want the warm, cushioning blanket of precedent and convention, it's a period of neurosis, madness, ulcers and misery. The whole history of the world is gone; it was a convention and a precedent, based on things that existed only because knowledge was missing. The knowledge destroys the vacuum in which those things could exist. A man who knows that such drugs as penicillin are possible will nevermore accept the world wherein people died regularly of pneumonia and simple wound infection.

The workman who has lived on a diet of air-freighted California fruit, fresh-frozen vegetables from last-year's crop, and fresh-frozen fish caught six months ago in Danish waters, the man used to this diet no King of old could imagine, will not settle for black bread and salt meat. However great his unhappiness that his customs cannot remain customary, that the best and truest answers of yesteryear are nonsense today, still he demands the technological triumphs. In essence, he is cursing not the fact that he can't have his cake and eat it too, but that he must accept the cake in order to eat it, and the cake leaves his fingers sticky.

Science fiction is the literature of the Technological Era. It, unlike other literatures, assumes that change is the natural order of things, that there are goals ahead larger than those we know. That the motto of the technical civilization is true: "There must be a better way of doing this!"

"This," however, doesn't refer solely to gadgets and machines. Only in its early childhood did science fiction consider that facet solely, or even primarily. "This" is a method of living together; a method of government, a method of thinking, or a method of human relations. Machines and gadgets aren't the end and the goal; they are the means to the true goal, which is a better way of living with each other and with ourselves.

Once, ninety per cent of man's tasks were handled by routines and traditions, so that his energies could all be directed at the hard and terrible labor of forcing Nature to surrender a living. The goal now is to harness Nature so that natural law and the machine will do ninety per cent of the work of providing a living. But that is a fruitless effort, unless man then devotes the great energies he has to the higher task of learning how to enjoy that living, learning how to live with each other.

The caveman had no time to spend understanding his fellows; he had to get a living, and leave understanding to a pattern of customary responses.

The eventual goal of man is to understand man—but to do it, he must devise nonhuman servitors that can understand and manipulate Nature for him.

Science fiction, in its earliest days, considered the machine. In its adolescence it considers the effect of the machine and the technology on Man. And in its more mature forms it considers Man's proper relationship to Man and the Universe. You see but short horizons when your nose is hard against the grindstone; when you get a robot to keep the grindstone happy, you have time to look at the far horizons—the planets rising in the East, and the far, bright stars overhead.

These are tales of Far Horizons, in the days when Man can build the robots that free him of the grinding labor—and can accept change freely and well. These are tales written by minds that ranged free and deep and wide—and loved it. They're written with zest and enthusiasm, conviction and sincerity. They're written by the men who have shaped a new literature—even though some of them, such as T. L. Sherred, have written only one story in the field. For science fiction is young, and its strength is in its concepts and its thoughts, not in its polish and routine and formula. One strong, penetrating thought, thrown into the field, influences all the stories written thereafter.

The strongest influences in the field have been such men as Robert A. Heinlein, Isaac Asimov, Lewis Padgett—to single out arbitrarily a few of the many who have, time and again, thrown in important new thoughts. It should be noted that other highly significant writers can be only inadequately represented here because of the space limitations of the anthology: Jack Williamson is one whose strength is—unfortunately for the purposes of this volume—in his novels; he cannot be fairly represented by a short story, yet he is one of the oldest hands in the field in point of time, though still a young man. A. E. van Vogt, another of the great shapers of the literature, is another who has done nearly all his work, and all his truly significant work, in novel form. Eric Frank Russell, on the other hand, is a prolific and powerful writer who, fortunately, has worked largely at the novelette length.

The stories herein are, then, stories I feel are genuinely intriguing, important, and good—though not necessarily "the very best" of each author's works.

This volume is, I believe, representative of the moods and forces at work in the development of the new literature of the Technological Era. It is essential in the nature of things that there is, at such a period of change-over, two different literatures. One, the old, will at this period be bitter, confused, disillusioned, and angry. Those novelists dealing with broad themes will have stories of neurotic, confused and essentially homeless-ghost people: people who are trying to live by conventions that have been shattered and haven't been able to build new ones, who have seen every effort to build a new stable society wrecked by new forces.

The new literature will tend to be filled with a touch of unreality, but will tell of goals and directions and solid hopes. Naturally it has a touch of unreality; the old goals are gone, the new ones not yet here. Therein is the implicit unreality of any hopeful, optimistic literature of such a period; it asserts that the goal is real, but not yet achieved. Most people want goals that someone has already achieved and reported on fully.

Herein, I suggest, is just such a goal. There are two kinds of stability the engineer recognizes: the stability demonstrated by Cheops' Pyramid—static stability; and the immense stability of the planet Earth itself, the spinning, revolving Earth, the dynamic stability that lies in going instead of in being. The stability of the compass needle that points always to the pole it never attains, but knows surely is there, instead of the stability of a fallen tree that points the way a long-gone wind blew it. The compass, if deflected from its goal, returns to its original direction. That's a far

higher, longer-range stability than the stolid, solid stability of The Glory
That Was Rome, *the Law Giver.*

Science fiction isn't as yet the mature literature it should be, and will
be. But the science-fictioneer doesn't find that too troublesome; he recognizes that he hasn't reached his goal—and recognizes also that that does
nothing to prove his goal is either unattainable or undesirable. Whatever
his failures, he maintains with a cheerful stubbornness: "No—it hasn't
been done . . . yet!"

Basically, of course, the science-fictioneer is simply the citizen of the
Technological Era, whose concern is, say, the political effect of a United
States base on the Moon. The technical achievement of such a base he
knows full well he can assume; the engineering knowledge of how to
handle the technical problem is on hand. But the political knowledge of
how to handle the consequences definitely isn't.

Science fiction has a place that never existed before—but will exist
forevermore.

John W. Campbell, Jr.

Mountainside, N. J.
October, 1951

THE

Astounding

SCIENCE FICTION

ANTHOLOGY

First published: 1940

BLOWUPS HAPPEN *

by Robert Heinlein

"PUT DOWN THAT WRENCH!"

The man addressed turned slowly around and faced the speaker. His expression was hidden by a grotesque helmet, part of a heavy, leaden armor which shielded his entire body, but the tone of voice in which he answered showed nervous exasperation.

"What the hell's eating on you, doc?" He made no move to replace the tool in question.

They faced each other like two helmeted, arrayed fencers, watching for an opening. The first speaker's voice came from behind his mask a shade higher in key and more peremptory in tone. "You heard me, Harper. Put down that wrench at once, and come away from that 'trigger.' Erickson!"

A third armored figure came around the shield which separated the uranium bomb proper from the control room in which the first two stood. "Whatcha want, doc?"

"Harper is relieved from watch. You take over as engineer-of-the-watch. Send for the stand-by engineer."

"Very well." His voice and manner were phlegmatic, as he accepted the situation without comment. The atomic engineer, whom he had just relieved, glanced from one to the other, then carefully replaced the wrench in its rack.

"Just as you say, Dr. Silard—but send for your relief, too. I shall demand

* This is the original magazine version of Blowups Happen, based entirely on information available to the author in late 1939. A rewritten version, incorporating post-war knowledge, has appeared elsewhere. Since one purpose of this collection is to indicate changing styles and emphases in science fiction in the past dozen years, none of the stories have been altered or rewritten for their publication here. Thus no effort has been made to ferret out possible small factual discrepancies in any of them that may have been uncovered by the findings of later years.—J. W. C., Jr.

an immediate hearing!" Harper swept indignantly out, his lead-sheathed boots clumping on the floor plates.

Dr. Silard waited unhappily for the ensuing twenty minutes until his own relief arrived. Perhaps he had been hasty. Maybe he was wrong in thinking that Harper had at last broken under the strain of tending the most dangerous machine in the world—an atomic power plant. But if he had made a mistake, it had to be on the safe side—slips *must not happen* in this business; not when a slip might result in the atomic detonation of two and a half tons of uranium.

He tried to visualize what that would mean, and failed. He had been told that uranium was potentially forty million times as explosive as TNT. The figure was meaningless that way. He thought of it, instead, as a hundred million tons of high explosive, two hundred million aircraft bombs as big as the biggest ever used. It still did not mean anything. He had once seen such a bomb dropped, when he had been serving as a temperament analyst for army aircraft pilots. The bomb had left a hole big enough to hide an apartment house. He could not imagine the explosion of a thousand such bombs, much, much less a hundred million of them.

Perhaps these atomic engineers could. Perhaps, with their greater mathematical ability and closer comprehension of what actually went on inside the nuclear fission chamber—the "bomb"—they had some vivid glimpse of the mind-shattering horror locked up beyond that shield. If so, no wonder they tended to blow up—

He sighed. Erickson looked up from the linear resonant accelerator on which he had been making some adjustment. "What's the trouble, doc?"

"Nothing. I'm sorry I had to relieve Harper."

Silard could feel the shrewd glance of the big Scandinavian. "Not getting the jitters yourself, are you, doc? Sometimes you squirrel sleuths blow up, too—"

"Me? I don't think so. I'm scared of that thing in there—I'd be crazy if I weren't."

"So am I," Erickson told him soberly, and went back to his work.

The accelerator's snout disappeared in the shield between them and the bomb, where it fed a steady stream of terrifically speeded up subatomic bullets to the beryllium target located within the bomb itself. The tortured beryllium yielded up neutrons, which shot out in all directions through the uranium mass. Some of these neutrons struck uranium atoms squarely on their nuclei and split them in two. The fragments were new elements, barium, xenon, rubidium—depending on the proportions in which each atom split. The new elements were usually unstable isotopes and broke down into a dozen more elements by radioactive disintegration in a progressive chain reaction.

But these chain reactions were comparatively unimportant; it was the original splitting of the uranium nucleus, with the release of the awe-inspiring energy that bound it together—an incredible two hundred million electron-volts—that was important—and perilous.

For, while uranium isotope 235 may be split by bombarding it with neutrons from an outside source, the splitting itself gives up more neutrons which, in turn, may land in other uranium nuclei and split them. If conditions are favorable to a progressively increasing reaction of this sort, it may get out of hand, build up in an unmeasurable fraction of a micro-second into a complete atomic explosion—an explosion which would dwarf the eruption of Krakatoa to popgun size; an explosion so far beyond all human experience as to be as completely incomprehensible as the idea of personal death. It could be feared, but not understood.

But a self-perpetuating sequence of nuclear splitting, *just under the level of complete explosion,* was necessary to the operation of the power plant. To split the first uranium nucleus by bombarding it with neutrons from the beryllium target took more power than the death of the atom gave up. In order that the output of power from the system should exceed the power input in useful proportion it was imperative that each atom split by a neutron from the beryllium target should cause the splitting of many more.

It was equally imperative that this chain of reactions should always tend to dampen, to die out. It must not build up, or the entire mass would explode within a time interval too short to be measured by any means whatsoever.

Nor would there be anyone left to measure it.

The atomic engineer on duty at the bomb could control this reaction by means of the "trigger," a term the engineers used to include the linear resonant accelerator, the beryllium target, and the adjacent controls, instrument board, and power sources. That is to say, he could vary the bombardment on the beryllium target to increase or decrease the power output of the plant, and he could tell from his instruments that the internal reaction was dampened—or, rather, that it had been dampened the split second before. He could not possibly know what was actually happening *now* within the bomb—subatomic speeds are too great and the time intervals too small. He was like the bird that flew backward; he could see where he had been, but he never knew where he was going.

Nevertheless, it was his responsibility, and his alone, not only to maintain the bomb at a high input-output efficiency, but to see that the reaction never passed the critical point and progressed into mass explosion.

But that was impossible. He could not be sure; he could never be sure.

He could bring to the job all of the skill and learning of the finest technical education, and use it to reduce the hazard to the lowest mathematical probability, but the blind laws of chance which appear to rule in subatomic action might turn up a royal flush against him and defeat his most skillful play.

And each atomic engineer knew it, knew that he gambled not only with his own life, but with the lives of countless others, perhaps with the lives of every human being on the planet. Nobody knew quite what such an explosion would do. The most conservative estimate assumed that, in addition to destroying the plant and its personnel completely, it would tear a chunk out of the populous and heavily traveled Los Angeles-Oklahoma Road City a hundred miles to the north.

That was the official, optimistic viewpoint on which the plant had been authorized, and based on mathematics which predicted that a mass of uranium would itself be disrupted on a molar scale, and thereby rendered comparatively harmless, before progressive and accelerated atomic explosion could infect the entire mass.

The atomic engineers, by and large, did not place faith in the official theory. They judged theoretical mathematical prediction for what it was worth—precisely nothing, until confirmed by experiment.

But even from the official viewpoint, each atomic engineer while on watch carried not only his own life in his hands, but the lives of many others—how many, it was better not to think about. No pilot, no general, no surgeon ever carried such a daily, inescapable, ever-present weight of responsibility for the lives of other people as these men carried every time they went on watch, every time they touched a vernier screw or read a dial.

They were selected not alone for their intelligence and technical training, but quite as much for their characters and sense of social responsibility. Sensitive men were needed—men who could fully appreciate the importance of the charge intrusted to them; no other sort would do. But the burden of responsibility was too great to be borne indefinitely by a sensitive man.

It was, of necessity, a psychologically unstable condition. Insanity was an occupational disease.

Dr. Cummings appeared, still buckling the straps of the armor worn to guard against stray radiation. "What's up?" he asked Silard.

"I had to relieve Harper."

"So I guessed. I met him coming up. He was sore as hell—just glared at me."

"I know. He wants an immediate hearing. That's why I had to send for you."

Cummings grunted, then nodded toward the engineer, anonymous in all-inclosing armor. "Who'd I draw?"

"Erickson."

"Good enough. Squareheads can't go crazy—eh, Gus?"

Erickson looked up momentarily and answered, "That's your problem," and returned to his work.

Cummings turned back to Silard and commented: "Psychiatrists don't seem very popular around here. O. K.—I relieve you, sir."

"Very well, sir."

Silard threaded his way through the zigzag in the tanks of water which surrounded the disintegration room. Once outside this outer shield, he divested himself of the cumbersome armor, disposed of it in the locker room provided, and hurried to a lift. He left the lift at the tube station, underground, and looked around for an unoccupied capsule. Finding one, he strapped himself in, sealed the gasketed door, and settled the back of his head into the rest against the expected surge of acceleration.

Five minutes later he knocked at the door of the office of the general superintendent, twenty miles away.

The power plant proper was located in a bowl of desert hills on the Arizona plateau. Everything not necessary to the immediate operation of the plant—administrative offices, television station and so forth—lay beyond the hills. The buildings housing these auxiliary functions were of the most durable construction technical ingenuity could devise. It was hoped that, if *der tag* ever came, occupants would stand approximately the chance of survival of a man going over Niagara Falls in a barrel.

Silard knocked again. He was greeted by a male secretary, Steinke. Silard recalled reading his case history. Formerly one of the most brilliant of the young engineers, he had suffered a blanking out of the ability to handle mathematical operations. A plain case of *fugue*, but there had been nothing that the poor devil could do about it—he had been anxious enough with his conscious mind to stay on duty. He had been rehabilitated as an office worker.

Steinke ushered him into the superintendent's private office. Harper was there before him, and returned his greeting with icy politeness. The superintendent was cordial, but Silard thought he looked tired, as if the twenty-four-hour-a-day strain was too much for him.

"Come in, doctor, come in. Sit down. Now tell me about this. I'm a little surprised. I thought Harper was one of my steadiest men."

"I don't say he isn't, sir."

"Well?"

"He may be perfectly all right, but your instructions to me are not to take any chances."

"Quite right." The superintendent gave the engineer, silent and tense in his chair, a troubled glance, then returned his attention to Silard. "Suppose you tell me about it."

Silard took a deep breath. "While on watch as psychological observer at the control station I noticed that the engineer of the watch seemed preoccupied and less responsive to stimuli than usual. During my off-watch observation of this case, over a period of the past several days, I have suspected an increasing lack of attention. For example, while playing contract bridge, he now occasionally asks for a review of the bidding, which is contrary to his former behavior pattern.

"Other similar data are available. To cut it short, at 3:11 today, while on watch, I saw Harper, with no apparent reasonable purpose in mind, pick up a wrench used only for operating the valves of the water shield and approach the trigger. I relieved him of duty and sent him out of the control room."

"Chief!" Harper calmed himself somewhat and continued: "If this witch doctor knew a wrench from an oscillator, he'd known what I was doing. The wrench was on the wrong rack. I noticed it, and picked it up to return it to its proper place. On the way, I stopped to check the readings!"

The superintendent turned inquiringly to Dr. Silard.

"That may be true. Granting that it is true," answered the psychiatrist doggedly, "my diagnosis still stands. Your behavior pattern has altered; your present actions are unpredictable, and I can't approve you for responsible work without a complete check-up."

General Superintendent King drummed on the desk top and sighed. Then he spoke slowly to Harper: "Cal, you're a good boy, and, believe me, I know how you feel. But there is no way to avoid it—you've got to go up for the psychometricals, and accept whatever disposition the board makes of you." He paused, but Harper maintained an expressionless silence. "Tell you what, son—why don't you take a few days leave? Then, when you come back, you can go up before the board, or transfer to another department away from the bomb, whichever you prefer." He looked to Silard for approval, and received a nod.

But Harper was not mollified. "No, chief," he protested. "It won't do. Can't you see what's wrong? It's this constant supervision. Somebody always watching the back of your neck, *expecting* you to go crazy. A man can't even shave in private. We're jumpy about the most innocent acts, for fear some head doctor, half batty himself, will see it and decide it's a sign we're slipping. Good grief, what do you expect?" His outburst having run its course, he subsided into a flippant cynicism that did not quite jell. "O. K.—never mind the strait jacket; I'll go quietly. You're a good Joe in spite of it, chief, and I'm glad to have worked under you. Good-by."

King kept the pain in his eyes out of his voice. "Wait a minute, Cal— you're not through here. Let's forget about the vacation. I'm transferring you to the radiation laboratory. You belong in research, anyhow; I'd never have spared you from it to stand watches if I hadn't been short on No. 1 men.

"As for the constant psychological observation, I hate it as much as you do. I don't suppose you know that they watch me about twice as hard as they watch you duty engineers." Harper showed his surprise, but Silard nodded in sober confirmation. "But we have to have this supervision. Do you remember Manning? No, he was before your time. We didn't have psychological observers then. Manning was able and brilliant. Furthermore, he was always cheerful; nothing seemed to bother him.

"I was glad to have him on the bomb, for he was always alert, and never seemed nervous about working with it—in fact, he grew more buoyant and cheerful the longer he stood control watches. I should have known that was a very bad sign, but I didn't, and there was no observer to tell me so.

"His technician had to slug him one night. He found him dismounting the safety interlocks on the trigger. Poor old Manning never pulled out of it—he's been violently insane ever since. After Manning cracked up, we worked out the present system of two qualified engineers and an observer for every watch. It seemed the only thing to do."

"I suppose so, chief," Harper mused, his face no longer sullen, but still unhappy. "It's a hell of a situation just the same."

"That's putting it mildly." King rose and put out his hand. "Cal, unless you're dead set on leaving us, I'll expect to see you at the radiation laboratory tomorrow. Another thing—I don't often recommend this, but it might do you good to get drunk tonight."

King had signed to Silard to remain after the young man left. Once the door was closed he turned back to the psychiatrist. "There goes another one—and one of the best. Doctor, what am I going to do?"

Silard pulled at his cheek. "I don't know," he admitted. "The hell of it is, Harper's absolutely right. It does increase the strain on them to know that they are being watched—and yet they have to be watched. Your psychiatric staff isn't doing too well, either. It makes us nervous to be around the bomb—the more so because we don't understand it. And it's a strain on us to be hated and despised as we are. Scientific detachment is difficult under such conditions; I'm getting jumpy myself."

King ceased pacing the floor and faced the doctor. "But there must be *some* solution—" he insisted.

Silard shook his head. "It's beyond me, superintendent. I see no solution from the standpoint of psychology."

"No? Hm-m-m. Doctor, who is the top man in your field?"

"Eh?"

"Who is the recognized No. 1 man in handling this sort of thing?"

"Why, that's hard to say. Naturally, there isn't any one leading psychiatrist in the world; we specialize too much. I know what you mean, though. You don't want the best industrial-temperament psychometrician; you want the best all-around man for psychoses nonlesional and situational. That would be Lentz."

"Go on."

"Well— He covers the whole field of environmental adjustment. He's the man who correlated the theory of optimum tonicity with the relaxation technique that Korzybski had developed empirically. He actually worked under Korzybski himself, when he was a young student—it's the only thing he's vain about."

"He did? Then he must be pretty old; Korzybski died in— What year did he die?"

"I started to say that you must know his work in symbology—theory of abstraction and calculus of statement, all that sort of thing—because of its applications to engineering and mathematical physics."

"*That* Lentz—yes, of course. But I had never thought of him as a psychiatrist."

"No, you wouldn't, in your field. Nevertheless, we are inclined to credit him with having done as much to check and reduce the pandemic neuroses of the Crazy Years as any other man, and more than any man left alive."

"Where is he?"

"Why, Chicago, I suppose. At the Institute."

"Get him here."

"Eh?"

"Get him down here. Get on that visiphone and locate him. Then have Steinke call the Port of Chicago, and hire a stratocar to stand by for him. I want to see him as soon as possible—before the day is out." King sat up in his chair with the air of a man who is once more master of himself and the situation. His spirit knew that warming replenishment that comes only with reaching a decision. The harassed expression was gone.

Silard looked dumfounded. "But, superintendent," he expostulated, "you can't ring for Dr. Lentz as if he were a junior clerk. He's . . . he's *Lentz*."

"Certainly—that's why I want him. But I'm not a neurotic clubwoman looking for sympathy, either. He'll come. If necessary, turn on the heat from Washington. Have the White House call him. But get him here at once. Move!" King strode out of the office.

When Erickson came off watch he inquired around and found that Harper had left for town. Accordingly, he dispensed with dinner at the base, shifted into "drinkin' clothes," and allowed himself to be dispatched via tube to Paradise.

Paradise, Arizona, was a hard little boom town, which owed its existence to the power plant. It was dedicated exclusively to the serious business of detaching the personnel of the plant from their inordinate salaries. In this worthy project they received much co-operation from the plant personnel themselves, each of whom was receiving from twice to ten times as much money each pay day as he had ever received in any other job, and none of whom was certain of living long enough to justify saving for old age. Besides, the company carried a sinking fund in Manhattan for their dependents; why be stingy?

It was said, with some truth, that any entertainment or luxury obtainable in New York City could be purchased in Paradise. The local chamber of commerce had appropriated the slogan of Reno, Nevada, "Biggest Little City in the World." The Reno boosters retaliated by claiming that, while any town that close to the atomic power plant undeniably brought thoughts of death and the hereafter, Hell's Gates would be a more appropriate name than Paradise.

Erickson started making the rounds. There were twenty-seven places licensed to sell liquor in the six blocks of the main street of Paradise. He expected to find Harper in one of them, and, knowing the man's habits and tastes, he expected to find him in the first two or three he tried.

He was not mistaken. He found Harper sitting alone at a table in the rear of DeLancey's Sans Souci Bar. DeLancey's was a favorite of both of them. There was an old-fashioned comfort about its chrome-plated bar and red leather furniture that appealed to them more than did the spectacular fittings of the up-to-the-minute places. DeLancey was conservative; he stuck to indirect lighting and soft music; his hostesses were required to be fully clothed, even in the evening.

The fifth of Scotch in front of Harper was about two thirds full. Erickson shoved three fingers in front of Harper's face and demanded, "Count!"

"Three," announced Harper. "Sit down, Gus."

"That's correct," Erickson agreed, sliding his big frame into a low-slung chair. "You'll do—for now. What was the outcome?"

"Have a drink. Not," he went on, "that this Scotch is any good. I think Lance has taken to watering it. I surrendered, horse and foot."

"Lance wouldn't do that—stick to that theory and you'll sink in the sidewalk up to your knees. How come you capitulated? I thought you planned to beat 'em about the head and shoulders, at least."

"I did," mourned Harper, "but, cripes, Gus, the chief is right. If a brain mechanic says you're punchy, he has *got* to back him up and take you off the bomb. The chief can't afford to take a chance."

"Yeah, the chief's all right, but I can't learn to love our dear psychiatrists. Tell you what—let's find us one, and see if he can feel pain. I'll hold him while you slug 'im."

"Oh, forget it, Gus. Have a drink."

"A pious thought—but not Scotch. I'm going to have a martini; we ought to eat pretty soon."

"I'll have one, too."

"Do you good." Erickson lifted his blond head and bellowed, "Israfel!"

A large, black person appeared at his elbow. "Mistuh Erickson! Yes, suh!"

"Izzy, fetch two martinis. Make mine with Italian." He turned back to Harper. "What are you going to do now, Cal?"

"Radiation laboratory."

"Well, that's not so bad. I'd like to have a go at the matter or rocket fuels myself. I've got some ideas."

Harper looked mildly amused. "You mean atomic fuel for interplanetary flight? That problem's pretty well exhausted. No, son, the stratosphere is the ceiling until we think up something better than rockets. Of course, you *could* mount the bomb in a ship, and figure out some jury rig to convert its radiant output into push, but where does that get you? One bomb, one ship—and twenty years of mining in Little America has only produced enough pitchblende to make one bomb.

That's disregarding the question of getting the company to lend you their one bomb for anything that doesn't pay dividends."

Erickson looked balky. "I don't concede that you've covered all the alternatives. What have we got? The early rocket boys went right ahead trying to build better rockets, serene in the belief that, by the time they could build rockets good enough to fly to the Moon, a fuel would be perfected that would do the trick. And they did build ships that were good enough—you could take any ship that makes the antipodes run, and refit it for the Moon—*if* you had a fuel that was sufficiently concentrated to maintain the necessary push for the whole run. But they haven't got it.

"And why not? Because we let 'em down, that's why. Because they're still depending on molecular energy, on chemical reactions, with atomic power sitting right here in our laps. It's not their fault—old D. D. Harriman had Rockets Consolidated underwrite the whole first issue of Antarctic Pitchblende, and took a big slice of it himself, in the expectation that we would produce something usable in the way of a concentrated rocket fuel. Did we do it? Like hell! The company went hog-wild for immediate commercial exploitation, and there's no fuel yet."

"But you haven't stated it properly," Harper objected. "There are just two forms of atomic power available, radioactivity and atomic disintegration. The first is too slow; the energy is there, but you can't wait years for it to come out—not in a rocketship. The second we can only manage in a large mass of uranium. There has only been enough uranium mined for one bomb. There you are—stymied."

Erickson's Scandinavian stubbornness was just gathering for another try at the argument when the waiter arrived with the drinks. He set them down with a triumphant flourish. "There you are, suh!"

"Want to roll for them, Izzy?" Harper inquired.

"Don' mind if I do."

The Negro produced a leather dice cup, and Harper rolled. He selected his combinations with care and managed to get four aces and a jack in three rolls. Israfel took the cup. He rolled in the grand manner with a backward twist to his wrist. His score finished at five kings, and he courteously accepted the price of six drinks. Harper stirred the engraved cubes with his forefinger.

"Izzy," he asked, "are these the same dice I rolled with?"

"Why, Mistuh Harper!" The Negro's expression was pained.

"Skip it," Harper conceded. "I should know better than to gamble with you. I haven't won a roll from you in six weeks. What did you start to say, Gus?"

"I was just going to say that there ought to be a better way to get energy out of—"

But they were joined again, this time by something very seductive in an evening gown that appeared to have been sprayed on her lush figure. She was young, perhaps nineteen or twenty. "You boys lonely?" she asked as she flowed into a chair.

"Nice of you to ask, but we're not," Erickson denied with patient politeness. He jerked a thumb at a solitary figure seated across the room. "Go talk to Hannigan; he's not busy."

She followed his gesture with her eyes, and answered with faint scorn: "Him? He's no use. He's been like that for three weeks—hasn't spoken to a soul. If you ask me, I'd say that he was cracking up."

"That so?" he observed noncommittally. "Here"—he fished out a five-dollar bill and handed it to her— "buy yourself a drink. Maybe we'll look you up later."

"Thanks, boys." The money disappeared under her clothing, and she stood up. "Just ask for Edith."

"Hannigan does look bad," Harper considered, noting the brooding stare and apathetic attitude, "and he has been awfully stand-offish lately, for him. Do you suppose we're obliged to report him?"

"Don't let it worry you," advised Erickson. "There's a spotter on the job now. Look." Harper followed his companion's eyes and recognized Dr. Mott of the psychological staff. He was leaning against the far end of the bar, and nursing a tall glass, which gave him protective coloration. But his stance was such that his field of vision included not only Hannigan, but Erickson and Harper as well.

"Yeah, and he's studying us as well," Harper added. "Damn it to hell, why does it make my back hair rise just to lay eyes on one of them?"

The question was rhetorical; Erickson ignored it. "Let's get out of here," he suggested, "and have dinner somewhere else."

"O. K."

DeLancey himself waited on them as they left. "Going so soon, gentlemen?" he asked, in a voice that implied that their departure would leave him no reason to stay open. "Beautiful lobster thermidor tonight. If you do not like it, you need not pay." He smiled brightly.

"Not sea food, Lance," Harper told him, "not tonight. Tell me—why do you stick around here when you know that the bomb is bound to get you in the long run? Aren't you afraid of it?"

The tavernkeeper's eyebrows shot up. "Afraid of the bomb? But it is my friend!"

"Makes you money, eh?"

"Oh, I do not mean that." He leaned toward them confidentially. "Five years ago I come here to make some money quickly for my family before my cancer of the stomach, it kills me. At the clinic, with the wonderful new radiants you gentlemen make with the aid of the bomb, I am cured—I live again. No, I am not afraid of the bomb; it is my good friend."

"Suppose it blows up?"

"When the good Lord needs me, He will take me." He crossed himself quickly.

As they turned away, Erickson commented in a low voice to Harper, "There's your answer, Cal—if all us engineers had his faith, the bomb wouldn't get us down."

Harper was unconvinced. "I don't know," he mused. "I don't think it's faith; I think it's lack of imagination—and knowledge."

Notwithstanding King's confidence, Lentz did not show up until the next day. The superintendent was subconsciously a little surprised at his visitor's appearance. He had pictured a master psychologist as wearing flowing hair, an imperial, and having piercing black eyes. But this man was not very tall, was heavy in his framework, and fat—almost gross. He might have been a butcher. Little, piggy, faded-blue eyes peered merrily out from beneath shaggy blond brows. There was no hair anywhere else on the enormous skull, and the apelike jaw was smooth and pink. He was dressed in mussed pajamas of unbleached linen. A long cigarette holder jutted permanently from one corner of a wide mouth, widened still more by a smile which suggested unmalicious amusement at the worst that life, or men, could do. He had gusto.

King found him remarkably easy to talk to.

At Lentz's suggestion the superintendent went first into the history of the atomic power plant, how the fission of the uranium atom by Dr. Otto Hahn in December, 1938, had opened up the way to atomic power. The door was opened just a crack; the process to be self-perpetuating and commercially usable required an enormously greater mass of uranium than there was available in the entire civilized world at that time.

But the discovery, fifteen years later, of enormous deposits of pitchblende in the old rock underlying Little America removed that obstacle. The deposits were similar to those previously worked at Great Bear Lake in the arctic north of Canada, but so much more extensive that the eventual possibility of accumulating enough uranium to build an atomic power plant became evident.

The demand for commercially usable, cheap power had never been satiated. Even the Douglas-Martin sunpower screens, used to drive the roaring road cities of the period and for a myriad other industrial purposes, were not sufficient to fill the ever-growing demand. They had saved the country from impending famine of oil and coal, but their maximum output of approximately one horsepower per square yard of sun-illuminated surface put a definite limit to the power from that source available in any given geographical area.

Atomic power was needed—was demanded.

But theoretical atomic physics predicted that a uranium mass sufficiently large to assist in its own disintegration might assist too well—blow up instantaneously, with such force that it would probably wreck every man-made structure on the globe and conceivably destroy the entire human race as well. They dared not build the bomb, even though the uranium was available.

"It was Destry's mechanics of infinitesimals that showed a way out of the dilemma," King went on. "His equations appeared to predict that an atomic explosion, once started, would disrupt the molar mass inclosing it so rapidly that neutron loss through the outer surface of the fragments would dampen the progression of the atomic explosion to zero before complete explosion could be reached.

"For the mass we use in the bomb, his equations predict a possible force of explosion one seventh of one percent of the force of complete explosion. That alone, of course, would be incomprehensibly destructive—about the equivalent of a hundred and forty thousand tons of TNT—enough to wreck this end of the State. Personally, I've never been sure that is all that would happen."

"Then why did you accept this job?" inquired Lentz.

King fiddled with items on his desk before replying. "I couldn't turn it down, doctor—I *couldn't*. If I had refused, they would have gotten someone else—and it was an opportunity that comes to a physicist once in history."

Lentz nodded. "And probably they would have gotten someone not as competent. I understand, Dr. King—you were compelled by the 'truth-tropism' of the scientist. He must go where the data is to be found, even if it kills him. But about this fellow Destry, I've never liked his mathematics; he postulates too much."

King looked up in quick surprise, then recalled that this was the man who had refined and given rigor to the calculus of statement. "That's just the hitch," he agreed. "His work is brilliant, but I've never been sure that his predictions were worth the paper they were written on. Nor, apparently," he added bitterly, "do my junior engineers."

He told the psychiatrist of the difficulties they had had with personnel, of how the most carefully selected men would, sooner or later, crack under the strain. "At first I thought it might be some degenerating effect from the hard radiation that leaks out of the bomb, so we improved the screening and the personal armor. But it didn't help. One young fellow who had joined us after the new screening was installed became violent at dinner one night, and insisted that a pork chop was about to explode. I hate to think of what might have happened if he had been on duty at the bomb when he blew up."

The inauguration of the system of constant psychological observation had greatly reduced the probability of acute danger resulting from a watch engineer cracking up, but King was forced to admit that the system was not a success; there had actually been a marked increase in psychoneuroses, dating from that time.

"And that's the picture, Dr. Lentz. It gets worse all the time. It's getting me now. The strain is telling on me; I can't sleep, and I don't think my judgment is as good as it used to be—I have trouble making up my mind, of coming to a decision. Do you think you can do anything for us?"

But Lentz had no immediate relief for his anxiety. "Not so fast, superintendent," he countered. "You have given me the background, but I have no real data as yet. I must look around for a while, smell out the situation for myself, talk to your engineers, perhaps have a few drinks with them, and get acquainted. That is possible, is it not? Then in a few days, maybe, we'll know where we stand."

King had no alternative but to agree.

"And it is well that your young men do not know what I am here for. Suppose I am your old friend, a visiting physicist, eh?"

"Why, yes—of course. I can see to it that that idea gets around. But say—" King was reminded again of something that had bothered him from the time Silard had first suggested Lentz's name, "may I ask a personal question?"

The merry eyes were undisturbed. "Go ahead."

"I can't help but be surprised that one man should attain eminence in two such widely differing fields as psychology and mathematics. And right now I'm perfectly convinced of your ability to pass yourself off as a physicist. I don't understand it."

The smile was more amused, without being in the least patronizing, nor offensive. "Same subject," he answered.

"Eh? How's that—"

"Or rather, both mathematical physics and psychology are branches of the same subject, symbology. You are a specialist; it would not necessarily come to your attention."

"I still don't follow you."

"No? Man lives in a world of ideas. Any phenomenon is so complex that he cannot possibly grasp the whole of it. He abstracts certain characteristics of a given phenomenon as an idea, then represents that idea as a symbol, be it a word or a mathematical sign. Human reaction is almost entirely reaction to symbols, and only negligibly to phenomena. As a matter of fact," he continued, removing the cigarette holder from his mouth and settling into his subject, "it can be demonstrated that the human mind can think only in terms of symbols.

"When we think, we let symbols operate on other symbols in certain, set fashions—rules of logic, or rules of mathematics. If the symbols have been abstracted so that they are structurally similar to the phenomena they stand for, and if the symbol operations are similar in structure and order to the operations of phenomena in the real world, we think sanely. If our logic-mathematics, or our word-symbols, have been poorly chosen, we think not sanely.

"In mathematical physics you are concerned with making your symbology fit physical phenomena. In psychiatry I am concerned with precisely the same thing, except that I am more immediately concerned with the man who does the thinking than with the phenomena he is thinking about. But the same subject, always the same subject."

"We're not getting any place, Gus." Harper put down his slide rule and frowned.

"Seems like it, Cal," Erickson grudgingly admitted. "Damn it, though —there ought to be some reasonable way of tackling the problem. What do we need? Some form of concentrated, controllable power for rocket fuel. What have we got? Power galore in the bomb. There must be some way to bottle that power, and serve it out when we need it—and the answer is some place in one of the radioactive series. I *know* it." He stared glumly around the laboratory as if expecting to find the answer written somewhere on the lead-sheathed walls.

"Don't be so down in the mouth about it. You've got me convinced there is an answer; let's figure out how to find it. In the first place the three natural radioactive series are out, aren't they?"

"Yes—at least we had agreed that all that ground had been fully covered before."

"O. K.; we have to assume that previous investigators have done what their notes show they have done—otherwise we might as well not believe anything, and start checking on everybody from Archimedes to date. Maybe that is indicated, but Methuselah himself couldn't carry out such an assignment. What have we got left?"

"Artificial radioactives."

"All right. Let's set up a list of them, both those that have been made up to now, and those that might possibly be made in the future. Call that our group—or rather, field, if you want to be pedantic about definitions. There are a limited number of operations that can be performed on each member of the group, and on the members in combination. Set it up."

Erickson did so, using the curious curlicues of the calculus of statement. Harper nodded. "All right—expand it."

Erickson looked up after a few moments, and asked, "Cal, have you any idea how many terms there are in the expansion?"

"No—hundreds, maybe thousands, I suppose."

"You're conservative. It reaches four figures without considering possible new radioactives. We couldn't finish such a research in a century." He chucked his pencil down and looked morose.

Cal Harper looked at him curiously, but with sympathy. "Gus," he said gently, "the bomb isn't getting you, too, is it?"

"I don't think so. Why?"

"I never saw you so willing to give up anything before. Naturally you and I will never finish any such job, but at the very worst we will have eliminated a lot of wrong answers for somebody else. Look at Edison—sixty years of experimenting, twenty hours a day, yet he never found out the one thing he was most interested in knowing. I guess if he could take it, we can."

Erickson pulled out of his funk to some extent. "I suppose so," he agreed. "Anyhow, maybe we could work out some techniques for carrying a lot of experiments simultaneously."

Harper slapped him on the shoulder. "That's the ol' fight. Besides—we may not need to finish the research, or anything like it, to find a satisfactory fuel. The way I see it, there are probably a dozen, maybe a hundred, right answers. We may run across one of them any day. Anyhow, since you're willing to give me a hand with it in your off-watch time, I'm game to peck away at it till hell freezes."

Lentz puttered around the plant and the administration center for several days, until he was known to everyone by sight. He made himself pleasant and asked questions. He was soon regarded as a harmless nuisance, to be tolerated because he was a friend of the superintendent. He even poked his nose into the commercial power end of the plant, and had the mercury-steam-turbogenerator sequence explained to him in detail. This alone would have been sufficient to disarm any suspicion that he might be a psychiatrist, for the staff psychiatrists paid no attention to the hard-bitten technicians of the power-conversion unit. There was no need to; mental instability on their part could not affect the bomb, nor were they subject to the man-killing strain of social responsibility. Theirs was simply a job personally dangerous, a type of strain strong men have been inured to since the jungle.

In due course he got around to the unit of the radiation laboratory set aside for Calvin Harper's use. He rang the bell and waited. Harper answered the door, his antiradiation helmet shoved back from his face like a grotesque sunbonnet. "What is it?" he asked. "Oh—it's you, Dr. Lentz. Did you want to see me?"

"Why, yes and no," the older man answered. "I was just looking around the experimental station, and wondered what you do in here. Will I be in the way?"

"Not at all. Come in. Gus!"

Erickson got up from where he had been fussing over the power leads to their trigger—a modified cyclotron rather than a resonant accelerator. "Hello."

"Gus, this is Dr. Lentz—Gus Erickson."

"We've met," said Erickson, pulling off his gauntlet to shake hands. He had had a couple of drinks with Lentz in town and considered him a "nice old duck." "You're just between shows, but stick around and we'll start another run—not that there is much to see."

While Erickson continued with the set-up, Harper conducted Lentz around the laboratory, explaining the line of research they were conducting, as happy as a father showing off twins. The psychiatrist listened with one ear and made appropriate comments while he studied the young scientist for signs of the instability he had noted to be recorded against him.

"You see," Harper explained, oblivious to the interest in himself, "we are testing radioactive materials to see if we can produce disintegration of the sort that takes place in the bomb, but in a minute, almost microscopic mass. If we are successful, we can use the power of the bomb to make a safe, convenient, atomic fuel for rockets." He went on to explain their schedule of experimentation.

"I see," Lentz observed politely. "What metal are you examining now?"

Harper told him. "But it's not a case of examining one element—we've finished Isotope II with negative results. Our schedule calls next for running the same test on Isotope V. Like this." He hauled out a lead capsule, and showed the label to Lentz, who saw that it was, indeed, marked with the symbol of the fifth isotope. He hurried away to the shield around the target of the cyclotron, left open by Erickson. Lentz saw that he had opened the capsule, and was performing some operation on it in a gingerly manner, having first lowered his helmet. Then he closed and clamped the target shield.

"O. K., Gus?" he called out. "Ready to roll?"

"Yeah, I guess so," Erickson assured him, coming around from behind the ponderous apparatus, and rejoining them. They crowded behind a thick metal shield that cut them off from direct sight of the set-up.

"Will I need to put on armor?" inquired Lentz.

"No," Erickson reassured him, "we wear it because we are around the stuff day in and day out. You just stay behind the shield and you'll be all right. It's lead—backed up by eight inches of case-hardened armor plate."

Erickson glanced at Harper, who nodded, and fixed his eyes on a panel of instruments mounted behind the shield. Lentz saw Erickson press a push button at the top of the board, then heard a series of relays click on the far side of the shield. There was a short moment of silence.

The floor slapped his feet like some incredible bastinado. The concussion that beat on his ears was so intense that it paralyzed the auditory nerve almost before it could be recorded as sound. The air-conducted concussion wave flailed every inch of his body with a single, stinging, numbing blow. As he picked himself up, he found he was trembling uncontrollably and realized, for the first time, that he was getting old.

Harper was seated on the floor and had commenced to bleed from the nose. Erickson had gotten up; his cheek was cut. He touched a hand to the wound, then stood there, regarding the blood on his fingers with a puzzled expression on his face.

"Are you hurt?" Lentz inquired inanely. "What happened?"

Harper cut in. "Gus, we've done it! We've done it! Isotope V's turned the trick!"

Erickson looked still more bemused. "Five?" he said stupidly. "But that wasn't Five; that was Isotope II. I put it in myself."

"*You* put it in? *I* put it in! It was Five, I tell you!"

They stood staring at each other, still confused by the explosion, and each a little annoyed at the boneheaded stupidity the other displayed in the face of the obvious. Lentz diffidently interceded.

"Wait a minute, boys," he suggested. "Maybe there's a reason—Gus, you placed a quantity of the second isotope in the receiver?"

"Why, yes, certainly. I wasn't satisfied with the last run, and I wanted to check it."

Lentz nodded. "It's my fault, gentlemen," he admitted ruefully. "I came in and disturbed your routine, and both of you charged the receiver. I know Harper did, for I saw him do it—with Isotope V. I'm sorry."

Understanding broke over Harper's face, and he slapped the older man on the shoulder. "Don't be sorry," he laughed; "you can come around to our lab and help us make mistakes any time you feel in the mood. Can't he, Gus? This is the answer, Dr. Lentz; this is it!"

"But," the psychiatrist pointed out, "you don't know which isotope blew up."

"Nor care," Harper supplemented. "Maybe it was both, taken together. But we *will* know—this business is cracked now; we'll soon have it open." He gazed happily around at the wreckage.

In spite of Superintendent King's anxiety, Lentz refused to be hurried in passing judgment on the situation. Consequently, when he did present himself at King's office, and announced that he was ready to report, King was pleasantly surprised as well as relieved. "Well, I'm delighted," he said. "Sit down, doctor, sit down. Have a cigar. What do we do about it?"

But Lentz stuck to his perennial cigarette and refused to be hurried. "I must have some information first. How important," he demanded, "is the power from your plant?"

King understood the implication at once. "If you are thinking about shutting down the bomb for more than a limited period, it can't be done."

"Why not? If the figures supplied me are correct, your output is less than thirteen percent of the total power used in the country."

"Yes, that is true, but you haven't considered the items that go in to make up the total. A lot of it is domestic power, which householders get from sunscreens located on their own roofs. Another big slice is power for the moving roadways—that's sun-power again. The portion we provide here is the main power source for most of the heavy industries—steel, plastics, lithics, all kinds of manufacturing and processing. You might as well cut the heart out of a man—"

"But the food industry isn't basically dependent on you?" Lentz persisted.

"No. Food isn't basically a power industry—although we do supply a certain percentage of the power used in processing. I see your point, and will go on and concede that transportation—that is to say, distribution of food—could get along without us. But, good heavens, doctor, you can't stop atomic power without causing the biggest panic this country has ever seen. It's the keystone of our whole industrial system."

"The country has lived through panics before, and we got past the oil shortage safely."

"Yes—because atomic power came along to take the place of oil. You don't realize what this would mean, doctor. It would be worse than a war; in a system like ours, one thing depends on another. If you cut off the heavy industries all at once, everything else stops, too."

"Nevertheless, you had better dump the bomb." The uranium in the bomb was molten, its temperature being greater than twenty-four hundred degrees centigrade. The bomb could be dumped into a group of small containers, when it was desired to shut it down. The mass in any one container was too small to maintain progressive atomic disintegration.

King glanced involuntarily at the glass-inclosed relay mounted on his office wall, by which he, as well as the engineer on duty, could dump the bomb, if need be. "But I couldn't do that—or rather, if I did, the plant wouldn't stay shut down. The directors would simply replace me with someone who *would* operate the bomb."

"You're right, of course." Lentz silently considered the situation for some time, then said, "Superintendent, will you order a car to fly me back to Chicago?"

"You're going, doctor?"

"Yes." He took the cigarette holder from his face, and, for once, the smile of Olympian detachment was gone completely. His entire manner was sober, even tragic. "Short of shutting down the bomb, there is no solution to your problem—none whatsoever!"

"I owe you a full explanation," Lentz continued, at length. "You are confronted here with recurring instances of situational psychoneurosis. Roughly, the symptoms manifest themselves as anxiety neurosis or some form of hysteria. The partial amnesia of your secretary, Steinke, is a good example of the latter. He might be cured with shock technique, but it would hardly be a kindness, as he has achieved a stable adjustment which puts him beyond the reach of the strain he could not stand.

"That other young fellow, Harper, whose blowup was the immediate cause of your sending for me, is an anxiety case. When the cause of the anxiety was eliminated from his matrix, he at once regained full sanity. But keep a close watch on his friend, Erickson—

"However, it is the cause, and prevention, of situational psychoneurosis we are concerned with here, rather than the forms in which it is manifested. In plain language, psychoneurosis situational simply refers to the common fact that, if you put a man in a situation that worries him more than he can stand, in time he blows up, one way or another.

"That is precisely the situation here. You take sensitive, intelligent young men, impress them with the fact that a single slip on their part, or even some fortuitous circumstance beyond their control, will result in the death of God knows how many other people, and then expect them to remain sane. It's ridiculous—impossible!"

"But good heavens, doctor, there must be some answer! There must!" He got up and paced around the room. Lentz noted, with pity, that King himself was riding the ragged edge of the very condition they were discussing.

"No," he said slowly. "No. Let me explain. You don't dare intrust the bomb to less sensitive, less socially conscious men. You might as well turn the controls over to a mindless idiot. And to psychoneurosis situational there are but two cures. The first obtains when the psychosis results from a misevaluation of environment. That cure calls for semantic readjustment. One assists the patient to evaluate correctly his environment. The worry disappears because there never was a real reason for worry in the situation itself, but simply in the wrong meaning the patient's mind had assigned to it.

"The second case is when the patient has correctly evaluated the situation, and rightly finds in it cause for extreme worry. His worry is perfectly sane and proper, but he can not stand up under it indefinitely; it drives him crazy. The only possible cure is to change the situation. I have stayed here long enough to assure myself that such is the condition here. Your engineers have correctly evaluated the public danger of this bomb, and it will, with dreadful certainty, drive all of you crazy!

"The only possible solution is to dump the bomb—and leave it dumped."

King had continued his nervous pacing of the floor, as if the walls of the room itself were the cage of his dilemma. Now he stopped and appealed once more to the psychiatrist. "Isn't there *anything* I can do?"

"Nothing to cure. To alleviate—well, possibly."

"How?"

"Situational psychosis results from adrenalin exhaustion. When a man is placed under a nervous strain, his adrenal glands increase their secretion to help compensate for the strain. If the strain is too great and lasts too long, the adrenals aren't equal to the task, and he cracks. That is what you have here. Adrenalin therapy might stave off a mental breakdown, but it most assuredly would hasten a physical breakdown. But that would be safer from a viewpoint of public welfare—even though it assumes that physicists are expendable!

"Another thing occurs to me: If you selected any new watch engineers from the membership of churches that practice the confessional, it would increase the length of their usefulness."

King was plainly surprised. "I don't follow you."

"The patient unloads most of his worry on his confessor, who is not himself actually confronted by the situation, and can stand it. That is simply an ameliorative, however. I am convinced that, in this situation, eventual insanity is inevitable. But there is a lot of good sense in the confessional," he added. "It fills a basic human need. I think that is why the early psychoanalysts were so surprisingly successful, for all their limited knowledge." He fell silent for a while, then added, "If you will be so kind as to order a stratocab for me—"

"You've nothing more to suggest?"

"No. You had better turn your psychological staff loose on means of alleviation; they're able men, all of them."

King pressed a switch and spoke briefly to Steinke. Turning back to Lentz, he said, "You'll wait here until your car is ready?"

Lentz judged correctly that King desired it and agreed.

Presently the tube delivery on King's desk went *ping!* The superintendent removed a small white pasteboard, a calling card. He studied it with surprise and passed it over to Lentz. "I can't imagine why he should be calling on me," he observed, and added, "Would you like to meet him?"

Lentz read:

THOMAS P. HARRINGTON

CAPTAIN (MATHEMATICS)

UNITED STATES NAVY

DIRECTOR,

U. S. NAVAL OBSERVATORY

"But I do know him," he said. "I'd be very pleased to see him."

Harrington was a man with something on his mind. He seemed relieved when Steinke had finished ushering him in, and had returned to the outer office. He commenced to speak at once, turning to Lentz, who was nearer to him than King. "You're King? . . . Why, Dr. Lentz! What are you doing here?"

"Visiting," answered Lentz, accurately but incompletely, as he shook hands. "This is Superintendent King over here. Superintendent King— Captain Harrington."

"How do you do, captain—it's a pleasure to have you here."

"It's an honor to be here, sir."

"Sit down?"

"Thanks." He accepted a chair and laid a brief case on a corner of King's desk. "Superintendent, you are entitled to an explanation as to why I have broken in on you like this—"

"Glad to have you." In fact, the routine of formal politeness was an anodyne to King's frayed nerves.

"That's kind of you, but— That secretary chap, the one that brought me in here, would it be too much to ask you to tell him to forget my name? I know it seems strange—"

"Not at all." King was mystified, but willing to grant any reasonable request of a distinguished colleague in science. He summoned Steinke to the interoffice visiphone and gave him his orders.

Lentz stood up and indicated that he was about to leave. He caught Harrington's eye. "I think you want a private palaver, captain."

King looked from Harrington to Lentz and back to Harrington. The astronomer showed momentary indecision, then protested: "I have no objection at all myself; it's up to Dr. King. As a matter of fact," he added, "it might be a very good thing if you did sit in on it."

"I don't know what it is, captain," observed King, "that you want to see me about, but Dr. Lentz is already here in confidential capacity."

"Good! Then that's settled. I'll get right down to business. Dr. King, you know Destry's mechanics of infinitesimals?"

"Naturally." Lentz cocked a brow at King, who chose to ignore it.

"Yes, of course. Do you remember theorem six and the transformation between equations thirteen and fourteen?"

"I think so, but I'd want to see them." King got up and went over to a bookcase. Harrington stayed him with a hand.

"Don't bother. I have them here." He hauled out a key, unlocked his brief case, and drew out a large, much-thumbed, loose-leaf notebook. "Here. You, too, Dr. Lentz. Are you familiar with this development?"

Lentz nodded. "I've had occasion to look into them."

"Good—I think it's agreed that the step between thirteen and fourteen is the key to the whole matter. Now, the change from thirteen to fourteen looks perfectly valid—and would be, in some fields. But suppose we expand it to show every possible phase of the matter, every link in the chain of reasoning."

He turned a page and showed them the same two equations broken down into nine intermediate equations. He placed a finger under an associated group of mathematical symbols. "Do you see that? Do you see what that implies?" He peered anxiously at their faces.

King studied it, his lips moving. "Yes . . . I believe I do see. Odd . . . I never looked at it just that way before—yet I've studied those equations until I've dreamed about them." He turned to Lentz. "Do you agree, doctor?"

Lentz nodded slowly. "I believe so. . . . Yes, I think I may say so."

Harrington should have been pleased; he wasn't. "I had hoped you could tell me I was wrong," he said, almost petulantly, "but I'm afraid there is no further doubt about it. Dr. Destry included an assumption valid in molar physics, but for which we have absolutely no assurance in atomic physics. I suppose you realize what this means to you, Dr. King?"

King's voice was a dry whisper. "Yes," he said, "yes— It means that if that bomb out there ever blows up, we must assume that it will go up all at once, rather than the way Destry predicted—and God help the human race!"

Captain Harrington cleared his throat to break the silence that followed. "Superintendent," he said, "I would not have ventured to call had it been simply a matter of disagreement as to interpretation of theoretical predictions—"

"You have something more to go on?"

"Yes and no. Probably you gentlemen think of the Naval Observatory as being exclusively preoccupied with ephemerides and tide tables. In a way you would be right—but we still have some time to devote to research as long as it doesn't cut into the appropriation. My special interest has always been lunar theory.

"I don't mean lunar ballistics," he continued. "I mean the much more interesting problem of its origin and history, the problem the younger Darwin struggled with, as well as my illustrious predecessor, Captain T. J. J. See. I think that it is obvious that any theory of lunar origin and history must take into account the surface features of the Moon—especially the mountains, the craters, that mark its face so prominently."

He paused momentarily, and Superintendent King put in: "Just a minute, captain—I may be stupid, or perhaps I missed something, but—

is there a connection between what we were discussing before and lunar theory?"

"Bear with me for a few moments, Dr. King," Harrington apologized. "There is a connection—at least, I'm *afraid* there is a connection—but I would rather present my points in their proper order before making my conclusions." They granted him an alert silence; he went on:

"Although we are in the habit of referring to the 'craters' of the Moon, we know they are not volcanic craters. Superficially, they follow none of the rules of terrestrial volcanoes in appearance or distribution, but when Rutter came out in 1952 with his monograph on the dynamics of vulcanology, he proved rather conclusively that the lunar craters could not be caused by anything that we know as volcanic action.

"That left the bombardment theory as the simplest hypothesis. It looks good, on the face of it, and a few minutes spent throwing pebbles into a patch of mud will convince anyone that the lunar craters could have been formed by falling meteors.

"But there are difficulties. If the Moon was struck so repeatedly, why not the Earth? It hardly seems necessary to mention that the Earth's atmosphere would be no protection against masses big enough to form craters like Endymion or Plato. And if they fell after the Moon was a dead world while the Earth was still young enough to change its face and erase the marks of bombardment, why did the meteors avoid so nearly completely the great dry basins we call lunar seas?

"I want to cut this short; you'll find the data and the mathematical investigations from the data here in my notes. There is one other major objection to the meteor-bombardment theory: the great rays that spread from Tycho across almost the entire surface of the Moon. It makes the Moon look like a crystal ball that had been struck with a hammer, and impact from outside seems evident, but there are difficulties. The striking mass, our hypothetical meteor, must be small enough to have formed the crater of Tycho, but it must have the mass and speed to crack an entire planet.

"Work it out for yourself—you must either postulate a chunk out of the core of a dwarf star, or speeds such as we have never observed within the system. It's conceivable but a farfetched explanation."

He turned to King. "Doctor, does anything occur to you that might account for a phenomenon like Tycho?"

The superintendent grasped the arms of his chair, then glanced at his palms. He fumbled for a handkerchief, and wiped them. "Go ahead," he said, almost inaudibly.

"Very well then." Harrington drew out of his brief case a large photograph of the Moon—a beautiful full-Moon portrait made at Lick. "I want you to imagine the Moon as she might have been sometime in the past. The dark areas we call the 'seas' are actual oceans. It has an atmosphere, perhaps a heavier gas than oxygen and nitrogen, but an active gas, capable of supporting some conceivable form of life.

"For this is an inhabited planet, inhabited by intelligent beings, beings capable of discovering atomic power and exploiting it!"

He pointed out on the photograph, near the southern limb, the lime-white circle of Tycho, with its shining, incredible, thousand-mile-long rays spreading, thrusting, jutting out from it. "Here . . . here at Tycho was located their main power plant." He moved his finger to a point near the equator and somewhat east of meridian—the point where three great dark areas merged, *Mare Nubium, Mare Imbrium, Oceanus Procellarum* —and picked out two bright splotches surrounded, also, by rays, but shorter, less distinct, and wavy. "And here at Copernicus and at Kepler, on islands at the middle of a great ocean, were secondary power stations."

He paused, and interpolated soberly: "Perhaps they knew the danger they ran, but wanted power so badly that they were willing to gamble the life of their race. Perhaps they were ignorant of the ruinous possibilities of their little machines, or perhaps their mathematicians assured them that it could not happen.

"But we will never know—no one can ever know. For it blew up and killed them—and it killed their planet.

"It whisked off the grassy envelope and blew it into outer space. It blasted great chunks off the planet's crust. Perhaps some of that escaped completely, too, but all that did not reach the speed of escape fell back down in time and splashed great ring-shaped craters in the land.

"The oceans cushioned the shock; only the more massive fragments formed craters through the water. Perhaps some life still remained in those ocean depths. If so, it was doomed to die—for the water, unprotected by atmospheric pressure, could not remain liquid and must inevitably escape in time to outer space. Its lifeblood drained away. The planet was dead—dead by suicide!"

He met the grave eyes of his two silent listeners with an expression almost of appeal. "Gentlemen . . . this is only a theory, I realize . . . only a theory, a dream, a nightmare . . . but it has kept me awake so many nights that I had to come tell you about it, and see if you saw it the same way I do. As for the mechanics of it, it's all in there in my notes. You can check it—and I pray that you find some error! But it is the only lunar theory I have examined which included all of the known data and accounted for all of them."

He appeared to have finished. Lentz spoke up. "Suppose, captain, suppose we check your mathematics and find no flaw—what then?"

Harrington flung out his hands. "That's what I came here to find out!"

Although Lentz had asked the question, Harrington directed the appeal to King. The superintendent looked up; his eyes met the astronomer's, wavered and dropped again. "There's nothing to be done," he said dully, "nothing at all."

Harrington stared at him in open amazement. "But good God, man!" he burst out. "Don't you see it? That bomb has *got* to be disassembled—at once!"

"Take it easy, captain." Lentz's calm voice was a spray of cold water. "And don't be too harsh on poor King—this worries him even more than it does you. What he means is this: we're not faced with a problem in physics, but with a political and economic situation. Let's put it this way: King can no more dump the bomb than a peasant with a vineyard on the slopes of Mount Vesuvius can abandon his holdings and pauperize his family simply because there will be an eruption some day.

"King doesn't own that bomb out there; he's only the custodian. If he dumps it against the wishes of the legal owners, they'll simply oust him and put in someone more amenable. No, we have to convince the owners."

"The president could do it," suggested Harrington. "I could get to the president—"

"No doubt you could, through the navy department. And you might even convince him. But could he help much?"

"Why, of course he could. He's the *president*!"

"Wait a minute. You're director of the Naval Observatory; suppose you took a sledge hammer and tried to smash the big telescope—how far would you get?"

"Not very far," Harrington conceded. "We guard the big fellow pretty closely."

"Nor can the president act in an arbitrary manner," Lentz persisted. "He's not an unlimited monarch. If he shuts down this plant without due process of law, the Federal courts will tie him in knots. I admit that Congress isn't helpless, but—would you like to try to give a congressional committee a course in the mechanics of infinitesimals?"

Harrington readily stipulated the point. "But there is another way," he pointed out. "Congress is responsive to public opinion. What we need to do is to convince the public that the bomb is a menace to everybody. That could be done without ever trying to explain things in terms of higher mathematics."

"Certainly it could," Lentz agreed. "You could go on the air with it and scare everybody half to death. You could create the damnedest panic this slightly slug-nutty country has ever seen. No, thank you. I, for one, would rather have us all take the chance of being quietly killed than bring on a mass psychosis that would destroy the culture we are building up. I think one taste of the Crazy Years is enough."

"Well, then, what do *you* suggest?"

Lentz considered shortly, then answered: "All I see is a forlorn hope. We've got to work on the board of directors and try to beat some sense into their heads."

King, who had been following the discussion with attention in spite of his tired despondency, interjected a remark: "How would you go about that?"

"I don't know," Lentz admitted. "It will take some thinking. But it seems the most fruitful line of approach. If it doesn't work, we can always fall back on Harrington's notion of publicity—I don't insist that the world commit suicide to satisfy my criteria of evaluation."

Harrington glanced at his wrist watch—a bulky affair—and whistled. "Good heavens!" he exclaimed. "I forgot the time! I'm supposed officially to be at the Flagstaff Observatory."

King had automatically noted the time shown by the captain's watch as it was displayed. "But it can't be that late," he had objected. Harrington looked puzzled, then laughed.

"It isn't—not by two hours. We are in zone plus-seven; this shows zone plus-five—it's radio-synchronized with the master clock at Washington."

"Did you say radio-synchronized?"

"Yes. Clever, isn't it?" He held it out for inspection. "I call it a tele-chronometer; it's the only one of its sort to date. My nephew designed it for me. He's a bright one, that boy. He'll go far. That is"—his face clouded, as if the little interlude had only served to emphasize the tragedy that hung over them—"if any of us live that long!"

A signal light glowed at King's desk, and Steinke's face showed on the communicator screen. King answered him, then said, "Your car is ready, Dr. Lentz."

"Let Captain Harrington have it."

"Then you're not going back to Chicago?"

"No. The situation has changed. If you want me, I'm stringing along."

The following Friday, Steinke ushered Lentz into King's office. King looked almost happy as he shook hands. "When did you ground, doctor? I didn't expect you back for another hour or so."

"Just now. I hired a cab instead of waiting for the shuttle."

"Any luck?"

"None. The same answer they gave you: 'The company is assured by independent experts that Destry's mechanics is valid, and sees no reason to encourage an hysterical attitude among its employees.'"

King tapped on his desk top, his eyes unfocused. Then, hitching himself around to face Lentz directly, he said, "Do you suppose the chairman is right?"

"How?"

"Could the three of us—you, me and Harrington—have gone off the deep end—slipped mentally?"

"No."

"You're sure?"

"Certain. I looked up some independent experts of my own, not retained by the company, and had them check Harrington's work. It checks." Lentz purposely neglected to mention that he had done so partly because he was none too sure of King's present mental stability.

King sat up briskly, reached out and stabbed a push button. "I am going to make one more try," he explained, "to see if I can't throw a scare into Dixon's thick head. Steinke," he said to the communicator, "get me Mr. Dixon on the screen."

"Yes, sir."

In about two minutes the visiphone screen came to life and showed the features of Chairman Dixon. He was transmitting, not from his office, but from the board room of the company in Jersey City. "Yes?" he said. "What is it, superintendent?" His manner was somehow both querulous and affable.

"Mr. Dixon," King began, "I've called to try to impress on you the seriousness of the company's action. I stake my scientific reputation that Harrington has proved completely that—"

"Oh, that? Mr. King, I thought you understood that that was a closed matter."

"But, Mr. Dixon—"

"Superintendent, please! If there were any possible legitimate cause to fear, do you think I would hesitate? I have children, you know, and grandchildren."

"That is just why—"

"We try to conduct the affairs of the company with reasonable wisdom and in the public interest. But we have other responsibilities, too. There are hundreds of thousands of little stockholders who expect us to show a reasonable return on their investment. You must not expect us to jettison a billion-dollar corporation just because you've taken up astrology! Moon theory!" He sniffed.

"Very well, Mr. Chairman." King's tone was stiff.

"Don't take it that way, Mr. King. I'm glad you called—the board has just adjourned a special meeting. They have decided to accept you for retirement—with full pay, of course."

"I did not apply for retirement!"

"I know, Mr. King, but the board feels that—"

"I understand. Good-by!"

"Mr. King—"

"Good-by!" He switched him off, and turned to Lentz. " '—with full pay,' " he quoted, "which I can enjoy in any way that I like for the rest of my life—just as happy as a man in the death house!"

"Exactly," Lentz agreed. "Well, we've tried our way. I suppose we should call up Harrington now and let him try the political and publicity method."

"I suppose so," King seconded absent-mindedly. "Will you be leaving for Chicago now?"

"No," said Lentz. "No. . . . I think I will catch the shuttle for Los Angeles and take the evening rocket for the antipodes."

King looked surprised, but said nothing. Lentz answered the unspoken comment. "Perhaps some of us on the other side of the Earth will survive. I've done all that I can here. I would rather be a live sheep-herder in Australia than a dead psychiatrist in Chicago."

King nodded vigorously. "That shows horse sense. For two cents, I'd dump the bomb now and go with you."

"Not horse sense, my friend—a horse will run back into a burning barn, which is exactly *not* what I plan to do. Why don't you do it and come along? If you did, it would help Harrington to scare 'em to death."

"I believe I will!"

Steinke's face appeared again on the screen. "Harper and Erickson are here, chief."

"I'm busy."

"They are pretty urgent about seeing you."

"Oh . . . all right," King said in a tired voice, "show them in. It doesn't matter."

They breezed in, Harper in the van. He commenced talking at once, oblivious to the superintendent's morose preoccupation. "We've got it, chief, we've got it—and it all checks out to the umpteenth decimal!"

"You've got what? Speak English."

Harper grinned. He was enjoying his moment of triumph, and was stretching it out to savor it. "Chief, do you remember a few weeks back when I asked for an additional allotment—a special one without specifying how I was going to spend it?"

"Yes. Come on—get to the point."

"You kicked at first, but finally granted it. Remember? Well, we've got something to show for it, all tied up in pink ribbon. It's the greatest advance in radioactivity since Hahn split the nucleus. Atomic fuel, chief, atomic fuel, safe, concentrated, and controllable. Suitable for rockets, for power plants, for any damn thing you care to use it for."

King showed alert interest for the first time. "You mean a power source that doesn't require the bomb?"

"The bomb? Oh, no, I didn't say that. You use the bomb to make the fuel, then you use the fuel anywhere and anyhow you like, with something like ninety-two percent recovery of the energy of the bomb. But you could junk the mercury-steam sequence, if you wanted to."

King's first wild hope of a way out of his dilemma was dashed; he subsided. "Go ahead. Tell me about it."

"Well—it's a matter of artificial radioactives. Just before I asked for that special research allotment, Erickson and I—Dr. Lentz had a finger in it, too—found two isotopes of a radioactive that seemed to be mutually antagonistic. That is, when we goosed 'em in the presence of each other they gave up their latent energy all at once—blew all to hell. The important point is, we were using just a gnat's whisker of mass of each—the reaction didn't require a big mass like the bomb to maintain it."

"I don't see," objected King, "how that could—"

"Neither do we, quite—but it works. We've kept it quiet until we were sure. We checked on what we had, and we found a dozen other fuels. Probably we'll be able to tailor-make fuels for any desired purpose. But here it is." Harper handed King a bound sheaf of typewritten notes which he had been carrying under his arm. "That's your copy. Look it over."

King started to do so. Lentz joined him, after a look that was a silent request for permission, which Erickson had answered with his only verbal contribution, "Sure, doc."

As King read, the troubled feelings of an acutely harassed executive left him. His dominant personality took charge, that of the scientist. He enjoyed the controlled and cerebral ecstasy of the impersonal seeker for the elusive truth. The emotions felt in the throbbing thalamus were permitted only to form a sensuous obbligato for the cold flame of cortical activity. For the time being, he was sane, more nearly completely sane than most men ever achieve at any time.

For a long period there was only an occasional grunt, the clatter of turned pages, a nod of approval. At last he put it down.

"It's the stuff," he said. "You've done it, boys. It's great; I'm proud of you."

Erickson glowed a bright pink and swallowed. Harper's small, tense figure gave the ghost of a wriggle, reminiscent of a wire-haired terrier receiving approval. "That's fine, chief. We'd rather hear you say that than get the Nobel Prize."

"I think you'll probably get it. However"—the proud light in his eyes died down—"I'm not going to take any action in this matter."

"Why not, chief?" Harper's tone was bewildered.

"I'm being retired. My successor will take over in the near future; this is too big a matter to start just before a change in administration."

"*You* being *retired*! Blazes!"

"About the same reason I took you off the bomb—at least, the directors think so."

"But that's nonsense! You were right to take me off the bomb; I *was* getting jumpy. But you're another matter—we all depend on you."

"Thanks, Cal—but that's how it is; there's nothing to be done about it." He turned to Lentz. "I think this is the last ironical touch needed to make the whole thing pure farce," he observed bitterly. "This thing is big, bigger than we can guess at this stage—and I have to give it a miss."

"Well," Harper burst out, "I can think of something to do about it!" He strode over to King's desk and snatched up the manuscript. "Either you superintend the exploitation or the company can damn well get along without our discovery!" Erickson concurred belligerently.

"Wait a minute." Lentz had the floor. "Dr. Harper, have you already achieved a practical rocket fuel?"

"I said so. We've got it on hand now."

"An escape-speed fuel?" They understood his verbal shorthand—a fuel that would lift a rocket free of the Earth's gravitational pull.

"Sure. Why, you could take any of the Clipper rockets, refit them a trifle, and have breakfast on the Moon."

"Very well. Bear with me—" He obtained a sheet of paper from King and commenced to write. They watched in mystified impatience. He continued briskly for some minutes, hesitating only momentarily. Presently he stopped and spun the paper over to King. "Solve it!" he demanded.

King studied the paper. Lentz had assigned symbols to a great number of factors, some social, some psychological, some physical, some economic.

He had thrown them together into a structural relationship, using the symbols of calculus of statement. King understood the paramathematical operations indicated by the symbols, but he was not as used to them as he was to the symbols and operations of mathematical physics. He plowed through the equations, moving his lips slightly in unconscious subvocalization.

He accepted a pencil from Lentz and completed the solution. It required several more lines, a few more equations, before the elements canceled out, or rearranged themselves, into a definite answer.

He stared at this answer while puzzlement gave way to dawning comprehension and delight.

He looked up. "Erickson! Harper!" he rapped out. "We will take your new fuel, refit a large rocket, install the bomb in it, and throw it into an orbit around the Earth, far out in space. There we will use it to make more fuel, safe fuel, for use on Earth, with the danger from the bomb itself limited to the operators actually on watch!"

There was no applause. It was not that sort of an idea; their minds were still struggling with the complex implications.

"But, chief," Harper finally managed, "how about your retirement? We're still not going to stand for it."

"Don't worry," King assured him. "It's all in there, implicit in those equations, you two, me, Lentz, the board of directors—and just what we all have to do to accomplish it."

"All except the matter of time," Lentz cautioned.

"Eh?"

"You'll note that elapsed time appears in your answer as an undetermined unknown."

"Yes . . . yes, of course. That's the chance we have to take. Let's get busy!"

Chairman Dixon called the board of directors to order. "This being a special meeting, we'll dispense with minutes and reports," he announced. "As set forth in the call we have agreed to give the retiring superintendent three hours of our time."

"Mr. Chairman—"

"Yes, Mr. Thornton?"

"I thought we had settled that matter."

"We have, Mr. Thornton, but in view of Superintendent King's long and distinguished service, if he asks a hearing, we are honor bound to grant it. You have the floor, Dr. King."

King got up and stated briefly, "Dr. Lentz will speak for me." He sat down.

Lentz had to wait till coughing, throat clearing and scraping of chairs subsided. It was evident that the board resented the outsider.

Lentz ran quickly over the main points in the argument which contended that the bomb presented an intolerable danger anywhere on the face of the Earth. He moved on at once to the alternative proposal that the bomb should be located in a rocketship, an artificial moonlet flying in a free orbit around the Earth at a convenient distance—say, fifteen thousand miles—while secondary power stations on Earth burned a safe fuel manufactured by the bomb.

He announced the discovery of the Harper-Erickson technique and dwelt on what it meant to them commercially. Each point was presented as persuasively as possible, with the full power of his engaging personality. Then he paused and waited for them to blow off steam.

They did. "Visionary—" "Unproved—" "No essential change in the situation—" The substance of it was that they were very happy to hear of the new fuel, but not particularly impressed by it. Perhaps in another twenty years, after it had been thoroughly tested and proved commercially, and provided enough uranium had been mined to build another bomb, they might consider setting up another power station outside the atmosphere. In the meantime there was no hurry.

Lentz patiently and politely dealt with their objections. He emphasized the increasing incidence of occupational psychoneurosis among the engineers and the grave danger to everyone near the bomb even under the orthodox theory. He reminded them of their insurance and indemnity-bond costs, and of the "squeeze" they paid State politicians.

Then he changed his tone and let them have it directly and brutally. "Gentlemen," he said, "we believe that we are fighting for our lives—our own lives, our families and every life on the globe. If you refuse this compromise, we will fight as fiercely and with as little regard for fair play as any cornered animal." With that he made his first move in attack.

It was quite simple. He offered for their inspection the outline of a propaganda campaign on a national scale, such as any major advertising firm could carry out as a matter of routine. It was complete to the last detail, television broadcasts, spot plugs, newspaper and magazine coverage with planted editorials, dummy "citizens' committees" and—most important—a supporting whispering campaign and a letters-to-Congress organization. Every businessman there knew from experience how such things worked.

But its object was to stir up fear of the bomb and to direct that fear, not into panic, but into rage against the board of directors personally, and into a demand that the government take action to have the bomb removed to outer space.

"This is blackmail! We'll stop you!"

"I think not," Lentz replied gently. "You may be able to keep us out of some of the newspapers, but you can't stop the rest of it. You can't even keep us off the air—ask the Federal Communications Commission." It was true. Harrington had handled the political end and had performed his assignment well; the president was convinced.

Tempers were snapping on all sides; Dixon had to pound for order. "Dr. Lentz," he said, his own temper under taut control, "you plan to make every one of us appear a black-hearted scoundrel with no other thought than personal profit, even at the expense of the lives of others. You know that is not true; this is a simple difference of opinion as to what is wise."

"I did not say it was true," Lentz admitted blandly, "but you will admit that I can convince the public that you are deliberate villains. As to it being a difference of opinion—you are none of you atomic physicists; you are not entitled to hold opinions in this matter.

"As a matter of fact," he went on callously, "the only doubt in my mind is whether or not an enraged public will destroy your precious power plant before Congress has time to exercise eminent domain and take it away from you!"

Before they had time to think up arguments in answer and ways of circumventing him, before their hot indignation had cooled and set as stubborn resistance, he offered his gambit. He produced another layout for a propaganda campaign—an entirely different sort.

This time the board of directors was to be built up, not torn down. All of the same techniques were to be used; behind-the-scenes feature articles with plenty of human interest would describe the functions of the company, describe it as a great public trust, administered by patriotic, unselfish statesmen of the business world. At the proper point in the campaign, the Harper-Erickson fuel would be announced, not as a semi-accidental result of the initiative of two employees, but as the long-expected end product of years of systematic research conducted under a fixed policy of the board of directors, a policy growing naturally out of their humane determination to remove forever the menace of explosion from even the sparsely settled Arizona desert.

No mention was to be made of the danger of complete, planet-embracing catastrophe.

Lentz discussed it. He dwelt on the appreciation that would be due them from a grateful world. He invited them to make a noble sacrifice and, with subtle misdirection, tempted them to think of themselves as heroes. He deliberately played on one of the most deep-rooted of simian instincts, the desire for approval from one's kind, deserved or not.

All the while he was playing for time, as he directed his attention from one hard case, one resistant mind, to another. He soothed and he tickled and he played on personal foibles. For the benefit of the timorous and the devoted family men, he again painted a picture of the suffering, death and destruction that might result from their well-meant reliance on the unproved and highly questionable predictions of Destry's mathematics. Then he described in glowing detail a picture of a world free from worry but granted almost unlimited power, safe power from an invention which was theirs for this one small concession.

It worked. They did not reverse themselves all at once, but a committee was appointed to investigate the feasibility of the proposed spaceship power plant. By sheer brass Lentz suggested names for the committee and Dixon confirmed his nominations, not because he wished to, particularly, but because he was caught off guard and could not think of a reason to refuse without affronting those colleagues.

The impending retirement of King was not mentioned by either side. Privately, Lentz felt sure that it never would be mentioned.

It worked, but there was left much to do. For the first few days after the victory in committee, King felt much elated by the prospect of an early release from the soul-killing worry. He was buoyed up by pleasant demands of manifold new administrative duties. Harper and Erickson were detached to Goddard Field to collaborate with the rocket engineers there in design of firing chambers, nozzles, fuel stowage, fuel metering and the like. A schedule had to be worked out with the business office to permit as much power of the bomb as possible to be diverted to making atomic fuel, and a giant combustion chamber for atomic fuel had to be designed and ordered to replace the bomb itself during the interim between the time it was shut down on Earth and the later time when sufficient local, smaller plants could be built to carry the commercial load. He was busy.

When the first activity had died down and they were settled in a new routine, pending the shutting down of the bomb and its removal to outer space, King suffered an emotional reaction. There was, by then, nothing to do but wait, and tend the bomb, until the crew at Goddard Field smoothed out the bugs and produced a space-worthy rocketship.

They ran into difficulties, overcame them, and came across more difficulties. They had never used such high reaction velocities; it took many trials to find a nozzle shape that would give reasonably high efficiency. When that was solved, and success seemed in sight, the jets burned out on a time-trial ground test. They were stalemated for weeks over that hitch.

Back at the power plant Superintendent King could do nothing but chew his nails and wait. He had not even the release of running over to Goddard Field to watch the progress of the research, for, urgently as he desired to, he felt an even stronger, an overpowering compulsion to watch over the bomb more lest it—heartbreakingly!—blow up at the last minute.

He took to hanging around the control room. He had to stop that; his unease communicated itself to his watch engineers; two of them cracked up in a single day—one of them on watch.

He must face the fact—there had been a grave upswing in psychoneurosis among his engineers since the period of watchful waiting had commenced. At first, they had tried to keep the essential facts of the plan a close secret, but it had leaked out, perhaps through some member of the investigating committee. He admitted to himself now that it had been a mistake ever to try to keep it secret—Lentz had advised against it, and the engineers not actually engaged in the change-over were bound to know that something was up.

He took all of the engineers into confidence at last, under oath of secrecy. That had helped for a week or more, a week in which they were all given a spiritual lift by the knowledge, as he had been. Then it had worn off, the reaction had set in, and the psychological observers had started disqualifying engineers for duty almost daily. They were even reporting each other as mentally unstable with great frequency; he might even be faced with a shortage of psychiatrists if that kept up, he thought to himself with bitter amusement. His engineers were already standing four hours in every sixteen. If one more dropped out, he'd put himself on watch. That would be a relief, to tell himself the truth.

Somehow, some of the civilians around about and the nontechnical employees were catching on to the secret. That mustn't go on—if it spread any farther there might be a nation-wide panic. But how the hell could he stop it? He couldn't.

He turned over in bed, rearranged his pillow, and tried once more to get to sleep. No soap. His head ached, his eyes were balls of pain, and his brain was a ceaseless grind of useless, repetitive activity, like a disk recording stuck in one groove.

God! This was unbearable! He wondered if he were cracking up—if he already had cracked up. This was worse, many times worse, than the old routine when he had simply acknowledged the danger and tried to forget it as much as possible. Not that the bomb was any different—it was this five-minutes-to-armistice feeling, this waiting for the curtain to go up, this race against time with nothing to do to help.

He sat up, switched on his bed lamp, and looked at the clock. Three thirty. Not so good. He got up, went into his bathroom, and dissolved a sleeping powder in a glass of whiskey and water, half and half. He gulped it down and went back to bed. Presently he dozed off.

He was running, fleeing down a long corridor. At the end lay safety —he knew that, but he was so utterly exhausted that he doubted his ability to finish the race. The thing pursuing him was catching up; he forced his leaden, aching legs into greater activity. The thing behind him increased its pace, and actually touched him. His heart stopped, then pounded again. He became aware that he was screaming, shrieking in mortal terror.

But he had to reach the end of that corridor; more depended on it than just himself. He had to. He had to! *He had to!*

Then the sound hit him, and he realized that he had lost, realized it with utter despair and utter, bitter defeat. He had failed; the bomb had blown up.

The sound was the alarm going off; it was seven o'clock. His pajamas were soaked, dripping with sweat, and his heart still pounded. Every ragged nerve throughout his body screamed for release. It would take more than a cold shower to cure this case of the shakes.

He got to the office before the janitor was out of it. He sat there, doing nothing, until Lentz walked in on him, two hours later. The psychiatrist came in just as he was taking two small tablets from a box in his desk.

"Easy . . . easy, old man," Lentz said in a slow voice. "What have you there?" He came around and gently took possession of the box.

"Just a sedative."

Lentz studied the inscription on the cover. "How many have you had today?"

"Just two, so far."

"You don't need a sedative; you need a walk in the fresh air. Come, take one with me."

"You're a fine one to talk—you're smoking a cigarette that isn't lighted!"

"Me? Why, so I am! We both need that walk. Come."

Harper arrived less than ten minutes after they had left the office. Steinke was not in the outer office. He walked on through and pounded on the door of King's private office, then waited with the man who accompanied him—a hard young chap with an easy confidence to his bearing. Steinke let them in.

Harper brushed on past him with a casual greeting, then checked himself when he saw that there was no one else inside.

"Where's the chief?" he demanded.

"Gone out. Should be back soon."

"I'll wait. Oh—Steinke, this is Greene. Greene—Steinke."

The two shook hands. "What brings you back, Cal?" Steinke asked, turning back to Harper.

"Well . . . I guess it's all right to tell you—"

The communicator screen flashed into sudden activity, and cut him short. A face filled most of the frame. It was apparently too close to the pickup, as it was badly out of focus. "Superintendent!" it yelled in an agonized voice. "The bomb—"

A shadow flashed across the screen, they heard a dull *smack*, and the face slid out of the screen. As it fell it revealed the control room behind it. Someone was down on the floor plates, a nameless heap. Another figure ran across the field of pickup and disappeared.

Harper snapped into action first. "That was Silard!" he shouted, "in the control room! Come on, Steinke!" He was already in motion himself.

Steinke went dead-white, but hesitated only an unmeasurable instant. He pounded sharp on Harper's heels. Greene followed without invitation, in a steady run that kept easy pace with them.

They had to wait for a capsule to unload at the tube station. Then all three of them tried to crowd into a two-passenger capsule. It refused to start, and moments were lost before Greene piled out and claimed another car.

The four-minute trip at heavy acceleration seemed an interminable crawl. Harper was convinced that the system had broken down, when the familiar click and sigh announced their arrival at the station under the bomb. They jammed each other trying to get out at the same time.

The lift was up; they did not wait for it. That was unwise; they gained no time by it, and arrived at the control level out of breath. Nevertheless, they speeded up when they reached the top, zigzagged frantically around the outer shield, and burst into the control room.

The limp figure was still on the floor, and another, also inert, was near it. The second's helmet was missing.

The third figure was bending over the trigger. He looked up as they came in, and charged them. They hit him together, and all three went down. It was two to one, but they got in each other's way. The man's heavy armor protected him from the force of their blows. He fought with senseless, savage violence.

Harper felt a bright, sharp pain; his right arm went limp and useless. The armored figure was struggling free of them.

There was a shout from somewhere behind them, "Hold still!"

Harper saw a flash with the corner of one eye, a deafening crack hurried on top of it, and re-echoed painfully in the restricted space.

The armored figure dropped back to his knees, balanced there, and then fell heavily on his face. Greene stood in the entrance, a service pistol balanced in his hand.

Harper got up and went over to the trigger. He tried to reduce the dampening adjustment, but his right hand wouldn't carry out his orders, and his left was too clumsy. "Steinke," he called, "come here! Take over."

Steinke hurried up, nodded as he glanced at the readings, and set busily to work.

It was thus that King found them when he bolted in a very few minutes later.

"Harper!" he shouted, while his quick glance was still taking in the situation. "What's happened?"

Harper told him briefly. He nodded. "I saw the tail end of the fight from my office— Steinke!" He seemed to grasp for the first time who was on the trigger. "He can't manage the controls—" He hurried toward him.

Steinke looked up at his approach. "Chief!" he called out. "Chief! *I've got my mathematics back!*"

King looked bewildered, then nodded vaguely, and let him be. He turned back to Harper. "How does it happen you're here?"

"Me? I'm here to report—we've done it, chief!"

"Eh?"

"We've finished; it's all done. Erickson stayed behind to complete the power-plant installation on the big ship. I came over in the ship we'll use to shuttle between Earth and the big ship, the power plant. Four minutes from Goddard Field to here in her. That's the pilot over there." He pointed to the door, where Greene's solid form partially hid Lentz.

"Wait a minute. You say that everything is ready to install the bomb in the ship? You're sure?"

"Positive. The big ship has already flown with our fuel—longer and faster than she will have to fly to reach station in her orbit; I was in it— out in space, chief! We're all set, six ways from zero."

King stared at the dumping switch, mounted behind glass at the top of the instrument board. "There's fuel enough," he said softly, as if he were alone and speaking only to himself; "there's been fuel enough for weeks."

He walked swiftly over to the switch, smashed the glass with his fist, and pulled it.

The room rumbled and shivered as two and a half tons of molten, massive metal, heavier than gold, coursed down channels, struck against baffles, split into a dozen dozen streams, and plunged to rest in leaden receivers—to rest, safe and harmless, until it should be reassembled far out in space.

First published: 1940

HINDSIGHT

by Jack Williamson

SOMETHING WAS WRONG WITH THE CIGAR.

But Brek Veronar didn't throw it away. Earth-grown tobacco was precious, here on Ceres. He took another bite off the end, and pressed the lighter cone again. This time, imperfectly, the cigar drew—with an acrid, puzzling odor of scorching paper.

Brek Veronar—born William Webster, Earthman—was sitting in his big, well-furnished office, adjoining the arsenal laboratory. Beyond the perdurite windows, magnified in the crystalline clarity of the asteroid's synthetic atmosphere, loomed a row of the immense squat turret forts that guarded the Astrophon base—their mighty twenty-four-inch rifles, coupled to the Veronar autosight, covered with their theoretical range everything within Jupiter's orbit. A squadron of the fleet lay on the field beyond, seven tremendous dead-black cigar shapes. Far off, above the rugged red palisades of a second plateau, stood the many-colored domes and towers of Astrophon itself, the Astrarch's capital.

A tall, gaunt man, Brek Veronar wore the bright, close-fitting silks of the Astrarchy. Dyed to conceal the increasing streaks of gray, his hair was perfumed and curled. In abrupt contrast to the force of his gray, wide-set eyes, his face was white and smooth from cosmetic treatments. Only the cigar could have betrayed him as a native of Earth, and Brek Veronar never smoked except here in his own locked laboratory.

He didn't like to be called the Renegade.

Curiously, that whiff of burning paper swept his mind away from the intricate drawing of a new rocket-torpedo gyropilot pinned to a board on the desk before him, and back across twenty years of time. It returned him to the university campus, on the low yellow hills beside the ancient Martian city of Toran—to the fateful day when Bill Webster had renounced allegiance to his native Earth, for the Astrarch.

Tony Grimm and Elora Ronee had both objected. Tony was the

43

freckled, irresponsible redhead who had come out from Earth with him six years before, on the other of the two annual engineering scholarships. Elora Ronee was the lovely dark-eyed Martian girl—daughter of the professor of geodesics, and a proud descendant of the first colonists—whom they both loved.

He walked with them, that dry, bright afternoon, out from the yellow adobe buildings, across the rolling, stony, ocher-colored desert. Tony's sunburned, blue-eyed face was grave for once, as he protested.

"You can't do it, Bill. No Earthman could."

"No use talking," said Bill Webster, shortly. "The Astrarch wants a military engineer. His agents offered me twenty thousand eagles a year, with raises and bonuses—ten times what any research scientist could hope to get, back on Earth."

The tanned, vivid face of Elora Ronee looked hurt. "Bill—what about your own research?" the slender girl cried. "Your new reaction tube! You promised you were going to break the Astrarch's monopoly on space transport. Have you forgotten?"

"The tube was just a dream," Bill Webster told her, "but probably it's the reason he offered the contract to me, and not Tony. Such jobs don't go begging."

Tony caught his arm. "You can't turn against your own world, Bill," he insisted. "You can't give up everything that means anything to an Earthman. Just remember what the Astrarch is—a superpirate."

Bill Webster's toe kicked up a puff of yellow dust. "I know history," he said. "I know that the Astrarchy had its beginnings from the space pirates who established their bases in the asteroids, and gradually turned to commerce instead of raiding."

His voice was injured and defiant. "But, so far as I'm concerned, the Astrarchy is just as respectable as such planet nations as Earth and Mars and the Jovian Federation. And it's a good deal more wealthy and powerful than any of them."

Tense-faced, the Martian girl shook her dark head. "Don't blind yourself, Bill," she begged urgently. "Can't you see that the Astrarch really is no different from any of the old pirates? His fleets still seize any independent vessel, or make the owners ransom it with his space-patrol tax."

She caught an indignant breath. "Everywhere—even here on Mars—the agents and residents and traders of the Astrarchy have brought graft and corruption and oppression. The Astrarch is using his wealth and his space power to undermine the government of every independent planet. He's planning to conquer the system!"

Her brown eyes flashed. "You won't aid him, Bill. You—couldn't!"

Bill Webster looked into the tanned, intent loveliness of her face—
he wanted suddenly to kiss the smudge of yellow dust on her impudent
little nose. He had loved Elora Ronee, had once hoped to take her back
to Earth. Perhaps he still loved her. But now it was clear that she had
always wanted Tony Grimm.

Half angrily, he kicked an iron-reddened pebble. "If things had been
different, Elora, it might have been—" With an abrupt little shrug, he
looked back at Tony. "Anyhow," he said flatly, "I'm leaving for Astrophon
tonight."

That evening, after they had helped him pack, he made a bonfire of
his old books and papers. They burned palely in the thin air of Mars,
with a cloud of acrid smoke.

That sharp odor was the line that had drawn Brek Veronar back across
the years, when his nostrils stung to the scorched-paper scent. The cigar
came from a box that had just arrived from Cuba, Earth—made to his
special order.

He could afford such luxuries. Sometimes, in fact, he almost regretted
the high place he had earned in the Astrarch's favor. The space officers,
and even his own jealous subordinates in the arsenal laboratory, could
never forget that he was an Earthman—the Renegade.

The cigar's odor puzzled him.

Deliberately, he crushed out the smoldering tip, peeled off the brown
wrapper leaves. He found a tightly rolled paper cylinder. Slipping off
the rubber bands, he opened it. A glimpse of the writing set his heart to
thudding.

It was the hand of Elora Ronee!

Brek Veronar knew that fine graceful script. For once Bill Webster
had treasured a little note that she had written him, when they were
friends at school. He read it eagerly:

DEAR BILL: This is the only way we can hope to get word to you, past
the Astrarch's spies. Your old name, Bill, may seem strange to you. But
we—Tony and I—want you to remember that you are an Earthman.

You can't know the oppression that Earth now is suffering, under the
Astrarch's heel. But independence is almost gone. Weakened and corrupted, the government yields everywhere. Every Earthman's life is
choked with taxes and unjust penalties and the unfair competition of
the Astrarch traders.

But Earth, Bill, has not completely yielded. We are going to strike
for liberty. Many years of our lives—Tony's and mine—have gone into

the plan. And the toil and the sacrifices of millions of our fellow Earthmen. We have at least a chance to recover our lost freedom.

But we need you, Bill—desperately.

For your own world's sake, come back. Ask for a vacation trip to Mars. The Astrarch will not deny you that. On April 8th, a ship will be waiting for you in the desert outside Toran—where we walked the day you left.

Whatever your decision, Bill, we trust you to destroy this letter and keep its contents secret. But we believe that you will come back. For Earth's sake, and for your old friends,   TONY AND ELORA.

Brek Veronar sat for a long time at his desk, staring at the charred, wrinkled sheet. His eyes blurred a little, and he saw the tanned vital face of the Martian girl, her brown eyes imploring. At last he sighed and reached slowly for the lighter cone. He held the letter until the flame had consumed it.

Next day four space officers came to the laboratory. They were insolent in the gaudy gold and crimson of the Astrarch, and the voice of the captain was suave with a triumphant hate:

"Earthman, you are under technical arrest, by the Astrarch's order. You will accompany us at once to his quarters aboard the *Warrior Queen.*"

Brek Veronar knew that he was deeply disliked, but very seldom had the feeling been so openly shown. Alarmed, he locked his office and went with the four.

Flagship of the Astrarch's space fleets, the *Warrior Queen* lay on her cradle, at the side of the great field beyond the low gray forts. A thousand feet and a quarter of a million tons of fighting metal, with sixty-four twenty-inch rifles mounted in eight bulging spherical turrets, she was the most powerful engine of destruction the system had ever seen.

Brek Veronar's concern was almost forgotten in a silent pride, as a swift electric car carried them across the field. It was his autosight—otherwise the Veronar achronic field detector geodesic achron-integration self-calculating range finder—that directed the fire of those mighty guns. It was the very fighting brain of the ship—of all the Astrarch's fleet.

No wonder these men were jealous.

"Come, Renegade!" The bleak-faced captain's tone was ominous. "The Astrarch is waiting."

Bright-uniformed guards let them into the Astrarch's compact but luxurious suite, just aft the console room and forward of the autosight installation, deep in the ship's armored bowels. The Astrarch turned from a chart projector, and crisply ordered the two officers to wait outside.

"Well, Veronar?"

A short, heavy, compact man, the dictator of the Astrarchy was vibrant with a ruthless energy. His hair was waved and perfumed, his face a rouged and powdered mask, his silk-swathed figure loaded with jewels. But nothing could hide the power of his hawklike nose and his burning black eyes.

The Astrarch had never yielded to the constant pressure of jealousy against Brek Veronar. The feeling between them had grown almost to friendship. But now the Earthman sensed, from the cold inquiry of those first words, and the probing flash of the ruler's eyes, that his position was gravely dangerous.

Apprehension strained his voice. "I'm under arrest?"

The Astrarch smiled, gripped his hand. "My men are overzealous, Veronar." The voice was warm, yet Brek Veronar could not escape the sense of something sharply critical, deadly. "I merely wish to talk with you, and the impending movements of the fleet allowed little time."

Behind that smiling mask, the Astrarch studied him. "Veronar, you have served me loyally. I am leaving Astrophon for a cruise with the fleet, and I feel that you, also, have earned a holiday. Do you want a vacation from your duties here—let us say, to Mars?"

Beneath those thrusting eyes, Brek Veronar flinched. "Thank you, Gorro," he gulped—he was among the few privileged to call the Astrarch by name. "Later, perhaps. But the torpedo guide isn't finished. And I've several ideas for improving the autosight. I'd much prefer to stay in the laboratory."

For an instant, the short man's smile seemed genuine. "The Astrarchy is indebted to you for the autosight. The increased accuracy of fire has in effect quadrupled our fleets." His eyes were sharp again, doubtful. "Are further improvements possible?"

Brek Veronar caught his breath. His knees felt a little weak. He knew that he was talking for his life. He swallowed, and his words came at first unsteadily.

"Geodesic analysis and integration is a completely new science," he said desperately. "It would be foolish to limit the possibilities. With a sufficiently delicate pick-up, the achronic detector fields ought to be able to trace the world lines of any object almost indefinitely. Into the future—"

He paused for emphasis. "Or into the past!"

An eager interest flashed in the Astrarch's eyes. Brek felt confidence returning. His breathless voice grew smoother.

"Remember, the principle is totally new. The achronic field can be made a thousand times more sensitive than any telescope—I believe, a million times! And the achronic beam eliminates the time lag of all electromagnetic methods of observation. Timeless, paradoxically it facilitates the exploration of time."

"Exploration?" questioned the dictator. "Aren't you speaking rather wildly, Veronar?"

"Any range finder, in a sense, explores time," Brek assured him urgently. "It analyzes the past to predict the future—so that a shell fired from a moving ship and deflected by the gravitational fields of space may move thousands of miles to meet another moving ship, minutes in the future.

"Instruments depending on visual observation and electromagnetic transmission of data were not very successful. One hit in a thousand used to be good gunnery. But the autosight has solved the problem—now you reprimand gunners for failing to score two hits in a hundred."

Brek caught his breath. "Even the newest autosight is just a rough beginning. Good enough, for a range finder. But the detector fields can be made infinitely more sensitive, the geodesic integration infinitely more certain.

"It ought to be possible to unravel the past for years, instead of minutes. It ought to be possible to foretell the position of a ship for weeks ahead—to anticipate every maneuver, and even watch the captain eating his breakfast!"

The Earthman was breathless again, his eyes almost feverish. "From geodesic analysis," he whispered, "there is one more daring step—control. You are aware of the modern view that there is no absolute fact, but only probability. I can prove it! And probability can be manipulated, through pressure of the achronic field.

"It is possible, even, I tell you—"

Brek's rushing voice faltered. He saw that doubt had drowned the flash of interest in the Astrarch's eyes. The dictator made an impatient gesture for silence. In a flat, abrupt voice he stated: "Veronar, you are an Earthman."

"Once I was an Earthman."

The black, flashing eyes probed into him. "Veronar," the Astrarch said, "trouble is coming with Earth. My agents have uncovered a dangerous plot. The leader of it is an engineer named Grimm, who has a Martian wife. The fleet is moving to crush the rebellion." He paused. "Now, do you want the vacation?"

Before those ruthless eyes, Brek Veronar stood silent. Life, he was now certain, depended on his answer. He drew a long, unsteady breath. "No," he said.

Still the Astrarch's searching tension did not relax. "My officers," he said, "have protested against serving with you, against Earth. They are suspicious."

Brek Veronar swallowed. "Grimm and his wife," he whispered hoarsely, "once were friends of mine. I had hoped that it would not be necessary to betray them. But I have received a message from them."

He gulped again, caught his breath. "To prove to your men that I am no longer an Earthman—a ship that they have sent for me will be waiting, on April 8th, Earth calendar, in the desert south of the Martian city of Toran."

The white, lax mask of the Astrarch smiled. "I'm glad you told me, Veronar," he said. "You have been very useful—and I like you. Now I can tell you that my agents read the letter in the cigar. The rebel ship was overtaken and destroyed by the space patrol, just a few hours ago."

Brek Veronar swayed to a giddy weakness.

"Entertain no further apprehensions." The Astrarch touched his arm. "You will accompany the fleet, in charge of the autosight. We take off in five hours."

The long black hull of the *Warrior Queen* lifted on flaring reaction tubes, leading the squadron. Other squadrons moved from the bases on Pallas, Vesta, Thule, and Eros. The Second Fleet came plunging Sunward from its bases on the Trojan planets. Four weeks later, at the rendezvous just within the orbit of Mars, twenty-nine great vessels had come together.

The armada of the Astrarchy moved down upon Earth.

Joining the dictator in his chartroom, Brek was puzzled. "Still I don't see the reason for such a show of strength," he said. "Why have you gathered three fourths of your space forces, to crush a handful of plotters?"

"We have to deal with more than a handful of plotters." Behind the pale mask of the Astrarch's face, Brek could sense a tension of worry. "Millions of Earthmen have labored for years to prepare for this rebellion. Earth has built a space fleet."

Brek was astonished. "A fleet?"

"The parts were manufactured secretly, mostly in underground mills," the Astrarch told him. "The ships were assembled by divers, under the surface of fresh-water lakes. Your old friend, Grimm, is clever and dangerous. We shall have to destroy his fleet, before we can bomb the planet into submission."

Steadily, Brek met the Astrarch's eyes. "How many ships?" he asked. "Six."

"Then we outnumber them five to one." Brek managed a confident smile. "Without considering the further advantage of the autosight. It will be no battle at all."

"Perhaps not," said the Astrarch, "but Grimm is an able man. He has invented a new type reaction tube, in some regards superior to our own." His dark eyes were somber. "It is Earthman against Earthman," he said softly. "And one of you shall perish."

Day after day, the armada dropped Earthward.

The autosight served also as the eyes of the fleet, as well as the fighting brain. In order to give longer base lines for the automatic triangulations, additional achronic-field pick-ups had been installed upon half a dozen ships. Tight achronic beams brought their data to the immense main instrument, on the *Warrior Queen*. The autosight steered every ship, by achronic beam control, and directed the fire of its guns.

The *Warrior Queen* led the fleet. The autosight held the other vessels in accurate line behind her, so that only one circular cross section might be visible to the telescopes of Earth.

The rebel planet was still twenty million miles ahead, and fifty hours at normal deceleration, when the autosight discovered the enemy fleet. Brek Veronar sat at the curving control table.

Behind him, in the dim-lit vastness of the armored room, bulked the main instrument. Banked thousands of green-painted cases—the intricate cells of the mechanical brain—whirred with geodesic analyzers and integrators. The achronic field pick-ups—sense organs of the brain—were housed in insignificant black boxes. And the web of achronic transmission beams—instantaneous, ultrashort, nonelectromagnetic waves of the subelectronic order—the nerve fibers that joined the busy cells—was quite invisible.

Before Brek stood the twenty-foot cube of the stereoscreen, through which the brain communicated its findings. The cube was black, now, with the crystal blackness of space. Earth, in it, made a long misty crescent of wavering crimson splendor. The Moon was a smaller scimitar, blue with the dazzle of its artificial atmosphere.

Brek touched intricate controls. The Moon slipped out of the cube.

Earth grew—and turned. So far had the autosight conquered time and space. It showed the planet's Sunward side.

Earth filled the cube, incredibly real. The vast white disk of one low-pressure area lay upon the Pacific's glinting blue. Another, blotting out the winter brown of North America, reached to the bright gray cap of the arctic.

Softly, in the dim room, a gong clanged. Numerals of white fire flickered against the image in the cube. An arrow of red flame pointed. At its point was a tiny fleck of black.

The gong throbbed again, and another black mote came up out of the clouds. A third followed. Presently there were six. Watching, Brek Veronar felt a little stir of involuntary pride, a dim numbness of regret.

Those six vessels were the mighty children of Tony Grimm and Elora, the fighting strength of Earth. Brek felt an aching tenseness in his throat, and tears stung his eyes. It was too bad that they had to be destroyed.

Tony would be aboard one of those ships. Brek wondered how he would look, after twenty years. Did his freckles still show? Had he grown stout? Did concentration still plow little furrows between his blue eyes?

Elora—would she be with him? Brek knew she would. His mind saw the Martian girl, slim and vivid and intense as ever. He tried to thrust away the image. Time must have changed her. Probably she looked worn from the years of toil and danger; her dark eyes must have lost their sparkle.

Brek had to forget that those six little blots represented the lives of Tony and Elora, and the independence of the Earth. They were only six little lumps of matter, six targets for the autosight.

He watched them, rising, swinging around the huge, luminous curve of the planet. They were only six mathematical points, tracing world lines through the continuum, making a geodesic pattern for the analyzers to unravel and the integrators to project against the future—

The gong throbbed again.

Tense with abrupt apprehension, Brek caught up a telephone.

"Give me the Astrarch. . . . An urgent report. . . . No, the admiral won't do. . . . Gorro, the autosight has picked up the Earth fleet . . . Yes, only six ships, just taking off from the Sunward face. But there is one alarming thing."

Brek Veronar was hoarse, breathless. "Already, behind the planet, they have formed a cruising line. The axis extends exactly in our direction. That means that they know our precise position, before they have come into telescopic view. That suggests that Tony Grimm has invented an autosight of his own!"

Strained hours dragged by. The Astrarch's fleet decelerated, to circle and bombard the mother world, after the battle was done. The Earth ships came out at full normal acceleration.

"They must stop," the Astrarch said. "That is our advantage. If they go by us at any great velocity, we'll have the planet bombed into submission before they can return. They must turn back—and then we'll pick them off."

Puzzlingly, however, the Earth fleet kept up acceleration, and a slow apprehension grew in the heart of Brek Veronar. There was but one explanation. The Earthmen were staking the life of their planet on one brief encounter.

As if certain of victory!

The hour of battle neared. Tight achronic beams relayed telephoned orders from the Astrarch's chartroom, and the fleet deployed into battle formation—into the shape of an immense shallow bowl, so that every possible gun could be trained upon the enemy.

The hour—and the instant!

Startling in the huge dim space that housed the autosight, crackling out above the whirring of the achron-integrator, the speaker that was the great brain's voice counted off the minutes.

"Minus four—"

The autosight was set, the pick-ups tuned, the director relays tested, a thousand details checked. Behind the control table, Brek Veronar tried to relax. His part was done.

A space battle was a conflict of machines. Human beings were too puny, too slow, even to comprehend the play of the titanic forces they had set loose. Brek tried to remember that he was the autosight's inventor; he fought an oppression of helpless dread.

"Minus three—"

Sodium bombs filled the void ahead with vast silver plumes and streamers—for the autosight removed the need of telescopic eyes, and enabled ships to fight from deep smoke screens.

"Minus two—"

The two fleets came together at a relative velocity of twelve hundred thousand miles an hour. Maximum useful range of twenty-inch guns, even with the autosight, was only twenty thousand miles in free space.

Which meant, Brek realized, that the battle could last just two minutes.

In that brief time lay the destinies of Astrarchy and Earth—and Tony Grimm's and Elora's and his own.

"Minus one—"

The sodium screens made little puffs and trails of silver in the great black cube. The six Earth ships were visible behind them, through the magic of the achronic field pick-ups, now spaced in a close ring, ready for action.

Brek Veronar looked down at the jeweled chronometer on his wrist— a gift from the Astrarch. Listening to the rising hum of the achron-integrators, he caught his breath, tensed instinctively.

"Zero!"

The *Warrior Queen* began quivering to her great guns, a salvo of four firing every half-second. Brek breathed again, watching the chronometer. That was all he had to do. And in two minutes—

The vessel shuddered, and the lights went out. Sirens wailed, and air valves clanged. The lights came on, went off again. And abruptly the cube of the stereo screen was dark. The achron-integrators clattered and stopped.

The guns ceased to thud.

"Power!" Brek gasped into a telephone. "Give me power! Emergency! The autosight has stopped and—"

But the telephone was dead.

There were no more hits. Smothered in darkness, the great room remained very silent. After an eternal time, feeble emergency lights came on. Brek looked again at his chronometer, and knew that the battle was ended.

But who the victor?

He tried to hope that the battle had been won before some last chance broadside crippled the flagship—until the Astrarch came stumbling into the room, looking dazed and pale.

"Crushed," he muttered. "You failed me, Veronar."

"What are the losses?" whispered Brek.

"Everything." The shaken ruler dropped wearily at the control table. "Your achronic beams are dead. Five ships remain able to report defeat by radio. Two of them hope to make repairs.

"The *Queen* is disabled. Reaction batteries shot away, and main power plant dead. Repair is hopeless. And our present orbit will carry us far too close to the Sun. None of our ships able to undertake rescue. We'll be baked alive."

His perfumed dark head sank hopelessly. "In those two minutes, the

Astrarchy was destroyed." His hollow, smoldering eyes lifted resentfully to Brek. "Just two minutes!" He crushed a soft white fist against the table. "If time could be recaptured—"

"How were we beaten?" demanded Brek. "I can't understand!"

"Marksmanship," said the tired Astrarch. "Tony Grimm has something better than your autosight. He shot us to pieces before we could find the range." His face was a pale mask of bitterness. "If my agents had employed him, twenty years ago, instead of you—" He bit blood from his lip. "But the past cannot be changed."

Brek was staring at the huge, silent bulk of the autosight. "Perhaps" —he whispered—"it can be!"

Trembling, the Astrarch rose to clutch his arm. "You spoke of that before," gasped the agitated ruler. "Then I wouldn't listen. But now— try anything you can, Veronar. To save us from roasting alive, at perihelion. Do you really think—"

The Astrarch shook his pale head. "I'm the madman," he whispered. "To speak of changing even two minutes of the past!" His hollow eyes clung to Brek. "Though you have done amazing things, Veronar."

The Earthman continued to stare at his huge creation. "The autosight itself brought me one clue, before the battle," he breathed slowly. "The detector fields caught a beam of Tony Grimm's, and analyzed the frequencies. He's using achronic radiation a whole octave higher than anything I've tried. That must be the way to the sensitivity and penetration I have hoped for."

Hope flickered in the Astrarch's eyes. "You believe you can save us? How?"

"If the high-frequency beam can search out the determiner factors," Brek told him, "it might be possible to alter them, with a sufficiently powerful field. Remember that we deal with probabilities, not with absolutes. And that small factors can determine vast results.

"The pick-ups will have to be rebuilt. And we'll have to have power. Power to project the tracer fields. And a river of power—if we can trace out a decisive factor and attempt to change it. But the power plants are dead."

"Rebuild your pick-ups," the Astrarch told him. "And you'll have power —if I have to march every man aboard into the conversion furnaces, for fuel."

Calm again, and confident, the short man surveyed the tall, gaunt Earthman with wondering eyes.

"You're a strange individual, Veronar," he said. "Fighting time and destiny to crush the planet of your birth! It isn't strange that men call you the Renegade."

Silent for a moment, Brek shook his haggard head. "I don't want to be baked alive," he said at last. "Give me power—and we'll fight that battle again."

The wreck dropped Sunward. A score of expert technicians toiled, under Brek's expert direction, to reconstruct the achronic pick-ups. And a hundred men labored, beneath the ruthless eye of the Astrarch himself, to repair the damaged atomic converters.

They had crossed the orbit of Venus, when the autosight came back to humming life. The Astrarch was standing beside Brek, at the curved control table. The shadow of doubt had returned to his reddened, sleepless eyes. "Now," he demanded, "what can you do about the battle?"

"Nothing, directly," Brek admitted. "First we must search the past. We must find the factor that caused Tony Grimm to invent a better autosight than mine. With the high-frequency field—and the full power of the ship's converters, if need be—we must reverse that factor. Then the battle should have a different outcome."

The achron-integrators whirred, as Brek manipulated the controls, and the huge black cube began to flicker with the passage of ghostly images. Symbols of colored fire flashed and vanished within it.

"Well?" anxiously rasped the Astrarch.

"It works!" Brek assured him. "The tracer fields are following all the world lines that intersected at the battle, back across the months and years. The analyzers will isolate the smallest—and hence most easily altered—essential factor."

The Astrarch gripped his shoulder. "There—in the cube—yourself!"

The ghostly shape of the Earthman flickered out, and came again. A hundred times, Brek Veronar glimpsed himself in the cube. Usually the scene was the great arsenal laboratory, at Astrophon. Always he was differently garbed, always younger.

Then the background shifted. Brek caught his breath as he recognized glimpses of barren, stony, ocher-colored hills, and low, yellow adobe buildings. He gasped to see a freckled, red-haired youth and a slim, tanned, dark-eyed girl.

"That's on Mars!" he whispered. "At Toran. He's Tony Grimm. And she's Elora Ronee—the Martian girl we loved."

The racing flicker abruptly stopped, upon one frozen tableau. A bench on the dusty campus, against a low adobe wall. Elora Ronee, with a pile of books propped on her knees to support pen and paper. Her dark eyes were staring away across the campus, and her sun-brown face looked tense and troubled.

In the huge dim room aboard the wrecked warship, a gong throbbed softly. A red arrow flamed in the cube, pointing down at the note on the girl's knee. Cryptic symbols flashed above it. And Brek realized that the humming of the achron-integrators had stopped.

"What's this?" rasped the anxious Astrarch. "A schoolgirl writing a note—what has she to do with a space battle?"

Brek scanned the fiery symbols. "She was deciding the battle—that day twenty years ago!" His voice rang with elation. "You see, she had a date to go dancing in Toran with Tony Grimm that night. But her father was giving a special lecture on the new theories of achronic force. Tony broke the date, to attend the lecture."

As Brek watched the motionless image in the cube, his voice turned a little husky. "Elora was angry—that was before she knew Tony very well. I had asked her for a date. And, at the moment you see, she has just written a note, to say that she would go dancing with me."

Brek gulped. "But she is undecided, you see. Because she loves Tony. A very little would make her tear up the note to me, and write another to Tony, to say that she would go to the lecture with him."

The Astrarch stared cadaverously. "But how could that decide the battle?"

"In the past that we have lived," Brek told him, "Elora sent the note to me. I went dancing with her, and missed the lecture. Tony attended it—and got the germ idea that finally caused his autosight to be better than mine.

"But, if she had written to Tony instead, he would have offered, out of contrition, to cut the lecture—so the analyzers indicate. I should have attended the lecture in Tony's place, and my autosight would have been superior in the end."

The Astrarch's waxen head nodded slowly. "But—can you really change the past?"

Brek paused for a moment, solemnly. "We have all the power of the ship's converters," he said at last. "We have the high-frequency achronic field, as a lever through which to apply it. Surely, with the millions of kilowatts to spend, we can stimulate a few cells in a schoolgirl's brain. We shall see."

His long, pale fingers moved swiftly over the control keys. At last, deliberately, he touched a green button. The converters whispered again through the silent ship. The achron-integrators whirred again. Beyond, giant transformers began to whine.

And that still tableau came to sudden life.

Elora Ronee tore up the note that began, "Dear Bill—" Brek and the Astrarch leaned forward, as her trembling fingers swiftly wrote: "Dear Tony—I'm so sorry that I was angry. May I come with you to father's lecture? Tonight—"

The image faded.

"Minus four—"

The metallic rasp of the speaker brought Brek Veronar to himself with a start. Could he have been dozing—with contact just four minutes away? He shook himself. He had a queer, unpleasant feeling—as if he had forgotten a nightmare dream in which the battle was fought and lost.

He rubbed his eyes, scanned the control board. The autosight was set, the pick-ups were tuned, the director relays tested. His part was done. He tried to relax the puzzling tension in him.

"Minus three—"

Sodium bombs filled the void ahead with vast silver plumes and streamers. Staring into the black cube of the screen, Brek found once more the six tiny black motes of Tony Grimm's ships. He couldn't help an uneasy shake of his head.

Was Tony mad? Why didn't he veer aside, delay the contact? Scattered in space, his ships could harry the Astrarchy's commerce, and interrupt bombardment of the Earth. But, in a head-on battle, they were doomed.

Brek listened to the quiet hum of the achron-integrators. Under these conditions, the new autosight gave an accuracy of fire of forty percent. Even if Tony's gunnery was perfect, the odds were still two to one against him.

"Minus two—"

Two minutes! Brek looked down at the jeweled chronometer on his wrist. For a moment he had an odd feeling that the design was unfamiliar. Strange, when he had worn it for twenty years.

The dial blurred a little. He remembered the day that Tony and Elora gave it to him—the day he left the university to come to Astrophon. It was too nice a gift. Neither of them had much money.

He wondered if Tony had ever guessed his love for Elora. Probably it was better that she had always declined his attentions. No shadow of jealousy had ever come over their friendship.

"Minus one—"

This wouldn't do! Half angrily, Brek jerked his eyes back to the screen. Still, however, in the silvery sodium clouds, he saw the faces of Tony and Elora. Still he couldn't forget the oddly unfamiliar pressure of the chronometer on his wrist—it was like the soft touch of Elora's fingers, when she had fastened it there.

Suddenly the black flecks in the screen were not targets any more. Brek caught a long gasping breath. After all, he was an Earthman. After twenty years in the Astrarch's generous pay, this timepiece was still his most precious possession.

His gray eyes narrowed grimly. Without the autosight, the Astrarch's fleet would be utterly blind in the sodium clouds. Given any sort of achronic range finder, Tony Grimm could wipe it out.

Brek's gaunt body trembled. Death, he knew, would be the sure penalty. In the battle or afterward—it didn't matter. He knew that he would accept it without regret.

"Zero!"

The achron-integrators were whirring busily, and the *Warrior Queen* quivered to the first salvo of her guns. Then Brek's clenched fists came down on the carefully set keyboard. The autosight stopped humming. The guns ceased to fire.

Brek picked up the Astrarch's telephone. "I've stopped the autosight." His voice was quiet and low. "It is quite impossible to set it again in two minutes."

The telephone clicked and was dead.

The vessel shuddered and the lights went out. Sirens wailed. Air valves clanged. The lights came on, went off again. Presently, there were no more hits. Smothered in darkness, the great room remained very silent.

The tiny racing tick of the chronometer was the only sound.

After an eternal time, feeble emergency lights came on. The Astrarch came stumbling into the room, looking dazed and pale.

A group of spacemen followed him. Their stricken, angry faces made an odd contrast with their gay uniforms. Before their vengeful hatred, Brek felt cold and ill. But the Astrarch stopped their ominous advance.

"The Earthman has doomed himself as well," the shaken ruler told them. "There's not much more that you can do. And certainly no haste about it."

He left them muttering at the door and came slowly to Brek.

"Crushed," he whispered. "You destroyed me, Veronar." A trembling hand wiped at the pale waxen mask of his face. "Everything is lost. The *Queen* disabled. None of our ships able to undertake rescue. We'll be baked alive."

His hollow eyes stared dully at Brek. "In those two minutes, you destroyed the Astrarchy." His voice seemed merely tired, strangely without bitterness. "Just two minutes," he murmured wearily. "If time could be recaptured—"

"Yes," Brek said, "I stopped the autosight." He lifted his gaunt shoulders defiantly, and met the menacing stares of the spacemen. "And they can do nothing about it?"

"Can you?" Hope flickered in the Astrarch's eyes.

"Once you told me, Veronar, that the past could be changed. Then I wouldn't listen. But now—try anything you can. You might be able to save yourself from the unpleasantness that my men are planning."

Looking at the muttering men, Brek shook his head. "I was mistaken," he said deliberately. "I failed to take account of the two-way nature of time. But the future, I see now, is as real as the past. Aside from the direction of entropy change and the flow of consciousness, future and past cannot be distinguished.

"The future determines the past, as much as the past does the future. It is possible to trace out the determiner factors, and even, with sufficient power, to cause a local deflection of the geodesics. But world lines are fixed in the future, as rigidly as in the past. However the factors are rearranged, the end result will always be the same."

The Astrarch's waxen face was ruthless. "Then, Veronar, you are doomed."

Slowly, Brek smiled. "Don't call me Veronar," he said softly. "I remembered, just in time, that I am William Webster, Earthman. You can kill me in any way you please. But the defeat of the Astrarchy and the new freedom of Earth are fixed in time—forever."

First published: 1940

VAULT OF THE BEAST

by A. E. van Vogt

THE CREATURE CREPT. IT WHIMPERED FROM FEAR AND PAIN, A THING, slobbering sound horrible to hear. Shapeless, formless thing yet changing shape and form with every jerky movement.

It crept along the corridor of the space freighter, fighting the terrible urge of its elements to take the shape of its surroundings. A gray blob of disintegrating stuff, it crept, it cascaded, it rolled, flowed, dissolved, every movement an agony of struggle against the abnormal need to become a stable shape.

Any shape! The hard, chilled-blue metal wall of the Earth-bound freighter, the thick, rubbery floor. The floor was easy to fight. It wasn't like the metal that pulled and pulled. It would be easy to become metal for all eternity.

But something prevented it. An implanted purpose. A purpose that drummed from electron to electron, vibrated from atom to atom with an unvarying intensity that was like a special pain: *Find the greatest mathematical mind in the Solar System, and bring it to the vault of the Martian ultimate metal. The Great One must be freed! The prime number time lock must be opened!*

That was the purpose that hummed with unrelenting agony through its elements. That was the thought that had been seared into its fundamental consciousness by the great and evil minds that had created it.

There was movement at the far end of the corridor. A door opened. Footsteps sounded. A man whistling to himself. With a metallic hiss, almost a sigh, the creature dissolved, looking momentarily like diluted mercury. Then it turned brown like the floor. It became the floor, a slightly thicker stretch of dark-brown rubber spread out for yards.

It was ecstasy just to lie there, to be flat and to have shape, and to be so nearly dead that there was no pain. Death was so sweet, so utterly desirable. And life such an unbearable torment of agony, such a throbbing, piercing nightmare of anguished convulsion. If only the life that was approaching would pass swiftly. If the life stopped, it would pull it into shape. Life could do that. Life was stronger than metal, stronger than anything. The approaching life meant torture, struggle, pain.

The creature tensed its now flat, grotesque body—the body that could develop muscles of steel—and waited in terror for the death struggle.

Spacecraftsman Parelli whistled happily as he strode along the gleaming corridor that led from the engine room. He had just received a wireless from the hospital. His wife was doing well, and it was a boy. Eight pounds, the radiogram had said. He suppressed a desire to whoop and dance. A boy. Life sure was good.

Pain came to the thing on the floor. Primeval pain that sucked through its elements like acid burning, burning. The brown floor shuddered in every atom as Parelli strode over it. The aching urge to pull toward him, to take his shape. The thing fought its horrible desire, fought with anguish and shivering dread, more consciously now that it could think with Parelli's brain. A ripple of floor rolled after the man.

Fighting didn't help. The ripple grew into a blob that momentarily seemed to become a human head. Gray, hellish nightmare of demoniac shape. The creature hissed metallically in terror, then collapsed palpitating, slobbering with fear and pain and hate as Parelli strode on rapidly—too rapidly for its creeping pace.

The thin, horrible sound died; the thing dissolved into brown floor, and lay quiescent yet quivering in every atom from its unquenchable, uncontrollable urge to live—live in spite of pain, in spite of abysmal terror and primordial longing for stable shape. To live and fulfill the purpose of its lusting and malignant creators.

Thirty feet up the corridor, Parelli stopped. He jerked his mind from its thoughts of child and wife. He spun on his heels, and stared uncertainly along the passageway from the engine room.

"Now, what the devil was that?" he pondered aloud.

A sound—a queer, faint yet unmistakably horrid sound was echoing and re-echoing through his consciousness. A shiver ran the length of his spine. That sound—that devilish sound.

He stood there, a tall, magnificently muscled man, stripped to the waist, sweating from the heat generated by the rockets that were decelerating the craft after its meteoric flight from Mars. Shuddering, he clenched his fists, and walked slowly back the way he had come.

The creature throbbed with the pull of him, a gnawing, writhing, tormenting struggle that pierced into the deeps of every restless, agitated cell, stabbing agonizingly along the alien nervous system; and then became terrifyingly aware of the inevitable, the irresistible need to take the shape of the life.

Parelli stopped uncertainly. The floor moved under him, a visible wave that reared brown and horrible before his incredulous eyes and grew into a bulbous, slobbering, hissing mass. A venomous demon head reared on twisted, half-human shoulders. Gnarled hands on apelike, malformed arms clawed at his face with insensate rage—and changed even as they tore at him.

"Good God!" Parelli bellowed.

The hands, the arms that clutched him grew more normal, more human, brown, muscular. The face assumed familiar lines, sprouted a nose, eyes, a red gash of mouth. The body was suddenly his own, trousers and all, sweat and all.

"—God!" his image echoed; and pawed at him with letching fingers and an impossible strength.

Gasping, Parelli fought free, then launched one crushing blow straight into the distorted face. A drooling scream of agony came from the thing. It turned and ran, dissolving as it ran, fighting dissolution, uttering strange half-human cries.

And, struggling against horror, Parelli chased it, his knees weak and trembling from sheer funk and incredulity. His arm reached out, and plucked at the disintegrating trousers. A piece came away in his hand, a cold, slimy, writhing lump like wet clay.

The feel of it was too much. His gorge rising in disgust, he faltered in his stride. He heard the pilot shouting ahead:

"What's the matter?"

Parelli saw the open door of the storeroom. With a gasp, he dived in, came out a moment later, wild-eyed, an ato-gun in his fingers. He saw the pilot, standing with staring, horrified brown eyes, white face and rigid body, facing one of the great windows.

"There it is!" the man cried.

A gray blob was dissolving into the edge of the glass, becoming glass. Parelli rushed forward, ato-gun poised. A ripple went through the glass, darkening it; and then, briefly, he caught a glimpse of a blob emerging on the other side of the glass into the cold of space.

The officer stood gaping beside him; the two of them watched the gray, shapeless mass creep out of sight along the side of the rushing freight liner.

Parelli sprang to life. "I got a piece of it!" he gasped. "Flung it down on the floor of the storeroom."

It was Lieutenant Morton who found it. A tiny section of floor reared up, and then grew amazingly large as it tried to expand into human shape. Parelli with distorted, crazy eyes scooped it up in a shovel. It hissed; it nearly became a part of the metal shovel, but couldn't because Parelli was so close. Changing, fighting for shape, it slobbered and hissed as Parelli staggered with it behind his superior officer. He was laughing hysterically. "I touched it," he kept saying, "I touched it."

A large blister of metal on the outside of the space freighter stirred into sluggish life, as the ship tore into the Earth's atmosphere. The metal walls of the freighter grew red, then white-hot, but the creature, un-affected, continued its slow transformation into gray mass. Vague thought came to the thing, realization that it was time to act.

Suddenly, it was floating free of the ship, falling slowly, heavily, as if somehow the gravitation of Earth had no serious effect upon it. A minute distortion in its electrons started it falling faster, as in some alien way it suddenly became more allergic to gravity.

The Earth was green below; and in the dim distance a gorgeous and tremendous city of spires and massive buildings glittered in the sinking Sun. The thing slowed, and drifted like a falling leaf in a breeze toward the still-distant Earth. It landed in an arroyo beside a bridge at the outskirts of the city.

A man walked over the bridge with quick, nervous steps. He would have been amazed, if he had looked back, to see a replica of himself climb from the ditch to the road, and start walking briskly after him.

Find the—greatest mathematician!

It was an hour later; and the pain of that throbbing thought was a dull, continuous ache in the creature's brain, as it walked along the crowded street. There were other pains, too. The pain of fighting the pull of the pushing, hurrying mass of humanity that swarmed by with unseeing eyes. But it was easier to think, easier to hold form now that it had the brain and body of a man.

Find—mathematician!

"Why?" asked the man's brain of the thing; and the whole body shook with startled shock at such heretical questioning. The brown eyes darted in fright from side to side, as if expecting instant and terrible doom. The face dissolved a little in that brief moment of mental chaos, became successively the man with the hooked nose who swung by, the tanned face of the tall woman who was looking into the shop window, the—

With a second gasp, the creature pulled its mind back from fear, and fought to readjust its face to that of the smooth-shaven young man who sauntered idly in from a side street. The young man glanced at him, looked away, then glanced back again startled. The creature echoed the thought in the man's brain: "Who the devil is that? Where have I seen that fellow before?"

Half a dozen women in a group approached. The creature shrank aside as they passed, its face twisted with the agony of the urge to become woman. Its brown suit turned just the faintest shade of blue, the color of the nearest dress, as it momentarily lost control of its outer atoms. Its mind hummed with the chatter of clothes and "My dear, didn't she look dreadful in that awful hat?"

There was a solid cluster of giant buildings ahead. The thing shook its human head consciously. So many buildings meant metal; and the forces that held metal together would pull and pull at its human shape. The creature comprehended the reason for this with the understanding of the slight man in a dark suit who wandered by dully. The slight man was a clerk; the thing caught his thought. He was thinking enviously of his boss who was Jim Brender, of the financial firm of J. P. Brender & Co.

The overtones of that thought struck along the vibrating elements of the creature. It turned abruptly and followed Lawrence Pearson, book-keeper. If people ever paid attention to other people on the street, they would have been amazed after a moment to see two Lawrence Pearsons proceeding down the street, one some fifty feet behind the other. The second Lawrence Pearson had learned from the mind of the first that Jim Brender was a Harvard graduate in mathematics, finance and political economy, the latest of a long line of financial geniuses, thirty years old, and the head of the tremendously wealthy J. P. Brender & Co. Jim Brender had just married the most beautiful girl in the world; and this was the reason for Lawrence Pearson's discontent with life.

"Here I'm thirty, too," his thoughts echoed in the creature's mind, "and I've got nothing. He's got everything—everything while all I've got to look forward to is the same old boardinghouse till the end of time."

It was getting dark as the two crossed the river. The creature quickened its pace, striding forward with aggressive alertness that Lawrence Pearson in the flesh could never have managed. Some glimmering of its terrible purpose communicated itself in that last instant to the victim. The slight man turned; and let out a faint squawk as those steel-muscled fingers jerked at his throat, a single, fearful snap.

The creature's brain went black with dizziness as the brain of Lawrence Pearson crashed into the night of death. Gasping, whimpering, fighting dissolution, it finally gained control of itself. With one sweeping movement, it caught the dead body and flung it over the cement railing. There was a splash below, then a sound of gurgling water.

The thing that was now Lawrence Pearson walked on hurriedly, then more slowly till it came to a large, rambling brick house. It looked anxiously at the number, suddenly uncertain if it had remembered rightly. Hesitantly, it opened the door.

A streamer of yellow light splashed out, and laughter vibrated in the thing's sensitive ears. There was the same hum of many thoughts and many brains, as there had been in the street. The creature fought against the inflow of thought that threatened to crowd out the mind of Lawrence Pearson. A little dazed by the struggle, it found itself in a large, bright hall, which looked through a door into a room where a dozen people were sitting around a dining table.

"Oh, it's you, Mr. Pearson," said the landlady from the head of the table. She was a sharp-nosed, thin-mouthed woman at whom the creature stared with brief intentness. From her mind, a thought had come. She had a son who was a mathematics teacher in a high school. The creature shrugged. In one penetrating glance, the truth throbbed along the intricate atomic structure of its body. This woman's son was as much of an intellectual lightweight as his mother.

"You're just in time," she said incuriously. "Sarah, bring Mr. Pearson's plate."

"Thank you, but I'm not feeling hungry," the creature replied; and its human brain vibrated to the first silent, ironic laughter that it had ever known. "I think I'll just lie down."

All night long it lay on the bed of Lawrence Pearson, bright-eyed, alert, becoming more and more aware of itself. It thought:

"I'm a machine, without a brain of my own. I use the brains of other people, but somehow my creators made it possible for me to be more than just an echo. I use people's brains to carry out my purpose."

It pondered about those creators, and felt a surge of panic sweeping along its alien system, darkening its human mind. There was a vague physiological memory of pain unutterable, and of tearing chemical action that was frightening.

The creature rose at dawn, and walked the streets till half past nine. At that hour, it approached the imposing marble entrance of J. P. Brender & Co. Inside, it sank down in the comfortable chair initialed L. P.; and began painstakingly to work at the books Lawrence Pearson had put away the night before.

At ten o'clock, a tall young man in a dark suit entered the arched hallway and walked briskly through the row after row of offices. He smiled with easy confidence to every side. The thing did not need the chorus of "Good morning, Mr. Brender" to know that its prey had arrived.

Terrible in its slow-won self-confidence, it rose with a lithe, graceful movement that would have been impossible to the real Lawrence Pearson, and walked briskly to the washroom. A moment later, the very image of Jim Brender emerged from the door and walked with easy confidence to the door of the private office which Jim Brender had entered a few minutes before.

The thing knocked and walked in—and simultaneously became aware of three things: The first was that it had found the mind after which it had been sent. The second was that its image mind was incapable of imitating the finer subtleties of the razor-sharp brain of the young man who was staring up from dark-gray eyes that were a little startled. And the third was the large metal bas-relief that hung on the wall.

With a shock that almost brought chaos, it felt the overpowering tug of that metal. And in one flash it knew that this was ultimate metal, product of the fine craft of the ancient Martians, whose metal cities, loaded with treasures of furniture, art and machinery, were slowly being dug up by enterprising human beings from the sands under which they had been buried for thirty or fifty million years.

The ultimate metal! The metal that no heat would even warm, that no diamond or other cutting device, could scratch, never duplicated by human beings, as mysterious as the *ieis* force which the Martians made from apparent nothingness.

All these thoughts crowded the creature's brain, as it explored the memory cells of Jim Brender. With an effort that was a special pain, the thing wrenched its mind from the metal, and fastened its eyes on Jim Brender. It caught the full flood of the wonder in his mind, as he stood up.

"Good lord," said Jim Brender, "who are you?"

"My name's Jim Brender," said the thing, conscious of grim amusement, conscious, too, that it was progress for it to be able to feel such an emotion.

The real Jim Brender had recovered himself. "Sit down, sit down," he said heartily. "This is the most amazing coincidence I've ever seen."

He went over to the mirror that made one panel of the left wall. He stared, first at himself, then at the creature. "Amazing," he said. "Absolutely amazing."

"Mr. Brender," said the creature, "I saw your picture in the paper, and I thought our astounding resemblance would make you listen, where otherwise you might pay no attention. I have recently returned from Mars, and I am here to persuade you to come back to Mars with me."

"That," said Jim Brender, "is impossible."

"Wait," the creature said, "until I have told you why. Have you ever heard of the Tower of the Beast?"

"The Tower of the Beast!" Jim Brender repeated slowly. He went around his desk and pushed a button.

A voice from an ornamental box said: "Yes, Mr. Brender?"

"Dave, get me all the data on the Tower of the Beast and the legendary city of Li in which it is supposed to exist."

"Don't need to look it up," came the crisp reply. "Most Martian histories refer to it as the beast that fell from the sky when Mars was young —some terrible warning connected with it—the beast was unconscious when found—said to be the result of its falling out of sub-space. Martians read its mind; and were so horrified by its subconscious intentions they tried to kill it, but couldn't. So they built a huge vault, about fifteen hundred feet in diameter and a mile high—and the beast, apparently of these dimensions, was locked in. Several attempts have been made to find the city of Li, but without success. Generally believed to be a myth. That's all, Jim."

"Thank you!" Jim Brender clicked off the connection, and turned to his visitor. "Well?"

"It is not a myth. I know where the Tower of the Beast is; and I also know that the beast is still alive."

"Now, see here," said Brender good-humoredly, "I'm intrigued by your resemblance to me; and as a matter of fact I'd like Pamela—my wife —to see you. How about coming over to dinner? But don't, for Heaven's sake, expect me to believe such a story. The beast, if there is such a thing, fell from the sky when Mars was young. There are some authorities who maintain that the Martian race died out a hundred million years ago, though twenty-five million is the conservative estimate. The only things remaining of their civilization are their constructions of ultimate metal. Fortunately, toward the end they built almost everything from that indestructible metal."

"Let me tell you about the Tower of the Beast," said the thing quietly. "It is a tower of gigantic size, but only a hundred feet or so projected above the sand when I saw it. The whole top is a door, and that door is geared to a time lock, which in turn has been integrated along a line of ieis to the ultimate prime number."

Jim Brender stared; and the thing caught his startled thought, the first uncertainty, and the beginning of belief.

"Ultimate prime number!" Brender ejaculated. "What do you mean?" He caught himself. "I know of course that a prime number is a number divisible only by itself and by one."

He snatched at a book from the little wall library beside his desk, and rippled through it. "The largest known prime is—ah, here it is—is 230-584300921393951. Some others, according to this authority, are 77-843839397, 182521213001, and 78875943472201."

He frowned. "That makes the whole thing ridiculous. The ultimate prime would be an indefinite number." He smiled at the thing. "If there is a beast, and it is locked up in a vault of ultimate metal, the door of which is geared to a time lock, integrated along a line of ieis to the ultimate prime number—then the beast is caught. Nothing in the world can free it."

"To the contrary," said the creature. "I have been assured by the beast that it is within the scope of human mathematics to solve the problem, but that what is required is a born mathematical mind, equipped with all the mathematical training that Earth science can afford. You are that man."

"You expect me to release this evil creature—even if I could perform this miracle of mathematics."

"Evil nothing!" snapped the thing. "That ridiculous fear of the unknown which made the Martians imprison it has resulted in a very grave wrong. The beast is a scientist from another space, accidentally caught in one of his experiments. I say 'his' when of course I do not know whether this race has a sexual differentiation."

"You actually talked with the beast?"

"It communicated with me by mental telepathy."

"It has been proven that thoughts cannot penetrate ultimate metal."

"What do humans know about telepathy? They cannot even communicate with each other except under special conditions." The creature spoke contemptuously.

"That's right. And if your story is true, then this is a matter for the Council."

"This is a matter for two men, you and I. Have you forgotten that the vault of the beast is the central tower of the great city of Li—billions of dollars' worth of treasure in furniture, art and machinery? The beast demands release from its prison before it will permit anyone to mine that treasure. You can release it. We can share the treasure."

"Let me ask you a question," said Jim Brender. "What is your real name?"

"P-Pierce Lawrence!" the creature stammered. For the moment, it could think of no greater variation of the name of its first victim than reversing the two words, with a slight change on "Pearson." Its thoughts darkened with confusion as the voice of Brender pounded:

"On what ship did you come from Mars?"

"O-on $F4961$," the thing stammered chaotically, fury adding to the confused state of its mind. It fought for control, felt itself slipping, suddenly felt the pull of the ultimate metal that made up the bas-relief on the wall, and knew by that tug that it was dangerously near dissolution.

"That would be a freighter," said Jim Brender. He pressed a button. "Carltons, find out if the $F\ 4961$ had a passenger or person aboard, named Pierce Lawrence. How long will it take?"

"About a minute, sir."

"You see," said Jim Brender, leaning back, "this is mere formality. If you were on that ship, then I shall be compelled to give serious attention to your statements. You can understand, of course, that I could not possibly go into a thing like this blindly. I—"

The buzzer rang. "Yes?" said Jim Brender.

"Only the crew of two was on the $F4961$ when it landed yesterday. No such person as Pierce Lawrence was aboard."

"Thank you." Jim Brender stood up. He said coldly, "Good-by, Mr. Lawrence. I cannot imagine what you hoped to gain by this ridiculous story. However, it has been most intriguing, and the problem you presented was very ingenious indeed—"

The buzzer was ringing. "What is it?"

"Mr. Gorson to see you, sir."

"Very well, send him right in."

The thing had greater control of its brain now, and it saw in Brender's mind that Gorson was a financial magnate, whose business ranked with the Brender firm. It saw other things, too; things that made it walk out of the private office, out of the building, and wait patiently until Mr. Gorson emerged from the imposing entrance. A few minutes later, there were two Mr. Gorsons walking down the street.

Mr. Gorson was a vigorous man in his early fifties. He had lived a clean, active life; and the hard memories of many climates and several planets were stored away in his brain. The thing caught the alertness of this man on its sensitive elements, and followed him warily, respectfully, not quite decided whether it would act.

It thought: "I've come a long way from the primitive life that couldn't hold its shape. My creators, in designing me, gave to me powers of learning, developing. It is easier to fight dissolution, easier to be human. In handling this man, I must remember that my strength is invincible when properly used."

With minute care, it explored in the mind of its intended victim the exact route of his walk to his office. There was the entrance to a large building clearly etched on his mind. Then a long, marble corridor, into an automatic elevator up to the eighth floor, along a short corridor with two doors. One door led to the private entrance of the man's private office. The other to a storeroom used by the janitor. Gorson had looked into the place on various occasions; and there was in his mind, among other things, the memory of a large chest—

The thing waited in the storeroom till the unsuspecting Gorson was past the door. The door creaked. Gorson turned, his eyes widening. He didn't have a chance. A fist of solid steel smashed his face to a pulp, knocking the bones back into his brain.

This time, the creature did not make the mistake of keeping its mind tuned to that of its victim. It caught him viciously as he fell, forcing its steel fist back to a semblance of human flesh. With furious speed, it stuffed the bulky and athletic form into the large chest, and clamped the lid down tight.

Alertly, it emerged from the storeroom, entered the private office of Mr. Gorson, and sat down before the gleaming desk of oak. The man who responded to the pressing of a button saw John Gorson sitting there, and heard John Gorson say:

"Crispins, I want you to start selling these stocks through the secret channels right away. Sell until I tell you to stop, even if you think it's crazy. I have information of something big on."

Crispins glanced down the row after row of stock names; and his eyes grew wider and wider. "Good lord, man!" he gasped finally, with that familiarity which is the right of a trusted adviser, "these are all the gilt-edged stocks. Your whole fortune can't swing a deal like this."

"I told you I'm not in this alone."

"But it's against the law to break the market," the man protested.

"Crispins, you heard what I said. I'm leaving the office. Don't try to get in touch with me. I'll call you."

The thing that was John Gorson stood up, paying no attention to the bewildered thoughts that flowed from Crispins. It went out of the door by which it had entered. As it emerged from the building, it was thinking: "All I've got to do is kill half a dozen financial giants, start their stocks selling, and then—"

By one o'clock it was over. The exchange didn't close till three, but at one o'clock, the news was flashed on the New York tickers. In London, where it was getting dark, the papers brought out an extra. In Hankow and Shanghai, a dazzling new day was breaking as the newsboys ran along the streets in the shadows of skyscrapers, and shouted that J. P. Brender & Co. had assigned; and that there was to be an investigation—

"We are facing," said the chairman of the investigation committee, in his opening address the following morning, "one of the most astounding coincidences in all history. An ancient and respected firm, with world-wide affiliations and branches, with investments in more than a thousand companies of every description, is struck bankrupt by an unexpected crash in every stock in which the firm was interested. It will require months to take evidence on the responsibility for the short-selling which brought about this disaster. In the meantime, I see no reason, regrettable as the action must be to all the old friends of the late J. P. Brender, and of his son, why the demands of the creditors should not be met, and the properties liquidated through auction sales and such other methods as may be deemed proper and legal—"

"Really, I don't blame her," said the first woman, as they wandered through the spacious rooms of the Brenders' Chinese palace. "I have no doubt she does love Jim Brender, but no one could seriously expect her to remain married to him *now*. She's a woman of the world, and it's utterly impossible to expect her to live with a man who's going to be a mere pilot or space hand or something on a Martian spaceship—"

Commander Hughes of Interplanetary Spaceways entered the office of his employer truculently. He was a small man, but extremely wiry; and the thing that was Louis Dyer gazed at him tensely, conscious of the force and power of this man.

Hughes began: "You have my report on this Brender case?"

The thing twirled the mustache of Louis Dyer nervously; then picked up a small folder, and read out loud:

"Dangerous for psychological reasons . . . to employ Brender. . . . So many blows in succession. Loss of wealth, position and wife. . . . No normal man could remain normal under . . . circumstances. Take him into office . . . befriend him . . . give him a sinecure, or position where his undoubted great ability . . . but not on a spaceship, where the utmost hardiness, both mental, moral, spiritual and physical is required—"

Hughes interrupted: "Those are exactly the points which I am stressing. I knew you would see what I meant, Louis."

"Of course, I see," said the creature, smiling in grim amusement, for it was feeling very superior these days. "Your thoughts, your ideas, your code and your methods are stamped irrevocably on your brain and"— it added hastily—"you have never left me in doubt as to where you stand. However, in this case I must insist. Jim Brender will not take an ordinary position offered by his friends. And it is ridiculous to ask him to subordinate himself to men to whom he is in every way superior. He has commanded his own space yacht; he knows more about the mathematical end of the work than our whole staff put together; and that is no reflection on our staff. He knows the hardships connected with space flying, and believes that it is exactly what he needs. I, therefore, command you, for the first time in our long association, Peter, to put him on space freighter *F4961* in the place of Spacecraftsman Parelli who collapsed into a nervous breakdown after that curious affair with the creature from space, as Lieutenant Morton described it— By the way, did you find the . . . er . . . sample of that creature yet?"

"No, sir, it vanished the day you came in to look at it. We've searched the place high and low—queerest stuff you ever saw. Goes through glass as easy as light; you'd think it was some form of light-stuff—scares me, too. A pure sympodial development—actually more adaptable to environment than anything hitherto discovered; and that's putting it mildly. I tell you, sir— But see here, you can't steer me off the Brender case like that."

"Peter, I don't understand your attitude. This is the first time I've interfered with your end of the work and—"

"I'll resign," groaned that sorely beset man.

The thing stifled a smile. "Peter, you've built up the staff of Spaceways. It's your child, your creation; you can't give it up, you know you can't—"

The words hissed softly into alarm; for into Hughes' brain had flashed the first real intention of resigning. Just hearing of his accomplishments and the story of his beloved job brought such a rush of memories, such a realization of how tremendous an outrage was this threatened interference. In one mental leap, the creature saw what this man's resignation would mean: The discontent of the men; the swift perception of the situation by Jim Brender; and his refusal to accept the job. There was only one way out—that Brender would get to the ship without finding out what had happened. Once on it, he must carry through with one trip to Mars; and that was all that was needed.

The thing pondered the possibility of imitating Hughes' body; then agonizingly realized that it was hopeless. Both Louis Dyer and Hughes must be around until the last minute.

"But, Peter, listen!" the creature began chaotically. Then it said, "Damn!" for it was very human in its mentality; and the realization that Hughes took its words as a sign of weakness was maddening. Uncertainty descended like a black cloud over its brain.

"I'll tell Brender when he arrives in five minutes how I feel about all this!" Hughes snapped; and the creature knew that the worst had happened. "If you forbid me to tell him then I resign. I— Good God, man, your face!"

Confusion and horror came to the creature simultaneously: It knew abruptly that its face had dissolved before the threatened ruin of its plans. It fought for control, leaped to its feet, seeing the incredible danger. The large office just beyond the frosted glass door—Hughes' first outcry would bring help—

With a half sob, it sought to force its arm into an imitation of a metal fist, but there was no metal in the room to pull it into shape. There was only the solid maple desk. With a harsh cry, the creature leaped completely over the desk, and sought to bury a pointed shaft of stick into Hughes' throat.

Hughes cursed in amazement, and caught at the stick with furious strength. There was sudden commotion in the outer office, raised voices, running feet—

It was quite accidental the way it happened. The surface cars swayed to a stop, drawing up side by side as the red light blinked on ahead. Jim Brender glanced at the next car.

A girl and a man sat in the rear of the long, shiny, streamlined affair, and the girl was desperately striving to crouch down out of his sight, striving with equal desperation not to be too obvious in her intention. Realizing that she was seen, she smiled brilliantly, and leaned out of the window.

"Hello, Jim, how's everything?"

"Hello, Pamela!" Jim Brender's fingers tightened on the steering wheel till the knuckles showed white, as he tried to keep his voice steady. He couldn't help adding: "When does the divorce become final?"

"I get my papers tomorrow," she said, "but I suppose you won't get yours till you return from your first trip. Leaving today, aren't you?"

"In about fifteen minutes." He hesitated. "When is the wedding?"

The rather plump, white-faced man who had not participated in the conversation so far, leaned forward.

"Next week," he said. He put his fingers possessively over Pamela's hand. "I wanted it tomorrow but Pamela wouldn't—er, good-by."

His last words were hastily spoken, as the traffic lights switched, and the cars rolled on, separating at the first corner.

The rest of the drive to the spaceport was a blur. He hadn't expected the wedding to take place so soon. Hadn't, when he came right down to it, expected it to take place at all. Like a fool, he had hoped blindly—

Not that it was Pamela's fault. Her training, her very life made this the only possible course of action for her. But—*one week!* The spaceship would be one fourth of the long trip to Mars—

He parked his car. As he paused beside the runway that led to the open door of $F4961$—a huge globe of shining metal, three hundred feet in diameter—he saw a man running toward him. Then he recognized Hughes.

The thing that was Hughes approached, fighting for calmness. The whole world was a flame of cross-pulling forces. It shrank from the thoughts of the people milling about in the office it had just left. Everything had gone wrong. It had never intended to do what it now had to do. It had intended to spend most of the trip to Mars as a blister of metal on the outer shield of the ship. With an effort, it controlled its funk, its terror, its brain.

"We're leaving right away," it said.

Brender looked amazed. "But that means I'll have to figure out a new orbit under the most difficult—"

"Exactly," the creature interrupted. "I've been hearing a lot about your marvelous mathematical ability. It's time the words were proved by deeds."

Jim Brender shrugged. "I have no objection. But how is it that you're coming along?"

"I always go with a new man."

It sounded reasonable. Brender climbed the runway, closely followed by Hughes. The powerful pull of the metal was the first real pain the creature had known for days. For a long month, it would now have to fight the metal, fight to retain the shape of Hughes—and carry on a thousand duties at the same time.

That first stabbing pain tore along its elements, and smashed the confidence that days of being human had built up. And then, as it followed Brender through the door, it heard a shout behind it. It looked back hastily. People were streaming out of several doors, running toward the ship.

Brender was several yards along the corridor. With a hiss that was almost a sob, the creature leaped inside, and pulled the lever that clicked the great door shut.

There was an emergency lever that controlled the antigravity plates. With one jerk, the creature pulled the heavy lever hard over. There was a sensation of lightness and a sense of falling.

Through the great plate window, the creature caught a flashing glimpse of the field below, swarming with people. White faces turning upward, arms waving. Then the scene grew remote, as a thunder of rockets vibrated through the ship.

"I hope," said Brender, as Hughes entered the control room, "you wanted me to start the rockets."

"Yes," the thing replied, and felt brief panic at the chaos in its brain, the tendency of its tongue to blur. "I'm leaving the mathematical end entirely in your hands."

It didn't dare to stay so near the heavy metal engines, even with Brender's body there to help it keep its human shape. Hurriedly, it started up the corridor. The best place would be the insulated bedroom—

Abruptly, it stopped in its headlong walk, teetered for an instant on tiptoes. From the control room it had just left, a thought was trickling—a thought from Brender's brain. The creature almost dissolved in terror as it realized that Brender was sitting at the radio, answering an insistent call from Earth—

It burst into the control room, and braked to a halt, its eyes widening with humanlike dismay. Brender whirled from before the radio with a single twisting step. In his fingers, he held a revolver. In his mind, the creature read a dawning comprehension of the whole truth. Brender cried:

"You're the . . . thing that came to my office, and talked about prime numbers and the vault of the beast."

He took a step to one side to cover an open doorway that led down another corridor. The movement brought the telescreen into the vision of the creature. In the screen was the image of the real Hughes. Simultaneously, Hughes saw the thing.

"Brender," he bellowed, "it's the monster that Morton and Parelli saw on their trip from Mars. It doesn't react to heat or any chemicals, but we never tried bullets. Shoot, you fool!"

It was too much, there was too much metal, too much confusion. With a whimpering cry, the creature dissolved. The pull of the metal twisted it horribly into thick half metal; the struggle to be human left it a malignant structure of bulbous head, with one eye half gone, and two snakelike arms attached to the half metal of the body.

Instinctively, it fought closer to Brender, letting the pull of his body make it more human. The half metal became fleshlike stuff that sought to return to its human shape.

"Listen, Brender!" Hughes' voice came urgently. "The fuel vats in the engine room are made of ultimate metal. One of them is empty. We caught a part of this thing once before, and it couldn't get out of the small jar of ultimate metal. If you could drive it into the vat while it's lost control of itself, as it seems to do very easily—"

"I'll see what lead can do!" Brender rapped in a brittle voice.

Bang! The half-human creature screamed from its half-formed slit of mouth, and retreated, its legs dissolving into gray dough.

"It hurts, doesn't it?" Brender ground out. "Get over into the engine room, you damned thing, into the vat!"

"Go on, go on!" Hughes was screaming from the telescreen.

Brender fired again. The creature made a horrible slobbering sound, and retreated once more. But it was bigger again, more human; and in one caricature hand a caricature of Brender's revolver was growing.

It raised the unfinished, unformed gun. There was an explosion, and a shriek from the thing. The revolver fell, a shapeless, tattered blob, to the floor. The little gray mass of it scrambled frantically toward the parent body, and attached itself like some monstrous canker to the right foot.

And then, for the first time, the mighty and evil brains that had created the thing, sought to dominate their robot. Furious, yet conscious that the game must be carefully played, the Controller forced the terrified and utterly beaten thing to its will. Scream after agonized scream rent the air, as the change was forced upon the unstable elements. In an instant, the thing stood in the shape of Brender, but instead of a revolver, there grew from one browned, powerful hand a pencil of shining metal. Mirror bright, it glittered in every facet like some incredible gem.

The metal glowed ever so faintly, an unearthly radiance. And where the radio had been, and the screen with Hughes' face on it, there was a gaping hole. Desperately, Brender pumped bullets into the body before him, but though the shape trembled, it stared at him now, unaffected. The shining weapon swung toward him.

"When you are quite finished," it said, "perhaps we can talk."

It spoke so mildly that Brender, tensing to meet death, lowered his gun in amazement. The thing went on:

"Do not be alarmed. This which you hear and see is a robot, designed by us to cope with your space and number world. Several of us are working here under the most difficult conditions to maintain this connection, so I must be brief.

"We exist in a time world immeasurably more slow than your own. By a system of synchronization, we have geared a number of these spaces in such fashion that, though one of our days is millions of your years, we can communicate. Our purpose is to free our colleague, Kalorn, from the Martian vault. Kalorn was caught accidentally in a time warp of his own making and precipitated onto the planet you know as Mars. The Martians, needlessly fearing his great size, constructed a most diabolical prison, and we need your knowledge of the mathematics peculiar to your space and number world—and to it alone—in order to free him."

The calm voice continued, earnest but not offensively so, insistent but friendly. He regretted that their robot had killed human beings. In greater detail, he explained that every space was constructed on a different numbers system, some all negative, some all positive, some a mixture of the two, the whole an infinite variety, and every mathematic interwoven into the very fabric of the space it ruled.

Ieis force was not really mysterious. It was simply a flow from one space to another, the result of a difference in potential. This flow, however, was one of the universal forces, which only one other force could affect, the one he had used a few minutes before. Ultimate metal was *actually* ultimate.

In their space they had a similar metal, built up from negative atoms. He could see from Brender's mind that the Martians had known nothing about minus numbers, so that they must have built it up from ordinary atoms. It could be done that way, too, though not so easily. He finished:

"The problem narrows down to this: Your mathematics must tell us how, with our universal force, we can short-circuit the ultimate prime number—that is, factor it—so that the door will open any time. You may ask how a prime can be factored when it is divisible only by itself and by one. That problem is, for your system, solvable only by your mathematics. Will you do it?"

Brender realized with a start that he was still holding his revolver. He tossed it aside. His nerves were calm as he said:

"Everything you have said sounds reasonable and honest. If you were desirous of making trouble, it would be the simplest thing in the world to send as many of your kind as you wished. Of course, the whole affair must be placed before the Council—"

"Then it is hopeless—the Council could not possibly accede—"

"And you expect me to do what you do not believe the highest governmental authority in the System would do?" Brender exclaimed.

"It is inherent in the nature of a democracy that it cannot gamble with the lives of its citizens. We have such a government here; and its members have already informed us that, in a similar condition, they would not consider releasing an unknown beast upon their people. Individuals, however, can gamble where governments must not. You have agreed that our argument is logical. What system do men follow if not that of logic?"

The Controller, through its robot, watched Brender's thoughts alertly. It saw doubt and uncertainty, opposed by a very human desire to help, based upon the logical conviction that it was safe. Probing his mind, it saw swiftly that it was unwise, in dealing with men, to trust too much to logic. It pressed on:

"To an individual we can offer—everything. In a minute, with your permission, we shall transfer this ship to Mars; not in thirty days, but in thirty seconds. The knowledge of how this is done will remain with you. Arrived at Mars, you will find yourself the only living person who knows the whereabouts of the ancient city of Li, of which the vault of the beast is the central tower. In this city will be found literally billions of dollars' worth of treasure made of ultimate metal; and according to the laws of Earth, fifty percent will be yours. Your fortune re-established, you will be able to return to Earth this very day, and reclaim your former wife, and your position. Poor silly child, she loves you still, but the iron conventions and training of her youth leave her no alternative. If she were older, she would have the character to defy those conventions. You must save her from herself. Will you do it?"

Brender was as white as a sheet, his hands clenching and unclenching. Malevolently, the thing watched the flaming thought sweeping through his brain—the memory of a pudgy white hand closing over Pamela's fingers, watched the reaction of Brender to its words, those words that expressed exactly what he had always thought. Brender looked up with tortured eyes.

"Yes," he said, "I'll do what I can."

A bleak range of mountains fell away into a valley of reddish gray sand. The thin winds of Mars blew a mist of sand against the building. *Such* a building! At a distance, it had looked merely big. A bare hundred feet projected above the desert, a hundred feet of length and *fifteen hundred feet of diameter*. Literally thousands of feet must extend beneath the restless ocean of sand to make the perfect balance of form, the graceful flow, the fairylike beauty, which the long-dead Martians demanded of all their constructions, however massive. Brender felt suddenly small and insignificant as the rockets of his spacesuit pounded him along a few feet above the sand toward that incredible building.

At close range the ugliness of sheer size was miraculously lost in the wealth of the decorative. Columns and pilasters assembled in groups and clusters, broke up the façades, gathered and dispersed again restlessly. The flat surfaces of wall and roof melted into a wealth of ornaments and imitation stucco work, vanished and broke into a play of light and shade.

The creature floated beside Brender; and its Controller said: "I see that you have been giving considerable thought to the problem, but this robot seems incapable of following abstract thoughts, so I have no means of knowing the source of your speculations. I see however that you seem to be satisfied."

"I think I've got the answer," said Brender, "but first I wish to see the time lock. Let's climb."

They rose into the sky, dipping over the lip of the building. Brender saw a vast flat expanse; and in the center— He caught his breath!

The meager light from the distant sun of Mars shone down on a structure located at what seemed the exact center of the great door. The structure was about fifty feet high, and seemed nothing less than a series of quadrants coming together at the center, which was a metal arrow pointing straight up.

The arrow head was not solid metal. Rather it was as if the metal had divided in two parts, then curved together again. But not quite together. About a foot separated the two sections of metal. But that foot was bridged by a vague, thin, green flame of ieis force.

"The time lock!" Brender nodded. "I thought it would be something like that, though I expected it would be bigger, more substantial."

"Do not be deceived by its fragile appearance," answered the thing. "Theoretically, the strength of ultimate metal is infinite; and the ieis force can only be affected by the universal I have mentioned. Exactly what the effect will be, it is impossible to say as it involves the temporary derangement of the whole number system upon which that particular area of space is built. But now tell us what to do."

"Very well." Brender eased himself onto a bank of sand, and cut off his antigravity plates. He lay on his back, and stared thoughtfully into the blue-black sky. For the time being all doubts, worries and fears were gone from him, forced out by sheer will power. He began to explain:

"The Martian mathematic, like that of Euclid and Pythagoras, was based on endless magnitude. Minus numbers were beyond their philosophy. On Earth, however, beginning with Descartes, an analytical mathematic was evolved. Magnitude and perceivable dimensions were replaced by that of variable relation-values between positions in space.

"For the Martians, there was only one number between 1 and 3. Actually, the totality of such numbers is an infinite aggregate. And with the introduction of the idea of the square root of minus one—or *i*—and the complex numbers, mathematics definitely ceased to be a simple thing of magnitude, perceivable in pictures. Only the intellectual step from the infinitely small quantity to the lower limit of every possible finite magnitude brought out the conception of a variable number which oscillated beneath any assignable number that was not zero.

"The prime number, being a conception of pure magnitude, had no reality in *real* mathematics, but in this case was rigidly bound up with the reality of the ieis force. The Martians knew ieis as a pale-green flow about a foot in length and developing say a thousand horsepower. (It was actually 12.171 inches and 1021.23 horsepower, but that was unimportant.) The power produced never varied, the length never varied, from year end to year end, for tens of thousands of years. The Martians took the length as their basis of measurement, and called it one 'el'; they took the power as their basis of power and called it one 'rb.' And because of the absolute invariability of the flow they knew it was eternal.

"They knew furthermore that nothing could be eternal without being prime; their whole mathematic was based on numbers which could be factored, that is, disintegrated, destroyed, rendered less than they had been; and numbers which could not be factored, disintegrated or divided into smaller groups.

"Any number which could be factored was incapable of being infinite. Contrariwise, the infinite number must be prime.

"Therefore, they built a lock and integrated it along a line of ieis, to operate when the ieis ceased to flow—which would be at the end of Time, provided it was not interfered with. To prevent interference, they buried the motivating mechanism of the flow in ultimate metal, which could not be destroyed or corroded in any way. According to their mathematic, that settled it."

"But you have the answer," said the voice of the thing eagerly.

"Simply this: The Martians set a value on the flow of one 'rb.' If you interfere with that flow to no matter what small degree, you no longer have an 'rb.' You have something less. The flow, which is a universal, becomes automatically less than a universal, less than infinite. The prime number ceases to be prime. Let us suppose that you interfere with it to the extent of *infinity minus one*. You will then have a number divisible by two. As a matter of fact, the number, like most large numbers, will immediately break into thousands of pieces, i.e., it will be divisible by tens of thousands of smaller numbers. If the present time falls anywhere near one of those breaks, the door would open then. In other words, the door will open immediately if you can so interfere with the flow that one of the factors occurs in immediate time."

"That is very clear," said the Controller with satisfaction and the image of Brender was smiling triumphantly. "We shall now use this robot to manufacture a universal; and Kalorn shall be free very shortly." He laughed aloud. "The poor robot is protesting violently at the thought of being destroyed, but after all it is only a machine, and not a very good one at that. Besides, it is interfering with my proper reception of your thoughts. Listen to it scream, as I twist it into shape."

The cold-blooded words chilled Brender, pulled him from the heights of his abstract thought. Because of the prolonged intensity of his thinking, he saw with sharp clarity something that had escaped him before.

"Just a minute," he said. "How is it that the robot, introduced from your world, is living at the same time rate as I am, whereas Kalorn continues to live at your time rate?"

"A very good question." The face of the robot was twisted into a triumphant sneer, as the Controller continued. "Because, my dear Brender, you have been duped. It is true that Kalorn is living in our time rate, but that was due to a shortcoming in our machine. The machine which Kalorn built, while large enough to transport him, was not large enough in its adaptive mechanism to adapt him to each new space as he entered it. With the result that he was transported but not adapted. It was possible of course for us, his helpers, to transport such a small thing as the robot, though we have no more idea of the machine's construction than you have.

"In short, we can use what there is of the machine, but the secret of its construction is locked in the insides of our own particular ultimate metal, and in the brain of Kalorn. Its invention by Kalorn was one of those accidents which, by the law of averages, will not be repeated in millions of our years. Now that you have provided us with the method of bringing Kalorn back, we shall be able to build innumerable interspace machines. Our purpose is to control all spaces, all worlds—particularly those which are inhabited. We intend to be absolute rulers of the entire Universe."

The ironic voice ended; and Brender lay in his prone position the prey of horror. The horror was twofold, partly due to the Controller's monstrous plan, and partly due to the thought that was pulsing in his brain. He groaned, as he realized that warning thought must be ticking away on the automatic receiving brain of the robot. "Wait," his thought was saying, "that adds a new factor. Time—"

There was a scream from the creature as it was forcibly dissolved. The scream choked to a sob, then silence. An intricate machine of shining metal lay there on that great gray-brown expanse of sand and ultimate metal.

The metal glowed; and then the machine was floating in the air. It rose to the top of the arrow, and settled over the green flame of ieis.

Brender jerked on his antigravity screen, and leaped to his feet. The violent action carried him some hundred feet into the air. His rockets sputtered into staccato fire, and he clamped his teeth against the pain of acceleration.

Below him, the great door began to turn, to unscrew, faster and faster, till it was like a flywheel. Sand flew in all directions in a miniature storm.

At top acceleration, Brender darted to one side.

Just in time. First, the robot machine was flung off that tremendous wheel by sheer centrifugal power. Then the door came off, and, spinning now at an incredible rate, hurtled straight into the air, and vanished into space.

A puff of black dust came floating up out of the blackness of the vault. Suppressing his horror, yet perspiring from awful relief, he rocketed to where the robot had fallen into the sand.

Instead of glistening metal, a time-dulled piece of junk lay there. The dull metal flowed sluggishly and assumed a quasi-human shape. The flesh remained gray and in little rolls as if it were ready to fall apart from old age. The thing tried to stand up on wrinkled, horrible legs, but finally lay still. Its lips moved, mumbled:

"I caught your warning thought, but I didn't let them know. Now, Kalorn is dead. They realized the truth as it was happening. End of Time came—"

It faltered into silence; and Brender went on: "Yes, end of Time came when the flow became momentarily less than eternal—came at the factor point which occurred a few minutes ago."

"I was . . . only partly . . . within its . . . influence, Kalorn all the way. . . . Even if they're lucky . . . will be years before . . . they invent another machine . . . and one of their years is billions . . . of yours. . . . I didn't tell them. . . . I caught your thought . . . and kept it . . . from them—"

"But why did you do it? Why?"

"Because they were hurting me. They were going to destroy me. Because . . . I liked . . . being human. I was . . . somebody!"

The flesh dissolved. It flowed slowly into a pool of lavalike gray. The lava crinkled, split into dry, brittle pieces. Brender touched one of the pieces. It crumbled into a fine powder of gray dust. He gazed out across that grim, deserted valley of sand, and said aloud, pityingly:

"Poor Frankenstein."

He turned toward the distant spaceship, toward the swift trip to Earth. As he climbed out of the ship a few minutes later, one of the first persons he saw was Pamela.

She flew into his arms. "Oh, Jim, Jim," she sobbed. "What a fool I've been. When I heard what had happened, and realized you were in danger, I— Oh, Jim!"

Later, he would tell her about their new fortune.

First published: 1940

THE EXALTED

by L. Sprague de Camp

THE STORKLIKE MAN WITH THE GRAY GOATEE SHUFFLED THE TWELVE black billets about on the table top. "Try it again," he said.

The undergraduate sighed. "O. K., Professor Methuen." He looked apprehensively at Johnny Black, sitting across the table with one claw on the button of the stop clock. Johnny returned the look impassively through the spectacles perched on his yellowish muzzle.

"Go," said Ira Methuen.

Johnny depressed the button. The undergraduate started the second run of his wiggly-block test. The twelve billets formed a kind of three-dimensional jigsaw puzzle; when assembled they would make a cube. But the block had originally been sawn apart on wavy, irregular lines, so that the twelve billets had to be put together just so.

The undergraduate fiddled with the billets, trying this one and that one against one he held in his hand. The clock ticked round. In four minutes he had all but one in place. This one, a corner piece, simply would not fit. The undergraduate wiggled it and pushed it. He looked at it closely and tried again. But its maladjustment remained.

The undergraduate gave up. "What's the trick?" he asked.

Methuen reversed the billet end for end. It fitted.

"Oh, heck," said the undergraduate. "I could have gotten it if it hadn't been for Johnny."

Instead of being annoyed, Johnny Black twitched his mouth in a bear's equivalent of a grin. Methuen asked the student why.

"He distracts me somehow. I know he's friendly and all that, but . . . it's this way, sort of. Here I come to Yale to get to be a psychologist. I hear all about testing animals, chimps and bears and such. And when I get here I find a bear testing *me*. It's kind of upsetting."

"That's all right," said Methuen. "Just what we wanted. We're after, not your wiggly-block score by itself, but the effect of Johnny's presence

84

on people taking the test. We're getting Johnny's distraction factor—his ability to distract people. We're also getting the distraction factor of a lot of other things, such as various sounds and smells. I didn't tell you sooner because the knowledge might have affected your performance."

"I see. Do I still get my five bucks?"

"Of course. Good day, Kitchell. Come on, Johnny; we've just got time to make Psychobiology 100. We'll clean up the stuff later."

On the way out of Methuen's office, Johnny asked: "Hey, boss! Do you feer any effec' yet?"

"Not a bit," said Methuen. "I think my original theory was right: that the electrical resistance of the gaps between human neurons is already as low as it can be, so the Methuen injections won't have any appreciable effect on a human being. Sorry, Johnny, but I'm afraid your boss won't become any great genius as a result of trying a dose of his own medicine."

The Methuen treatment had raised Johnny's intelligence from that of a normal black bear to that of—or more exactly to the equivalent of that of—a human being. It had enabled him to carry out those spectacular coups in the Virgin Islands and the Central Park Zoo. It had also worked on a number of other animals in the said zoo, with regrettable results.

Johnny grumbled in his urso-American accent: "Stirr, I don't sink it is smart to teach a crass when you are furr of zat stuff. You never know—"

But they had arrived. The class comprised a handful of grave graduate students, on whom Johnny's distraction factor had little effect.

Ira Methuen was not a good lecturer. He put in too many uh's and er's, and tended to mumble. Besides, Psychobiology 100 was an elementary survey, and Johnny was pretty well up in the field himself. So he settled himself to a view of the Grove Street Cemetery across the street, and to melancholy reflections on the short life span of his species compared with that of men.

"*Ouch!*"

R. H. Wimpus, B.S., '68, jerked his backbone from its normally nonchalant arc into a quivering reflex curve. His eyes were wide with mute indignation.

Methuen was saying: "—whereupon it was discovered that the . . . uh . . . paralysis of the pes resulting from excision of the corresponding motor area of the cortex was much more lasting among the Simiidae than among the other catarrhine primates; that it was more lasting among these than among the platyrrhines— Mr. Wimpus?"

"Nothing," said Wimpus. "I'm sorry."

"And that the platyrrhines, in turn, suffered more than the lemuroids and tarsioids. When—"

"*Unh!*" Another graduate student jerked upright. While Methuen paused with his mouth open, a third man picked a small object off the floor and held it up.

"Really, gentlemen," said Methuen, "I thought you'd outgrown such amusements as shooting rubber bands at each other. As I was saying when—"

Wimpus gave another grunt and jerk. He glared about him. Methuen tried to get his lecture going again. But, as rubber bands from nowhere continued to sting the necks and ears of the listeners, the classroom organization visibly disintegrated like a lump of sugar in a cup of weak tea.

Johnny had put on his spectacles and was peering about the room. But he was no more successful than the others in locating the source of the bombardment.

He slid off his chair and shuffled over to the light switch. The daylight through the windows left the rear end of the classroom dark. As soon as the lights went on, the source of the elastics was obvious. A couple of the graduates pounced on a small wooden box on the shelf beside the projector.

The box gave out a faint whir, and spat rubber bands through a slit, one every few seconds. They brought it up and opened it on Methuen's lecture table. Inside was a mass of machinery apparently made of the parts of a couple of alarm clocks and a lot of hand-whittled wooden cams and things.

"My, my," said Methuen. "A most ingenious contraption, isn't it?"

The machine ran down with a click. While they were still examining it, the bell rang.

Methuen looked out the window. A September rain was coming up. Ira Methuen pulled on his topcoat and his rubbers and took his umbrella from the corner. He never wore a hat. He went out and headed down Prospect Street, Johnny padding behind.

"Hi!" said a young man, a fat young man in need of a haircut. "Got any news for us, Professor Methuen?"

"I'm afraid not, Bruce," replied Methuen. "Unless you call Ford's giant mouse news."

"What? What giant mouse?"

"Dr. Ford has produced a three-hundred-pound mouse by orthogonal mutation. He had to alter its morphological characteristics—"

"Its *what?*"

"Its shape, to you. He had to alter it to make it possible for it to live—"

"Where? Where is it?"

"Osborn Labs. If—" But Bruce Inglehart was gone up the hill toward the science buildings. Methuen continued: "With no war on, and New Haven as dead a town as it always has been, they have to come to us for news, I suppose. Come on, Johnny. Getting garrulous in my old age."

A passing dog went crazy at the sight of Johnny, snarling and yelping. Johnny ignored it. They entered Woodbridge Hall.

Dr. Wendell Cook, president of Yale University, had Methuen sent in at once. Johnny, excluded from the sanctum, went up to the president's secretary. He stood up and put his paws on her desk. He leered—you have to see a bear leer to know how it is done—and said: "How about it, kid?"

Miss Prescott, an unmistakable Boston spinster, smiled at him. "Suttinly, Johnny. Just a moment." She finished typing a letter, opened a drawer, and took out a copy of Hecht's "Fantazius Mallare." This she gave Johnny. He curled up on the floor, adjusted his glasses, and read.

After a while he looked up, saying: "Miss Prescott, I am halfway srough zis, and I stirr don't see why zey cawr it obscene. I sink it is just durr. Can't you get me a *rearry* dirty book?"

"Well, really, Johnny, I don't run a pornography shop, you know. Most people find that quite strong enough."

Johnny sighed. "Peopre get excited over ze funnies' sings."

Meanwhile, Methuen was closeted with Cook and Dalrymple, the prospective endower, in another of those interminable and indecisive conferences. R. Hanscom Dalrymple looked like a statue that the sculptor had never gotten around to finishing. The only expression the steel chairman ever allowed himself was a canny, secretive smile. Cook and Methuen had a feeling he was playing them on the end of a long and well-knit fish line made of U. S. Federal Reserve notes. It was not because he wasn't willing to part with the damned endowment, but because he enjoyed the sensation of power over these oh-so-educated men. And in the actual world, one doesn't lose one's temper and tell Croesus what to do with his loot. One says: "Yes, Mr. Dalrymple. My, my, that *is* a brilliant suggestion, Mr. Dalrymple! Why didn't we think of it ourselves?" Cook and Methuen were both old hands at this game. Methuen, though otherwise he considered Wendell Cook a pompous ass, admired the president's endowment-snagging ability. After all, wasn't Yale University named after a retired merchant on the basis of a gift of five hundred and sixty-two pounds twelve shillings?

"Say, Dr. Cook," said Dalrymple, "why don't you come over to the Taft and have lunch on me for a change? You, too, Professor Methuen."

The academics murmured their delight and pulled on their rubbers. On the way out Dalrymple paused to scratch Johnny behind the ears. Johnny put his book away, keeping the title on the cover out of sight, and restrained himself from snapping at the steel man's hand. Dalrymple meant well enough, but Johnny did not like people to take such liberties with his person.

So three men and a bear slopped down College Street. Cook paused now and then, ignoring the sprinkle, to make studied gestures toward one or another of the units of the great soufflé of Georgian and Collegiate Gothic architecture. He explained this and that. Dalrymple merely smiled his blank little smile.

Johnny, plodding behind, was the first to notice that passing undergraduates were pausing to stare at the president's feet. The word "feet" is meant literally. For Cook's rubbers were rapidly changing into a pair of enormous pink bare feet.

Cook himself was quite unconscious of it, until quite a group of undergraduates had collected. These gave forth the catarrhal snorts of men trying unsuccessfully not to laugh. By the time Cook had followed their stares and looked down, the metamorphosis was complete. That he should be startled was only natural. The feet were startling enough. His face gradually matched the feet in redness, making a cheerful note of color in the gray landscape.

R. Hanscom Dalrymple lost his reserve for once. His howls did nothing to save prexy's now-apoplectic face. Cook finally stooped and pulled off the rubbers. It transpired that the feet had been painted on the outside of the rubbers and covered over with lampblack. The rain had washed the lampblack off.

Wendell Cook resumed his walk to the Hotel Taft in gloomy silence. He held the offensive rubbers between thumb and finger as if they were something unclean and loathsome. He wondered who had done this dastardly deed. There hadn't been any undergraduates in his office for some days, but you never wanted to underestimate the ingenuity of undergraduates. He noticed that Ira Methuen was wearing rubbers of the same size and make as his own. But he put suspicion in that direction out of his mind before it had fully formed. Certainly Methuen wouldn't play practical jokes with Dalrymple around, when he'd be the head of the new Department of Biophysics when—if—Dalrymple came through with the endowment.

The next man to suspect that the Yale campus was undergoing a severe pixilation was John Dugan, the tall thin one of the two campus cops. He was passing Christ Church—which is so veddy high-church Episcopal that they refer to Charles I of England as St. Charles the Martyr—on his way to his lair in Phelps Tower. A still small voice spoke in his ear: "Beware, John Dugan! Your sins will find you out!"

Dugan jumped and looked around. The voice repeated its message. There was nobody within fifty feet of Dugan. Moreover, he could not think of any really serious sins he had committed lately. The only people in sight were a few undergraduates and Professor Methuen's educated black bear, trailing after his boss as usual. There was nothing for John Dugan to suspect but his own sanity.

R. Hanscom Dalrymple was a bit surprised at the grim earnestness of the professors in putting away their respective shares of the James Pierpont dinner. They were staying the eternal gnaw of hunger that afflicts those who depend on a college commissary for sustenance. Many of them suspected a conspiracy among college cooks to see that the razor edge wasn't taken off students' and instructors' intellects by overfeeding. They knew that conditions were much the same in most colleges.

Dalrymple sipped his coffee and looked at his notes. Presently Cook would get up and say a few pleasant nothings. Then he would announce Dalrymple's endowment, which was to be spent in building a Dalrymple Biophysical Laboratory and setting up a new department. Everybody would applaud and agree that biophysics had floated in the void between the domains of the departments of zoölogy, psychology, and the physiological sciences long enough. Then Dalrymple would get up and clear his throat and say—though in much more dignified language: "Shucks, fellas, it really isn't nothing."

Dr. Wendell Cook duly got up, beamed out over the ranked shirt fronts, and said his pleasant nothings. The professors exchanged nervous looks when he showed signs of going off into his favorite oration, there-is-no-conflict-between-science-and-religion. They had heard it before.

He was well launched into Version 3A of this homily, when he began to turn blue in the face. It was not the dark purplish-gray called loosely "blue" that appears on the faces of stranglees, but a bright, cheerful cobalt. Now, such a color is all very well in a painting of a ship sailing under a clear blue sky, or in the uniform of a movie-theater doorman. But it is distinctly out of place in the face of a college president. Or so felt the professors. They leaned this way and that, their boiled shirts bulging, popping and gaping as they did so, and whispered.

Cook frowned and continued. He was observed to sniff the air as if he smelled something. Those at the speakers' table detected a slight smell of acetone. But that seemed hardly an adequate explanation of the robin's-egg hue of their prexy's face. The color was now quite solid on the face proper. It ran up into the area where Cook's hair would have been if he had had some. His collar showed a trace of it, too.

Cook, on his part, had no idea of why the members of his audience were swaying in their seats like saplings in a gale and whispering. He thought it very rude of them. But his frowns had no effect. So presently he cut Version 3A short. He announced the endowment in concise, businesslike terms, and paused for the expected thunder of applause.

There was none. To be exact, there was a feeble patter that nobody in his right mind would call a thunder of anything.

Cook looked at R. Hanscom Dalrymple, hoping that the steel man would not be insulted. Dalrymple's face showed nothing. Cook assumed that this was part of his general reserve. The truth was that Dalrymple was too curious about the blue face to notice the lack of applause. When Cook introduced him to the audience, it took him some seconds to pull himself together.

He started rather lamely: "Gentlemen and members of the Yale faculty . . . uh . . . I mean, of course, you're *all* gentlemen . . . I am reminded of a story about the poultry farmer who got married— I mean, I'm not reminded of *that* story, but the one about the divinity student who died and went to—" Here Dalrymple caught the eye of the dean of the divinity school. He tacked again: "Maybe I'd . . . uh . . . better tell the one about the Scotchman who got lost on his way home and—"

It was not a bad story, as such things go. But it got practically no laughter. Instead, the professors began swaying, like a roomful of boiled-shirted Eastern ascetics at their prayers, and whispering again.

Dalrymple could put two and two together. He leaned over and hissed into Cook's ear: "Is there anything wrong with me?"

"Yes, your face has turned green."

"Green?"

"Bright green. Like grass. Nice young grass."

"Well, you might like to know that yours is blue."

Both men felt their faces. There was no doubt; they were masked with coatings of some sort of paint, still wet.

Dalrymple whispered: "What kind of gag is this?"

"I don't know. Better finish your speech."

Dalrymple tried. But his thoughts were scattered beyond recovery. He made a few remarks about how glad he was to be there amid the elms and ivy and traditions of old Eli, and sat down. His face looked rougher-hewn than ever. If a joke had been played on him—well, he hadn't signed any checks yet.

The lieutenant governor of the State of Connecticut was next on the list. Cook shot a question at him. He mumbled: "But if I'm going to turn a funny color when I get up—"

The question of whether his honor should speak was never satisfactorily settled. For at that moment a thing appeared on one end of the speakers' table. It was a beast the size of a St. Bernard. It looked rather the way a common bat would look if, instead of wings, it had arms with disk-shaped pads on the ends of the fingers. Its eyes were as big around as luncheon plates.

There was commotion. The speaker sitting nearest the thing fell over backward. The lieutenant govenor crossed himself. An English zoölogist put on his glasses and said: "By Jove, a spectral tarsier! But a bit large, what?"

A natural-sized tarsier would fit in your hand comfortably, and is rather cute if a bit spooky. But a tarsier the size of this one is not the kind of thing one can glance at and then go on reading the adventures of Alley Oop. It breaks one's train of thought. It disconcerts one. It may give one the screaming meemies.

This tarsier walked gravely down the twenty feet of table. The diners were too busy going away from there to observe that it upset no tumblers and kicked no ashtrays about; that it was, in fact, slightly transparent. At the other end of the table it vanished.

Johnny Black's curiosity wrestled with his better judgment. His curiosity told him that all these odd happenings had taken place in the presence of Ira Methuen. Therefore, Ira Methuen was at least a promising suspect. "So what?" said his better judgment. "He's the only man you have a real affection for. If you learned that he was the pixie in the case, you wouldn't expose him, would you? Better keep your muzzle out of this."

But in the end his curiosity won, as usual. The wonder was that his better judgment kept on trying.

He got hold of Bruce Inglehart. The young reporter had a reputation for discretion.

Johnny explained: "He gave himserf ze Messuen treatment—you know, ze spinar injection—to see what it would do to a man. Zat was a week ago. Should have worked by now. But he says it had no effec'. Maybe not. But day after ze dose, awr zese sings start happening. Very eraborate jokes. Kind a crazy scientific genius would do. If it's him, I mus' stop him before he makes rear troubre. You wirr he'p me?"

"Sure, Johnny. Shake on it."

Johnny extended his paw.

It was two nights later that Durfee Hall caught fire. Yale had been discussing the erasure of this singularly ugly and useless building for forty years. It had been vacant for some time, except for the bursar's office in the basement.

About ten o'clock an undergraduate noticed little red tongues of flame crawling up the roof. He gave the alarm at once. The New Haven fire department was not to be blamed for the fact that the fire spread as fast as if the building had been soaked in kerosene. By the time they, and about a thousand spectators, had arrived, the whole center of the building was going up with a fine roar and crackle. The assistant bursar bravely dashed into the building and reappeared with an armful of papers, which later turned out to be a pile of quite useless examination forms. The fire department squirted enough water onto the burning section to put out Mount Vesuvius. Some of them climbed ladders at the ends of the building to chop holes in the roof.

The water seemed to have no effect. So the fire department called for some more apparatus, connected up more hoses, and squirted more water. The undergraduates yelled:

"Rah, rah, fire department! Rah, rah, fire! Go get 'em, department! Hold that line, fire!"

Johnny Black bumped into Bruce Inglehart, who was dodging about in the crowd with a pad and pencil, trying to get information for his New Haven *Courier*. Inglehart asked Johnny whether he knew anything.

Johnny, in his deliberate manner, said: "I know one sing. Zat is ze firs' hetress fire I have seen."

Inglehart looked at Johnny, then at the conflagration. "My gosh!" he said. "We ought to feel the radiation here, oughtn't we? Heatless fire is right. Another superscientific joke, you suppose?"

"We can rook around," said Johnny. Turning their backs on the conflagration, they began searching among the shrubbery and railings along Elm Street.

"Woof!" said Johnny. "Come here, Bruce!"

In a patch of shadow stood Professor Ira Methuen and a tripod whereon was mounted a motion-picture projector. It took Johnny a second to distinguish which was which.

Methuen seemed uneasily poised on the verge of flight. He said:

"Why, hello, Johnny, why aren't you asleep? I just found this . . . uh . . . this projector—"

Johnny, thinking fast, slapped the projector with his paw. Methuen caught it as it toppled. Its whir ceased. At the same instant the fire went out, vanished utterly. The roar and crackle still came from the place where the fire had been. But there was no fire. There was not even a burned place in the roof, off which gallons of water were still pouring. The fire department looked at one another foolishly.

While Johnny's and Inglehart's pupils were still expanding in the sudden darkness, Methuen and his projector vanished. They got a glimpse of him galloping around the College Street corner, lugging the tripod. They ran after him. A few undergraduates ran after Johnny and Inglehart, being moved by the instinct that makes dogs chase automobiles.

They caught sight of Methuen, lost him, and caught sight of him again. Inglehart was not built for running, and Johnny's eyesight was an affair of limited objectives. Johnny opened up when it became evident that Methuen was heading for the old Phelps mansion, where he, Johnny, and several unmarried instructors lived. Everybody in the house had gone to see the fire. Methuen dashed in the front door three jumps ahead of Johnny and slammed it in the bear's face.

Johnny padded around in the dark with the idea of attacking a window. But while he was making up his mind, something happened to the front steps under him. They became slicker than the smoothest ice. Down the steps went Johnny, *bump-bump-bump*.

Johnny picked himself up in no pleasant mood. So this was the sort of treatment he got from the one man— But then, he reflected, if Methuen was really crazy, you couldn't blame him.

Some of the undergraduates caught up with them. These crowded toward the mansion—until their feet went out from under them as if they were wearing invisible roller skates. They tried to get up, and fell again, sliding down the slight grade of the crown of the road into heaps in the gutter. They retired on hands and knees, their clothes showing large holes.

A police car drove up and tried to stop. Apparently neither brakes nor tires would hold. It skidded about, banged against the curb once, and finally stopped down the street beyond the slippery zone. The cop—he was a fairly important cop, a captain—got out and charged the mansion.

He fell down, too. He tried to keep going on hands and knees. But every time he applied a horizontal component of force to a hand or knee, the hand or knee simply slid backward. The sight reminded Johnny of the efforts of those garter snakes to crawl on the smooth concrete floor of the Central Park Zoo monkey house.

When the police captain gave up and tried to retreat, the laws of friction came back on. But when he stood up, all his clothes below the waist, except his shoes, disintegrated into a cloud of textile fibers.

"My word!" said the English zoölogist, who had just arrived. "Just like one of those Etruscan statues, don't you know!"

The police captain bawled at Bruce Inglehart: "Hey, you, for gossakes gimmie a handkerchief!"

"What's the matter; got a cold?" asked Inglehart innocently.

"No, you dope! You know what I want it for!"

Inglehart suggested that a better idea would be for the captain to use his coat as an apron. While the captain was knotting the sleeves behind his back, Inglehart and Johnny explained their version of the situation to him.

"Hm-m-m," said the captain. "We don't want nobody to get hurt, or the place to get damaged. But suppose he's got a death ray or sumpm?"

"I don't sink so," said Johnny. "He has not hurt anybody. Jus' prayed jokes."

The captain thought for a few seconds of ringing up headquarters and having them send an emergency truck. But the credit for overpowering a dangerous maniac singlehanded was too tempting. He said: "How'll we get into the place, if he can make everything so slippery?"

They thought. Johnny said: "Can you get one of zose sings wiss a wood stick and a rubber cup on end?"

The captain frowned. Johnny made motions. Inglehart said: "Oh, you mean the plumber's friend! Sure. You wait. I'll get one. See if you can find a key to the place."

The assault on Methuen's stronghold was made on all fours. The captain, in front, jammed the end of the plumber's friend against the rise of the lowest front step. If Methuen could abolish friction, he had not discovered how to get rid of barometric pressure. The rubber cup held, and the cop pulled himself, Inglehart and Johnny after him. By using the instrument on successive steps, they mounted them. Then the captain anchored them to the front door and pulled them up to it. He hauled himself to his feet by the door handle, and opened the door with a key borrowed from Dr. Wendell Cook.

At one window, Methuen crouched behind a thing like a surveyor's transit. He swiveled the thing toward them, and made adjustments. The captain and Inglehart, feeling their shoes grip the floor, gathered themselves to jump. But Methuen got the contraption going, and their feet went out from under them.

Johnny used his head. He was standing next to the door. He lay down, braced his hind feet against the door frame, and kicked out. His body whizzed across the frictionless floor and bowled over Methuen and his contraption.

The professor offered no more resistance. He seemed more amused than anything, despite the lump that was growing on his forehead. He said: "My, my, you fellows *are* persistent. I suppose you're going to take me off to some asylum. I thought you and you"—he indicated Inglehart and Johnny—"were friends of mine. Oh, well, it doesn't matter."

The captain growled: "What did you do to my pants?"

"Simple. My telelubricator here neutralizes the interatomic bonds on the surface of any solid on which the beam falls. So the surface, to a depth of a few molecules, is put in the condition of a supercooled liquid as long as the beam is focused on it. Since the liquid form of any compound will wet the solid form, you have perfect lubrication."

"But my pants—"

"They were held together by friction between the fibers, weren't they? And I have a lot more inventions like that. My soft-speaker and my three-dimensional projector, for instance, are—"

Inglehart interrupted: "Is that how you made that phony fire, and that whatchamacallit that scared the people at the dinner? With a three-dimensional projector?"

"Yes, of course, though, to be exact, it took two projectors at right angles, and a phonograph and amplifier to give the sound effect. It was amusing, wasn't it?"

"But," wailed Johnny, "why do you *do* zese sings? You trying to ruin your career?"

Methuen shrugged. "It doesn't matter. Nothing matters. Johnny, as you'd know if you were in my . . . uh . . . condition. And now, gentlemen, where do you want me to go? Wherever it is, I'll find something amusing there."

Dr. Wendell Cook visited Ira Methuen on the first day of his incarceration in the New Haven Hospital. In ordinary conversation Methuen seemed sane enough, and quite agreeable. He readily admitted that he had been the one responsible for the jokes. He explained: "I painted your and Dalrymple's face with a high-powered needle sprayer I invented. It's a most amusing little thing. Fits in your hand and discharges through a ring on your finger. With your thumb you can regulate the amount of acetone mixed in with the water, which in turn controls the surface tension and therefore the point at which the needle spray breaks up into droplets. I made the spray break up just before it reached your face. You were a sight, Cook, especially when you found out what was wrong with you. You looked almost as funny as the day I painted those feet on my rubbers and substituted them for yours. You react so beautifully to having your dignity pricked. You always were a pompous ass, you know."

Cook puffed out his cheeks and controlled himself. After all, the poor man was mad. These absurd outbursts about Cook's pompousness proved it. He said sadly: "Dalrymple's leaving tomorrow night. He was most displeased about the face-painting episode, and when he found that you were under observation, he told me that no useful purpose would be served by his remaining here. I'm afraid that's the end of our endowment. Unless you can pull yourself together and tell us what's happened to you and how to cure it."

Ira Methuen laughed. "Pull myself together? I am all in one piece, I assure you. And I've told you what's the matter with me, as you put it. I gave myself my own treatment. As for curing it, I wouldn't tell you how even if I knew. I wouldn't give up my present condition for anything. I at last realize that nothing really matters, including endowments. I shall be taken care of, and I will devote myself to amusing myself as I see fit."

Johnny had been haunting Cook's office all day. He waylaid the president when the latter returned from the hospital.

Cook told Johnny what had happened. He said: "He seems to be completely irresponsible. We'll have to get in touch with his son, and have a guardian appointed. And we'll have to do something about you, Johnny."

Johnny didn't relish the prospect of the "something." He knew he had no legal status other than that of a tamed wild animal. The fact that Methuen technically owned him was his only protection if somebody took a notion to shoot him during bear-hunting season. And he was not enthusiastic about Ralph Methuen. Ralph was a very average young schoolteacher without his father's scientific acumen or whimsical humor. Finding Johnny on his hands, his reaction would be to give Johnny to a zoo or something.

He put his paws on Miss Prescott's desk and asked: "Hey, good-rooking, wirr you cawr up Bruce Ingrehart at ze *Courier?*"

"Johnny," said the president's secretary, "you get fresher every day."

"Ze bad infruence of ze undergraduates. Wirr you cawr Mr. Ingrehart, beautifur?" Miss Prescott, who was not, did so.

Bruce Inglehart arrived at the Phelps mansion to find Johnny taking a shower. Johnny was also making a horrible bawling noise. *"Waaaaa!"* he howled. *"Hoooooooo! Yrrrrrrr! Waaaaaaa!"*

"Whatcha doing?" yelled Inglehart.

"Taking a bass," replied Johnny. *"Wuuuuuuh!"*

"Are you sick?"

"No. Jus' singing in bass. People sing whire taking bass; why shouldn't I? *Yaaaaaaaaaaa!*"

"Well, for Pete's sake don't. It sounds like you were having your throat cut. What's the idea of these bath towels spread all over the floor?"

"I show you." Johnny came out of the shower, lay down on the bath towels and rolled. When he was more or less dry, he scooped the towels up in his forepaws and hove them into a corner. Neatness was not one of Johnny's strong points.

He told Inglehart about the Methuen situation. "Rook here, Bruce," he said, "I sink I can fix him, but you wirr have to he'p me."

"O. K. Count me in."

Pop!

The orderly looked up from his paper. But none of the buttons showed a light. So, presumably, none of the patients wanted attention. He went back to his reading.

Pop!

It sounded a little like a breaking light bulb. The orderly sighed, put away his paper, and began prowling. As he approached the room of the mad professor, No. 14, he noticed a smell of limburger.

Pop!

There was no doubt that the noise came from No. 14. The orderly stuck his head in.

At one side of the room sat Ira Methuen. He held a contraption made of a length of glass rod and assorted wires. At the other side of the room, on the floor, lay a number of crumbs of cheese. A cockroach scuttled out of the shadows and made for the crumbs. Methuen sighted along his glass rod and pressed a button. *Pop!* A flash, and there was no more cockroach.

Methuen swung the rod toward the orderly. "Stand back, sir! I'm Buck Rogers, and this is my disintegrator!"

"Hey," said the orderly feebly. The old goof might be crazy, but after what happened to the roach— He ducked out and summoned a squad of interns.

But the interns had no trouble with Methuen. He tossed the contraption on the bed, saying: "If I thought it mattered, I'd raise a hell of a stink about cockroaches in a supposedly sanitary hospital."

One of the interns protested: "But I'm sure there aren't any here."

"What do you call that?" asked Methuen dryly, pointing at the shattered remains of one of his victims.

"It must have been attracted in from the outside by the smell of that cheese. *Phew!* Judson, clean up the floor. What *is* this, professor?" He picked up the rod and the flashlight battery attached to it.

Methuen waved a deprecating hand. "Nothing important. Just a little gadget I thought up. By applying the right e.m.f. to pure crown glass, it's possible to raise its index of refraction to a remarkable degree. The result is that light striking the glass is so slowed up that it takes weeks to pass through it in the ordinary manner. The light that is thus trapped can be released by making a small spark near the glass. So I simply lay the rod on the window sill all afternoon to soak up sunlight, a part of which is released by making a spark with that button. Thus I can shoot an hour's accumulated light-energy out the front end of the rod in a very small fraction of a second. Naturally when this beam hits an opaque object, it raises its temperature. So I've been amusing myself by luring the roaches in here and exploding them. You may have the thing; its charge is about exhausted."

The intern was stern. "That's a dangerous weapon. We can't let you play with things like that."

"Oh, can't you? Not that it matters, but I'm only staying here because I'm taken care of. I can walk out any time I like."

"No you can't, professor. You're under a temporary commitment for observation."

"That's all right, son. I still say I can walk out whenever I feel like it. I just don't care much whether I do or not." With which Methuen began tuning the radio by his bed, ignoring the interns.

Exactly twelve hours later, at 10 A.M., Ira Methuen's room in the hospital was found to be vacant. A search of the hospital failed to locate him. The only clue to his disappearance was the fact that his radio had been disemboweled. Tubes, wires, and condensers lay in untidy heaps on the floor.

The New Haven police cars received instructions to look for a tall, thin man with gray hair and goatee, probably armed with death rays, disintegrators, and all the other advanced weapons of fact and fiction.

For hours they scoured the city with screaming sirens. They finally located the menacing madman, sitting placidly on a park bench three blocks from the hospital and reading a newspaper. Far from resisting, he grinned at them and looked at his watch. "Three hours and forty-eight minutes. Not bad, boys, not bad, considering how carefully I hid myself."

One of the cops pounced on a bulge in Methuen's pocket. The bulge was made by another wire contraption. Methuen shrugged. "My hyperbolic solenoid. Gives you a conical magnetic field, and enables you to manipulate ferrous objects at a distance. I picked the lock of the door to the elevators with it."

When Bruce Inglehart arrived at the hospital about four, he was told Methuen was asleep. That was amended to the statement that Methuen was getting up, and could see a visitor in a few minutes. He found Methuen in a dressing gown.

Methuen said: "Hello, Bruce. They had me wrapped up in a wet sheet, like a mummy. It's swell for naps; relaxes you. I told 'em they could do it whenever they liked. I think they were annoyed about my getting out."

Inglehart was slightly embarrassed.

Methuen said: "Don't worry; I'm not mad at you. I realize that nothing matters, including resentments. And I've had a most amusing time here. Just watch them fizz the next time I escape."

"But don't you care about your future?" said Inglehart. "They'll transfer you to a padded cell at Middletown—"

Methuen waved a hand. "That doesn't bother me. I'll have fun there, too."

"But how about Johnny Black, and Dalrymple's endowment?"

"I don't give a damn what happens to them."

Here the orderly stuck his head in the door briefly to check up on this unpredictable patient. The hospital, being short-handed, was unable to keep a continuous watch on him.

Methuen continued: "Not that I don't like Johnny. But when you get a real sense of proportion, like mine, you realize that humanity is nothing but a sort of skin disease on a ball of dirt, and that no effort beyond subsistence, shelter, and casual amusement is worth while. The State of Connecticut is willing to provide the first two for me, so I shall devote myself to the third. What's that you have there?"

Inglehart thought, "They're right; he's become a childishly irresponsible scientific genius." Keeping his back to the door, the reporter brought out his family heirloom: a big silver pocket flask dating back to the fabulous prohibition period. His aunt Martha had left it to him, and he himself expected to will it to a museum.

"Apricot brandy," he murmured. Johnny had tipped him off to Methuen's tastes.

"Now, Bruce, that's something sensible. Why didn't you bring it out sooner, instead of making futile appeals to my sense of duty?"

The flask was empty. Ira Methuen sprawled in his chair. Now and then he passed a hand across his forehead. He said: "I can't believe it. I can't believe that I felt that way half an hour ago. O Lord, what have I done?"

"Plenty," said Inglehart.

Methuen was not acting at all drunk. He was full of sober remorse.

"I remember everything—those inventions that popped out of my mind, everything. But I didn't care. How did you know alcohol would counteract the Methuen injection?"

"Johnny figured it out. He looked up its effects, and discovered that in massive doses it coagulates the proteins in the nerve cells. He guessed it would lower their conductivity to counteract the increased conductivity through the gaps between them that your treatment causes."

"So," said Methuen, "when I'm sober I'm drunk, and when I'm drunk I'm sober. But what'll we do about the endowment—my new department and the laboratory and everything?"

"I don't know. Dalrymple's leaving tonight; he had to stay over a day on account of some trustee business. And they won't let you out for a while yet, even when they know about the alcohol counter-treatment. Better think of something quick, because the visiting period is pretty near up."

Methuen thought. He said: "I remember how all those inventions work, though I couldn't possibly invent any more of them unless I went back to the other condition." He shuddered. "There's the soft-speaker, for instance—"

"What's that?"

"It's like a loud-speaker, only it doesn't speak loudly. It throws a supersonic beam, modulated by the human voice to give the effect of audible sound-frequencies when it hits the human ear. Since you can throw a supersonic beam almost as accurately as you can throw a light beam, you can turn the soft-speaker on a person, who will then hear a still small voice in his ear apparently coming from nowhere. I tried it on Dugan one day. It worked. Could you do anything with that?"

"I don't know. Maybe."

"I hope you can. This is terrible. I thought I was perfectly sane and rational. Maybe I was— Maybe nothing *is* important. But I don't feel that way now, and I don't want to feel that way again—"

The omnipresent ivy, of which Yale is so proud, affords splendid handholds for climbing. Bruce Inglehart, keeping an eye peeled for campus cops, swarmed up the big tower at the corner of Bingham Hall. Below, in the dark, Johnny waited.

Presently the end of a clothesline came dangling down. Johnny inserted the hook in the end of the rope ladder into the loop in the end of the line. Inglehart hauled the ladder up and secured it, wishing that he and Johnny could change bodies for a while. That climb up the ivy had scared him and winded him badly. But he could climb ivy and Johnny couldn't.

The ladder creaked under Johnny's five hundred pounds. A few minutes later it slid slowly, jerkily up the wall, like a giant centipede. Then Inglehart, Johnny, ladder, and all were on top of the tower.

Inglehart got out the soft-speaker and trained the telescopic sight on the window of Dalrymple's room in the Taft, across the intersection of College and Chapel Streets. He found the yellow rectangle of light. He could see into about half the room. His heart skipped a few beats until a stocky figure moved into his field of vision. Dalrymple had not yet left. But he was packing a couple of suitcases.

Inglehart slipped the transmitter clip around his neck, so that the transmitter nestled against his larynx. The next time Dalrymple appeared, Inglehart focused the crosshairs on the steel man's head. He spoke: "Hanscom Dalrymple!" He saw the man stop suddenly. He repeated: "Hanscom Dalrymple!"

"Huh?" said Dalrymple. "Who the hell are you? Where the hell are you?" Inglehart could not hear him, of course, but he could guess.

Inglehart said, in solemn tones: "I am your conscience."

By now Dalrymple's agitation was evident even at that distance. Inglehart continued: "Who squeezed out all the common stockholders of Hephaestus Steel in that phony reorganization?" Pause. "You did, Hanscom Dalrymple!

"Who bribed a United States senator to swing the vote for a higher steel tariff, with fifty thousand dollars and a promise of fifty thousand more, which was never paid?" Pause. "You did, Hanscom Dalrymple!

"Who promised Wendell Cook the money for a new biophysics building, and then let his greed get the better of him and backed out on the thin excuse that the man who was to have headed the new department had had a nervous breakdown?" Pause, while Inglehart reflected that "nervous breakdown" was merely a nice way of saying "gone nuts." "You did, Hanscom Dalrymple!

"Do you know what'll happen to you if you don't atone, Dalrymple? You'll be reincarnated as a spider, and probably caught by a wasp and used as live fodder for her larvæ. How will you like that, *heh-heh?*

"What can you do to atone? Don't be a sap. Call up Cook. Tell him you've changed your mind, and are renewing your offer!" Pause. "Well, what are you waiting for? Tell him you're not only renewing it, but doubling it!" Pause. "Tell him—"

But at this point Dalrymple moved swiftly to the telephone. Inglehart said, "Ah, that's better, Dalrymple," and shut off the machine.

Johnny asked: "How did you know awr zose sings about him?"

"I got his belief in reincarnation out of his obit down at the shop. And one of our rewrite men who used to work in Washington says everybody down there knows about the other things. Only you can't print a thing like that unless you have evidence to back it up."

They lowered the rope ladder and reversed the process by which they had come up. They gathered up their stuff and started for the Phelps mansion. But as they rounded the corner of Bingham they almost ran into a familiar storklike figure. Methuen was just setting up another contraption at the corner of Welch.

"Hello," he said.

Man and bear gaped at him. Inglehart asked: "Did you escape again?"

"Uh-huh. When I sobered up and got my point of view back. It was easy, even though they'd taken my radio away. I invented a hypnotizer, using a light bulb and a rheostat made of wire from my mattress, and hypnotized the orderly into giving me his uniform and opening the doors for me. My, my, that *was* amusing."

"What are you doing now?" Inglehart became aware that Johnny's black pelt had melted off into the darkness.

"This? Oh, I dropped around home and knocked together an improved soft-speaker. This one'll work through masonry walls. I'm going to put all the undergraduates to sleep and tell 'em they're monkeys. When they wake up, it will be most amusing to see them running around on all fours and scratching and climbing the chandeliers. They're practically monkeys to begin with, so it shouldn't be difficult."

"But you can't, professor! Johnny and I just went to a lot of trouble getting Dalrymple to renew his offer. You don't want to let us down, do you?"

"What you and Johnny do doesn't matter to me in the slightest. Nothing matters. I'm going to have my fun. And don't try to interfere, Bruce." Methuen pointed another glass rod at Inglehart's middle. "You're a nice young fellow, and it would be too bad if I had to let you have three hours' accumulation of sun-ray energy all at once."

"But this afternoon you said—"

"I know what I said this afternoon. I was drunk and back in my old state of mind, full of responsibility and conscientiousness and such bunk. I'll never touch the stuff again if it has that effect on me. Only a man who has received the Methuen treatment can appreciate the futility of all human effort."

Methuen shrank back into the shadows as a couple of undergraduates passed. Then he resumed work on his contraption, using one hand and keeping Inglehart covered with the other. Inglehart, not knowing what else to do, asked him questions about the machine. Methuen responded with a string of technical jargon. Inglehart wondered desperately what to do. He was not an outstandingly brave young man, especially in the face of a gun or its equivalent. Methuen's bony hand never wavered. He made the adjustments on his machine mostly by feel.

"Now," he said, "that ought to be about right. This contains a tonic metronome that will send them a note of frequency of 349 cycles a second, with 68.4 pulses of sound a minute. This, for various technical reasons, has the maximum hypnotic effect. From here I can rake the colleges along College Street—" He made a final adjustment. "This will be the most amusing joke yet. And the cream of it is that, since Connecticut is determined to consider me insane, they can't do anything to me for it! Here goes, Bruce— *Phew*, has somebody started a still here, or what? I've been smelling and tasting alcohol for the last five minutes—*ouch!*"

The glass rod gave one dazzling flash, and then Johnny's hairy black body catapulted out of the darkness. Down went Ira Methuen, all the wind knocked out of him.

"Quick, Bruce!" barked Johnny. "Pick up zat needre sprayer I dropped. Unscrew ze container on ze bottom. Don't spirr it. Zen come here and pour it down his sroat!"

This was done, with Johnny holding Methuen's jaws apart with his claws, like Sampson slaying the lion, only conversely.

They waited a few minutes for the alcohol to take effect, listening for sounds that they had been discovered. But the colleges were silent save for the occasional tick of a typewriter.

Johnny explained: "I ran home and got ze needre sprayer from his room. Zen I got Webb, ze research assistant in biophysics, to ret me in ze raboratory for ze arcohor. Zen I try to sneak up and squirt a spray in his mouse whire he talks. I get some in, but I don't get ze sprayer adjusted right, and ze spray hit him before it breaks up, and stings him. I don't have fingers, you know. So we have to use what ze books cawr brute force."

Methuen began to show signs of normalcy. As without his glass rod he was just a harmless old professor, Johnny let him up. His words tumbled out: "I'm so glad you did, Johnny—you saved my reputation, maybe my life. Those fatheads at the hospital wouldn't believe I had to be kept full of alcohol, so, of course, I sobered up and went crazy again—maybe they'll believe now. Come on; let's get back there quickly. If they haven't discovered my absence, they might be willing to keep this last escape quiet. When they let me out, I'll work on a permanent cure for the Methuen treatment. I'll find it, if I don't die of stomach ulcers from all the alcohol I'll have to drink."

Johnny waddled up Temple Street to his home, feeling rather smug about his ability as a fixer. Maybe Methuen, sober, was right about the futility of it all. But if such a philosophy led to the upsetting of Johnny's pleasant existence, Johnny preferred Methuen drunk.

He was glad Methuen would soon be well and coming home. Methuen was the only man he had any sentimental regard for. But as long as Methuen was shut up, Johnny was going to take advantage of that fact. When he reached the Phelps mansion, instead of going directly in, he thrust a foreleg around behind the hedge next to the wall. It came out with a huge slab of chewing tobacco. Johnny bit off about half the slab, thrust the rest back in its cache, and went in, drooling happily a little at each step. Why not?

First published: 1941

NIGHTFALL

by Isaac Asimov

If the stars should appear one night in a thousand years, how would men believe and adore, and preserve for many generations the remembrance of the city of God!—Emerson

ATON 77, DIRECTOR OF SARO UNIVERSITY, THRUST OUT A BELLIGERENT lower lip and glared at the young newspaperman in a hot fury.

Theremon 762 took that fury in his stride. In his earlier days, when his now widely syndicated column was only a mad idea in a cub reporter's mind, he had specialized in "impossible" interviews. It had cost him bruises, black eyes, and broken bones; but it had given him an ample supply of coolness and self-confidence.

So he lowered the outthrust hand that had been so pointedly ignored and calmly waited for the aged director to get over the worst. Astronomers were queer ducks, anyway, and if Aton's actions of the last two months meant anything, this same Aton was the queer-duckiest of the lot.

Aton 77 found his voice, and though it trembled with restrained emotion, the careful, somewhat pedantic, phraseology, for which the famous astronomer was noted, did not abandon him.

"Sir," he said, "you display an infernal gall in coming to me with that impudent proposition of yours."

The husky telephotographer of the Observatory, Beenay 25, thrust a tongue's tip across dry lips and interposed nervously, "Now, sir, after all—"

The director turned to him and lifted a white eyebrow. "Do not interfere, Beenay. I will credit you with good intentions in bringing this man here; but I will tolerate no insubordination now."

Theremon decided it was time to take a part. "Director Aton, if you'll let me finish what I started saying I think—"

"I don't believe, young man," retorted Aton, "that anything you could say now would count much as compared with your daily columns of these last two months. You have led a vast newspaper campaign against the efforts of myself and my colleagues to organize the world against the menace which it is now too late to avert. You have done your best with your highly personal attacks to make the staff of this Observatory objects of ridicule."

The director lifted the copy of the Saro City *Chronicle* on the table and shook it at Theremon furiously. "Even a person of your well-known impudence should have hesitated before coming to me with a request that he be allowed to cover today's events for his paper. Of all newsmen, you!"

Aton dashed the newspaper to the floor, strode to the window and clasped his arms behind his back.

"You may leave," he snapped over his shoulder. He stared moodily out at the skyline where Gamma, the brightest of the planet's six suns, was setting. It had already faded and yellowed into the horizon mists, and Aton knew he would never see it again as a sane man.

He whirled. "No, wait, come here!" He gestured peremptorily. "I'll give you your story."

The newsman had made no motion to leave, and now he approached the old man slowly. Aton gestured outward, "Of the six suns, only Beta is left in the sky. Do you see it?"

The question was rather unnecessary. Beta was almost at zenith; its ruddy light flooding the landscape to an unusual orange as the brilliant rays of setting Gamma died. Beta was at aphelion. It was small; smaller than Theremon had ever seen it before, and for the moment it was undisputed ruler of Lagash's sky.

Lagash's own sun, Alpha, the one about which it revolved, was at the antipodes; as were the two distant companion pairs. The red dwarf Beta—Alpha's immediate companion—was alone, grimly alone.

Aton's upturned face flushed redly in the sunlight. "In just under four hours," he said, "civilization, as we know it, comes to an end. It will do so because, as you see, Beta is the only sun in the sky." He smiled grimly. "Print that! There'll be no one to read it."

"But if it turns out that four hours pass—and another four—and nothing happens?" asked Theremon softly.

"Don't let that worry you. Enough will happen."

"Granted! And *still*—if nothing happens?"

For a second time, Beenay 25 spoke, "Sir, I think you ought to listen to him."

Theremon said, "Put it to a vote, Director Aton."

There was a stir among the remaining five members of the Observatory staff, who till now had maintained an attitude of wary neutrality.

"That," stated Aton flatly, "is not necessary." He drew out his pocket watch. "Since your good friend, Beenay, insists so urgently, I will give you five minutes. Talk away."

"Good! Now, just what difference would it make if you allowed me to take down an eyewitness account of what's to come? If your prediction comes true, my presence won't hurt; for in that case my column would never be written. On the other hand, if nothing comes of it, you will just have to expect ridicule or worse. It would be wise to leave that ridicule to friendly hands."

Aton snorted. "Do you mean yours when you speak of friendly hands?"

"Certainly!" Theremon sat down and crossed his legs. "My columns may have been a little rough at times, but I gave you people the benefit of the doubt every time. After all, this is not the century to preach 'the end of the world is at hand' to Lagash. You have to understand that people don't believe the 'Book of Revelations' any more, and it annoys them to have scientists turn about face and tell us the Cultists are right after all—"

"No such thing, young man," interrupted Aton. "While a great deal of our data has been supplied us by the Cult, our results contain none of the Cult's mysticism. Facts are facts, and the Cult's so-called 'mythology' *has* certain facts behind it. We've exposed them and ripped away their mystery. I assure you that the Cult hates us now worse than you do."

"I don't hate you. I'm just trying to tell you that the public is in an ugly humor. They're angry."

Aton twisted his mouth in derision. "Let them be angry."

"Yes, but what about tomorrow?"

"There'll be no tomorrow!"

"But if there is. Say that there is—just to see what happens. That anger might take shape into something serious. After all, you know, business has taken a nose dive these last two months. Investors don't really believe the world is coming to an end, but just the same they're being cagy with their money until it's all over. Johnny Public doesn't believe you, either, but the new spring furniture might as well wait a few months—just to make sure.

"You see the point. Just as soon as this is all over, the business interests will be after your hide. They'll say that if crackpots—begging your pardon —can upset the country's prosperity any time they want simply by making some cockeyed prediction—it's up to the planet to prevent them. The sparks will fly, sir."

The director regarded the columnist sternly. "And just what were you proposing to do to help the situation?"

"Well," grinned Theremon, "I was proposing to take charge of the publicity. I can handle things so that only the ridiculous side will show. It would be hard to stand, I admit, because I'd have to make you all out to be a bunch of gibbering idiots, but if I can get people laughing at you, they might forget to be angry. In return for that, all my publisher asks is an exclusive story."

Beenay nodded and burst out, "Sir, the rest of us think he's right. These last two months we've considered everything but the million-to-one chance that there is an error somewhere in our theory or in our calculations. We ought to take care of that, too."

There was a murmur of agreement from the men grouped about the table, and Aton's expression became that of one who found his mouth full of something bitter and couldn't get rid of it.

"You may stay if you wish, then. You will kindly refrain, however, from hampering us in our duties in any way. You will also remember that I am in charge of all activities here, and in spite of your opinions as expressed in your columns, I will expect full co-operation and full respect—"

His hands were behind his back, and his wrinkled face thrust forward determinedly as he spoke. He might have continued indefinitely but for the intrusion of a new voice.

"Hello, hello, hello!" It came in a high tenor, and the plump cheeks of the newcomer expanded in a pleased smile. "What's this morgue-like atmosphere about here? No one's losing his nerve, I hope."

Aton started in consternation and said peevishly, "Now what the devil are you doing here, Sheerin? I thought you were going to stay behind in the Hideout."

Sheerin laughed and dropped his tubby figure into a chair. "Hideout be blowed! The place bored me. I wanted to be here, where things are getting hot. Don't you suppose I have my share of curiosity? I want to see these Stars the Cultists are forever speaking about." He rubbed his hands and added in a soberer tone, "It's freezing outside. The wind's enough to hang icicles on your nose. Beta doesn't seem to give any heat at all, at the distance it is."

The white-haired director ground his teeth in sudden exasperation,

"Why do you go out of your way to do crazy things, Sheerin? What kind of good are you around here?"

"What kind of good am I around there?" Sheerin spread his palms in comical resignation. "A psychologist isn't worth his salt in the Hideout. They need men of action and strong, healthy women that can breed children. Me? I'm a hundred pounds too heavy for a man of action, and I wouldn't be a success at breeding children. So why bother them with an extra mouth to feed? I feel better over here."

Theremon spoke briskly, "Just what is the Hideout, sir?"

Sheerin seemed to see the columnist for the first time. He frowned and blew his ample cheeks out, "And just who in Lagash are you, redhead?"

Aton compressed his lips and then muttered sullenly, "That's Theremon 762, the newspaper fellow. I suppose you've heard of him."

The columnist offered his hand. "And, of course, you're Sheerin 501 of Saro University. I've heard of *you*." Then he repeated, "What is this Hideout, sir?"

"Well," said Sheerin, "we have managed to convince a few people of the validity of our prophecy of—er—doom, to be spectacular about it, and those few have taken proper measures. They consist mainly of the immediate members of the families of the Observatory staff, certain of the faculty of Saro University and a few outsiders. Altogether, they number about three hundred, but three quarters are women and children."

"I see! They're supposed to hide where the Darkness and the—er— Stars can't get at them, and then hold out when the rest of the world goes poof."

"If they can. It won't be easy. With all of mankind insane; with the great cities going up in flames—environment will not be conducive to survival. But they have food, water, shelter, and weapons—"

"They've got more," said Aton. "They've got all our records, except for what we will collect today. Those records will mean everything to the next cycle, and *that's* what must survive. The rest can go hang."

Theremon whistled a long, low whistle and sat brooding for several minutes. The men about the table had brought out a multichess board and started a six-member game. Moves were made rapidly and in silence. All eyes bent in furious concentration on the board. Theremon watched them intently and then rose and approached Aton, who sat apart in whispered conversation with Sheerin.

"Listen," he said, "let's go somewhere where we won't bother the rest of the fellows. I want to ask some questions."

The aged astronomer frowned sourly at him, but Sheerin chirped up, "Certainly. It will do me good to talk. It always does. Aton was telling me

about your ideas concerning world reaction to a failure of the prediction—
and I agree with you. I read your column pretty regularly, by the way,
and as a general thing I like your views."

"Please, Sheerin," growled Aton.

"Eh? Oh, all right. We'll go into the next room. It has softer chairs,
anyway."

There *were* softer chairs in the next room. There were also thick red
curtains on the windows and a maroon carpet on the floor. With the
bricky light of Beta pouring in, the general effect was one of dried blood.

Theremon shuddered, "Say, I'd give ten credits for a decent dose of
white light for just a second. I wish Gamma or Delta were in the sky."

"What are your questions?" asked Aton. "Please remember that our
time is limited. In a little over an hour and a quarter we're going upstairs,
and after that there will be no time for talk."

"Well, here it is." Theremon leaned back and folded his hands on
his chest. "You people seem so all-fired serious about this that I'm beginning to believe you. Would you mind explaining what it's all about?"

Aton exploded, "Do you mean to sit there and tell me that you've been
bombarding us with ridicule without even finding out what we've been
trying to say?"

The columnist grinned sheepishly. "It's not that bad, sir. I've got the
general idea. You say that there is going to be a world-wide Darkness
in a few hours and that all mankind will go violently insane. What I
want now is the science behind it."

"No, you don't. No, you don't," broke in Sheerin. "If you ask Aton
for that—supposing him to be in the mood to answer at all—he'll trot out
pages of figures and volumes of graphs. You won't make head or tail of it.
Now if you were to ask *me*, I could give you the layman's standpoint."

"All right; I ask you."

"Then first I'd like a drink." He rubbed his hands and looked at Aton.

"Water?" grunted Aton.

"Don't be silly!"

"Don't you be silly. No alcohol today. It would be too easy to get my
men drunk. I can't afford to tempt them."

The psychologist grumbled wordlessly. He turned to Theremon, im-
paled him with his sharp eyes, and began.

"You realize, of course, that the history of civilization on Lagash displays a cyclic character—but I mean, *cyclic!*"

"I know," replied Theremon cautiously, "that that is the current
archæological theory. Has it been accepted as a fact?"

"Just about. In this last century it's been generally agreed upon. This cyclic character is—or, rather, was—one of *the* great mysteries. We've located series of civilizations, nine of them definitely, and indications of others as well, all of which have reached heights comparable to our own, and all of which, without exception, were destroyed by fire at the very height of their culture.

"And no one could tell why. All centers of culture were thoroughly gutted by fire, with nothing left behind to give a hint as to the cause."

Theremon was following closely. "Wasn't there a Stone Age, too?"

"Probably, but as yet, practically nothing is known of it, except that men of that age were little more than rather intelligent apes. We can forget about that."

"I see. Go on!"

"There have been explanations of these recurrent catastrophes, all of a more or less fantastic nature. Some say that there are periodic rains of fire; some that Lagash passes through a sun every so often; some even wilder things. But there is one theory, quite different from all of these, that has been handed down over a period of centuries."

"I know. You mean this myth of the 'Stars' that the Cultists have in their 'Book of Revelations.' "

"Exactly," rejoined Sheerin with satisfaction. "The Cultists said that every two thousand and fifty years Lagash entered a huge cave, so that all the suns disappeared, and there came *total darkness all over the world!* And then, they say, things called Stars appeared, which robbed men of their souls and left them unreasoning brutes, so that they destroyed the civilization they themselves had built up. Of course, they mix all this up with a lot of religio-mystic notions, but that's the central idea."

There was a short pause in which Sheerin drew a long breath. "And now we come to the Theory of Universal Gravitation." He pronounced the phrase so that the capital letters sounded—and at that point Aton turned from the window, snorted loudly, and stalked out of the room.

The two stared after him, and Theremon said, "What's wrong?"

"Nothing in particular," replied Sheerin. "Two of the men were due several hours ago and haven't shown up yet. He's terrifically short-handed, of course, because all but the really essential men have gone to the Hideout."

"You don't think the two deserted, do you?"

"Who? Faro and Yimot? Of course not. Still, if they're not back within the hour, things would be a little sticky." He got to his feet suddenly, and his eyes twinkled. "Anyway, as long as Aton is gone—"

Tiptoeing to the nearest window, he squatted, and from the low window box beneath withdrew a bottle of red liquid that gurgled suggestively when he shook it.

"I *thought* Aton didn't know about this," he remarked as he trotted back to the table. "Here! We've only got one glass so, as the guest, you can have it. I'll keep the bottle." And he filled the tiny cup with judicious care.

Theremon rose to protest, but Sheerin eyed him sternly. "Respect your elders, young man."

The newsman seated himself with a look of pain and anguish on his face. "Go ahead, then, you old villain."

The psychologist's Adam's apple wobbled as the bottle upended, and then, with a satisfied grunt and a smack of the lips, he began again. "But what do you know about gravitation?"

"Nothing, except that it is a very recent development, not too well established, and that the math is so hard that only twelve men in Lagash are supposed to understand it."

"*Tcha!* Nonsense! Boloney! I can give you all the essential math in a sentence. The Law of Universal Gravitation states that there exists a cohesive force among all bodies of the universe, such that the amount of this force between any two given bodies is proportional to the product of their masses divided by the square of the distance between them."

"Is that all?"

"That's enough! It took four hundred years to develop it."

"Why that long? It sounded simple enough, the way you said it."

"Because great laws are not divined by flashes of inspiration, whatever you may think. It usually takes the combined work of a world full of scientists over a period of centuries. After Genovi 41 discovered that Lagash rotated about the sun Alpha, rather than vice versa—and that was four hundred years ago—astronomers have been working. The complex motions of the six suns were recorded and analyzed and unwoven. Theory after theory was advanced and checked and counter-checked and modified and abandoned and revived and converted to something else. It was a devil of a job."

Theremon nodded thoughtfully and held out his glass for more liquor. Sheerin grudgingly allowed a few ruby drops to leave the bottle.

"It was twenty years ago," he continued after remoistening his own throat, "that it was finally demonstrated that the Law of Universal Gravitation accounted exactly for the orbital motions of the six suns. It was a great triumph."

Sheerin stood up and walked to the window, still clutching his bottle,

"And now we're getting to the point. In the last decade, the motions of Lagash about Alpha were computed according to gravity, and *it did not account for the orbit observed*; not even when all perturbations due to the other suns were included. Either the law was invalid, or there was another, as yet unknown, factor involved."

Theremon joined Sheerin at the window and gazed out past the wooded slopes to where the spires of Saro City gleamed bloodily on the horizon. The newsman felt the tension of uncertainty grow within him as he cast a short glance at Beta. It glowered redly at zenith, dwarfed and evil.

"Go ahead, sir," he said softly.

Sheerin replied, "Astronomers stumbled about for years, each proposed theory more untenable than the one before—until Aton had the inspiration of calling in the Cult. The head of the Cult, Sor 5, had access to certain data that simplified the problem considerably. Aton set to work on a new track.

"What if there were another nonluminous planetary body such as Lagash? If there were, you know, it would shine only by reflected light, and if it were composed of bluish rock, as Lagash itself largely is, then, in the redness of the sky, the eternal blaze of the suns would make it invisible—drown it out completely."

Theremon whistled, "What a screwy idea!"

"You think *that's* screwy? Listen to this: Suppose this body rotated about Lagash at such a distance and in such an orbit and had such a mass that its attraction would exactly account for the deviations of Lagash's orbit from theory—do you know what would happen?"

The columnist shook his head.

"Well, sometimes this body would get in the way of a sun." And Sheerin emptied what remained in the bottle at a draft.

"And it does, I suppose," said Theremon flatly.

"Yes! But only one sun lies in its plane of revolutions." He jerked a thumb at the shrunken sun above. "Beta! And it has been shown that the eclipse will occur only when the arrangement of the suns is such that Beta is alone in its hemisphere and at maximum distance, at which time the moon is invariably at minimum distance. The eclipse that results, with the moon seven times the apparent diameter of Beta, covers all of Lagash and lasts well over half a day, so that no spot on the planet escapes the effects. *That eclipse comes once every two thousand and forty-nine years.*"

Theremon's face was drawn into an expressionless mask. "And that's my story?"

The psychologist nodded. "That's all of it. First the eclipse—which will start in three quarters of an hour—then universal Darkness, and, maybe, these mysterious Stars—then madness, and end of the cycle."

He brooded. "We had two months' leeway—we at the Observatory—and that wasn't enough time to persuade Lagash of the danger. Two centuries might not have been enough. But our records are at the Hideout, and today we photograph the eclipse. The next cycle will *start off* with the truth, and when the *next* eclipse comes, mankind will at last be ready for it. Come to think of it, that's part of your story, too."

A thin wind ruffled the curtains at the window as Theremon opened it and leaned out. It played coldly with his hair as he stared at the crimson sunlight on his hand. Then he turned in sudden rebellion.

"What is there in Darkness to drive *me* mad?"

Sheerin smiled to himself as he spun the empty liquor bottle with abstracted motions of his hand. "Have you ever experienced Darkness, young man?"

The newsman leaned against the wall and considered. "No. Can't say I have. But I know what it is. Just—uh—" He made vague motions with his fingers, and then brightened. "Just no light. Like in caves."

"Have you ever been in a cave?"

"In a *cave*! Of course not!"

"I thought not. *I* tried last week—just to see—but I got out in a hurry. I went in until the mouth of the cave was just visible as a blur of light, with black everywhere else. I never thought a person my weight could run that fast."

Theremon's lip curled. "Well, if it comes to that, I guess I wouldn't have run, if I had been there."

The psychologist studied the young man with an annoyed frown. "My, don't you talk big! I dare you to draw the curtain."

Theremon looked his surprise and said, "What for? If we had four or five suns out there we might want to cut the light down a bit for comfort, but now we haven't enough light as it is."

"That's the point. Just draw the curtain; then come here and sit down."

"All right." Theremon reached for the tasseled string and jerked. The red curtain slid across the wide window, the brass rings hissing their way along the crossbar, and a dusk-red shadow clamped down on the room.

Theremon's footsteps sounded hollowly in the silence as he made his way to the table, and then they stopped halfway. "I can't see you, sir," he whispered.

"Feel your way," ordered Sheerin in a strained voice.

"But I can't see you, sir." The newsman was breathing harshly. "I can't see anything."

"What did you expect?" came the grim reply. "Come here and sit down!"

The footsteps sounded again, waveringly, approaching slowly. There was the sound of someone fumbling with a chair. Theremon's voice came thinly, "Here I am. I feel . . . *ulp* . . . all right."

"You like it, do you?"

"N-no. It's pretty awful. The walls seem to be—" He paused. "They seem to be closing in on me. I keep wanting to push them away. But I'm not going *mad*! In fact, the feeling isn't as bad as it was."

"All right. Draw the curtain back again."

There were cautious footsteps through the dark, the rustle of Theremon's body against the curtain as he felt for the tassel, and then the triumphant *ro-o-o-osh* of the curtain slithering back. Red light flooded the room, and with a cry of joy Theremon looked up at the sun.

Sheerin wiped the moisture off his forehead with the back of a hand and said shakily, "And that was just a dark room."

"It can be stood," said Theremon lightly.

"Yes, a dark room can. But were you at the Jonglor Centennial Exposition two years ago?"

"No, it so happens I never got around to it. Six thousand miles was just a bit too much to travel, even for the exposition."

"Well, I was there. You remember hearing about the 'Tunnel of Mystery' that broke all records in the amusement area—for the first month or so, anyway?"

"Yes. Wasn't there some fuss about it?"

"Very little. It was hushed up. You see, that Tunnel of Mystery was just a mile-long tunnel—with no lights. You got into a little open car and jolted along through Darkness for fifteen minutes. It was very popular—while it lasted."

"Popular?"

"Certainly. There's a fascination in being frightened *when it's part of a game*. A baby is born with three instinctive fears: of loud noises, of falling, and of the absence of light. That's why it's considered so funny to jump at someone and shout 'Boo!' That's why it's such fun to ride a roller coaster. And that's why that Tunnel of Mystery started cleaning up. People came out of that Darkness shaking, breathless, half dead with fear, but they kept on paying to get in."

"Wait a while, I remember now. Some people came out dead, didn't they? There were rumors of that after it shut down."

The psychologist snorted. "Bah! Two or three died. That was nothing! They paid off the families of the dead ones and argued the Jonglor City Council into forgetting it. After all, they said, if people with weak hearts want to go through the tunnel, it was at their own risk—and besides, it wouldn't happen again. So they put a doctor in the front office and had every customer go through a physical examination before getting into the car. That actually *boosted* ticket sales."

"Well, then?"

"But, you see, there was something else. People sometimes came out in perfect order, except that they refused to go into buildings—any buildings; including palaces, mansions, apartment houses, tenements, cottages, huts, shacks, lean-tos, and tents."

Theremon looked shocked. "You mean they refused to come in out of the open. Where'd they sleep?"

"In the open."

"They should have *forced* them inside."

"Oh, they did, they did. Whereupon these people went into violent hysterics and did their best to bat their brains out against the nearest wall. Once you got them inside, you couldn't keep them there without a strait jacket and a shot of morphine."

"They must have been crazy."

"Which is exactly what they were. One person out of every ten who went into that tunnel came out that way. They called in the psychologists, and we did the only thing possible. We closed down the exhibit." He spread his hands.

"What was the matter with these people?" asked Theremon finally.

"Essentially the same thing that was the matter with you when you thought the walls of the room were crushing in on you in the dark. There is a psychological term for mankind's instinctive fear of the absence of light. We call it 'claustrophobia,' because the lack of light is always tied up with inclosed places, so that fear of one is fear of the other. You see?"

"And those people of the tunnel?"

"Those people of the tunnel consisted of those unfortunates whose mentality did not quite possess the resiliency to overcome the claustrophobia that overtook them in the Darkness. Fifteen minutes without light is a long time; you only had two or three minutes, and I believe you were fairly upset.

"The people of the tunnel had what is called a 'claustrophobic fixation.'

Their latent fear of Darkness and inclosed places had crystallized and become active, and, as far as we can tell, permanent. *That's* what fifteen minutes in the dark will do."

There was a long silence, and Theremon's forehead wrinkled slowly into a frown. "I don't believe it's that bad."

"You mean you don't want to believe," snapped Sheerin. "You're afraid to believe. Look out the window!"

Theremon did so, and the psychologist continued without pausing, "Imagine Darkness—everywhere. No light, as far as you can see. The houses, the trees, the fields, the earth, the sky—*black*! And Stars thrown in, for all I know—whatever *they* are. Can you conceive it?"

"Yes, I can," declared Theremon truculently.

And Sheerin slammed his fist down upon the table in sudden passion. "You lie! You can't conceive that. Your brain wasn't built for the conception any more than it was built for the conception of infinity or of eternity. You can only talk about it. A fraction of the reality upsets you, and when the real thing comes, your brain is going to be presented with a phenomenon outside its limits of comprehension. You will go mad, completely and permanently! There is no question of it!"

He added sadly, "And another couple of millenniums of painful struggle comes to nothing. Tomorrow there won't be a city standing unharmed in all Lagash."

Theremon recovered part of his mental equilibrium. "That doesn't follow. I still don't see that I can go loony just because there isn't a Sun in the sky—but even if I did, and everyone else did, how does that harm the cities? Are we going to blow them down?"

But Sheerin was angry, too. "If you were in Darkness, what would you want more than anything else; what would it be that every instinct would call for? Light, damn you, *light*!"

"Well?"

"And how would you get light?"

"I don't know," said Theremon flatly.

"What's the *only* way to get light, short of the sun?"

"How should I know?"

They were standing face to face and nose to nose.

Sheerin said, "You burn something, mister. Ever see a forest fire? Ever go camping and cook a stew over a wood fire? Heat isn't the only thing burning wood gives off, you know. It gives off light, and people know that. And when it's dark they want light, and they're going to *get it*."

"So they burn wood?"

"So they burn whatever they can get. They've got to have light. They've got to burn something, and wood isn't handy—so they'll burn whatever is nearest. They'll have their light—and every center of habitation goes up in flames!"

Eyes held each other as though the whole matter were a personal affair of respective will powers, and then Theremon broke away wordlessly. His breathing was harsh and ragged, and he scarcely noted the sudden hubbub that came from the adjoining room behind the closed door.

Sheerin spoke, and it was with an effort that he made it sound matter-of-fact. "I think I heard Yimot's voice. He and Faro are probably back. Let's go in and see what kept them."

"Might as well!" muttered Theremon. He drew a long breath and seemed to shake himself. The tension was broken.

The room was in an uproar, with members of the staff clustering about two young men who were removing outer garments even as they parried the miscellany of questions being thrown at them.

Aton bustled through the crowd and faced the newcomers angrily. "Do you realize that it's less than half an hour before deadline. Where have you two been?"

Faro 24 seated himself and rubbed his hands. His cheeks were red with the outdoor chill. "Yimot and I have just finished carrying through a little crazy experiment of our own. We've been trying to see if we couldn't construct an arrangement by which we could simulate the appearance of Darkness and Stars so as to get an advance notion as to how it looked."

There was a confused murmur from the listeners, and a sudden look of interest entered Aton's eyes. "There wasn't anything said of this before. How did you go about it?"

"Well," said Faro, "the idea came to Yimot and myself long ago, and we've been working it out in our spare time. Yimot knew of a low one-story house down in the city with a domed roof—it had once been used as a museum, I think. Anyway, we bought it—"

"Where did you get the money?" interrupted Aton peremptorily.

"Our bank accounts," grunted Yimot 70. "It cost two thousand credits." Then, defensively, "Well, what of it? Tomorrow, two thousand credits will be two thousand pieces of paper. That's all."

"Sure," agreed Faro. "We bought the place and rigged it up with black velvet from top to bottom so as to get as perfect a Darkness as possible. Then we punched tiny holes in the ceiling and through the roof and covered them with little metal caps, all of which could be shoved aside simultaneously at the close of a switch. At least, we didn't do that part ourselves; we got a carpenter and an electrician and some others—money didn't count. The point was that we could get the light to shine through those holes in the roof, so that we could get a starlike effect."

Not a breath was drawn during the pause that followed. Aton said stiffly:

"You had no right to make a private—"

Faro seemed abashed. "I know, sir—but, frankly, Yimot and I thought the experiment was a little dangerous. If the effect really worked, we half expected to go mad—from what Sheerin says about all this, we thought that would be rather likely. We wanted to take the risk ourselves. Of course, if we found we could retain sanity, it occurred to us that we might develop immunity to the real thing, and then expose the rest of you to the same thing. But things didn't work out at all—"

"Why, what happened?"

It was Yimot who answered. "We shut ourselves in and allowed our eyes to get accustomed to the dark. It's an extremely creepy feeling because the total Darkness makes you feel as if the walls and ceiling are crushing in on you. But we got over that and pulled the switch. The caps fell away and the roof glittered all over with little dots of light—"

"Well?"

"Well—nothing. That was the whacky part of it. Nothing happened. It was just a roof with holes in it, and that's just what it looked like. We tried it over and over again—that's what kept us so late—but there just isn't any effect at all."

There followed a shocked silence, and all eyes turned to Sheerin, who sat motionless, mouth open.

Theremon was the first to speak. "You know what this does to this whole theory you've built up, Sheerin, don't you?" He was grinning with relief.

But Sheerin raised his hand. "Now wait a while. Just let me think this through." And then he snapped his fingers, and when he lifted his head there was neither surprise nor uncertainty in his eyes. "Of course—"

He never finished. From somewhere up above there sounded a sharp clang, and Beenay, starting to his feet, dashed up the stairs with a "What the devil!"

The rest followed after.

Things happened quickly. Once up in the dome, Beenay cast one horrified glance at the shattered photographic plates and at the man bending over them; and then hurled himself fiercely at the intruder, getting a death grip on his throat. There was a wild threshing, and as others of the staff joined in, the stranger was swallowed up and smothered under the weight of half a dozen angry men.

Aton came up last, breathing heavily. "Let him up!"

There was a reluctant unscrambling and the stranger, panting harshly, with his clothes torn and his forehead bruised, was hauled to his feet. He had a short yellow beard curled elaborately in the style affected by the Cultists.

Beenay shifted his hold to a collar grip and shook the man savagely. "All right, rat, what's the idea? These plates—"

"I wasn't after *them*," retorted the Cultist coldly. "That was an accident."

Beenay followed his glowering stare and snarled, "I see. You were after the cameras themselves. The accident with the plates was a stroke of luck for you, then. If you had touched Snapping Bertha or any of the others, you would have died by slow torture. As it is—" He drew his fist back.

Aton grabbed his sleeve. "Stop that! Let him go!"

The young technician wavered, and his arm dropped reluctantly. Aton pushed him aside and confronted the Cultist. "You're Latimer, aren't you?"

The Cultist bowed stiffly and indicated the symbol upon his hip. "I am Latimer 25, adjutant of the third class to his serenity, Sor 5."

"And"—Aton's white eyebrows lifted—"you were with his serenity when he visited me last week, weren't you?"

Latimer bowed a second time.

"Now, then, what do you want?"

"Nothing that you would give me of your own free will."

"Sor 5 sent you, I suppose—or is this your own idea?"

"I won't answer that question."

"Will there be any further visitors?"

"I won't answer that, either."

Aton glanced at his timepiece and scowled. "Now, man, what is it your master wants of me. I have fulfilled my end of the bargain."

Latimer smiled faintly, but said nothing.

"I asked him," continued Aton angrily, "for data only the Cult could supply, and it was given to me. For that, thank you. In return, I promised to prove the essential truth of the creed of the Cult."

"There was no need to prove that," came the proud retort. "It stands proven by the 'Book of Revelations.'"

"For the handful that constitute the Cult, yes. Don't pretend to mistake my meaning. I offered to present scientific backing for your beliefs. And I did!"

The Cultist's eyes narrowed bitterly. "Yes, you did—with a fox's subtlety, for your pretended explanation backed our beliefs, and at the same time removed all necessity for them. You made of the Darkness and of the Stars a natural phenomenon, and removed all its real significance. That was blasphemy."

"If so, the fault isn't mine. The facts exist. What can I do but state them?"

"Your 'facts' are a fraud and a delusion."

Aton stamped angrily. "How do *you* know?"

And the answer came with the certainty of absolute faith. "I *know!*"

The director purpled and Beenay whispered urgently. Aton waved him silent. "And what does Sor 5 want us to do. He still thinks, I suppose, that in trying to warn the world to take measures against the menace of madness, we are placing innumerable souls in jeopardy. We aren't succeeding, if that means anything to him."

"The attempt itself has done harm enough, and your vicious effort to gain information by means of your devilish instruments must be stopped. We obey the will of the Stars, and I only regret that my clumsiness prevented me from wrecking your infernal devices."

"It wouldn't have done you too much good," returned Aton. "All our data, except for the direct evidence, we intend collecting right now, is already safely cached and well beyond possibility of harm." He smiled grimly. "But that does not affect your present status as an attempted burglar and criminal."

He turned to the men behind him. "Someone call the police at Saro City."

There was a cry of distaste from Sheerin. "Damn it, Aton, what's wrong with you? There's no time for that. Here"—he bustled his way forward—"let me handle this."

Aton stared down his nose at the psychologist. "This is not the time for your monkeyshines, Sheerin. Will you please let me handle this my own way? Right now you are a complete outsider here, and don't forget it."

Sheerin's mouth twisted eloquently. "Now why should we go to the impossible trouble of calling the police—with Beta's eclipse a matter of minutes from now—when this young man here is perfectly willing to pledge his word of honor to remain and cause no trouble whatsoever."

The Cultist answered promptly, "I will do no such thing. You're free to do what you want, but it's only fair to warn you that just as soon as I get my chance I'm going to finish what I came out here to do. If it's my word of honor you're relying on, you'd better call the police."

Sheerin smiled in a friendly fashion. "You're a determined cuss, aren't you? Well, I'll explain something. Do you see that young man at the window? He's a strong, husky fellow, quite handy with his fists, and he's an outsider besides. Once the eclipse starts there will be nothing for him to do except keep an eye on you. Besides him, there will be myself—a little too stout for active fisticuffs, but still able to help."

"Well, what of it?" demanded Latimer frozenly.

"Listen and I'll tell you," was the reply. "Just as soon as the eclipse starts, we're going to take you, Theremon and I, and deposit you in a little closet with one door, to which is attached one giant lock and no windows. You will remain there for the duration."

"And afterward," breathed Latimer fiercely, "there'll be no one to let me out. I know as well as you do what the coming of the Stars means—I know it far better than you. With all your minds gone, you are not likely to free me. Suffocation or slow starvation, is it? About what I might have expected from a group of scientists. But I don't give my word. It's a matter of principle, and I won't discuss it further."

Aton seemed perturbed. His faded eyes were troubled. "Really, Sheerin, locking him—"

"Please!" Sheerin motioned him impatiently to silence. "I don't think for a moment things will go that far. Latimer has just tried a clever little bluff, but I'm not a psychologist just because I like the sound of the word." He grinned at the Cultist. "Come now, you don't really think I'm trying anything as crude as slow starvation. My dear Latimer, if I lock you in the closet, you are not going to see the Darkness, and you are not going to see the Stars. It does not take much of a knowledge of the fundamental creed of the Cult to realize that for you to be hidden from the Stars when they appear means the loss of your immortal soul. Now, I believe you to be an honorable man. I'll accept your word of honor to make no further effort to disrupt proceedings if you'll offer it."

A vein throbbed in Latimer's temple, and he seemed to shrink within himself as he said thickly, "You have it!" And then he added with swift fury, "But it is my consolation that you will all be damned for your deeds of today." He turned on his heel and stalked to the high three-legged stool by the door.

Sheerin nodded to the columnist. "Take a seat next to him, Theremon —just as a formality. Hey, Theremon!"

But the newspaperman didn't move. He had gone pale to the lips.

"Look at that!" The finger he pointed toward the sky shook, and his voice was dry and cracked.

There was one simultaneous gasp as every eye followed the pointing finger and, for one breathless moment, stared frozenly.

Beta was chipped on one side!

The tiny bit of encroaching blackness was perhaps the width of a finger-nail, but to the staring watchers it magnified itself into the crack of doom.

Only for a moment they watched, and after that there was a shrieking confusion that was even shorter of duration and which gave way to an orderly scurry of activity—each man at his prescribed job. At the crucial moment there was no time for emotion. The men were merely scientists with work to do. Even Aton had melted away.

Sheerin said prosaically, "First contact must have been made fifteen minutes ago. A little early, but pretty good considering the uncertainties involved in the calculation." He looked about him and then tiptoed to Theremon, who still remained staring out the window, and dragged him away gently.

"Aton is furious," he whispered, "so stay away. He missed first contact on account of this fuss with Latimer, and if you get in his way he'll have you thrown out the window."

Theremon nodded shortly and sat down. Sheerin stared in surprise at him.

"The devil, man," he exclaimed, "you're shaking."

"Eh?" Theremon licked dry lips and then tried to smile. "I don't feel very well, and that's a fact."

The psychologist's eyes hardened. "You're not losing your nerve?"

"No!" cried Theremon in a flash of indignation. "Give me a chance, will you? I haven't really believed this rigmarole—not way down beneath, anyway—till just this minute. Give me a chance to get used to the idea. *You've* been preparing yourself for two months or more."

"You're right, at that," replied Sheerin thoughtfully. "Listen! Have you got a family—parents, wife, children?"

Theremon shook his head. "You mean the Hideout, I suppose. No, you don't have to worry about that. I have a sister, but she's two thousand miles away. I don't even know her exact address."

"Well, then, what about yourself? You've got time to get there, and they're one short anyway, since I left. After all, you're not needed here, and you'd make a darned fine addition—"

Theremon looked at the other wearily. "You think I'm scared stiff, don't you? Well, get this, mister, I'm a newspaperman and I've been assigned to cover a story. I intend covering it."

There was a faint smile on the psychologist's face. "I see. Professional honor, is that it?"

"You might call it that. But, man, I'd give my right arm for another bottle of that sockeroo juice even half the size of the one *you* hogged. If ever a fellow needed a drink, I do."

He broke off. Sheerin was nudging him violently. "Do you hear that? Listen!"

Theremon followed the motion of the other's chin and stared at the Cultist, who, oblivious to all about him, faced the window, a look of wild elation on his face, droning to himself the while in singsong fashion.

"What's he saying?" whispered the columnist.

"He's quoting 'Book of Revelations,' fifth chapter," replied Sheerin. Then, urgently, "Keep quiet and listen, I tell you."

The Cultist's voice had risen in a sudden increase of fervor:

" 'And it came to pass that in those days the Sun, Beta, held lone vigil in the sky for ever longer periods as the revolutions passed; until such time as for full half a revolution, it alone, shrunken and cold, shone down upon Lagash.

" 'And men did assemble in the public squares and in the highways, there to debate and to marvel at the sight, for a strange depression had seized them. Their minds were troubled and their speech confused, for the souls of men awaited the coming of the Stars.

" 'And in the city of Trigon, at high noon, Vendret 2 came forth and said unto the men of Trigon, "Lo, ye sinners! Though ye scorn the ways of righteousness, yet will the time of reckoning come. Even now the Cave approaches to swallow Lagash; yea, and all it contains."

" 'And even as he spoke the lip of the Cave of Darkness passed the edge of Beta so that to all Lagash it was hidden from sight. Loud were the cries of men as it vanished, and great the fear of soul that fell upon them.

" 'It came to pass that the Darkness of the Cave fell upon Lagash, and there was no light on all the surface of Lagash. Men were even as blinded, nor could one man see his neighbor, though he felt his breath upon his face.

" 'And in this blackness there appeared the Stars, in countless numbers, and to the strains of ineffable music of a beauty so wondrous that the very leaves of the trees turned to tongues that cried out in wonder.

" 'And in that moment the souls of men departed from them, and their abandoned bodies became even as beasts; yea, even as brutes of the wild; so that through the blackened streets of the cities of Lagash they prowled with wild cries.

" 'From the Stars there then reached down the Heavenly Flame, and where it touched, the cities of Lagash flamed to utter destruction, so that of man and of the works of man nought remained.

" 'Even then—' "

There was a subtle change in Latimer's tone. His eyes had not shifted, but somehow he had become aware of the absorbed attention of the other two. Easily, without pausing for breath, the timber of his voice shifted and the syllables became more liquid.

Theremon, caught by surprise, stared. The words seemed on the border of familiarity. There was an elusive shift in the accent, a tiny change in the vowel stress; nothing more—yet Latimer had become thoroughly unintelligible.

Sheerin smiled slyly. "He shifted to some old-cycle tongue, probably their traditional second cycle. That was the language in which the 'Book of Revelations' had originally been written, you know."

"It doesn't matter; I've heard enough." Theremon shoved his chair back and brushed his hair back with hands that no longer shook. "I feel much better now."

"You do?" Sheerin seemed mildly surprised.

"I'll say I do. I had a bad case of jitters just a while back. Listening to you and your gravitation and seeing that eclipse start almost finished me. But this"—he jerked a contemptuous thumb at the yellow-bearded Cultist—"*this* is the sort of thing my nurse used to tell me. I've been laughing at that sort of thing all my life. I'm not going to let it scare me *now*."

He drew a deep breath and said with a hectic gaiety, "But if I expect to keep on the good side of myself, I'm going to turn my chair away from the window."

Sheerin said, "Yes, but you'd better talk lower. Aton just lifted his head out of that box he's got it stuck into and gave you a look that should have killed you."

Theremon made a mouth. "I forgot about the old fellow." With elaborate care he turned the chair from the window, cast one distasteful look over his shoulder and said, "It has occurred to me that there must be considerable immunity against this Star madness."

The psychologist did not answer immediately. Beta was past its zenith now, and the square of bloody sunlight that outlined the window upon the floor had lifted into Sheerin's lap. He stared at its dusky color thoughtfully and then bent and squinted into the sun itself.

The chip in its side had grown to a black encroachment that covered a third of Beta. He shuddered, and when he straightened once more his florid cheeks did not contain quite as much color as they had had previously.

With a smile that was almost apologetic, he reversed his chair also. "There are probably two million people in Saro City that are all trying to join the Cult at once in one gigantic revival." Then, ironically, "The Cult is in for an hour of unexampled prosperity. I trust they'll make the most of it. Now, what was it you said?"

"Just this. How do the Cultists manage to keep the 'Book of Revelations' going from cycle to cycle, and how on Lagash did it get written in the first place? There must have been some sort of immunity, for if everyone had gone mad, who would be left to write the book?"

Sheerin stared at his questioner ruefully. "Well, now, young man, there isn't any eyewitness answer to that, but we've got a few damned good notions as to what happened. You see, there are three kinds of people who might remain relatively unaffected. First, the very few who don't see the Stars at all; the blind, those who drink themselves into a stupor at the beginning of the eclipse and remain so to the end. We leave them out—because they aren't really witnesses.

"Then there are children below six, to whom the world as a whole is too new and strange for them to be *too* frightened at Stars and Darkness. They would be just another item in an already surprising world. You see that, don't you?"

The other nodded doubtfully. "I suppose so."

"Lastly, there are those whose minds are too coarsely grained to be entirely toppled. The very insensitive would be scarcely affected—oh, such people as some of our older, work-broken peasants. Well, the children would have fugitive memories, and that, combined with the confused, incoherent babblings of the half-mad morons, formed the basis for the 'Book of Revelations.'

"Naturally, the book was based, in the first place, on the testimony of those least qualified to serve as historians; that is, children and morons; and was probably extensively edited and re-edited through the cycles."

"Do you suppose," broke in Theremon, "that they carried the book through the cycles the way we're planning on handing on the secret of gravitation?"

Sheerin shrugged. "Perhaps, but their exact method is unimportant. They do it, somehow. The point I was getting at was that the book can't help but be a mass of distortion, even if it is based on fact. For instance, do you remember the experiment with the holes in the roof that Faro and Yimot tried—the one that didn't work?"

"Yes."

"You know why it didn't w—" He stopped and rose in alarm, for Aton was approaching, his face a twisted mask of consternation. *"What's happened?"*

Aton drew him aside and Sheerin could feel the fingers on his elbow twitching.

"Not so loud!" Aton's voice was low and tortured. "I've just gotten word from the Hideout on the private line."

Sheerin broke in anxiously, "They are in trouble?"

"Not *they*." Aton stressed the pronoun significantly. "They sealed themselves off just a while ago, and they're going to stay buried till day after tomorrow. They're safe. But the *city*, Sheerin—it's a shambles. You have no idea—" He was having difficulty in speaking.

"Well?" snapped Sheerin impatiently. "What of it? It will get worse. What are you shaking about?" Then, suspiciously, "How do you feel?"

Aton's eyes sparked angrily at the insinuation, and then faded to anxiety once more. "You don't understand. The Cultists are active. They're rousing the people to storm the Observatory—promising them immediate entrance into grace, promising them salvation, promising them anything. What are we to do, Sheerin?"

Sheerin's head bent, and he stared in long abstraction at his toes. He tapped his chin with one knuckle, then looked up and said crisply, "Do? What is there to do? Nothing at all! Do the men know of this?"

"No, of course not!"

"Good! Keep it that way. How long till totality?"

"Not quite an hour."

"There's nothing to do but gamble. It will take time to organize any really formidable mob, and it will take more time to get them out here. We're a good five miles from the city—"

He glared out the window, down the slopes to where the farmed patches gave way to clumps of white houses in the suburbs; down to where the metropolis itself was a blur on the horizon—a mist in the waning blaze of Beta.

He repeated without turning, "It will take time. Keep on working and pray that totality comes first."

Beta was cut in half, the line of division pushing a slight concavity into the still-bright portion of the Sun. It was like a gigantic eyelid shutting slantwise over the light of a world.

The faint clatter of the room in which he stood faded into oblivion, and he sensed only the thick silence of the fields outside. The very insects seemed frightened mute. And things were dim.

He jumped at the voice in his ear. Theremon said, "Is something wrong?"

"Eh? Er—no. Get back to the chair. We're in the way." They slipped back to their corner, but the psychologist did not speak for a time. He lifted a finger and loosened his collar. He twisted his neck back and forth but found no relief. He looked up suddenly.

"Are you having any difficulty in breathing?"

The newspaperman opened his eyes wide and drew two or three long breaths. "No. Why?"

"I looked out the window too long, I suppose. The dimness got me. Difficulty in breathing is one of the first symptoms of a claustrophobic attack."

Theremon drew another long breath. "Well, it hasn't got me yet. Say, here's another of the fellows."

Beenay had interposed his bulk between the light and the pair in the corner, and Sheerin squinted up at him anxiously. "Hello, Beenay."

The astronomer shifted his weight to the other foot and smiled feebly. "You won't mind if I sit down awhile and join in on the talk. My cameras are set, and there's nothing to do till totality." He paused and eyed the Cultist, who fifteen minutes earlier had drawn a small, skin-bound book from his sleeve and had been poring intently over it ever since. "That rat hasn't been making trouble, has he?"

Sheerin shook his head. His shoulders were thrown back and he frowned his concentration as he forced himself to breathe regularly. He said, "Have you had any trouble breathing, Beenay?"

Beenay sniffed the air in his turn. "It doesn't seem stuffy to me."

"A touch of claustrophobia," explained Sheerin apologetically.

"Oh-h-h! It worked itself differently with me. I get the impression that my eyes are going back on me. Things seem to blur and—well, nothing is clear. And it's cold, too."

"Oh, it's cold, all right. That's no illusion." Theremon grimaced. "My toes feel as if I've been shipping them cross country in a refrigerating car."

"What we need," put in Sheerin, "is to keep our minds busy with extraneous affairs. I was telling you a while ago, Theremon, why Faro's experiments with the holes in the roof came to nothing."

"You were just beginning," replied Theremon. He encircled a knee with both arms and nuzzled his chin against it.

"Well, as I started to say, they were misled by taking the 'Book of Revelations' literally. There probably wasn't any sense in attaching any physical significance to the Stars. It might be, you know, that in the presence of total Darkness, the mind finds it absolutely necessary to create light. This illusion of light might be all the Stars there really are."

"In other words," interposed Theremon, "you mean the Stars are the results of the madness and not one of the causes. Then, what good will Beenay's photographs be?"

"To prove that it is an illusion, maybe; or to prove the opposite, for all I know. Then again—"

But Beenay had drawn his chair closer, and there was an expression of sudden enthusiasm on his face. "Say, I'm glad you two got on to this subject." His eyes narrowed and he lifted one finger. "I've been thinking about these Stars and I've got a really cute notion. Of course, it's strictly ocean foam, and I'm not trying to advance it seriously, but I think it's interesting. Do you want to hear it?"

He seemed half reluctant, but Sheerin leaned back and said, "Go ahead! I'm listening."

"Well, then, supposing there were other suns in the universe." He broke off a little bashfully. "I mean suns that are so far away that they're too dim to see. It sounds as if I've been reading some of that fantastic fiction, I suppose."

"Not necessarily. Still, isn't that possibility eliminated by the fact that, according to the Law of Gravitation, they would make themselves evident, by their attractive forces?"

"Not if they were far enough off," rejoined Beenay, "really far off— maybe as much as four light years, or even more. We'd never be able to detect perturbations then, because they'd be too small. Say that there were a lot of suns that far off; a dozen or two, maybe."

Theremon whistled melodiously. "What an idea for a good Sunday supplement article. Two dozen suns in a universe eight light years across. Wow! That would shrink *our* universe into insignificance. The readers would eat it up."

"Only an idea," said Beenay with a grin, "but you see the point. During eclipse, these dozen suns would become visible, because there'd be no *real* sunlight to drown them out. Since they're so far off, they'd appear small, like so many little marbles. Of course, the Cultists talk of millions of Stars, but that's probably exaggeration. There just isn't any place in the universe you could put a million suns—unless they touch each other."

Sheerin had listened with gradually increasing interest. "You've hit something there, Beenay. And exaggeration is just exactly what would happen. Our minds, as you probably know, can't grasp directly any number higher than five; above that there is only the concept of 'many.' A dozen would become a million just like that. A damn good idea!"

"And I've got another cute little notion," Beenay said. "Have you ever thought what a simple problem gravitation would be if only you had a sufficiently simple system? Supposing you had a universe in which there was a planet with only one sun. The planet would travel in a perfect ellipse and the exact nature of the gravitational force would be so evident it could be accepted as an axiom. Astronomers on such a world would start off with gravity probably before they even invent the telescope. Naked-eye observation would be enough."

"But would such a system be dynamically stable?" questioned Sheerin doubtfully.

"Sure! They call it the 'one-and-one' case. It's been worked out mathematically, but it's the philosophical implications that interest me."

"It's nice to think about," admitted Sheerin, "as a pretty abstraction—like a perfect gas or absolute zero."

"Of course," continued Beenay, "there's the catch that life would be impossible on such a planet. It wouldn't get enough heat and light, and if it rotated there would be total Darkness half of each day. You couldn't expect life—which is fundamentally dependent upon light—to develop under those conditions. Besides—"

Sheerin's chair went over backward as he sprang to his feet in a rude interruption. "Aton's brought out the lights."

Beenay said, "Huh," turned to stare, and then grinned halfway around his head in open relief.

There were half a dozen foot-long, inch-thick rods cradled in Aton's arms. He glared over them at the assembled staff members.

"Get back to work, all of you. Sheerin, come here and help me!"

Sheerin trotted to the older man's side and, one by one, in utter silence, the two adjusted the rods in makeshift metal holders suspended from the walls.

With the air of one carrying through the most sacred item of a religious ritual, Sheerin scraped a large, clumsy match into spluttering life and passed it to Aton, who carried the flame to the upper end of one of the rods.

It hesitated there a while, playing futilely about the tip, until a sudden, crackling flare cast Aton's lined face into yellow highlights. He withdrew the match and a spontaneous cheer rattled the window.

The rod was topped by six inches of wavering flame! Methodically, the other rods were lighted, until six independent fires turned the rear of the room yellow.

The light was dim, dimmer even than the tenuous sunlight. The flames reeled crazily, giving birth to drunken, swaying shadows. The torches smoked devilishly and smelled like a bad day in the kitchen. But they emitted yellow light.

There is something *to* yellow light—after four hours of somber, dimming Beta. Even Latimer had lifted his eyes from his book and stared in wonder.

Sheerin warmed his hands at the nearest, regardless of the soot that gathered upon them in a fine, gray powder, and muttered ecstatically to himself. "Beautiful! Beautiful! I never realized before what a wonderful color yellow is."

But Theremon regarded the torches suspiciously. He wrinkled his nose at the rancid odor, and said, "What are those things?"

"Wood," said Sheerin shortly.

"Oh, no, they're not. They aren't burning. The top inch is charred and the flame just keeps shooting up out of nothing."

"That's the beauty of it. This is a really efficient artificial-light mechanism. We made a few hundred of them, but most went to the Hideout, of course. You see"—he turned and wiped his blackened hands upon his handkerchief—"you take the pithy core of coarse water reeds, dry them thoroughly and soak them in animal grease. Then you set fire to it and the grease burns, little by little. These torches will burn for almost half an hour without stopping. Ingenious, isn't it? It was developed by one of our own young men at Saro University."

After the momentary sensation, the dome had quieted. Latimer had carried his chair directly beneath a torch and continued reading, lips moving in the monotonous recital of invocations to the Stars. Beenay had drifted away to his cameras once more, and Theremon seized the opportunity to add to his notes on the article he was going to write for the Saro City *Chronicle* the next day—a procedure he had been following for the last two hours in a perfectly methodical, perfectly conscientious and, as he was well aware, perfectly meaningless fashion.

But, as the gleam of amusement in Sheerin's eyes indicated, careful note taking occupied his mind with something other than the fact that the sky was gradually turning a horrible deep purple-red, as if it were one gigantic, freshly peeled beet; and so it fulfilled its purpose.

The air grew, somehow, denser. Dusk, like a palpable entity, entered the room, and the dancing circle of yellow light about the torches etched itself into ever-sharper distinction against the gathering grayness beyond. There was the odor of smoke and the presence of little chuckling sounds that the torches made as they burned; the soft pad of one of the men circling the table at which he worked, on hesitant tiptoes; the occasional indrawn breath of someone trying to retain composure in a world that was retreating into the shadow.

It was Theremon who first heard the extraneous noise. It was a vague, unorganized *impression* of sound that would have gone unnoticed but for the dead silence that prevailed within the dome.

The newsman sat upright and replaced his notebook. He held his breath and listened; then, with considerable reluctance, threaded his way between the solaroscope and one of Beenay's cameras and stood before the window.

The silence ripped to fragments at his startled shout:

"Sheerin!"

Work stopped! The psychologist was at his side in a moment. Aton joined him. Even Yimot 70, high in his little lean-back seat at the eyepiece of the gigantic solaroscope, paused and looked downward.

Outside, Beta was a mere smoldering splinter, taking one last desperate look at Lagash. The eastern horizon, in the direction of the city, was lost in Darkness, and the road from Saro to the Observatory was a dull-red line bordered on both sides by wooded tracts, the trees of which had somehow lost individuality and merged into a continuous shadowy mass.

But it was the highway itself that held attention, for along it there surged another, and infinitely menacing, shadowy mass.

Aton cried in a cracked voice, "The madmen from the city! They've come!"

"How long to totality?" demanded Sheerin.

"Fifteen minutes, but . . . but they'll be here in five."

"Never mind, keep the men working. We'll hold them off. This place is built like a fortress. Aton, keep an eye on our young Cultist just for luck. Theremon, come with me."

Sheerin was out the door, and Theremon was at his heels. The stairs stretched below them in tight, circular sweeps about the central shaft, fading into a dank and dreary grayness.

The first momentum of their rush had carried them fifty feet down, so that the dim, flickering yellow from the open door of the dome had disappeared and both up above and down below the same dusky shadow crushed in upon them.

Sheerin paused, and his pudgy hand clutched at his chest. His eyes bulged and his voice was a dry cough. "I can't ... breath ... go down ... yourself. Close all doors—"

Theremon took a few downward steps, then turned. "Wait! Can you hold out a minute?" He was panting himself. The air passed in and out his lungs like so much molasses, and there was a little germ of screeching panic in his mind at the thought of making his way into the mysterious Darkness below by himself.

Theremon, after all, was afraid of the dark!

"Stay here," he said. "I'll be back in a second." He dashed upward two steps at a time, heart pounding—not altogether from the exertion—tumbled into the dome and snatched a torch from its holder. It was foul smelling, and the smoke smarted his eyes almost blind, but he clutched that torch as if he wanted to kiss it for joy, and its flame streamed backward as he hurtled down the stairs again.

Sheerin opened his eyes and moaned as Theremon bent over him. Theremon shook him roughly. "All right, get a hold on yourself. We've got light."

He held the torch at tiptoe height and, propping the tottering psychologist by an elbow, made his way downward in the middle of the protecting circle of illumination.

The offices on the ground floor still possessed what light there was, and Theremon felt the horror about him relax.

"Here," he said brusquely, and passed the torch to Sheerin. "You can hear *them* outside."

And they could. Little scraps of hoarse, wordless shouts.

But Sheerin was right; the Observatory *was* built like a fortress. Erected in the last century, when the neo-Gavottian style of architecture was at its ugly height, it had been designed for stability and durability, rather than for beauty.

The windows were protected by the grillework of inch-thick iron bars sunk deep into the concrete sills. The walls were solid masonry that an earthquake couldn't have touched, and the main door was a huge oaken slab reinforced with iron at the strategic points. Theremon shot the bolts and they slid shut with a dull clang.

At the other end of the corridor, Sheerin cursed weakly. He pointed to the lock of the back door which had been neatly jimmied into uselessness.

"That must be how Latimer got in," he said.

"Well, don't stand there," cried Theremon impatiently. "Help drag up the furniture—and keep that torch out of my eyes. The smoke's killing me."

He slammed the heavy table up against the door as he spoke, and in two minutes had built a barricade which made up for what it lacked in beauty and symmetry by the sheer inertia of its massiveness.

Somewhere, dimly, far off, they could hear the battering of naked fists upon the door; and the screams and yells from outside had a sort of half reality.

That mob had set off from Saro City with only two things in mind: the attainment of Cultist salvation by the destruction of the Observatory, and a maddening fear that all but paralyzed them. There was no time to think of ground cars, or of weapons, or of leadership, or even of organization. They made for the Observatory on foot and assaulted it with bare hands.

And now that they were there, the last flash of Beta, the last ruby-red drop of flame, flickered feebly over a humanity that had left only stark, universal fear!

Theremon groaned, "Let's get back to the dome!"

In the dome, only Yimot, at the solaroscope, had kept his place. The rest were clustered about the cameras, and Beenay was giving his instructions in a hoarse, strained voice.

"Get it straight, all of you. I'm snapping Beta just before totality and changing the plate. That will leave one of you to each camera. You all know about . . . about times of exposure—"

There was a breathless murmur of agreement.

Beenay passed a hand over his eyes. "Are the torches still burning? Never mind, I see them!" He was leaning hard against the back of a chair. "Now remember, don't . . . don't try to look for good shots. Don't waste time trying to get t-two stars at a time in the scope field. One is enough. And . . . and if you feel yourself going, *get away from the camera.*"

At the door, Sheerin whispered to Theremon, "Take me to Aton. I don't see him."

The newsman did not answer immediately. The vague forms of the astronomers wavered and blurred, and the torches overhead had become only yellow splotches.

"It's dark," he whimpered.

Sheerin held out his hand, "Aton." He stumbled forward. "Aton!"

Theremon stepped after and seized his arm. "Wait, I'll take you."

Somehow he made his way across the room. He closed his eyes against the Darkness and his mind against the chaos within it.

No one heard them or paid attention to them. Sheerin stumbled against the wall. "Aton!"

The psychologist felt shaking hands touching him, then withdrawing, and a voice muttering, "Is that you, Sheerin?"

"Aton!" He strove to breathe normally. "Don't worry about the mob. The place will hold them off."

Latimer, the Cultist, rose to his feet, and his face twisted in desperation. His word was pledged, and to break it would mean placing his soul in mortal peril. Yet that word had been forced from him and had not been given freely. The Stars would come soon; he could not stand by and allow— And yet his word was pledged.

Beenay's face was dimly flushed as it looked upward at Beta's last ray, and Latimer, seeing him bend over his camera, made his decision. His nails cut the flesh of his palms as he tensed himself.

He staggered crazily as he started his rush. There was nothing before him but shadows; the very floor beneath his feet lacked substance. And then someone was upon him and he went down with clutching fingers at his throat.

He doubled his knee and drove it hard into his assailant. "Let me up or I'll kill you."

Theremon cried out sharply and muttered through a blinding haze of pain, "You double-crossing rat!"

The newsman seemed conscious of everything at once. He heard Beenay croak, "I've got it. At your cameras, men!" and then there was the strange awareness that the last thread of sunlight had thinned out and snapped.

Simultaneously he heard one last choking gasp from Beenay, and a queer little cry from Sheerin, a hysterical giggle that cut off in a rasp— and a sudden silence, a strange, deadly silence from outside.

And Latimer had gone limp in his loosening grasp. Theremon peered into the Cultist's eyes and saw the blankness of them, staring upward, mirroring the feeble yellow of the torches. He saw the bubble of froth upon Latimer's lips and heard the low animal whimper in Latimer's throat.

With the slow fascination of fear, he lifted himself on one arm and turned his eyes toward the blood-curdling blackness of the window.

Through it shone the Stars!

Not Earth's feeble thirty-six hundred Stars visible to the eye—Lagash was in the center of a giant cluster. Thirty thousand mighty suns shone down in a soul-searing splendor that was more frighteningly cold in its awful indifference than the bitter wind that shivered across the cold, horribly bleak world.

Theremon staggered to his feet, his throat constricting him to breathlessness, all the muscles of his body writhing in a tensity of terror and sheer fear beyond bearing. He was going mad, and knew it, and somewhere deep inside a bit of sanity was screaming, struggling to fight off the hopeless flood of black terror. It was very horrible to go mad and know that you were going mad—to know that in a little minute you would be here physically and yet all the real essence would be dead and drowned in the black madness. For this was the Dark—the Dark and the Cold and the Doom. The bright walls of the universe were shattered and their awful black fragments were falling down to crush and squeeze and obliterate him.

He jostled someone crawling on hands and knees, but stumbled somehow over him. Hands groping at his tortured throat, he limped toward the flame of the torches that filled all his mad vision.

"Light!" he screamed.

Aton, somewhere, was crying, whimpering horribly like a terribly frightened child. "Stars—all the Stars—we didn't know at all. We didn't know anything. We thought six stars is a universe is something the Stars didn't notice is Darkness forever and ever and ever and the walls are breaking in and we didn't know we couldn't know and anything—"

Someone clawed at the torch, and it fell and snuffed out. In the instant, the awful splendor of the indifferent Stars leaped nearer to them.

On the horizon outside the window, in the direction of Saro City, a crimson glow began growing, strengthening in brightness, that was not the glow of a sun.

The long night had come again.

First published: 1941

WHEN THE BOUGH BREAKS

by Lewis Padgett

THEY WERE SURPRISED AT GETTING THE APARTMENT, WHAT WITH HIGH rents and written-in clauses in the lease, and Joe Calderon felt himself lucky to be only ten minutes' subway ride from the University. His wife, Myra, fluffed up her red hair in a distracted fashion and said that landlords presumably expected parthenogenesis in their tenants, if that was what she meant. Anyhow, it was where an organism split in two and the result was two mature specimens. Calderon grinned, said, "Binary fission, chump," and watched young Alexander, aged eighteen months, backing up on all fours across the carpet, preparatory to assuming a standing position on his fat bowlegs.

It was a pleasant apartment, at that. The sun came into it at times, and there were more rooms than they had any right to expect, for the price. The next-door neighbor, a billowy blonde who talked of little except her migraine, said that it was hard to keep tenants in 4-D. It wasn't exactly haunted, but it had the queerest visitors. The last lessee, an insurance man who drank heavily, moved out one day talking about little men who came ringing the bell at all hours asking for a Mr. Pott, or somebody like that. Not until some time later did Joe identify Pott with Cauldron—or Calderon.

They were sitting on the couch in a pleased manner, looking at Alexander. He was quite a baby. Like all infants, he had a collar of fat at the back of his neck, and his legs, Calderon said, were like two vast and trunkless limbs of stone—at least they gave that effect. The eyes stopped at their incredible bulging pinkness, fascinated. Alexander laughed like a fool, rose to his feet, and staggered drunkenly toward his parents, muttering unintelligible gibberish. "Madman," Myra said fondly, and tossed the child a floppy velvet pig of whom he was enamored.

"So we're all set for the winter," Calderon said. He was a tall, thin, harassed-looking man, a fine research physicist, and very much interested in his work at the University. Myra was a rather fragile red-head, with a tilted nose and sardonic red-brown eyes. She made deprecatory noises.

"If we can get a maid. Otherwise I'll char."

"You sound like a lost soul," Calderon said. "What do you mean, you'll char?"

"Like a charwoman. Sweep, cook, clean. Babies are a great trial. Still, they're worth it."

"Not in front of Alexander. He'll get above himself."

The doorbell rang. Calderon uncoiled himself, wandered vaguely across the room, and opened the door. He blinked at nothing. Then he lowered his gaze somewhat, and what he saw was sufficient to make him stare a little.

Four tiny men were standing in the hall. That is, they were tiny below the brows. Their craniums were immense, watermelon large and watermelon shaped, or else they were wearing abnormally huge helmets of glistening metal. Their faces were wizened, peaked tiny masks that were nests of lines and wrinkles. Their clothes were garish, unpleasantly colored, and seemed to be made of paper.

"Oh?" Calderon said blankly.

Swift looks were exchanged among the four. One of them said, "Are you Joseph Calderon?"

"Yeah."

"We," said the most wrinkled of the quartet, "are your son's descendents. He's a super child. We're here to educate him."

"Yes," Calderon said. "Yes, of course. I . . . *listen!*"

"To what?"

"Super—"

"There he is," another dwarf cried. "It's Alexander! We've hit the right time at last!" He scuttled past Calderon's legs and into the room. Calderon made a few futile snatches, but the small men easily evaded him. When he turned, they were gathered around Alexander. Myra had drawn up her legs under her and was watching with an amazed expression.

"Look at that," a dwarf said. "See his potential tefeetzie?" It sounded like tefeetzie.

"But his skull, Bordent," another put in. "That's the important part. The vyrings are almost perfectly coblastably."

"Beautiful," Bordent acknowledged. He leaned forward. Alexander reached forward into the nest of wrinkles, seized Bordent's nose, and twisted painfully. Bordent bore it stoically until the grip relaxed.

"Undeveloped," he said tolerantly. "We'll develop him."

Myra sprang from the couch, picked up her child, and stood at bay, facing the little men. "Joe," she said, "are you going to stand for this? Who are these bad-mannered goblins?"

"Lord knows," Calderon said. He moistened his lips. "What kind of a gag is that? Who sent you?"

"Alexander," Bordent said. "From the year . . . ah . . . about 2450, reckoning roughly. He's practically immortal. Only violence can kill one of the Supers, and there's none of that in 2450."

Calderon sighed. "No, I mean it. A gag's a gag. But—"

"Time and again we've tried. In 1940, 1944, 1947—all around this era. We were either too early or too late. But now we've hit on the right time-sector. It's our job to educate Alexander. You should feel proud of being his parents. We worship you, you know. Father and mother of the new race."

"Tuh!" Calderon said. "Come off it!"

"They need proof, Dobish," someone said. "Remember, this is their first inkling that Alexander is homo superior."

"Homo nuts," Myra said. "Alexander's a perfectly normal baby."

"He's perfectly supernormal," Dobish said. "We're his descendents."

"That makes you a superman," Calderon said skeptically, eyeing the small man.

"Not in toto. There aren't many of the X Free type. The biological norm is specialization. Only a few are straight-line super. Some specialize in logic, others in vervainity, others—like us—are guides. If we were X Free supers, you couldn't stand there and talk to us. Or look at us. We're only parts. Those like Alexander are the glorious whole."

"Oh, send them away," Myra said, getting tired of it. "I feel like a Thurber woman."

Calderon nodded. "O.K. Blow, gentlemen. Take a powder. I mean it."

"Yes," Dobish said, "they need proof. What'll we do? Skyskinate?"

"Too twisty," Bordent objected. "Object lesson, eh? The stiller."

"Stiller?" Myra asked.

Bordent took an object from his paper clothes and spun it in his hands. His fingers were all double-jointed. Calderon felt a tiny electric shock go through him.

"Joe," Myra said, white-faced. "I can't move."

"Neither can I. Take it easy. This is . . . it's—" He slowed and stopped.

"Sit down," Bordent said, still twirling the object. Calderon and Myra backed up to the couch and sat down. Their tongues froze with the rest of them.

Dobish came over, clambered up, and pried Alexander out of his mother's grip. Horror moved in her eyes.

"We won't hurt him," Dobish said. "We just want to give him his first lesson. Have you got the basics, Finn?"

"In the bag." Finn extracted a foot-long bag from his garments. Things came out of that bag. They came out incredibly. Soon the carpet was littered with stuff—problematical in design, nature, and use. Calderon recognized a tesseract.

The fourth dwarf, whose name, it turned out, was Quat, smiled consolingly at the distressed parents. "You watch. You can't learn; you've not got the potential. You're homo saps. But Alexander, now—"

Alexander was in one of his moods. He was diabolically gay. With the devil-possession of all babies, he refused to collaborate. He crept rapidly backwards. He burst into loud, squalling sobs. He regarded his feet with amazed joy. He stuffed his fist into his mouth and cried bitterly at the result. He talked about invisible things in a soft, cryptic monotone. He punched Dobish in the eye.

The little men had inexhaustible patience. Two hours later they were through. Calderon couldn't see that Alexander had learned much.

Bordent twirled the object again. He nodded affably, and led the retreat. The four little men went out of the apartment, and a moment later Calderon and Myra could move.

She jumped up, staggering on numbed legs, seized Alexander, and collapsed on the couch. Calderon rushed to the door and flung it open. The hall was empty.

"Joe—" Myra said, her voice small and afraid. Calderon came back and smoothed her hair. He looked down at the bright fuzzy head of Alexander.

"Joe. We've got to do—do something."

"I don't know," he said. "If it happened—"

"It happened. They took those things with them. Alexander. Oh!"

"They didn't try to hurt him," Calderon said hesitatingly.

"Our *baby*! He's no superchild."

"Well," Calderon said, "I'll get out my revolver. What else can I do?"

"I'll do something," Myra promised. "Nasty little goblins! I'll do something, just wait."

And yet there wasn't a great deal they could do.

Tacitly they ignored the subject the next day. But at 4 P.M., the same time as the original visitation, they were with Alexander in a theater, watching the latest technicolor film. The four little men could scarcely find them here—

Calderon felt Myra stiffen, and even as he turned, he suspected the worst. Myra sprang up, her breath catching. Her fingers tightened on his arm.

"He's gone!"

"G-gone?"

"He just vanished. I was holding him . . . let's get out of here."

"Maybe you dropped him," Calderon said inanely, and lit a match. There were cries from behind. Myra was already pushing her way toward the aisle. There were no babies under the seat, and Calderon caught up with his wife in the lobby.

"He disappeared," Myra was babbling. "Like that. Maybe he's in the future. Joe, what'll we do?"

Calderon, through some miracle, got a taxi. "We'll go home. That's the most likely place. I hope."

"Yes. Of course it is. Give me a cigarette."

"He'll be in the apartment—"

He was, squatting on his haunches, taking a decided interest in the gadget Quat was demonstrating. The gadget was a gayly-colored egg beater with four-dimensional attachments, and it talked in a thin, high voice. Not in English.

Bordent flipped out the stiller and began to twirl it as the couple came in. Calderon got hold of Myra's arms and held her back. "Hold on," he said urgently. "That isn't necessary. We won't try anything."

"Joe!" Myra tried to wriggle free. "Are you going to let them—"

"Quiet!" he said. "Bordent, put that thing down. We want to talk to you."

"Well—if you promise not to interrupt—"

"We promise." Calderon forcibly led Myra to the couch and held her there. "Look, darling. Alexander's all right. They're not hurting him."

"Hurt him, indeed!" Finn said. "He'd skin us alive in the future if we hurt him in the past."

"Be quiet," Bordent commanded. He seemed to be the leader of the four. "I'm glad you're co-operating, Joseph Calderon. It goes against my grain to use force on a demigod. After all, you're *Alexander's* father."

Alexander put out a fat paw and tried to touch the whirling rainbow egg beater. He seemed to be fascinated. Quat said, "The kivelish is sparking. Shall I vastinate?"

"Not too fast," Bordent said. "He'll be rational in a week, and then we can speed up the process. Now, Calderon, please relax. Anything you want?"

"A drink."

"They mean alcohol," Finn said. "The Rubaiyat mentions it, remember?"

"Rubaiyat?"

"The singing red gem in Twelve Library."

"Oh, yes," Bordent said. "That one. I was thinking of the Yahveh slab, the one with the thunder effects. Do you want to make some alcohol, Finn?"

Calderon swallowed. "Don't bother. I have some in that sideboard. May I—"

"You're not *prisoners*." Bordent's voice was shocked. "It's just that we've got to make you listen to a few explanations, and after that—well, it'll be different."

Myra shook her head when Calderon handed her a drink, but he scowled at her meaningly. "You won't feel it. Go ahead."

She hadn't once taken her gaze from Alexander. The baby was imitating the thin noise of the egg beater now. It was subtly unpleasant.

"The ray is working," Quat said. "The viewer shows some slight cortical resistance, though."

"Angle the power," Bordent told him.

Alexander said, "Modjewabba?"

"What's that?" Myra asked in a strained voice. "Super language?"

Bordent smiled at her. "No, just baby talk."

Alexander burst into sobs. Myra said, "Super baby or not, when he cries like that, there's a good reason. Does your tutoring extend to that point?"

"Certainly," Quat said calmly. He and Finn carried Alexander out. Bordent smiled again.

"You're beginning to believe," he said. "That helps."

Calderon drank, feeling the hot fumes of whiskey along the backs of his cheeks. His stomach was crawling with cold uneasiness.

"If you were human—" he said doubtfully.

"If we were, we wouldn't be here. The old order changeth. It had to start sometime. Alexander is the first homo superior."

"But why us?" Myra asked.

"Genetics. You've both worked with radioactivity and certain short-wave radiations that effected the germ plasm. The mutation just happened. It'll happen again from now on. But you happen to be the first. You'll die, but Alexander will live on. Perhaps a thousand years."

Calderon said, "This business of coming from the future . . . you say Alexander sent you?"

"The adult Alexander. The mature superman. It's a different culture, of course—beyond your comprehension. Alexander is one of the X Frees. He said to me, through the interpreting-machine, of course, 'Bordent, I wasn't recognized as a super till I was thirty years old. I had only ordinary homo sap development till then. I didn't know my potential myself. And that's bad.' It *is* bad, you know," Bordent digressed. "The full capabilities of an organism can't emerge unless it's given the fullest chance of expansion from birth on. Or at least from infancy. Alexander said to me, 'It's about five hundred years ago that I was born. Take a few guides and go into the past. Locate me as an infant. Give me specialized training, from the beginning. I think it'll expand me.'"

"The past," Calderon said. "You mean it's plastic?"

"Well, it affects the future. You can't alter the past without altering the future, too. But things tend to drift back. There's a temporal norm, a general level. In the original time sector, Alexander wasn't visited by us. Now that's changed. So the future will be changed. But not tremendously. No crucial temporal apexes are involved, no keystones. The only result will be that the mature Alexander will have his potential more fully realized."

Alexander was carried back into the room, beaming. Quat resumed his lesson with the egg beater.

"There isn't a great deal you can do about it," Bordent said. "I think you realize that now."

Myra said, "Is Alexander going to look like you?" Her face was strained.

"Oh, no. He's a perfect physical specimen. I've never seen him, of course, but—"

Calderon said, "Heir to all the ages. Myra, are you beginning to get the idea?"

"Yes. A superman. But he's our baby."

"He'll remain so," Bordent put in anxiously. "We don't want to remove him from the beneficial home and parental influence. An infant needs that. In fact, tolerance for the young is an evolutionary trait aimed at providing for the superman's appearance, just as the vanishing appendix is such a preparation. At certain eras of history mankind is receptive to the preparation of the new race. It's never been quite successful before—there were anthropological miscarriages, so to speak. My squeevers, it's *important*! Infants are awfully irritating. They're helpless for a very long time, a great trial to the patience of the parents—the lower the order of the animal, the faster the infant develops. With mankind, it takes years for the young to reach an independent state. So the parental tolerance increases in proportion. The superchild won't mature, actually, till he's about twenty."

Myra said, "Alexander will still be a baby then?"

"He'll have the physical standards of an eight-year-old specimen of homo sap. Mentally . . . well, call it irrationality. He won't be leveled out to an intellectual or emotional norm. He won't be sane, any more than any baby is. Selectivity takes quite a while to develop. But his peaks will be far, far above the peaks of, say, *you* as a child."

"Thanks," Calderon said.

"His horizons will be broader. His mind is capable of grasping and assimilating far more than yours. The world is really his oyster. He won't be limited. But it'll take a while for his mind, his personality, to shake down."

"I want another drink," Myra said.

Calderon got it. Alexander inserted his thumb in Quat's eye and tried to gouge it out. Quat submitted passively.

"Alexander!" Myra said.

"Sit still," Bordent said. "Quat's tolerance in this regard is naturally higher developed than yours."

"If he puts Quat's eye out," Calderon said, "it'll be just too bad."

"Quat isn't important, compared to Alexander. He knows it, too."

Luckily for Quat's binocular vision, Alexander suddenly tired of his new toy and fell to staring at the egg beater again. Dobish and Finn leaned over the baby and looked at him. But there was more to it than that, Calderon felt.

"Induced telepathy," Bordent said. "It takes a long time to develop, but we're starting now. I tell you, it was a relief to hit the right time at last. I've rung this doorbell at least a hundred times. But never till now—"

"Move," Alexander said clearly. "Real. Move."

Bordent nodded. "Enough for today. We'll be here again tomorrow. You'll be ready?"

"As ready," Myra said, "as we'll ever be, I suppose." She finished her drink.

They got fairly high that night and talked it over. Their arguments were biased by their realization of the four little men's obvious resources. Neither doubted any more. They knew that Bordent and his companions had come from five hundred years in the future, at the command of a future Alexander who had matured into a fine specimen of superman.

"Amazing, isn't it?" Myra said. "That fat little blob in the bedroom turning into a twelfth-power Quiz Kid."

"Well, it's got to start somewhere. As Bordent pointed out."

"And as long as he isn't going to look like those goblins—ugh!"

"He'll be super. Deucalion and what's-her-name—that's us. Parents of a new race."

"I feel funny," Myra said. "As though I'd given birth to a moose."

"That could never happen," Calderon said consolingly. "Have another slug."

"It might as well have happened. Alexander is a swoose."

"Swoose?"

"I can use that goblin's doubletalk, too. Vopishly woggle in the grand foyer. So there."

"It's a language to them," Calderon said.

"Alexander's going to talk English. I've got my rights."

"Well, Bordent doesn't seem anxious to infringe on them. He said Alexander needed a home environment."

"That's the only reason I haven't gone crazy," Myra said. "As long as he . . . they . . . don't take our baby away from us—"

A week later it was thoroughly clear that Bordent had no intention of encroaching on parental rights—at least, any more than was necessary, for two hours a day. During that period the four little men fulfilled their orders by cramming Alexander with all the knowledge his infantile but super brain could hold. They did not depend on blocks or nursery rhymes or the abacus. Their weapons in the battle were cryptic, futuristic, but effective. And they taught Alexander, there was no doubt of that. As B-1 poured on a plant's roots forces growth, so the vitamin teaching of the dwarfs soaked into Alexander, and his potentially superhuman brain responded, expanding with brilliant, erratic speed.

He had talked intelligibly on the fourth day. On the seventh day he was easily able to hold conversations, though his baby muscles, lingually undeveloped, tired easily. His cheeks were still sucking-disks; he was not yet fully human, except in sporadic flashes. Yet those flashes came oftener now, and closer together.

The carpet was a mess. The little men no longer took their equipment back with them; they left it for Alexander to use. The infant crept—he no longer bothered to walk much, for he could crawl with more efficiency—among the Objects, selected some of them, and put them together. Myra had gone out to shop. The little men wouldn't show up for half an hour. Calderon, tired from his day's work at the University, fingered a highball and looked at his offspring.

"Alexander," he said.

Alexander didn't answer. He fitted a gadget to a Thing, inserted it peculiarly in a Something Else, and sat back with an air of satisfaction. Then—"Yes?" he said. It wasn't perfect pronunciation, but it was unmistakable. Alexander talked somewhat like a toothless old man.

"What are you doing?" Calderon said.

"No."

"What's that?"

"No."

"No?"

"I understand it," Alexander said. "That's enough."

"I see." Calderon regarded the prodigy with faint apprehension. "You don't want to tell me."

"No."

"Well, all right."

"Get me a drink," Alexander said. For a moment Calderon had a mad idea that the infant was demanding a highball. Then he sighed, rose, and returned with a bottle.

"Milk," Alexander said, refusing the potation.

"You said a drink. Water's a drink, isn't it?" My God, Calderon thought, I'm arguing with the kid. I'm treating him like . . . like an adult. But he isn't. He's a fat little baby squatting on his behind on the carpet, playing with a tinkertoy.

The tinkertoy said something in a thin voice. Alexander murmured, "Repeat." The tinkertoy did.

Calderon said, "What was that?"

"No."

"Nuts." Calderon went out to the kitchen and got milk. He poured himself another shot. This was like having relatives drop in suddenly—relatives you hadn't seen for ten years. How the devil did you *act* with a superchild?

He stayed in the kitchen, after supplying Alexander with his milk. Presently Myra's key turned in the outer door. Her cry brought Calderon hurrying.

Alexander was vomiting, with the air of a research man absorbed in a fascinating phenomenon.

"Alexander!" Myra cried. "Darling, are you sick?"

"No," Alexander said. "I'm testing my regurgitative processes. I must learn to control my digestive organs."

Calderon leaned against the door, grinning crookedly. "Yeah. You'd better start now, too."

"I'm finished," Alexander said. "Clean it up."

Three days later the infant decided that his lungs needed developing. He cried. He cried at all hours, with interesting variations—whoops, squalls, wails, and high-pitched bellows. Nor would he stop till he was satisfied. The neighbors complained. Myra said, "Darling, is there a pin sticking you? Let me look—"

"Go away," Alexander said. "You're too warm. Open the window. I want fresh air."

"Yes, d-darling. Of course." She came back to bed and Calderon put his arm around her. He knew there would be shadows under her eyes in the morning. In his crib Alexander cried on.

So it went. The four little men came daily and gave Alexander his lessons. They were pleased with the infant's progress. They did not complain when Alexander indulged in his idiosyncrasies, such as batting them heavily on the nose or ripping their paper garments to shreds. Bordent tapped his metal helmet and smiled triumphantly at Calderon.

"He's coming along. He's developing."

"I'm wondering. What about discipline?"

Alexander looked up from his rapport with Quat. "Homo sap discipline doesn't apply to me, Joseph Calderon."

"Don't call me Joseph Calderon. I'm your father, after all."

"A primitive biological necessity. You are not sufficiently well developed to provide the discipline I require. Your purpose is to give me parental care."

"Which makes me an incubator," Calderon said.

"But a deified one," Bordent soothed him. "Practically a logos. The father of the new race."

"I feel more like Prometheus," the father of the new race said dourly. "He was helpful, too. And he ended up with a vulture eating his liver."

"You will learn a great deal from Alexander."

"He says I'm incapable of understanding it."

"Well, aren't you?"

"Sure. I'm just the papa bird," Calderon said, and subsided into a sad silence, watching Alexander, under Quat's tutelary eye, put together a gadget of shimmering glass and twisted metal. Bordent said suddenly, "Quat! Be careful of the egg!" And Finn seized a bluish ovoid just before Alexander's chubby hand could grasp it.

"It isn't dangerous," Quat said. "It isn't connected."

"He might have connected it."

"I want that," Alexander said. "Give it to me."

"Not yet, Alexander," Bordent refused. "You must learn the correct way of connecting it first. Otherwise it might harm you."

"I could do it."

"You are not logical enough to balance your capabilities and lacks as yet. Later it will be safe. I think now, perhaps, a little philosophy, Dobish—eh?"

Dobish squatted and went en rapport with Alexander. Myra came out of the kitchen, took a quick look at the tableau, and retreated. Calderon followed her out.

"I will never get used to it if I live a thousand years," she said with slow emphasis, hacking at the doughy rim of a pie. "He's my baby only when he's asleep."

"We won't live a thousand years," Calderon told her. "Alexander will, though. I wish we could get a maid."

"I tried again today," Myra said wearily. "No use. They're all in war plants. I mention a baby—"

"You can't do all this alone."

"You help," she said, "when you can. But you're working hard too, fella. It won't be forever."

"I wonder if we had another baby . . . if—"

Her sober gaze met his. "I've wondered that, too. But I should think mutations aren't as cheap as that. Once in a lifetime. Still, we don't know."

"Well, it doesn't matter now, anyway. One infant's enough for the moment."

Myra glanced toward the door. "Everything all right in there? Take a look. I worry."

"It's all right."

"I know, but that blue egg—Bordent said it was dangerous, you know. I heard him."

Calderon peeped through the door-crack. The four dwarfs were sitting facing Alexander, whose eyes were closed. Now they opened. The infant scowled at Calderon.

"Stay out," he requested. "You're breaking the rapport."

"I'm so sorry," Calderon said, retreating. "He's O. K., Myra. His own dictatorial little self."

"Well, he *is* a superman," she said doubtfully.

"No. He's a super-baby. There's all the difference."

"His latest trick," Myra said, busy with the oven, "is riddles. Or something like riddles. I feel so small when he catches me up. But he says it's good for his ego. It compensates for his physical frailness."

"Riddles, eh? I know a few too."

"They won't work on Alexander," Myra said, with grim assurance.

Nor did they. "What goes up a chimney up?" was treated with the contempt it deserved; Alexander examined his father's riddles, turned them over in his logical mind, analyzed them for flaws in semantics and logic, and rejected them. Or else he answered them, with such fine accuracy that Calderon was too embarrassed to give the correct answers. He was reduced to asking why a raven was like a writing desk, and since not even the Mad Hatter had been able to answer his own riddle, was slightly terrified to find himself listening to a dissertation on comparative ornithology. After that, he let Alexander needle him with infantile gags about the relations of gamma rays to photons, and tried to be philosophical. There are few things as irritating as a child's riddles. His mocking triumph pulverizes itself into the dust in which you grovel.

"Oh, leave your father alone," Myra said, coming in with her hair disarranged. "He's trying to read the paper."

"That news is unimportant."

"I'm reading the comics," Calderon said. "I want to see if the Katzenjammers get even with the Captain for hanging them under a waterfall."

"The formula for the humor of an incongruity predicament," Alexander began learnedly, but Calderon disgustedly went into the bedroom, where Myra joined him. "He's asking me riddles again," she said. "Let's see what the Katzenjammers did."

"You look rather miserable. Got a cold?"

"I'm not wearing make-up. Alexander says the smell makes him ill."

"So what? He's no petunia."

"Well," Myra said, "he does get ill. But of course he does it on purpose."

"Listen. There he goes again. What now?"

But Alexander merely wanted an audience. He had found a new way of making imbecilic noises with his fingers and lips. At times the child's normal phases were more trying than his super periods. After a month had passed, however, Calderon felt that the worst was yet to come. Alexander had progressed into fields of knowledge hitherto untouched by homo sap, and he had developed a leechlike habit of sucking his father's brains dry of every scrap of knowledge the wretched man possessed.

It was the same with Myra. The world was indeed Alexander's oyster. He had an insatiable curiosity about everything, and there was no longer any privacy in the apartment. Calderon took to locking the bedroom door against his son at night—Alexander's crib was now in another room —but furious squalls might waken him at any hour.

In the midst of preparing dinner, Myra would be forced to stop and explain the caloric mysteries of the oven to Alexander. He learned all she knew, took a jump into more abstruse aspects of the matter, and sneered at her ignorance. He found out Calderon was a physicist, a fact which the man had hitherto kept carefully concealed, and thereafter pumped his father dry. He asked questions about geodetics and geopolitics. He inquired about monotremes and monorails. He was curious about biremes and biology. And he was skeptical, doubting the depth of his father's knowledge. "But," he said, "you and Myra Calderon are my closest contacts with homo sap as yet, and it's a beginning. Put out that cigarette. It isn't good for my lungs."

"All right," Calderon said. He rose wearily, with his usual feeling these days of being driven from room to room of the apartment, and went in search of Myra. "Bordent's about due. We can go out somewhere. O. K.?"

"Swell." She was at the mirror, fixing her hair, in a trice. "I need a permanent. If I only had the time—!"

"I'll take off tomorrow and stay here. You need a rest."

"Darling, no. The exams are coming up. You simply can't do it."

Alexander yelled. It developed that he wanted his mother to sing for him. He was curious about the tonal range of homo sap and the probable emotional and soporific effect of lullabies. Calderon mixed himself a drink, sat in the kitchen and smoked, and thought about the glorious destiny of his son. When Myra stopped singing, he listened for Alexander's wails, but there was no sound till a slightly hysterical Myra burst in on him, dithering and wide-eyed.

"Joe!" She fell into Calderon's arms. "Quick, give me a drink or . . . or hold me tight or something."

"What is it?" He thrust the bottle into her hands, went to the door, and looked out. "Alexander? He's quiet. Eating candy."

Myra didn't bother with a glass. The bottle's neck clicked against her teeth. "Look at me. Just look at me. I'm a mess."

"What happened?"

"Oh, nothing. Nothing at all. Alexander's turned into a black magician, that's all." She dropped into a chair and passed a palm across her forehead. "Do you know what that genius son of ours just did?"

"Bit you," Calderon hazarded, not doubting it for a minute.

"Worse, far worse. He started asking me for candy. I said there wasn't any in the house. He told me to go down to the grocery for some. I said I'd have to get dressed first, and I was too tired."

"Why didn't you ask me to go?"

"I didn't have the chance. Before I could say boo that infantile Merlin waved a magic wand or something. I . . . I was down at the grocery. Behind the candy counter."

Calderon blinked. "Induced amnesia?"

"There wasn't any time-lapse. It was just *phweet*—and there I was. In this rag of a dress, without a speck of make-up on, and my hair coming down in tassels. Mrs. Busherman was there, too, buying a chicken—that cat across the hall. She was kind enough to tell me I ought to take more care of myself. Meow," Myra ended furiously.

"Good Lord."

"Teleportation. That's what Alexander says it is. Something new he's picked up. I'm not going to stand for it, Joe. I'm not a rag doll, after all." She was half hysterical.

Calderon went into the next room and stood regarding his child. There was chocolate smeared around Alexander's mouth.

"Listen, wise guy," he said. "You leave your mother alone, hear me?"

"I didn't hurt her," the prodigy pointed out, in a blobby voice. "I was simply being efficient."

"Well, don't be so efficient. Where did you learn that trick, anyhow?"

"Teleportation? Quat showed me last night. He can't do it himself, but I'm X Free super, so I can. The power isn't disciplined yet. If I'd tried to teleport Myra Calderon over to Jersey, say, I might have dropped her in the Hudson by mistake."

Calderon muttered something uncomplimentary. Alexander said, "Is that an Anglo-Saxon derivative?"

"Never mind about that. You shouldn't have all that chocolate, anyway. You'll make yourself sick. You've already made your mother sick. And you nauseate me."

"Go away," Alexander said. "I want to concentrate on the taste."

"No. I said you'd make yourself sick. Chocolate's too rich for you. Give it here. You've had enough." Calderon reached for the paper sack. Alexander disappeared. In the kitchen Myra shrieked.

Calderon moaned despondently, and turned. As he had expected, Alexander was in the kitchen, on top of the stove, hoggishly stuffing candy into his mouth. Myra was concentrating on the bottle.

"What a household," Calderon said. "The baby teleporting himself all over the apartment, you getting stewed in the kitchen, and me heading for a nervous breakdown." He started to laugh. "O.K., Alexander. You can keep the candy. I know when to shorten my defensive lines strategically."

"Myra Calderon," Alexander said. "I want to go back into the other room."

"Fly in," Calderon suggested. "Here, I'll carry you."

"Not you. Her. She has a better rhythm when she walks."

"Staggers, you mean," Myra said, but she obediently put aside the bottle, got up, and laid hold of Alexander. She went out. Calderon was not much surprised to hear her scream a moment later. When he joined the happy family, Myra was sitting on the floor, rubbing her arms and biting her lips. Alexander was laughing.

"What now?"

"H-he sh-shocked me," Myra said in a child's voice. "He's like an electric eel. He d-did it on purpose, too. Oh, Alexander, will you *stop* laughing!"

"You fell down," the infant crowed in triumph. "You yelled and fell down."

Calderon looked at Myra, and his mouth tightened. "Did you do that on purpose?" he asked.

"Yes. She fell down. She looked funny."

"You're going to look a lot funnier in a minute. X Free super or not, what you need is a good paddling."

"Joe—" Myra said.

"Never mind. He's got to learn to be considerate of the rights of others."

"I'm homo superior," Alexander said, with the air of one clinching an argument.

"It's homo posterior I'm going to deal with," Calderon announced, and attempted to capture his son. There was a stinging blaze of jolting nervous energy that blasted up through his synapses; he went backwards ignominiously, and slammed into the wall, cracking his head hard against it. Alexander laughed like an idiot.

"You fell down, too," he crowed. "You look funny."

"Joe," Myra said. "Joe. Are you hurt?"

Calderon said sourly that he supposed he'd survive. Though, he added, it would probably be wise to lay in a few splints and a supply of blood plasma. "In case he gets interested in vivisection."

Myra regarded Alexander with troubled speculation. "You're kidding, I hope."

"I hope so, too."

"Well—here's Bordent. Let's talk to him."

Calderon answered the door. The four little men came in solemnly. They wasted no time. They gathered about Alexander, unfolded fresh apparatus from the recesses of their paper clothes, and set to work. The infant said, "I teleported *her* about eight thousand feet."

"That far, eh?" Quat said. "Were you fatigued at all?"

"Not a bit."

Calderon dragged Bordent aside. "I want to talk to you. I think Alexander needs a spanking."

"By voraster!" the dwarf said, shocked. "But he's *Alexander!* He's X Free type super!"

"Not yet. He's still a baby."

"But a superbaby. No, no, Joseph Calderon. I must tell you again that disciplinary measures can be applied only by sufficiently intelligent authorities."

"You?"

"Oh, not yet," Bordent said. "We don't want to overwork him. There's a limit even to super brain power, especially in the very formative period. He's got enough to do, and his attitudes for social contacts won't need forming for a while yet."

Myra joined them. "I don't agree with you there. Like all babies, he's antisocial. He may have superhuman powers but he's subhuman as far as mental and emotional balance go."

"Yeah," Calderon agreed. "This business of giving us electric shocks—"

"He's only playing," Bordent said.

"And teleportation. Suppose he teleports me to Times Square when I'm taking a shower?"

"It's only his play. He's a baby still."

"But what about us?"

"You have the hereditary characteristic of parental tolerance," Bordent explained. "As I told you before, Alexander and his race are the reason why tolerance was created in the first place. There's no great need for it with homo sap. I mean there's a wide space between normal tolerance and normal provocation. An ordinary baby may try his parents severely for a few moments at a time, but that's about all. The provocation is far too small to require the tremendous store of tolerance the parents have. But with the X Free type, it's a different matter."

"There's a limit even to tolerance," Calderon said. "I'm wondering about a crèche."

Bordent shook his shiny metallic-sheathed head. "He needs you."

"But," Myra said, "but! Can't you give him just a little discipline?"

"Oh, it isn't necessary. His mind's still immature, and he must concentrate on more important things. You'll tolerate him."

"It's not as though he's our baby any more," she murmured. "He's not Alexander."

"But he is. That's just it. *He's Alexander!*"

"Look, it's normal for a mother to want to hug her baby. But how can she do that if she expects him to throw her halfway across the room?"

Calderon was brooding. "Will he pick up more . . . more super powers as he goes along?"

"Why, yes. Naturally."

"He's a menace to life and limb. I still say he needs discipline. Next time I'll wear rubber gloves."

"That won't help," Bordent said, frowning. "Besides, I must insist . . . no, Joseph Calderon, it won't do. You mustn't interfere. You're not capable of giving him the right sort of discipline—which he doesn't need yet anyway."

"Just one spanking," Calderon said wistfully. "Not for revenge. Only to show him he's got to consider the rights of others."

"He'll learn to consider the rights of other X Free supers. You must not attempt anything of the sort. A spanking—even if you succeeded, which is far from probable—might warp him psychologically. We are his tutors, his mentors. We must *protect* him. You understand?"

"I think so," Calderon said slowly. "That's a threat."

"You are Alexander's parents, but it's Alexander who is important. If I must apply disciplinary measures to you, I must."

"Oh, forget it," Myra sighed. "Joe, let's go out and walk in the park while Bordent's here."

"Be back in two hours," the little man said. "Good-by."

As time went past, Calderon could not decide whether Alexander's moronic phases or his periods of keen intelligence were more irritating. The prodigy had learned new powers; the worst of that was that Calderon never knew what to expect, or when some astounding gag would be sprung on him. Such as the time when a mess of sticky taffy had materialized in his bed, filched from the grocery by deft teleportation. Alexander thought it was very funny. He laughed.

And, when Calderon refused to go to the store to buy candy because he said he had no money—"Now don't try to teleport me. I'm broke."—Alexander had utilized mental energy, warping gravity lines shockingly. Calderon found himself hanging upside-down in midair, being shaken, while loose coins cascaded out of his pocket. He went after the candy.

Humor is a developed sense, stemming basically from cruelty. The more primitive a mind, the less selectivity exists. A cannibal would probably be profoundly amused by the squirmings of his victim in the seething kettle. A man slips on a banana peel and breaks his back. The adult stops laughing at that point, the child does not. And a civilized ego finds embarrassment as acutely distressing as physical pain. A baby, a child, a moron, is incapable of practicing empathy. He cannot identify himself with another individual. He is regrettably autistic; his own rules are arbitrary, and garbage strewn around the bedroom was funny to neither Myra nor Calderon.

There was a little stranger in the house. Nobody rejoiced. Except Alexander. He had a lot of fun.

"No privacy," Calderon said. "He materializes everywhere, at all hours. Darling, I wish you'd see a doctor."

"What would he advise?" Myra asked. "Rest, that's all. Do you realize it's been two months since Bordent took over?"

"And we've made marvelous progress," Bordent said, coming over to them. Quat was en rapport with Alexander on the carpet, while the other two dwarfs prepared the makings of a new gadget. "Or, rather, Alexander has made remarkable progress."

"We need a rest," Calderon growled. "If I lose my job, who'll support that genius of yours?" Myra looked at her husband quickly, noting the possessive pronoun he had used.

Bordent was concerned. "You are in difficulty?"

"The Dean's spoken to me once or twice. I can't control my classes any more. I'm too irritable."

"You don't need to expend tolerance on your students. As for money, we can keep you supplied. I'll arrange to get some negotiable currency for you."

"But I want to work. I like my job."

"Alexander is your job."

"I need a maid," Myra said, looking hopeless. "Can't you make me a robot or something? Alexander scares every maid I've managed to hire. They won't stay a day in this madhouse."

"A mechanical intelligence would have a bad effect on Alexander," Bordent said. "No."

"I wish we could have guests in once in a while. Or go out visiting. Or just be alone," Myra sighed.

"Some day Alexander will be mature, and you'll reap your reward. The parents of Alexander. Did I ever tell you that we have images of you two in the Great Fogy Hall?"

"They must look terrible," Calderon said. "I know we do now."

"Be patient. Consider the destiny of your son."

"I do. Often. But he gets a little wearing sometimes. That's quite an understatement."

"Which is where tolerance comes in," Bordent said. "Nature planned well for the new race."

"Mm-m-m."

"He is working on sixth-dimensional abstractions now. Everything is progressing beautifully."

"Yeah," Calderon said. And he went away, muttering, to join Myra in the kitchen.

Alexander worked with facility at his gadgets, his pudgy fingers already stronger and surer. He still had an illicit passion for the blue ovoid, but under Bordent's watchful eye he could use it only along the restricted lines laid out by his mentors. When the lesson was finished, Quat selected a few of the objects and locked them in a cupboard, as was his custom. The rest he left on the carpet to provide exercise for Alexander's ingenuity.

"He develops," Bordent said. "Today we've made a great step."

Myra and Calderon came in in time to hear this. "What goes?" he asked.

"A psychic bloc-removal. Alexander will no longer need to sleep."

"What?" Myra said.

"He won't require sleep. It's an artificial habit anyway. The super race has no need of it."

"He won't sleep any more, eh?" Calderon said. He had grown a little pale.

"Correct. He'll develop faster now, twice as fast."

At 3:30 a. m. Calderon and Myra lay in bed, wide awake, looking through the open door into the full blaze of light where Alexander played. Seen there clearly, as if upon a lighted stage, he did not look quite like himself any more. The difference was subtle, but it was there. Under the golden down his head had changed shape slightly, and there was a look of intelligence and purpose upon the blobby features. It was not an attractive look. It didn't belong there. It made Alexander look less like a super-baby than a debased oldster. All a child's normal cruelty and selfishness—perfectly healthy, natural traits in the developing infant—flickered across Alexander's face as he played absorbedly with solid crystal blocks which he was fitting into one another like a Chinese puzzle. It was quite a shocking face to watch.

Calderon heard Myra sigh beside him.

"He isn't our Alexander any more," she said. "Not a bit."

Alexander glanced up and his face suddenly suffused. The look of paradoxical age and degeneracy upon it vanished as he opened his mouth and bawled with rage, tossing the blocks in all directions. Calderon watched one roll through the bedroom door and come to rest upon the carpet, spilling out of its solidity a cascade of smaller and smaller solid blocks that tumbled winking toward him. Alexander's cries filled the apartment. After a moment windows began to slam across the court, and presently the phone rang. Calderon reached for it, sighing.

When he hung up he looked across at Myra and grimaced. Above the steady roars he said, "Well, we have notice to move."

Myra said, "Oh. Oh, well."

"That about covers it."

They were silent for a moment. Then Calderon said, "Nineteen years more of it. I thing we can expect about that. They did say he'd mature at twenty, didn't they?"

"He'll be an orphan long before then," Myra groaned. "Oh, my head! I think I caught cold when he teleported us up to the roof just before dinner. Joe, do you suppose we're the first parents who ever got . . . got caught like this?"

"What do you mean?"

"I mean, was there ever another super-baby before Alexander? It does seem like a waste of a lot of tolerance if we're the first to need it."

"We could use a lot more. We'll need a lot." He said nothing more for awhile, but he lay there thinking and trying not to hear his super-child's rhythmic howling. Tolerance. Every parent needed a great deal of it. Every child was intolerable from time to time. The race had certainly needed parental love in vast quantities to permit its infants to survive. But no parents before had ever been tried consistently up to the very last degree of tolerance. No parents before had ever had to face twenty years of it, day and night, strained to the final notch. Parental love is a great and all-encompassing emotion, but—

"I wonder," he said thoughtfully. "I wonder if we *are* the first."

Myra's speculations had been veering. "I suppose it's like tonsils and appendix," she murmured. "They've outlived their use, but they still hang on. This tolerance is vestigial in reverse. It's been hanging on all these millenniums, waiting for Alexander."

"Maybe. I wonder— Still, if there ever had been an Alexander before now, we'd have heard of him. So—"

Myra rose on one elbow and looked at her husband. "You think so?" she said softly. "I'm not so sure. I think it might have happened before."

Alexander suddenly quieted. The apartment rang with silence for a moment. Then a familiar voice, without words, spoke in both their brains simultaneously.

"Get me some more milk. And I want it just warm, not hot."

Joe and Myra looked at one another again, speechless. Myra sighed and pushed the covers back. "I'll go this time," she said. "Something new, eh? I—"

"Don't dawdle," said the wordless voice, and Myra jumped and gave a little shriek. Electricity crackled audibly through the room, and Alexander's bawling laughter was heard through the doorway.

"He's about as civilized now as a well-trained monkey, I suppose," Joe remarked, getting out of bed. "I'll go. You crawl back in. And in another year he may reach the elevation of a bushman. After that, if we're still alive, we'll have the pleasure of living with a super-powered cannibal. Eventually he may work up to the level of practical joker. That ought to be interesting." He went out, muttering to himself.

Ten minutes later, returning to bed, Joe found Myra clasping her knees and looking into space.

"We aren't the first, Joe," she said, not glancing at him. "I've been thinking. I'm pretty sure we aren't."

"But we've never heard of any supermen developing—"

She turned her head and gave him a long, thoughtful look. "No," she said.

They were silent. Then, "Yes, I see what you mean," he nodded.

Something crashed in the living room. Alexander chuckled and the sound of splintering wood was loud in the silence of the night. Another window banged somewhere outside.

"There's a breaking point," Myra said quietly. "There's got to be."

"Saturation," Joe murmured. "Tolerance saturation—or something. It could have happened."

Alexander trundled into sight, clutching something blue. He sat down and began to fiddle with bright wires. Myra rose suddenly.

"Joe, he's got that blue egg! He must have broken into the cupboard."

Calderon said, "But Quat told him—"

"It's dangerous!"

Alexander looked at them, grinned, and bent the wires into a cradle-shape the size of the egg.

Calderon found himself out of bed and halfway to the door. He stopped before he reached it. "You know," he said slowly, "he might hurt himself with that thing."

"We'll have to get it away from him," Myra agreed, heaving herself up with tired reluctance.

"Look at him," Calderon urged. "Just look."

Alexander was dealing competently with the wires, his hands flickering into sight and out again as he balanced a tesseract beneath the cradle. That curious veil of knowledge gave his chubby face the debased look of senility which they had come to know so well.

"This will go on and on, you know," Calderon murmured. "Tomorrow he'll look a little less like himself than today. Next week—next month—what will he be like in a year?"

"I know." Myra's voice was an echo. "Still, I suppose we'll have to—" Her voice trailed to a halt. She stood barefoot beside her husband, watching.

"I suppose the gadget will be finished," she said, "once he connects up that last wire. We ought to take it away from him."

"Think we could?"

"We ought to try."

They looked at each other. Calderon said, "It looks like an Easter egg. I never heard of an Easter egg hurting anybody."

"I suppose we're doing him a favor, really," Myra said in a low voice. "A burnt child dreads the fire. Once a kid burns himself on a match, he stays away from matches."

They stood in silence, watching.

It took Alexander about three more minutes to succeed in his design, whatever it was. The results were phenomenally effective. There was a flash of white light, a crackle of split air, and Alexander vanished in the dazzle, leaving only a faint burnt smell behind him.

When the two could see again, they blinked distrustfully at the empty place. "Teleportation?" Myra whispered dazedly.

"I'll make sure." Calderon crossed the floor and stood looking down at a damp spot on the carpet, with Alexander's shoes in it. He said, "No. Not teleportation." Then he took a long breath. "He's gone, all right. So he never grew up and sent Bordent back in time to move in on us. It never happened."

"We weren't the first," Myra said in an unsteady, bemused voice. "There's a breaking point, that's all. How sorry I feel for the first parents who don't reach it!"

She turned away suddenly, but not so suddenly that he could not see she was crying. He hesitated, watching the door. He thought he had better not follow her just yet.

First published: 1943

CLASH BY NIGHT

by Lawrence O'Donnell

INTRODUCTION

A half mile beneath the shallow Venusian Sea the black impervium dome that protects Montana Keep rests frowningly on the bottom. Within the Keep is carnival, for the Montanans celebrate the four-hundred-year anniversary of Earthman's landing on Venus. Under the great dome that houses the city all is light and color and gaiety. Masked men and women, bright in celoflex and silks, wander through the broad streets, laughing, drinking the strong native wines of Venus. The sea bottom has been combed, like the hydroponic tanks, for rare delicacies to grace the tables of the nobles.

Through the festival grim shadows stalk, men whose faces mark them unmistakably as members of a Free Company. Their finery cannot disguise that stamp, hard-won through years of battle. Under the domino masks their mouths are hard and harsh. Unlike the undersea dwellers, their skins are burned black with the ultraviolet rays that filter through the cloud layer of Venus. They are skeletons at the feast. They are respected but resented. They are Free Companions—

We are on Venus, nine hundred years ago, beneath the Sea of Shoals, not much north of the equator. But there is a wide range in time and space. All over the cloud planet the underwater Keeps are dotted, and life will not change for many centuries. Looking back, as we do now, from the civilized days of the Thirty-fourth Century, it is too easy to regard the men of the Keeps as savages, groping, stupid and brutal. The Free Companies have long since vanished. The islands and continents of Venus have been tamed, and there is no war.

But in periods of transition, of desperate rivalry, there is always war. The Keeps fought among themselves, each striving to draw the fangs of the others by depriving them of their reserves of korium, the power source of the day. Students of that era find pleasure in sifting the legends and winnowing out the basic social and geopolitical truths. It is fairly well known that only one factor saved the Keeps from annihilating one another—the gentlemen's agreement that left war to the warriors, and allowed the undersea cities to develop their science and social cultures. That particular compromise was, perhaps, inevitable. And it caused the organization of the Free Companies, the roving bands of mercenaries, highly trained for their duties, who hired themselves out to fight for whatever Keeps were attacked or wished to attack.

Ap Towrn, in his monumental "Cycle of Venus," tells the saga through symbolic legends. Many historians have recorded the sober truth, which, unfortunately, seems often Mars-dry. But it is not generally realized that the Free Companions were almost directly responsible for our present high culture. War, because of them, was not permitted to usurp the place of peace-time social and scientific work. Fighting was highly specialized, and, because of technical advances, manpower was no longer important. Each band of Free Companions numbered a few thousand, seldom more.

It was a strange, lonely life they must have led, shut out from the normal life of the Keeps. They were vestigian but necessary, like the fangs of the marsupians who eventually evolved into Homo sapiens. But without those warriors, the Keeps would have been plunged completely into total war, with fatally destructive results.

Harsh, gallant, indomitable, serving the god of battles so that it might be destroyed—working toward their own obliteration—the Free Companies roar down the pages of history, the banner of Mars streaming above them in the misty air of Venus. They were doomed as Tyrannosaur Rex was doomed, and they fought on as he did, serving, in their strange way, the shape of Minerva that stood behind Mars.

Now they are gone. We can learn much by studying the place they held in the Undersea Period. For, because of them, civilization rose again to the heights it had once reached on Earth, and far beyond.

> "These lords shall light the mystery
> Of mastery or victory,
> And these ride high in history,
> But these shall not return."

The Free Companions hold their place in interplanetary literature. They are a legend now, archaic and strange. For they were fighters, and war has gone with unification. But we can understand them a little more than could the people of the Keeps.

This story, built on legends and fact, is about a typical warrior of the *period—Captain Brian Scott of Doone's Free Companions. He may never have existed—*

I.

O, it's Tommy this, an' Tommy that, an' "Tommy, go away";
But it's "Thank you, Mr. Atkins," when the band begins to play,
The band begins to play, my boys, the band begins to play—
O, it's "Thank you, Mr. Atkins," when the band begins to play.
—R. Kipling circa 1900

SCOTT DRANK STINGING UISQUEPLUS AND GLOWERED ACROSS THE SMOKY tavern. He was a hard, stocky man, with thick gray-shot brown hair and the scar of an old wound crinkling his chin. He was thirty-odd, looking like the veteran he was, and he had sense enough to wear a plain suit of blue celoflex, rather than the garish silks and rainbow fabrics that were all around him.

Outside, through the transparent walls, a laughing throng was carried to and fro along the movable ways. But in the tavern it was silent, except for the low voice of a harpman as he chanted some old ballad, accompanying himself on his complicated instrument. The song came to an end. There was scattered applause, and from the hot-box overhead the blaring music of an orchestra burst out. Instantly the restraint was gone. In the booths and at the bar men and women began to laugh and talk with casual unrestraint. Couples were dancing now.

The girl beside Scott, a slim, tan-skinned figure with glossy black ringlets cascading to her shoulders, turned inquiring eyes to him.

"Want to, Brian?"

Scott's mouth twisted in a wry grimace. "Suppose so, Jeana. Eh?" He rose, and she came gracefully into his arms. Brian did not dance too well, but what he lacked in practice he made up in integration. Jeana's heart-shaped face, with its high cheekbones and vividly crimson lips, lifted to him.

"Forget Bienne. He's just trying to ride you."

Scott glanced toward a distant booth, where two girls sat with a man— Commander Fredric Bienne of the Doones. He was a gaunt, tall, bitter-faced man, his regular features twisted into a perpetual sneer, his eyes somber under heavy dark brows. He was pointing, now, toward the couple on the floor.

"I know," Scott said. "He's doing it, too. Well, the hell with him. So I'm a captain now and he's still a commander. That's tough. Next time he'll obey orders and not send his ship out of the line, trying to ram."

"That was it, eh?" Jeana asked. "I wasn't sure. There's plenty of talk."

"There always is. Oh, Bienne's hated me for years. I reciprocate. We simply don't get on together. Never did. Every time I got a promotion, he chewed his nails. Figured he had a longer service record than I had, and deserved to move up faster. But he's too much of an individualist—at the wrong times."

"He's drinking a lot," Jeana said.

"Let him. Three months we've been in Montana Keep. The boys get tired of inaction—being treated like this." Scott nodded toward the door, where a Free Companion was arguing with the keeper. "No noncoms allowed in here. Well, the devil with it."

They could not hear the conversation above the hubbub, but its importance was evident. Presently the soldier shrugged, his mouth forming a curse, and departed. A fat man in scarlet silks shouted encouragement.

"—want any . . . Companions here!"

Scott saw Commander Bienne, his eyes half closed, get up and walk toward the fat man's booth. His shoulder moved in an imperceptible shrug. The hell with civilians, anyhow. Serve the lug right if Bienne smashed his greasy face. And that seemed the probable outcome. For the fat man was accompanied by a girl, and obviously wasn't going to back down, though Bienne, standing too close to him, was saying something insulting, apparently.

The auxiliary hot-box snapped some quick syllables, lost in the general tumult. But Scott's trained ear caught the words. He nodded to Jeana, made a significant clicking noise with his tongue, and said, "This is it."

She, too, had heard. She let Scott go. He headed toward the fat man's booth just in time to see the beginning of a brawl. The civilian, red as a turkey cock, had struck out suddenly, landing purely by accident on Bienne's gaunt cheek. The commander, grinning tightly, stepped back a pace, his fist clenching. Scott caught the other's arm.

"Hold it, commander."

Bienne swung around, glaring. "What business is it of yours? Let—"

The fat man, seeing his opponent's attention distracted, acquired more courage and came in swinging. Scott reached past Bienne, planted his open hand in the civilian's face, and pushed hard. The fat man almost fell backward on his table.

As he rebounded, he saw a gun in Scott's hand. The captain said curtly, " 'Tend to your knitting, mister."

The civilian licked his lips, hesitated, and sat down. Under his breath he muttered something about too-damn-cocky Free Companions.

Bienne was trying to break free, ready to swing on the captain. Scott holstered his gun. "Orders," he told the other, jerking his head toward the hot-box. "Get it?"

"—mobilization. Doonemen report to headquarters. Captain Scott to Administration. Immediate mobilization—"

"Oh," Bienne said, though he still scowled. "O.K. I'll take over. There was time for me to take a crack at that louse, though."

"You know what instant mobilization means," Scott grunted. "We may have to leave at an instant's notice. Orders, commander."

Bienne saluted halfheartedly and turned away. Scott went back to his own booth. Jeana had already gathered her purse and gloves and was applying lip juice.

She met his eyes calmly enough.

"I'll be at the apartment, Brian. Luck."

He kissed her briefly, conscious of a surging excitement at the prospect of a new venture. Jeana understood his emotion. She gave him a quick, wry smile, touched his hair lightly, and rose. They went out into the gay tumult of the ways.

Perfumed wind blew into Scott's face. He wrinkled his nose disgustedly. During carnival seasons the Keeps were less pleasant to the Free Companions than otherwise; they felt more keenly the gulf that lay between them and the undersea dwellers. Scott pushed his way through the crowd and took Jeana across the ways to the center fast-speed strip. They found seats.

At a clover-leaf intersection Scott left the girl, heading toward Administration, the cluster of taller buildings in the city's center. The technical and political headquarters were centered here, except for the laboratories, which were in the suburbs near the base of the Dome. There were a few small test-domes a mile or so distant from the city, but these were used only for more precarious experiments. Glancing up, Scott was reminded of the catastrophe that had unified science into something like a freemasonry. Above him, hanging without gravity over a central plaza, was the globe of the Earth, half shrouded by the folds of a black plastic pall. In every Keep on Venus there was a similar ever-present reminder of the lost mother planet.

Scott's gaze went up farther, to the Dome, as though he could penetrate the impervium and the mile-deep layer of water and the clouded atmosphere to the white star that hung in space, one quarter as brilliant as the Sun. A star—all that remained of Earth, since atomic power had been unleashed there two centuries ago. The scourge had spread like flame, melting continents and leveling mountains. In the libraries there were wire-tape pictorial records of the Holocaust. A religious cult—Men of the New Judgment—had sprung up, and advocated the complete destruction of science; followers of that dogma still existed here and there. But the cult's teeth had been drawn when technicians unified, outlawing experiments with atomic power forever, making use of that force punishable by death, and permitting no one to join their society without taking the Minervan Oath.

"—to work for the ultimate good of mankind . . . taking all precaution against harming humanity and science . . . requiring permission from those in authority before undertaking any experiment involving peril to the race . . . remembering always the extent of the trust placed in us and remembering forever the death of the mother planet through misuse of knowledge—"

The Earth. A strange sort of world it must have been, Scott thought. Sunlight, for one thing, unfiltered by the cloud layer. In the old days, there had been few unexplored areas left on Earth. But here on Venus, where the continents had not yet been conquered—there was no need, of course, since everything necessary to life could be produced under the Domes—here on Venus, there was still a frontier. In the Keeps, a highly specialized social culture. Above the surface, a primeval world, where only the Free Companions had their fortresses and navies—the navies for fighting, the forts to house the technicians who provided the latter-day sinews of war, science instead of money. The Keeps tolerated visits from the Free Companions, but would not offer them headquarters, so violent the feeling, so sharp the schism, in the public mind, between war and cultural progress.

Under Scott's feet the sliding way turned into an escalator, carrying him into the Administration Building. He stepped to another way which took him to a lift, and, a moment or two later, was facing the door-curtain bearing the face of President Dane Crosby of Montana Keep.

Crosby's voice said, "Come in, captain," and Scott brushed through the curtain, finding himself in a medium-sized room with muraled walls and a great window overlooking the city. Crosby, a white-haired, thin figure in blue silks, was at his desk. He looked like a tired old clerk out of Dickens, Scott thought suddenly, entirely undistinguished and ordinary. Yet Crosby was one of the greatest socio-politicians on Venus.

Cinc Rhys, leader of Doone's Free Companions, was sitting in a relaxer, the apparent antithesis of Crosby. All the moisture in Rhys' body seemed to have been sucked out of him years ago by ultraviolet actinic, leaving a mummy of brown leather and whipcord sinew. There was no softness in the man. His smile was a grimace. Muscles lay like wire under the swarthy cheeks.

Scott saluted. Rhys waved him to a relaxer. The look of subdued eagerness in the cinc's eyes was significant—an eagle poising himself, smelling blood. Crosby sensed that, and a wry grin showed on his pale face.

"Every man to his trade," he remarked, semi-ironically. "I suppose I'd be bored stiff if I had too long a vacation. But you'll have quite a battle on your hands this time, Cinc Rhys."

Scott's stocky body tensed automatically. Rhys glanced at him.

"Virginia Keep is attacking, captain. They've hired the Helldivers—Flynn's outfit."

There was a pause. Both Free Companions were anxious to discuss the angles, but unwilling to do so in the presence of a civilian, even the president of Montana Keep. Crosby rose.

"The money settlement's satisfactory, then?"

Rhys nodded. "Yes, that's all right. I expect the battle will take place in a couple of days. In the neighborhood of Venus Deep, at a rough guess."

"Good. I've a favor to ask, so if you'll excuse me for a few minutes, I'll—" He left the sentence unfinished and went out through the door-curtain. Rhys offered Scott a cigarette.

"You get the implications, captain—the Helldivers?"

"Yes, sir. Thanks. We can't do it alone."

"Right. We're short on manpower and armament both. And the Helldivers recently merged with O'Brien's Legion, after O'Brien was killed in that polar scrap. They're a strong outfit, plenty strong. Then they've got their specialty—submarine attack. I'd say we'll have to use H-plan 7."

Scott closed his eyes, remembering the files. Each Free Company kept up-to-date plans of attack suited to the merits of every other Company of Venus. Frequently revised as new advances were made, as groups merged, and as the balance of power changed on each side, the plans were so detailed that they could be carried into action at literally a moment's notice. H-plan 7, Scott recalled, involved enlisting the aid of the Mob, a small but well-organized band of Free Companions led by Cinc Tom Mendez.

"Right," Scott said. "Can you get him?"

"I think so. We haven't agreed yet on the bonus. I've been telaudioing him on a tight beam, but he keeps putting me off—waiting till the last moment, when he can dictate his own terms."

"What's he asking, sir?"

"Fifty thousand cash and a fifty percent cut on the loot."

"I'd say thirty percent would be about right."

Rhys nodded. "I've offered him thirty-five. I may send you to his fort—carte blanche. We can get another Company, but Mendez has got beautiful sub-detectors—which would come in handy against the Helldivers. Maybe I can settle things by audio. If not, you'll have to fly over to Mendez and buy his services, at less than fifty per if you can."

Scott rubbed the old scar on his chin with a calloused forefinger. "Meantime Commander Bienne's in charge of mobilization. When—"

"I telaudioed our fort. Air transports are on the way now."

"It'll be quite a scrap," Scott said, and the eyes of the two men met in perfect understanding. Rhys chuckled dryly.

"And good profits. Virginia Keep has a big supply of korium . . . dunno how much, but plenty."

"What started the fracas this time?"

"The usual thing, I suppose," Rhys said disinterestedly. "Imperialism. Somebody in Virginia Keep worked out a new plan for annexing the rest of the Keeps. Same as usual."

They stood up as the door-curtain swung back, admitting President Crosby, another man, and a girl. The man looked young, his boyish face not yet toughened under actinic burn. The girl was lovely in the manner of a plastic figurine, lit from within by vibrant life. Her blond hair was cropped in the prevalent mode, and her eyes, Scott saw, were an unusual shade of green. She was more than merely pretty—she was instantly exciting.

Crosby said, "My niece, Ilene Kane—and my nephew, Norman Kane." He performed introductions, and they found seats.

"What about drinks?" Ilene suggested. "This is rather revoltingly formal. The fight hasn't started yet, after all."

Crosby shook his head at her. "You weren't invited here anyway. Don't try to turn this into a party—there isn't too much time, under the circumstances."

"O.K.," Ilene murmured. "I can wait." She eyed Scott interestedly.

Norman Kane broke in. "I'd like to join Doone's Free Companions, sir. I've already applied, but now that there's a battle coming up, I hate to wait till my application's approved. So I thought—"

Crosby looked at Cinc Rhys. "A personal favor, but the decision's up to you. My nephew's a misfit—a romanticist. Never liked the life of a Keep. A year ago he went off and joined Starling's outfit."

Rhys raised an eyebrow. "That gang? It's not a recommendation, Kane. They're not even classed as Free Companions. More like a band of guerrillas, and entirely without ethics. There've even been rumors they're messing around with atomic power."

Crosby looked startled. "I hadn't heard that."

"It's no more than a rumor. If it's ever proved, the Free Companions—all of them—will get together and smash Starling in a hurry."

Norman Kane looked slightly uncomfortable. "I suppose I was rather a fool. But I wanted to get in the fighting game, and Starling's group appealed to me—"

The cinc made a sound in his throat. "They would. Swashbuckling romantics, with no idea of what war means. They've not more than a dozen technicians. And they've no discipline—it's like a pirate outfit. War today, Kane, isn't won by romantic animals dashing at forlorn hopes. The modern soldier is a tactician who knows how to think, integrate, and obey. If you join our Company, you'll have to forget what you learned with Starling."

"Will you take me, sir?"

"I think it would be unwise. You need the training course."

"I've had experience—"

Crosby said, "It would be a favor, Cinc Rhys, if you'd skip the red tape. I'd appreciate it. Since my nephew wants to be a soldier, I'd much prefer to see him with the Doones."

Rhys shrugged. "Very well. Captain Scott will give you your orders, Kane. Remember that discipline is vitally important with us."

The boy tried to force back a delighted grin. "Thank you, sir."

"Captain—"

Scott rose and nodded to Kane. They went out together. In the anteroom was a telaudio set, and Scott called the Doone's local headquarters in Montana Keep. An integrator answered, his face looking inquiringly from the screen.

"Captain Scott calling, subject induction."

"Yes, sir. Ready to record."

Scott drew Kane forward. "Photosnap this man. He'll report to headquarters immediately. Name, Norman Kane. Enlist him without training course—special orders from Cinc Rhys."

"Acknowledged, sir."

Scott broke the connection. Kane couldn't quite repress his grin.

"All right," the captain grunted, a sympathetic gleam in his eyes. "That fixes it. They'll put you in my command. What's your specialty."

"Flitterboats, sir."

"Good. One more thing. Don't forget what Cinc Rhys said, Kane. Discipline is damned important, and you may not have realized that yet. This isn't a cloak-and-sword war. There are no Charges of Light Brigades. No grandstand plays—that stuff went out with the Crusades. Just obey orders, and you'll have no trouble. Good luck."

"Thank you, sir." Kane saluted and strode out with a perceptible swagger. Scott grinned. The kid would have *that* knocked out of him pretty soon.

A voice at his side made him turn quickly. Ilene Kane was standing there, slim and lovely in her celoflex gown.

"You seem pretty human after all, captain," she said. "I heard what you told Norman."

Scott shrugged. "I did that for his own good—and the good of the Company. One man off the beam can cause plenty of trouble, Mistress Kane."

"I envy Norman," she said. "It must be a fascinating life you lead. I'd like it—for a while. Not for long. I'm one of the useless offshoots of this civilization, not much good for anything. So I've perfected one talent."

"What's that?"

"Oh, hedonism, I suppose you'd call it. I enjoy myself. It's not often too boring. But I'm a bit bored now. I'd like to talk to you, captain."

"Well, I'm listening," Scott said.

Ilene Kane made a small grimace. "Wrong semantic term. I'd like to get inside of you psychologically. But painlessly. Dinner and dancing. Can do?"

"There's no time," Scott told her. "We may get our orders any moment." He wasn't sure he wanted to go out with this girl of the Keeps, though there was definitely a subtle fascination for him, an appeal he could not analyze. She typified the most pleasurable part of a world he did not know. The other facets of that world could not impinge on him; geopolitics or nonmilitary science held no appeal, were too alien. But all worlds touch at one point—pleasure. Scott could understand the relaxations of the undersea groups, as he could not understand or feel sympathy for their work or their social impulses.

Cinc Rhys came through the door-curtain, his eyes narrowed. "I've some telaudioing to do, captain," he said. Scott knew what implications the words held: the incipient bargain with Cinc Mendez. He nodded.

"Yes, sir. Shall I report to headquarters?"

Rhys' harsh face seemed to relax suddenly as he looked from Ilene to

Scott. "You're free till dawn. I won't need you till then, but report to me at six a.m. No doubt you've a few details to clean up."

"Very well, sir." Scott watched Rhys go out. The cinc had meant Jeana, of course. But Ilene did not know that.

"So?" she asked. "Do I get a turn-down? You might buy me a drink, anyway."

There was plenty of time. Scott said, "It'll be a pleasure," and Ilene linked her arm with his. They took the dropper to ground-level.

As they came out on one of the ways, Ilene turned her head and caught Scott's glance. "I forgot something, captain. You may have a previous engagement. I didn't realize—"

"There's nothing," he said. "Nothing important."

It was true; he felt a mild gratitude toward Jeana at the realization. His relationship with her was the peculiar one rendered advisable by his career. Free-marriage was the word for it; Jeana was neither his wife nor his mistress, but something midway between. The Free Companions had no firmly grounded foundation for social life; in the Keeps they were visitors, and in their coastal forts they were—well, soldiers. One would no more bring a woman to a fort than aboard a ship of the line. So the women of the Free Companions lived in the Keeps, moving from one to another as their men did; and because of the ever-present shadow of death, ties were purposely left loose. Jeana and Scott had been free-married for five years now. Neither made demands on the other. No one expected fidelity of a Free Companion. Soldiers lived under such iron disciplines that when they were released, during the brief peacetimes, the pendulum often swung far in the opposite direction.

To Scott, Ilene Kane was a key that might unlock the doors of the Keep —doors that opened to a world of which he was not a part, and which he could not quite understand.

II.

I, a stranger and afraid
In a world I never made.
                    —Housman

There were nuances, Scott found, which he had never known existed. A hedonist like Ilene devoted her life to such nuances; they were her career. Such minor matters as making the powerful, insipid Moonflower Cocktails more palatable by filtering them through lime-soaked sugar held between the teeth. Scott was a uisqueplus man, having the average soldier's contempt for what he termed hydroponic drinks, but the cocktails Ilene suggested were quite as effective as acrid, burning amber uisqueplus. She taught him, that night, such tricks as pausing between glasses to sniff lightly at happy-gas, to mingle sensual excitement with mental by trying the amusement rides designed to give one the violent physical intoxication of breathless speed. Nuances all, which only a girl with Ilene's background could know. She was not representative of Keep life. As she had said, she was an offshoot, a casual and useless flower on the great vine that struck up inexorably to the skies, its strength in its tough, reaching tendrils—scientists and technicians and socio-politicians. She was doomed in her own way, as Scott was in his. The undersea folk served Minerva; Scott served Mars; and Ilene served Aphrodite—not purely the sexual goddess, but the patron of arts and pleasure. Between Scott and Ilene was the difference between Wagner and Strauss; the difference between crashing chords and tinkling arpeggios. In both was a muted bittersweet sadness, seldom realized by either. But that undertone was brought out by their contact. The sense of dim hopelessness in each responded to the other.

It was carnival, but neither Ilene nor Scott wore masks. Their faces were masks enough, and both had been trained to reserve, though in different ways. Scott's hard mouth kept its tight grimness even when he smiled. And Ilene's smiles came so often that they were meaningless.

Through her, Scott was able to understand more of the undersea life than he had ever done before. She was for him a catalyst. A tacit understanding grew between them, not needing words. Both realized that, in the course of progress, they would eventually die out. Mankind tolerated them because that was necessary for a little time. Each responded differently. Scott served Mars; he served actively; and the girl, who was passive, was attracted by the antithesis.

Scott's drunkenness struck psychically deep. He did not show it. His stiff silver-brown hair was not disarranged, and his hard, burned face was impassive as ever. But when his brown eyes met Ilene's green ones a spark of—something—met between them.

Color and light and sound. They began to form a pattern now, were not quite meaningless to Scott. They were, long past midnight, sitting in an Olympus, which was a private cosmos. The walls of the room in which they were seemed nonexistent. The gusty tides of gray, faintly luminous clouds seemed to drive chaotically past them, and, dimly, they could hear the muffled screaming of an artificial wind. They had the isolation of the gods.

And the Earth was without form, and void; and darkness was upon the face of the deep— That was, of course, the theory of the Olympus room. No one existed, no world existed, outside of the chamber; values automatically shifted, and inhibitions seemed absurd.

Scott relaxed on a translucent cushion like a cloud. Beside him, Ilene lifted the bit of a happy-gas tube to his nostrils. He shook his head.

"Not now, Ilene."

She let the tube slide back into its reel. "Nor I. Too much of anything is unsatisfactory, Brian. There should always be something untasted, some anticipation left— You have that. I haven't."

"How?"

"Pleasures—well, there's a limit. There's a limit to human endurance. And eventually I build up a resistance psychically, as I do physically, to everything. With you, there's always the last adventure. You never know when death will come. You can't plan. Plans are dull; it's the unexpected that's important."

Scott shook his head slightly. "Death isn't important either. It's an automatic cancellation of values. Or, rather—" He hesitated, seeking words. "In this life you can plan, you can work out values, because they're all based on certain conditions. On—let's say—arithmetic. Death is a change to a different plane of conditions, quite unknown. Arithmetical rules don't apply as such to geometry."

"You think death has its rules?"

"It may be a lack of rules, Ilene. One lives realizing that life is subject to death; civilization is based on that. That's why civilization concentrates on the race instead of the individual. Social self-preservation."

She looked at him gravely. "I didn't think a Free Companion could theorize that way."

Scott closed his eyes, relaxing. "The Keeps know nothing about Free Companions. They don't want to. We're men. Intelligent men. Our technicians are as great as the scientists under the Domes."

"But they work for war."

"War's necessary," Scott said. "Now, anyway."

"How did you get into it? Should I ask?"

He laughed a little at that. "Oh, I've no dark secrets in my past. I'm not a runaway murderer. One—drifts. I was born in Australia Keep. My father was a tech, but my grandfather had been a soldier. I guess it was in my blood. I tried various trades and professions. Meaningless. I wanted something that . . . hell, I don't know. Something, maybe, that needs all of a man. Fighting does. It's like a religion. Those cultists—Men of the

New Judgment—they're fanatics, but you can see that their religion is the only thing that matters to them."

"Bearded, dirty men with twisted minds, though."

"It happens to be a religion based on false premises. There are others, appealing to different types. But religion was too passive for me, in these days."

Ilene examined his harsh face. "You'd have preferred the church militant—the Knights of Malta, fighting Saracens."

"I suppose. I had no values. Anyhow, I'm a fighter."

"Just how important is it to you? The Free Companions?"

Scott opened his eyes and grinned at the girl. He looked unexpectedly boyish.

"Damn little, really. It has emotional appeal. Intellectually, I know that it's a huge fake. Always has been. As absurd as the Men of the New Judgment. Fighting's doomed. So we've no real purpose. I suppose most of us know there's no future for the Free Companions. In a few hundred years —well!"

"And still you go on. Why? It isn't money."

"No. There is a . . . a drunkenness to it. The ancient Norsemen had their berserker madness. We have something similar. To a Dooneman, his group is father, mother, child, and God Almighty. He fights the other Free Companions when he's paid to do so, but he doesn't hate the others. They serve the same toppling idol. And it *is* toppling, Ilene. Each battle we win or lose brings us closer to the end. We fight to protect the culture that eventually will wipe us out. The Keeps—when they finally unify, will they need a military arm? I can see the trend. If war was an essential part of civilization, each Keep would maintain its own military. But they shut us out—a necessary evil. If they would end war now!" Scott's fist unconsciously clenched. "So many men would find happier places in Venus —undersea. But as long as the Free Companions exist, there'll be new recruits."

Ilene sipped her cocktail, watching the gray chaos of clouds flow like a tide around them. In the dimly luminous light Scott's face seemed like dark stone, flecks of brightness showing in his eyes. She touched his hand gently.

"You're a soldier, Brian. You wouldn't change."

His laugh was intensely bitter. "Like hell I wouldn't, Mistress Ilene Kane! Do you think fighting's just pulling a trigger? I'm a military strategist. That took ten years. Harder cramming than I'd have had in a Keep

Tech-Institute. I have to know everything about war from trajectories to mass psychology. This is the greatest science the System has ever known, and the most useless. Because war will die in a few centuries at most. Ilene —you've never seen a Free Company's fort. It's science, marvelous science, aimed at military ends only. We have our psych-specialists. We have our engineers, who plan everything from ordnance to the frictional quotient on flitterboats. We have the foundries and mills. Each fortress is a city made for war, as the Keeps are made for social progress."

"As complicated as that?"

"Beautifully complicated and beautifully useless. There are so many of us who realize that. Oh, we fight—it's a poison. We worship the Company—that is an emotional poison But we live only during wartime. It's an incomplete life. Men in the Keeps have full lives; they have their work, and their relaxations are geared to fit them. We don't fit."

"Not all the undersea races," Ilene said. "There's always the fringe that doesn't fit. At least you have a *raison d'être*. You're a soldier. I can't make a lifework out of pleasure. But there's nothing else for me."

Scott's fingers tightened on hers. "You're the product of a civilization, at least. I'm left out."

"With you, Brian, it might be better. For a while. I don't think it would last for long."

"It might."

"You think so now. It's quite a horrible thing, feeling yourself a shadow."

"I know."

"I want you, Brian," Ilene said, turning to face him. "I want you to come to Montana Keep and stay here. Until our experiment fails. I think it'll fail presently. But, perhaps, not for some time. I need your strength. I can show you how to get the most out of this sort of life—how to enter into it. True hedonism. You can give me—companionship perhaps. For me the companionship of hedonists who know nothing else isn't enough."

Scott was silent. Ilene watched him for a while.

"Is war so important?" she asked at last.

"No," he said, "it isn't at all. It's a balloon. And it's empty, I know that. Honor of the regiment!" Scott laughed. "I'm not hesitating, really. I've been shut out for a long time. A social unit shouldn't be founded on an obviously doomed fallacy. Men and women are important, nothing else, I suppose."

"Men and women—or the race?"

"Not the race," he said with abrupt violence. "Damn the race! It's done nothing for me. I can fit myself into a new life. Not necessarily hedonism.

I'm an expert in several lines; I have to be. I can find work in Montana Keep."

"If you like. I've never tried. I'm more of a fatalist, I suppose. But . . . what about it, Brian?"

Her eyes were almost luminous, like shining emerald, in the ghostly light.

"Yes," Scott said. "I'll come back. To stay."

Ilene said, "Come back? Why not stay now?"

"Because I'm a complete fool, I guess. I'm a key man, and Cinc Rhys needs me just now."

"Is it Rhys or the Company?"

Scott smiled crookedly. "Not the Company. It's just a job I have to do. When I think how many years I've been slaving, pretending absurdities were important, knowing that I was bowing to a straw dummy— *No!* I want your life—the sort of life I didn't know could exist in the Keeps. I'll be back, Ilene. It's something more important than love. Separately we're halves. Together we may be a complete whole."

She didn't answer. Her eyes were steady on Scott's. He kissed her.

Before morning bell he was back in the apartment. Jeana had already packed the necessary light equipment. She was asleep, her dark hair cascading over the pillow, and Scott did not waken her. Quietly he shaved, showered, and dressed. A heavy, waiting silence seemed to fill the city like a cup brimmed with stillness.

As he emerged from the bathroom, buttoning his tunic, he saw the table had been let down and two places set at it. Jeana came in, wearing a cool morning frock. She set cups down and poured coffee.

"Morning, soldier," she said. "You've time for this, haven't you?"

"Uh-huh." Scott kissed her, a bit hesitantly. Up till this moment, the breaking with Jeana had seemed easy enough. She would raise no objections. That was the chief reason for free-marriage. However—

She was sitting in the relaxer, sweeting the coffee, opening a fresh celo-pack of cigarettes. "Hung over?"

"No. I vitamized. Feel pretty good." Most bars had a vitamizing chamber to nullify the effects of too much stimulant. Scott was, in fact, feeling fresh and keenly alert. He was wondering how to broach the subject of Ilene to Jeana.

She saved him the trouble.

"If it's a girl, Brian, just take it easy. No use doing anything till this war's over. How long will it take?"

"Oh, not long. A week at most. One battle may settle it, you know. The girl—"

"She's not a Keep girl."

"Yes."

Jeana looked up, startled. "You're crazy."

"I started to tell you," Scott said impatiently. "It isn't just—her. I'm sick of the Doones. I'm going to quit."

"Hm-m-m. Like that?"

"Like that."

Jeana shook her head. "Keep women aren't tough."

"They don't need to be. Their men aren't soldiers."

"Have it your own way. I'll wait till you get back. Maybe I've got a hunch. You see, Brian, we've been together for five years. We fit. Not because of anything like philosophy or psychology—it's a lot more personal. It's just us. As man and woman, we get along comfortably. There's love, too. Those close emotional feelings are more important, really, than the long view. You can get excited about futures, but you can't live them."

Scott shrugged. "Could be I'm starting to forget about futures. Concentrating on Brian Scott."

"More coffee . . . there. Well, for five years now I've gone with you from Keep to Keep, waiting every time you went off to war, wondering if you'd come back, knowing that I was just a part of your life, but—I sometimes thought—the most important part. Soldiering's seventy-five percent. I'm the other quarter. I think you need that quarter—you need the whole thing, in that proportion, actually. You could find another woman, but she'd have to be willing to take twenty-five percent."

Scott didn't answer. Jeana blew smoke through her nostrils.

"O.K., Brian. I'll wait."

"It isn't the girl so much. She happens to fit into the pattern of what I want. You—"

"I'd never be able to fit that pattern," Jeana said softly. "The Free Companions need women who are willing to be soldiers' wives. Freewives, if you like. Chiefly it's a matter of not being too demanding. But there are other things. No, Brian. Even if you wanted that, I couldn't make myself over into one of the Keep people. It wouldn't be me. I wouldn't respect myself, living a life that'd be false to me; and you wouldn't like me that way either. I couldn't and wouldn't change. I'll have to stay as I am. A soldier's wife. As long as you're a Dooneman, you'll need me. But if *you* change—" She didn't finish.

Scott lit a cigarette, scowling. "It's hard to know, exactly."

"I may not understand you, but I don't ask questions and I don't try to change you. As long as you want that, you can have it from me. I've nothing else to offer you. It's enough for a Free Companion. It's not enough—or too much—for a Keep-dweller."

"I'll miss you," he said.

"That'll depend, too. I'll miss you." Under the table her fingers writhed together, but her face did not change. "It's getting late. Here, let me check your chronometer." Jeana leaned across the table, lifted Scott's wrist, and compared his watch with the central-time clock on the wall. "O.K. On your way, soldier."

Scott stood up, tightening his belt. He bent to kiss Jeana, and, though she began to turn her face away, after a moment she raised her lips to his.

They didn't speak. Scott went out quickly, and the girl sat motionless, the cigarette smoldering out unheeded between her fingers. Somehow it did not matter so much, now, that Brian was leaving her for another woman and another life. As always, the one thing of real importance was that he was going into danger.

Guard him from harm, she thought, not knowing that she was praying. *Guard him from harm!*

And now there would be silence, and waiting. That, at least, had not changed. Her eyes turned to the clock.

Already the minutes were longer.

III.

'E's the kind of a giddy harumfrodite—soldier an' sailor too!
—Kipling

Commander Bienne was superintending the embarkation of the last Dooneman when Scott arrived at headquarters. He saluted the captain briskly, apparently untired by his night's work of handling the transportation routine.

"All checked, sir."

Scott nodded. "Good. Is Cinc Rhys here?"

"He just arrived." Bienne nodded toward a door-curtain. As Scott moved away, the other followed.

"What's up, commander?"

Bienne pitched his voice low. "Bronson's laid up with endemic fever." He forgot to say "sir." "He was to handle the left wing of the fleet. I'd appreciate that job."

"I'll see if I can do it."

Bienne's lips tightened, but he said nothing more. He turned back to his men, and Scott went on into the cinc's office. Rhys was at the telaudio. He looked up, his eyes narrowed.

"Morning, captain. I've just heard from Mendez."

"Yes, sir?"

"He's still holding out for a fifty percent cut on the korium ransom from Virginia Keep. You'll have to see him. Try and get the Mob for less than fifty if you can. Telaudio me from Mendez's fort."

"Check, sir."

"Another thing. Bronson's in sick bay."

"I heard that. If I may suggest Commander Bienne to take his place at left-wing command—"

But Cinc Rhys raised his hand. "Not this time. We can't afford individualism. The commander tried to play a lone hand in the last war. You know we can't risk it till he's back in line—thinking of the Doones instead of Fredric Bienne."

"He's a good man, sir. A fine strategist."

"But not yet a good integrating factor. Perhaps next time. Put Commander Geer on the left wing. Keep Bienne with you. He needs discipline. And—take a flitterboat to Mendez."

"Not a plane?"

"One of the technicians just finished a new tight-beam camouflager for communications. I'm having it installed immediately on all our planes and gliders. Use the boat; it isn't far to the Mob's fort—that long peninsula on the coast of Southern Hell."

Even on the charts that continent was named Hell—for obvious reasons. Heat was only one of them. And, even with the best equipment, a party exploring the jungle there would soon find itself suffering the tortures of the damned. On the land of Venus, flora and fauna combined diabolically to make the place uninhabitable to Earthmen. Many of the plants even exhaled poisonous gases. Only the protected coastal forts of the Free Companies could exist—and that was because they *were* forts.

Cinc Rhys frowned at Scott. "We'll use H-plan 7 if we can get the Mob. Otherwise we'll have to fall back on another outfit, and I don't want to do that. The Helldivers have too many subs, and we haven't enough detectors. So do your damnedest."

Scott saluted. "I'll do that, sir." Rhys waved him away, and he went out into the next room, finding Commander Bienne alone. The officer turned an inquiring look toward him.

"Sorry," Scott said. "Geer gets the left-wing command this time."

Bienne's sour face turned dark red. "I'm sorry I didn't take a crack at you before mobilization," he said. "You hate competition, don't you?"

Scott's nostrils flared. "If it had been up to me, you'd have got that command, Bienne."

"Sure. I'll bet. All right, captain. Where's my bunk? A flitterboat?"

"You'll be on right wing, with me. Control ship *Flintlock*."

"With you. Under you, you mean," Bienne said tightly. His eyes were blazing. "Yeah."

Scott's dark cheeks were flushed too. "Orders, commander," he snapped. "Get me a flitterboat pilot. I'm going topside."

Without a word Bienne turned to the telaudio. Scott, a tight, furious knot in his stomach, stamped out of headquarters, trying to fight down his anger. Bienne was a jackass. A lot he cared about the Doones—

Scott caught himself and grinned sheepishly. Well, he cared little about the Doones himself. But while he was in the Company, discipline was important—integration with the smoothly running fighting machine. No place for individualism. One thing he and Bienne had in common; neither had any sentiment about the Company.

He took a lift to the ceiling of the Dome. Beneath him Montana Keep dropped away, shrinking to doll size. Somewhere down there, he thought, was Ilene. He'd be back. Perhaps this war would be a short one—not that they were ever much longer than a week, except in unusual cases where a Company developed new strategies.

He was conducted through an air lock into a bubble, a tough, transparent sphere with a central vertical core through which the cable ran. Except for Scott, the bubble was empty. After a moment it started up with a slight jar. Gradually the water outside the curving walls changed from black to deep green, and thence to translucent chartreuse. Sea creatures were visible, but they were nothing new to Scott; he scarcely saw them.

The bubble broke surface. Since air pressure had been constant, there was no possibility of the bends, and Scott opened the panel and stepped out on one of the buoyant floats that dotted the water above Montana Keep. A few sightseers crowded into the chamber he had left, and presently it was drawn down, out of sight.

In the distance Free Companions were embarking from a larger float to an air ferry. Scott glanced up with a weather eye. No storm, he saw, though the low ceiling was, as usual, torn and twisted into boiling currents by the winds. He remembered, suddenly, that the battle would probably take place over Venus Deep. That would make it somewhat harder for the gliders—there would be few of the thermals found, for instance, above the Sea of Shallows here.

A flitterboat, low, fast, and beautifully maneuverable, shot in toward the quay. The pilot flipped back the overhead shell and saluted Scott. It was Norman Kane, looking shipshape in his tight-fitting gray uniform, and apparently ready to grin at the slightest provocation.

Scott jumped lightly down into the craft and seated himself beside the pilot. Kane drew the transparent shell back over them. He looked at Scott.

"Orders, captain?"

"Know where the Mob's fort is? Good. Head there. Fast."

Kane shot the flitterboat out from the float with a curtain of v-shaped spray rising from the bow. Drawing little water, maneuverable, incredibly fast, these tiny craft were invaluable in naval battle. It was difficult to hit one, they moved so fast. They had no armor to slow them down. They carried high-explosive bullets fired from small-caliber guns, and were, as a rule, two-man craft. They complemented the heavier ordnance of the battlewagons and destroyers.

Scott handed Kane a cigarette. The boy hesitated.

"We're not under fire," the captain chuckled. "Discipline clamps down during a battle, but it's O. K. for you to have a smoke with me. Here!" He lit the white tube for Kane.

"Thanks, sir. I guess I'm a bit—over-anxious?"

"Well, war has its rules. Not many, but they mustn't be broken." Both men were silent for a while, watching the blank gray surface of the ocean ahead. A transport plane passed them, flying low.

"Is Ilene Kane your sister?" Scott asked presently.

Kane nodded. "Yes, sir."

"Thought so. If she'd been a man, I imagine she'd have been a Free Companion."

The boy shrugged. "Oh, I don't know. She doesn't have the— I don't know. She'd consider it too much effort. She doesn't like discipline."

"Do you?"

"It's fighting that's important to me. Sir." That was an afterthought. "Winning, really."

"You can lose a battle even though you win it," Scott said rather somberly.

"Well, I'd rather be a Free Companion than do anything else I know of. Not that I've had much experience—"

"You've had experience of war with Starling's outfit, but you probably learned some dangerous stuff at the same time. War isn't swashbuckling piracy these days. If the Doones tried to win battles by that sort of thing, there'd be no more Doones in a week or so."

"But—" Kane hesitated. "Isn't that sort of thing rather necessary? Taking blind chances, I mean—"

"There are desperate chances," Scott told him, "but there are no blind chances in war—not to a good soldier. When I was green in the service, I ran a cruiser out of the line to ram. I was demoted, for a very good reason. The enemy ship I rammed wasn't as important to the enemy as our cruiser was to us. If I'd stayed on course, I'd have helped sink three or four ships instead of disabling one and putting my cruiser out of action. It's the great god integration we worship, Kane. It's much more important now than it ever was on Earth, because the military has consolidated. Army, navy, air, undersea—they're all part of one organization now. I suppose the only important change was in the air."

"Gliders, you mean? I knew powered planes couldn't be used in battle."

"Not in the atmosphere of Venus," Scott agreed. "Once powered planes get up in the cloud strata, they're fighting crosscurrents and pockets so much they've got no time to do accurate firing. If they're armored, they're slow. If they're light, detectors can spot them and antiaircraft can smash them. Unpowered gliders are valuable not for bombing but for directing attacks. They get into the clouds, stay hidden, and use infrared tele-cameras which are broadcast on a tight beam back to the control ships. They're the eyes of the fleet. They can tell us— *White water ahead, Kane! Swerve!*"

The pilot had already seen the ominous boiling froth foaming out in front of the bow. Instinctively he swung the flitterboat in a wrenching turn. The craft heeled sidewise, throwing its occupants almost out of their seats.

"Sea beast?" Scott asked, and answered his own question. "No, not with those spouts. It's volcanic. And it's spreading fast."

"I can circle it, sir," Kane suggested.

Scott shook his head. "Too dangerous. Backtrack."

Obediently the boy sent the flitterboat racing out of the area of danger. Scott had been right about the extent of the danger; the boiling turmoil was widening almost faster than the tiny ship could flee. Suddenly the line of white water caught up with them. The flitterboat jounced like a chip, the wheel being nearly torn from Kane's grip. Scott reached over and helped steady it. Even with two men handling the wheel, there was a possibility that it might wrench itself free. Steam rose in veils beyond the transparent shell. The water had turned a scummy brown under the froth.

Kane jammed on the power. The flitterboat sprang forward like a ricocheting bullet, dancing over the surface of the seething waves. Once they plunged head-on into a swell, and a screaming of outraged metal vibrated through the craft. Kane, tight-lipped, instantly slammed in the auxiliary, cutting out the smashed motor unit. Then, unexpectedly, they were in clear water, cutting back toward Montana Keep.

Scott grinned. "Nice handling. Lucky you didn't try to circle. We'd never have made it."

"Yes, sir." Kane took a deep breath. His eyes were bright with excitement.

"Circle now. Here." He thrust a lighted cigarette between the boy's lips. "You'll be a good Dooneman, Kane. Your reactions are good and fast."

"Thanks, sir."

Scott smoked silently for a while. He glanced toward the north, but, with the poor visibility, he could not make out the towering range of volcanic peaks that were the backbone of Southern Hell. Venus was a comparatively young planet, the internal fires still bursting forth unexpectedly. Which was why no forts were ever built on islands—they had an unhappy habit of disappearing without warning!

The flitterboat rode hard, at this speed, despite the insulating system of springs and shock absorbers. After a ride in one of these "spankers"— the irreverent name the soldiers had for them—a man needed arnica if not a chiropractor. Scott shifted his weight on the soft air cushions under him, which felt like cement.

Under his breath he hummed:

> *"It ain't the 'eavy 'aulin' that 'urts the 'orses' 'oofs,*
> *It's the 'ammer, 'ammer, 'ammer on the 'ard 'ighway!"*

The flitterboat scooted on, surrounded by monotonous sea and cloud, till finally the rampart of the coast grew before the bow, bursting suddenly from the fog-veiled horizon. Scott glanced at his chronometer and sighed with relief. They had made good time, in spite of the slight delay caused by the subsea volcano.

The fortress of the Mob was a huge metal and stone castle on the tip of the peninsula. The narrow strip that separated it from the mainland had been cleared, and the pockmarks of shell craters showed where guns had driven back onslaughts from the jungle—the reptilian, ferocious giants of Venus, partially intelligent but absolutely untractable because of the gulf that existed between their methods of thinking and the culture of mankind. Overtures had been made often enough; but it had been found that the reptile-folk were better left alone. They would not parley. They were blindly bestial savages, with whom it was impossible to make truce. They stayed in the jungle, emerging only to hurl furious attacks at the forts—attacks doomed to failure, since fang and talon were matched against lead-jacketed bullet and high explosive.

As the flitterboat shot in to a jetty, Scott kept his eyes straight ahead—it was not considered good form for a Free Companion to seem too curious when visiting the fort of another Company. Several men were on the quay, apparently waiting for him. They saluted as Scott stepped out of the boat.

He gave his name and rank. A corporal stepped forward.

"Cinc Mendez is expecting you, sir. Cinc Rhys telaudioed an hour or so back. If you'll come this way—"

"All right, corporal. My pilot—"

"He'll be taken care of, sir. A rubdown and a drink, perhaps, after a spanker ride."

Scott nodded and followed the other into the bastion that thrust out from the overhanging wall of the fort. The sea gate was open, and he walked swiftly through the courtyard in the corporal's wake, passing a door-curtain, mounting an escalator, and finding himself, presently, before another curtain that bore the face of Cinc Mendez, plump, hoglike, and bald as a bullet.

Entering, he saw Mendez himself at the head of a long table, where nearly a dozen officers of the Mob were also seated. In person Mendez was somewhat more prepossessing than in effigy. He looked like a boar rather than a pig—a fighter, not a gourmand. His sharp black eyes seemed to drive into Scott with the impact of a physical blow.

He stood up, his officers following suit. "Sit down, captain. There's a place at the foot of the table. No reflections on rank, but I prefer to be face to face with the man I'm dealing with. But first—you just arrived? If you'd like a quick rubdown, we'll be glad to wait."

Scott took his place. "Thank you, no, Cinc Mendez. I'd prefer not to lose time."

"Then we'll waste none on introductions. However, you can probably stand a drink." He spoke to the orderly at the door, and presently a filled glass stood at Scott's elbow.

His quick gaze ran along the rows of faces. Good soldiers, he thought—tough, well trained, and experienced. They had been under fire. A small outfit, the Mob, but a powerful one.

Cinc Mendez sipped his own drink. "To business. The Doonemen wish to hire our help in fighting the Helldivers. Virginia Keep has bought the services of the Helldivers to attack Montana Keep." He enumerated on stubby fingers. "You offer us fifty thousand cash and thirty-five percent of the korium ransom. So?"

"That's correct."

"We ask fifty percent."

"It's high. The Doones have superior manpower and equipment."

"To us, not to the Helldivers. Besides, the percentage is contingent. If we should lose, we get only the cash payment."

Scott nodded. "That's correct, but the only real danger from the Helldivers is their submarine corps. The Doones have plenty of surface and air equipment. We might lick the Helldivers without you."

"I don't think so." Mendez shook his bald head. "They have some new underwater torpedoes that make hash out of heavy armor plate. But *we* have new sub-detectors. We can blast the Helldivers' subs for you before they get within torpedo range."

Scott said bluntly, "You've been stalling, Cinc Mendez. We're not that bad off. If we can't get you, we'll find another outfit."

"With sub-detectors?"

"Yardley's Company is good at undersea work."

A major near the head of the table spoke up. "That's true, sir. They have suicide subs—not too dependable, but they have them."

Cinc Mendez wiped his bald head with his palms in a slow circular motion. "Hm-m-m. Well, captain, I don't know. Yardley's Company isn't as good as ours for this job."

"All right," Scott said, "I've *carte blanche*. We don't know how much korium Virginia Keep has in her vaults. How would this proposition strike you: the Mob gets fifty percent of the korium ransom up to a quarter of a million; thirty-five percent above that."

"Forty-five."

"Forty, above a quarter of a million; forty-five below that sum."

"Gentlemen?" Cinc Mendez asked, looking down the table. "Your vote?"

There were several ayes, and a scattering of nays. Mendez shrugged. "Then I have the deciding vote. Very well. We get forty-five percent of the Virginia Keep ransom up to a quarter of a million; forty percent on any amount above that. Agreed. We'll drink to it."

Orderlies served drinks. As Mendez rose, the others followed his example. The cinc nodded to Scott.

"Will you propose a toast, captain?"

"With pleasure. Nelson's toast, then—a willing foe and sea room!"

They drank to that, as Free Companions had always drunk that toast on the eve of battle. As they seated themselves once more, Mendez said, "Major Matson, please telaudio Cinc Rhys and arrange details. We must know his plans."

"Yes, sir."

Mendez glanced at Scott. "Now how else may I serve you?"

"Nothing else. I'll get back to our fort. Details can be worked out on the telaudio, on tight beam."

"If you're going back in that flitterboat," Mendez said sardonically, "I strongly advise a rubdown. There's time to spare, now we've come to an agreement."

Scott hesitated. "Very well. I'm ... uh ... starting to ache." He stood up. "Oh, one thing I forgot. We've heard rumors that Starling's outfit is using atomic power."

Mendez's mouth twisted into a grimace of distaste. "Hadn't heard that. Know anything about it, gentlemen?"

Heads were shaken. One officer said, "I've heard a little talk about it, but only talk, so far."

Mendez said, "After this war, we'll investigate further. If there's truth in the story, we'll join you, of course, in mopping up the Starlings. No court-martial is necessary for *that* crime!"

"Thanks. I'll get in touch with other Companies and see what they've heard. Now, if you'll excuse me—"

He saluted and went out, exultation flaming within him. The bargain had been a good one—for the Doonemen badly needed the Mob's help against the Helldivers. Cinc Rhys would be satisfied with the arrangement.

An orderly took him to the baths, where a rubdown relaxed his aching muscles. Presently he was on the quay again, climbing into the flitterboat. A glance behind him showed that the gears of war were beginning to grind. There was little he could see, but men were moving about through the courtyard with purposeful strides, to the shops, to administration, to the laboratories. The battlewagons were anchored down the coast, Scott knew, in a protected bay, but they would soon move out to their rendezvous with the Doones.

Kane, at the controls of the flitterboat, said, "They repaired the auxiliary unit for us, sir."

"Courtesies of the trade." Scott lifted a friendly hand to the men on the quay as the boat slid toward open water. "The Doone fort, now. Know it?"

"Yes, sir. Are . . . are the Mob fighting with us, if I may ask?"

"They are. And they're a grand lot of fighters. You're going to see action, Kane. When you hear battle stations next, it's going to mean one of the sweetest scraps that happened on Venus. Push down that throttle —we're in a hurry!"

The flitterboat raced southwest at top speed, its course marked by the flying V of spray.

"One last fight," Scott thought to himself. "I'm glad it's going to be a good one."

IV.

We eat and drink our own damnation.
—The Book of Common Prayer

The motor failed when they were about eight miles from the Doone fort.

It was a catastrophe rather than merely a failure. The overstrained and overheated engine, running at top speed, blew back. The previous accident, at the subsea volcano, had brought out hidden flaws in the alloy which the Mob's repair men had failed to detect, when they replaced the smashed single unit. Sheer luck had the flitterboat poised on a swell when the crack-up happened. The engine blew out and down, ripping the bow to shreds. Had they been bow-deep, the blast would have been unfortunate for Scott and the pilot—more so than it was.

They were perhaps a half mile from the shore. Scott was deafened by the explosion and simultaneously saw the horizon swinging in a drunken swoop. The boat turned turtle, the shell smacking into water with a loud cracking sound. But the plastic held. Both men were tangled together on what had been their ceiling, sliding forward as the flitterboat began to sink bow first. Steam sizzled from the ruined engine.

Kane managed to touch one of the emergency buttons. The shell was, of course, jammed, but a few of the segments slid aside, admitting a gush of acrid sea water. For a moment they struggled there, fighting the cross-currents till the air had been displaced. Scott, peering through cloudy green gloom, saw Kane's dark shadow twist and kick out through a gap. He followed.

Beneath him the black bulk of the boat dropped slowly and was gone.

His head broke surface, and he gasped for breath, shaking droplets from his lashes and glancing around. Where was Kane?

The boy appeared, his helmet gone, sleek hair plastered to his forehead. Scott caught his eye and pulled the trigger on his life vest, the inflatable undergarment which was always worn under the blouse on sea duty. As chemicals mixed, light gas rushed into the vest, lifting Scott higher in the water. He felt the collar cushion inflate against the back of his head—the skull-fitting pillow that allowed shipwrecked men to float and rest without danger of drowning in their sleep. But he had no need for this now.

Kane, he saw, had triggered his own life vest. Scott hurled himself up, searching for signs of life. There weren't any. The gray-green sea lay desolate to the misty horizon. A half mile away was a mottled chartreuse wall that marked the jungle. Above and beyond that dim sulphurous red lit the clouds.

Scott got out his leaf-bladed smatchet, gesturing for Kane to do the same. The boy did not seem worried. No doubt this was merely an exciting adventure for him, Scott thought wryly. Oh, well.

Gripping the smatchet between his teeth, the captain began to swim shoreward. Kane kept at his side. Once Scott warned his companion to stillness and bent forward, burying his face in the water and peering down at a great dim shadow that coiled away and was gone—a sea snake, but, luckily, not hungry. The oceans of Venus were perilous with teeming, ferocious life. Precautions were fairly useless. When a man was once in the water, it was up to him to get out of it as rapidly as possible.

Scott touched a small cylinder attached to his belt and felt bubbles rushing against his palm. He was slightly relieved. When he had inflated the vest, this tube of compressed gas had automatically begun to release, sending out a foul-smelling vapor that permeated the water for some distance around. The principle was that of the skunk adjusted to the environment of the squid, and dangerous undersea life was supposed to be driven away by the Mellison tubes; but it didn't work with carrion eaters like the snakes. Scott averted his nose. The gadgets were named Mellison tubes, but the men called them Stinkers, a far more appropriate term.

Tides on Venus are unpredictable. The clouded planet has no moon, but it is closer to the Sun than Earth. As a rule the tides are mild, except during volcanic activity, when tidal waves sweep the shores. Scott, keeping a weather eye out for danger, rode the waves in toward the beach, searching the strip of dull blackness for signs of life.

Nothing.

He scrambled out at last, shaking himself like a dog, and instantly changed the clip in his automatic for high explosive. The weapon, of course, was watertight—a necessity on Venus. As Kane sat down with a grunt and deflated his vest, Scott stood eying the wall of jungle thirty feet away. It stopped there abruptly, for nothing could grow on black sand.

The rush and whisper of the waves made the only sound. Most of the trees were liana-like, eking out a precarious existence, as the saying went, by taking in each other's washing. The moment one of them showed signs of solidity, it was immediately assailed by parasitic vines flinging themselves madly upward to reach the filtered sunlight of Venus. The leaves did not begin for thirty feet above the ground; they made a regular roof up there, lying like crazy shingles, and would have shut out all light had they not been of light translucent green. Whitish tendrils crawled like reaching serpents from tree to tree, tentacles of vegetable octopi. There were two types of Venusian fauna: the giants who could crash through the forest, and the supple, small ground-dwellers—insects and reptiles mostly—who depended on poison sacs for self-protection. Neither kind was pleasant company.

There were flying creatures, too, but these lived in the upper strata, among the leaves. And there were ambiguous horrors that lived in the deep mud and the stagnant pools under the forest, but no one knew much about these.

"Well," Scott said, "that's that."

Kane nodded. "I guess I should have checked the motors."

"You wouldn't have found anything. Latent flaws—it would have taken black night to bring 'em out. Just one of those things. Keep your gas mask handy, now. If we get anywhere near poison flowers and the wind's blowing this way, we're apt to keel over like that." Scott opened a waterproof wallet and took out a strip of sensitized litmus, which he clipped to his wrist. "If this turns blue, that means gas, even if we don't smell it."

"Yes, sir. What now?"

"We-el—the boat's gone. We can't telaudio for help." Scott fingered the blade of his smatchet and slipped it into the belt sheath. "We head for the fort. Eight miles. Two hours, if we can stick to the beach and if we don't run into trouble. More than that if Signal Rock's ahead of us, because we'll have to detour inland in that case." He drew out a collapsible single-lenser telescope and looked southwest along the shore. "Uh-huh. We detour."

A breath of sickening sweetness gusted down from the jungle roof. From above, Scott knew, the forest looked surprisingly lovely. It always reminded him of an antique candlewick spread he had once bought Jeana—immense rainbow flowers scattered over a background of pale green. Even among the flora competition was keen; the plants vied in producing colors and scents that would attract the winged carriers of pollen.

There would always be frontiers, Scott thought. But they might remain unconquered for a long time, here on Venus. The Keeps were enough for the undersea folk; they were self-sustaining. And the Free Companions had no need to carve out empires on the continents. They were fighters, not agrarians. Land hunger was no longer a part of the race. It might come again, but not in the time of the Keeps.

The jungles of Venus held secrets he would never know. Men can conquer lands from the air, but they cannot hold them by that method. It would take a long, slow period of encroachment, during which the forest and all it represented would be driven back, step by painful step— and that belonged to a day to come, a time Scott would not know. The savage world would be tamed. But not now—not yet.

At the moment it was untamed and very dangerous. Scott stripped off his tunic and wrung water from it. His clothing would not dry in this saturated air, despite the winds. His trousers clung to him stickily, clammy coldness in their folds.

"Ready, Kane?"

"Yes, sir."

"Then let's go."

They went southwest, along the beach, at a steady, easy lope that devoured miles. Speed and alertness were necessary in equal proportion. From time to time Scott scanned the sea with his telescope, hoping to sight a vessel. He saw nothing. The ships would be in harbor, readying for the battle; and planes would be grounded for installation of the new telaudio device Cinc Rhys had mentioned.

Signal Rock loomed ahead, an outthrust crag with eroded, unscalable sides towering two hundred feet and more. The black strip of sand ended there. From the rock there was a straight drop into deep water, cut up by a turmoil of currents. It was impossible to take the sea detour; there was nothing else for it but to swerve inland, a dangerous but inevitable course. Scott postponed the plunge as long as possible, till the scarp of Signal Rock, jet black with leprous silvery patches on its surface, barred the way. With a quizzical look at Kane he turned sharply to his right and headed for the jungle.

"Half a mile of forest equals a hundred miles of beach hiking," he remarked.

"That bad, sir? I've never tackled it."

"Nobody does, unless they have to. Keep your eyes open and your gun ready. Don't wade through water, even when you can see bottom. There are some little devils that are pretty nearly transparent—vampire fish. If a few of those fasten on you, you'll need a transfusion in less than a minute. I wish the volcanoes would kick up a racket. The beasties generally lie low when that happens."

Under a tree Scott stopped, seeking a straight, long limb. It took a while to find a suitable one, in that tangle of coiling lianas, but finally he succeeded, using his smatchet blade to hack himself a light five-foot pole. Kane at his heels, he moved on into the gathering gloom.

"We may be stalked," he told the boy. "Don't forget to guard the rear."

The sand had given place to sticky whitish mud that plastered the men to their calves before a few moments had passed. A patina of slickness seemed to overlay the ground. The grass was colored so much like the mud itself that it was practically invisible, except by its added slipperiness. Scott slowly advanced keeping close to the wall of rock on his left where the tangle was not so thick. Nevertheless he had to use the smatchet more than once to cut a passage through vines.

He stopped, raising his hand, and the squelch of Kane's feet in the mud paused. Silently Scott pointed. Ahead of them in the cliff base, was the mouth of a burrow.

The captain bent down, found a small stone, and threw it toward the den. He waited, one hand lightly on his gun, ready to see something flash out of that burrow and race toward them. In the utter silence a new sound made itself heard—tiny goblin drums, erratic and resonant in a faraway fashion. Water, dropping from leaf to leaf, in the soaked jungle ceiling above them. *Tink, tink, tink-tink, tink, tink-tink—*

"O. K.," Scott said quietly. "Watch it, though." He went on, gun drawn, till they were level with the mouth of the burrow. "Turn, Kane. Keep your eye on it till I tell you to stop." He gripped the boy's arm and guided him, holstering his own weapon. The pole, till now held between biceps and body, slipped into his hand. He used it to probe the slick surface of the mud ahead. Sinkhole and quicksands were frequent, and so were traps, camouflaged pits built by mud-wolves—which, of course, were not wolves, and belonged to no known genus. On Venus, the fauna had more subdivisions than on old Earth, and lines of demarcation were more subtle.

"All right now."

Kane, sighing with relief, turned his face forward again. "What was it?"

"You never know what may come out of those holes," Scott told him. "They come fast, and they're usually poisonous. So you can't take chances with the critters. Slow down here. I don't like the looks of that patch ahead."

Clearings were unusual in the forest. There was one here, twenty feet wide, slightly saucer-shaped. Scott gingerly extended the pole and probed. A faint ripple shook the white mud, and almost before it had appeared the captain had unholstered his pistol and was blasting shot after shot at the movement.

"Shoot, Kane!" he snapped. "Quick! Shoot at it!"

Kane obeyed, though he had to guess at his target. Mud geysered up, suddenly crimson-stained. Scott, still firing, gripped the boy's arm and ran him back at a breakneck pace.

The echoes died. Once more the distant elfin drums whispered through the green gloom.

"We got it," Scott said, after a pause.

"We did?" the other asked blankly. "What—"

"Mud-wolf, I think. The only way to kill those things is to get 'em before they get out of the mud. They're fast and they die hard. However—" He warily went forward. There was nothing to see. The mud had collapsed into a deeper saucer, but the holes blasted by the high-x bullets had filled in. Here and there were traces of thready crimson.

"Never a dull moment," Scott remarked. His crooked grin eased the tension. Kane chuckled and followed the captain's example in replacing his half-used clip with a full one.

The narrow spine of Signal Rock extended inland for a quarter mile before it became scalable. They reached that point finally, helping each other climb, and finding themselves, at the summit, still well below the leafy ceiling of the trees. The black surface of the rock was painfully hot, stinging their palms as they climbed, and even striking through their shoe soles.

"Halfway point, captain?"

"Yeah. But don't let that cheer you. It doesn't get any better till we hit the beach again. We'll probably need some fever shots when we reach the fort, just in case. Oh-oh. Mask, Kane, quick." Scott lifted his arm. On his wrist the band of litmus had turned blue.

With trained accuracy they donned the respirators. Scott felt a faint stinging on his exposed skin, but that wasn't serious. Still, it would be painful later. He beckoned to Kane, slid down the face of the rock, used the pole to test the mud below, and jumped lightly. He dropped in the sticky whiteness and rolled over hastily, plastering himself from head to foot. Kane did the same. Mud wouldn't neutralize the poison flowers' gas, but it would absorb most of it before it reached the skin.

Scott headed toward the beach, a grotesque figure. Mud dripped on the eye plate, and he scrubbed it away with a handful of white grass. He used the pole constantly to test the footing ahead.

Nevertheless the mud betrayed him. The pole broke through suddenly, and as Scott automatically threw his weight back, the ground fell away under his feet. He had time for a crazy feeling of relief that this was quicksand, not a mud-wolf's den, and then the clinging, treacherous stuff had sucked him down knee-deep. He fell back, keeping his grip on the pole and swinging the other end in an arc toward Kane.

The boy seized it in both hands and threw himself flat. His foot hooked over an exposed root. Scott, craning his neck at a painfully awkward angle and trying to see through the mud-smeared vision plates, kept a rattrap grip on his end of the pole, hoping its slickness would not slip through his fingers.

He was drawn down farther, and then Kane's anchorage began to help. The boy tried to pull the pole toward him, hand over hand. Scott shook his head. He was a good deal stronger than Kane, and the latter would need all his strength to keep a tight grip on the pole.

Something stirred in the shadows behind Kane. Scott instinctively let go with one hand, and, with the other, got out his gun. It had a sealed mechanism, so the mud hadn't harmed the firing, and the muzzle had a one-way trap. He fired at the movement behind Kane, heard a muffled tumult, and waited till it had died. The boy, after a startled look behind him, had not stirred.

After that, rescue was comparatively easy. Scott simply climbed along the pole, spreading his weight over the surface of the quicksand. The really tough part was pulling his legs free of that deadly grip. Scott had to rest for five minutes after that.

But he got out. That was the important thing.

Kane pointed inquiringly into the bushes where the creature had been shot, but Scott shook his head. The nature of the beast wasn't a question worth deciding, as long as it was apparently *hors de combat*. Readjusting his mask, Scott turned toward the beach, circling the quicksand, and Kane kept at his heels.

Their luck had changed. They reached the shore with no further difficulty and collapsed on the black sand to rest. Presently Scott used a litmus, saw that the gas had dissipated, and removed his mask. He took a deep breath.

"Thanks, Kane," he said. "You can take a dip now if you want to wash off that mud. But stay close inshore. No, don't strip. There's no time."

The mud clung like glue and the black sand scratched like pumice. Still, Scott felt a good deal cleaner after a few minutes in the surf, while Kane stayed on guard. Slightly refreshed, they resumed the march.

An hour later a convoy plane, testing, sighted them, telaudioed the fort, and a flitterboat came racing out to pick them up. What Scott appreciated most of all was the stiff shot of uisqueplus the pilot gave him.

Yeah. It was a dog's life, all right!

He passed the flask to Kane.

Presently the fort loomed ahead, guarding Doone Harbor. Large as the landlocked bay was, it could scarcely accommodate the fleet. Scott watched the activity visible with an approving eye. The flitterboat rounded the sea wall, built for protection against tidal waves, and shot toward a jetty. Its almost inaudible motor died; the shell swung back.

Scott got out, beckoning to an orderly.

"Yes, sir?"

"See that this soldier gets what he needs. We've been in the jungle."

The man didn't whistle sympathetically, but his mouth pursed. He saluted and helped Kane climb out of the flitterboat. As Scott hurried along the quay, he could hear an outburst of friendly profanity from the men on the dock, gathering around Kane.

He nodded imperceptibly. The boy would make a good Free Companion—always granted that he could stand the gaff under fire. That was the acid test. Discipline was tightened then to the snapping point. If it snapped—well, the human factor always remained a variable, in spite of all the psychologists could do.

He went directly to his quarters, switching on the telaudio to call Cinc Rhys. The cinc's seamed, leathery face resolved itself on the screen.

"Captain Scott reporting for duty, sir."

Rhys looked at him sharply. "What happened?"

"Flitterboat crack-up. Had to make it in here on foot."

The cinc called on his God in a mild voice. "Glad you made it. Any accident?"

"No, sir. The pilot's unharmed, too. I'm ready to take over, after I've cleaned up."

"Better take a rejuvenation—you probably need it. Everything's going like clockwork. You did a god job with Mendez—a better bargain than I'd hoped for. I've been talking with him on the telaudio, integrating our forces. We'll go into that later, though. Clean up and then make general inspection."

"Check, sir."

Rhys clicked off. Scott turned to face his orderly.

"Hello, Briggs. Help me off with these duds. You'll probably have to cut 'em off."

"Glad to see you back, sir. I don't think it'll be necessary to cut—" Blunt fingers flew deftly over zippers and clasps. "You were in the jungle?"

Scott grinned wryly. "Do I look as if I'd been gliding?"

"Not all the way, sir—no."

Briggs was like an old bulldog—one of those men who proved the truth of the saying: "Old soldiers never die; they only fade away." Briggs could have been pensioned off ten years ago, but he hadn't wanted that. There was always a place for old soldiers in the Free Companies, even those who were unskilled. Some became technicians; others, military instructors; the rest, orderlies. The forts were their homes. Had they retired to one of the Keeps, they would have died for lack of interests.

Briggs, now—he had never risen above the ranks, and knew nothing of military strategy, ordnance, or anything except plain fighting. But he had been a Dooneman for forty years, twenty-five of them on active service. He was sixty-odd now, his squat figure slightly stooped like an elderly bear, his ugly face masked with scar tissue.

"All right. Start the shower, will you?"

Briggs stumped off, and Scott, stripped of his filthy, sodden garments, followed. He luxuriated under the stinging spray, first hot soapy water, then alcomix, and after that plain water, first hot, then cold. That was the last task he had to do himself. Briggs took over, as Scott relaxed on the slab, dropping lotion into the captain's burning eyes, giving him a deft but murderous rubdown, combining osteopathic and chiropractic treatment, adjusting revitalizing lamps, and measuring a hypo shot to nullify fatigue toxins. When the orderly was finished, Scott was ready to resume his duties with a clear brain and a refreshed body.

Briggs appeared with fresh clothing. "I'll have the old uniform cleaned, sir. No use throwing it away."

"You can't clean that," Scott remarked, slipping into a singlet. "Not after I rolled in mud. But suit yourself. I won't be needing it for long."

The orderly's fingers, buttoning Scott's tunic, stopped briefly and then resumed their motion. "Is that so, sir?"

"Yeah. I'm taking out discharge papers."

"Another Company, sir?"

"Don't get on your high horse," Scott told the orderly. "It's not that. What would you do if it were? Court-martial me yourself and shoot me at sunrise?"

"No, sir. Begging your pardon, sir, I'd just think you were crazy."

"Why I stand you only the Lord knows," Scott remarked. "You're too damn independent. There's no room for new ideas in that plastic skull of yours. You're the quintessence of dogmatism."

Briggs nodded. "Probably, sir. When a man's lived by one set of rules for as long as I have, and those rules work out, I suppose he might get dogmatic."

"Forty years for you—about twelve for me."

"You came up fast, captain. You'll be cinc here yet."

"That's what you think."

"You're next in line after Cinc Rhys."

"But I'll be out of the Doones," Scott pointed out. "Keep that under your belt, Briggs."

The orderly grunted. "Can't see it, sir. If you don't join another Company, where'll you go?"

"Ever heard of the Keeps?"

Briggs permitted himself a respectful snort. "Sure. They're fine for a binge, but—"

"I'm going to live in one. Montana Keep."

"The Keeps were built with men and machines. I helped at the building of Doone fort. Blood's mixed with the plastic here. We had to hold back the jungle while the technicians were working. Eight months, sir, and never a day passed without some sort of attack. And attacks always meant casualties then. We had only breastworks. The ships laid down a barrage, but barrages aren't impassable. That was a fight, captain."

Scott thrust out a leg so that Briggs could lace his boots. "And a damn good one. I know." He looked down at the orderly's baldish, brown head where white hairs straggled.

"You know, but you weren't there, captain. I was. First we dynamited. We cleared a half circle where we could dig in behind breastworks. Behind us were the techs, throwing up a plastic wall as fast as they could. The guns were brought in on barges. Lying offshore were the battle-wagons. We could hear the shells go whistling over our heads—it sounded pretty good, because we knew things were O. K. as long as the barrage kept up. But it couldn't be kept up day and night. The jungle broke through. For months the smell of blood hung here, and that drew the enemy."

"But you held them off."

"Sure, we did. Addison Doone was cinc then—he'd formed the Company years before, but we hadn't a fort. Doone fought with us. Saved my life once, in fact. Anyhow—we got the fort built, or rather the techs did. I won't forget the kick I got out of it when the first big gun blasted off from the wall behind us. There was a lot to do after that, but when that shell was fired, we knew we'd done the job."

Scott nodded. "You feel a proprietary interest in the fort, I guess."

Briggs looked puzzled. "The fort? Why, that doesn't mean much, captain. There are lots of forts. It's something more than that; I don't quite know what it is. It's seeing the fleet out there—breaking in the rookies—giving the old toasts at mess—knowing that—" He stopped, at a loss.

Scott's lips twisted wryly. "You don't really know, do you, Briggs?"

"Know what, sir?"

"Why you stay here. Why you can't believe I'd quit."

Briggs gave a little shrug. "Well—it's the Doones," he said. "That's all, captain. It's just that."

"And what the devil will it matter, in a few hundred years?"

"I suppose it won't. No, sir. But it isn't our business to think about that. We're Doonemen, that's all."

Scott didn't answer. He could easily have pointed out the fallacy of Briggs' argument, but what was the use? He stood up, the orderly whisking invisible dust off his tunic.

"All set, sir. Shipshape."

"Check, Briggs. Well, I've one more scrap, anyhow. I'll bring you back a souvenir, eh?"

The orderly saluted, grinning. Scott went out, feeling good. Inwardly he was chuckling rather sardonically at the false values he was supposed to take seriously. Of course many men had died when Doone fort had been built. But did that, in itself, make a tradition? What good was the fort? In a few centuries it would have outlived its usefulness. Then it would be a relic of the past. Civilization moved on, and, these days, civilization merely tolerated the military.

So—what was the use? Sentiment needed a valid reason for its existence. The Free Companions fought, bitterly, doggedly, with insane valor, in order to destroy themselves. The ancient motives for war had vanished.

What was the use? All over Venus the lights of the great forts were going out—and, this time, they would never be lit again—not in a thousand lifetimes!

V.

And we are here as on a darkling plain
Swept with confused alarms of struggle and flight,
Where ignorant armies clash by night.
—*Arnold circa* 1870

The fort was a completely self-contained unit, military rather than social. There was no need for any agrarian development, since a state of complete siege never existed. Food could be brought in from the Keeps by water and air.

But military production was important, and, in the life of the fort, the techs played an important part, from the experimental physicist to the spot welder. There were always replacements to be made, for, in battle, there were always casualties. And it was necessary to keep the weapons up-to-date, continually striving to perfect new ones. But strategy and armament were of equal importance. An outnumbered fleet had been known to conquer a stronger one by the use of practical psychology.

Scott found Commander Bienne at the docks, watching the launching of a new sub. Apparently Bienne hadn't yet got over his anger, for he turned a scowling, somber face to the captain as he saluted.

"Hello, commander," Scott said. "I'm making inspection. Are you free?"

Bienne nodded. "There's not much to do."

"Well—routine. We got that sub finished just in time, eh?"

"Yes." Bienne couldn't repress his pleasure at sight of the trim, sleek vessel beginning to slide down the ways. Scott, too, felt his pulses heighten as the sub slipped into the water, raising a mighty splash, and then settling down to a smooth, steady riding on the waves. He looked out to where the great battlewagons stood at anchor, twelve of them, gray-green monsters of plated metal. Each of them carried launching equipment for gliders, but the collapsible aircraft were stowed away out of sight as yet. Smaller destroyers lay like lean-flanked wolves among the battleships. There were two fast carriers, loaded with gliders and flitterboats. There were torpedo boats and one low-riding monitor, impregnable, powerfully armed, but slow. Only a direct hit could disable a monitor, but the behemoths had their disadvantages. The battle was usually over before they lumbered into sight. Like all monitors, this one—the *Armaged-*

don—was constructed on the principle of a razorback hog, covered, except for the firing ports, by a tureen-shaped shield, strongly braced from within. The *Armageddon* was divided into groups of compartments and had several auxiliary engines, so that, unlike the legendary *Rover*, when a monitor died, it did *not* die all over. It was, in effect, a dinosaur. You could blow off the monster's head, and it would continue to fight with talons and lashing tail. Its heavy guns made up in mobility for the giant's unwieldiness—but the trouble was to get the monitor into battle. It was painfully slow.

Scott scowled. "We're fighting over Venus Deep, eh?"

"Yes," Bienne nodded. "That still goes. The Helldivers are already heading toward Montana Keep, and we'll intercept them over the Deep."

"When's zero hour?"

"Midnight tonight."

Scott closed his eyes, visualizing their course on a mental chart. Not so good. When battle was joined near island groups, it was sometimes possible for a monitor to slip up under cover of the islets, but that trick wouldn't work now. Too bad—for the Helldivers were a strong outfit, more so since their recent merger with O'Brien's Legion. Even with the Mob to help, the outcome of the scrap would be anyone's guess. The *Armageddon* might be the decisive factor.

"I wonder—" Scott said. "No. It'd be impossible."

"What?"

"Camouflaging the *Armageddon*. If the Helldivers see the monitor coming, they'll lead the fight away from it, faster than that tub can follow. I was thinking we might get her into the battle without the enemy realizing it."

"She's camouflaged now."

"Paint, that's all. She can be spotted. I had some screwy idea about disguising her as an island or a dead whale."

"She's too big for a whale and floating islands look a bit suspicious."

"Yeah. But if we *could* slip the *Armageddon* in without scaring off the enemy— Hm-m-m. Monitors have a habit of turning turtle, don't they?"

"Right. They're top-heavy. But a monitor can't fight upside down. It's not such a bright idea, captain." Briefly Bienne's sunken eyes gleamed with sneering mockery. Scott grunted and turned away.

"All right. Let's take a look around."

The fleet was shipshape. Scott went to the shops. He learned that several new hulls were under way, but would not be completed by zero hour. With Bienne, he continued to the laboratory offices. Nothing new. No slip-ups; no surprises. The machine was running smoothly.

By the time inspection was completed, Scott had an idea. He told Bienne to carry on and went to find Cinc Rhys. The cinc was in his office, just clicking off the telaudio as Scott appeared.

"That was Mendez," Rhys said. "The Mob's meeting our fleet a hundred miles off the coast. They'll be under our orders, of course. A good man, Mendez, but I don't entirely trust him."

"You're not thinking of a double cross, sir?"

Cinc Rhys made disparaging noises. "Brutus is an honorable man. No, he'll stick to his bargain. But I wouldn't cut cards with Mendez. As a Free Companion, he's trustworthy. Personally— Well, how do things look?"

"Very good, sir. I've an idea about the *Armageddon*."

"I wish I had," Rhys said frankly. "We can't get that damned scow into the battle in any way I can figure out. The Helldivers will see it coming, and lead the fight away."

"I'm thinking of camouflage."

"A monitor's a monitor. It's unmistakable. You can't make it look like anything else."

"With one exception, sir. You can make it look like a disabled monitor."

Rhys sat back, giving Scott a startled glance. "That's interesting. Go on."

"Look here, sir." The captain used a stylo to sketch the outline of a monitor on a convenient pad. "Above the surface, the *Armageddon's* dome-shaped. Below, it's a bit different, chiefly because of the keel. Why can't we put a fake superstructure on the monitor—build a false keel on it, so it'll seem capsized?"

"It's possible."

"Everybody knows a monitor's weak spot—that it turns turtle under fire sometimes. If the Helldivers saw an apparently capsized *Armageddon* drifting toward them, they'd naturally figure the tub was disabled."

"It's crazy," Rhys said. "One of those crazy ideas that might work." He used the local telaudio to issue crisp orders. "Got it? Good. Get the *Armageddon* under way as soon as the equipment's aboard. Alterations will be made at sea. We can't waste time. If we had them made in the yards, she'd never catch up with the fleet."

The cinc broke the connection, his seamed, leathery face twisting into a grin. "I hope it works. We'll see."

He snapped his fingers. "Almost forgot. President Crosby's nephew—Kane?—he was with you when you cracked up, wasn't he? I've been wondering whether I should have waived training for him. How did he show up in the jungle?"

"Quite well," Scott said. "I had my eye on him. He'll make a good soldier."

Rhys looked keenly at the captain. "What about discipline? I felt that was his weak spot."

"I've no complaint to make."

"So. Well, maybe. Starling's outfit is bad training for anyone—especially a raw kid. Speaking of Starling, did Cinc Mendez know anything about his using atomic power?"

"No, sir. If Starling's doing that, he's keeping it plenty quiet."

"We'll investigate after the battle. Can't afford that sort of thing—we don't want another holocaust. It was bad enough to lose Earth. It decimated the race. If it happened again, it'd wipe the race out."

"I don't think there's much danger of that. On Earth, it was the big atomic-power stations that got out of control. At worst, Starling can't have more than hand weapons."

"True. You can't blow up a world with those. But you know the law—no atomic power on Venus."

Scott nodded.

"Well, that's all." Rhys waved him away. "Clear weather."

Which, on this perpetually clouded world, had a tinge of irony.

After mess Scott returned to his quarters, for a smoke and a brief rest. He waved away Briggs' suggestion of a rubdown and sent the orderly to the commissary for fresh tobacco. "Be sure to get Twenty Star," he cautioned. "I don't want that green hydroponic cabbage."

"I know the brand, sir." Briggs looked hurt and departed. Scott settled back in his relaxer, sighing.

Zero hour at twelve. The last zero hour he'd ever know. All through the day he had been conscious that he was fulfilling his duties for the last time.

His mind went back to Montana Keep. He was living again those other-worldly moments in the cloud-wrapped Olympus with Ilene. Curiously, he found it difficult to visualize the girl's features. Perhaps she was a symbol—her appearance did not matter. Yet she was very lovely.

In a different way from Jeana. Scott glanced at Jeana's picture on the desk, three-dimensional and tinted after life. By pressing a button on the frame, he could have given it sound and motion. He leaned forward and touched the tiny stud. In the depths of the picture the figure of Jeana stirred, smiling. The red lips parted.

Her voice, though soft, was quite natural.

"Hello, Brian," the recording said. "Wish I were with you now. Here's a present, darling." The image blew him a kiss, and then faded back to immobility.

Scott sighed again. Jeana was a comfortable sort of person. But— Oh, hell! She wasn't willing to change. Very likely she couldn't. Ilene perhaps was equally dogmatic, but she represented the life of the Keeps— and that was what Scott wanted now.

It was an artificial life Ilene lived, but she was honest about it. She knew its values were false. At least she didn't pretend, like the Free Companions, that there were ideals worth dying for. Scott remembered Briggs. The fact that men had been killed during the building of Doone fort meant a lot to the old orderly. He never asked himself—*why*? Why had they died? Why was Doone fort built in the first place? For war. And war was doomed.

One had to believe in an ideal before devoting one's life to it. One had to feel he was helping the ideal to survive—watering the plant with his blood so eventually it would come to flower. The red flower of Mars had long since blown. How did that old poem go?

> *One thing is certain, and the rest is lies;*
> *The flower that once has blown forever dies.*

It was true. But the Free Companions blindly pretended that the flower was still in blazing scarlet bloom, refusing to admit that even the roots were withered and useless, scarcely able now to suck up the blood sacrificed to its hopeless thirst.

New flowers bloomed; new buds opened. But in the Keeps, not in the great doomed forts. It was the winter cycle, and, as the last season's blossoms faded, the buds of the next stirred into life. Life questing and intolerant. Life that fed on the rotting petals of the rose of war.

But the pretense went on, in the coastal forts that guarded the Keeps. Scott made a grimace of distaste. Blind, stupid folly! He was a man first, not a soldier. And man is essentially a hedonist, whether he identifies himself with the race or not.

Scott could not. He was not part of the undersea culture, and he could never be. But he could lose himself in the hedonistic backwash of the Keeps, the froth that always overlies any social unit. With Ilene, he could, at least, seek happiness, without the bitter self-mockery he had known for so long. Mockery at his own emotional weaknesses in which he did not believe.

Ilene was honest. She knew she was damned, because unluckily she had intelligence.

So—Scott thought—they would make a good pair.

Scott looked up as Commander Bienne came into the room. Bienne's sour, mahogany face was flushed deep red under the bronze. His lids were heavy over angry eyes. He swung the door-curtain shut after him and stood rocking on his heels, glowering at Scott.

He called Scott something unprintable.

The captain rose, an icy knot of fury in his stomach. Very softly he said, "You're drunk, Bienne. Get out. Get back to your quarters."

"Sure—you little tinhorn soldier. You like to give orders, don't you? You like to chisel, too. The way you chiseled me out of that left-wing command today. I'm pretty sick of it, Captain Brian Scott."

"Don't be a damned fool! I don't like you personally any more than you like me, but that's got nothing to do with the Company. I recommended you for that command."

"You lie," Bienne said, swaying. "And I hate your guts."

Scott went pale, the scar on his cheek flaming red. Bienne came forward. He wasn't too drunk to co-ordinate. His fist lashed out suddenly and connected agonizingly with Scott's molar.

The captain's reach was less than Bienne's. He ducked inside of the next swing and carefully smashed a blow home on the point of the other's jaw. Bienne was driven back, crashing against the wall and sliding down in a limp heap, his head lolling forward.

Scott, rubbing his knuckles, looked down, considering. Presently he knelt and made a quick examination. A knockout, that was all.

Oh, well.

Briggs appeared, showing no surprise at sight of Bienne's motionless body. The perfect orderly walked across to the table and began to refill the humidor with the tobacco he had brought.

Scott almost chuckled.

"Briggs."

"Yes, sir?"

"Commander Bienne's had a slight accident. He—slipped. Hit his chin on something. He's a bit tight, too. Fix him up, will you?"

"With pleasure, sir." Briggs hoisted Bienne's body across his brawny shoulders.

"Zero hour's at twelve. The commander must be aboard the *Flintlock* by then. And sober. Can do?"

"Certainly, sir," Briggs said, and went out.

Scott returned to his chair, filling his pipe. He should have confined Bienne to his quarters, of course. But—well, this was a personal matter. One could afford to stretch a point, especially since Bienne was a valuable man to have aboard during action. Scott vaguely hoped the commander would get his thick head blown off.

After a time he tapped the dottle from his pipe and went off for a final inspection.

At midnight the fleet hoisted anchor.

By dawn the Doones were nearing the Venus Deep.

The ships of the Mob had already joined them, seven battleships, and assorted cruisers, destroyers, and one carrier. No monitor. The Mob didn't own one—it had capsized two months before, and was still undergoing repairs.

The combined fleets sailed in crescent formation, the left wing, commanded by Scott, composed of his own ship, the *Flintlock*, and the *Arquebus*, the *Arrow*, and the *Misericordia*, all Doone battlewagons. There were two Mob ships with him, the *Navaho* and the *Zuni*, the latter commanded by Cinc Mendez. Scott had one carrier with him, the other being at right wing. Besides these, there were the lighter craft.

In the center were the battleships *Arbalest*, *Lance*, *Gatling*, and *Mace*, as well as three of Mendez's. Cinc Rhys was aboard the *Lance*, controlling operations. The camouflaged monitor *Armageddon* was puffing away valiantly far behind, well out of sight in the mists.

Scott was in his control room, surrounded by telaudio screens and switchboards. Six operators were perched on stools before the controls, ready to jump to action when orders came through their earphones. In the din of battle spoken commands often went unheard, which was why Scott wore a hush-mike strapped to his chest.

His eyes roved over the semicircle of screens before him.

"Any report from the gliders yet?"

"No, sir."

"Get me air-spotting command."

One of the screens flamed to life; a face snapped into view on it.

"Report."

"Nothing yet, captain. Wait." There was a distant thunder. "Detectors clamped on a telaudio tight-beam directly overhead."

"Enemy glider in the clouds?"

"Apparently. It's out of the focus now."

"Try to relocate it."

A lot of good that would do. Motored planes could easily be detected overhead, but a glider was another matter. The only way to spot one was by clamping a detector focus directly on the glider's telaudio beam— worse than a needle in a haystack. Luckily the crates didn't carry bombs.

"Report coming in, sir. One of our gliders."

Another screen showed a face. "Pilot reporting, sir. Located enemy."

"Good. Switch in the telaudio, infra. What sector?"

"V. D. eight hundred seven northwest twenty-one."

Scott said into his hush-mike, "Get Cinc Rhys and Commander Geer on tight-beam. And Cinc Mendez."

Three more screens lit up, showing the faces of the three officers.

"Cut in the pilot."

Somewhere over Venus Deep the glider pilot was arcing his plane through the cloud-layer, the automatic telaudio-camera, lensed to infra-red, penetrating the murk and revealing the ocean below. On the screen ships showed, driving forward in battle formation.

Scott recognized and enumerated them mentally. The *Orion*, the *Sirius*, the *Vega*, the *Polaris*—uh-huh. Lighter ships. Plenty of them. The scanner swept on.

Cinc Rhys said, "We're outnumbered badly. Cinc Mendez, are your sub-detectors in operation?"

"They are. Nothing yet."

"We'll join battle in half an hour, I judge. We've located them, and they've no doubt located us."

"Check."

The screens blanked out. Scott settled back, alertly at ease. Nothing to do now but wait, keeping ready for the unexpected. The *Orion* and the *Vega* were the Helldivers' biggest battleships, larger than anything in the line of the Doones—or the Mob. Cinc Flynn was no doubt aboard the *Orion*. The Helldivers owned a monitor, but it had not showed on the infrared aërial scanner. Probably the behemoth wouldn't even show up in time for the battle.

But even without the monitor, the Helldivers had an overwhelming surface display. Moreover, their undersea fleet was an important factor. The sub-detectors of Cinc Mendez might—probably would—cut down the odds. But possibly not enough.

The *Armageddon*, Scott thought, might be the point of decision, the ultimate argument. And, as yet, the camouflaged monitor was lumbering through the waves far in the wake of the Doones.

Commander Bienne appeared on a screen. He had frozen into a disciplined, trained robot, personal animosities forgotten for the time. Active duty did that to a man.

Scott expected nothing different, however, and his voice was completely impersonal as he acknowledged Bienne's call.

"The flitterboats are ready to go, captain."

"Send them out in fifteen minutes. Relay to left wing, all ships carrying flitters."

"Check."

For a while there was silence. A booming explosion brought Scott to instant alertness. He glanced up at the screens.

A new face appeared. "Helldivers opening up. Testing for range. They must have gliders overhead. We can't spot 'em."

"Get the men under cover. Send up a test barrage. Prepare to return fire. Contact our pilots over the Helldivers."

It was beginning now—the incessant, racking thunder that would continue till the last shot was fired. Scott cut in to Cinc Rhys as the latter signaled.

"Reporting, sir."

"Harry the enemy. We can't do much yet. Change to R-8 formation."

Cinc Mendez said, "We've got three enemy subs. Our detectors are tuned up to high pitch."

"Limit the range so our subs will be outside the sphere of influence."

"Already did that. The enemy's using magnetic depth charges, laying an undersea barrage as they advance."

"I'll talk to the sub command." Rhys cut off. Scott listened to the increasing fury of explosions. He could not yet hear the distinctive *clap-clap* of heat rays, but the quarters were not yet close enough for those undependable, though powerful, weapons. It took time for a heat ray to warm up, and during that period a well-aimed bullet could smash the projector lens.

"Casualty, sir. Direct hit aboard destroyer *Bayonet*."

"Extent of damage?"

"Not disabled. Complete report later."

After a while a glider pilot came in on the beam.

"Shell landed on the *Polaris*, sir."

"Use the scanner."

It showed the Helldivers' battlewagon, part of the superstructure carried away, but obviously still in fighting trim. Scott nodded. Both sides were getting the range now. The hazy clouds still hid each fleet from the other, but they were nearing.

The sound of artillery increased. Problems of trajectory were increased by the violent winds of Venus, but accurate aiming was possible. Scott nodded grimly as a crash shook the *Flintlock*.

They were getting it now. Here, in the brain of the ship, he was as close to the battle as any member of a firing crew. The screens were his eyes.

They had the advantage of being able to use infrared, so that Scott, buried here, could see more than he could have on deck, with his naked eye. Something loomed out of the murk and Scott's breath stopped before he recognized the lines of the Doone battlewagon *Misericordia*. She was off course. The captain used his hush-mike to snap a quick reprimand.

Flitterboats were going out now, speedy hornets that would harry the enemy fleet. In one of them, Scott remembered, was Norman Kane. He thought of Ilene and thrust the thought back, out of his mind. No time for that now.

Battle stations allowed no time for wool gathering.

The distant vanguard of the Helldivers came into sight on the screens. Cinc Mendez called.

"Eleven more subs. One got through. Seems to be near the *Flintlock*. Drop depth bombs."

Scott nodded and obeyed. Shuddering concussions shook the ship. Presently a report came in: fuel slick to starboard.

Good. A few well-placed torpedoes could do a lot of damage.

The *Flintlock* heeled incessantly under the action of the heavy guns. Heat rays were lancing out. The big ships could not easily avoid the searing blasts that could melt solid metal, but the flitterboats, dancing around like angry insects, sent a rain of bullets at the projectors. But even that took integration. The rays themselves were invisible, and could only be traced from their targets. The camera crews were working overtime, snapping shots of the enemy ships, tracing the rays' points of origin, and telaudioing the information to the flitterboats.

"Helldivers' *Rigel* out of action."

On the screen the big destroyer swung around, bow pointing forward. She was going to ram. Scott snapped orders. The *Flintlock* went hard over, guns pouring death into the doomed *Rigel*.

The ships passed, so close that men on the *Flintlock's* decks could see the destroyer lurching through the haze. Scott judged her course and tried desperately to get Mendez. There was a delay.

"QM—QM—emergency! Get the *Zuni!*"

"Here she answers, sir."

Scott snapped, "Change course. QM. Destroyer *Rigel* bearing down on you."

"Check." The screen blanked. Scott used a scanner. He groaned at the sight. The *Zuni* was swinging fast, but the *Rigel* was too close—too damned close.

She rammed.

Scott said, "Hell." That put the *Zuni* out of action. He reported to Cinc Rhys.

"All right, captain. Continue R-8 formation."

Mendez appeared on a screen. "Captain Scott. We're disabled. I'm coming aboard. Have to direct sub-strafing operations. Can you give me a control board?"

"Yes, sir. Land at Port Sector 7."

Hidden in the mist, the fleets swept on in parallel courses, the big battlewagons keeping steady formation, pouring heat rays and shells across the gap. The lighter ships strayed out of line at times, but the flitterboats swarmed like midges, dog-fighting when they were not harrying the larger craft. Gliders were useless now, at such close quarters.

The thunder crashed and boomed. Shudders rocked the *Flintlock.*

"Hit on Helldivers' *Orion.* Hit on *Sirius.*"

"Hit on Mob ship *Apache.*"

"Four more enemy subs destroyed."

"Doone sub *X-16* fails to report."

"Helldivers' *Polaris* seems disabled."

"Send out auxiliary flitterboats, units nine and twenty."

Cinc Mendez came in, breathing hard. Scott waved him to an auxiliary control unit seat.

"Hit on *Lance.* Wait a minute. Cinc Rhys a casualty, sir."

Scott froze. "Details."

"One moment— Dead, sir."

"Very well," Scott said after a moment. "I'm assuming command. Pass it along."

He caught a sidelong glance from Mendez. When a Company's cinc was killed, one of two things happened—promotion of a new cinc, or a merger with another Company. In this case Scott was required, by his rank, to assume temporarily the fleet's command. Later, at the Doone fort, there would be a meeting and a final decision.

He scarcely thought of that now. Rhys dead! Tough, unemotional old

Rhys, killed in action. Rhys had a free-wife in some Keep, Scott remembered. The Company would pension her. Scott had never seen the woman. Oddly, he wondered what she was like. The question had never occurred to him before.

The screens were flashing. Double duty now—or triple. Scott forgot everything else in directing the battle.

It was like first-stage anæsthesia—it was difficult to judge time. It might have been an hour or six since the battle had started. Or less than an hour, for that matter.

"Destroyer disabled. Cruiser disabled. Three enemy subs out of action—"

It went on, endlessly. At the auxiliaries Mendez was directing sub-strafing operations. Where in hell's the *Armageddon*, Scott thought? The fight would be over before that overgrown tortoise arrived.

Abruptly a screen flashed QM. The lean, beak-nosed face of Cinc Flynn of the Helldivers showed.

"Calling Doone command."

"Acknowledging," Scott said. "Captain Scott, emergency command."

Why was Flynn calling? Enemy fleets in action never communicated, except to surrender.

Flynn said curtly, "You're using atomic power. Explanation, please."

Mendez jerked around. Scott felt a tight band around his stomach.

"Done without my knowledge or approval, of course, Cinc Flynn. My apologies. Details?"

"One of your flitterboats fired an atomic-powered pistol at the *Orion*."

"Damage?"

"One seven-unit gun disabled."

"One of ours, of the same caliber, will be taken out of action immediately. Further details, sir?"

"Use your scanner, captain, on Sector Mobile 18 south *Orion*. Your apology is accepted. The incident will be erased from our records."

Flynn clicked off. Scott used the scanner, catching a Doone flitterboat in its focus. He used the enlarger.

The little boat was fleeing from enemy fire, racing back toward the Doone fleet, heading directly toward the *Flintlock*, Scott saw. Through the transparent shell he saw the bombardier slumped motionless, his head blown half off. The pilot, still gripping an atomic-fire pistol in one hand, was Norman Kane. Blood streaked his boyish, strained face.

So Starling's outfit did have atomic power, then. Kane must have smuggled the weapon out with him when he left. And, in the excitement of battle, he had used it against the enemy.

Scott said coldly, "Gun crews starboard. Flitterboat Z-19-4. Blast it."

Almost immediately a shell burst near the little craft. On the screen Kane looked up, startled by his own side firing upon him. Comprehension showed on his face. He swung the flitterboat off course, zigzagging, trying desperately to dodge the barrage.

Scott watched, his lips grimly tight. The flitterboat exploded in a rain of spray and debris.

Automatic court-martial.

After the battle, the Companies would band together and smash Starling's outfit.

Meantime, this was action. Scott returned to his screens, erasing the incident from his mind.

Very gradually, the balance of power was increasing with the Helldivers. Both sides were losing ships, put out of action rather than sunk, and Scott thought more and more often of the monitor *Armageddon*. She could turn the battle now. But she was still far astern.

Scott never felt the explosion that wrecked the control room. His senses blacked out without warning.

He could not have been unconscious for long. When he opened his eyes, he stared up at a shambles. He seemed to be the only man left alive. But it could not have been a direct hit, or he would not have survived either.

He was lying on his back, pinned down by a heavy crossbeam. But no bones were broken. Blind, incredible luck had helped him there. The brunt of the damage had been borne by the operators. They were dead, Scott saw at a glance.

He tried to crawl out from under the beam, but that was impossible. In the thunder of battle his voice could not be heard.

There was a movement across the room, halfway to the door. Cinc Mendez stumbled up and stared around, blinking. Red smeared his plump cheeks.

He saw Scott and stood, rocking back and forth, staring.

Then he put his hand on the butt of his pistol.

Scott could very easily read the other's mind. If the Doone captain died now, the chances were that Mendez could merge with the Doones and assume control. The politico-military balance lay that way.

If Scott lived, it was probable that he would be elected cinc.

It was, therefore, decidedly to Mendez's advantage to kill the emprisoned man.

A shadow crossed the doorway. Mendez, his back to the newcomer, did not see Commander Bienne halt on the threshold, scowling at the tableau. Scott knew that Bienne understood the situation as well as he himself did. The commander realized that in a very few moments Mendez would draw his gun and fire.

Scott waited. The cinc's fingers tightened on his gun butt.

Bienne, grinning crookedly, said, "I thought that shell had finished you, sir. Guess it's hard to kill a Dooneman."

Mendez took his hand off the gun, instantly regaining his poise. He turned to Bienne.

"I'm glad you're here, commander. It'll probably take both of us to move that beam."

"Shall we try, sir?"

Between the two of them, they managed to shift the weight off Scott's torso. Briefly the latter's eyes met Bienne's. There was still no friendliness in them, but there was a look of wry self-mockery.

Bienne hadn't saved Scott's life, exactly. It was, rather, a question of being a Dooneman. For Bienne was, first of all, a soldier, and a member of the Free Company.

Scott tested his limbs; they worked.

"How long was I out, commander?"

"Ten minutes, sir. The *Armageddon's* in sight."

"Good. Are the Helldivers veering off?"

Bienne shook his head. "So far they're not suspicious."

Scott grunted and made his way to the door, the others at his heels. Mendez said, "We'll need another control ship."

"All right. The *Arquebus*. Commander, take over here. Cinc Mendez—"

A flitterboat took them to the *Arquebus*, which was still in good fighting trim. The monitor *Armageddon*, Scott saw, was rolling helplessly in the trough of the waves. In accordance with the battle plan, the Doone ships were leading the Helldivers toward the apparently capsized giant. The technicians had done a good job; the false keel looked shockingly convincing.

Aboard the *Arquebus*, Scott took over, giving Mendez the auxiliary control for his substrafers. The Cinc beamed at Scott over his shoulder.

"Wait till that monitor opens up, captain."

"Yeah . . . we're in bad shape, though."

Neither man mentioned the incident that was in both their minds. It was tacitly forgotten—the only thing to do now.

Guns were still bellowing. The Helldivers were pouring their fire into the Doone formation, and they were winning. Scott scowled at the screens. If he waited too long, it would be just too bad.

Presently he put a beam on the *Armageddon*. She was in a beautiful position now, midway between two of the Helldivers' largest battleships.

"Unmask. Open fire."

Firing ports opened on the monitor. The sea titan's huge guns snouted into view. Almost simultaneously they blasted, the thunder drowning out the noise of the lighter guns.

"All Doone ships attack," Scott said. "Plan R-7."

This was it. *This was it!*

The Doones raced in to the kill. Blasting, bellowing, shouting, the guns tried to make themselves heard above the roaring of the monitor. They could not succeed, but that savage, invincible onslaught won the battle.

It was nearly impossible to maneuver a monitor into battle formation, but, once that was accomplished, the only thing that could stop the monster was atomic power.

But the Helldivers fought on, trying strategic formation. They could not succeed. The big battlewagons could not get out of range of the *Armageddon's* guns. And that meant—

Cinc Flynn's face showed on the screen.

"Capitulation, sir. Cease firing."

Scott gave orders. The roar of the guns died into humming, incredible silence.

"You gave us a great battle, cinc."

"Thanks. So did you. Your strategy with the monitor was excellent."

So—that was that. Scott felt something go limp inside of him. Flynn's routine words were meaningless; Scott was drained of the vital excitement that had kept him going till now.

The rest was pure formula.

Token depth charges would be dropped over Virginia Keep. They would not harm the Dome, but they were the rule. There would be the ransom, paid always by the Keep which backed the losing side. A supply of korium, or its negotiable equivalent. The Doone treasury would be swelled. Part of the money would go into replacements and new keels. The life of the forts would go on.

Alone at the rail of the *Arquebus*, heading for Virginia Keep, Scott watched slow darkness change the clouds from pearl to gray, and then to invisibility. He was alone in the night. The wash of waves came up to him softly as the *Arquebus* rushed to her destination, three hundred miles away.

Warm yellow lights gleamed from ports behind him, but he did not turn. This, he thought, was like the cloud-wrapped Olympus in Montana Keep, where he had promised Ilene—many things.

Yet there was a difference. In an Olympus a man was like a god, shut away completely from the living world. Here, in the unbroken dark, there was no sense of alienage. Nothing could be seen—Venus has no moon, and the clouds hid the stars, And the seas are not phosphorescent.

Beneath these waters stand the Keeps, Scott thought. They hold the future. Such battles as were fought today are fought so that the Keeps may not be destroyed.

And men will sacrifice. Men have always sacrificed, for a social organization or a military unit. Man must create his own ideal. "If there had been no God, man would have created Him."

Bienne had sacrificed today, in a queer, twisted way of loyalty to his fetish. Yet Bienne still hated him, Scott knew.

The Doones meant nothing. Their idea was a false one. Yet, because men were faithful to that ideal, civilization would rise again from the guarded Keeps. A civilization that would forget its doomed guardians, the watchers of the seas of Venus, the Free Companions yelling their mad, futile battle cry as they drove on—as this ship was driving—into a night that would have no dawn.

Ilene.

Jeana.

It was no such simple choice. It was, in fact, no real choice at all. For Scott knew, very definitely, that he could never, as long as he lived, believe wholeheartedly in the Free Companions. Always a sardonic devil deep within him would be laughing in bitter self-mockery.

The whisper of the waves drifted up.

It wasn't sensible. It was sentimental, crazy, stupid, sloppy thinking. But Scott knew, now, that he wasn't going back to Ilene.

He was a fool.

But he was a soldier.

First published: 1944

INVARIANT

by John Pierce

YOU KNOW THE GENERAL FACTS CONCERNING HOMER GREEN, SO I DON'T need to describe him or his surroundings. I knew as much and more, yet it was an odd sensation, which you don't get through reading, actually to dress in that primitive fashion, to go among strange surroundings, and to see him.

The house is no more odd than the pictures. Hemmed in by other twentieth century buildings, it must be indistinguishable from the original structure and its surroundings. To enter it, to tread on rugs, to see chairs covered in cloth with a nap, to see instruments for smoking, to see and hear a primitive radio, even though operating really from a variety of authentic transcriptions, and above all to see an open fire; all this gave me a sense of unreality, prepared though I was. Green sat by the fire in a chair, as we almost invariably find him, with a dog at his feet. He is perhaps the most valuable man in the world, I thought. But I could not shake off the sense of unreality concerning the substantial surroundings. He, too, seemed unreal, and I pitied him.

The sense of unreality continued through the form of self-introduction. How many have there been? I could, of course, examine the records.

"I'm Carew, from the Institute," I said. "We haven't met before, but they told me you'd be glad to see me."

Green rose and extended his hand. I took it obediently, making the unfamiliar gesture.

"Glad to see you," he said. "I've been dozing here. It's a little of a shock, the treatment, and I thought I'd rest a few days. I hope it's really permanent.

"Won't you sit down?" he added.

We seated ourselves before the fire. The dog, which had risen, lay down, pressed against his master's feet.

"I suppose you want to test my reactions?" Green asked.

"Later," I replied. "There's no hurry. And it's so very comfortable here."

213

Green was easily distracted. He relaxed, staring at the fire. This was an opportunity, and I spoke in a somewhat purposeful voice.

"It seems more a time for politics, here," I said. "What the Swede intends, and what the French—"

"Drench our thoughts in mirth—" Green replied.

I had thought from the records the quotation would have some effect.

"But one doesn't leave politics to drench his thoughts in mirth," he continued. "One studies them—"

I won't go into the conversation. You've seen it in Appendix A of my thesis, "An Aspect of Twentieth Century Politics and Speech." It was brief, as you know. I had been very lucky to get to see Green. I was more lucky to hit on the right thread directly. Somehow, it had never occurred to me before that twentieth century politicians had meant, or had thought that they meant, what they said; that indeed, they had in their own minds attached a sense of meaning or relevancy to what seem to us meaningless or irrelevant phrases. It's hard to explain so foreign an idea; perhaps an example would help.

For instance, would you believe that a man accused of making a certain statement would seriously reply, "I'm not in the habit of making such statements?" Would you believe that this might even mean that he had not made the statement? Or would you further believe that even if he had made the statement, this would seem to him to classify it as some sort of special instance, and his reply as not truly evasive? I think these conjectures plausible, that is, when I struggle to immerse myself in the twentieth century. But I would never have dreamed them before talking with Green. How truly invaluable the man is!

I have said that the conversation recorded in Appendix A is very short. There was no need to continue along political lines after I had grasped the basic idea. Twentieth century records are much more complete than Green's memory, and that itself has been thoroughly catalogued. It is not the dry bones of information, but the personal contact, the infinite variation in combinations, the stimulation of the warm human touch, that are helpful and suggestive.

So I was with Green, and most of a morning was still before me. You know that he is given meal times free, and only one appointment between meals, so that there will be no overlapping. I was grateful to the man, and sympathetic, and I was somewhat upset in his presence. I wanted to talk to him of the thing nearest his heart. There was no reason I shouldn't. I've recorded the rest of the conversation, but not published it. It's not new. Perhaps it is trivial, but it means a great deal to me. Maybe it's only my very personal memory of it. But I thought you might like to know.

"What led to your discovery?" I asked him.

"Salamanders," he replied without hesitation. "Salamanders."

The account I got of his perfect regeneration experiments was, of course, the published story. How many thousands of times has it been told? Yet, I swear I detected variations from the records. How nearly infinite the possible combinations are! But the chief points came in the usual order. How the regeneration of limbs in salamanders led to the idea of perfect regeneration of human parts. How, say, a cut heals, leaving not a scar, but a perfect replica of the damaged tissue. How in normal metabolism tissue can be replaced not imperfectly, as in an aging organism, but perfectly, indefinitely. You've seen it in animals, in compulsory biology. The chick whose metabolism replaces its tissues, but always in an exact, invariant form, never changing. It's disturbing to think of it in a man. Green looked so young, as young as I. Since the twentieth century—

When Green had concluded his description, including that of his own inoculation in the evening, he ventured to prophesy.

"I feel confident," he said, "that it will work, indefinitely."

"It does work, Dr. Green," I assured him. "Indefinitely."

"We mustn't be premature," he said. "After all, a short time—"

"Do you recall the date, Dr. Green?" I asked.

"September 11th," he said. "1943, if you want that, too."

"Dr. Green, today is August 4, 2170," I told him earnestly.

"Look here," Green said. "If it were, I wouldn't be here dressed this way, and you wouldn't be there dressed that way."

The impasse could have continued indefinitely. I took my communicator from my pocket and showed it to him. He watched with growing wonder and delight as I demonstrated, finally with projection, binaural and stereo. Not simple, but exactly the sort of electronic development which a man of Green's era associated with the future. Green seemed to have lost all thought of the conversation which had led to my production of the communicator.

"Dr. Green," I said, "the year is 2170. This is the twenty-second century."

He looked at me baffled, but this time not with disbelief. A strange sort of terror was spread over his features.

"An accident?" he asked. "My memory?"

"There has been no accident," I said. "Your memory is intact, as far as it goes. Listen to me. Concentrate."

Then I told him, simply and briefly, so that his thought processes would not lag. As I spoke to him he stared at me apprehensively, his mind apparently racing. This is what I said:

"Your experiment succeeded, beyond anything you had reason to hope. Your tissues took on the ability to reform themselves in exactly the same pattern year after year. Their form became invariant.

"Photographs and careful measurements show this, from year to year, yes, from century to century. You are just as you were over two hundred years ago.

"Your life has not been devoid of accident. Minor, even major, wounds have left no trace in healing. Your tissues are invariant.

"Your brain is invariant, too; that is, as far as the cell patterns are concerned. A brain may be likened to an electrical network. Memory is the network, the coils and condensers, and their interconnections. Conscious thought is the pattern of voltages across them and currents flowing through them. The pattern is complicated, but transitory—transient. Memory is changing the network of the brain, affecting all subsequent thoughts, or patterns in the network. The network of your brain never changes. It is invariant.

"Or thought is like the complicated operation of the relays and switches of a telephone exchange of your century, but memory is the interconnections of elements. The interconnections on other people's brains change in the process of thought, breaking down, building up, giving them new memories. The pattern of connections in your brain never changes. It is invariant.

"Other people can adapt themselves to new surroundings, learning where objects of necessity are, the pattern of rooms, adapting themselves unconsciously, without friction. You cannot; your brain is invariant. Your habits are keyed to a house, your house as it was the day before you treated yourself. It has been preserved, replaced through two hundred years so that you could live without friction. In it, you live, day after day, the day after the treatment which made your brain invariant.

"Do not think you give no return for this care. You are perhaps the most valuable man in the world. Morning, afternoon, evening; you have three appointments a day, when the lucky few who are judged to merit or need your help are allowed to seek it.

"I am a student of history. I came to see the twentieth century through the eyes of an intelligent man of that century. You are a very intelligent, a brilliant man. Your mind has been analyzed in a detail greater than that of any other. Few brains are better. I came to learn from this powerful observant brain what politics meant to a man of your period. I learned from a fresh new source, your brain, which is not overlaid, not changed by the intervening years, but is just as it was in 1943.

"But I am not very important. Important workers: psychologists, come to see you. They ask you questions, then repeat them a little differently, and observe your reactions. One experiment is not vitiated by your memory of an earlier experiment. When your train of thought is interrupted, it leaves no memory behind. Your brain remains invariant. And these men, who otherwise could draw only general conclusions from simple experiments on multitudes of different, differently constituted and differently prepared individuals, can observe undisputable differences of response due to the slightest changes in stimulus. Some of these men have driven you to a frenzy. You do not go mad. Your brain cannot change; it is invariant.

"You are so valuable it seems that the world could scarcely progress without your invariant brain. And yet, we have not asked another to do as you did. With animals, yes. Your dog is an example. What you did was willingly, and you did not know the consequences. You did the world this greatest service unknowingly. But we know."

Green's head had sunk to his chest. His face was troubled, and he seemed to seek solace in the warmth of the fire. The dog at his feet stirred, and he looked down, a sudden smile on his face. I knew that his train of thought had been interrupted. The transients had died from his brain. Our whole meeting was gone from his processes of thought.

I rose and stole away before he looked up. Perhaps I wasted the remaining hour of the morning.

First published: 1945

FIRST CONTACT

by Murray Leinster

I.

TOMMY DORT WENT INTO THE CAPTAIN'S ROOM WITH HIS LAST PAIR OF stereophotos and said:

"I'm through, sir. These are the last two pictures I can take."

He handed over the photographs and looked with professional interest at the visiplates which showed all space outside the ship. Subdued, deep-red lighting indicated the controls and such instruments as the quartermaster on duty needed for navigation of the spaceship *Llanvabon*. There was a deeply cushioned control chair. There was the little gadget of oddly angled mirrors—remote descendant of the back-view mirrors of twentieth century motorists—which allowed a view of all the visiplates without turning the head. And there were the huge plates which were so much more satisfactory for a direct view of space.

The *Llanvabon* was a long way from home. The plates, which showed every star of visual magnitude and could be stepped up to any desired magnification, portrayed stars of every imaginable degree of brilliance, in the startlingly different colors they show outside of atmosphere. But every one was unfamiliar. Only two constellations could be recognized as seen from Earth, and they were shrunken and distorted. The Milky Way seemed vaguely out of place. But even such oddities were minor compared to a sight in the forward plates.

There was a vast, vast mistiness ahead. A luminous mist. It seemed motionless. It took a long time for any appreciable nearing to appear in the vision plates, though the spaceship's velocity indicator showed an incredible speed. The mist was the Crab Nebula, six light-years long, three and a half light-years thick, with outward-reaching members that in the telescopes of Earth gave it some resemblance to the creature for which it was named. It was a cloud of gas, infinitely tenuous, reaching half again as far as from Sol to its nearest neighbor-sun. Deep within it

218

burned two stars; a double star; one component the familiar yellow of the sun of Earth, the other an unholy white.

Tommy Dort said meditatively:

"We're heading into a deep, sir?"

The skipper studied the last two plates of Tommy's taking, and put them aside. He went back to his uneasy contemplation of the vision plates ahead. The *Llanvabon* was decelerating at full force. She was a bare half light-year from the nebula. Tommy's work was guiding the ship's course, now, but the work was done. During all the stay of the exploring ship in the nebula, Tommy Dort would loaf. But he'd more than paid his way so far.

He had just completed a quite unique first—a complete photographic record of the movement of a nebula during a period of four thousand years, taken by one individual with the same apparatus and with control exposures to detect and record any systematic errors. It was an achievement in itself worth the journey from Earth. But in addition, he had also recorded four thousand years of the history of a double star, and four thousand years of the history of a star in the act of degenerating into a white dwarf.

It was not that Tommy Dort was four thousand years old. He was, actually, in his twenties. But the Crab Nebula is four thousand light-years from Earth, and the last two pictures had been taken by light which would not reach Earth until the sixth millennium A. D. On the way here—at speeds incredible multiples of the speed of light—Tommy Dort had recorded each aspect of the nebula by the light which had left it from forty centuries since to a bare six months ago.

The *Llanvabon* bored on through space. Slowly, slowly, slowly, the incredible luminosity crept across the vision plates. It blotted out half the universe from view. Before was glowing mist, and behind was a star-studded emptiness. The mist shut off three-fourths of all the stars. Some few of the brightest shone dimly through it near its edge, but only a few. Then there was only an irregularly shaped patch of darkness astern against which stars shone unwinking. The *Llanvabon* dived into the nebula, and it seemed as if it bored into a tunnel of darkness with walls of shining fog.

Which was exactly what the spaceship was doing. The most distant photographs of all had disclosed structural features in the nebula. It was not amorphous. It had form. As the *Llanvabon* drew nearer, indications of structure grew more distinct, and Tommy Dort had argued for a curved approach for photographic reasons. So the spaceship had come up to the nebula on a vast logarithmic curve, and Tommy had been able to take successive photographs from slightly different angles and get stereo-pairs which showed the nebula in three dimensions; which disclosed billowings and hollows and an actually complicated shape. In places, the nebula displayed convolutions like those of a human brain. It was into one of those hollows that the spaceship now plunged. They had been called "deeps" by analogy with crevasses in the ocean floor. And they promised to be useful.

The skipper relaxed. One of a skipper's functions, nowadays, is to think of things to worry about, and then worry about them. The skipper of the *Llanvabon* was conscientious. Only after a certain instrument re-mained definitely nonregistering did he ease himself back in his seat.

"It was just barely possible," he said heavily, "that those deeps might be nonluminous gas. But they're empty. So we'll be able to use over-drive as long as we're in them."

It was a light-year-and-a-half from the edge of the nebula to the neigh-borhood of the double star which was its heart. That was the problem. A nebula is a gas. It is so thin that a comet's tail is solid by comparison, but a ship traveling on overdrive—above the speed of light—does not want to hit even a merely hard vacuum. It needs pure emptiness, such as exists between the stars. But the *Llanvabon* could not do much in this expanse of mist if it was limited to speeds a merely hard vacuum will permit.

The luminosity seemed to close in behind the spaceship, which slowed and slowed and slowed. The overdrive went off with the sudden *pinging* sensation which goes all over a person when the overdrive field is released.

Then, almost instantly, bells burst into clanging, strident uproar all through the ship. Tommy was almost deafened by the alarm bell which rang in the captain's room before the quartermaster shut it off with a flip of his hand. But other bells could be heard ringing throughout the rest of the ship, to be cut off as automatic doors closed one by one.

Tommy Dort stared at the skipper. The skipper's hands clenched. He was up and staring over the quartermaster's shoulder. One indicator was apparently having convulsions. Others strained to record their find-ings. A spot on the diffusedly bright mistiness of a bow-quartering visi-plate grew brighter as the automatic scanner focused on it. That was the direction of the object which had sounded collision-alarm. But the object locator itself—. According to its reading, there was one solid object some eighty thousand miles away—an object of no great size. But there was another object whose distance varied from extreme range to zero, and whose size shared its impossible advance and retreat.

"Step up the scanner," snapped the skipper.

The extra-bright spot on the scanner rolled outward, obliterating the undifferentiated image behind it. Magnification increased. But nothing appeared. Absolutely nothing. Yet the radio locator insisted that something monstrous and invisible made lunatic dashes toward the *Llanvabon*, at speeds which inevitably implied collision, and then fled coyly away at the same rate.

The visiplate went up to maximum magnification. Still nothing. The skipper ground his teeth. Tommy Dort said meditatively:

"D'you know, sir, I saw something like this on a liner on the Earth-Mars run once, when we were being located by another ship. Their locator beam was the same frequency as ours, and every time it hit, it registered like something monstrous, and solid."

"That," said the skipper savagely, "is just what's happening now. There's something like a locator beam on us. We're getting that beam and our own echo besides. But the other ship's invisible! Who is out here in an invisible ship with locator devices? Not men, certainly!"

He pressed the button in his sleeve communicator and snapped:

"Action stations! Man all weapons! Condition of extreme alert in all departments immediately!"

His hands closed and unclosed. He stared again at the visiplate which showed nothing but a formless brightness.

"Not men?" Tommy Dort straightened sharply. "You mean—"

"How many solar systems in our galaxy?" demanded the skipper bitterly. "How many planets fit for life? And how many kinds of life could there be? If this ship isn't from Earth—and it isn't—it has a crew that isn't human. And things that aren't human but are up to the level of deep-space travel in their civilization could mean anything!"

The skipper's hands were actually shaking. He would not have talked so freely before a member of his own crew, but Tommy Dort was of the observation staff. And even a skipper whose duties include worrying may sometimes need desperately to unload his worries. Sometimes, too, it helps to think aloud.

"Something like this has been talked about and speculated about for years," he said softly. "Mathematically, it's been an odds-on bet that somewhere in our galaxy there'd be another race with a civilization equal to or further advanced than ours. Nobody could ever guess where or when we'd meet them. But it looks like we've done it now!"

Tommy's eyes were very bright.

"D'you suppose they'll be friendly, sir?"

The skipper glanced at the distance indicator. The phantom object still made its insane, nonexistent swoops toward and away from the

Llanvabon. The secondary indication of an object at eighty thousand miles stirred ever so slightly.

"It's moving," he said curtly. "Heading for us. Just what we'd do if a strange spaceship appeared in our hunting grounds! Friendly? Maybe! We're going to try to contact them. We have to. But I suspect this is the end of this expedition. Thank God for the blasters!"

The blasters are those beams of ravening destruction which take care of recalcitrant meteorites in a spaceship's course when the deflectors can't handle them. They are not designed as weapons, but they can serve as pretty good ones. They can go into action at five thousand miles, and draw on the entire power output of a whole ship. With automatic aim and a traverse of five degrees, a ship like the *Llanvabon* can come very close to blasting a hole through a small-sized asteroid which gets in its way. But not on overdrive, of course.

Tommy Dort had approached the bow-quartering visiplate. Now he jerked his head around.

"Blasters, sir? What for?"

The skipper grimaced at the empty visiplate.

"Because we don't know what they're like and can't take a chance! I know!" he added bitterly. "We're going to make contacts and try to find out all we can about them—especially where they come from. I suppose we'll try to make friends—but we haven't much chance. We can't trust them the fraction of an inch. We daren't! They've locators. Maybe they've tracers better than any we have. Maybe they could trace us all the way home without our knowing it! We can't risk a nonhuman race knowing where Earth is unless we're sure of them! And how can we be sure? They could come to trade, of course—or they could swoop down on overdrive with a battle fleet that could wipe us out before we knew what happened. We wouldn't know which to expect, or when!"

Tommy's face was startled.

"It's all been thrashed out over and over, in theory," said the skipper. "Nobody's ever been able to find a sound answer, even on paper. But you know, in all their theorizing, no one considered the crazy, rank impossibility of a deep-space contact, with neither side knowing the other's home world! But we've got to find an answer in fact! What are we going to do about them? Maybe these creatures will be aesthetic marvels, nice and friendly and polite—and underneath with the sneaking brutal ferocity of a Japanese. Or maybe they'll be crude and gruff as a Swedish farmer—and just as decent underneath. Maybe they're something in between. But am I going to risk the possible future of the human race on a guess that it's safe to trust them? God knows it would be worth while to make friends with a new civilization! It would be bound to stimulate our own, and maybe we'd gain enormously. But I can't take chances. The one thing I won't risk is having them know how to find Earth! Either I know they can't follow me, or I don't go home! And they'll probably feel the same way!"

He pressed the sleeve-communicator button again.

"Navigation officers, attention! Every star map on this ship is to be prepared for instant destruction. This includes photographs and diagrams from which our course or starting point could be deduced. I want all astronomical data gathered and arranged to be destroyed in a split second, on order. Make it fast and report when ready!"

He released the button. He looked suddenly old. The first contact of humanity with an alien race was a situation which had been foreseen in many fashions, but never one quite so hopeless of solution as this. A solitary Earth-ship and a solitary alien, meeting in a nebula which must be remote from the home planet of each. They might wish peace, but the line of conduct which best prepared a treacherous attack was just the seeming of friendliness. Failure to be suspicious might doom the human race,—and a peaceful exchange of the fruits of civilization would be the greatest benefit imaginable. Any mistake would be irreparable, but a failure to be on guard would be fatal.

The captain's room was very, very quiet. The bow-quartering visiplate was filled with the image of a very small section of the nebula. A very small section indeed. It was all diffused, featureless, luminous mist. But suddenly Tommy Dort pointed.

"There, sir!"

There was a small shape in the mist. It was far away. It was a black shape, not polished to mirror-reflection like the hull of the *Llanvabon*. It was bulbous—roughly pear-shaped. There was much thin luminosity between, and no details could be observed, but it was surely no natural object. Then Tommy looked at the distance indicator and said quietly:

"It's headed for us at very high acceleration, sir. The odds are that they're thinking the same thing, sir, that neither of us will dare let the other go home. Do you think they'll try a contact with us, or let loose with their weapons as soon as they're in range?"

The *Llanvabon* was no longer in a crevasse of emptiness in the nebula's thin substance. She swam in luminescence. There were no stars save the two fierce glows in the nebula's heart. There was nothing but an all-enveloping light, curiously like one's imagining of underwater in the tropics of Earth.

The alien ship had made one sign of less than lethal intention. As it drew near the *Llanvabon,* it decelerated. The *Llanvabon* itself had advanced for a meeting and then come to a dead stop. Its movement had been a recognition of the nearness of the other ship. Its pausing was both a friendly sign and a precaution against attack. Relatively still, it could swivel on its own axis to present the least target to a slashing assault, and it would have a longer firing-time than if the two ships flashed past each other at their combined speeds.

The moment of actual approach, however, was tenseness itself. The *Llanvabon's* needle-pointed bow aimed unwaveringly at the alien bulk. A relay to the captain's room put a key under his hand which would fire the blasters with maximum power. Tommy Dort watched, his brow wrinkled. The aliens must be of a high degree of civilization if they had spaceships, and civilization does not develop without the development of foresight. These aliens must recognize all the implications of this first contact of two civilized races as fully as did the humans on the *Llanvabon.*

The possibility of an enormous spurt in the development of both, by peaceful contact and exchange of their separate technologies, would probably appeal to them as to the man. But when dissimilar human cultures are in contact, one must usually be subordinate or there is war. But subordination between races arising on separate planets could not be peacefully arranged. Men, at least, would never consent to subordination, nor was it likely that any highly developed race would agree. The benefits to be derived from commerce could never make up for a condition of inferiority. Some races—men, perhaps—would prefer commerce to conquest. Perhaps—perhaps!—these aliens would also. But some types even of human beings would have craved red war. If the alien ship now approaching the *Llanvabon* returned to its home base with news of humanity's existence and of ships like the *Llanvabon,* it would give its race the choice of trade or battle. They might want trade, or they might want war. But it takes two to make trade, and only one to make war. They could not be sure of men's peacefulness, nor could men be sure of theirs. The only safety for either civilization would lie in the destruction of one or both of the two ships here and now.

But even victory would not be really enough. Men would need to know where this alien race was to be found, for avoidance if not for battle. They would need to know its weapons, and its resources, and if it could be a menace and how it could be eliminated in case of need. The aliens would feel the same necessities concerning humanity.

So the skipper of the *Llanvabon* did not press the key which might possibly have blasted the other ship to nothingness. He dared not. But he dared not fire either. Sweat came out on his face.

A speaker muttered. Someone from the range room.

"The other ship's stopped, sir. Quite stationary. Blasters are centered on it, sir."

It was an urging to fire. But the skipper shook his head, to himself. The alien ship was no more than twenty miles away. It was dead-black. Every bit of its exterior was an abysmal, nonreflecting sable. No details could be seen except by minor variations in its outline against the misty nebula.

"It's stopped dead, sir," said another voice. "They've sent a modulated short wave at us, sir. Frequency modulated. Apparently a signal. Not enough power to do any harm."

The skipper said through tight-locked teeth:

"They're doing something now. There's movement on the outside of their hull. Watch what comes out. Put the auxiliary blasters on it."

Something small and round came smoothly out of the oval outline of the black ship. The bulbous hulk moved.

"Moving away, sir," said the speaker. "The object they let out is stationary in the place they've left."

Another voice cut in:

"More frequency modulated stuff, sir. Unintelligible."

Tommy Dort's eyes brightened. The skipper watched the visiplate, with sweat-droplets on his forehead.

"Rather pretty, sir," said Tommy, meditatively. "If they sent anything toward us, it might seem a projectile or a bomb. So they came close, let out a lifeboat, and went away again. They figure we can send a boat or a man to make contact without risking our ship. They must think pretty much as we do."

The skipper said, without moving his eyes from the plate:

"Mr. Dort, would you care to go out and look the thing over? I can't order you, but I need all my operating crew for emergencies. The observation staff—"

"Is expendable. Very well, sir," said Tommy briskly. "I won't take a lifeboat, sir. Just a suit with a drive in it. It's smaller and the arms and legs will look unsuitable for a bomb. I think I should carry a scanner, sir."

The alien ship continued to retreat. Forty, eighty, four hundred miles. It came to a stop and hung there, waiting. Climbing into his atomic-driven spacesuit just within the *Llanvabon's* air lock, Tommy heard the reports as they went over the speakers throughout the ship. That the other ship had stopped its retreat at four hundred miles was encouraging. It might not have weapons effective at a greater distance than that, and so felt safe. But just as the thought formed itself in his mind, the alien retreated precipitately still farther. Which, as Tommy reflected as he emerged from the lock, might be because the aliens had realized they were giving themselves away, or might be because they wanted to give the impression that they had done so.

He swooped away from the silvery-mirror *Llanvabon*, through a brightly glowing emptiness which was past any previous experience of the human race. Behind him, the *Llanvabon* swung about and darted away. The skipper's voice came in Tommy's helmet phones.

"We're pulling back, too, Mr. Dort. There is a bare possibility that they've some explosive atomic reaction they can't use from their own ship, but which might be destructive even as far as this. We'll draw back. Keep your scanner on the object."

The reasoning was sound, if not very comforting. An explosive which would destroy anything within twenty miles was theoretically possible, but humans didn't have it yet. It was decidedly safest for the *Llanvabon* to draw back.

But Tommy Dort felt very lonely. He sped through emptiness toward the tiny black speck which hung in incredible brightness. The *Llanvabon* vanished. Its polished hull would merge with the glowing mist at a relatively short distance, anyhow. The alien ship was not visible to the naked eye, either. Tommy swam in nothingness, four thousand light-years from home, toward a tiny black spot which was the only solid object to be seen in all of space.

It was a slightly distorted sphere, not much over six feet in diameter. It bounced away when Tommy landed on it, feet-first. There were small tentacles, or horns, which projected in every direction. They looked rather like the detonating horns of a submarine mine, but there was a glint of crystal at the tip-end of each.

"I'm here," said Tommy into his helmet phone.

He caught hold of a horn and drew himself to the object. It was all metal, dead-black. He could feel no texture through his space gloves, of course, but he went over and over it, trying to discover its purpose.

"Deadlock, sir," he said presently. "Nothing to report that the scanner hasn't shown you."

Then, through his suit, he felt vibrations. They translated themselves as clankings. A section of the rounded hull of the object opened out. Two sections. He worked his way around to look in and see the first nonhuman civilized beings that any man had ever looked upon.

But what he saw was simply a flat plate on which dim-red glows crawled here and there in seeming aimlessness. His helmet phones emitted a startled exclamation. The skipper's voice:

"Very good, Mr. Dort. Fix your scanner to look into that plate. They dumped out a robot with an infrared visiplate for communication. Not risking any personnel. Whatever we might do would damage only machinery. Maybe they expect us to bring it on board—and it may have a bomb charge that can be detonated when they're ready to start for home. I'll send a plate to face one of its scanners. You return to the ship."

"Yes, sir," said Tommy. "But which way is the ship, sir?"

There were no stars. The nebula obscured them with its light. The only thing visible from the robot was the double star at the nebula's center. Tommy was no longer oriented. He had but one reference point.

"Head straight away from the double star," came the order in his helmet phone. "We'll pick you up."

He passed another lonely figure, a little later, headed for the alien sphere with a vision plate to set up. The two spaceships, each knowing that it dared not risk its own race by the slightest lack of caution, would communicate with each other through this small round robot. Their separate vision systems would enable them to exchange all the information they dared give, while they debated the most practical way of making sure that their own civilization would not be endangered by this first contact with another. The truly most practical method would be the destruction of the other ship in a swift and deadly attack—in self-defense.

II.

The *Llanvabon*, thereafter, was a ship in which there were two separate enterprises on hand at the same time. She had come out from Earth to make close-range observations on the smaller component of the double star at the nebula's center. The nebula itself was the result of the most titanic explosion of which men have any knowledge. The explosion took place sometime in the year 2946 B. C., before the first of the seven cities of long-dead Ilium was even thought of. The light of that explosion reached Earth in the year 1054 A. D., and was duly recorded in ecclesiastic annals and somewhat more reliably by Chinese court astronomers. It was bright enough to be seen in daylight for twenty-three successive days. Its light—and it was four thousand light-years away—was brighter than that of Venus.

From these facts, astronomers could calculate nine hundred years later the violence of the detonation. Matter blown away from the center of the explosion would have traveled outward at the rate of two million three hundred thousand miles an hour; more than thirty-eight thousand miles a minute; something over six hundred thirty-eight miles per second. When twentieth-century telescopes were turned upon the scene of this vast explosion, only a double star remained—and the nebula. The brighter star of the doublet was almost unique in having so high a surface temperature that it showed no spectrum lines at all. It had a continuous spectrum. Sol's surface temperature is about 7,000° Absolute. That of the hot white star is 500,000 degrees. It has nearly the mass of the sun, but only one fifth its diameter, so that its density is one hundred seventy-three times that of water, sixteen times that of lead, and eight times that of iridium— the heaviest substance known on Earth. But even this density is not that of a dwarf white star like the companion of Sirius. The white star in the Crab Nebula is an incomplete dwarf; it is a star still in the act of collapsing. Examination—including the survey of a four-thousand-year column of its light—was worth while. The *Llanvabon* had come to make that examination. But the finding of an alien spaceship upon a similar errand had implications which overshadowed the original purpose of the expedition.

A tiny bulbous robot floated in the tenuous nebular gas. The normal operating crew of the *Llanvabon* stood at their posts with a sharp alertness which was productive of tense nerves. The observation staff divided itself, and a part went half-heartedly about the making of the observations for which the *Llanvabon* had come. The other half applied itself to the problem the spaceship offered.

It represented a culture which was up to space travel on an interstellar scale. The explosion of a mere five thousand years since must have blasted every trace of life out of existence in the area now filled by the nebula. So the aliens of the black spaceship came from another solar system. Their trip must have been, like that of the Earth ship, for purely scientific purposes. There was nothing to be extracted from the nebula.

They were, then, at least near the level of human civilization, which meant that they had or could develop arts and articles of commerce which men would want to trade for, in friendship. But they would necessarily realize that the existence and civilization of humanity was a potential menace to their own race. The two races could be friends, but also they could be deadly enemies. Each, even if unwillingly, was a monstrous menace to the other. And the only safe thing to do with a menace is to destroy it.

In the Crab Nebula the problem was acute and immediate. The future relationship of the two races would be settled here and now. If a process for friendship could be established, one race, otherwise doomed, would survive and both would benefit immensely. But that process had to be established, and confidence built up, without the most minute risk of danger from treachery. Confidence would need to be established upon a foundation of necessarily complete distrust. Neither dared return to its own base if the other could do harm to its race. Neither dared risk any of the necessities to trust. The only safe thing for either to do was destroy the other or be destroyed.

But even for war, more was needed than mere destruction of the other. With interstellar traffic, the aliens must have atomic power and some form of overdrive for travel above the speed of light. With radio location and visiplates and short-wave communication they had, of course, many other devices. What weapons did they have? How widely extended was their culture? What were their resources? Could there be a development of trade and friendship, or were the two races so unlike that only war could exist between them? If peace was possible, how could it be begun?

The men on the *Llanvabon* needed facts—and so did the crew of the other ship. They must take back every morsel of information they could. The most important information of all would be of the location of the other civilization, just in case of war. That one bit of information might be the decisive factor in an interstellar war. But other facts would be enormously valuable.

The tragic thing was that there could be no possible information which could lead to peace. Neither ship could stake its own race's existence upon any conviction of the good will or the honor of the other.

So there was a strange truce between the two ships. The alien went about its work of making observations, as did the *Llanvabon*. The tiny robot floated in bright emptiness. A scanner from the *Llanvabon* was focused upon a vision plate from the alien. A scanner from the alien regarded a vision plate from the *Llanvabon*. Communication began.

It progressed rapidly. Tommy Dort was one of those who made the first progress report. His special task on the expedition was over. He had now been assigned to work on the problem of communication with the alien entities. He went with the ship's solitary psychologist to the captain's room to convey the news of success. The captain's room, as usual, was a place of silence and dull-red indicator lights and the great bright visiplates on every wall and on the ceiling.

"We've established fairly satisfactory communication, sir," said the psychologist. He looked tired. His work on the trip was supposed to be that of measuring personal factors of error in the observation staff, for the reduction of all observations to the nearest possible decimal to the absolute. He had been pressed into service for which he was not especially fitted, and it told upon him. "That is, we can say almost anything we wish, to them, and can understand what they say in return. But of course we don't know how much of what they say is the truth."

The skipper's eyes turned to Tommy Dort.

"We've hooked up some machinery," said Tommy, "that amounts to a mechanical translator. We have vision plates, of course, and then short-wave beams direct. They use frequency-modulation plus what is probably variation in wave forms—like our vowel and consonant sounds in speech. We've never had any use for anything like that before, so our coils won't handle it, but we've developed a sort of code which isn't the language of either set of us. They shoot over short-wave stuff with frequency-modulation, and we record it as sound. When we shoot it back, it's reconverted into frequency-modulation."

The skipper said, frowning:

"Why wave-form changes in short waves? How do you know?"

"We showed them our recorder in the vision plates, and they showed us theirs. They record the frequency-modulation direct. I think," said Tommy carefully, "they don't use sound at all, even in speech. They've set up a communications room, and we've watched them in the act of communicating with us. They make no perceptible movement of anything that corresponds to a speech organ. Instead of a microphone, they simply stand near something that would work as a pick-up antenna. My guess, sir, is that they use microwaves for what you might call person-to-person conversation. I think they make short-wave trains as we make sounds."

The skipper stared at him:

"That means they have telepathy?"

"M-m-m. Yes, sir," said Tommy. "Also it means that we have telepathy too, as far as they are concerned. They're probably deaf. They've certainly no idea of using sound waves in air for communication. They simply don't use noises for any purpose."

The skipper stored the information away.

"What else?"

"Well, sir," said Tommy doubtfully, "I think we're all set. We agreed on arbitrary symbols for objects, sir, by way of the visiplates, and worked out relationships and verbs and so on with diagrams and pictures. We've a couple of thousand words that have mutual meanings. We set up an analyzer to sort out their short-wave groups, which we feed into a decoding machine. And then the coding end of the machine picks out recordings to make the wave groups we want to send back. When you're ready to talk to the skipper of the other ship, sir, I think we're ready."

"H-m-m. What's your impression of their psychology?" The skipper asked the question of the psychologist.

"I don't know, sir," said the psychologist harassedly. "They seem to be completely direct. But they haven't let slip even a hint of the tenseness we know exists. They act as if they were simply setting up a means of communication for friendly conversation. But there is . . . well . . . an overtone—"

The psychologist was a good man at psychological mensuration, which is a good and useful field. But he was not equipped to analyze a completely alien thought-pattern.

"If I may say so, sir—" said Tommy uncomfortably.

"What?"

"They're oxygen breathers," said Tommy, "and they're not too dissimilar to us in other ways. It seems to me, sir, that parallel evolution has been at work. Perhaps intelligence evolves in parallel lines, just as . . . well . . . basic bodily functions. I mean," he added conscientiously, "any living being of any sort must ingest, metabolize, and excrete. Perhaps any intelligent brain must perceive, apperceive, and find a personal reaction. I'm sure I've detected irony. That implies humor, too. In short, sir, I think they could be likable."

The skipper heaved himself to his feet.

"H-m-m." He said profoundly, "We'll see what they have to say."

He walked to the communications room. The scanner for the vision plate in the robot was in readiness. The skipper walked in front of it. Tommy Dort sat down at the coding machine and tapped at the keys. Highly improbable noises came from it, went into a microphone, and governed the frequency-modulation of a signal sent through space to the other spaceship. Almost instantly the vision screen which with one relay—in the robot—showed the interior of the other ship lighted up. An alien came before the scanner and seemed to look inquisitively out of the plate. He was extraordinarily manlike, but he was not human. The impression he gave was of extreme baldness and a somehow humorous frankness.

"I'd like to say," said the skipper heavily, "the appropriate things about this first contact of two dissimilar civilized races, and of my hopes that a friendly intercourse between the two peoples will result."

Tommy Dort hesitated. Then he shrugged and tapped expertly upon the coder. More improbable noises.

The alien skipper seemed to receive the message. He made a gesture which was wryly assenting. The decoder on the *Llanvabon* hummed to itself and word-cards dropped into the message frame. Tommy said dispassionately:

"He says, sir, 'That is all very well, but is there any way for us to let each other go home alive? I would be happy to hear of such a way if you can contrive one. At the moment it seems to me that one of us must be killed.'"

III.

The atmosphere was of confusion. There were too many questions to be answered all at once. Nobody could answer any of them. And all of them had to be answered.

The *Llanvabon* could start for home. The alien ship might or might not be able to multiply the speed of light by one more unit than the Earth vessel. If it could, the *Llanvabon* would get close enough to Earth to reveal its destination—and then have to fight. It might or might not win. Even if it did win, the aliens might have a communication system by which the *Llanvabon's* destination might have been reported to the aliens' home planet before battle was joined. But the *Llanvabon* might lose in such a fight. If she was to be destroyed, it would be better to be destroyed here, without giving any clue to where human beings might be found by a forewarned, forearmed alien battle fleet.

The black ship was in exactly the same predicament. It, too, could start for home. But the *Llanvabon* might be faster, and an overdrive field can be trailed, if you set to work on it soon enough. The aliens, also, would not know whether the *Llanvabon* could report to its home base without returning. If the alien was to be destroyed, it also would prefer to fight it out here, so that it could not lead a probable enemy to its own civilization.

Neither ship, then, could think of flight. The course of the *Llanvabon* into the nebula might be known to the black ship, but it had been the end of a logarithmic curve, and the aliens could not know its properties. They could not tell from that from what direction the Earth ship had started. As of the moment, then, the two ships were even. But the question was and remained, "What now?"

There was no specific answer. The aliens traded information for information—and did not always realize what information they gave. The humans traded information for information—and Tommy Dort sweated blood in his anxiety not to give any clue to the whereabouts of Earth.

The aliens saw by infrared light, and the vision plates and scanners in the robot communication-exchange had to adapt their respective images up and down an optical octave each, for them to have any meaning at all. It did not occur to the aliens that their eyesight told that their sun was a red dwarf, yielding light of greatest energy just below the part of the spectrum visible to human eyes. But after that fact was realized on the *Llanvabon,* it was realized that the aliens, also, should be able to deduce the Sun's spectral type by the light to which men's eyes were best adapted.

There was a gadget for the recording of short-wave trains which was as casually in use among the aliens as a sound-recorder is among men. The humans wanted that, badly. And the aliens were fascinated by the mystery of sound. They were able to perceive noise, of course, just as a man's palm will perceive infrared light by the sensation of heat it produces, but they could no more differentiate pitch or tone-quality than a man is able to distinguish between two frequencies of heat-radiation even half an octave apart. To them, the human science of sound was a remarkable discovery. They would find uses for noises which humans had never imagined—if they lived.

But that was another question. Neither ship could leave without first destroying the other. But while the flood of information was in passage, neither ship could afford to destroy the other. There was the matter of the outer coloring of the two ships. The *Llanvabon* was mirror-bright exteriorly. The alien ship was dead-black by visible light. It absorbed heat to perfection, and should radiate it away again as readily. But it did not. The black coating was not a "black body" color or lack of color. It was a perfect reflector of certain infrared wave lengths while simultaneously it fluoresced in just those wave bands. In practice, it absorbed the higher frequencies of heat, converted them to lower frequencies it did not radiate —and stayed at the desired temperature even in empty space.

Tommy Dort labored over his task of communications. He found the alien thought-processes not so alien that he could not follow them. The discussion of technics reached the matter of interstellar navigation. A star map was needed to illustrate the process. It would have been logical to use a star map from the chart room—but from a star map one could guess the point from which the map was projected. Tommy had a map made specially, with imaginary but convincing star images upon it. He translated directions for its use by the coder and decoder. In return, the aliens presented a star map of their own before the visiplate. Copied instantly by photograph, the Nav officers labored over it, trying to figure out from what spot in the galaxy the stars and Milky Way would show at such an angle. It baffled them.

It was Tommy who realized finally that the aliens had made a special star map for their demonstration too, and that it was a mirror-image of the faked map Tommy had shown them previously.

Tommy could grin, at that. He began to like these aliens. They were not human, but they had a very human sense of the ridiculous. In course of time Tommy essayed a mild joke. It had to be translated into code numerals, these into quite cryptic groups of short-wave, frequency-modulated impulses, and these went to the other ship and into heaven knew what to become intelligible. A joke which went through such formalities would not seem likely to be funny. But the aliens did see the point.

There was one of the aliens to whom communication became as normal a function as Tommy's own code-handlings. The two of them developed a quite insane friendship, conversing by coder, decoder and short-wave trains. When technicalities in the official messages grew too involved, that alien sometimes threw in strictly nontechnical interpolations akin to slang. Often, they cleared up the confusion. Tommy, for no reason whatever, had filed a code-name of "Buck" which the decoder picked out regularly when this particular operator signed his own symbol to a message.

In the third week of communication, the decoder suddenly presented Tommy with a message in the message frame.

You are a good guy. It is too bad we have to kill each other.—Buck.

Tommy had been thinking much the same thing. He tapped off the rueful reply:

We can't see any way out of it. Can you?

There was a pause, and the message frame filled up again.

If we could believe each other, yes. Our skipper would like it. But we can't believe you, and you can't believe us. We'd trail you home if we got a chance, and you'd trail us. But we feel sorry about it.—Buck.

Tommy Dort took the messages to the skipper.

"Look here, sir!" he said urgently. "These people are almost human, and they're likable cusses."

The skipper was busy about his important task of thinking things to worry about, and worrying about them. He said tiredly:

"They're oxygen breathers. Their air is twenty-eight per cent oxygen instead of twenty, but they could do very well on Earth. It would be a highly desirable conquest for them. And we still don't know what weapons they've got or what they can develop. Would you tell them how to find Earth?"

"N-no," said Tommy, unhappily.

"They probably feel the same way," said the skipper dryly. "And if we did manage to make a friendly contact, how long would it stay friendly? If their weapons were inferior to ours, they'd feel that for their own safety they had to improve them. And we, knowing they were planning to revolt, would crush them while we could—for our own safety! If it happened to be the other way about, they'd have to smash us before we could catch up to them."

Tommy was silent, but he moved restlessly.

"If we smash this black ship and get home," said the skipper, "Earth Government will be annoyed if we don't tell them where it came from. But what can we do? We'll be lucky enough to get back alive with our warning. It isn't possible to get out of those creatures any more information than we give them, and we surely won't give them our address! We've run into them by accident. Maybe—if we smash this ship—there won't be another contact for thousands of years. And it's a pity, because trade could mean so much! But it takes two to make a peace, and we can't risk trusting them. The only answer is to kill them if we can, and if we can't, to make sure that when they kill us they'll find out nothing that will lead them to Earth. I don't like it," added the skipper tiredly, "but there simply isn't anything else to do!"

IV.

On the *Llanvabon*, the technicians worked frantically in two divisions. One prepared for victory, and the other for defeat. The ones working for victory could do little. The main blasters were the only weapons with any promise. Their mountings were cautiously altered so that they were no longer fixed nearly dead ahead, with only a 5° traverse. Electronic controls which followed a radio-locator master-finder would keep them trained with absolute precision upon a given target regardless of its maneuverings. More; a hitherto unsung genius in the engine room devised a capacity-storage system by which the normal full-output of the ship's engines could be momentarily accumulated and released in surges of stored power far above normal. In theory, the range of the blasters should be multiplied and their destructive power considerably stepped up. But there was not much more that could be done.

The defeat crew had more leeway. Star charts, navigational instruments carrying telltale notations, the photographic record Tommy Dort had made on the six months' journey from Earth, and every other memorandum offering clues to Earth's position, were prepared for destruction. They were put in sealed files, and if any one of them was opened by one who did not know the exact, complicated process, the contents of all the files would flash into ashes and the ashes be churned past any hope of restoration. Of course, if the *Llanvabon* should be victorious, a carefully not-indicated method of reopening them in safety would remain.

There were atomic bombs placed all over the hull of the ship. If its human crew should be killed without complete destruction of the ship, the atomic-power bombs should detonate if the *Llanvabon* were brought alongside the alien vessel. There were no ready-made atomic bombs on board, but there were small spare atomic-power units on board. It was not hard to trick them so that when they were turned on, instead of yielding a smooth flow of power they would explode. And four men of the earth ship's crew remained always in spacesuits with closed helmets, to fight the ship should it be punctured in many compartments by an unwarned attack.

Such an attack, however, would not be treacherous. The alien skipper had spoken frankly. His manner was that of one who wryly admits the uselessness of lies. The skipper and the *Llanvabon*, in turn, heavily admitted the virtue of frankness. Each insisted—perhaps truthfully—that he wished for friendship between the two races. But neither could trust the other not to make every conceivable effort to find out the one thing he needed most desperately to conceal—the location of his home planet. And neither dared believe that the other was unable to trail him and find out. Because each felt it his own duty to accomplish that unbearable—to the other—act, neither could risk the possible extinction of his race by trusting the other. They must fight because they could not do anything else.

They could raise the stakes of the battle by an exchange of information beforehand. But there was a limit to the stake either would put up. No information on weapons, population, or resources would be given by either. Not even the distance of their home bases from the Crab Nebula would be told. They exchanged information, to be sure, but they knew a battle to the death must follow, and each strove to represent his own civilization as powerful enough to give pause to the other's ideas of possible conquest—and thereby increased its appearance of menace to the other, and made battle more unavoidable.

It was curious how completely such alien brains could mesh, however. Tommy Dort, sweating over the coding and decoding machines, found a personal equation emerging from the at first stilted arrays of word-cards which arranged themselves. He had seen the aliens only in the vision screen, and then only in light at least one octave removed from the light they saw by. They, in turn, saw him very strangely, by transposed illumination from what to them would be the far ultraviolet. But their brains worked alike. Amazingly alike. Tommy Dort felt an actual sympathy and even something close to friendship for the gill-breathing, bald, and dryly ironic creatures of the black space vessel.

Because of that mental kinship he set up—though hopelessly—a sort of table of the aspects of the problem before them. He did not believe that the aliens had any instinctive desire to destroy man. In fact, the study of communications from the aliens had produced on the *Llanvabon* a feeling of tolerance not unlike that between enemy soldiers during a truce on Earth. The men felt no enmity, and probably neither did the aliens. But they had to kill or be killed for strictly logical reasons.

Tommy's table was specific. He made a list of objectives the men must try to achieve, in the order of their importance. The first was the carrying back of news of the existence of the alien culture. The second was the location of that alien culture in the galaxy. The third was the carrying back of as much information as possible about that culture. The third was being worked on but the second was probably impossible. The first—and all—would depend on the result of the fight which must take place.

The aliens' objectives would be exactly similar, so that the men must prevent, first, news of the existence of Earth's culture from being taken back by the aliens, second, alien discovery of the location of Earth, and third, the acquiring by the aliens of information which would help them or encourage them to attack humanity. And again the third was in train, and the second was probably taken care of, and the first must await the battle.

There was no possible way to avoid the grim necessity of the destruction of the black ship. The aliens would see no solution to their problems but the destruction of the *Llanvabon*. But Tommy Dort, regarding his tabulation ruefully, realized that even complete victory would not be a perfect solution. The ideal would be for the *Llanvabon* to take back the alien ship for study. Nothing less would be a complete attainment of the third objective. But Tommy realized that he hated the idea of so complete a victory, even if it could be accomplished. He would hate the idea of killing even nonhuman creatures who understood a human joke. And beyond that, he would hate the idea of Earth fitting out a fleet of fighting ships to destroy an alien culture because its existence was dangerous. The pure accident of this encounter, between peoples who could like each other, had created a situation which could only result in wholesale destruction.

Tommy Dort soured on his own brain which could find no answer which would work. But there had to be an answer! The gamble was too big! It was too absurd that two spaceships should fight—neither one primarily designed for fighting—so that the survivor could carry back news which would set one side to frenzied preparation for war against the unwarned other.

If both races could be warned, though, and each knew that the other did not want to fight, and if they could communicate with each other but not locate each other until some grounds for mutual trust could be reached—

It was impossible. It was chimerical. It was a daydream. It was nonsense. But it was such luring nonsense that Tommy Dort ruefully put it into the coder to his gill-breathing friend Buck, then some hundred thousand miles off in the misty brightness of the nebula.

"Sure," said Buck, in the decoder's word-cards flicking into place in the message frame. "That is a good dream. But I like you and still won't believe you. If I said that first, you would like me but not believe me either. I tell you the truth more than you believe, and maybe you tell me the truth more than I believe. But there is no way to know. I am sorry."

Tommy Dort stared gloomily at the message. He felt a very horrible sense of responsibility. Everyone did, on the *Llanvabon*. If they failed in this encounter, the human race would run a very good chance of being exterminated in time to come. If they succeeded, the race of the aliens would be the one to face destruction, most likely. Millions or billions of lives hung upon the actions of a few men.

Then Tommy Dort saw the answer.

It would be amazingly simple, if it worked. At worst it might give a partial victory to humanity and the *Llanvabon*. He sat quite still, not daring to move lest he break the chain of thought that followed the first tenuous idea. He went over and over it, excitedly finding objections here and meeting them, and overcoming impossibilities there. It was the answer! He felt sure of it.

He felt almost dizzy with relief when he found his way to the captain's room and asked leave to speak.

It is the function of a skipper, among others, to find things to worry about. But the *Llanvabon's* skipper did not have to look. In the three weeks and four days since the first contact with the alien black ship, the skipper's face had grown lined and old. He had not only the *Llanvabon* to worry about. He had all of humanity.

"Sir," said Tommy Dort, his mouth rather dry because of his enormous earnestness, "may I offer a method of attack on the black ship? I'll undertake it myself, sir, and if it doesn't work our ship won't be weakened."

The skipper looked at him unseeingly.

"The tactics are all worked out, Mr. Dort," he said heavily. "They're being cut on tape now, for the ship's handling. It's a terrible gamble, but it has to be done."

"I think," said Tommy carefully, "I've worked out a way to take the gamble out. Suppose, sir, we send a message to the other ship, offering—"

His voice went on in the utterly quiet captain's room, with the visiplates showing only a vast mistiness outside and the two fiercely burning stars in the nebula's heart.

V.

The skipper himself went through the air lock with Tommy. For one reason, the action Tommy had suggested would need his authority behind it. For another, the skipper had worried more intensively than anybody else on the *Llanvabon*, and he was tired of it. If he went with Tommy, he would do the thing himself, and if he failed he would be the first one killed—and the taps for the Earth ship's maneuvering were already fed into the control board and correlated with the master-timer. If Tommy and the skipper were killed, a single control pushed home would throw the *Llanvabon* into the most furious possible all-out attack, which would end in the complete destruction of one ship or the other—or both. So the skipper was not deserting his post.

The outer airlock door swung wide. It opened upon that shining emptiness which was the nebula. Twenty miles away, the little round robot hung in space, drifting in an incredible orbit about the twin central suns, and floating ever nearer and nearer. It would never reach either of them, of course. The white star alone was so much hotter than Earth's sun that its heat-effect would produce Earth's temperature on an object five times as far from it as Neptune is from Sol. Even removed to the distance of Pluto, the little robot would be raised to cherry-red heat by the blazing white dwarf. And it could not possibly approach to the ninety-odd million miles which is the Earth's distance from the sun. So near, its metal would melt and boil away as vapor. But, half a light-year out, the bulbous object bobbed in emptiness.

The two spacesuited figures soared away from the *Llanvabon*. The small atomic drives which made them minute spaceships on their own had been subtly altered, but the change did not interfere with their functioning. They headed for the communication robot. The skipper, out in space, said gruffly:

"Mr. Dort, all my life I have longed for adventure. This is the first time I could ever justify it to myself."

His voice came through Tommy's space-phone receivers. Tommy wetted his lips and said:

"It doesn't seem like adventure to me, sir. I want terribly for the plan to go through. I thought adventure was when you didn't care."

"Oh, no," said the skipper. "Adventure is when you toss your life on the scales of chance and wait for the pointer to stop."

They reached the round object. They clung to its short, scanner-tipped horns.

"Intelligent, those creatures," said the skipper heavily. "They must want desperately to see more of our ship than the communications room, to agree to this exchange of visits before the fight."

"Yes, sir," said Tommy. But privately, he suspected that Buck—his gill-breathing friend—would like to see him in the flesh before one or both of them died. And it seemed to him that between the two ships had grown up an odd tradition of courtesy, like that between two ancient knights before a tourney, when they admired each other wholeheartedly before hacking at each other with all the contents of their respective armories.

They waited.

Then, out of the mist, came two other figures. The alien spacesuits were also power-driven. The aliens themselves were shorter than men, and their helmet openings were coated with a filtering material to cut off visible and ultraviolet rays which to them would be lethal. It was not possible to see more than the outline of the heads within.

Tommy's helmet phone said, from the communications room on the *Llanvabon*:

"They say that their ship is waiting for you, sir. The airlock door will be open."

The skipper's voice said heavily:

"Mr. Dort, have you seen their spacesuits before? If so, are you sure they're not carrying anything extra, such as bombs?"

"Yes, sir," said Tommy. "We've showed each other our space equipment. They've nothing but regular stuff in view, sir."

The skipper made a gesture to the two aliens. He and Tommy Dort plunged on for the black vessel. They could not make out the ship very clearly with the naked eye, but directions for change of course came from the communication room.

The black ship loomed up. It was huge; as long as the *Llanvabon* and vastly thicker. The air lock did stand open. The two spacesuited men moved in and anchored themselves with magnetic-soled boots. The outer door closed. There was a rush of air and simultaneously the sharp quick tug of artificial gravity. Then the inner door opened.

All was darkness. Tommy switched on his helmet light at the same instant as the skipper. Since the aliens saw by infrared, a white light would have been intolerable to them. The men's helmet lights were, therefore, of the deep-red tint used to illuminate instrument panels so there will be no dazzling of eyes that must be able to detect the minutest specks of white light on a navigating vision plate. There were aliens waiting to receive them. They blinked at the brightness of the helmet lights. The space-phone receivers said in Tommy's ear:

"They say, sir, their skipper is waiting for you."

Tommy and the skipper were in a long corridor with a soft flooring underfoot. Their lights showed details of which every one was exotic.

"I think I'll crack my helmet, sir," said Tommy.

He did. The air was good. By analysis it was thirty percent oxygen instead of twenty for normal air on Earth, but the pressure was less. It felt just right. The artificial gravity, too, was less than that maintained on the *Llanvabon*. The home planet of the aliens would be smaller than Earth, and—by the infrared data—circling close to a nearly dead, dull-red sun. The air had smells in it. They were utterly strange, but not unpleasant.

An arched opening. A ramp with the same soft stuff underfoot. Lights which actually shed a dim, dull-red glow about. The aliens had stepped up some of their illuminating equipment as an act of courtesy. The light might hurt their eyes, but it was a gesture of consideration which made Tommy even more anxious for his plan to go through.

The alien skipper faced them, with what seemed to Tommy a gesture of wryly humorous deprecation. The helmet phones said:

"He says, sir, that he greets you with pleasure, but he has been able to think of only one way in which the problem created by the meeting of these two ships can be solved."

"He means a fight," said the skipper. "Tell him I'm here to offer another choice."

The *Llanvabon's* skipper and the skipper of the alien ship were face to face, but their communication was weirdly indirect. The aliens used no sound in communication. Their talk, in fact, took place on microwaves and approximated telepathy. But they could not hear, in any ordinary sense of the word, so the skipper's and Tommy's speech approached telepathy, too, as far as they were concerned. When the skipper spoke, his space phone sent his words back to the *Llanvabon*, where the words were fed into the coder and short-wave equivalents sent back to the black ship. The alien skipper's reply went to the *Llanvabon* and through the decoder, and was retransmitted by space phone in words read from the message frame. It was awkward, but it worked.

The short and stocky alien skipper paused. The helmet phones relayed his translated, soundless reply.

"He is anxious to hear, sir."

The skipper took off his helmet. He put his hands at his belt in a belligerent pose.

"Look here!" he said truculently to the bald, strange creature in the unearthly red glow before him. "It looks like we have to fight and one batch of us get killed. We're ready to do it if we have to. But if you win, we've got it fixed so you'll never find out where Earth is, and there's a good chance we'll get you anyhow! If we win, we'll be in the same fix. And if we win and go back home, our government will fit out a fleet and start hunting your planet. And if we find it we'll be ready to blast it to hell! If you win, the same thing will happen to us! And it's all foolishness! We've stayed here a month, and we've swapped information, and we don't hate each other. There's no reason for us to fight except for the rest of our respective races!"

The skipper stopped for breath, scowling. Tommy Dort inconspicuously put his own hands on the belt of his spacesuit. He waited, hoping desperately that the trick would work.

"He says, sir," reported the helmet phones, "that all you say is true. But that his race has to be protected, just as you feel that yours must be."

"Naturally!" said the skipper angrily, "but the sensible thing to do is to figure out how to protect it! Putting its future up as a gamble in a fight is not sensible. Our races have to be warned of each other's existence. That's true. But each should have proof that the other doesn't want to fight, but wants to be friendly. And we shouldn't be able to find each other, but we should be able to communicate with each other to work out grounds for a common trust. If our governments want to be fools, let them! But we should give them the chance to make friends, instead of starting a space war out of mutual funk!"

Briefly, the space phone said:

"He says that the difficulty is that of trusting each other now. With the possible existence of his race at stake, he cannot take any chance, and neither can you, of yielding an advantage."

"But my race," boomed the skipper, glaring at the alien captain, "my race has an advantage now. We came here to your ship in atom-powered spacesuits! Before we left, we altered the drives! We can set off ten pounds of sensitized fuel apiece, right here in this ship, or it can be set off by remote control from our ship! It will be rather remarkable if your fuel store doesn't blow up with us! In other words, if you don't accept my proposal for a commonsense approach to this predicament, Dort and I blow up in an atomic explosion, and your ship will be wrecked if not destroyed—and the *Llanvabon* will be attacking with everything it's got within two seconds after the blast goes off!"

The captain's room of the alien ship was a strange scene, with its dull-red illumination and the strange, bald, gill-breathing aliens watching the skipper and waiting for the inaudible translation of the harangue they could not hear. But a sudden tensity appeared in the air. A sharp, savage feeling of strain. The alien skipper made a gesture. The helmet phones hummed.

"He says, sir, what is your proposal?"

"Swap ships!" roared the skipper. "Swap ships and go on home! We can fix our instruments so they'll do no trailing, he can do the same with his. We'll each remove our star maps and records. We'll each dismantle our weapons. The air will serve, and we'll take their ship and they'll take ours, and neither one can harm or trail the other, and each will carry home more information than can be taken otherwise! We can agree on this same Crab Nebula as a rendezvous when the double-star has made another circuit, and if our people want to meet them they can do it, and if they are scared they can duck it! That's my proposal! And he'll take it, or Dort and I blow up their ship and the *Llanvabon* blasts what's left!"

He glared about him while he waited for the translation to reach the tense small stocky figures about him. He could tell when it came because the tenseness changed. The figures stirred. They made gestures. One of them made convulsive movements. It lay down on the soft floor and kicked. Others leaned against its walls and shook.

The voice in Tommy Dort's helmet phones had been strictly crisp and professional, before, but now it sounded blankly amazed.

"He says, sir, that it is a good joke. Because the two crew members he sent to our ship, and that you passed on the way, have their spacesuits stuffed with atomic explosive too, sir, and he intended to make the very same offer and threat! Of course he accepts, sir. Your ship is worth more to him than his own, and his is worth more to you than the *Llanvabon*. It appears, sir, to be a deal."

Then Tommy Dort realized what the convulsive movements of the aliens were. They were laughter.

It wasn't quite as simple as the skipper had outlined it. The actual working-out of the proposal was complicated. For three days the crews of the two ships were intermingled, the aliens learning the workings of the *Llanvabon's* engines, and the men learning the controls of the black spaceship. It was a good joke—but it wasn't all a joke. There were men on the black ship, and aliens on the *Llanvabon*, ready at an instant's notice to blow up the vessels in question. And they would have done it in case of need, for which reason the need did not appear. But it was, actually, a better arrangement to have two expeditions return to two civilizations, under the current arrangement, than for either to return alone.

There were differences, though. There was some dispute about the removal of records. In most cases the dispute was settled by the destruction of the records. There was more trouble caused by the *Llanvabon's* books, and the alien equivalent of a ship's library, containing works which approximated the novels of Earth. But those items were valuable to possible friendship, because they would show the two cultures, each to the other, from the viewpoint of normal citizens and without propaganda.

But nerves were tense during those three days, Aliens unloaded and inspected the foodstuffs intended for the men on the black ship. Men transshipped the foodstuffs the aliens would need to return to their home. There were endless details, from the exchange of lighting equipment to suit the eyesight of the exchanging crews, to a final check-up of apparatus. A joint inspection party of both races verified that all detector devices had been smashed but not removed, so that they could not be used for trailing and had not been smuggled away. And of course, the aliens were anxious not to leave any useful weapon on the black ship, nor the men upon the *Llanvabon*. It was a curious fact that each crew was best qualified to take exactly the measures which made an evasion of the agreement impossible.

There was a final conference before the two ships parted, back in the communication room of the *Llanvabon*.

"Tell the little runt," rumbled the *Llanvabon*'s former skipper, "that he's got a good ship and he'd better treat her right."

The message frame flicked word-cards into position.

"I believe," it said on the alien skipper's behalf, "that your ship is just as good. I will hope to meet you here when the double star has turned one turn."

The last man left the *Llanvabon*. It moved away into the misty nebula before they had returned to the black ship. The vision plates in that vessel had been altered for human eyes, and human crewmen watched jealously for any trace of their former ship as their new craft took a crazy, evading course to a remote part of the nebula. It came to a crevasse of nothingness, leading to the stars. It rose swiftly to clear space. There was the instant of breathlessness which the overdrive field produces as it goes on, and then the black ship whipped away into the void at many times the speed of light.

Many days later, the skipper saw Tommy Dort poring over one of the strange objects which were the equivalent of books. It was fascinating to puzzle over. The skipper was pleased with himself. The technicians of the *Llanvabon*'s former crew were finding out desirable things about the ship almost momently. Doubtless the aliens were as pleased with their discoveries in the *Llanvabon*. But the black ship would be enormously worth while—and the solution that had been found was by any standard much superior even to a combat in which the Earthmen had been overwhelmingly victorious.

"Hm-m-m, Mr. Dort," said the skipper profoundly. "You've no equipment to make another photographic record on the way back. It was left on the *Llanvabon*. But fortunately, we have your record taken on the way out, and I shall report most favorably on your suggestion and your assistance in carrying it out. I think very well of you, sir."

"Thank you, sir," said Tommy Dort.

He waited. The skipper cleared his throat.

"You . . . ah . . . first realized the close similarity of mental processes between the aliens and ourselves," he observed. "What do you think of the prospects of a friendly arrangement if we keep a rendezvous with them at the nebula as agreed?"

"Oh, we'll get along all right, sir," said Tommy. "We've got a good start toward friendship. After all, since they see by infrared, the planets they'd want to make use of wouldn't suit us. There's no reason why we shouldn't get along. We're almost alike in psychology."

"Hm-m-m. Now just what do you mean by that?" demanded the skipper.

"Why, they're just like us, sir!" said Tommy. "Of course they breathe through gills and they see by heat waves, and their blood has a copper base instead of iron and a few little details like that. But otherwise we're just alike! There were only men in their crew, sir, but they have two sexes as we have, and they have families, and . . . er . . . their sense of humor— In fact—"

Tommy hesitated.

"Go on, sir," said the skipper.

"Well— There was the one I called Buck, sir, because he hasn't any name that goes into sound waves," said Tommy. "We got along very well. I'd really call him my friend, sir. And we were together for a couple of hours just before the two ships separated and we'd nothing in particular to do. So I became convinced that humans and aliens are bound to be good friends if they have only half a chance. You see, sir, we spent those two hours telling dirty jokes."

First published: 1946

MEIHEM IN CE KLASRUM

by Dolton Edwards

BECAUSE WE ARE STILL BEARING SOME OF THE SCARS OF OUR BRIEF SKIR-
mish with II-B English, it is natural that we should be enchanted by Mr.
George Bernard Shaw's current campaign for a simplified alphabet.

Obviously, as Mr. Shaw points out, English spelling is in much need
of a general overhauling and streamlining. However, our own resistance
to any changes requiring a large expenditure of mental effort in the near
future would cause us to view with some apprehension the possibility of
some day receiving a morning paper printed in—to us—Greek.

Our own plan would achieve the same end as the legislation proposed
by Mr. Shaw, but in a less shocking manner, as it consists merely of an
acceleration of the normal processes by which the language is continually
modernized.

As a catalytic agent, we would suggest that a National Easy Language
Week be proclaimed, which the President would inaugurate, outlining
some short cut to concentrate on during the week, and to be adopted during the ensuing year. All school children would be given a holiday, the
lost time being the equivalent of that gained by the spelling short cut.

In 1946, for example, we would urge the elimination of the soft "c,"
for which we would substitute "s." Sertainly, such an improvement
would be selebrated in all sivic-minded sircles as being suffisiently worth
the trouble, and students in all sities in the land would be reseptive toward any change eliminating the nesessity of learning the differense between the two letters.

In 1947, sinse only the hard "c" would be left, it would be possible to
substitute "k" for it, both letters being pronounsed identikally. Imagine
how greatly only two years of this prosess would klarify the konfusion in
the minds of students. Already we would have eliminated an entire letter
from the alphabet. Typewriters and linotypes, kould all be built with one
less letter, and all the manpower and materials previously devoted to

247

making "c's" kould be turned toward raising the national standard of living.

In the fase of so many notable improvements, it is easy to foresee that by 1948, "National Easy Language Week" would be a pronounsed sukses. All skhool tshildren would be looking forward with konsiderable exsitement to the holiday, and in a blaze of national publisity it would be announsed that the double konsonant "ph" no longer existed, and that the sound would henseforth be written "f" in all words. This would make sutsh words as "fonograf" twenty persent shorter in print.

By 1949, publik interest in a fonetik alfabet kan be expekted to have inkreased to the point where a more radikal step forward kan be taken without fear of undue kritisism. We would therefore urge the elimination, at that time of al unesesary double leters, whitsh, although quite harmles, have always ben a nuisanse in the language and a desided deterent to akurate speling. Try it yourself in the next leter you write, and se if both writing and reading are not fasilitated.

With so mutsh progres already made, it might be posible in 1950 to delve further into the posibilities of fonetik speling. After due konsideration of the reseption aforded the previous steps, it should be expedient by this time to spel al difthongs fonetikaly. Most students do not realize that the long "i" and "y," as in "time" and "by," are aktualy the difthong "ai," as it is writen in "aisle," and that the long "a" in "fate," is in reality the difthong "ei" as in "rein." Although perhaps not imediately aparent, the saving in taime and efort wil be tremendous when we leiter elimineite the sailent "e," as meide posible bai this last tsheinge.

For, as is wel known, the horible mes of "e's" apearing in our writen language is kaused prinsipaly bai the present nesesity of indikeiting whether a vowel is long or short. Therefore, in 1951 we kould simply elimineit al sailent "e's," and kontinu to read and wrait merily along as though we wer in an atomik ag of edukation.

In 1951 we would urg a greit step forward. Sins bai this taim it would have ben four years sins anywun had usd the leter "c," we would sugest that the "National Easy Languag Wek" for 1951 be devoted to substitution of "c" for "Th." To be sur it would be som taim befor peopl would bekom akustomd to reading ceir newspapers and buks wic sutsh sentenses in cem as "Ceodor caught he had cre cousand cistls crust crough ce cik of his cumb."

In ce seim maner, bai meiking eatsh leter hav its own sound and cat sound only, we kould shorten ce language stil mor. In 1952 we would elimineit ce "y"; cen in 1953 we kould us ce leter to indikeit ce "sh" sound, cerbai klarifaiing words laik yugar and yur, as wel as redusing bai wun

mor leter al words laik "yut," "yore," and so forc. Cink, cen, of al ce benefits to be geind bai ce distinktion whitsh wil cen be meid between words
laik:

ocean   now writen oyean
machine   "   "   mayin
racial   "   "   reiyial

Al sutsh divers weis of wraiting wun sound would no longer exist, and
whenever wun kaim akros a "y" sound he would know exaktli what to
wrait.

Kontinuing cis proses, year after year, we would eventuali hav a reali
sensibl writen langug. By 1975, wi ventyur tu sei, cer wud bi no mor uv
ces teribli trublsum difikultis, wic no tu leters usd to indikeit ce seim nois,
and laikwais no tu noises riten wic ce seim leter. Even Mr. Yaw, wi beliv,
wud be hapi in ce noleg cat his drims fainali keim tru.

First published: 1947

HOBBYIST

by Eric Frank Russell

THE SHIP ARCED OUT OF A GOLDEN SKY AND LANDED WITH A WHOOP AND a wallop that cut down a mile of lush vegetation. Another half mile of growths turned black and drooped to ashes under the final flicker of the tail rocket blasts. That arrival was spectacular, full of verve, and worthy of four columns in any man's paper. But the nearest sheet was distant by a goodly slice of a lifetime, and there was none to record what this far corner of the cosmos regarded as the pettiest of events. So the ship squatted tired and still at the foremost end of the ashy blast-track and the sky glowed down and the green world brooded solemnly all around.

Within the transpex control dome, Steve Ander sat and thought things over. It was his habit to think things over carefully. Astronauts were not the impulsive daredevils so dear to the stereopticon-loving public. They couldn't afford to be. The hazards of the profession required an infinite capacity for cautious, contemplative thought. Five minutes' consideration had prevented many a collapsed lung, many a leaky heart, many a fractured frame. Steve valued his skeleton. He wasn't conceited about it and he'd no reason to believe it in any way superior to anyone else's skeleton. But he'd had it a long time, found it quite satisfactory, and had an intense desire to keep it—intact.

Therefore, while the tail tubes cooled off with their usual creaking contractions, he sat in the control seat, stared through the dome with eyes made unseeing by deep preoccupation, and performed a few thinks.

Firstly, he'd made a rough estimate of this world during his hectic approach. As nearly as he could judge, it was ten times the size of Terra. But his weight didn't seem abnormal. Of course, one's notions of weight tended to be somewhat wild when for some weeks one's own weight has shot far up or far down in between periods of weightlessness. The most reasonable estimate had to be based on muscular reaction. If you felt as

250

sluggish as a Saturnian sloth, your weight was way up. If you felt as powerful as Angus McKittrick's bull, your weight was down.

Normal weight meant Terrestrial mass despite this planet's tenfold volume. That meant light plasma. And that meant lack of heavy elements. No thorium. No nickel. No nickel-thorium alloy. Ergo, no getting back. The Kingston-Kane atomic motors demanded fuel in the form of ten gauge nickel-thorium alloy wire fed directly into the vaporizers. Denatured plutonium would do, but it didn't occur in natural form, and it had to be made. He had three yards nine and a quarter inches of nickel-thorium left on the feed-spool. Not enough. He was here for keeps.

A wonderful thing, logic. You could start from the simple premise that when you were seated your behind was no flatter than usual, and work your way to the inevitable conclusion that you were a wanderer no more. You'd become a native. Destiny had you tagged as suitable for the status of oldest inhabitant.

Steve pulled an ugly face and said, "Darn!"

The face didn't have to be pulled far. Nature had given said pan a good start. That is to say, it wasn't handsome. It was a long, lean, nutbrown face with pronounced jaw muscles, prominent cheekbones, and a thin, hooked nose. This, with his dark eyes and black hair, gave him a hawklike appearance. Friends talked to him about tepees and tomahawks whenever they wanted him to feel at home.

Well, he wasn't going to feel at home any more; not unless this brooding jungle held intelligent life dopey enough to swap ten gauge nickelthorium wire for a pair of old boots. Or unless some dopey search party was intelligent enough to pick this cosmic dust mote out of a cloud of motes, and took him back. He estimated this as no less than a million-to-one chance. Like spitting at the Empire State hoping to hit a cent-sized mark on one of its walls.

Reaching for his everflo stylus and the ship's log, he opened the log, looked absently at some of the entries.

"Eighteenth day: The spatial convulsion has now flung me past rotalrange of Rigel. Am being tossed into uncharted regions.

"Twenty-fourth day: Arm of convulsion now tails back seven parsecs. Robot recorder now out of gear. Angle of throw changed seven times today.

"Twenty-ninth day: Now beyond arm of the convulsive sweep and regaining control. Speed far beyond range of the astrometer. Applying braking rockets cautiously. Fuel reserve: fourteen hundred yards.

"Thirty-seventh day: Making for planetary system now within reach."

He scowled, his jaw muscles lumped, and he wrote slowly and legibly, "Thirty-ninth day: Landed on planet unknown, primary unknown, galactic area standard reference and sector numbers unknown. No cosmic formations were recognizable when observed shortly before landing. Angles of offshoot and speed of transit not recorded, and impossible to estimate. Condition of ship: workable. Fuel reserve: three and one quarter yards."

Closing the log, he scowled again, rammed the stylus into its desk-grip, and muttered, "Now to check on the outside air and then see how the best girl's doing."

The Radson register had three simple dials. The first recorded outside pressure at thirteen point seven pounds, a reading he observed with much satisfaction. The second said that oxygen content was high. The third had a bi-colored dial, half white, half red, and its needle stood in the middle of the white.

"Breathable," he grunted, clipping down the register's lid. Crossing the tiny control room, he slid aside a metal panel, looked into the padded compartment behind. "Coming out, Beauteous?" he asked.

"Steve loves Laura?" inquired a plaintive voice.

"You bet he does!" he responded with becoming passion. He shoved an arm into the compartment, brought out a large, gaudily colored macaw. "Does Laura love Steve?"

"Hey-hey!" cackled Laura harshly. Climbing up his arm, the bird perched on his shoulder. He could feel the grip of its powerful claws. It regarded him with a beady and brilliant eye, then rubbed its crimson head against his left ear. "Hey-hey! Time flies!"

"Don't mention it," he reproved. "There's plenty to remind me of the fact without you chipping in."

Reaching up, he scratched her poll while she stretched and bowed with absurd delight. He was fond of Laura. She was more than a pet. She was a bona fide member of the crew, issued with her own rations and drawing her own pay. Every probe ship had a crew of two: one man, one macaw. When he'd first heard of it, the practice had seemed crazy—but when he got the reasons, it made sense.

"Lonely men, probing beyond the edge of the charts, get queer psychological troubles. They need an anchor to Earth. A macaw provides the necessary companionship—and more! It's the space-hardiest bird we've got, its weight is negligible, it can talk and amuse, it can fend for itself when necessary. On land, it will often sense dangers before you do. Any strange fruit or food it may eat is safe for you to eat. Many a man's life has been saved by his macaw. Look after yours, my boy, and it'll look after you!"

Yes, they looked after each other, Terrestrials both. It was almost a symbiosis of the spaceways. Before the era of astronavigation nobody had thought of such an arrangement, though it had been done before. Miners and their canaries.

Moving over to the miniature air lock, he didn't bother to operate the pump. It wasn't necessary with so small a difference between internal and external pressures. Opening both doors, he let a little of his higher-pressured air sigh out, stood on the rim of the lock, jumped down. Laura fluttered from his shoulder as he leaped, followed him with a flurry of wings, got her talons into his jacket as he staggered upright.

The pair went around the ship, silently surveying its condition. Front braking nozzles O.K., rear steering flares O.K., tail propulsion tubes O.K. All were badly scored but still usable. The skin of the vessel likewise was scored but intact. Three months supply of food and maybe a thousand yards of wire could get her home, theoretically. But only theoretically, Steve had no delusions about the matter. The odds were still against him even if given the means to move. How do you navigate from you-don't-know-where to you-don't-know-where? Answer: you stroke a rabbit's foot and probably arrive you-don't-know-where-else.

"Well," he said, rounding the tail, "it's something in which to live. It'll save us building a shanty. Way back on Terra they want fifty thousand smackers for an all-metal, streamlined bungalow, so I guess we're mighty lucky. I'll make a garden here, and a rockery there, and build a swimming pool out back. You can wear a pretty frock and do all the cooking."

"Yawk!" said Laura derisively.

Turning, he had a look at the nearest vegetation. It was of all heights, shapes and sizes, of all shades of green with a few tending toward blueness. There was something peculiar about the stuff but he was unable to decide where the strangeness lay. It wasn't that the growths were alien and unfamiliar—one expected that on every new world—but an underlying something which they shared in common. They had a vague, shadowy air of being not quite right in some basic respect impossible to define.

A plant grew right at his feet. It was green in color, a foot high, and monocotyledonous. Looked at as a thing in itself, there was nothing wrong with it. Near to it flourished a bush of darker hue, a yard high, with green, firlike needles in lieu of leaves, and pale, waxy berries scattered over it. That, too, was innocent enough when studied apart from its neighbors. Beside it grew a similar plant, differing only in that its needles were longer and its berries a bright pink. Beyond these towered a cactus-like object dragged out of somebody's drunken dreams, and beside it stood an umbrella-frame which had taken root and produced little purple pods. Individually, they were acceptable. Collectively, they made the discerning mind search anxiously for it knew not what.

That eerie feature had Steve stumped. Whatever it was, he couldn't nail it down. There was something stranger than the mere strangeness of new forms of plant life, and that was all. He dismissed the problem with a shrug. Time enough to trouble about such matters after he'd dealt with others more urgent such as, for example, the location and purity of the nearest water supply.

A mile away lay a lake of some liquid that might be water. He'd seen it glittering in the sunlight as he'd made his descent, and he'd tried to land fairly near to it. If it wasn't water, well, it'd be just his tough luck and he'd have to look someplace else. At worst, the tiny fuel reserve would be enough to permit one circumnavigation of the planet before the ship became pinned down forever. Water he must have if he wasn't going to end up imitating the mummy of Rameses the Second.

Reaching high, he grasped the rim of the port, dexterously muscled himself upward and through it. For a minute he moved around inside the ship, then reappeared with a four-gallon freezocan which he tossed to the ground. Then he dug out his popgun, a belt of explosive shells, and let down the folding ladder from lock to surface. He'd need that ladder. He could muscle himself up through a hole seven feet high, but not with fifty pounds of can and water.

Finally, he locked both the inner and outer air lock doors, skipped down the ladder, picked up the can. From the way he'd made his landing the lake should be directly bow-on relative to the vessel, and somewhere the other side of those distant trees. Laura took a fresh grip on his shoulder as he started off. The can swung from his left hand. His right hand rested warily on the gun. He was perpendicular on this world instead of horizontal on another because, on two occasions, his hand had been ready on the gun, and because it was the most nervous hand he possessed.

The going was rough. It wasn't so much that the terrain was craggy as the fact that impeding growths got in his way. At one moment he was stepping over an ankle-high shrub, the next he was facing a burly plant struggling to become a tree. Behind the plant would be a creeper, then a natural zareba of thorns, a fuzz of fine moss, followed by a giant fern. Progress consisted of stepping over one item, ducking beneath a second, going around a third, and crawling under a fourth.

It occurred to him, belatedly, that if he'd planted the ship tail-first to the lake instead of bow-on, or if he'd let the braking rockets blow after he'd touched down, he'd have saved himself much twisting and dodging. All this obstructing stuff would have been reduced to ashes for at least half the distance to the lake—together with any venomous life it might conceal.

That last thought rang like an alarm bell within his mind just as he doubled up to pass a low-swung creeper. On Venus were creepers that coiled and constricted, swiftly, viciously. Macaws played merry hell if taken within fifty yards of them. It was a comfort to know that, this time, Laura was riding his shoulder unperturbed—but he kept the hand on the gun.

The elusive peculiarity of the planet's vegetation bothered him all the more as he progressed through it. His inability to discover and name this unnamable queerness nagged at him as he went on. A frown of self-disgust was on his lean face when he dragged himself free of a clinging bush and sat on a rock in a tiny clearing.

Dumping the can at his feet, he glowered at it and promptly caught a glimpse of something bright and shining a few feet beyond the can. He raised his gaze. It was then he saw the beetle.

The creature was the biggest of its kind ever seen by human eyes. There were other things bigger, of course, but not of this type. Crabs, for instance. But this was no crab. The beetle ambling purposefully across the clearing was large enough to give any crab a severe inferiority complex, but it was a genuine, twenty-four-karat beetle. And a beautiful one. Like a scarab.

Except that he clung to the notion that little bugs were vicious and big ones companionable, Steve had no phobia about insects. The amiability of large ones was a theory inherited from schoolkid days when he'd been the doting owner of a three-inch stag-beetle afflicted with the name of Edgar.

So he knelt beside the creeping giant, placed his hand palm upward in its path. It investigated the hand with waving feelers, climbed onto his palm, paused there ruminatively. It shone with a sheen of brilliant metallic blue and it weighed about three pounds. He jogged it on his hand to get its weight, then put it down, let it wander on. Laura watched it go with a sharp but incurious eye.

"*Scarabaeus Anderii*," Steve said with glum satisfaction. "I pin my name on him—but nobody'll ever know it!"

"Dinna fash y'rsel'!" shouted Laura in a hoarse voice imported straight from Aberdeen. "Dinna fash! Stop chunnerin', wumman! Y' gie me a pain ahint ma sporran! Dinna—"

"Shut up!" Steve jerked his shoulder, momentarily unbalancing the bird. "Why d'you pick up that barbaric dialect quicker than anything else, eh?"

"McGillicuddy," shrieked Laura with ear-splitting relish. "McGilli-Gilli-Gillicuddy! The great black—!" It ended with a word that pushed Steve's eyebrows into his hair and surprised even the bird itself. Filming its eyes with amazement, it tightened its claw-hold on his shoulder, opened the eyes, emitted a couple of raucous clucks, and joyfully repeated, "The great black—"

It didn't get the chance to complete the new and lovely word. A violent jerk of the shoulder unseated it in the nick of time and it fluttered to the ground, squawking protestingly. *Scarabaeus Anderii* lumbered out from behind a bush, his blue armor glistening as if freshly polished, and stared reprovingly at Laura.

Then something fifty yards away released a snort like the trumpet of doom and took one step that shook the earth. *Scarabaeus Anderii* took refuge under a projecting root. Laura made an agitated swoop for Steve's shoulder and clung there desperately. Steve's gun was out and pointing northward before the bird had found its perch. Another step. The ground quivered.

Silence for awhile. Steve continued to stand like a statue. Then came a monstrous whistle more forceful than that of a locomotive blowing off steam. Something squat and wide and of tremendous length charged headlong through the half-concealing vegetation while the earth trembled beneath its weight.

Its mad onrush carried it blindly twenty yards to Steve's right, the gun swinging to cover its course, but not firing. Steve caught an extended glimpse of a slate-gray bulk with a serrated ridge on its back which, despite the thing's pace, took long to pass. It seemed several times the length of a fire ladder.

Bushes were flung roots topmost and small trees whipped aside as the creature pounded grimly onward in a straight line which carried it far past the ship and into the dim distance. It left behind a tattered swathe wide enough for a first-class road. Then the reverberations of its mighty tonnage died out, and it was gone.

Steve used his left hand to pull out a handkerchief and wipe the back of his neck. He kept the gun in his right hand. The explosive shells in that gun were somewhat wicked; any one of them could deprive a rhinoceros of a hunk of meat weighing two hundred pounds. If a man caught one, he just strewed himself over the landscape. By the looks of that slate-colored galloper, it would need half a dozen shells to feel incommoded. A seventy-five millimeter bazooka would be more effective for kicking it in the back teeth, but probe ship boys don't tote around such artillery. Steve finished the mopping, put the handkerchief back, picked up the can.

Laura said pensively, "I want my mother."

He scowled, made no reply, set out toward the lake. Her feathers still ruffled, Laura rode his shoulder and lapsed into surly silence.

The stuff in the lake was water, cold, faintly green and a little bitter to the taste. Coffee would camouflage the flavor. If anything, it might improve the coffee since he liked his java bitter, but the stuff would have to be tested before absorbing it in any quantity. Some poisons were accumulative. It wouldn't do to guzzle gayly while building up a death-dealing reserve of lead, for instance. Filling the freezocan, he lugged it to the ship in hundred yard stages. The swathe helped; it made an easier path to within short distance of the ship's tail. He was perspiring freely by the time he reached the base of the ladder.

Once inside the vessel, he relocked both doors, opened the air vents, started the auxiliary lighting-set and plugged in the percolator, using water out of his depleted reserve supply. The golden sky had dulled to orange, with violet streamers creeping upward from the horizon. Looking at it through the transpex dome, he found that the perpetual haze still effectively concealed the sinking sun. A brighter area to one side was all that indicated its position. He'd need his lights soon.

Pulling out the collapsible table, he jammed its supporting leg into place, plugged into its rim the short rod which was Laura's official seat. She claimed the perch immediately, watched him beadily as he set out her meal of water, melon seeds, sunflower seeds, pecans and unshelled oleo nuts. Her manners were anything but ladylike and she started eagerly, without waiting for him.

A deep frown lay across his brown, muscular features as he sat at the table, poured out his coffee and commenced to eat. It persisted through the meal, was still there when he lit a cigarette and stared speculatively up at the dome.

Presently, he murmured, "I've seen the biggest bug that ever was. I've seen a few other bugs. There were a couple of little ones under a creeper.

One was long and brown and many-legged, like an earwig. The other was round and black, with little red dots on its wing cases. I've seen a tiny purple spider and a tinier green one of different shape, also a bug that looked like an aphid. But not an ant."

"Ant, ant," hooted Laura. She dropped a piece of oleo nut, climbed down after it. "Yawk!" she added from the floor.

"Nor a bee."

"Bee," echoed Laura, companionably. "Bee-ant. Laura loves Steve." Still keeping his attention on the dome, he went on, "And what's cock-eyed about the plants is equally cockeyed about the bugs. I wish I could place it. Why can't I? Maybe I'm going nuts already."

"Laura loves nuts."

"I know it, you technicolored belly!" said Steve rudely.

And at that point night fell with a silent bang. The gold and orange and violet abruptly were swamped with deep, impenetrable blackness devoid of stars or any random gleam. Except for greenish glowings on the instrument panel, the control room was stygian, with Laura swearing steadily on the floor.

Putting out a hand, Steve switched on the indirect lighting. Laura got to her perch with the rescued titbit, concentrated on the job of dealing with it and let him sink back into his thoughts.

"*Scarabaeus Anderii* and a pair of smaller bugs and a couple of spiders, all different. At the other end of the scale, that gigantosaurus. But no ant, or bee. Or rather, no ants, no bees." The switch from singular to plural stirred his back hairs queerly. In some vague way, he felt that he'd touched the heart of the mystery. "No ant—no ants," he thought. "No bee—no bees." Almost he had it—but still it evaded him.

Giving it up for the time being, he cleared the table, did a few minor chores. After that, he drew a standard sample from the freezocan, put it through its paces. The bitter flavor he identified as being due to the presence of magnesium sulphate in quantity far too small to prove embarrassing. Drinkable—that was something! Food, drink and shelter were the three essentials of survival. He'd enough of the first for six or seven weeks. The lake and the ship were his remaining guarantees of life.

Finding the log, he entered the day's report, bluntly, factually, without any embroidery. Partway through, he found himself stuck for a name for the planet. *Ander*, he decided, would cost him dear if the million-to-one chance put him back among the merciless playmates of the Probe Service. O.K. for a bug, but not for a world. *Laura* wasn't so hot, either—especially when you knew Laura. It wouldn't be seemly to name a big, gold planet after an oversized parrot. Thinking over the golden aspect of this world's sky, he hit upon the name of *Oro*, promptly made the christening authoritative by entering it in his log.

By the time he'd finished, Laura had her head buried deep under one wing. Occasionally she teetered and swung erect again. It always fascinated him to watch how her balance was maintained even in her slumbers. Studying her fondly, he remembered that unexpected addition to her vocabulary. This shifted his thoughts to a fiery-headed and fierier-tongued individual named Menzies, the sworn foe of another volcano named McGillicuddy. If ever the opportunity presented itself, he decided, the educative work of said Menzies was going to be rewarded with a bust on the snoot.

Sighing, he put away the log, wound up the forty-day chronometer, opened his folding bunk and lay down upon it. His hand switched off the lights. Ten years back, a first landing would have kept him awake all night in dithers of excitement. He'd got beyond that now. He'd done it often enough to have grown phlegmatic about it. His eyes closed in preparation for a good night's sleep, and he did sleep—for two hours.

What brought him awake within that short time he didn't know, but suddenly he found himself sitting bolt upright on the edge of the bunk, his ears and nerves stretched to their utmost, his legs quivering in a way they'd never done before. His whole body fizzed with that queer mixture of palpitation and shock which follows narrow escape from disaster.

This was something not within previous experience. Sure and certain in the intense darkness, his hand sought and found his gun. He cuddled the butt in his palm while his mind strove to recall a possible nightmare, though he knew he was not given to nightmares.

Laura moved restlessly on her perch, not truly awake, yet not asleep, and this was unusual in her.

Rejecting the dream theory, he stood up on the bunk, looked out through the dome. Blackness, the deepest, darkest, most impenetrable blackness it was possible to conceive. And silence! The outside world slumbered in the blackness and the silence as in a sable shroud.

Yet never before had he felt so wide awake in this, his normal sleeping time. Puzzled, he turned slowly round to take in the full circle of unseeable view, and at one point he halted. The surrounding darkness was not complete. In the distance beyond the ship's tail moved a tall, stately glow. How far off it might be was not possible to estimate, but the sight of it stirred his soul and caused his heart to leap.

Uncontrollable emotions were not permitted to master his disciplined mind. Narrowing his eyes, he tried to discern the nature of the glow while his mind sought the reason why the mere sight of it should make him twang like a harp. Bending down, he felt at the head of the bunk, found a leather case, extracted a pair of powerful night glasses. The glow was still moving, slowly, deliberately, from right to left. He got the glasses on it, screwed the lenses into focus, and the phenomenon leaped into closer view.

The thing was a great column of golden haze much like that of the noonday sky except that small, intense gleams of silver sparkled within it. It was a shaft of lustrous mist bearing a sprinkling of tiny stars. It was like nothing known to or recorded by any form of life lower than the gods. But was it life?

It moved, though its mode of locomotion could not be determined. Self-motivation is the prime symptom of life. It could be life, conceivably though not credibly, from the Terrestrial viewpoint. Consciously, he preferred to think it a strange and purely local feature comparable with Saharan sand-devils. Subconsciously, he knew it was life, tall and terrifying.

He kept the glasses on it while slowly it receded into the darkness, foreshortening with increasing distance and gradually fading from view. To the very last the observable field shifted and shuddered as he failed to control the quiver in his hands. And when the sparkling haze had gone, leaving only a pall over his lenses, he sat down on the bunk and shivered with eerie cold.

Laura was dodging to and fro along her perch, now thoroughly awake and agitated, but he wasn't inclined to switch on the lights and make the dome a beacon in the night. His hand went out, feeling for her in the darkness, and she clambered eagerly onto his wrist, thence to his lap. She was fussy and demonstrative, pathetically yearning for comfort and companionship. He scratched her poll and fondled her while she pressed close against his chest with funny little crooning noises. For some time he soothed her and, while doing it, fell asleep. Gradually he slumped backward on the bunk. Laura perched on his forearm, clucked tiredly, put her head under a wing.

There was no further awakening until the outer blackness disappeared and the sky again sent its golden glow pouring through the dome. Steve got up, stood on the bunk, had a good look over the surrounding terrain. It remained precisely the same as it had been the day before. Things stewed within his mind while he got his breakfast; especially the jumpiness he'd experienced in the nighttime. Laura also was subdued and quiet. Only once before had she been like that—which was when he'd traipsed through the Venusian section of the Panplanetary Zoo and had shown her a crested eagle. The eagle had stared at her with contemptuous dignity.

Though he'd all the time in his life, he now felt a peculiar urge to hasten. Getting the gun and the freezocan, he made a full dozen trips to the lake, wasting no minutes, nor stopping to study the still enigmatic plants and bugs. It was late in the afternoon by the time he'd filled the ship's fifty-gallon reservoir, and had the satisfaction of knowing that he'd got a drinkable quota to match his food supply.

There had been no sign of gigantosaurus or any other animal. Once he'd seen something flying in the far distance, birdlike or batlike. Laura had cocked a sharp eye at it but betrayed no undue interest. Right now she was more concerned with a new fruit. Steve sat in the rim of the outer lock door, his legs dangling, and watched her clambering over a small tree thirty yards away. The gun lay in his lap; he was ready to take a crack at anything which might be ready to take a crack at Laura.

The bird sampled the tree's fruit, a crop resembling blue-shelled lychee nuts. She ate one with relish, grabbed another. Steve lay back in the lock, stretched to reach a bag, then dropped to the ground and went across to the tree. He tried a nut. Its flesh was soft, juicy, sweet and citrous. He filled the bag with the fruit, slung it into the ship.

Nearby stood another tree, not quite the same, but very similar. It bore nuts like the first except that they were larger. Picking one, he offered it to Laura who tried it, spat it out in disgust. Picking a second, he slit it, licked the flesh gingerly. As far as he could tell, it was the same. Evidently he couldn't tell far enough: Laura's diagnosis said it was not the same. The difference, too subtle for him to detect, might be sufficient to roll him up like a hoop and keep him that shape to the unpleasant end. He flung the thing away, went back to his seat in the lock, and ruminated.

That elusive, nagging feature of Oro's plants and bugs could be narrowed down to these two nuts. He felt sure of that. If he could discover why—parrotwise—one nut was a nut while the other nut was not, he'd have his finger right on the secret. The more he thought about those similar fruits the more he felt that, in sober fact, his finger was on the secret already—but he lacked the power to lift it and see what lay beneath.

Tantalizingly, his mulling-over the subject landed him the same place as before; namely, nowhere. It got his dander up, and he went back to the trees, subjected both to close examination. His sense of sight told him that they were different individuals of the same species. Laura's sense of whatchamacallit insisted that they were different species. Ergo, you can't believe the evidence of your eyes. He was aware of that fact, of course, since it was a platitude of the spaceways, but when you couldn't trust your optics it was legitimate to try to discover just why you couldn't trust 'em. And he couldn't discover even that!

It soured him so much that he returned to the ship, locked its doors, called Laura back to his shoulder and set off on a tailward exploration. The rules of first landings were simple and sensible. Go in slowly, come out quickly, and remember that all we want from you is evidence of suitability for human life. Thoroughly explore a small area rather than scout a big one—the mapping parties will do the rest. Use your ship as a base and centralize it where you can live—don't move it unnecessarily. Restrict your trips to a radius representing daylight-reach and lock yourself in after dark.

Was Oro suitable for human life? The unwritten law was that you don't jump to conclusions and say, "Of course! I'm still living, aren't I?" Cameron, who'd plonked his ship on Mithra, for instance, thought he'd found paradise until, on the seventeenth day, he'd discovered the fungoid plague. He'd left like a bat out of hell and had spent three sweaty, swearing days in the Lunar Purification Plant before becoming fit for society. The authorities had vaporized his ship. Mithra had been taboo ever since. Every world a potential trap baited with scenic delight. The job of the Probe Service was to enter the traps and jounce on the springs. Another dollop of real estate for Terra—if nothing broke your neck.

Maybe Oro was loaded for bear. The thing that walked in the night, Steve mused, bore awful suggestion of nonhuman power. So did a waterspout, and whoever heard of anyone successfully wrestling with a waterspout? If this Oro-spout were sentient, so much the worse for human prospects. He'd have to get the measure of it, he decided, even if he had to chase it through the blank avenues of night. Plodding steadily away from the tail, gun in hand, he pondered so deeply that he entirely overlooked the fact that he wasn't on a pukka probe job anyway, and that nothing else remotely human might reach Oro in a thousand years. Even space-boys can be creatures of habit. Their job: to look for death; they were liable to go on looking long after the need had passed, in bland disregard of the certainty that if you look for a thing long enough, ultimately you find it!

The ship's chronometer had given him five hours to darkness. Two and a half hours each way; say ten miles out and ten back. The water had consumed his time. On the morrow, and henceforth, he'd increase the radius to twelve and take it easier.

Then all thoughts fled from his mind as he came to the edge of the vegetation. The stuff didn't dribble out of existence with hardy spurs and offshoots fighting for a hold in rocky ground. It stopped abruptly, in light loam, as if cut off with a machete, and from where it stopped spread a different crop. The new growths were tiny and crystalline.

He accepted the crystalline crop without surprise, knowing that novelty was the inevitable feature of any new locale. Things were ordinary only by Terrestrial standards. Outside of Terra, nothing was supernormal or abnormal except insofar as they failed to jibe with their own peculiar conditions. Besides, there were crystalline growths on Mars. The one unacceptable feature of the situation was the way in which vegetable growths ended and crystalline ones began. He stepped back to the verge and made another startled survey of the borderline. It was so straight that the sight screwed his brain around. Like a field. A cultivated field. Dead straightness of that sort couldn't be other than artificial. Little beads of moisture popped out on his back.

Squatting on the heel of his right boot, he gazed at the nearest crystals and said to Laura, "Chicken, I think these things got planted. Question is, who planted 'em?"

"McGillicuddy," suggested Laura brightly.

Putting out a finger, he flicked the crystal sprouting near the toe of his boot, a green, branchy object an inch high.

The crystal vibrated and said, "*Zing!*" in a sweet, high voice.

He flicked its neighbor, and that said, "*Zang!*" in lower tone.

He flicked a third. It emitted no note, but broke into a thousand shards.

Standing up, he scratched his head, making Laura fight for a clawhole within the circle of his arm. One zinged and one zanged and one returned to dust. Two nuts. Zings and zangs and nuts. It was right in his grasp if only he could open his hand and look at what he'd got.

Then he lifted his puzzled and slightly ireful gaze, saw something fluttering erratically across the crystal field. It was making for the vegetation. Laura took off with a raucous cackle, her blue and crimson wings beating powerfully. She swooped over the object, frightening it so low that it dodged and sideslipped only a few feet above Steve's head. He saw that it was a large butterfly, frill-winged, almost as gaudy as Laura. The bird swooped again, scaring the insect but not menacing it. He called her back, set out to cross the area ahead. Crystals crunched to powder under his heavy boots as he tramped on.

Half an hour later he was toiling up a steep, crystal-coated slope when his thoughts suddenly jelled and he stopped with such abruptness that

Laura spilled from his shoulder and perforce took to wing. She beat round in a circle, came back to her perch, made bitter remarks in an unknown language.

"One of this and one of that," he said. "No twos or threes or dozens. Nothing I've seen has repeated itself. There's only one gigantosaurus, only one *Scarabaeus Anderii*, only one of every other danged thing. Every item is unique, original, and an individual creation in its own right. What does that suggest?"

"McGillicuddy," offered Laura.

"For Pete's sake, forget McGillicuddy."

"For Pete's sake, for Pete's sake," yelled Laura, much taken by the phrase. "The great black—"

Again he upset her in the nick of time, making her take to flight while he continued talking to himself. "It suggests constant and all-pervading mutation. Everything breeds something quite different from itself and there aren't any dominant strains." He frowned at the obvious snag in this theory. "But how the blazes does anything breed? What fertilizes which?"

"McGilli—," began Laura, then changed her mind and shut up.

"Anyway, if nothing breeds true, it'll be tough on the food problem," he went on. "What's edible on one plant may be a killer on its offspring. Today's fodder is tomorrow's poison. How's a farmer to know what he's going to get? Hey-hey, if I'm guessing right, this planet won't support a couple of hogs."

"No, sir. No hogs. Laura loves hogs."

"Be quiet," he snapped. "Now, what shouldn't support a couple of hogs demonstrably does support gigantosaurus—and any other fancy animals which may be mooching around. It seems crazy to me. On Venus or any other place full of consistent fodder, gigantosaurus would thrive, but here, according to my calculations, the big lunk has no right to be alive. He ought to be dead."

So saying, he topped the rise and found the monster in question sprawling right across the opposite slope. It *was* dead.

The way in which he determined its deadness was appropriately swift, simple and effective. Its enormous bulk lay draped across the full length of the slope and its dragon-head, the size of a lifeboat, pointed toward him. The head had two dull, lackluster eyes like dinner plates. He planted a shell smack in the right eye and a sizable hunk of noggin promptly splashed in all directions. The body did not stir.

There was a shell ready for the other eye should the creature leap to frantic, vengeful life, but the mighty hulk remained supine.

His boots continued to desiccate crystals as he went down the slope, curved a hundred yards off his route to get around the corpse, and trudged up the farther rise. Momentarily, he wasn't much interested in the dead beast. Time was short and he could come again tomorrow, bringing a full-color stereoscopic camera with him. Gigantosaurus would go on record in style, but would have to wait.

This second rise was a good deal higher, and more trying a climb. Its crest represented the approximate limit of this day's trip, and he felt anxious to surmount it before turning back. Humanity's characteristic urge to see what lay over the hill remained as strong as on the day determined ancestors topped the Rockies. He had to have a look, firstly because elevation gave range to the vision, and secondly because of that prowler in the night—and, nearly as he could estimate, the prowler had gone down behind this rise. A column of mist, sucked down from the sky, might move around aimlessly, going nowhere, but instinct maintained that this had been no mere column of mist, and that it was going somewhere.

Where?

Out of breath, he pounded over the crest, looked down into an immense valley, and found the answer.

The crystal growths gave out on the crest, again in a perfectly straight line. Beyond them the light loam, devoid of rock, ran gently down to the valley and up the farther side. Both slopes were sparsely dotted with queer, jellylike lumps of matter which lay and quivered beneath the sky's golden glow.

From the closed end of the valley jutted a great, glistening fabrication, flat-roofed, flat-fronted, with a huge, square hole gaping in its mid-section at front. It looked like a tremendous oblong slab of polished, milk-white plastic half-buried endwise in a sandy hill. No decoration disturbed its smooth, gleaming surface. No road led to the hole in front. Somehow, it had the new-old air of a house that struggles to look empty because it is full—of fiends.

Steve's back hairs prickled as he studied it. One thing was obvious—Oro bore intelligent life. One thing was possible—the golden column represented that life. One thing was probable—fleshly Terrestrials and hazy Orons would have difficulty in finding a basis for friendship and cooperation.

Whereas enmity needs no basis.

Curiosity and caution pulled him opposite ways. One urged him down into the valley while the other drove him back, back, while yet there was time. He consulted his watch. Less than three hours to go, within which he had to return to the ship, enter the log, prepare supper. That milky creation was at least two miles away, a good hour's journey there and back. Let it wait. Give it another day and he'd have more time for it, with the benefit of needful thought betweentimes.

Caution triumphed. He investigated the nearest jellyblob. It was flat, a yard in diameter, green, with bluish streaks and many tiny bubbles hiding in its semitransparency. The thing pulsated slowly. He poked it with the toe of his boot, and it contracted, humping itself in the middle, then sluggishly relaxed. No amoeba, he decided. A low form of life, but complicated withal. Laura didn't like the object. She skittered off as he bent over it, vented her anger by bashing a few crystals.

This jello dollop wasn't like its nearest neighbor, or like any other. One of each, only one. The same rule: one butterfly of a kind, one bug, one plant, one of these quivering things.

A final stare at the distant mystery down in the valley, then he retraced his steps. When the ship came into sight he speeded up like a gladsome voyager nearing home. There were new prints near the vessel, big, three-toed, deeply-impressed spoor which revealed that something large, heavy and two-legged had wandered past in his absence. Evidently an animal, for nothing intelligent would have meandered on so casually without circling and inspecting the nearby invader from space. He dismissed it from his mind. There was only one thingumbob, he felt certain of that.

Once inside the ship, he relocked the doors, gave Laura her feed, ate his supper. Then he dragged out the log, made his day's entry, had a look around from the dome. Violet streamers once more were creeping upward from the horizon. He frowned at the encompassing vegetation. What sort of stuff had bred all this in the past? What sort of stuff would this breed in the future? How did it progenerate, anyway?

Wholesale radical mutation presupposed modification of genes by hard radiation in persistent and considerable blasts. You shouldn't get hard radiation on lightweight planets—unless it poured in from the sky. Here, it didn't pour from the sky, or from any place else. In fact, there wasn't any.

He was pretty certain of that fact because he'd a special interest in it and had checked up on it. Hard radiation betokened the presence of radioactive elements which, at a pinch, might be usable as fuel. The ship was equipped to detect such stuff. Among the junk was a cosmiray counter, a radium hen, and a gold-leaf electroscope. The hen and the counter hadn't given so much as one heartening cluck, in fact the only clucks had been Laura's. The electroscope he'd charged on landing and its leaves still formed an inverted V. The air was dry, ionization negligible, and the leaves didn't look likely to collapse for a week.

"Something's wrong with my theorizing," he complained to Laura. "My think-stuff's not doing its job."

"Not doing its job," echoed Laura faithfully. She cracked a pecan with a grating noise that set his teeth on edge. "I tell you it's a hoodoo ship. I won't sail. No, not even if you pray for me. I won't, I won't, I won't. Nope. Nix. Who's drunk? That hairy Lowlander Mc—"

"Laura!" he said sharply.

"Gillicuddy," she finished with bland defiance. Again she rasped his teeth. "Rings bigger'n Saturn's. I saw them myself. Who's a liar? Yawk! She's down in Grayway Bay, on Tethis. Boy, what a torso!"

He looked at her hard and said, "You're nuts!"

"Sure! Sure, pal! Laura loves nuts. Have one on me."

"O.K.," he accepted, holding out his hand.

Cocking her colorful pate, she pecked at his hand, gravely selected a pecan and gave it to him. He cracked it, chewed on the kernel while starting up the lighting-set. It was almost as if night were waiting for him. Blackness fell even as he switched on the lights.

With the darkness came a keen sense of unease. The dome was the trouble. It blazed like a beacon and there was no way of blacking it out except by turning off the lights. Beacons attracted things, and he'd no desire to become a center of attraction in present circumstances. That is to say, not at night.

Long experience had bred fine contempt for alien animals, no matter how whacky, but outlandish intelligences were a different proposition. So filled was he with the strange inward conviction that last night's phenomenon was something that knew its onions that it didn't occur to him to wonder whether a glowing column possessed eyes or anything equivalent to a sense of sight. If it had occurred to him, he'd have derived no comfort from it. His desire to be weighed in the balance in some eerie, extrasensory way was even less than his desire to be gaped at visually in his slumbers.

An unholy mess of thoughts and ideas was still cooking in his mind when he extinguished the lights, bunked down and went to sleep. Nothing disturbed him this time, but when he awoke with the golden dawn his chest was damp with perspiration and Laura again had sought refuge on his arm.

Digging out breakfast, his thoughts began to marshal themselves as he kept his hands busy. Pouring out a shot of hot coffee, he spoke to Laura.

"I'm durned if I'm going to go scatty trying to maintain a three-watch system single-handed, which is what I'm supposed to do if faced by powers unknown when I'm not able to beat it. Those armchair warriors at head-quarters ought to get a taste of situations not precisely specified in the book of rules."

"Burp!" said Laura contemptuously.

"He who fights and runs away lives to fight another day," Steve quoted. "That's the Probe Law. It's a nice, smooth, lovely law—when you can run away. We can't!"

"Burrup!" said Laura with unnecessary emphasis.

"For a woman, your manners are downright disgusting," he told her. "Now I'm not going to spend the brief remainder of my life looking fear-fully over my shoulder. The only way to get rid of powers unknown is to convert 'em into powers known and understood. As Uncle Joe told Willie when dragging him to the dentist, the longer we put it off the worse it'll feel."

"Dinna fash y'rsel'," declaimed Laura. "Burp-gollop-bop!"

Giving her a look of extreme distaste, he continued, "So we'll try tossing the bull. Such techniques disconcert bulls sometimes." Standing up, he grabbed Laura, shoved her into her traveling compartment, slid the panel shut. "We're going to blow off forthwith."

Climbing up to the control seat, he stamped on the energizer stud. The tail rockets popped a few times, broke into a subdued roar. Juggling the controls to get the preparatory feel of them, he stepped up the boost until the entire vessel trembled and the rear venturis began to glow cherry-red. Slowly the ship commenced to edge its bulk forward and, as it did so, he fed it the take-off shot. A half-mile blast kicked backward and the probe ship plummeted into the sky.

Pulling it round in a wide and shallow sweep, he thundered over the borderline of vegetation, the fields of crystals and the hills beyond. In a flash he was plunging through the valley, braking rockets blazing from the nose. This was tricky. He had to co-ordinate forward shoot, backward thrust and downward surge, but like most of his kind he took pride in the stunts performable with these neat little vessels. An awe-inspired audience was all he lacked to make the exhibition perfect. The vessel landed fairly and squarely on the milk-white roof of the alien edifice, slid halfway to the cliff, then stopped.

"Boy," he breathed, "am I good!" He remained in his seat, stared around through the dome, and felt that he ought to add, "And too young to die." Occasionally eying the chronometer, he waited awhile. The boat must have handed that roof a thump sufficient to wake the dead. If anyone

were in, they'd soon hotfoot out to see who was heaving hundred-ton bottles at their shingles. Nobody emerged. He gave them half an hour, his
hawklike face strained, alert. Then he gave it up, said, "Ah, well," and
got out of the seat.

He freed Laura. She came out with ruffled dignity, like a dowager
who's paraded into the wrong room. Females were always curious critters,
in his logic, and he ignored her attitude, got his gun, unlocked the doors,
jumped down onto the roof. Laura followed reluctantly, came to his
shoulder as if thereby conferring a great favor.

Walking past the tail to the edge of the roof, he looked down. The
sheerness of the five-hundred-foot drop took him aback. Immediately
below his feet, the entrance soared four hundred feet up from the ground
and he was standing on the hundred-foot lintel surmounting it. The
only way down was to walk to the side of the roof and reach the earthy
slope in which the building was embedded, seeking a path down that.

He covered a quarter of a mile of roof to get to the slope, his eyes
examining the roof's surface as he went, and failing to find one crack
or joint in the uniformly smooth surface. Huge as it was, the erection
appeared to have been molded all in one piece—a fact which did nothing
to lessen inward misgivings. Whoever did this mighty job weren't Zulus!

From ground level the entrance loomed bigger than ever. If there
had been a similar gap at the other side of the building, and a clear way
through, he could have taken the ship in at one end and out at the other
as easily as threading a needle.

Absence of doors didn't seem peculiar; it was difficult to imagine any
sort of door huge enough to fill this opening yet sufficiently balanced to
enable anyone—or anything—to pull open or shut. With a final, cautious
look around which revealed nothing moving in the valley, he stepped
boldly through the entrance, blinked his eyes, found interior darkness
slowly fading as visual retention lapsed and gave up remembrance of the
golden glow outside.

There was a glow inside, a different one, paler, ghastlier, greenish. It
exuded from the floor, the walls, the ceiling, and the total area of radiation
was enough to light the place clearly, with no shadows. He sniffed as his
vision adjusted itself. There was a strong smell of ozone mixed with other,
unidentifiable odors.

To his right and left, rising hundreds of feet, stood great tiers of transparent cases. He went to the ones on his right and examined them. They
were cubes, about a yard each way, made of something like transpex.
Each contained three inches of loam from which sprouted a crystal. No

two crystals were alike; some small and branchy, others large and indescribably complicated.

Dumb with thought, he went around to the back of the monster tier, found another ten yards behind it. And another behind that. And another and another. All with crystals. The number and variety of them made his head whirl. He could study only the two bottom rows of each rack, but row on row stepped themselves far above his head to within short distance of the roof. Their total number was beyond estimation.

It was the same on the left. Crystals by the thousands. Looking more closely at one especially fine example, he noticed that the front plate of its case bore a small, inobtrusive pattern of dots etched upon the outer surface. Investigation revealed that all cases were similarly marked, differing only in the number and arrangement of the dots. Undoubtedly, some sort of cosmic code used for classification purposes.

"The Oron Museum of Natural History," he guessed, in a whisper.

"You're a liar," squawked Laura violently. "I tell you it's a hoodoo—" She stopped, dumfounded, as her own voice roared through the building in deep, organlike tones, "A hoodoo— A hoodoo—"

"Holy smoke, will you keep quiet!" hissed Steve. He tried to keep watch on the exit and the interior simultaneously. But the voice rumbled away in the distance without bringing anyone to dispute their invasion.

Turning, he paced hurriedly past the first blocks of tiers to the next batteries of exhibits. Jelly blobs in this lot. Small ones, no bigger than his wrist watch, numberable in thousands. None appeared to be alive, he noted.

Sections three, four and five took him a mile into the building as nearly as he could estimate. He passed mosses, lichens and shrubs, all dead but wondrously preserved. By this time he was ready to guess at section six—plants. He was wrong. The sixth layout displayed bugs, including moths, butterflies, and strange, unfamiliar objects resembling chitinous humming-birds. There was no sample of *Scarabaeus Anderii*, unless it were several hundred feet up. Or unless there was an empty box ready for it—when its day was done.

Who made the boxes? Had it prepared one for him? One for Laura? He visualized himself, petrified forever, squatting in the seventieth case of the twenty-fifth row of the tenth tier in section something-or-other, his front panel duly tagged with its appropriate dots. It was a lousy picture. It made his forehead wrinkle to think of it.

Looking for he knew not what, he plunged steadily on, advancing deeper and deeper into the heart of the building. Not a soul, not a sound, not a footprint. Only that all-pervading smell and the unvarying glow. He had a feeling that the place was visited frequently but never occupied for any worth-while period of time. Without bothering to stop and look, he passed an enormous case containing a creature faintly resembling a bison-headed rhinoceros, then other, still larger cases holding equally larger exhibits—all carefully dot-marked.

Finally, he rounded a box so tremendous that it sprawled across the full width of the hall. It contained the grand-pappy of all trees and the great-grand-pappy of all serpents. Behind, for a change, reared five hundred feet high racks of metal cupboards, each cupboard with a stud set in its polished door, each ornamented with more groups of mysteriously arranged dots.

Greatly daring, he pressed the stud on the nearest cupboard and its door swung open with a juicy click. The result proved disappointing. The cupboard was filled with stacks of small, glassy sheets each smothered with dots.

"Super filing-system," he grunted, closing the door. "Old Prof Heggarty would give his right arm to be here."

"Heggarty," said Laura, in a faltering voice. "For Pete's sake!"

He looked at her sharply. She was ruffled and fidgety, showing signs of increasing agitation.

"What's the matter, Chicken?"

She peeked at him, returned her anxious gaze the way they had come, side-stepped to and fro on his shoulder. Her neck feathers started to rise. A nervous cluck came from her beak and she cowered close to his jacket.

"Darn!" he muttered. Spinning on one heel, he raced past successive filing blocks, got into the ten yards' space between the end block and the wall. His gun was out and he kept watch on the front of the blocks while his free hand tried to soothe Laura. She snuggled up close, rubbing her head into his neck and trying to hide under the angle of his jaw.

"Quiet, Honey," he whispered. "Just you keep quiet and stay with Steve, and we'll be all right."

She kept quiet, though she'd begun to tremble. His heart speeded up in sympathy though he could see nothing, hear nothing to warrant it.

Then, while he watched and waited, and still in absolute silence, the interior brightness waxed, became less green, more golden. And suddenly he knew what it was that was coming. He *knew* what it was!

He sank on one knee to make himself as small and inconspicuous as possible. Now his heart was palpitating wildly and no coldness in his mind could freeze it down to slower, more normal beat. The silence, the awful silence of its approach was the unbearable feature. The crushing thud of a weighty foot or hoof would have been better. Colossi have no right to steal along like ghosts.

And the golden glow built up, drowning out the green radiance from floor to roof, setting the multitude of case-surfaces afire with its brilliance. It grew as strong as the golden sky, and stronger. It became all-pervading, unendurable, leaving no darkness in which to hide, no sanctuary for little things.

It flamed like the rising sun or like something drawn from the heart of a sun, and the glory of its radiance sent the cowering watcher's mind awhirl. He struggled fiercely to control his brain, to discipline it, to bind it to his fading will—and failed.

With drawn face beaded by sweat, Steve caught the merest fragmentary glimpse of the column's edge appearing from between the stacks of the center aisle. He saw a blinding strip of burnished gold in which glittered a pure white star, then a violent effervescence seemed to occur within his brain and he fell forward into a cloud of tiny bubbles.

Down, down he sank through myriad bubbles and swirls and sprays of iridescent froth and foam which shone and changed and shone anew with every conceivable color. And all the time his mind strove frantically to battle upward and drag his soul to the surface.

Deep into the nethermost reaches he went while still the bubbles whirled around in their thousands and their colors were of numberless hues. Then his progress slowed. Gradually the froth and the foam ceased to rotate upward, stopped its circling, began to swirl in the reverse direction and sink. He was rising! He rose for a lifetime, floating weightlessly, in a dreamlike trance.

The last of the bubbles drifted eerily away, leaving him in a brief hiatus of nonexistence—then he found himself sprawled full length on the floor with a dazed Laura clinging to his arm. He blinked his eyes, slowly, several times. They were strained and sore. His heart was still palpitating and his legs felt weak. There was a strange sensation in his stomach as if memory had sickened him with a shock from long, long ago.

He didn't get up from the floor right away; his body was too shaken and his mind too muddled for that. While his wits came back and his composure returned, he lay and noted that all the invading goldness had gone and that again the interior illumination was a dull, shadowless green. Then his eyes found his watch and he sat up, startled. Two hours had flown!

That fact brought him shakily to his feet. Peering around the end of the bank of filing cabinets, he saw that nothing had changed. Instinct told him that the golden visitor had gone and that once more he had this place to himself. Had it become aware of his presence? Had it made him lose consciousness or, if not, why had he lost it? Had it done anything about the ship on the roof?

Picking up his futile gun, he spun it by its stud guard and looked at it with contempt. Then he holstered it, helped Laura onto his shoulder where she perched groggily, went around the back of the racks and still deeper into the building.

"I reckon we're O.K., Honey," he told her. "I think we're too small to be noticed. We're like mice. Who bothers to trap mice when he's got bigger and more important things in mind?" He pulled a face, not liking the mouse comparison. It wasn't flattering either to him or his kind. But it was the best he could think of at the moment. "So, like little mice, let's for cheese. I'm not giving up just because a big hunk of something has sneaked past and put a scare into us. We don't scare off, do we, Sweetness?"

"No," said Laura unenthusiastically. Her voice was still subdued and her eyes perked apprehensively this way and that. "No scare. I won't sail, I tell you. Blow my sternpipes! Laura loves nuts!"

"Don't you call me a nut!"

"Nuts! Stick to farming—it gets you more eggs. McGillicuddy, the great—"

"Hey!" he warned.

She shut up abruptly. He put the pace on, refusing to admit that his system felt slightly jittery with nervous strain or that anything had got him bothered. But he knew that he'd no desire to be near that sparkling giant again. Once was enough, more than enough. It wasn't that he feared it, but something else, something he was quite unable to define.

Passing the last bank of cabinets, he found himself facing a machine. It was complicated and bizarre—and it was making a crystalline growth. Near it, another and different machine was manufacturing a small, horned lizard. There could be no doubt at all about the process of fabrication because both objects were half-made and both progressed slightly even as he watched. In a couple of hours' time, perhaps less, they'd be finished, and all they'd need would be . . . would be—

The hairs stiffened on the back of his neck and he commenced to run. Endless machines, all different, all making different things, plants, bugs, birds and fungoids. It was done by electroponics, atom fed to atom like brick after brick to build a house. It wasn't synthesis because that's only assembly, and this was assembly plus growth in response to unknown laws. In each of these machines, he knew, was some key or code or cipher, some weird master-control of unimaginable complexity, determining the patterns each was building—and the patterns were infinitely variable.

Here and there a piece of apparatus stood silent, inactive, their tasks complete. Here and there other monstrous layouts were in pieces, either under repair or readied for modification. He stopped by one which had finished its job. It had fashioned a delicately shaded moth which perched motionless like a jeweled statue within its fabrication jar. The creature was perfect as far as he could tell, and all it was waiting for was . . . was—

Beads of moisture popped out on his forehead. All that moth needed was the breath of life!

He forced a multitude of notions to get out of his mind. It was the only way to retain a hold on himself. Divert your attention—take it off this and place it on that! Firmly, he fastened his attention on one tremendous, partly disassembled machine lying nearby. Its guts were exposed, revealing great field coils of dull gray wire. Bits of similar wire lay scattered around on the floor.

Picking up a short piece, he found it surprisingly heavy. He took off his wrist watch, opened its back, brought the wire near to its works. The Venusian jargoon bearing fluoresced immediately. V-jargoons invariably glowed in the presence of near radiation. This unknown metal was a possible fuel. His heart gave a jump at the mere thought of it.

Should he drag out a huge coil and lug it up to the ship? It was very heavy, and he'd need a considerable length of the stuff—if it was usable as fuel. Supposing the disappearance of the coil caused mousetraps to be set before he returned to search anew?

It pays to stop and think whenever you've got time to stop and think; that was a fundamental of Probe Service philosophy. Pocketing a sample of the wire, he sought around other disassembled machines for more. The search took him still deeper into the building and he fought harder to keep his attention concentrated solely on the task. It wasn't easy. There was that dog, for instance, standing there, statuelike, waiting, waiting. If only it had been anything but indubitably and recognizably an Earth-type dog. It was impossible to avoid seeing it. It would be equally impossible to avoid seeing other, even more familiar forms—if they were there.

He'd gained seven samples of different radioactive wires when he gave up the search. A cockatoo ended his peregrinations. The bird stood steadfastly in its jar, its blue plumage smooth and bright, its crimson crest raised, its bright eye fixed in what was not death but not yet life. Laura shrieked at it hysterically and the immense hall shrieked back at her with long-drawn roars and rumbles that reverberated into dim distances. Laura's reaction was too much; he wanted no cause for similar reaction of his own.

He sped through the building at top pace, passing the filing cabinets and the mighty array of exhibition cases unheedingly. Up the loamy side slopes he climbed almost as rapidly as he'd gone down, and he was breathing heavily by the time he got into the ship.

His first action was to check the ship for evidence of interference. There wasn't any. Next, he checked the instruments. The Electroscope's leaves were collapsed. Charging them, he watched them flip open and flop together again. The counter showed radiation aplenty. The hen clucked energetically. He'd blundered somewhat—he should have checked up when first he landed on the roof. However, no matter. What lay beneath the roof was now known; the instruments would have advised him earlier but not as informatively.

Laura had her feed while he accompanied her with a swift meal. After that, he dug out his samples of wire. No two were the same gauge and one obviously was far too thick to enter the feed holes of the Kingston-Kanes. It took him half an hour to file it down to a suitable diameter. The original piece of dull gray wire took the first test. Feeding it in, he set the controls to minimum warming-up intensity, stepped on the energizer. Nothing happened.

He scowled to himself. Someday they'd have jobs better than the sturdy but finicky Kingston-Kanes, jobs that'd eat anything eatable. Density and radioactivity weren't enough for these motors; the stuff fed to them had to be right.

Going back to the Kingston-Kanes, he pulled out the wire, found its end fused into shapelessness. Definitely a failure. Inserting the second sample, another gray wire not so dull as the first, he returned to the controls, rammed the energizer. The tail rockets promptly blasted with a low, moaning note and the thrust dial showed sixty per cent normal surge.

Some people would have got mad at that point. Steve didn't. His lean, hawklike features quirked, he felt in his pocket for the third sample, tried that. No soap. The fourth likewise was a flop. The fifth produced a peculiar and rhythmic series of blasts which shook the vessel from end to end and caused the thrust-dial needle to waggle between one hundred twenty per cent and zero. He visualized the Probe patrols popping through space like outboard motors while he extracted the stuff and fed the sixth sample. The sixth roared joyously at one hundred seventy per cent. The seventh sample was another flop.

He discarded all but what was left of the sixth wire. The stuff was about twelve gauge and near enough for his purpose. It resembled deep-colored copper but was not as soft as copper nor as heavy. Hard, springy and light, like telephone wire. If there were at least a thousand yards of it below, and if he could manage to drag it up to the ship, and if the golden thing didn't come along and ball up the works, he might be able to blow free. Then he'd get to some place civilized—if he could find it. The future was based on an appalling selection of "ifs."

The easiest and most obvious way to salvage the needed treasure was to blow a hole in the roof, lower a cable through it, and wind up the wire with the aid of the ship's tiny winch. Problem: how to blow a hole without suitable explosives. Answer: drill the roof, insert unshelled pistol ammunition, say a prayer and pop the stuff off electrically. He tried it, using a hand drill. The bit promptly curled up as if gnawing on a diamond. He drew his gun, bounced a shell off the roof; the missile exploded with a sharp, hard crack and fragments of shell casing whined shrilly into the sky. Where it had struck, the roof bore a blast smudge and a couple of fine scratches.

There was nothing for it but to go down and heave on his shoulders as much loot as he could carry. And do it right away. Darkness would fall before long, and he didn't want to encounter that golden thing in the dark. It was fateful enough in broad light of day, or in the queer, green glow of the building's interior, but to have it stealing softly behind him as he struggled through the nighttime with his plunder was something of which he didn't care to think.

Locking the ship and leaving Laura inside, he returned to the building, made his way past the mile of cases and cabinets to the machine section at back. He stopped to study nothing on his way. He didn't wish to study anything. The wire was the thing, only the wire. Besides, mundane thoughts of mundane wire didn't twist one's mind around until one found it hard to concentrate.

Nevertheless, his mind was afire as he searched. Half of it was prickly with alertness, apprehensive of the golden column's sudden return; the other half burned with excitement at the possibility of release. Outwardly, his manner showed nothing of this; it was calm, assured, methodical.

Within ten minutes he'd found a great coil of the coppery metal, a huge ovoid, intricately wound, lying beside a disassembled machine. He tried to move it, could not shift it an inch. The thing was far too big, too heavy for one to handle. To get it onto the roof he'd have to cut it up and make four trips of it—and some of its inner windings were fused together.

So near, so far! Freedom depended upon his ability to move a lump of metal a thousand feet vertically. He muttered some of Laura's words to himself.

Although the wire cutters were ready in his hand, he paused to think, decided to look farther before tackling this job. It was a wise decision which brought its reward, for at a point a mere hundred yards away he came across another, differently shaped coil, wheel-shaped, in good condition, easy to unreel. This again was too heavy to carry, but with a tremendous effort which made his muscles crack he got it up on its rim and proceeded to roll it along like a monster tire.

Several times he had to stop and let the coil lean against the nearest case while he rested a moment. The last such case trembled under the impact of the weighty coil and its shining, spidery occupant stirred in momentary simulation of life. His dislike of the spider shot up with its motion, he made his rest brief, bowled the coil onward.

Violet streaks again were creeping from the horizon when he rolled his loot out of the mighty exit and reached the bottom of the bank. Here, he stopped, clipped the wire with his cutters, took the free end, climbed the bank with it. The wire uncoiled without hindrance until he reached the ship, where he attached it to the winch, wound the loot in, rewound it on the feed spool.

Night fell in one ominous swoop. His hands were trembling slightly but his hawklike face was firm, phlegmatic as he carefully threaded the wire's end through the automatic injector and into the feed hole of the Kingston-Kanes. That done, he slid open Laura's door, gave her some of the fruit they'd picked off the Oron tree. She accepted it morbidly, her manner still subdued, and not inclined for speech.

"Stay inside, Honey," he soothed. "We're getting out of this and going home."

Shutting her in, he climbed into the control seat, switched on the nose beam, saw it pierce the darkness and light up the facing cliff. Then he stamped on the energizer, warmed the tubes. Their bellow was violent and comforting. At seventy per cent better thrust he'd have to be a lot more careful in all his adjustments: it wouldn't do to melt his own tail off when success was within his grasp. All the same, he felt strangely impatient, as if every minute counted, aye, every second!

But he contained himself, got the venturis heated, gave a discreet puff on his starboard steering flare, watched the cliff glide sidewise past as the ship slewed around on its belly. Another puff, then another, and he had the vessel nose-on to the front edge of the roof. There seemed to be a faint aura in the gloom ahead and he switched off his nose beam to study it better.

It was a faint yellow haze shining over the rim of the opposite slope. His back hairs quivered as he saw it. The haze strengthened, rose higher. His eyes strained into the outer pall as he watched it fascinatedly, and his hands were frozen on the controls. There was dampness on his back. Behind him, in her traveling compartment, Laura was completely silent, not even shuffling uneasily as was her wont. He wondered if she were cowering.

With a mighty effort of will which strained him as never before, he shifted his control a couple of notches, lengthened the tail blast. Trembling in its entire fabric, the ship edged forward. Summoning all he'd got, Steve forced his reluctant hands to administer the take-off boost. With a tearing crash that thundered back from the cliffs, the little vessel leaped skyward on an arc of fire. Peering through the transpex, Steve caught a fragmentary and foreshortened glimpse of the great golden column advancing majestically over the crest, the next instant it had dropped far behind his tail and his bow was arrowing for the stars.

An immense relief flooded through his soul though he knew not what there had been to fear. But the relief was there and so great was it that he worried not at all about where he was bound or for how long. Somehow, he felt certain that if he swept in a wide, shallow curve he'd pick up a Probe beat-note sooner or later. Once he got a beat-note, from any source at all, it would lead him out of the celestial maze.

Luck remained with him, and his optimistic hunch proved correct, for while still among completely strange constellations he caught the faint throb of Hydra III on his twenty-seventh day of sweep. That throb was his cosmic lighthouse beckoning him home.

He let go a wild shriek of "Yipee!" thinking that only Laura heard him—but he was heard elsewhere.

Down on Oron, deep in the monster workshop, the golden giant paused blindly as if listening. Then it slid stealthily along the immense aisles, reached the filing system. A compartment opened, two glassy plates came out.

For a moment the plates contacted the Oron's strange, sparkling substance, became etched with an array of tiny dots. They were returned to the compartment, and the door closed. The golden glory with its imprisoned stars then glided quietly back to the machine section.

Something nearer to the gods had scribbled its notes. Nothing lower in the scale of life could have translated them or deduced their full purport.

In simplest sense, one plate may have been inscribed, "Biped, erect, pink, homo intelligens type P.739, planted on Sol III, Condensation Arm BDB—moderately successful."

Similarly, the other plate may have recorded, "Flapwing, large, hook-beaked, vari-colored, periquito macao type K.8, planted on Sol III, Condensation Arm BDB—moderately successful."

But already the sparkling hobbyist had forgotten his passing notes. He was breathing his essence upon a jeweled moth.

First published: 1947

E FOR EFFORT

by T. L. Sherred

THE CAPTAIN WAS MET AT THE AIRPORT BY A STAFF CAR. LONG AND FAST
it sped. In a narrow, silent room the general sat, ramrod-backed, tense.
The major waited at the foot of the gleaming steps shining frostily in the
night air. Tires screamed to a stop and together the captain and the
major raced up the steps. No words of greeting were spoken. The general
stood quickly, hand outstretched. The captain ripped open a dispatch
case and handed over a thick bundle of papers. The general flipped them
over eagerly and spat a sentence at the major. The major disappeared and
his harsh voice rang curtly down the outside hall. The man with glasses
came in and the general handed him the papers. With jerky fingers the
man with glasses sorted them out. With a wave from the general the captain left, a proud smile on his weary young face. The general tapped his
fingertips on the black glossy surface of the table. The man with glasses
pushed aside crinkled maps, and began to read aloud.

Dear Joe:
   I started this just to kill time, because I got tired of just looking out
the window. But when I got almost to the end I began to catch the
trend of what's going on. You're the only one I know that can come
through for me, and when you finish this you'll know why you must.
   I don't know who will get this to you. Whoever it is won't want you
to identify a face later. Remember that, and please, Joe—*hurry*!
                                                                    Ed.

It all started because I'm lazy. By the time I'd shaken off the sandman
and checked out of the hotel every seat in the bus was full. I stuck my bag
in a dime locker and went out to kill the hour I had until the next bus
left. You know the bus terminal: right across from the Book-Cadillac and
the Statler, on Washington Boulevard near Michigan Avenue. Michigan
Avenue. Like Main in Los Angeles, or maybe Sixty-third in its present

state of decay in Chicago, where I was going. Cheap movies, pawnshops and bars by the dozens, a penny arcade or two, restaurants that feature hamburg steak, bread and butter and coffee for forty cents. Before the War, a quarter.

I like pawnshops. I like cameras, I like tools, I like to look in windows crammed with everything from electric razors to sets of socket wrenches to upper plates. So, with an hour to spare, I walked out Michigan to Sixth and back on the other side of the street. There are a lot of Chinese and Mexicans around that part of town, the Chinese running the restaurants and the Mexicans eating Southern Home Cooking. Between Fourth and Fifth I stopped to stare at what passed for a movie. Store windows painted black, amateurish signs extolling in Spanish "Detroit premiere . . . cast of thousands . . . this week only . . . ten cents—" The few 8x10 glossy stills pasted on the windows were poor blowups, spotty and wrinkled; pictures of mailed cavalry and what looked like a good sized battle. All for ten cents. Right down my alley.

Maybe it's lucky that history was my major in school. Luck it must have been, certainly not cleverness, that made me pay a dime for a seat in an undertaker's rickety folding chair imbedded solidly—although the only other customers were a half-dozen Sons of the Order of Tortilla— in a cast of second-hand garlic. I sat near the door. A couple of hundred watt bulbs dangling naked from the ceiling gave enough light for me to look around. In front of me, in the rear of the store, was the screen, what looked like a white-painted sheet of beaverboard, and when over my shoulder I saw the battered sixteen millimeter projector I began to think that even a dime was no bargain. Still, I had forty minutes to wait.

Everyone was smoking. I lit a cigarette and the discouraged Mexican who had taken my dime locked the door and turned off the lights, after giving me a long, questioning look. I'd paid my dime, so I looked right back. In a minute the old projector started clattering. No film credits, no producer's name, no director, just a tentative flicker before a closeup of a bewhiskered mug labeled Cortez. Then a painted and feathered Indian with the title of Guatemotzin, successor to Montezuma; an aerial shot of a beautiful job of model-building tagged Ciudad de Méjico, 1521. Shots of old muzzle-loaded artillery banging away, great walls spurting stone splinters under direct fire, skinny Indians dying violently with the customary gyrations, smoke and haze and blood. The photography sat me right up straight. It had none of the scratches and erratic cuts that characterize an old print, none of the fuzziness, none of the usual mugging at the camera by the handsome hero. There wasn't any handsome hero. Did you ever see one of these French pictures, or a Russian, and comment on the reality and depth brought out by working on a small budget that can't afford famed actors? This, what there was of it, was as good, or better.

It wasn't until the picture ended with a pan shot of a dreary desolation that I began to add two and two. You can't, for pennies, really have a cast of thousands, or sets big enough to fill Central Park. A mock-up, even, of a thirty-foot fall costs enough to irritate the auditors, and there had been a lot of wall. That didn't fit with the bad editing and lack of sound track, not unless the picture had been made in the old silent days. And I knew it hadn't by the color tones you get with pan film. It looked like a well-rehearsed and badly-planned newsreel.

The Mexicans were easing out and I followed them to where the discouraged one was rewinding the reel. I asked him where he got the print.

"I haven't heard of any epics from the press agents lately, and it looks like a fairly recent print."

He agreed that it was recent, and added that he'd made it himself. I was polite to that, and he saw that I didn't believe him and straightened up from the projector.

"You don't believe that, do you?" I said that I certainly did, and I had to catch a bus. "Would you mind telling me why, exactly why?" I said that the bus— "I mean it. I'd appreciate it if you'd tell me just what's wrong with it."

"There's nothing wrong with it," I told him. He waited for me to go on. "Well, for one thing, pictures like that aren't made for the sixteen millimeter trade. You've got a reduction from a thirty-five millimeter master," and I gave him a few of the other reasons that separate home movies from Hollywood. When I finished he smoked quietly for a minute.

"I see." He took the reel off the projector spindle and closed the case. "I have beer in the back." I agreed beer sounded good, but the bus—well, just one. From in back of the beaverboard screen he brought paper cups and a Jumbo bottle. With a whimsical "Business suspended" he closed the open door and opened the bottle with an opener screwed on the wall. The store had likely been a grocery or restaurant. There were plenty of chairs. Two we shoved around and relaxed companionably. The beer was warm.

"You know something about this line," tentatively.

I took it as a question and laughed. "Not too much. Here's mud," and we drank. "Used to drive a truck for the Film Exchange." He was amused at that.

"Stranger in town?"

"Yes and no. Mostly yes. Sinus trouble chased me out and relatives bring me back. Not any more, though; my father's funeral was last week." He said that was too bad, and I said it wasn't. "He had sinus, too." That was a joke, and he refilled the cups. We talked awhile about Detroit climate.

Finally he said, rather speculatively, "Didn't I see you around here last night? Just about eight." He got up and went after more beer.

I called after him. "No more beer for me." He brought a bottle anyway, and I looked at my watch. "Well, just one."

"Was it you?"

"Was it me what?" I held out my paper cup.

"Weren't you around here—"

I wiped foam off my mustache. "Last night? No, but I wish I had. I'd have caught my bus. No, I was in the Motor Bar last night at eight. And I was still there at midnight."

He chewed his lip thoughtfully. "The Motor Bar. Just down the street?" And I nodded. "The Motor Bar. Hm-m-m." I looked at him. "Would you like . . . sure, you would." Before I could figure out what he was talking about he went to the back and from behind the beaverboard screen rolled out a big radio-phonograph and another Jumbo bottle. I held the bottle against the light. Still half full. I looked at my watch. He rolled the radio against the wall and lifted the lid to get at the dials.

"Reach behind you, will you? The switch on the wall." I could reach the switch without getting up, and I did. The lights went out. I hadn't expected that, and I groped at arm's length. Then the lights came on again, and I turned back, relieved. But the lights weren't on; I was looking at the street!

Now, all this happened while I was dripping beer and trying to keep my balance on a tottering chair—the street moved, I didn't and it was day and it was night and I was in front of the Book-Cadillac and I was going into the Motor Bar and I was watching myself order a beer and I knew I was wide awake and not dreaming. In a panic I scrabbled off the floor, shedding chairs and beer like an umbrella while I ripped my nails feeling frantically for that light switch. By the time I found it—and all the while I was watching myself pound the bar for the barkeep—I was really in fine fettle, just about ready to collapse. Out of thin air right into a nightmare. At last I found the switch.

The Mexican was looking at me with the queerest expression I've ever seen, like he'd baited a mousetrap and caught a frog. Me? I suppose I looked like I'd seen the devil himself. Maybe I had. The beer was all over the floor and I barely made it to the nearest chair.

"What," I managed to get out, "what was that?"

The lid of the radio went down. "I felt like that too, the first time. I'd forgotten."

My fingers were too shaky to get out a cigarette, and I ripped off the top of the package. "I said, what was that?"

He sat down. "That was you, in the Motor Bar, at eight last night." I must have looked blank as he handed me another paper cup. Automatically I held it out to be refilled.

"Look here—" I started.

"I suppose it is a shock. I'd forgotten what I felt like the first time I . . . I don't care much any more. Tomorrow I'm going out to Phillips Radio." That made no sense to me, and I said so. He went on.

"I'm licked. I'm flat broke. I don't give a care any more. I'll settle for cash and live off the royalties." The story came out, slowly at first, then faster until he was pacing the floor. I guess he was tired of having no one to talk to.

His name was Miguel Jose Zapata Laviada. I told him mine; Lefko. Ed Lefko. He was the son of sugar beet workers who had emigrated from Mexico somewhere in the Twenties. They were sensible enough not to quibble when their oldest son left the back-breaking Michigan fields to seize the chance provided by a NYA scholarship. When the scholarship ran out, he'd worked in garages, driven trucks, clerked in stores, and sold brushes door-to-door to exist and learn. The Army cut short his education with the First Draft to make him a radar technician, the Army had given him an honorable discharge and an idea so nebulous as to be almost merely a hunch. Jobs were plentiful then, and it wasn't too hard to end up with enough money to rent a trailer and fill it with Army surplus radio and radar equipment. One year ago he'd finished what he'd started, finished underfed, underweight, and overexcited. But successful, because he had it.

"It" he installed in a radio cabinet, both for ease in handling and for camouflage. For reasons that will become apparent, he didn't dare apply for a patent. I looked "it" over pretty carefully. Where the phonograph turntable and radio controls had been were vernier dials galore. One big one was numbered 1 to 24, a couple were numbered 1 to 60, and there were a dozen or so numbered 1 to 25, plus two or three with no numbers at all. Closest of all it resembled one of these fancy radio or motor testers found in a super super-service station. That was all, except that there was a sheet of heavy plywood hiding whatever was installed in place of the radio chassis and speaker. A perfectly innocent cache for—

Daydreams are swell. I suppose we've all had our share of mental wealth or fame or travel or fantasy. But to sit in a chair and drink warm beer and realize that the dream of ages isn't a dream any more, to feel like a god, to know that just by turning a few dials you can see and watch anything, anybody, anywhere, that has ever happened—it still bothers me once in a while.

I know this much, that it's high frequency stuff. And there's a lot of mercury and copper and wiring of metals cheap and easy to find, but what goes where, or how, least of all, why, is out of my line. Light has mass and energy, and that mass always loses part of itself and can be translated back to electricity, or something. Mike Laviada himself says that what he stumbled on and developed was nothing new, that long before the war it had been observed many times by men like Compton and Michelson and Pfeiffer, who discarded it as a useless laboratory effect. And, of course, that was before atomic research took precedence over everything.

When the first shock wore off—and Mike had to give me another demonstration—I must have made quite a sight. Mike tells me I couldn't sit down. I'd pop up and gallop up and down the floor of that ancient store kicking chairs out of my way or stumbling over them, all the time gobbling out words and disconnected sentences faster than my tongue could trip. Finally it filtered through that he was laughing at me. I didn't see where it was any laughing matter, and I prodded him. He began to get angry.

"I know what I have," he snapped. "I'm not the biggest fool in the world, as you seem to think. Here, watch this," and he went back to the radio. "Turn out the light." I did, and there I was watching myself at the Motor Bar again, a lot happier this time. "Watch this."

The bar backed away. Out in the street, two blocks down to the City Hall. Up the steps to the Council Room. No one there. Then Council was in session, then they were gone again. Not a picture, not a projection of a lantern slide, but a slice of life about twelve feet square. If we were close, the field of view was narrow. If we were further away, the background was just as much in focus as the foreground. The images, if you want to call them images, were just as real, just as lifelike as looking in the doorway of a room. Real they were, three-dimensional, stopped by only the back wall or the distance in the background. Mike was talking as he spun the dials, but I was too engrossed to pay much attention.

I yelped and grabbed and closed my eyes as you would if you were looking straight down with nothing between you and the ground except a lot of smoke and a few clouds. I winked my eyes open almost at the ends of what must have been a long racing vertical dive, and there I was, looking at the street again.

"Go any place up to the Heaviside Layer, go down as deep as any hole, anywhere, any time." A blur, and the street changed into a glade of sparse pines. "Buried treasure. Sure. Find it, with what?" The trees disappeared and I reached back for the light switch as he dropped the lid of the radio and sat down.

"How are you going to make any money when you haven't got it to start?" No answer to that from me. "I ran an ad in the paper offering to recover lost articles; my first customer was the Law wanting to see my private detective's license. I've seen every big speculator in the country sit in his office buying and selling and making plans; what do you think would happen if I tried to peddle advance market information? I've watched the stock market get shoved up and down while I had barely the money to buy the paper that told me about it. I watched a bunch of Peruvian Indians bury the second ransom of Atuahalpa; I haven't the fare to get to Peru, or the money to buy the tools to dig." He got up and brought two more bottles. He went on. By that time I was getting a few ideas.

"I've watched scribes indite the books that burnt at Alexandria; who would buy, or who would believe me, if I copied one? What would happen if I went over to the Library and told them to rewrite their histories? How many would fight to tie a rope around my neck if they knew I'd watched them steal and murder and take a bath? What sort of a padded cell would I get if I showed up with a photograph of Washington, or Caesar? Or Christ?"

I agreed that it was all probably true, but—

"Why do you think I'm here now? You saw the picture I showed for a dime. A dime's worth, and that's all, because I didn't have the money to buy film or to make the picture as I knew I should." His tongue began to get tangled. He was excited. "I'm doing this because I haven't the money to get the things I need to get the money I'll need—" He was so disgusted he booted a chair halfway across the room. It was easy to see that if I had been around a little later, Phillips Radio would have profited. Maybe I'd have been better off, too.

Now, although always I've been told that I'd never be worth a hoot, no one has ever accused me of being slow for a dollar. Especially an easy one. I saw money in front of me, easy money, the easiest and the quickest in the world. I saw, for a minute, so far in the future with me on top of the heap, that my head reeled and it was hard to breathe.

"Mike," I said, "let's finish that beer and go where we can get some more, and maybe something to eat. We've got a lot of talking to do." So we did.

Beer is a mighty fine lubricant; I have always been a pretty smooth talker, and by the time we left the gin mill I had a pretty good idea of just what Mike had on his mind. By the time we'd shacked up for the night behind that beaverboard screen in the store, we were full-fledged partners. I don't recall our even shaking hands on the deal, but that partnership still holds good. Mike is ace high with me, and I guess it's the other way around, too. That was six years ago; it only took me a year or so to discard some of the corners I used to cut.

Seven days after that, on a Tuesday, I was riding a bus to Grosse Pointe with a full briefcase. Two days after that I was riding back from Grosse Pointe in a shiny taxi, with an empty briefcase and a pocketful of folding money. It was easy.

"Mr. Jones—or Smith—or Brown—I'm with Aristocrat Studios, Personal and Candid Portraits. We thought you might like this picture of you and . . . no, this is just a test proof. The negative is in our files. . . . Now, if you're really interested, I'll be back the day after tomorrow with our files. . . . I'm sure you will, Mr. Jones. Thank you, Mr. Jones. . . ."

Dirty? Sure. Blackmail is always dirty. But if I had a wife and family and a good reputation, I'd stick to the roast beef and forget the Roquefort. Very smelly Roquefort, at that. Mike liked it less than I did. It took some talking, and I had to drag out the old one about the ends justifying the means, and they could well afford it, anyway. Besides, if there was a squawk, they'd get the negatives free. Some of them were pretty bad.

So we had the cash; not too much, but enough to start. Before we took the next step there was plenty to decide. There are a lot who earn a living by convincing millions that Sticko soap is better. We had a harder problem than that: we had, first, to make a salable and profitable product, and second, we had to convince many, many millions that our "Product" was absolutely honest and absolutely accurate. We all know that if you repeat something long enough and loud enough many—or most—will accept it as gospel truth. That called for publicity on an international scale. For the skeptics who know better than to accept advertising, no matter how blatant, we had to use another technique. And since we were going to get certainly only one chance, we had to be right the first time. Without Mike's machine the job would have been impossible; without it the job would have been unnecessary.

A lot of sweat ran under the bridge before we found what we thought—

and we still do!—the only workable scheme. We picked the only possible way to enter every mind in the world without a fight; the field of entertainment. Absolute secrecy was imperative, and it was only when we reached the last decimal point that we made a move. We started like this.

First we looked for a suitable building, or Mike did, while I flew east, to Rochester, for a month. The building he rented was an old bank. We had the windows sealed, a flossy office installed in the front—the bulletproof glass was my idea—air conditioning, a portable bar, electrical wiring of whatever type Mike's little heart desired, and a blond secretary who thought she was working for M-E Experimental Laboratories. When I got back from Rochester I took over the job of keeping happy the stone masons and electricians, while Mike fooled around in our suite in the Book where he could look out the window at his old store. The last I heard, they were selling snake oil there. When the Studio, as we came to call it, was finished, Mike moved in and the blonde settled down to a routine of reading love stories and saying no to all the salesmen that wandered by. I left for Hollywood.

I spent a week digging through the files of Central Casting before I was satisfied, but it took a month of snooping and some under-the-table cash to lease a camera that would handle Trucolor film. That took the biggest load from my mind. When I got back to Detroit the big view camera had arrived from Rochester, with a truckload of glass color plates. Ready to go.

We made quite a ceremony of it. We closed the Venetian blinds and I popped the cork on one of the bottles of champagne I'd bought. The blond secretary was impressed; all she'd been doing for her salary was to accept delivery of packages and crates and boxes. We had no wine glasses, but we made no fuss about that. Too nervous and excited to drink any more than one bottle, we gave the rest to the blonde and told her to take the rest of the afternoon off. After she left—and I think she was disappointed at breaking up what could have been a good party—we locked up after her, went into the studio itself, locked up again and went to work.

I've mentioned that the windows were sealed. All the inside wall had been painted dull black, and with the high ceiling that went with that old bank lobby, it was impressive. But not gloomy. Midway in the studio was planted the big Trucolor camera, loaded and ready. Not much could we see of Mike's machine, but I knew it was off to the side, set to throw on the back wall. Not *on* the wall, understand, because the images produced are projected into the air, like the meeting of the rays of two searchlights. Mike lifted the lid and I could see him silhouetted against the tiny lights that lit the dials.

"Well?" he said expectantly.

I felt pretty good just then, right down to my billfold.

"It's all yours, Mike," and a switch ticked over. There he was. There was a youngster, dead twenty-five hundred years, real enough, almost, to touch. Alexander. Alexander of Macedon.

Let's take that first picture in detail. I don't think I can ever forget what happened in the next year or so. First we followed Alexander through his life, from beginning to end. We skipped, of course, the little things he did, jumping ahead days and weeks and years at a time. Then we'd miss him, or find that he'd moved in space. That would mean we'd have to jump back and forth, like the artillery firing bracket or ranging shots, until we found him again. Helped only occasionally by his published lives, we were astounded to realize how much distortion has crept into his life. I often wonder why legends arise about the famous. Certainly their lives are as startling or appalling as fiction. And unfortunately we had to hold closely to the accepted histories. If we hadn't, every professor would have gone into his corner for a hearty sneer. We couldn't take that chance. Not at first.

After we knew approximately what had happened and where, we used our notes to go back to what had seemed a particularly photogenic section and work on that awhile. Eventually we had a fair idea of what we were actually going to film. Then we sat down and wrote an actual script to follow, making allowance for whatever shots we'd have to double in later. Mike used his machine as the projector, and I operated the Trucolor camera at a fixed focus, like taking moving pictures of a movie. As fast as we finished a reel it would go to Rochester for processing, instead of one of the Hollywood outfits that might have done it cheaper. Rochester is so used to horrible amateur stuff that I doubt if anyone ever looks at anything. When the reel was returned we'd run it ourselves to check our choice of scenes and color sense and so on.

For example, we had to show the traditional quarrels with his father, Philip. Most of that we figured on doing with doubles, later. Olympias, his mother, and the fangless snakes she affected, didn't need any doubling, as we used an angle and amount of distance that didn't call for actual conversation. The scene where Alexander rode the bucking horse no one else could ride came out of some biographer's head, but we thought it was so famous we couldn't leave it out. We dubbed the closeups later, and the actual horseman was a young Scythian that hung around the royal stables for his keep. Roxanne was real enough, like the rest of the Persians' wives that Alexander took over. Luckily most of them had enough poundage to look luscious. Philip and Parmenio and the rest of the characters were heavily bearded, which made easy the necessary doubling and dubbing-in the necessary speech. (If you ever saw them shave in those days, you'd know why whiskers were popular.)

The most trouble we had with the interior shots. Smoky wicks in a bowl of lard, no matter how plentiful, are too dim even for fast film. Mike got around that by running the Trucolor camera at a single frame a second, with his machine paced accordingly. That accounts for the startling clarity and depth of focus we got from a lens well stopped down. We had all the time in the world to choose the best possible scenes and camera angles; the best actors in the world, expensive camera booms, or repeated retakes under the most exacting director can't compete with us. We had a lifetime from which to choose.

Eventually we had on film about eighty per cent of what you saw in the finished picture. Roughly we spliced the reels together and sat there entranced at what we had actually done. Even more exciting, even more spectacular than we'd dared to hope, the lack of continuity and sound didn't stop us from realizing that we'd done a beautiful job. We'd done all we could, and the worst was yet to come. So we sent for more champagne and told the blonde we had cause for celebration. She giggled.

"What are you doing in there, anyway?" she asked. "Every salesman who comes to the door wants to know what you're making."

I opened the first bottle. "Just tell them you don't know."

"That's just what I've been telling them. They think I'm awfully dumb." We all laughed at the salesmen.

Mike was thoughtful. "If we're going to do this sort of thing very often, we ought to have some of these fancy hollow-stemmed glasses."

The blonde was pleased with that. "And we could keep them in my bottom drawer." Her nose wrinkled prettily. "These bubbles— You know, this is the only time I've ever had champagne, except at a wedding, and then it was only one glass."

"Pour her another," Mike suggested. "Mine's empty, too." I did. "What did you do with those bottles you took home last time?"

A blush and a giggle. "My father wanted to open them, but I told him you said to save it for a special occasion."

By that time I had my feet on her desk. "This is the special occasion, then," I invited. "Have another, Miss . . . what's your first name, anyway? I hate being formal after working hours."

She was shocked. "And you and Mr. Laviada sign my checks every week! It's Ruth."

"Ruth. Ruth." I rolled it around the piercing bubbles, and it sounded all right.

She nodded. "And your name is Edward, and Mr. Laviada's is Migwell. Isn't it?" And she smiled at him.

"MiGELL," he smiled back. "An old Spanish custom. Usually shortened to Mike."

"If you'll hand me another bottle," I offered, "shorten Edward to Ed." She handed it over.

By the time we got to the fourth bottle we were as thick as bugs in a rug. It seems that she was twenty-four, free, white, and single, and loved champagne.

"But," she burbled fretfully, "I wish I knew what you were doing in there all hours of the day and night. I know you're here at night sometimes because I've seen your car out in front."

Mike thought that over. "Well," he said a little unsteadily, "we take pictures." He blinked one eye. "Might even take pictures of you if we were approached properly."

I took over. "We take pictures of models."

"Oh, no."

"Yes. Models of things and people and what not. Little ones. We make it look like it's real." I think she was a trifle disappointed.

"Well, now I know, and that makes me feel better. I sign all those bills from Rochester and I don't know what I'm signing for. Except that they must be film or something."

"That's just what it is; film and things like that."

"Well, it bothered me— No, there's two more behind the fan."

Only two more. She had a capacity. I asked her how she would like a vacation. She hadn't thought about a vacation just yet.

I told her she'd better start thinking about it. "We're leaving day after tomorrow for Los Angeles, Hollywood."

"The day after tomorrow? Why—"

I reassured her. "You'll get paid just the same. But there's no telling how long we'll be gone, and there doesn't seem to be much use in your sitting around here with nothing to do."

From Mike "Let's have that bottle," and I handed it to him. I went on.

"You'll get your checks just the same. If you want, we'll pay you in advance so—"

I was getting full of champagne, and so were we all. Mike was humming softly to himself, happy as a taco. The blonde, Ruth, was having a little trouble with my left eye. I knew just how she felt, because I was having a little trouble watching where she overlapped the swivel chair. Blue eyes, sooo tall, fuzzy hair. Hm-m-m. All work and no play— She handed me the last bottle.

Demurely she hid a tiny hiccup. "I'm going to save all the corks— No I won't either. My father would want to know what I'm thinking of, drinking with my bosses."

I said it wasn't a good idea to annoy your father. Mike said why fool with bad ideas, when he had a good one. We were interested. Nothing like a good idea to liven things up.

Mike was expansive as the very devil. "Going to Los Angeles."

We nodded solemnly.

"Going to Los Angeles to work."

Another nod.

"Going to work in Los Angeles. What will we do for pretty blonde girl to write letters?"

Awful. No pretty blonde to write letters and drink champagne. Sad case.

"Gotta hire somebody to write letters anyway. Might not be blonde. No blondes in Hollywood. No good ones, anyway. So—"

I saw the wonderful idea, and finished for him. "So we take pretty blonde to Los Angeles to write letters!"

What an idea that was! One bottle sooner and its brilliancy would have been dimmed. Ruth bubbled like a fresh bottle and Mike and I sat there, smirking like mad.

"But I can't! I couldn't leave day after tomorrow just like that—!"

Mike was magnificent. "Who said day after tomorrow? Changed our minds. Leave right now."

She was appalled. "Right now! Just like that?"

"Right now. Just like that." I was firm.

"But—"

"No buts. Right now. Just like that."

"Nothing to wear—"

"Buy clothes any place. Best ones in Los Angeles."

"But my hair—"

Mike suggested a haircut in Hollywood, maybe?

I pounded the table. It felt solid. "Call the airport. Three tickets."

She called the airport. She intimidated easy.

The airport said we could leave for Chicago any time on the hour, and change there for Los Angeles. Mike wanted to know why she was wasting time on the telephone when we could be on our way. Holding up the wheels of progress, emery dust in the gears. One minute to get her hat.

"Call Pappy from the airport."

Her objections were easily brushed away with a few word-pictures of how much fun there was to be had in Hollywood. We left a sign on the door, "Gone to Lunch—Back in December," and made the airport in time for the four o'clock plane, with no time left to call Pappy. I told the parking attendant to hold the car until he heard from me and we made it up the steps and into the plane just in time. The steps were taken away, the motors snorted, and we were off, with Ruth holding fast her hat in an imaginary breeze.

There was a two-hour layover in Chicago. They don't serve liquor at the airport, but an obliging cab driver found us a convenient bar down the road, where Ruth made her call to her father. Cautiously we stayed away from the telephone booth, but from what Ruth told us, he must have read her the riot act. The bartender didn't have champagne, but gave us the special treatment reserved for those that order it. The cab driver saw that we made the liner two hours later.

In Los Angeles we registered at the Commodore, cold sober and ashamed of ourselves. The next day Ruth went shopping for clothes for herself, and for us. We gave her the sizes and enough money to soothe her hangover. Mike and I did some telephoning. After breakfast we sat around until the desk clerk announced a Mr. Lee Johnson to see us.

Lee Johnson was the brisk professional type, the high-bracket salesman. Tall, rather homely, a clipped way of talking. We introduced ourselves as embryo producers. His eyes brightened when we said that. His meat.

"Not exactly the way you think," I told him. "We have already eighty per cent or better of the final print."

He wanted to know where he came in.

"We have several thousand feet of Trucolor film. Don't bother asking where or when we got it. This footage is silent. We'll need sound and, in places, speech dubbed in."

He nodded. "Easy enough. What condition is the master?"

"Perfect condition. It's in the hotel vault right now. There are gaps in the story to fill. We'll need quite a few male and female characters. And all of these will have to do their doubling for cash, and not for screen credit."

Johnson raised his eyebrows. "And why? Out here screen credit is bread and butter."

"Several reasons. This footage was made—never mind where—with the understanding that film credit would favor no one."

"If you're lucky enough to catch your talent between pictures you might get away with it. But if your footage is worth working with, my boys will want screen credit. And I think they're entitled to it."

I said that was reasonable enough. The technical crews were essential, and I was prepared to pay well. Particularly to keep their mouths closed until the print was ready for final release. Maybe even after that.

"Before we go any further," Johnson rose and reached for his hat, "let's take a look at that print. I don't know if we can—"

I knew what he was thinking. Amateurs. Home movies. Feelthy peek-chures, mebbe?

We got the reels out of the hotel safe and drove to his laboratory, out Sunset. The top was down on his convertible and Mike hoped audibly that Ruth would have sense enough to get sport shirts that didn't itch.

"Wife?" Johnson asked carelessly.

"Secretary," Mike answered just as casually. "We flew in last night and she's out getting us some light clothes." Johnson's estimation of us rose visibly.

A porter came out of the laboratory to carry the suitcase containing the film reels. It was a long, low building, with the offices at the front and the actual laboratories tapering off at the rear. Johnson took us in the side door and called for someone whose name we didn't catch. The anonymous one was a projectionist who took the reels and disappeared into the back of the projection room. We sat for a minute in the soft easychairs until the projectionist buzzed ready. Johnson glanced at us and we nodded. He clicked a switch on the arm of his chair and the overhead lights went out. The picture started.

It ran a hundred and ten minutes as it stood. We both watched Johnson like a cat at a rathole. When the tag end showed white on the screen he signaled with the chair-side buzzer for lights. They came on. He faced us.

"Where did you get that print?"

Mike grinned at him. "Can we do business?"

"Do business?" He was vehement. "You bet your life we can do business. We'll do the greatest business you ever saw!"

The projection man came down. "Hey, that's all right. Where'd you get it?"

Mike looked at me. I said, "This isn't to go any further."

Johnson looked at his man, who shrugged. "None of my business."

I dangled the hook. "That wasn't made here. Never mind where."

Johnson rose and struck, hook, line and sinker. "Europe! Hm-m-m.

Germany. No, France. Russia, maybe, Einstein, or Eisenstein, or whatever his name is?"

I shook my head. "That doesn't matter. The leads are all dead, or out
of commission, but their heirs . . . well, you get what I mean."

Johnson saw what I meant. "Absolutely right. No point taking any
chances. Where's the rest—?"

"Who knows? We were lucky to salvage that much. Can do?"

"Can do." He thought for a minute. "Get Bernstein in here. Better
get Kessler and Marrs, too." The projectionist left. In a few minutes
Kessler, a heavy-set man, and Marrs, a young, nervous chain-smoker,
came in with Bernstein, the sound man. We were introduced all around
and Johnson asked if we minded sitting through another showing.

"Nope. We like it better than you do."

Not quite. Kessler and Marrs and Bernstein, the minute the film was
over, bombarded us with startled questions. We gave them the same
answers we'd given Johnson. But we were pleased with the reception,
and said so.

Kessler grunted. "I'd like to know who was behind that camera. Best
I've seen, by Cripes, since 'Ben Hur.' Better than 'Ben Hur.' The boy's
good."

I grunted right back at him. "That's the only thing I can tell you. The
photography was done by the boys you're talking to right now. Thanks
for the kind word."

All four of them stared.

Mike said, "That's right."

"Hey, hey!" from Marrs. They all looked at us with new respect. It
felt good.

Johnson broke into the silence when it became awkward. "What's next
on the score card?"

We got down to cases. Mike, as usual, was content to sit there with his
eyes half closed, taking it all in, letting me do all the talking.

"We want sound dubbed in all the way through."

"Pleasure," said Bernstein.

"At least a dozen, maybe more, of speaking actors with a close resemblance to the leads you've seen."

Johnson was confident. "Easy. Central Casting has everybody's picture
since the Year One."

"I know. We've already checked that. No trouble there. They'll have
to take the cash and let the credit go, for reasons I've already explained to
Mr. Johnson."

A moan from Marrs. "I bet I get that job."

Johnson was snappish. "You do. What else?" to me.

I didn't know. "Except that we have no plans for distribution as yet. That will have to be worked out."

"Like falling off a log." Johnson was happy about that. "One look at the rushes and United Artists would spit in Shakespeare's eye."

Marrs came in. "What about the other shots? Got a writer lined up?"

"We've got what will pass for the shooting script, or would have in a week or so. Want to go over it with us?"

He'd like that.

"How much time have we got?" interposed Kessler. "This is going to be a job. When do we want it?" Already it was "we."

"Yesterday is when we want it," snapped Johnson, and he rose. "Any ideas about music? No? We'll try for Werner Janssen and his boys. Bernstein, you're responsible for that print from now on. Kessler, get your crew in and have a look at it. Marrs, you'll go with Mr. Lefko and Mr. Laviada through the files at Central Casting at their convenience. Keep in touch with them at the Commodore. Now, if you'll step into my office, we'll discuss the financial arrangements—"

As easy as all that.

Oh, I don't say that it was easy work or anything like that, because in the next few months we were playing Busy Bee. What with running down the only one registered at Central Casting who looked like Alexander himself, he turned out to be a young Armenian who had given up hope of ever being called from the extra lists and had gone home to Santee—casting and rehearsing the rest of the actors and swearing at the costumers and the boys who built the sets, we were kept hopping. Even Ruth, who had reconciled her father with soothing letters, for once earned her salary. We took turns shooting dictation at her until we had a script that satisfied Mike and myself and young Marrs, who turned out to be clever as a fox on dialogue.

What I really meant is that it was easy, and immensely gratifying, to crack the shell of the tough boys who had seen epics and turkeys come and go. They were really impressed by what we had done. Kessler was disappointed when we refused to be bothered with photographing the rest of the film. We just batted our eyes and said that we were too busy, that we were perfectly confident that he would do as well as we could. He outdid himself, and us. I don't know what we would have done if he had asked us for any concrete advice. I suppose, when I think it all over, that the boys we met and worked with were so tired of working with the usual mine-run Grade B's, that they were glad to meet someone that knew the difference between glycerin tears and reality and didn't care if it cost two dollars extra. They had us placed as a couple of city slickers with plenty on the ball. I hope.

Finally it was all over with. We all sat in the projection room; Mike and I, Marrs and Johnson, Kessler and Bernstein, and all the lesser technicians that had split up the really enormous amount of work that had been done watched the finished product. It was terrific. Everyone had done his work well. When Alexander came on the screen, he *was* Alexander the Great. (The Armenian kid got a good bonus for that.) All that blazing color, all that wealth and magnificence and glamor seemed to flare right out of the screen and sear across your mind. Even Mike and I, who had seen the original, were on the edge of our seats.

The sheer realism and magnitude of the battle scenes, I think, really made the picture. Gore, of course, is glorious when it's all make-believe and the dead get up to go to lunch. But when Bill Mauldin sees a picture and sells a breathless article on the similarity of infantrymen of all ages— well, Mauldin knows what war is like. So did the infantrymen throughout the world who wrote letters comparing Alexander's Arbela to Anzio and the Argonne. The weary peasant, not stolid at all, trudging and trudging into mile after mile of those dust-laden plains and ending as a stinking, naked, ripped corpse peeping under a mound of flies isn't any different when he carries a sarissa instead of a rifle. That we'd tried to make obvious, and we succeeded.

When the lights came up in the projection room we knew we had a winner. Individually we shook hands all around, proud as a bunch of penguins, and with chests out as far. The rest of the men filed out and we retired to Johnson's office. He poured a drink all around and got down to business.

"How about releases?"

I asked him what he thought.

"Write your own ticket," he shrugged. "I don't know whether or not you know it, but the word has already gone around that you've got something."

I told him we'd had calls at the hotel from various sources, and named them.

"See what I mean? I know those babies. Kiss them out if you want to keep your shirt. And while I'm at it, you owe us quite a bit. I suppose you've got it."

"We've got it."

"I was afraid you would. If you didn't, I'd be the one that would have your shirt." He grinned, but we all knew he meant it. "All right, that's settled. Let's talk about release.

"There are two or three outfits around town that will want a crack at it. My boys will have the word spread around in no time; there's no point in trying to keep them quiet any longer. I know—they'll have sense enough not to talk about the things you want off the record. I'll see to that. But you're top dog right now. You got loose cash, you've got the biggest potential gross I've ever seen, and you don't have to take the first offer. That's important, in this game."

"How would you like to handle it yourself?"

"I'd like to try. The outfit I'm thinking of needs a feature right now, and they don't know I know it. They'll pay and pay. What's in it for me?"

"That," I said, "we can talk about later. And I think I know just what you're thinking. We'll take the usual terms and we don't care if you hold up whoever you deal with. What we don't know won't hurt us." That's what he was thinking, all right. That's a cutthroat game out there.

"Good. Kessler, get your setup ready for duplication."

"Always ready."

"Marrs, start the ball rolling on publicity . . . what do you want to do about that?" to us.

Mike and I had talked about that before. "As far as we're concerned," I said slowly, "do as you think best. Personal publicity, O.K. We won't look for it, but we won't dodge it. As far as that goes, we're the local yokels making good. Soft pedal any questions about where the picture was made, without being too obvious. You're going to have trouble when you talk about the nonexistent actors, but you ought to be able to figure out something."

Marrs groaned and Johnson grinned. "He'll figure out something."

"As far as technical credit goes, we'll be glad to see you get all you can, because you've done a swell job." Kessler took that as a personal compliment, and it was. "You might as well know now, before we go any further, that some of the work came right from Detroit." They all sat up at that.

"Mike and I have a new process of model and trick work." Kessler opened his mouth to say something but thought better of it. "We're not going to say what was done, or how much was done in the laboratory, but you'll admit that it defies detection."

About that they were fervent. "I'll say it defies detection. In the game this long and process work gets by me . . . where—"

"I'm not going to tell you that. What we've got isn't patented and won't be, as long as we can hold it up." There wasn't any griping there. These men knew process work when they saw it. If they didn't see it, it was good. They could understand why we'd want to keep a process that good a secret.

"We can practically guarantee there'll be more work for you to do later on." Their interest was plain. "We're not going to predict when, or make any definite arrangement, but we still have a trick or two in the deck. We like the way we've been getting along, and we want to stay that way. Now, if you'll excuse us, we have a date with a blonde."

Johnson was right about the bidding for the release. We—or rather Johnson—made a very profitable deal with United Amusement and the affiliated theaters. Johnson, the bandit, got his percentage from us and likely did better with United. Kessler and Johnson's boys took huge ads in the trade journals to boast about their connections with the Academy Award Winner. Not only the Academy, but every award that ever went to any picture. Even the Europeans went overboard. They're the ones that make a fetish of realism. They knew the real thing when they saw it, and so did everyone else.

Our success went to Ruth's head. In no time she wanted a secretary. At that, she needed one to fend off the screwballs that popped out of the woodwork. So we let her hire a girl to help out. She picked a good typist, about fifty. Ruth is a smart girl, in a lot of ways. Her father showed signs of wanting to see the Pacific, so we raised her salary on condition he'd stay away. The three of us were having too much fun.

The picture opened at the same time in both New York and Hollywood. We went to the premiere in great style with Ruth between us, swollen like a trio of bullfrogs. It's a great feeling to sit on the floor, early in the morning, and read reviews that make you feel like floating. It's a better feeling to have a mintful of money. Johnson and his men were right along with us. I don't think he could have been too flush in the beginning, and we all got a kick out of riding the crest.

It was a good-sized wave, too. We had all the personal publicity we wanted, and more. Somehow the word was out that we had a new gadget for process photography, and every big studio in town was after what they thought would be a mighty economical thing to have around. The studios that didn't have a spectacle scheduled looked at the receipts of "Alexander" and promptly scheduled a spectacle. We drew some very good offers, Johnson said, but we made a series of long faces and broke the news that we were leaving for Detroit the next day, and to hold the fort awhile. I don't think he thought we actually meant it, but we did. We left the next day.

Back in Detroit we went right to work, helped by the knowledge that we were on the right track. Ruth was kept busy turning away the countless would-be visitors. We admitted no reporters, no salesmen, no one. We had no time. We were using the view camera. Plate after plate we sent to Rochester for developing. A print of each was returned to us and the plate was held in Rochester for our disposal. We sent to New York for a representative of one of the biggest publishers in the country. We made a deal.

Your main library has a set of the books we published, if you're interested. Huge heavy volumes, hundreds of them, each page a razor-sharp blowup from an 8x10 negative. A set of those books went to every major library and university in the world. Mike and I got a real kick out of solving some of the problems that have had savants guessing for years. In the Roman volume, for example, we solved the trireme problem with a series of pictures, not only the interior of a trireme, but a line-of-battle quinquereme. (Naturally, the professors and amateur yachtsmen weren't convinced at all.) We had a series of aerial shots of the City of Rome taken a hundred years apart, over a millennium. Aerial views of Ravenna and Londinium, Palmyra and Pompeii, of Eboracum and Byzantium. Oh, we had the time of our lives! We had a volume for Greece and for Rome, for Persia and for Crete, for Egypt and for the Eastern Empire. We had pictures of the Parthenon and the Pharos, pictures of Hannibal and Caractacus and Vercingetorix, pictures of the Walls of Babylon and the building of the pyramids and the palace of Sargon, pages from the Lost Books of Livy and the plays of Euripides. Things like that.

Terrifically expensive, a second printing sold at cost to a surprising number of private individuals. If the cost had been less, historical interest would have become even more the fad of the moment.

When the flurry had almost died down, some Italian digging in the hitherto-unexcavated section of ash-buried Pompeii, dug right into a tiny buried temple right where our aerial shot had showed it to be. His budget was expanded and he found more ash-covered ruins that agreed with our aerial layout, ruins that hadn't seen the light of day for almost two thousand years. Everyone promptly wailed that we were the luckiest guessers in captivity; the head of some California cult suspected aloud that we were the reincarnations of two gladiators named Joe.

To get some peace and quiet Mike and I moved into our studio, lock, stock, and underwear. The old bank vault had never been removed, at our request, and it served well to store our equipment when we weren't around. All the mail Ruth couldn't handle we disposed of, unread; the old bank building began to look like a well-patronized soup kitchen. We hired burly private detectives to handle the more obnoxious visitors and subscribed to a telegraphic protective service. We had another job to do, another full-length feature.

We still stuck to the old historical theme. This time we tried to do what Gibbon did in *The Decline and Fall of the Roman Empire*. And, I think, we were rather successful, at that. In four hours you can't completely cover two thousand years, but you can, as we did, show the cracking up of a great civilization, and how painful the process can be. The criticism we drew for almost ignoring Christ and Christianity was unjust, we think, and unfair. Very few knew then, or know now, that we had included, as a kind of trial balloon, some footage of Christ Himself, and His times. This footage we had to cut. The Board of Review, as you know, is both Catholic and Protestant. They—the Board—went right up in arms. We didn't protest very hard when they claimed our "treatment" was irreverent, indecent, and biased and inaccurate "by any Christian standard." "Why," they wailed, "it doesn't even look like Him," and they were right; it didn't. Not any picture *they* ever saw. Right then and there we decided that it didn't pay to tamper with anyone's religious beliefs. That's why you've never seen anything emanating from us that conflicted even remotely with the accepted historical, sociological, or religious features of Someone Who Knew Better. That Roman picture, by the way,—but not accidentally—deviated so little from the textbooks you conned in school that only a few enthusiastic specialists called our attention to what they insisted were errors. We were still in no position to do any mass rewriting of history, because we were unable to reveal just where we got our information.

Johnson, when he saw the Roman epic, mentally clicked high his heels. His men went right to work, and we handled the job as we had the first. One day Kessler got me in a corner, dead earnest.

"Ed," he said, "I'm going to find out where you got that footage if it's the last thing I ever do."

I told him that some day he would.

"And I don't mean some day, either; I mean right now. That bushwa about Europe might go once, but not twice. I know better, and so does everyone else. Now, what about it?"

I told him I'd have to consult Mike and I did. We were up against it. We called a conference.

"Kessler tells me he has troubles. I guess you all know what they are." They all knew.

Johnson spoke up. "He's right, too. We know better. Where did you get it?"

I turned to Mike. "Want to do the talking?"

A shake of his head. "You're doing all right."

"All right." Kessler hunched a little forward and Marrs lit another cigarette. "We weren't lying and we weren't exaggerating when we said the actual photography was ours. Every frame of film was taken right here in this country, within the last few months. Just how—I won't mention why or where—we can't tell you just now." Kessler snorted in disgust. "Let me finish.

"We all know that we're cashing in, hand over fist. And we're going to cash in some more. We have, on our personal schedule, five more pictures. Three of that five we want you to handle as you did the others. The last two of the five will show you both the reason for all the childish secrecy, as Kessler calls it, and another motive that we have so far kept hidden. The last two pictures will show you both our motives and our methods; one is as important as the other. Now—is that enough? Can we go ahead on that basis?"

It wasn't enough for Kessler. "That doesn't mean a thing to me. What are we, a bunch of hacks?"

Johnson was thinking about his bank balance. "Five more. Two years, maybe four."

Marrs was skeptical. "Who do you think you're going to kid that long? Where's your studio? Where's your talent? Where do you shoot your exteriors? Where do you get your costumes and your extras? In one single shot you've got forty thousand extras, if you've got one! Maybe you can shut *me* up, but who's going to answer the questions that Metro and Fox and Paramount and RKO have been asking? Those boys aren't fools, they know their business. How do you expect me to handle any publicity when I don't know what the score is, myself?"

Johnson told him to pipe down for a while and let him think. Mike and I didn't like this one bit. But what could we do—tell the truth and end up in a strait-jacket?

"Can we do it this way?" he finally asked. "Marrs: these boys have an in with the Soviet Government. They work in some place in Siberia, maybe. Nobody gets within miles of there. No one ever knows what the Russians are doing—"

"Nope!" Marrs was definite. "Any hint that these came from Russia and we'd all be a bunch of Reds. Cut the gross in half."

Johnson began to pick up speed. "All right, not from Russia. From one of these little republics fringed around Siberia or Armenia or one of those places. They're not Russian-made films at all. In fact, they've been made by some of these Germans and Austrians the Russians took over and moved after the War. The war fever had died down enough for people to realize that the Germans knew their stuff occasionally. The old sympathy racket for these refugees struggling with faulty equipment, lousy climate, making super-spectacles and smuggling them out under the nose of the Gestapo or whatever they call it— That's it!"

Doubtfully, from Marrs: "And the Russians tell the world we're nuts, that they haven't got any loose Germans?"

That, Johnson overrode. "Who reads the back pages? Who pays any attention to what the Russians say? Who cares? They might even think we're telling the truth and start looking around their own backyard for something that isn't there! All right with you?" to Mike and myself.

I looked at Mike and he looked at me.

"O.K. with us."

"O.K. with the rest of you? Kessler? Bernstein?"

They weren't too agreeable, and certainly not happy, but they agreed to play games until we gave the word.

We were warm in our thanks. "You won't regret it."

Kessler doubted that very much, but Johnson eased them all out, back to work. Another hurdle leaped, or sidestepped.

"Rome" was released on schedule and drew the same friendly reviews. "Friendly" is the wrong word for reviews that stretched ticket line-ups blocks long. Marrs did a good job on the publicity. Even that chain of newspapers that afterward turned on us so viciously fell for Marrs' word wizardry and ran full-page editorials urging the reader to see "Rome."

With our third picture, "Flame Over France," we corrected a few misconceptions about the French Revolution, and began stepping on a few tender toes. Luckily, however, and not altogether by design, there happened to be in power in Paris a liberal government. They backed us to the hilt with the confirmation we needed. At our request they released a lot of documents that had hitherto conveniently been lost in the cavernous recesses of the Bibliotheque Nationale. I've forgotten the name of whoever happened to be the perennial pretender to the French throne. At, I'm sure, the subtle prodding of one of Marrs' ubiquitous publicity men, the pretender sued us for our whole net, alleging the defamation of the good name of the Bourbons. A lawyer Johnson dug up for us sucked the poor chump into a courtroom and cut him to bits. Not even six cents damages did he get. Samuels, the lawyer, and Marrs drew a good-sized bonus, and the pretender moved to Honduras.

Somewhere around this point, I believe, did the tone of the press begin to change. Up until then we'd been regarded as crosses between Shakespeare and Barnum. Since long obscure facts had been dredged into the light, a few well-known pessimists began to wonder *sotto voce* if we weren't just a pair of blasted pests. "Should leave well enough alone." Only our huge advertising budget kept them from saying more.

I'm going to stop right here and say something about our personal life while all this was going on. Mike I've kept in the background pretty well, mostly because he wants it that way. He lets me do all the talking and stick my neck out while he sits in the most comfortable chair in sight. I yell and I argue and he just sits there; hardly ever a word coming out of that dark-brown pan, certainly never an indication showing that behind those polite eyebrows there's a brain—and a sense of humor and wit—faster and as deadly as a bear trap. Oh, I know we've played around, sometimes with a loud bang, but we've been, ordinarily, too busy and too preoccupied with what we were doing to waste any time. Ruth, while she was with us, was a good dancing and drinking partner. She was young, she was almost what you'd call beautiful, and she seemed to like being with us. For a while I had a few ideas about her that might have developed into something serious. We both—I should say, all three of us—found out in time that we looked at a lot of things too differently. So we weren't too disappointed when she signed with Metro. Her contract meant what she thought was all the fame and money and happiness in the world, plus the personal attention she was doubtless entitled to have. They put her in Class B's and serials and she, financially, is better off than she ever expected to be. Emotionally, I don't know. We heard from her sometime ago, and I think she's about due for another divorce. Maybe it's just as well.

But let's get away from Ruth. I'm ahead of myself, anyway. All this time Mike and I had been working together, our approach to the final payoff had been divergent. Mike was hopped on the idea of making a better world, and doing that by making war impossible. "War," he's often said, "war of any kind is what has made man spend most of his history in merely staying alive. Now, with the atom to use, he has within himself the seed of self-extermination. So help me, Ed, I'm going to do my share of stopping that, or I don't see any point in living. I mean it!"

He did mean it. He told me that in almost the same words the first day we met. Then I tagged that idea as a pipe dream picked up on an empty stomach. I saw his machine only as a path to luxurious and personal Nirvana, and I thought he'd soon be going my way. I was wrong.

You can't live, or work, with a likable person without admiring some of the qualities that make that person likable. Another thing; it's a lot easier to worry about the woes of the world when you haven't any yourself. It's a lot easier to have a conscience when you can afford it. When I donned the rose-colored glasses half my battle was won; when I realized how grand a world this *could* be, the battle was over. That was about the time of "Flame Over France," I think. The actual time isn't important. What *is* important is that, from that time on, we became the tightest team possible. Since then the only thing we've differed on would be the time to knock off for a sandwich. Most of our leisure time, what we had of it, has been spent in locking up for the night, rolling out the portable bar, opening just enough beer to feel good, and relaxing. Maybe, after one or two, we might diddle the dials of the machine, and go rambling.

Together we've been everywhere and seen anything. It might be a good night to check up on François Villon, the faker, or maybe we might chase around with Haroun-el-Rashid. (If there was ever a man born a few hundred years too soon, it was that careless caliph.) Or if we were in a bad or discouraged mood we might follow the Thirty Years' War for a while, or if we were real raffish we might inspect the dressing rooms at Radio City. For Mike the crackup of Atlantis has always had an odd fascination, probably because he's afraid that man will do it again, now that he's rediscovered nuclear energy. And if I doze off he's quite apt to go back to the very Beginning, back to the start of the world as we know it now. (It wouldn't do any good to tell you what went before that.)

When I stop to think, it's probably just as well that neither of us married. We, of course, have hopes for the future, but at present we're both tired of the whole human race; tired of greedy faces and hands. With a world that puts a premium on wealth and power and strength, it's no wonder what decency there is stems from fear of what's here now, or fear of what's hereafter. We've seen so much of the hidden actions of the world—call it snooping, if you like—that we've learned to disregard the surface indications of kindness and good. Only once did Mike and I ever look into the private life of someone we knew and liked and respected. Once was enough. From that day on we made it a point to take people as they seemed. Let's get away from that.

The next two pictures we released in rapid succession; the first, "Freedom for Americans," the American Revolution, and "The Brothers and the Guns," the American Civil War. Bang! Every third politician, a lot of so-called "educators," and all the professional patriots started after our scalps. Every single chapter of the DAR, the Sons of Union Veterans, and the Daughters of the Confederacy pounded their collective heads against the wall. The South went frantic; every state in the Deep South and one state on the border flatly banned both pictures, the second because it was truthful, and the first because censorship is a contagious disease. They stayed banned until the professional politicians got wise. The bans were revoked, and the choke-collar and string-tie brigade pointed to both pictures as horrible examples of what some people actually believed and thought, and felt pleased that someone had given them an opportunity to roll out the barrel and beat the drums that sound sectional and racial hatred.

New England was tempted to stand on its dignity, but couldn't stand the strain. North of New York both pictures were banned. In New York state the rural representatives voted en bloc, and the ban was clamped on statewide. Special trains ran to Delaware, where the corporations were too busy to pass another law. Libel suits flew like spaghetti, and although the extras blared the filing of each new suit, very few knew that we lost not one. Although we had to appeal almost every suit to higher courts, and in some cases request a change of venue which was seldom granted, the documentary proof furnished by the record cleared us once we got to a judge, or series of judges, with no fences to mend.

It was a mighty rasp we drew over wounded ancestral pride. We had shown that not all the mighty had haloes of purest gold, that not all the Redcoats were strutting bullies—nor angels, and the British Empire, except South Africa, refused entry to both pictures and made violent passes at the State Department. The spectacle of Southern and New England congressmen approving the efforts of a foreign ambassador to suppress free speech drew hilarious hosannas from certain quarters. H. L. Mencken gloated in the clover, doing loud nip-ups, and the newspapers hung on the triple-horned dilemma of anti-foreign, pro-patriotic, and quasi-logical criticism. In Detroit the Ku Klux Klan fired an anemic cross on our doorstep, and the Friendly Sons of St. Patrick, the NAACP, and the WCTU passed flattering resolutions. We forwarded the most vicious and obscene letters—together with a few names and addresses that hadn't been originally signed—to our lawyers and the Post Office Department. There were no convictions south of Illinois.

Johnson and his boys made hay. Johnson had pyramided his bets into an international distributing organization, and pushed Marrs into hiring every top press agent either side of the Rockies. What a job they did! In no time at all there were two definite schools of thought that overflowed into the public letter boxes. One school held that we had no business raking up old mud to throw, that such things were better left forgotten and forgiven, that nothing wrong had ever happened, and if it had, we were liars anyway. The other school reasoned more to our liking. Softly and slowly at first, then with a triumphant shout, this fact began to emerge; such things had actually happened, and could happen again, were possibly happening even now; had happened because twisted truth had too long left its imprint on international, sectional, and racial feelings. It pleased us when many began to agree, with us, that it is important to forget the past, but that it is even more important to understand and evaluate it with a generous and unjaundiced eye. That was what we were trying to bring out.

The banning that occurred in the various states hurt the gross receipts only a little, and we were vindicated in Johnson's mind. He had dolefully predicted loss of half the national gross because "you can't tell the truth in a movie and get away with it. Not if the house holds over three hundred." Not even on the stage? "Who goes to anything but a movie?"

So far things had gone just about as we'd planned. We'd earned and received more publicity, favorable and otherwise, than anyone living. Most of it stemmed from the fact that our doing had been newsworthy. Some, naturally, had been the ninety-day-wonder material that fills a thirsty newspaper. We had been very careful to make our enemies in the strata that can afford to fight back. Remember the old saw about knowing a man by the enemies he makes? Well, publicity was our ax. Here's how we put an edge on it.

I called Johnson in Hollywood. He was glad to hear from us. "Long time no see. What's the pitch, Ed?"

"I want some lip readers. And I want them yesterday, like you tell your boys."

"Lip readers? Are you nuts? What do you want with lip readers?"

"Never mind why. I want lip readers. Can you get them?"

"How should I know? What do you want them for?"

"I said, can you get them?"

He was doubtful. "I think you've been working too hard."

"Look—"

"Now, I didn't say I couldn't. Cool off. When do you want them? And how many?"

"Better write this down. Ready? I want lip readers for these languages: English, French, German, Russian, Chinese, Japanese, Greek, Belgian, Dutch and Spanish."

"Ed Lefko, have you gone crazy?"

I guess it didn't sound very sensible, at that. "Maybe I have. But those languages are essential. If you run across any who can work in any other language, hang on to them. I might need them, too." I could see him sitting in front of his telephone, wagging his head like mad. Crazy. The heat must have got Lefko, good old Ed. "Did you hear what I said?"

"Yes, I heard you. If this is a rib—"

"No rib. Dead serious."

He began to get mad. "Where you think I'm going to get lip readers, out of my hat?"

"That's your worry. I'd suggest you start with the local School for the Deaf." He was silent. "Now, get this into your head; this isn't a rib, this is the real thing. I don't care what you do, or where you go, or what you spend—I want those lip readers in Hollywood when we get there or I want to know they're on the way."

"When are you going to get here?"

I said I wasn't sure. "Probably a day or two. We've got a few loose ends to clean up."

He swore a blue streak at the iniquities of fate. "You'd better have a good story when you do—" I hung up.

Mike met me at the studio. "Talk to Johnson?" I told him, and he laughed. "Does sound crazy, I suppose. But he'll get them, if they exist and like money. He's the Original Resourceful Man."

I tossed my hat in a corner. "I'm glad this is about over. Your end caught up?"

"Set and ready to go. The films and the notes are on the way, the real estate company is ready to take over the lease, and the girls are paid up to date, with a little extra."

I opened a bottle of beer for myself. Mike had one. "How about the office files? How about the bar, here?"

"The files go to the bank to be stored. The bar? Hadn't thought about it."

The beer was cold. "Have it crated and send it to Johnson."

We grinned, together. "Johnson it is. He'll need it."

I nodded at the machine. "What about that?"

"That goes with us on the plane as air express." He looked closely at me. "What's the matter with you—jitters?"

"Nope. Willies. Same thing."

"Me, too. Your clothes and mine left this morning."

"Not even a clean shirt left?"

"Not even a clean shirt. Just like—"

I finished it. "—the first trip with Ruth. A little different, maybe."

Mike said slowly, "A lot different." I opened another beer. "Anything you want around here, anything else to be done?" I said no. "O.K. Let's get this over with. We'll put what we need in the car. We'll stop at the Courville Bar before we hit the airport."

I didn't get it. "There's still beer left—"

"But no champagne."

I got it. "O.K. I'm dumb, at times. Let's go."

We loaded the machine into the car, and the bar, left the studio keys at the corner grocery for the real estate company, and headed for the airport by way of the Courville Bar. Ruth was in California, but Joe had champagne. We got to the airport late.

Marrs met us in Los Angeles. "What's up? You've got Johnson running around in circles."

"Did he tell you why?"

"Sounds crazy to me. Couple of reporters inside. Got anything for them?"

"Not right now. Let's get going."

In Johnson's private office we got a chilly reception. "This better be good. Where do you expect to find someone to lipread in Chinese? Or Russian, for that matter?"

We all sat down. "What have you got so far?"

"Besides a headache?" He handed me a short list.

I scanned it. "How long before you can get them here?"

An explosion. "How long before I can get them here? Am I your errand boy?"

"For all practical purposes you are. Quit the fooling. How about it?" Marrs snickered at the look on Johnson's face.

"What are you smirking at, you moron?" Marrs gave in and laughed outright, and I did, too. "Go ahead and laugh. This isn't funny. When I called the State School for the Deaf they hung up. Thought I was some practical joker. We'll skip that.

"There's three women and a man on that list. They cover English, French, Spanish, and German. Two of them are working in the East, and I'm waiting for answers to telegrams I sent them. One lives in Pomona and one works for the Arizona School for the Deaf. That's the best I could do."

We thought that over. "Get on the phone. Talk to every state in the union if you have to, or overseas."

Johnson kicked the desk. "And what are you going to do with them, if I'm that lucky?"

"You'll find out. Get them on planes and fly them here, and we'll talk turkey when they get here. I want a projection room, not yours, and a good bonded court reporter."

He asked the world to appreciate what a life he led.

"Get in touch with us at the Commodore." To Marrs: "Keep the reporters away for a while. We'll have something for them later." Then we left.

Johnson never did find anyone who could lipread Greek. None, at least, that could speak English. The expert on Russian he dug out of Ambridge, in Pennsylvania, the Flemish and Holland Dutch expert came from Leyden, in the Netherlands, and at the last minute he stumbled upon a Korean who worked in Seattle as an inspector for the Chinese Government. Five women and two men. We signed them to an ironclad contract drawn by Samuels, who now handled all our legal work. I made a little speech before they signed.

"These contracts, as far as we've been able to make sure, are going to control your personal and business life for the next year, and there's a clause that says we can extend that period for another year if we so desire. Let's get this straight. You are to live in a place of your own, which we will provide. You will be supplied with all necessities by our buyers. Any attempt at unauthorized communication will result in abrogation of the contract. Is that clear?

"Good. Your work will not be difficult, but it will be tremendously important. You will, very likely, be finished in three months, but you will be ready to go any place at any time at our discretion, naturally at our expense. Mr. Sorenson, as you are taking this down, you realize that this goes for you, too." He nodded.

"Your references, your abilities, and your past work have been thoroughly checked, and you will continue under constant observation. You will be required to verify and notarize every page, perhaps every line, of your transcripts, which Mr. Sorenson here will supply. Any questions?"

No questions. Each was getting a fabulous salary, and each wanted to appear eager to earn it. They all signed.

Resourceful Johnson bought for us a small rooming house, and we paid an exorbitant price to a detective agency to do the cooking and cleaning and chauffering required. We requested that the lipreaders refrain from discussing their work among themselves, especially in front of the house employees, and they followed instructions very well.

One day, about a month later, we called a conference in the projection room of Johnson's laboratory. We had a single reel of film.

"What's that for?"

"That's the reason for all the cloak-and-dagger secrecy. Never mind calling your projection man. This I'm going to run through myself. See what you think of it."

They were all disgusted. "I'm getting tired of all this kid stuff," said Kessler.

As I started for the projection booth I heard Mike say, "You're no more tired of it than I am."

From the booth I could see what was showing on the downstairs screen, but nothing else. I ran through the reel, rewound, and went back down.

I said, "One more thing, before we go any further read this. It's a certified and notarized transcript of what has been read from the lips of the characters you just saw. They weren't, incidentally, 'characters,' in that sense of the word." I handed the crackling sheets around, a copy for each. "Those 'characters' are real people. You've just seen a newsreel. This transcript will tell you what they were talking about. Read it. In the trunk of the car Mike and I have something to show you. We'll be back by the time you've read it."

Mike helped me carry in the machine from the car. We came in the door in time to see Kessler throw the transcript as far as he could. He bounced to his feet as the sheets fluttered down.

He was furious. "What's going on here?" We paid no attention to him, nor to the excited demands of the others until the machine had been plugged into the nearest outlet.

Mike looked at me. "Any ideas?"

I shook my head and told Johnson to shut up for a minute. Mike lifted the lid and hesitated momentarily before he touched the dials. I pushed Johnson into his chair and turned off the lights myself. The room went black. Johnson, looking over my shoulder, gasped. I heard Bernstein swear softly, amazed.

I turned to see what Mike had shown them.

It was impressive, all right. He had started just over the roof of the laboratory and continued straight up in the air. Up, up, up, until the city of Los Angeles was a tiny dot on a great ball. On the horizon were the Rockies. Johnson grabbed my arm. He hurt.

"What's that? What's that? Stop it!" He was yelling. Mike turned off the machine.

You can guess what happened next. No one believed their eyes, nor Mike's patient explanation. He had to twice turn on the machine again, once going far back into Kessler's past. Then the reaction set in.

Marrs smoked one cigarette after another, Bernstein turned a gold pencil over and over in his nervous fingers, Johnson paced like a caged tiger, and burly Kessler stared at the machine, saying nothing at all. Johnson was muttering as he paced. Then he stopped and shook his fist under Mike's nose.

"Man! Do you know what you've got there? Why waste time playing around here? Can't you see you've got the world by the tail on a down-hill pull? If I'd ever known this—"

Mike appealed to me. "Ed, talk to this wildman."

I did. I can't remember exactly what I said, and it isn't important. But I did tell him how we'd started, how we'd plotted our course, and what we were going to do. I ended by telling him the idea behind the reel of film I'd run off a minute before.

He recoiled as though I were a snake. "You can't get away with that! You'd be hung—if you weren't lynched first!"

"Don't you think we know that? Don't you think we're willing to take that chance?"

He tore his thinning hair. Marrs broke in. "Let me talk to him." He came over and faced us squarely.

"Is this on the level? You going to make a picture like that and stick your neck out? You're going to turn that . . . that thing over to the people of the world?"

I nodded. "Just that."

"And toss over everything you've got?" He was dead serious, and so was I. He turned to the others. "He means it!"

Bernstein said, "Can't be done!"

Words flew. I tried to convince them that we had followed the only possible path. "What kind of a world do you want to live in? Or don't you want to live?"

Johnson grunted. "How long do you think we'd live if we ever made a picture like that? You're crazy! I'm not. I'm not going to put my head in a noose."

"Why do you think we've been so insistent about credit and responsi-bility for direction and production? You'll be doing only what we hired you for. Not that we want to twist your arm, but you've made a fortune, all of you, working for us. Now, when the going gets heavy, you want to back out!"

Marrs gave in. "Maybe you're right, maybe you're wrong. Maybe you're crazy, maybe I am. I always used to say I'd try anything once. Bernie, you?"

Bernstein was quietly cynical. "You saw what happened in the last war. This might help. I don't know if it will. I don't know—but I'd hate to think I didn't try. Count me in!"

Kessler?

He swiveled his head. "Kid stuff! Who wants to live forever? Who wants to let a chance go by?"

Johnson threw up his hands. "Let's hope we get a cell together. Let's all go crazy." And that was that.

We went to work in a blazing drive of mutual hope and understanding. In four months the lipreaders were through. There's no point in detailing here their reactions to the dynamite they daily dictated to Sorenson. For their own good we kept them in the dark about our final purpose, and when they were through we sent them across the border into Mexico, to a small ranch Johnson had leased. We were going to need them later.

While the print duplicators worked overtime Marrs worked harder. The press and the radio shouted the announcement that, in every city of the world we could reach, there would be held the simultaneous premieres of our latest picture. It would be the last we needed to make. Many wondered aloud at our choice of the word "needed." We whetted curiosity by refusing any advance information about the plot, and Johnson so well infused the men with their own now-fervent enthusiasm that not much could be pried out of them but conjecture. The day we picked for release was Sunday. Monday, the storm broke.

I wonder how many prints of that picture are left today. I wonder how many escaped burning or confiscation. Two World Wars we covered, covered from the unflattering angles that, up until then, had been represented by only a few books hidden in the dark corners of libraries. We showed and *named* the war-makers, the cynical ones who signed and laughed and lied, the blatant patriots who used the flare of headlines and the ugliness of atrocity to hide behind their flag while life turned to death for millions. Our own and foreign traitors were there, the hidden ones with Janus faces. Our lipreaders had done their work well; no guesses these, no deduced conjectures from the broken records of a blasted past, but the exact words that exposed treachery disguised as patriotism.

In foreign lands the performances lasted barely the day. Usually, in retaliation for the imposed censorship, the theaters were wrecked by the raging crowds. (Marrs, incidentally, had spent hundreds of thousands bribing officials to allow the picture to be shown without previous censorship. Many censors, when that came out, were shot without trial.) In the Balkans, revolutions broke out, and various embassies were stormed by mobs. Where the film was banned or destroyed written versions spontaneously appeared on the streets or in coffeehouses. Bootlegged editions were smuggled past customs guards, who looked the other way. One royal family fled to Switzerland.

Here in America it was a racing two weeks before the Federal Government, prodded into action by the raging of press and radio, in an unprecedented move closed all performances "to promote the common welfare, insure domestic tranquillity, and preserve foreign relations." Murmurs—and one riot—rumbled in the Midwest and spread until it was realized by the powers that be that something had to be done, and done quickly, if every government in the world were not to collapse of its own weight.

We were in Mexico, at the ranch Johnson had rented for the lipreaders. While Johnson paced the floor, jerkily fraying a cigar, we listened to a special broadcast of the attorney general himself:

". . . furthermore, this message was today forwarded to the Government of the United States of Mexico. I read: 'the Government of the United States of America requests the immediate arrest and extradition of the following:

" 'Edward Joseph Lefkowicz, known as Lefko.' " First on the list. Even a fish wouldn't get into trouble if he kept his mouth shut.

" 'Miguel Jose Zapata Laviada.' " Mike crossed one leg over the other.

" 'Edward Lee Johnson.' " He threw his cigar on the floor and sank into a chair.

" 'Robert Chester Marrs.' " He lit another cigarette. His face twitched.

" 'Benjamin Lionel Bernstein.' " He smiled a twisted smile and closed his eyes.

" 'Carl Wilhelm Kessler.' " A snarl.

"These men are wanted by the Government of the United States of America, to stand trial on charges ranging from criminal syndicalism, incitement to riot, suspicion of treason—"

I clicked off the radio. "Well?", to no one in particular.

Bernstein opened his eyes. "The rurales are probably on their way. Might as well go back and face the music—" We crossed the border at Juarez. The FBI was waiting.

Every press and radio chain in the world must have had coverage at that trial, every radio system, even the new and imperfect television chain. We were allowed to see no one but our lawyer. Samuels flew from the West Coast and spent a week trying to get past our guards. He told us not to talk to reporters, if we ever saw them.

"You haven't seen the newspapers? Just as well— How did you ever get yourselves into this mess, anyway? You ought to know better."

I told him.

He was stunned. "Are you all crazy?"

He was hard to convince. Only the united effort and concerted stories of all of us made him believe that there was such a machine in existence. (He talked to us separately, because we were kept isolated.) When he got back to me he was unable to think coherently.

"What kind of defense do you call that?"

I shook my head. "No. That is, we know that we're guilty of practically everything under the sun if you look at it one way. If you look at it another—"

He rose. "Man, you don't need a lawyer, you need a doctor. I'll see you later. I've got to get this figured out in my mind before I can do a thing."

"Sit down. What do you think of this?" and I outlined what I had in mind.

"I think . . . I don't know what I think. I don't know. I'll talk to you later. Right now I want some fresh air," and he left.

As most trials do, this one began with the usual blackening of the defendant's character, or lack of it. (The men we'd blackmailed at the beginning had long since had their money returned, and they had sense enough to keep quiet. That might have been because they'd received a few hints that there might still be a negative or two lying around. Compounding a felony? Sure.) With the greatest of interest we sat in that great columned hall and listened to a sad tale.

We had, with malice aforethought, libeled beyond repair great and unselfish men who had made a career of devotion to the public weal, imperiled needlessly relations traditionally friendly by falsely reporting mythical events, mocked the courageous sacrifices of those who had *dulce et gloria mori*, and completely upset everyone's peace of mind. Every new accusation, every verbal lance drew solemn agreement from the dignitary-packed hall. Against someone's better judgment, the trial had been transferred from the regular courtroom to the Hall of Justice. Packed with influence, brass, and pompous legates from all over the world, only the congressmen from the biggest states, or with the biggest votes were able to crowd the newly installed seats. So you can see it was a hostile audience that faced Samuels when the defense had its say. We had spent the previous night together in the guarded suite to which we had been transferred for the duration of the trial, perfecting, as far as we could, our planned defense. Samuels has the arrogant sense of humor that usually goes with supreme self-confidence, and I'm sure he enjoyed standing there among all those bemedaled and bejowled bigwigs, knowing the bombshell he was going to hurl. He made a good grenadier. Like this:

"We believe there is only one defense possible, we believe there is only one defense necessary. We have gladly waived, without prejudice, our inalienable right of trial by jury. We shall speak plainly and bluntly, to the point.

"You have seen the picture in question. You have remarked, possibly, upon what has been called the startling resemblance of the actors in that picture to the characters named and portrayed. You have remarked, possibly, upon the apparent verisimilitude to reality. That I will mention again. The first witness will, I believe, establish the trend of our rebuttal of the allegations of the prosecution." He called the first witness.

"Your name, please?"

"Mercedes Maria Gomez."

"A little louder, please."

"Mercedes Maria Gomez."

"Your occupation?"

"Until last March I was a teacher at the Arizona School for the Deaf. Then I asked for and obtained a leave of absence. At present I am under personal contract to Mr. Lefko."

"If you see Mr. Lefko in this courtroom, Miss . . . Mrs.—"

"Miss."

"Thank you. If Mr. Lefko is in this court will you point him out? Thank you. Will you tell us the extent of your duties at the Arizona School?"

"I taught children born totally deaf to speak. And to read lips."

"You read lips yourself, Miss Gomez?"

"I have been totally deaf since I was fifteen."

"In English only?"

"English and Spanish. We have . . . had many children of Mexican descent."

Samuels asked for a designated Spanish-speaking interpreter. An officer in the back immediately volunteered. He was identified by his ambassador, who was present.

"Will you take this book to the rear of the courtroom, sir?" To the Court: "If the prosecution wishes to examine that book, they will find that it is a Spanish edition of the Bible." The prosecution didn't wish to examine it.

"Will the officer open the Bible at random and read aloud?" He opened the Bible at the center and read. In dead silence the Court strained to hear. Nothing could be heard the length of that enormous hall.

Samuels: "Miss Gomez. Will you take these binoculars and repeat, to the Court, just what the officer is reading at the other end of the room?"

She took the binoculars and focused them expertly on the officer, who had stopped reading and was watching alertly. "I am ready."

Samuels: "Will you please read, sir?"

He did, and the Gomez woman repeated aloud, quickly and easily, a section that sounded as though it might be anything at all. I can't speak Spanish. The officer continued to read for a minute or two.

Samuels: "Thank you, sir. And thank you, Miss Gomez. Your pardon, sir, but since there are several who have been known to memorize the Bible, will you tell the Court if you have anything on your person that is written, anything that Miss Gomez has had no chance of viewing?" Yes, the officer had. "Will you read that as before? Will you, Miss Gomez—"

She read that, too. Then the officer came to the front to listen to the court reporter read Miss Gomez' words.

"That's what I read," he affirmed.

Samuels turned her over to the prosecution, who made more experiments that served only to convince that she was equally good as an interpreter and lipreader in either language.

In rapid succession Samuels put the rest of the lipreaders on the stand. In rapid succession they proved themselves as able and as capable as Miss Gomez, in their own linguistic specialty. The Russian from Ambridge generously offered to translate into his broken English any other Slavic language handy, and drew scattered grins from the press box. The Court was convinced, but failed to see the purpose of the exhibition. Samuels, glowing with satisfaction and confidence, faced the Court.

"Thanks to the indulgence of the Court, and despite the efforts of the distinguished prosecution, we have proved the almost amazing accuracy of lipreading in general, and these lipreaders in particular." One Justice absently nodded in agreement. "Therefore, our defense will be based on that premise, and on one other which we have had until now found necessary to keep hidden—the picture in question was and is definitely not a fictional representation of events of questionable authenticity. Every scene in that film contained, not polished professional actors, but the original person named and portrayed. Every foot, every inch of film was not the result of an elaborate studio reconstruction but an actual collection of pictures, an actual collection of newsreels—if they can be called that—edited and assembled in story form!"

Through the startled spurt of astonishment we heard one of the prosecution: "That's ridiculous! No newsreel—"

Samuels ignored the objections and the tumult to put me on the stand. Beyond the usual preliminary questions I was allowed to say things my own way. At first hostile, the Court became interested enough to overrule the repeated objections that flew from the table devoted to the prosecution. I felt that at least two of the Court, if not outright favorable, were friendly. As far as I can remember, I went over the maneuvers of the past years, and ended something like this:

"As to why we arranged the cards to fall as they did; both Mr. Laviada and myself were unable to face the prospect of destroying his discovery, because of the inevitable penalizing of needed research. We were, and we are, unwilling to better ourselves or a limited group by the use and maintenance of secrecy, if secrecy were possible. As to the only other alternative," and I directed this straight at Judge Bronson, the well-known liberal on the bench, "since the last war all atomic research and activity has been under the direction of a Board nominally civilian, but actually under the 'protection and direction' of the Army and Navy. This 'direction and protection,' as any competent physicist will gladly attest, has proved to be nothing but a smothering blanket serving to conceal hidebound antiquated reasoning, abysmal ignorance, and inestimable amounts of fumbling. As of right now, this country, or any country that was foolish enough to place any confidence in the rigid regime of the military mind, is years behind what would otherwise be the natural course of discovery and progress in nuclear and related fields.

"We were, and we are, firmly convinced that even the slightest hint of the inherent possibilities and scope of Mr. Laviada's discovery would have meant, under the present regime, instant and mandatory confiscation of even a supposedly secure patent. Mr. Laviada has never applied for a patent, and never will. We both feel that such a discovery belongs not to an individual, a group, a corporation, or even to a nation, but to the world and those who live in it.

"We know, and are eager and willing to prove, that the domestic and external affairs of not only this nation, but of every nation are influenced, sometimes controlled, by esoteric groups warping political theories and human lives to suit their own ends." The Court was smothered in sullen silence, thick and acid with hate and disbelief.

"Secret treaties, for example, and vicious, lying propaganda have too long controlled human passions and made men hate; honored thieves have too long rotted secretly in undeserved high places. The machine can make treachery and untruth impossible. It *must,* if atomic war is not to sear the face and fate of the world.

"Our pictures were all made with that end in view. We needed, first, the wealth and prominence to present to an international audience what we knew to be the truth. We have done as much as we can. From now on, this Court takes over the burden we have carried. We are guilty of no treachery, guilty of no deceit, guilty of nothing but deep and true humanity. Mr. Laviada wishes me to tell the Court and the world that he has been unable till now to give his discovery to the world, free to use as it wills."

The Court stared at me. Every foreign representative was on the edge of his seat waiting for the Justices to order us shot without further ado, the sparkling uniforms were seething, and the pressmen were racing their pencils against time. The tension dried my throat. The speech that Samuels and I had rehearsed the previous night was strong medicine. Now what?

Samuels filled the breach smoothly. "If the Court pleases; Mr. Lefko has made some startling statements. Startling, but certainly sincere, and certainly either provable or disprovable. And proof it shall be!"

He strode to the door of the conference room that had been allotted us. As the hundreds of eyes followed him it was easy for me to slip down from the witness stand, and wait, ready. From the conference room Samuels rolled the machine, and Mike rose. The whispers that curdled the air seemed disappointed, unimpressed. Right in front of the Bench he trundled it.

He moved unobtrusively to one side as the television men trained their long-snouted cameras. "Mr. Laviada and Mr. Lefko will show you . . . I trust there will be no objection from the prosecution?" He was daring them.

One of the prosecution was already on his feet. He opened his mouth hesitantly, but thought better, and sat down. Heads went together in conference as he did. Samuels was watching the Court with one eye, and the courtroom with the other.

"If the Court pleases, we will need a cleared space. If the bailiff will . . . thank you, sir." The long tables were moved back, with a raw scraping. He stood there, with every eye in the courtroom glued on him. For two long breaths he stood there, then he spun and went to his table. "Mr. Lefko," and he bowed formally. He sat.

The eyes swung to me, to Mike, as he moved to his machine and stood there silently. I cleared my throat and spoke to the Bench as though I did not see the directional microphones trained at my lips.

"Justice Bronson."

He looked steadily at me and then glanced at Mike. "Yes, Mr. Lefko?"

"Your freedom from bias is well known." The corners of his mouth went down as he frowned. "Will you be willing to be used as proof that there can be no trickery?" He thought that over, then nodded slowly. The prosecution objected, and was waved down. "Will you tell me exactly where you were at any given time? Any place where you are absolutely certain and can verify that there were no concealed cameras or observers?"

He thought. Seconds. Minutes. The tension twanged, and I swallowed dust. He spoke quietly. "1918. November 11th."

Mike whispered to me. I said, "Any particular time?"

Justice Bronson looked at Mike. "Exactly eleven. Armistice time." He paused, then went on. "Niagara Falls. Niagara Falls, New York."

I heard the dials tick in the stillness, and Mike whispered again. I said, "The lights should be off." The bailiff rose. "Will you please watch the left wall, or in that direction? I think that if Justice Kassel will turn a little . . . we are ready."

Bronson looked at me, and at the left wall. "Ready."

The lights flicked out overhead and I heard the television crews mutter. I touched Mike on the shoulder. "Show them, Mike!"

We're all showmen at heart, and Mike is no exception. Suddenly out of nowhere and into the depths poured a frozen torrent. Niagara Falls. I've mentioned, I think, that I've never got over my fear of heights. Few people ever do. I heard long, shuddery gasps as we started straight down. Down, until we stopped at the brink of the silent cataract, weird in its frozen majesty. Mike had stopped time at exactly eleven, I knew. He shifted to the American bank. Slowly he moved along. There were a few tourists standing in almost comic attitudes. There was snow on the ground, flakes in the air. Time stood still, and hearts slowed in sympathy.

Bronson snapped, "Stop!"

A couple, young. Long skirts, high-buttoned army collar, dragging army overcoat, facing, arms about each other. Mike's sleeve rustled in the darkness and they moved. She was sobbing and the soldier was smiling. She turned away her head, and he turned it back. Another couple seized them gayly, and they twirled breathlessly.

Bronson's voice was harsh. "That's enough!" The view blurred for seconds.

Washington. The White House. The President. Someone coughed like a small explosion. The President was watching a television screen. He jerked erect suddenly, startled. Mike spoke for the first time in court.

"That is the President of the United States. He is watching the trial that is being broadcast and televised from this courtroom. He is listening to what I am saying right now, and he is watching, in his television screen, as I use my machine to show him what he was doing one second ago."

The President heard those fateful words. Stiffly he threw an unconscious glance around his room at nothing and looked back at his screen in time to see himself do what he just had done, one second ago. Slowly, as if against his will, his hand started toward the switch of his set.

"Mr. President, don't turn off that set." Mike's voice was curt, almost rude. "You must hear this, you of all people in the world. You must understand!

"This is not what we wanted to do, but we have no recourse left but to appeal to you, and to the people of this twisted world." The President might have been cast in iron. "You must see, you must understand that you have in your hands the power to make it impossible for greed-born war to be bred in secrecy and rob man of his youth or his old age or whatever he prizes." His voice softened, pleaded. "That is all we have to say. That is all we want. That is all anyone could want, ever." The President, unmoving, faded into blackness. "The lights, please," and almost immediately the Court adjourned. That was over a month ago.

Mike's machine has been taken from us, and we are under military guard. Probably it's just as well we're guarded. We understand there have been lynching parties, broken up only as far as a block or two away. Last week we watched a white-haired fanatic scream about us, on the street below. We couldn't catch what he was shrieking, but we did catch a few air-borne epithets.

"Devils! Anti-Christs! Violation of the Bible! Violations of this and that!" Some, right here in the city, I suppose, would be glad to build a bonfire to cook us right back to the flames from which we've sprung. I wonder what the various religious groups are going to do now that the truth can be seen. Who can read lips in Aramaic, or Latin, or Coptic? And is a mechanical miracle a miracle?

This changes everything. We've been moved. Where, I don't know, except that the weather is warm, and we're on some type of military reservation, by the lack of civilians. Now we know what we're up against. What started out to be just a time-killing occupation, Joe, has turned out to be a necessary preface to what I'm going to ask you to do. Finish this, and then move fast! We won't be able to get this to you for a while yet, so I'll go on for a bit the way I started, to kill time. Like our clippings:
TABLOID:
. . . Such a weapon cannot, must not be loosed in unscrupulous hands. The last professional production of the infamous pair proves what distortions can be wrested from isolated and misunderstood events. In the hands of perpetrators of heretical isms, no property, no business deal, no personal life could be sacrosanct, no foreign policy could be . . .

TIMES:

... colonies stand with us firmly ... liquidation of the Empire ... white man's burden ...

LE MATIN:

... rightful place ... restore proud France ...

PRAVDA:

... democratic imperialist plot ... our glorious scientists ready to announce ...

NICHI-NICHI:

... incontrovertibly prove divine descent ...

LA PRENSA:

... oil concessions ... dollar diplomacy ...

DETROIT JOURNAL:

... under our noses in a sinister fortress on East Warren ... under close Federal supervision ... perfection by our production-trained technicians a mighty aid to law-enforcement agencies ... tirades against politicians and business common-sense carried too far ... tomorrow revelations by ...

L'OSSERVATORE ROMANO:

Council of Cardinals ... announcement expected hourly ...

JACKSON STAR-CLARION:

... proper handling will prove the fallacy of race equality ...

Almost unanimously the press screamed; Pegler frothed, Winchell leered. We got the surface side of the situation from the press. But a military guard is composed of individuals, hotel rooms must be swept by maids, waiters must serve food, and a chain is as strong— We got what we think the truth from those who work for a living.

There are meetings on street corners and homes, two great veterans' groups have arbitrarily fired their officials, seven governors have resigned, three senators and over a dozen representatives have retired with "ill health," and the general temper is ugly. International travelers report the same of Europe, Asia is bubbling, and transport planes with motors running stud the airports of South America. A general whisper is that a Constitutional Amendment is being rammed through to forbid the use of any similar instrument by any individual, with the manufacture and leasing by the Federal government to law-enforcement agencies or financially-responsible corporations suggested; it is whispered that motor caravans are forming throughout the country for a Washington march to demand a decision by the Court on the truth of our charges; it is generally suspected that all news disseminating services are under direct Federal—

Army—control; wires are supposed to be sizzling with petitions and demands to Congress, which are seldom delivered.

One day the chambermaid said: "And the whole hotel might as well close up shop. The whole floor is blocked off, there're MP's at every door, and they're clearing out all the other guests as fast as they can be moved. The whole place wouldn't be big enough to hold the letters and wires addressed to you, or the ones that are trying to get in to see you. Fat chance they have," she added grimly. "The joint is lousy with brass."

Mike glanced at me and I cleared my throat. "What's your idea of the whole thing?"

Expertly she spanked and reversed a pillow. "I saw your last picture before they shut it down. I saw all your pictures. When I wasn't working I listened to your trial. I heard you tell them off. I never got married because my boy friend never came back from Burma. Ask *him* what he thinks," and she jerked her head at the young private that was supposed to keep her from talking. "Ask him if he wants some bunch of stinkers to start him shooting at some other poor chump. See what he says, and then ask me if I want an atom bomb dropped down my neck just because some chiselers want more than they got." She left suddenly, and the soldier left with her. Mike and I had a beer and went to bed. Next week the papers had headlines a mile high.

U. S. KEEPS MIRACLE RAY

CONSTITUTION AMENDMENT

AWAITS STATES OKAY

LAVIADA-LEFKO FREED

We were freed all right, Bronson and the President being responsible for that. But the President and Bronson don't know, I'm sure, that we were rearrested immediately. We were told that we'll be held in "protective custody" until enough states have ratified the proposed constitutional amendment. The Man Without a Country was in what you might call "protective custody," too. We'll likely be released the same way he was.

We're allowed no newspapers, no radio, allowed no communication coming or going, and we're given no reason, as if that were necessary. They'll never, never let us go, and they'd be fools if they did. They think that if we can't communicate, or if we can't build another machine, our fangs are drawn, and when the excitement dies, we fall into oblivion, six feet of it. Well, we can't build another machine. But, communicate?

Look at it this way. A soldier is a soldier because he wants to serve his country. A soldier doesn't want to die unless his country is at war. Even then death is only a last resort. And war isn't necessary any more, not with our machine. In the dark? Try to plan or plot in absolute darkness, which is what would be needed. Try to plot or carry on a war without putting things in writing. O.K. Now—

The Army has Mike's machine. The Army has Mike. They call it military expediency, I suppose. Bosh! Anyone beyond the grade of moron can see that to keep that machine, to hide it, is to invite the world to attack, and attack in self-defense. If every nation, or if every man, had a machine, each would be equally open, or equally protected. But if only one nation, or only one man can see, the rest will not long be blind. Maybe we did this all wrong. God knows that we thought about it often. God knows we did our best to make an effort at keeping man out of his own trap.

There isn't much time left. One of the soldiers guarding us will get this to you, I hope, in time.

A long time ago we gave you a key, and hoped we would never have to ask you to use it. But now is the time. That key fits a box at the Detroit Savings Bank. In that box are letters. Mail them, not all at once, or in the same place. They'll go all over the world, to men we know, and have watched well; clever, honest, and capable of following the plans we've enclosed.

But you've got to hurry! One of these bright days someone is going to wonder if we've made more than one machine. We haven't, of course. That would have been foolish. But if some smart young lieutenant gets hold of that machine long enough to start tracing back our movements they'll find that safety deposit box, with the plans and letters ready to be scattered broadside. You can see the need for haste—if the rest of the world, or any particular nation, wants that machine bad enough, they'll fight for it. And they will! They must! Later on, when the Army gets used to the machine and its capabilities, it will become obvious to everyone, as it already has to Mike and me, that, with every plan open to inspection as soon as it's made, no nation or group of nations would have a chance in open warfare. So if there is to be an attack, it will have to be deadly, and fast, and sure. Please God that we haven't shoved the world into a war we tried to make impossible. With all the atom bombs and rockets that have been made in the past few years—*Joe, you've got to hurry!*

GHQ TO 9TH ATTK GRP

Report report report report report report report report report report

CMDR 9TH ATTK GRP TO GHQ

BEGINS: No other manuscript found. Searched body of Lefko immediately upon landing. According to plan Building Three untouched. Survivors insist both were moved from Building Seven previous day defective plumbing. Body of Laviada identified definitely through fingerprints. Request further instructions. ENDS

GHQ TO CMDR 32ND SHIELDED RGT

BEGINS: Seal area Detroit Savings Bank. Advise immediately condition safety deposit boxes. Afford coming technical unit complete co-operation. ENDS

LT. COL. TEMP. ATT. 32ND SHIELDED RGT

BEGINS: Area Detroit Savings Bank vaporized direct hit. Radioactivity lethal. Impossible boxes or any contents survive. Repeat, direct hit. Request permission proceed Washington Area. ENDS

GHQ. TO LT. COL. TEMP. ATT. 32ND SHIELDED RGT

BEGINS: Request denied. Sift ashes if necessary regardless cost. Repeat, regardless cost. ENDS

GHQ. TO ALL UNITS REPEAT ALL UNITS

BEGINS: Lack of enemy resistance explained misdirected atom rocket seventeen miles SSE Washington. Lone survivor completely destroyed special train claims all top officials left enemy capital two hours preceding attack. Notify local governments where found necessary and obvious cessation hostilities. Occupy present areas Plan Two. Further orders follow. ENDS

First published: 1947

CHILD'S PLAY

by William Tenn

AFTER THE MAN FROM THE EXPRESS COMPANY HAD GIVEN THE DOOR AN
untipped slam, Sam Weber decided to move the huge crate under the one
light bulb in his room. It was all very well for the messenger to drawl, "I
dunno. We don't send 'em; we just deliver 'em, mister"—but there must
be some mildly lucid explanation.

With a grunt that began as an anticipatory reflex and ended on a note
of surprised annoyance, Sam shoved the box forward the few feet necessary. It was heavy enough; he wondered how the messenger had carried
it up the three flights of stairs.

He straightened and frowned down at the garish card which contained
his name and address as well as the legend—"Merry Christmas, 2153."

A joke? He didn't know anyone who'd think it funny to send a card
dated over two hundred years in the future. Unless one of the comedians
in his law school graduating class meant to record his opinion as to when
Weber would be trying his first case. Even so—

The letters were shaped strangely, come to think of it, sort of green
streaks instead of lines. And the card was a sheet of gold!

Sam decided he was really interested. He ripped the card aside, tore
off the flimsy wrapping material—and stopped. He whistled. Then he
gulped.

"Well clip my ears and call me streamlined!"

There was no top to the box, no slit in its side, no handle anywhere
in sight. It seemed to be a solid, cubical mass of brown stuff. Yet he was
positive something had rattled inside when it was moved.

He seized the corners and strained and grunted till it lifted. The underside was as smooth and innocent of opening as the rest. He let it thump
back to the floor.

"Ah, well," he said, philosophically, "it's not the gift; it's the principle
involved."

326

Many of his gifts still required appreciative notes. He'd have to work up something special for Aunt Maggie. Her neckties were things of cubistic horror, but he hadn't even sent her a lone handkerchief this Christmas. Every cent had gone into buying that brooch for Tina. Not quite a ring, but maybe she'd consider that under the circumstances—

He turned to walk to his bed which he had drafted into the additional service of desk and chair. He kicked at the great box disconsolately. "Well, if you won't open, you won't open."

As if smarting under the kick, the box opened. A cut appeared on the upper surface, widened rapidly and folded the top back and down on either side like a valise. Sam clapped his forehead and addressed a rapid prayer to every god from Set to Father Divine. Then he remembered what he'd said.

"Close," he suggested.

The box closed, once more as smooth as a baby's anatomy.

"Open."

The box opened.

So much for the sideshow, Sam decided. He bent down and peered into the container.

The interior was a crazy mass of shelving on which rested vials filled with blue liquids, jars filled with red solids, transparent tubes showing yellow and green and orange and mauve and other colors which Sam's eyes didn't quite remember. There were seven pieces of intricate apparatus on the bottom which looked as if tube-happy radio hams had assembled them. There was also a book.

Sam picked the book off the bottom and noted numbly that while all its pages were metallic, it was lighter than any paper book he'd ever held.

He carried the book over to the bed and sat down. Then he took a long, deep breath and turned to the first page. "Gug," he said, exhaling his long, deep breath.

In mad, green streaks of letters:

Bild-A-Man Set #3. This set is intended solely for the uses of children between the ages of eleven and thirteen. The equipment, much more advanced than Bild-A-Man Sets 1 and 2, will enable the child of this age-group to build and assemble complete adult humans in perfect working order. The retarded child may also construct the babies and mannikins of the earlier kits. Two disassembleators are provided so that the set can be used again and again with profit. As with Sets 1 and 2, the aid of a Census Keeper in all disassembling is advised. Refills and additional parts may be acquired from The Bild-A-Man Company, 928

Diagonal Level, Glunt City, Ohio. Remember—only with a Bild-A-Man can you build a man!

Weber slammed his eyes shut. What was that gag in the movie he'd seen last night? Terrific gag. Terrific picture, too. Nice technicolor. Wonder how much the director made a week? The cameraman? Five hundred? A thousand?

He opened his eyes warily. The box was still a squat cube in the center of his room. The book was still in his shaking hand. And the page read the same.

"Only with a Bild-A-Man can you build a man!" Heaven help a neurotic young lawyer at a time like this!

There was a price list on the next page for "refills and additional parts." Things like one liter of hemoglobin and three grams of assorted enzymes were offered for sale in terms of one slunk fifty and three slunks forty-five. A note on the bottom advertised Set #4: "The thrill of building your first live Martian!"

Fine print announced *pat. pending* 2148.

The third page was a table of contents. Sam gripped the edge of the mattress with one sweating hand and read:

Chapter   I—A child's garden of biochemistry.
"   II—Making simple living things indoors and out.
"   III—Mannikins and what makes them do the world's work.
"   IV—Babies and other small humans.
"   V—Twins for every purpose, twinning yourself and your friends.
"   VI—What you need to build a man.
"   VII—Completing the man.
"   VIII—Disassembling the man.
          IX—New kinds of life for your leisure moments.

Sam dropped the book back into the box and ran for the mirror. His face was still the same, somewhat like bleached chalk, but fundamentally the same. He hadn't twinned or grown himself a mannikin or devised a new kind of life for his leisure moments. Everything was snug as a bug in a bughouse.

Very carefully he pushed his eyes back into their proper position in their sockets.

"Dear Aunt Maggie," he began writing feverishly. "Your ties made the most beautiful gift of my Christmas. My only regret is—"

My only regret is that I have but one life to give for my Christmas present. Who could have gone to such fantastic lengths for a practical joke? Lew Knight? Even Lew must have some reverence in his insensitive body for the institution of Christmas. And Lew didn't have the brains or the patience for a job so involved.

Tina? Tina had the fine talent for complication, all right. But Tina, while possessing a delightful abundance of all other physical attributes, was sadly lacking in funnybone.

Sam drew the leather envelope forth and caressed it. Tina's perfume seemed to cling to the surface and move the world back into focus.

The metallic greeting card glinted at him from the floor. Maybe the reverse side contained the sender's name. He picked it up, turned it over.

Nothing but blank gold surface. He was sure of the gold; his father had been a jeweler. The very value of the sheet was rebuttal to the possibility of a practical joke. Besides, again, what was the point?

"Merry Christmas, 2153." Where would humanity be in two hundred years? Traveling to the stars, or beyond—to unimaginable destinations? Using little mannikins to perform the work of machines and robots? Providing children with—

There might be another card or note inside the box. Weber bent down to remove its contents. His eye noted a large grayish jar and the label etched into its surface: *Dehydrated Neurone Preparation, for human construction only*.

He backed away and glared. "Close!"

The thing melted shut. Weber sighed his relief at it and decided to go to bed.

He regretted while undressing that he hadn't thought to ask the messenger the name of his firm. Knowing the delivery service involved would be useful in tracing the origin of this gruesome gift.

"But then," he repeated as he fell asleep, "it's not the gift—it's the principle! Merry Christmas, me."

The next morning when Lew Knight breezed in with his "Good morning, counselor," Sam waited for the first sly ribbing to start. Lew wasn't the man to hide his humor behind a bushel. But Lew buried his nose in "The New York State Supplement" and kept it there all morning. The other five young lawyers in the communal office appeared either too bored or too busy to have Bild-A-Man sets on their conscience. There were no sly grins, no covert glances, no leading questions.

Tina walked in at ten o'clock, looking like a pin-up girl caught with her clothes on.

"Good morning, counselors," she said.

Each in his own way, according to the peculiar gland secretions he was enjoying at the moment, beamed, drooled or nodded a reply. Lew Knight drooled. Sam Weber beamed.

Tina took it all in and analyzed the situation while she fluffed her hair about. Her conclusions evidently involved leaning markedly against Lew Knight's desk and asking what he had for her to do this morning.

Sam bit savagely into Hackleworth "On Torts." Theoretically, Tina was employed by all seven of them as secretary, switchboard operator and receptionist. Actually, the most faithful performance of her duties entailed nothing more daily than the typing and addressing of two envelopes with an occasional letter to be sealed inside. Once a week there might be a wistful little brief which was never to attain judicial scrutiny. Tina therefore had a fair library of fashion magazines in the first drawer of her desk and a complete cosmetics laboratory in the other two; she spent one third of her working day in the ladies' room swapping stocking prices and sources with other secretaries; she devoted the other two thirds religiously to that one of her employers who as of her arrival seemed to be in the most masculine mood. Her pay was small but her life was full.

Just before lunch, she approached casually with the morning's mail. "Didn't think we'd be too busy this morning, counselor—" she began.

"You thought incorrectly, Miss Hill," he informed her with a brisk irritation that he hoped became him well; "I've been waiting for you to terminate your social engagements so that we could get down to what occasionally passes for business."

She was as startled as an uncushioned kitten. "But—this isn't Monday. Somerset & Ojack only send you stuff on Mondays."

Sam winced at the reminder that if it weren't for the legal drudgework he received once a week from Somerset & Ojack he would be a lawyer in name only, if not in spirit only. "I have a letter, Miss Hill," he replied steadily. "Whenever you assemble the necessary materials, we can get on with it."

Tina returned in a head-shaking moment with stenographic pad and pencils.

"Regular heading, today's date," Sam began. "Address it to Chamber of Commerce, Glunt City, Ohio. Gentlemen: Would you inform me if you have registered currently with you a firm bearing the name of the Bild-A-Man Company or a firm with any name at all similar? I am also interested in whether a firm bearing the above or related name has recently made known its intention of joining your community. This inquiry is being made informally on behalf of a client who is interested in a product of this organization whose address he has mislaid. Signature and then this P.S.—My client is also curious as to the business possibilities of a street known as Diagonal Avenue or Diagonal Level. Any data on this address and the organizations presently located there will be greatly appreciated."

Tina batted wide blue eyes at him. "Oh, Sam," she breathed, ignoring the formality he had introduced, "Oh, Sam, you have another client. I'm so glad. He looked a little sinister, but in *such* a distinguished manner that I was certain—"

"Who? Who looked a little sinister?"

"Why your new cli-ent." Sam had the uncomfortable feeling that she had almost added "stu-pid." "When I came in this morning, there was this terribly tall old man in a long black overcoat talking to the elevator operator. He turned to me—the elevator operator, I mean—and said, 'This is Mr. Weber's secretary. She'll be able to tell you anything you want to know.' Then he sort of winked which I thought was sort of impolite, you know, considering. Then this old man looked at me hard and I felt distinctly uncomfortable and he walked away muttering, 'Either disjointed or predatory personalities. Never normal. Never balanced.' Which I didn't think was very polite, either, I'll have you know, if he *is* your new client!" She sat back and began breathing again.

Tall, sinister old men in long, black overcoats pumping the elevator operator about him. Hardly a matter of business. He had no skeletons in his personal closet. Could it be connected with his unusual Christmas present? Sam hmmmed mentally.

"—but she is my favorite aunt, you know," Tina was saying. "And she came in so unexpectedly."

The girl was explaining about their Christmas date. Sam felt a rush of affection for her as she leaned forward.

"Don't bother," he told her. "I knew you couldn't help breaking the date. I was a little sore when you called me, but I got over it; never-hold-a-grudge-against-a-pretty-girl-Sam, I'm known as. How about lunch?"

"Lunch?" She flew distress signals. "I promised Lew, Mr. Knight, that is— But he wouldn't mind if you came along."

"Fine. Let's go." This would be helping Lew to a spoonful of his own annoying medicine.

Lew Knight took the business of having a crowd instead of a party for lunch as badly as Sam hoped he would. Unfortunately, Lew was able to describe details of his forthcoming case, the probable fees and possible distinction to be reaped thereof. After one or two attempts to bring an interesting will he was rephrasing for Somerset & Ojack into the conversation, Sam subsided into daydreams. Lew immediately dropped Rosenthal vs. Rosenthal and leered at Tina conversationally.

Outside the restaurant, snow discolored into slush. Most of the stores were removing Christmas displays. Sam noticed construction sets for children, haloed by tinsel and glittering with artificial snow. Build a radio, a skyscraper, an airplane. But "Only with a Bild-A-Man can you—"

"I'm going home," he announced suddenly. "Something important I just remembered. If anything comes up, call me there."

He was leaving Lew a clear field, he told himself, as he found a seat on the subway. But the bitter truth was that the field was almost as clear when he was around as when he wasn't. Lupine Lew Knight, he had been called in Law School; since the day when he had noticed that Tina had the correct proportions of dress-filling substance, Sam's chances had been worth a crowbar at Fort Knox.

Tina hadn't been wearing his brooch today. Her little finger, right hand, however, had sported an unfamiliar and garish little ring. "Some got it," Sam philosophized. "Some don't got it. I don't got it."

But it would have been nice, with Tina, to have "got it."

As he unlocked the door of his room he was surprised by an unmade bed telling with rumpled stoicism of a chambermaid who'd never come. This hadn't happened before— Of course! He'd never locked his room before. The girl must have thought he wanted privacy.

Maybe he had.

Aunt Maggie's ties glittered obscenely at the foot of the bed. He chucked them into the closet as he removed his hat and coat. Then he went over to the washstand and washed his hands, slowly. He turned around.

This was it. At last the great cubical bulk that had been lurking quietly in the corner of his vision was squarely before him. It was there and it undoubtedly contained all the outlandish collection he remembered.

"Open," he said, and the box opened.

The book, still open to the metallic table of contents, was lying at the bottom of the box. Part of it had slipped into the chamber of a strange piece of apparatus. Sam picked both out gingerly.

He slipped the book out and noticed the apparatus consisted mostly of some sort of binoculars, supported by a coil and tube arrangement and bearing on a flat green plate. He turned it over. The underside was lettered in the same streaky way as the book. "Combination Electron Microscope and Workbench."

Very carefully he placed it on the floor. One by one, he removed the others, from the "Junior Biocalibrator" to the "Jiffy Vitalizer." Very respectfully he ranged against the box in five multi-colored rows the phials of lymph and the jars of basic cartilage. The walls of the chest were lined with indescribably thin and wrinkled sheets; a slight pressure along their edges expanded them into three-dimensional outlines of human organs whose shape and size could be varied with pinching any part of their surface—most indubitably molds.

Quite an assortment. If there was anything solidly scientific to it, that box might mean unimaginable wealth. Or some very useful publicity. Or —well, it should mean something!

If there was anything solidly scientific to it.

Sam flopped down to the bed and opened to "A Child's Garden Of Biochemistry."

At nine that night he squatted next to the Combination Electron Microscope and Workbench and began opening certain small bottles. At nine forty-seven Sam Weber made his first simple living thing.

It wasn't much, if you used the first chapter of Genesis as your standard. Just a primitive brown mold that, in the field of the microscope, fed diffidently on a piece of pretzel, put forth a few spores and died in about twenty minutes. But *he* had made it. He had constructed a specific lifeform to feed on the constituents of a specific pretzel; it could survive nowhere else.

He went out to supper with every intention of getting drunk. After just a little alcohol, however, the *deiish* feeling returned and he scurried back to his room.

Never again that evening did he recapture the exultation of the brown mold, though he constructed a giant protein molecule and a whole slew of filterable viruses.

He called the office in the little corner drugstore which was his breakfast nook. "I'll be home all day," he told Tina.

She was a little puzzled. So was Lew Knight who grabbed the phone. "Hey, counselor, you building up a neighborhood practice? Kid Blackstone is missing out on a lot of cases. Two ambulances have already clanged past the building."

"Yeah," said Sam. "I'll tell him when he comes in."

The week end was almost upon him, so he decided to take the next day off as well. He wouldn't have any real work till Monday when the Somerset & Ojack basket would produce his lone egg.

Before he returned to his room, he purchased a copy of an advanced bacteriology. It was amusing to construct—with improvements!—uni-cellular creatures whose very place in the scheme of classification was a matter for argument among scientists of his own day. The Bild-A-Man manual, of course, merely gave a few examples and general rules; but with the descriptions in the bacteriology, the world was his oyster.

Which was an idea: he made a few oysters. The shells weren't hard enough, and he couldn't quite screw his courage up to the eating point, but they were most undeniably bivalves. If he cared to perfect his technique, his food problem would be solved.

The manual was fairly easy to follow and profusely illustrated with pictures that expanded into solidity as the page was opened. Very little was taken for granted; involved explanations followed simpler ones. Only the allusions were occasionally obscure—"This is the principle used in the phanphophlink toys," "When your teeth are next yokekkled or demortoned, think of the *Bacterium cyanogenum* and the humble part it plays," "If you have a rubicular mannikin around the house, you needn't bother with the chapter on mannikins."

After a brief search had convinced Sam that whatever else he now had in his apartment he didn't have a rubicular mannikin, he felt justified in turning to the chapter on mannikins. He had conquered completely this feeling of being Pop playing with Junior's toy train: already he had done more than the world's top biologists ever dreamed of for the next generation and what might not lie ahead—what problems might he not yet solve?

"Never forget that mannikins are constructed for one purpose and one purpose only." I won't, Sam promised. "Whether they are sanitary mannikins, tailoring mannikins, printing mannikins or even sunevviarry mannikins, they are each constructed with one operation of a given process in view. When you make a mannikin that is capable of more than one function, you are committing a crime so serious as to be punishable by public admonition."

"To construct an elementary mannikin—"

It was very difficult. Three times he tore down developing monstrosities and began anew. It wasn't till Sunday afternoon that the mannikin was complete—or rather, incomplete.

Long arms it had—although by an error, one was slightly longer than the other—a faceless head and a trunk. No legs. No eyes or ears, no organs of reproduction. It lay on his bed and gurgled out of the red rim of a mouth that was supposed to serve both for ingress and excretion of food. It waved the long arms, designed for some one simple operation not yet invented, in slow circles.

Sam, watching it, decided that life could be as ugly as an open field latrine in midsummer.

He had to disassemble it. Its length—three feet from almost boneless fingers to tapering, sealed-off trunk—precluded the use of the tiny disassembleator with which he had taken apart the oysters and miscellaneous small creations. There was a bright yellow notice on the large disassembleator, however—"To be used only under the direct supervision of a Census Keeper. Call formula A76 or unstable your *id*."

"Formula A76" meant about as much as "sunevviarry," and Sam decided his *id* was already sufficiently unstabled, thank you. He'd have to make out without a Census Keeper. The big disassembleator probably used the same general principles as the small one.

He clamped it to a bedpost and adjusted the focus. He snapped the switch set in the smooth underside.

Five minutes later the mannikin was a bright, gooey mess on his bed.

The large disassembleator, Sam was convinced as he tidied his room, did require the supervision of a Census Keeper. Some sort of keeper anyway. He rescued as many of the legless creature's constituents as he could, although he doubted he'd be using the set for the next fifty years or so. He certainly wouldn't ever use the disassembleator again; much less spectacular and disagreeable to shove the whole thing into a meat grinder and crank the handle as it squashed inside.

As he locked the door behind him on his way to a gentle binge, he made a mental note to purchase some fresh sheets the next morning. He'd have to sleep on the floor tonight.

Wrist-deep in Somerset & Ojack minutiae, Sam was conscious of Lew Knight's stares and Tina's puzzled glances. If they only knew, he exulted! But Tina would probably just think it "marr-vell-ouss!" and Lew Knight might make some crack like "Hey! Kid Frankenstein himself!" Come to think of it though Lew would probably have worked out some method of duplicating, to a limited extent, the contents of the Bild-A-Man set and marketing it commercially. Whereas he—well, there were other things you could do with the gadget. Plenty of other things.

"Hey, counselor," Lew Knight was perched on the corner of his desk, "what are these long week ends we're taking? You might not make as much money in the law, but does it look right for an associate of mine to sell magazine subscriptions on the side?"

Sam stuffed his ears mentally against the emery-wheel voice. "I've been writing a book."

"A law book? Weber 'On Bankruptcy'?"

"No, a juvenile. 'Lew Knight, The Neanderthal Nitwit.'"

"Won't sell. The title lacks punch. Something like 'Knights, Knaves and Knobheads' is what the public goes for these days. By the way, Tina tells me you two had some sort of understanding about New Year's Eve and she doesn't think you'd mind if I took her out instead. I don't think you'd mind either, but I may be prejudiced. Especially since I have a table reservation at Cigale's where there's usually less of a crowd of a New Year's Eve than at the automat."

"I don't mind."

"Good," said Knight approvingly as he moved away. "By the way, I won that case. Nice juicy fee, too. Thanks for asking."

Tina also wanted to know if he objected to the new arrangements when she brought the mail. Again, he didn't. Where had he been for over two days? He had been busy, very busy. Something entirely new. Something important.

She stared down at him as he separated offers of used cars guaranteed not to have been driven over a quarter of a million miles from caressing reminders that he still owed half the tuition for the last year of law school and when was he going to pay it?

Came a letter that was neither bill nor ad. Sam's heart momentarily lost interest in the monotonous round of pumping that was its lot as he stared at a strange postmark: Glunt City, Ohio.

Dear Sir:

There is no firm in Glunt City at the present time bearing any name similar to "Bild-A-Man Company" nor do we know of any such organization planning to join our little community. We also have no thoroughfare called "Diagonal"; our north-south streets are named after Indian tribes while our east-west avenues are listed numerically in multiples of five.

Glunt City is a restricted residential township; we intend to keep it that. Only small retailing and service establishments are permitted here. If you are interested in building a home in Glunt City and can furnish proof of white, Christian, Anglo-Saxon ancestry on both sides of your family for fifteen generations, we would be glad to furnish further information.

Thomas H. Plantagenet, Mayor

P.S. An airfield for privately owned jet- and propeller-driven aircraft is being built outside the city limits.

That was sort of that. He would get no refills on any of the vials and bottles even if he had a loose slunk or two with which to pay for the stuff. Better go easy on the material and conserve it as much as possible. But no disassembling!

Would the "Bild-A-Man Company" begin manufacturing at Glunt City some time in the future when it had developed into an industrial metropolis against the constricted wills of its restricted citizenry? Or had his package slid from some different track in the human time stream, some era to be born on an other-dimensional earth? There would have to be a common origin to both, else why the English wordage? And could there be a purpose in his having received it, beneficial—or otherwise?

Tina had been asking him a question. Sam detached his mind from shapeless speculation and considered her quite-the-opposite features.

"So if you'd still like me to go out with you New Year's Eve, all I have to do is tell Lew that my mother expects to suffer from her gallstones and I have to stay home. Then I think you could buy the Cigale reservations from him cheap."

"Thanks a lot, Tina, but very honestly I don't have the loose cash right now. You and Lew make a much more logical couple anyhow."

Lew Knight wouldn't have done that. Lew cut throats with carefree zest. But Tina did seem to go with Lew as a type.

Why? Until Lew had developed a raised eyebrow where Tina was concerned, it had been Sam all the way. The rest of the office had accepted the fact and moved out of their path. It wasn't only a question of Lew's greater success and financial well-being: just that Lew had decided he wanted Tina and had got her.

It hurt. Tina wasn't special; she was no cultural companion, no intellectual equal; but he wanted her. He liked being with her. She was the woman he desired, rightly or wrongly, whether or not there was a sound basis to their relationship. He remembered his parents before a railway accident had orphaned him: they were theoretically incompatible, but they had been terribly happy together.

He was still wondering about it the next night as he flipped the pages of "Twinning yourself and your friends." It would be interesting to twin Tina.

"One for me, one for Lew."

Only the horrible possibility of an error was there. His mannikin had not been perfect: its arms had been of unequal length. Think of a physically lopsided Tina, something he could never bring himself to disassemble, limping extraneously through life.

And then the book warned: "Your constructed twin, though resembling you in every obvious detail, has not had the slow and guarded maturity you have enjoyed. He or she will not be as stable mentally, much less able to cope with unusual situations, much more prone to neurosis. Only a professional carnuplicator, using the finest equipment, can make an exact copy of a human personality. Yours will be able to live and even reproduce, but never to be accepted as a valid and responsible member of society."

Well, he could chance that. A little less stability in Tina would hardly be noticeable; it might be more desirable.

There was a knock. He opened the door, guarding the box from view with his body. His landlady.

"Your door has been locked for the past week, Mr. Weber. That's why the chambermaid hasn't cleaned the room. We thought you didn't want anyone inside."

"Yes." He stepped into the hall and closed the door behind him. "I've been doing some highly important legal work at home."

"Oh." He sensed a murderous curiosity and changed the subject.

"Why all the fine feathers, Mrs. Lipanti—New Year's Eve party?"

She smoothed her frilled black dress self-consciously. "Y-yes. My sister and her husband came in from Springfield today and we were going to make a night of it. Only . . . only the girl who was supposed to come over and mind their baby just phoned and said she isn't feeling well. So I guess we won't go unless somebody else, I mean unless we can get someone else to take care . . . I mean, somebody who doesn't have a previous engagement and who wouldn't—" Her voice trailed away in assumed embarrassment as she realized the favor was already asked.

Well, after all, he wasn't doing anything tonight. And she had been remarkably pleasant those times when he had had to operate on the basis of "Of course I'll have the rest of the rent in a day or so." But why did any one of the earth's two billion humans, when in the possession of an unpleasant buck, pass it automatically to Sam Weber?

Then he remembered Chapter IV on babies and other small humans. Since the night when he had separated the mannikin from its constituent parts, he'd been running through the manual as an intellectual exercise. He didn't feel quite up to making some weird error on a small human. But twinning wasn't supposed to be as difficult.

Only by Gog and by Magog, by Aesculapius the Physician and Kildare the Doctor, he would not disassemble this time. There must be other methods of disposal possible in a large city on a dark night. He'd think of something.

"I'd be glad to watch the baby for a few hours." He started down the hall to anticipate her polite protest. "Don't have a date tonight myself. No, don't mention it, Mrs. Lipanti. Glad to do it."

In the landlady's apartment, her nervous sister briefed him doubtfully.

"And that's the only time she cries in a low, steady way so if you move fast there won't be much damage done. Not much, anyway."

He saw them to the door. "I'll be fast enough," he assured the mother. "Just so I get a hint."

Mrs. Lipanti paused at the door. "Did I tell you about the man who was asking after you this afternoon?"

Again? "A sort of tall, old man in a long, black overcoat?"

"With the most frightening way of staring into your face and talking under his breath. Do you know him?"

"Not exactly. What did he want?"

"Well, he asked if there was a Sam Weaver living here who was a lawyer and had been spending most of his time in his room for the past week. I told him we had a Sam Weber—your first name *is* Sam?—who answered to that description, but that the last Weaver had moved out over a year ago. He just looked at me for a while and said, 'Weaver, Weber —they might have made an error,' and walked out without so much as a good-by or excuse me. Not what I call a polite gentleman."

Thoughtfully Sam walked back to the child. Strange how sharp a mental picture he had formed of this man! Possibly because the two women who had met him thus far had been very impressionable, although to hear their stories the impression was there to be received.

He doubted there was any mistake: the man had been looking for him on both occasions; his knowledge of Sam's vacation from foolscap this past week proved that. It did seem as if he weren't interested in meeting him until some moot point of identity should be established beyond the least shadow of a doubt. Something of a legal mind, that.

The whole affair centered around the "Bild-A-Man" set he was positive. This skulking investigation hadn't started until after the gift from 2153 had been delivered—and Sam had started using it.

But till the character in the long, black overcoat paddled up to Sam Weber personally and stated his business, there wasn't very much he could do about it.

Sam went upstairs for his Junior Biocalibrator.

He propped the manual open against the side of the bed and switched the instrument on to full scanning power. The infant gurgled thickly as the calibrator was rolled slowly over its fat body and a section of metal tape unwound from the slot with, according to the manual, a completely detailed physiological description.

It was detailed. Sam gasped as the tape, running through the enlarging viewer, gave information on the child for which a pediatrician would have taken out at least three mortgages on his immortal soul. Thyroid capacity, chromosome quality, cerebral content. All broken down into neat subheads of data for construction purposes. Rate of skull expansion in minutes for the next ten hours; rate of cartilage transformation; changes in hormone secretions while active and at rest.

This was a blueprint; it was like taking canons from a baby.

Sam left the child to a puzzled contemplation of its navel and sped upstairs. With the tape as a guide, he clipped sections of the molds into the required smaller sizes. Then, almost before he knew it consciously, he was constructing a small human.

He was amazed at the ease with which he worked. Skill was evidently acquired in this game; the mannikin had been much harder to put together. The matter of duplication and working from an informational tape simplified his problems, though.

The child took form under his eyes.

He was finished just an hour and a half after he had taken his first measurements. All except the vitalizing.

A moment's pause, here. The ugly prospect of disassembling stopped him for a moment, but he shook it off. He had to see how well he had done the job. If this child could breathe, what was not possible to him! Besides he couldn't keep it suspended in an inanimate condition very long without running the risk of ruining his work and the materials.

He started the vitalizer.

The child shivered and began a low, steady cry. Sam tore down to the landlady's apartment again and scooped up a square of white linen left on the bed for emergencies. Oh well, some more clean sheets.

After he had made the necessary repairs, he stood back and took a good look at it. He was in a sense a papa. He felt as proud.

It was a perfect little creature, glowing and round with health.

"I have twinned," he said happily.

Every detail correct. The two sides of the face correctly unexact, the duplication of the original child's lunch at the very same point of digestion. Same hair, same eyes—or was it? Sam bent over the infant. He could have sworn the other was a blonde. This child had dark hair which seemed to grow darker as he looked.

He grabbed it with one hand and picked up the junior biocalibrator with the other.

Downstairs, he placed the two babies side by side on the big bed. No doubt about it. One was blonde; the other, his plagiarism, was now a definite brunette.

The biocalibrator showed other differences: Slightly faster pulse for his model. Lower blood count. Minutely higher cerebral capacity, although the content was the same. Adrenalin and bile secretions entirely unalike.

It added up to error. His child might be the superior specimen, or the inferior one, but he had not made a true copy. He had no way of knowing at the moment whether or not the infant he had built could grow into a human maturity. The other could.

Why? He had followed directions faithfully, had consulted the calibrator tape at every step. And this had resulted. Had he waited too long before starting the vitalizer? Or was it just a matter of insufficient skill?

Close to midnight, his watch delicately pointed out. It would be necessary to remove evidences of baby-making before the Sisters Lipanti came home. Sam considered possibilities swiftly.

He came down in a few moments with an old tablecloth and a cardboard carton. He wrapped the child in the tablecloth, vaguely happy that the temperature had risen that night, then placed it in the carton.

The child gurgled at the adventure. Its original on the bed gooed in return. Sam slipped quietly out into the street.

Male and female drunks stumbled along tootling on tiny trumpets. People wished each other a *hic* Happy New Year as he strode down the necessary three blocks.

As he turned left, he saw the sign: "Urban Foundling Home." There was a light burning over a side door. Convenient, but that was a big city for you.

Sam shrank into the shadow of an alley for a moment as a new idea occurred to him. This had to look genuine. He pulled a pencil out of his breast pocket and scrawled on the side of the carton in as small handwriting as he could manage:

Please take good care of my darling little girl. I am not married.

Then he deposited the carton on the doorstep and held his finger on the bell until he heard movement inside. He was across the street and in the alley again by the time a nurse had opened the door.

It wasn't until he walked into the boarding house that he remembered about the navel. He stopped and tried to recall. No, he had built his little girl without a navel! Her belly had been perfectly smooth. That's what came of hurrying! Shoddy workmanship.

There might be a bit of to-do in the foundling home when they unwrapped the kid. How could they explain it?

Sam slapped his forehead. "Me and Michelangelo. He adds a navel, I forget one!"

Except for an occasional groan, the office was fairly quiet the second day of the New Year.

He was going through the last intriguing pages of the book when he was aware of two people teetering awkwardly near his desk. His eyes left the manual reluctantly: "New kinds of life for your leisure moments" was really stuff!

Tina and Lew Knight.

Sam digested the fact that neither of them were perched on his desk.

Tina wore the little ring she'd received for Christmas on the third finger of her left hand; Lew was experimenting with a sheepish look and finding it difficult.

"Oh, Sam. Last night, Lew . . . Sam, we wanted you to be the first—Such a surprise, like that I mean! Why I almost—Naturally we thought this would be a little difficult . . . Sam, we're going, I mean we expect—"

"—to be married," Lew Knight finished in what was almost an undertone. For the first time since Sam had known him he looked uncertain and suspicious of life, like a man who finds a newly-hatched octopus in his breakfast orange juice.

"You'd adore the way Lew proposed," Tina was gushing. "So roundabout. And so shy. I told him afterwards that I thought for a moment he was talking of something else entirely. I did have trouble understanding you, didn't I dear?"

"Huh? Oh yeah, you had trouble understanding me." Lew stared at his former rival. "Much of a surprise?"

"Oh, no. No surprise at all. You two fit together so perfectly that I knew it right from the first." Sam mumbled his felicitations, conscious of Tina's searching glances. "And now, if you'll excuse me, there's something I have to take care of immediately. A special sort of wedding present."

Lew was disconcerted. "A wedding present. This early?"

"Why certainly," Tina told him. "It isn't very easy to get just the right thing. And a special friend like Sam naturally wants a very special gift."

Sam decided he had taken enough. He grabbed the manual and his coat and dodged through the door.

By the time he came to the red stone steps of the boarding house, he had reached the conclusion that the wound, while painful, had definitely missed his heart. He was in fact chuckling at the memory of Lew Knight's face when his landlady plucked at his sleeve.

"That man was here again today, Mr. Weber. He said he wanted to see you."

"Which man? The tall, old fellow?"

Mrs. Lipanti nodded, her arms folded complacently across her chest. "Such an unpleasant person! When I told him you weren't in, he insisted I take him up to your room. I said I couldn't do that without your permission and he looked at me fit to kill. I've never believed in the evil eye myself—although I always say where there is smoke there must be fire—but if there is such a thing as an evil eye, he has it."

"Will he be back?"

"Yes. He asked me when you usually return and I said about eight o'clock, figuring that if you didn't want to meet him it would give you time to change your clothes and wash up and leave before he gets here. And, Mr. Weber, if you'll excuse me for saying this, I don't think you want to meet him."

"Thanks. But when he comes in at eight, show him up. If he's the right person, I'm in illegal possession of his property. I want to know where this property originates."

In his room, he put the manual away carefully and told the box to open. The Junior Biocalibrator was not too bulky and newspaper would suffice to cover it. He was on his way uptown in a few minutes with the strangely shaped parcel under his arm.

Did he still want to duplicate Tina, he pondered? Yes, in spite of everything. She was still the woman he desired more than any he had ever known; and with the original married to Lew, the replica would have no choice but himself. Only—the replica would have Tina's characteristics up to the moment the measurements were taken; she might insist on marrying Lew as well.

That would make for a bit of a sitcheeayshun. But he was still miles from that bridge. It might even be amusing—

The possibility of error was more annoying. The Tina he would make might be off-center in a number of ways: reds might overlap pinks; like an imperfectly reproduced color photograph she might, in time, come to digest her own stomach; there could very easily be a streak of strange and incurable insanity implicit in his model which would not assert itself until a deep mutual affection had flowered and borne fruit. As yet, he was no great shakes as a twinner and human mimeographer; the errors he had made on Mrs. Lipanti's niece demonstrated his amateur standing.

Sam knew he would never be able to dismantle Tina if she proved defective. Outside of the chivalrous concepts and almost superstitious reverence for womankind pressed into him by a small town boyhood, there was the unmitigated horror he felt at the idea of such a beloved object going through the same disintegrating process as—well, the manni-kin. But if he overlooked an essential in his construction, what other recourse would there be?

Solution: nothing must be overlooked. Sam grinned bitterly as the ancient elevator swayed up to his office. If he only had time for a little more practice with a person whose reactions he knew so exactly that any deviation from the norm would be instantly obvious! But the strange, old man would be calling tonight, and, if his business concerned "Bild-A-Man" sets, Sam's experiments might be abruptly curtailed. And where would he find such a person—he had few real friends and no intimate ones. And, to be at all valuable, it would have to be someone he knew as well as himself.

Himself!

"Floor, sir." The elevator operator was looking at him reproachfully. Sam's exultant shout had caused him to bring the carrier to a spasmodic stop six inches under the floor level, something he had not done since that bygone day when he had first nervously reached for the controls. He felt his craftsmanship was under a shadow as he morosely closed the door behind the lawyer.

And why not himself? He knew his own physical attributes better than he knew Tina's; any mental instability on the part of his reproduced self would be readily discernible long before it reached the point of psychosis or worse. And the beauty of it was that he would have no compunction in disassembling a superfluous Sam Weber. Quite the contrary: the horror in that situation would be the continued existence of a duplicate personality; its removal would be a relief.

Twinning himself would provide the necessary practice in a familiar medium. Ideal. He'd have to take careful notes so that if anything went wrong he'd know just where to avoid going off the track in making his own personal Tina.

And maybe the old geezer wasn't interested in the set at all. Even if he were, Sam could take his landlady's advice and not be at home when he called. Silver linings wherever he looked.

Lew Knight stared at the instrument in Sam's hands. "What in the sacred name of Blackstone and all his commentaries is that? Looks like a lawn mower for a window box!"

"It's uh, sort of a measuring gadget. Gives the right size for one thing and another and this and that. Won't be able to get you the wedding present I have in mind unless I know the right size. Or sizes. Tina, would you mind stepping out into the hall?"

"Nooo." She looked dubiously at the gadget. "It won't hurt?"

It wouldn't hurt a bit, Sam assured her. "I just want to keep this a secret from Lew till after the ceremony."

She brightened at that and preceded Sam through the door. "Hey counselor," one of the other young lawyers called at Lew as they left. "Hey counselor, don't let him do that. Possession is nine points, Sam always says. He'll never bring her back."

Lew chuckled weakly and bent over his work.

"Now I want you to go into the ladies' room," Sam explained to a bewildered Tina. "I'll stand guard outside and tell the other customers that the place is out of order. If another woman is inside wait until she leaves. Then strip."

"Strip?" Tina squealed.

He nodded. Then very carefully, emphasizing every significant detail of operation, he told her how to use the Junior Biocalibrator. How she must be careful to kick the switch and set the tape running. How she must cover every external square inch of her body. "This little arm will enable you to lower it down your back. No questions now. Git." She gat.

She was back in fifteen minutes, fluffing her dress into place and studying the tape with a rapt frown. "This is the *strangest* thing— According to the spool, my iodine content—"

Sam snaffled the Biocalibrator hurriedly. "Don't give it another thought. It's a code, kind of. Tells me just what size and how many of what kind. You'll be crazy about the gift when you see it."

"I know I will." She bent over him as he kneeled and examined the tape to make certain she had applied the instrument correctly. "You know, Sam, I always felt your taste was perfect. I want you to come and visit us often after we're married. You can have such beautiful ideas! Lew is a bit too . . . too businesslike, isn't he? I mean it's necessary for success and all that, but success isn't everything. I mean you have to have culture, too. You'll help me keep cultured, won't you, Sam?"

"Sure," Sam said vaguely. The tape was complete. Now to get started! "Anything I can do—glad to help."

He rang for the elevator and noticed the forlorn uncertainty with which she watched him. "Don't worry, Tina. You and Lew will be very happy together. And you'll love this wedding present." But not as much as I will, he told himself as he stepped into the elevator.

Back in his room, he emptied the machine and undressed. In a few moments he had another tape on himself. He would have liked to consider it for a while, but being this close to the goal made him impatient. He locked the door, cleaned his room hurriedly of accumulated junk—remembering to sniff in annoyance at Aunt Maggie's ties: the blue and red one almost lighted up the room—ordered the box to open—and he was ready to begin.

First the water. With the huge amount of water necessary to the human body, especially in the case of an adult, he might as well start collecting it now. He had bought several pans and it would take his lone faucet some time to fill them all.

As he placed the first pot under the tap, Sam wondered suddenly if its chemical impurities might affect the end product. Of course it might! These children of 2153 would probably take absolutely pure H_2O as a matter of daily use; the manual hadn't mentioned the subject, but how did he know what kind of water they had available? Well, he'd boil this batch over his chemical stove; when he got to making Tina he could see about getting *aqua* completely *pura*.

Score another point for making a simulacrum of Sam first.

While waiting for the water to boil, he arranged his supplies to positions of maximum availability. They were getting low. That baby had taken up quite a bit of useful ingredients; too bad he hadn't seen his way clear to disassembling it. That meant if there were any argument in favor of allowing the replica of himself to go on living, it was now invalid. He'd have to take it apart in order to have enough for Tina II. Or Tina prime?

He leafed through Chapters VI, VII and VIII on the ingredients, completion and disassembling of a man. He'd been through this several times before but he'd passed more than one law exam on the strength of a last-minute review.

The constant reference to mental instability disturbed him. "The humans constructed with this set will, at the very best, show most of the superstitious tendencies, and neurosis-compulsions of medieval mankind. In the long run they are not normal; take great care not to consider them such." Well, it wouldn't make too much difference in Tina's case—and that was all that was important.

When he had finished adjusting the molds to the correct sizes, he fastened the vitalizer to the bed. Then—very, very slowly and with repeated glances at the manual, he began to duplicate Sam Weber. He learned more of his physical limitations and capabilities in the next two hours than any man had ever known since the day when an inconspicuous primate had investigated the possibilities of ground locomotion upon the nether extremities alone.

Strangely enough, he felt neither awe nor exultation. It was like building a radio receiver for the first time. Child's play.

Most of the vials and jars were empty when he had finished. The damp molds were stacked inside the box, still in their three-dimensional outline. The manual lay neglected on the floor.

Sam Weber stood near the bed looking down at Sam Weber on the bed.

All that remained was vitalizing. He daren't wait too long or imperfections might set in and the errors of the baby be repeated. He shook off a nauseating feeling of unreality, made certain that the big disassembleator was within reach and set the Jiffy Vitalizer in motion.

The man on the bed coughed. He stirred. He sat up.

"Wow!" he said. "Pretty good, if I do say so myself!"

And then he had leaped off the bed and seized the disassembleator. He tore great chunks of wiring out of the center, threw it to the floor and kicked it into shapelessness. "No Sword of Damocles going to hang over *my* head," he informed an open-mouthed Sam Weber. "Although, I could have used it on you, come to think of it."

Sam eased himself to the mattress and sat down. His mind stopped rearing and whinnied to a halt. He had been so impressed with the helplessness of the baby and the mannikin that he had never dreamed of the possibility that his duplicate would enter upon life with such enthusiasm. He should have, though; this was a full-grown man, created at a moment of complete physical and mental activity.

"This is bad," he said at last in a hoarse voice. "You're unstable. You can't be admitted into normal society."

"I'm unstable?" his image asked. "Look who's talking! The guy who's been mooning his way through his adult life, who wants to marry an overdressed, conceited collection of biological impulses that would come crawling on her knees to any man sensible enough to push the right buttons—"

"You leave Tina's name out of this," Sam told him, feeling acutely uncomfortable at the theatrical phrase.

His double looked at him and grinned. "O.K., I will. But not her body! Now, look here, Sam or Weber or whatever you want me to call you, you can live your life and I'll live mine. I won't even be a lawyer if that'll make you happy. But as far as Tina is concerned, now that there are no ingredients to make a copy—that was a rotten escapist idea, by the way—I have enough of your likes and dislikes to want her badly. And I can have her, whereas you can't. You don't have the gumption."

Sam leaped to his feet and doubled his fists. Then he saw the other's entirely equal size and slightly more assured twinkle. There was no point in fighting—that would end in a draw, at best. He went back to reason.

"According to the manual," he began, "you are prone to neurosis—"

"The manual! The manual was written for children of two centuries hence, with quite a bit of selective breeding and scientific education behind them. Personally, I think I'm a—"

There was a double knock on the door. "Mr. Weber."

"Yes," they both said simultaneously.

Outside, the landlady gasped and began speaking in an uncertain voice. "Th-that gentleman is downstairs. He'd like to see you. Shall I tell him you're in?"

"No, I'm not at home," said the double.

"Tell him I left an hour ago," said Sam at exactly the same moment.

There was another, longer gasp and the sound of footsteps receding hurriedly.

"That's one clever way to handle a situation," Sam's facsimile exploded. "Couldn't you keep your mouth shut? The poor woman's probably gone off to have a fit."

"You forget that this is my room and you are just an experiment that went wrong," Sam told him hotly. "I have just as much right, in fact more right . . . hey, what do you think you're doing?"

The other had thrown open the closet door and was stepping into a pair of pants. "Just getting dressed. You can wander around in the nude if you find it exciting, but I want to look a bit respectable."

"I undressed to take my measurements . . . or your measurements. Those are my clothes, this is my room—"

"Look, take it easy. You could never prove it in a court of law. Don't make me go into that *cliché* about what's yours is mine and so forth."

Heavy feet resounded through the hall. They stopped outside the room. Cymbals seemed to clash all around them and there was a panic-stricken sense of unendurable heat. Then shrill echoes fled into the distance. The walls stopped shuddering.

Silence and a smell of burning wood.

They whirled in time to see a terribly tall, terrible old man in a long black overcoat walking through the smoldering remains of the door. Much too tall for the entrance, he did not stoop as he came in; rather he drew his head down into his garment and shot it up again. Instinctively, they moved close together.

His eyes, all shiny black iris without any whites, were set back deep in the shadow of his head. They reminded Sam Weber of the scanners on the Biocalibrator: they tabulated, deduced, rather than saw.

"I was afraid I would be too late," he rumbled at last in weird, clipped tones. "You have already duplicated yourself, Mr. Weber, making necessary unpleasant rearrangements. And the duplicate has destroyed the disassembleator. Too bad. I shall have to do it manually. An ugly job."

He came further into the room until they could almost breathe their fright upon him. "This affair has already dislocated four major programs, but we had to move in accepted cultural grooves and be absolutely certain of the recipient's identity before we could act to withdraw the set. Mrs. Lipanti's collapse naturally stimulated emergency measures."

The duplicate cleared his throat. "You are—?"

"Not exactly human. A humble civil servant of precision manufacture. I am Census Keeper for the entire twenty-ninth oblong. You see, your set was intended for the Thregander children who are on a field trip in this oblong. One of the Threganders who has a Weber chart requested the set through the chrondromos which, in an attempt at the supernormal, unstabled without carnuplicating. You therefore received the package instead. Unfortunately, the unstabling was so complete that we were forced to locate you by indirect methods."

The Census Keeper paused and Sam's double hitched his pants nervously. Sam wished he had anything—even a fig leaf—to cover his nakedness. He felt like a character in the Garden of Eden trying to build up a logical case for apple eating. He appreciated glumly how much more than "Bild-A-Man" sets clothes had to do with the making of a man.

"We will have to recover the set, of course," the staccato thunder continued, "and readjust any discrepancies it has caused. Once the matter has been cleared up, however, your life will be allowed to resume its normal progression. Meanwhile, the problem is which of you is the original Sam Weber?"

"I am," they both quavered—and turned to glare at each other.

"Difficulties," the old man rumbled. He sighed like an arctic wind. "I always have difficulties! Why can't I ever have a simple case like a carnuplicator?"

"Look here," the duplicate began. "The original will be—"

"Less unstable and of better emotional balance than the replica," Sam interrupted. "Now, it seems—"

"That you should be able to tell the difference," the other concluded breathlessly. "From what you see and have seen of us, can't you decide which is the more valid member of society?"

What a pathetic confidence, Sam thought, the fellow was trying to display! Didn't he know he was up against someone who could really discern mental differences? This was no fumbling psychiatrist of the present; here was a creature who could see through externals to the most coherent personality beneath.

"I can, naturally. Now, just a moment." He studied them carefully, his eyes traveling with judicious leisure up and down their bodies. They waited, fidgeting, in a silence that pounded.

"Yes," the old man said at last. "Yes. Quite."

He walked forward.

A long thin arm shot out.

He started to disassemble Sam Weber.

"But listennnnn—" began Weber in a yell that turned into a high scream and died in a liquid mumble.

"It would be better for your sanity if you didn't watch," the Census Keeper suggested.

The duplicate exhaled slowly, turned away and began to button a shirt. Behind him the mumbling continued, rising and falling in pitch.

"You see," came the clipped, rumbling accents, "it's not the gift we're afraid of letting you have—it's the principle involved. Your civilization isn't ready for it. You understand."

"Perfectly," replied the counterfeit Weber, knotting Aunt Maggie's blue and red tie.

First published: 1947

THUNDER AND ROSES

by Theodore Sturgeon

WHEN PETE MAWSER LEARNED ABOUT THE SHOW, HE TURNED AWAY FROM the GHQ bulletin board, touched his long chin, and determined to shave, in spite of the fact that the show would be video, and he would see it in his barracks. He had an hour and a half. It felt good to have a purpose again—even the small matter of shaving before eight o'clock. Eight o'clock Tuesday, just the way it used to be. Everyone used to say, Wednesday morning, "How about the way Starr sang *The Breeze and I* last night?"

That was a while ago, before the attack, before all those people were dead, before the country was dead. Starr Anthim—an institution, like Crosby, like Duse, like Jenny Lind, like the Statue of Liberty. (Liberty had been one of the first to get it, her bronze beauty volatilized, radio-activated, and even now being carried about in vagrant winds, spreading over the earth . . .)

Pete Mawser grunted and forced his thoughts away from the drifting, poisonous fragments of a blasted liberty. Hate was first. Hate was ubiquitous, like the increasing blue glow in the air at night, like the tension that hung over the base.

Gunfire crackled sporadically far to the right, swept nearer. Pete stepped out to the street and made for a parked truck. There was a Wac sitting on the short running-board.

At the corner a stocky figure backed into the intersection. The man carried a tommy-gun in his arms, and he was swinging it to and fro with the gentle, wavering motion of a weather-vane. He staggered toward them, his gun-muzzle hunting. Someone fired from a building and the man swiveled and blasted wildly at the sound.

"He's—blind," said Pete Mawser, and added, "he ought to be," looking at the tattered face.

A siren keened. An armored jeep slewed into the street. The full-

351

throated roar of a brace of .50-caliber machine-guns put a swift and shocking end to the incident.

"Poor crazy kid," Pete said softly. "That's the fourth I've seen today." He looked down at the Wac. She was smiling. "Hey!"

"Hello, Sarge." She must have identified him before, because now she did not raise her eyes nor her voice. "What happened?"

"You know what happened. Some kid got tired of having nothing to fight and nowhere to run to. What's the matter with you?"

"No," she said. "I don't mean that." At last she looked up at him. "I mean all of this. I can't seem to remember."

"You—well, it's not easy to forget. We got hit. We got hit everywhere at once. All the big cities are gone. We got it from both sides. We got too much. The air is becoming radioactive. We'll all—" He checked himself. She didn't know. She'd forgotten. There was nowhere to escape to, and she'd escaped inside herself, right here. Why tell her about it? Why tell her that everyone was going to die? Why tell her that other, shameful thing: that we hadn't struck back?

But she wasn't listening. She was still looking at him. Her eyes were not quite straight. One held his, but the other was slightly shifted and seemed to be looking at his temple. She was smiling again. When his voice trailed off she didn't prompt him. Slowly, he moved away. She did not turn her head, but kept looking up at where he had been, smiling a little. He turned away, wanting to run, walking fast.

How long could a guy hold out? When you were in the army they tried to make you be like everybody else. What did you do when everybody else was cracking up?

He blanked out the mental picture of himself as the last one left sane. He'd followed that one through before. It always led to the conclusion that it would be better to be one of the first. He wasn't ready for that yet. Then he blanked that out, too. Every time he said to himself that he wasn't ready for that yet, something within him asked "Why not?" and he never seemed to have an answer ready.

How long could a guy hold out?

He climbed the steps of the QM Central and went inside. There was nobody at the reception switchboard. It didn't matter. Messages were carried by jeep, or on motor-cycles. The Base Command was not insisting that anybody stick to a sitting job these days. Ten desk-men could crack up for every one on a jeep, or on the soul-sweat squads. Pete made up his mind to put in a little stretch on a squad tomorrow. Do him good. He just hoped that this time the adjutant wouldn't burst into tears in the middle of the parade ground. You could keep your mind on the manual of arms just fine until something like that happened.

He bumped into Sonny Weisefreund in the barracks corridor. The Tech's round young face was as cheerful as ever. He was naked and glowing, and had a towel thrown over his shoulder.

"Hi, Sonny. Is there plenty of hot water?"

"Why not?" grinned Sonny. Pete grinned back, wondering if anybody could say anything about anything at all without one of these reminders. Of course, there was hot water. The QM barracks had hot water for three hundred men. There were three dozen left. Men dead, men gone to the hills, men locked up so they wouldn't—

"Starr Anthim's doing a show tonight."

"Yeah. Tuesday night. Not funny, Pete. Don't you know there's a war—"

"No kidding," Pete said swiftly. "She's here—right here on the base."

Sonny's face was joyful. "Gee." He pulled the towel off his shoulder and tied it around his waist. "Starr Anthim here! Where are they going to put on the show?"

"HQ, I imagine. Video only. You know about public gatherings."

"Yeah. And a good thing, too," said Sonny. "Somebody'd be sure to crack up. I wouldn't want her to see anything like that. How'd she happen to come here, Pete?"

"Drifted in on the last gasp of a busted-up Navy helicopter."

"Yeah, but why?"

"Search me. Get your head out of that gift-horse's mouth."

He went into the washroom, smiling and glad that he still could. He undressed and put his neatly folded clothes down on a bench. There were a soap-wrapper and an empty tooth-paste tube lying near the wall. He picked them up and put them in the catchall, took the mop that leaned against the partition and mopped the floor where Sonny had splashed after shaving. Someone had to keep things straight. He might have worried if it were anyone else but Sonny. But Sonny wasn't cracking up. Sonny always had been like that. Look there. Left his razor out again.

Pete started his shower, meticulously adjusting the valves until the pressure and temperature exactly suited him. He did nothing carelessly these days. There was so much to feel, and taste, and see now. The impact of water on his skin, the smell of soap, the consciousness of light and heat, the very pressure of standing on the soles of his feet . . . he wondered vaguely how the slow increase of radioactivity in the air, as the nitrogen transmuted to Carbon Fourteen, would affect him if he kept carefully healthy in every way. What happens first? Blindness? Headaches? Perhaps a loss of appetite or slow fatigue?

Why not look it up?

On the other hand, why bother? Only a very small percentage of the men would die of radioactive poisoning. There were too many other things that killed more quickly, which was probably just as well. That razor, for example. It lay gleaming in a sunbeam, curved and clean in the yellow light. Sonny's father and grandfather had used it, or so he said, and it was his pride and joy.

Pete turned his back on it, and soaped under his arms, concentrating on the tiny kisses of bursting bubbles. In the midst of a recurrence of disgust at himself for thinking so often of death, a staggering truth struck him. He did not think of such things because he was morbid, after all! It was the very familiarity of things that brought death-thoughts. It was either "I shall never do this again" or "This is one of the last times I shall do this." You might devote yourself completely to doing things in different ways, he thought madly. You might crawl across the floor this time, and next time walk across on your hands. You might skip dinner tonight, and have a snack at two in the morning instead, and eat grass for breakfast.

But you had to breathe. Your heart had to beat. You'd sweat and you'd shiver, the same as always. You couldn't get away from that. When those things happened, they would remind you. Your heart wouldn't beat out its *wunklunk, wunklunk* any more. It would go *one-less, one-less,* until it yelled and yammered in your ears and you had to make it stop.

Terrific polish on that razor.

And your breath would go on, same as before. You could sidle through this door, back through the next one and the one after, and figure out a totally new way to go through the one after that, but your breath would keep on sliding in and out of your nostrils like a razor going through whiskers, making a sound like a razor being stropped.

Sonny came in. Pete soaped his hair. Sonny picked up the razor and stood looking at it. Pete watched him, soap ran into his eyes, he swore, and Sonny jumped.

"What are you looking at, Sonny? Didn't you ever see it before?"

"Oh, sure. Sure. I just was—" He shut the razor, opened it, flashed light from its blade, shut it again. "I'm tired of using this, Pete. I'm going to get rid of it. Want it?"

Want it? In his foot-locker, maybe. Under his pillow. "Thanks, no, Sonny. Couldn't use it."

"I like safety razors," Sonny mumbled. "Electrics, even better. What are we going to do with it?"

"Throw it in the—no." Pete pictured the razor turning end over end in the air, half open, gleaming in the maw of the catchall. "Throw it out the—" No. Curving out into the long grass. He might want it. He might crawl around in the moonlight looking for it. He might find it.

"I guess maybe I'll break it up."

"No," Pete said. "The pieces—" Sharp little pieces. Hollow-ground fragments. "I'll think of something. Wait'll I get dressed."

He washed briskly, toweled, while Sonny stood looking at the razor. It was a blade now, and if it were broken it would be shards and glittering splinters, still razor sharp. If it were ground dull with an emery wheel, somebody could find it and put another edge on it because it was so obviously a razor, a fine steel razor, one that would slice so—

"I know. The laboratory. We'll get rid of it," Pete said confidently.

He stepped into his clothes, and together they went to the laboratory wing. It was very quiet there. Their voices echoed.

"One of the ovens," said Pete, reaching for the razor.

"Bake-ovens? You're crazy!"

Pete chuckled. "You don't know this place, do you? Like everything else on the base, there was a lot more went on here than most people knew about. They kept calling it the bakeshop. Well, it *was* research headquarters for new high-nutrient flours. But there's lots else here. We tested utensils and designed vegetable-peelers and all sorts of things like that. There's an electric furnace in there that—" He pushed open a door.

They crossed a long, quiet, cluttered room to the thermal equipment. "We can do everything here from annealing glass, through glazing ceramics, to finding the melting point of frying pans." He clicked a switch tentatively. A pilot light glowed. He swung open a small, heavy door and set the razor inside. "Kiss it goodbye. In twenty minutes it'll be a puddle."

"I want to see that," said Sonny. "Can I look around until it's cooked?"

"Why not?"

They walked through the laboratories. Beautifully equipped they were, and too quiet. Once they passed a major who was bent over a complex electronic hook-up on one of the benches. He was watching a little amber light flicker, and he did not return their salute. They tiptoed past him, feeling awed at his absorption, envying it. They saw the models of the automatic kneaders, the vitaminizers, the remote signal thermostats and timers and controls.

"What's in there?"

"I dunno. I'm over the edge of my territory. I don't think there's anybody left for this section. They were mostly mechanical and electronic theoreticians. Hey!"

Sonny followed the pointing hand. "What?"

"That wall-section. It's loose, or—well, what do you know!"

He pushed at the section of wall which was very slightly out of line. There was a dark space beyond.

"What's in there?"

"Nothing, or some semi-private hush-hush job. These guys used to get away with murder."

Sonny said, with an uncharacteristic flash of irony, "Isn't that the Army theoretician's business?"

Cautiously they peered in, then entered.

"Wh—*hey*! The door!"

It swung swiftly and quietly shut. The soft click of the latch was accompanied by a blaze of light.

The room was small and windowless. It contained machinery—a "trickle" charger, a bank of storage batteries, an electric-powered dynamo, two small self-starting gas-driven light plants and a diesel complete with sealed compressed-air starting cylinders. In the corner was a relay rack with its panel-bolts spot-welded. Protruding from it was a red-topped lever.

They looked at the equipment wordlessly for a time and then Sonny said, "Somebody wanted to make awful sure he had power for something."

"Now, I wonder what—" Pete walked over to the relay rack. He looked at the lever without touching it. It was wired up; behind the handle, on the wire, was a folded tag. He opened it cautiously. "To be used only on specific orders of the Commanding Officer."

"Give it a yank and see what happens."

Something clicked behind them. They whirled. "What was that?"

"Seemed to come from that rig beside the door."

They approached it cautiously. There was a spring-loaded solenoid attached to a bar which was hinged to drop across the inside of the secret door, where it would fit into steel gudgeons on the panel. It clicked again.

"A Geiger counter," said Pete disgustedly.

"Now why," mused Sonny, "would they design a door to stay locked unless the general radioactivity went beyond a certain point? That's what it is. See the relays? And the overload switch there? And this?"

"It has a manual lock, too," Pete pointed out. The counter clicked again. "Let's get out of here. I got one of those things built into my head these days."

The door opened easily. They went out, closing it behind them. The keyhole was cleverly concealed in the crack between two boards.

They were silent as they made their way back to the QM labs. The small thrill of violation was gone.

Back at the furnace, Pete glanced at the temperature dial, then kicked the latch control. The pilot winked out, and then the door swung open. They blinked and started back from the raging heat within. They bent and peered. The razor was gone. A pool of brilliance lay on the floor of the compartment.

"Ain't much left. Most of it oxidized away," Pete grunted.

They stood together for a time with their faces lit by the small shimmering ruin. Later, as they walked back to the barracks, Sonny broke his long silence with a sigh. "I'm glad we did that, Pete. I'm awful glad we did that."

At a quarter to eight they were waiting before the combination console in the barracks. All hands except Pete and Sonny and a wiry-haired, thick-set corporal named Bonze had elected to see the show on the big screen in the mess-hall. The reception was better there, of course, but, as Bonze put it, "You don't get close enough in a big place like that."

"I hope she's the same," said Sonny, half to himself.

Why should she be? thought Pete morosely as he turned on the set and watched the screen begin to glow. There were many more of the golden speckles that had killed reception for the past two weeks . . . Why should anything be the same, ever again?

He fought a sudden temptation to kick the set to pieces. It, and Starr Anthim, were part of something that was dead. The country was dead, a once real country—prosperous, sprawling, laughing, grabbing, growing, and changing, mostly healthy, leprous in spots with poverty and injustice, but systemically healthy enough to overcome any ill. He wondered how the murderers would like it. They were welcome to it, now. Nowhere to go. No one to fight. That was true for every soul on earth now.

"You hope she's the same," he muttered.

"The show, I mean," said Sonny mildly. "I'd like to just sit here and have it like—like—"

Oh, thought Pete mistily. Oh—that. Somewhere to go, that's what it is, for a few minutes . . . "I know," he said, all the harshness gone from his voice.

Noise receded from the audio as the carrier swept in. The light on the screen swirled and steadied into a diamond pattern. Pete adjusted the focus, chromic balance and intensity. "Turn out the lights, Bonze. I don't want to see anything but Starr Anthim."

It *was* the same, at first. Starr Anthim had never used the usual fanfares, fade-ins, color and clamor of her contemporaries. A black screen, then *click!* a blaze of gold. It was all there, in focus; tremendously intense, it did not change. Rather, the eye changed to take it in. She never moved for seconds after she came on; she was there, a portrait, a still face and a white throat. Her eyes were open and sleeping. Her face was alive and still.

Then, in the eyes which seemed green but were blue flecked with gold, an awareness seemed to gather, and they came awake. Only then was it noticeable that her lips were parted. Something in the eyes made the lips be seen, though nothing moved yet. Not until she bent her head slowly, so that some of the gold flecks seemed captured in the golden brows. The eyes were not, then, looking out at an audience. They were looking at me, and at *me*, and at ME.

"Hello—you," she said. She was a dream, with a kid sister's slightly irregular teeth.

Bonze shuddered. The cot on which he lay began to squeak rapidly. Sonny shifted in annoyance. Pete reached out in the dark and caught the leg of the cot. The squeaking subsided.

"May I sing a song?" Starr asked. There was music, very faint. "It's an old one, and one of the best. It's an easy song, a deep song, one that comes from the part of men and women that is mankind—the part that has in it no greed, no hate, no fear. This song is about joyousness and strength. It's—my favorite. Is it yours?"

The music swelled. Pete recognized the first two notes of the introduction and swore quietly. This was wrong. This song was not for—this song was part of—

Sonny sat raptly. Bonze lay still.

Starr Anthim began to sing. Her voice was deep and powerful, but soft, with the merest touch of vibrato at the ends of the phrases. The song flowed from her, without noticeable effort, seeming to come from her face, her long hair, her wide-set eyes. Her voice, like her face, was shadowed and clean, round, blue and green but mostly gold.

> When you gave me your heart, you gave me the world,
> You gave me the night and the day,
> And thunder, and roses, and sweet green grass,
> The sea, and soft wet clay.

I drank the dawn from a golden cup,
From a silver one, the dark,
The steed I rode was the wild west wind,
My song was the brook and the lark.

The music spiraled, caroled, slid into a somber cry of muted hungry sixths and ninths; rose, blared, and cut, leaving her voice full and alone:

With thunder I smote the evil of earth,
With roses I won the right,
With the sea I washed, and with clay I built,
And the world was a place of light!

The last note left a face perfectly composed again, and there was no movement in it; it was sleeping and vital while the music curved off and away to the places where music rests when it is not heard.

Starr smiled.

"It's so easy," she said. "So simple. All that is fresh and clean and strong about mankind is in that song, and I think that's all that need concern us about mankind." She leaned forward. "Don't you see?"

The smile faded and was replaced with a gentle wonder. A tiny furrow appeared between her brows; she drew back quickly. "I can't seem to talk to you tonight," she said, her voice small. "You hate something."

Hate was shaped like a monstrous mushroom. Hate was the random speckling of a video plate.

"What has happened to us," said Starr abruptly, impersonally, "is simple too. It doesn't matter who did it—do you understand that? *It* doesn't matter. We were attacked. We were struck from the east and from the west. Most of the bombs were atomic—there were blast-bombs and there were dust-bombs. We were hit by about five hundred and thirty bombs altogether, and it has killed us."

She waited.

Sonny's fist smacked into his palm. Bonze lay with his eyes open, open, quiet. Pete's jaws hurt.

"We have more bombs than both of them put together. We *have* them. We are not going to use them. *Wait!*" She raised her hands suddenly, as if she could see into each man's face. They sank back, tense.

"So saturated is the atmosphere with Carbon Fourteen that all of us in this hemisphere are going to die. Don't be afraid to say it. Don't be afraid to think it. It is a truth, and it must be faced. As the transmutation effect spreads from the ruins of our cities, the air will become increasingly radioactive, and then we must die. In months, in a year or so, the effect will be strong overseas. Most of the people there will die too. None will escape completely. A worse thing will come to them than anything they have given us, because there will be a wave of horror and madness which is impossible to us. We are merely going to die. They will live and burn and sicken, and the children that will be born to them—" She shook her head, and her lower lip grew full. She visibly pulled herself together.

"Five hundred and thirty bombs . . . I don't think either of our attackers knew just how strong the other was. There has been so much secrecy." Her voice was sad. She shrugged slightly. "They have killed us, and they have ruined themselves. As for us—we are not blameless, either. Neither are we helpless to do anything—yet. But what we must do is hard. We must die—without striking back."

She gazed briefly at each man in turn, from the screen. "We must *not* strike back. Mankind is about to go through a hell of his own making. We can be vengeful—or merciful, if you like—and let go with the hundreds of bombs we have. That would sterilize the planet so that not a microbe, not a blade of grass could escape, and nothing new could grow. We would reduce the earth to a bald thing, dead and deadly.

"No—it just won't do. We can't do it.

"Remember the song? *That* is humanity. That's in all humans. A disease made other humans our enemies for a time, but as the generations march past, enemies become friends and friends enemies. The enmity of those who have killed us is such a tiny, temporary thing in the long sweep of history!"

Her voice deepened. "Let us die with the knowledge that we have done the one noble thing left to us. The spark of humanity can still live and grow on this planet. It will be blown and drenched, shaken and all but extinguished, but it will live if that song is a true one. It will live if we are human enough to discount the fact that the spark is in the custody of our temporary enemy. Some—a few—of his children will live to merge with the new humanity that will gradually emerge from the jungles and the wilderness. Perhaps there will be ten thousand years of beastliness; perhaps man will be able to rebuild while he still has his ruins."

She raised her head, her voice tolling. "And even if this is the end of humankind, we dare not take away the chances some other life-form might have to succeed where we failed. If we retaliate, there will not be a dog, a deer, an ape, a bird or fish or lizard to carry the evolutionary torch In the name of justice, if we must condemn and destroy ourselves, let us not condemn all other life along with us! Mankind is heavy enough with sins. If we must destroy, let us stop with destroying ourselves!"

There was a shimmering flicker of music. It seemed to stir her hair like a breath of wind. She smiled.

"That's all," she whispered. And to each man listening she said, "Good night . . ."

The screen went black. As the carrier cut off (there was no announcement) the ubiquitous speckles began to swarm across it.

Pete rose and switched on the lights. Bonze and Sonny were quite still. It must have been minutes later when Sonny sat up straight, shaking himself like a puppy. Something besides the silence seemed to tear with the movement.

He said, softly, "You're not allowed to fight anything, or to run away, or to live, and now you can't even hate any more, because Starr says no."

There was bitterness in the sound of it, and a bitter smell to the air.

Pete Mawser sniffed once, which had nothing to do with the smell. He sniffed again. "What's that smell, Son?"

Sonny tested it. "I don't— Something familiar. Vanilla—no . . . No."

"Almonds. Bitter— Bonze!"

Bonze lay still with his eyes open, grinning. His jaw muscles were knotted, and they could see almost all his teeth. He was soaking wet.

"Bonze!"

"It was just when she came on and said 'Hello—you,' remember?" whispered Pete. "Oh, the poor kid. That's why he wanted to catch the show here instead of in the mess-hall."

"Went out looking at her," said Sonny through pale lips. "I—can't say I blame him much. Wonder where he got the stuff."

"Never mind that!" Pete's voice was harsh. "Let's get out of here."

They left to call the ambulance. Bonze lay watching the console with his dead eyes and his smell of bitter almonds.

Pete did not realize where he was going, or exactly why, until he found himself on the dark street near GHQ and the communications shack, reflecting that it might be nice to be able to hear Starr, and see her, whenever he felt like it. Maybe there weren't any recordings; yet her musical background was recorded, and the signal corps might have recorded the show.

He stood uncertainly outside the GHQ building. There was a cluster of men outside the main entrance. Pete smiled briefly. Rain, nor snow, nor sleet, nor gloom of night could stay the stage-door Johnnie.

He went down the side street and up the delivery ramp in the back. Two doors along the platform was the rear exit of the Communications section.

There was a light on in the communications shack. He had his hand out to the screen door when he noticed someone standing in the shadows beside it. The light played daintily on the golden margins of a head and face.

He stopped. "S—Starr Anthim!"

"Hello, soldier. Sergeant."

He blushed like an adolescent. "I—" His voice left him. He swallowed, reached up to whip off his hat. He had no hat. "I saw the show," he said. He felt clumsy. It was dark, and yet he was very conscious of the fact that his dress-shoes were indifferently shined.

She moved toward him into the light, and she was so beautiful that he had to close his eyes. "What's your name?"

"Mawser. Pete Mawser."

"Like the show?"

Not looking at her, he said stubbornly, "No."

"Oh?"

"I mean—I liked it some. The song."

"I—think I see."

"I wondered if I could maybe get a recording."

"I think so," she said. "What kind of reproducer have you got?"

"Audiovid."

"A disc. Yes; we dubbed off a few. Wait, I'll get you one."

She went inside, moving slowly. Pete watched her, spellbound. She was a silhouette, crowned and haloed; and then she was a framed picture, vivid and golden. He waited, watching the light hungrily. She returned with a large envelope, called good night to someone inside, and came out on the platform.

"Here you are, Pete Mawser."

"Thanks very—" he mumbled. He wet his lips. "It was very good of you."

"Not really. The more it circulates, the better." She laughed suddenly. "That isn't meant quite as it sounds. I'm not exactly looking for new publicity these days."

The stubbornness came back. "I don't know that you'd get it, if you put on that show in normal times."

Her eyebrows went up. "Well!" she smiled. "I seem to have made quite an impression."

"I'm sorry," he said warmly. "I shouldn't have taken that tack. Everything I think and say these days is exaggerated."

"I know what you mean." She looked around. "How is it here?"

"It's okay. I used to be bothered by the secrecy, and being buried miles away from civilization." He chuckled bitterly. "Turned out to be lucky after all."

"You sound like the first chapter of *One World or None*."

He looked up quickly. "What do you use for a reading list—the Government's own *Index Expurgatorius*?"

She laughed. "Come now, it isn't as bad as all that. The book was never banned. It was just—"

"Unfashionable," he filled in.

"Yes, more's the pity. If people had paid more attention to it in the 'forties, perhaps this wouldn't have happened."

He followed her gaze to the dimly pulsating sky. "How long are you going to be here?"

"Until—as long as—I'm not leaving."

"You're not?"

"I'm finished," she said simply. "I've covered all the ground I can. I've been everywhere that . . . anyone knows about."

"With this show?"

She nodded. "With this particular message."

He was quiet, thinking. She turned to the door, and he put out his hand, not touching her. "Please—"

"What is it?"

"I'd like to—I mean, if you don't mind, I don't often have a chance to talk to—maybe you'd like to walk around a little before you turn in."

"Thanks, no, Sergeant. I'm tired." She did sound tired. "I'll see you around."

He stared at her, a sudden fierce light in his brain. "I know where it is. It's got a red-topped lever and a tag referring to orders of the commanding officer. It's really camouflaged."

She was quiet so long that he thought she had not heard him. Then, "I'll take that walk."

They went down the ramp together and turned toward the dark parade ground.

"How did you know?" she asked quietly.

"Not too tough. This 'message' of yours; the fact that you've been all over the country with it; most of all, the fact that somebody finds it necessary to persuade us not to strike back. Who are you working for?" he asked bluntly.

Surprisingly, she laughed.

"What's that for?"

"A moment ago you were blushing and shuffling your feet."

His voice was rough. "I wasn't talking to a human being. I was talking to a thousand songs I've heard, and a hundred thousand blonde pictures I've seen pinned up. You'd better tell me what this is all about."

She stopped. "Let's go up and see the colonel."

He took her elbow. "No. I'm just a sergeant, and he's high brass, and that doesn't make any difference at all now. You're a human being, and so am I, and I'm supposed to respect your rights as such. I don't. You'd better tell me about it."

"All right," she said, with a tired acquiescence that frightened something inside him. "You seem to have guessed right, though. It's true. There are master firing keys for the launching sites. We have located and dismantled all but two. It's very likely that one of the two was vaporized. The other one is—lost."

"Lost?"

"I don't have to tell you about the secrecy," she said. "You know how it developed between nation and nation. You must know that it existed between State and Union, between department and department, office and office. There were only three or four men who knew where all the keys were. Three of them were in the Pentagon when it went up. That was the third blast-bomb, you know. If there was another, it could only have been Senator Vanercook, and he died three weeks ago without talking."

"An automatic radio key, *hm*?"

"That's right. Sergeant, must we walk? I'm so tired."

"I'm sorry," he said impulsively. They crossed to the reviewing stand and sat on the lonely benches. "Launching racks all over, all hidden, and all armed?"

"Most of them are armed. There's a timing mechanism in them that will disarm them in a year or so. But in the meantime, they are armed—and aimed."

"Aimed where?"

"It doesn't matter."

"I think I see. What's the optimum number again?"

"About six hundred and forty; a few more or less. At least five hundred and thirty have been thrown so far. We don't know exactly."

"Who are *we*?" he asked furiously.

"Who? Who?" She laughed weakly. "I could say, 'The Government,' perhaps. If the President dies, the Vice-President takes over, and then the Secretary of State, and so on and on. How far can you go? Pete Mawser, don't you realize yet what's happened?"

"I don't know what you mean."

"How many people do you think are left in this country?"

"I don't know. Just a few million, I guess."

"How many are here?"

"About nine hundred."

"Then, as far as I know, this is the largest city left."

He leaped to his feet. *"No!"* The syllable roared away from him, hurled itself against the dark, empty buildings, came back to him in a series of lower-case echoes: nonono*no* . . . *no*-no.

Starr began to speak rapidly, quietly. "They're scattered all over the fields and the roads. They sit in the sun and die. They run in packs, they tear at each other. They pray and starve and kill themselves and die in the fires. The fires—everywhere, if anything stands, it's burning. Summer, and the leaves all down in the Berkshires, and the blue grass burnt brown; you can see the grass dying from the air, the death going out wider and wider from the bald-spots. Thunder and roses. . . . I saw roses, new ones, creeping from the smashed pots of a greenhouse. Brown petals, alive and sick, and the thorns turned back on themselves, growing into the stems, killing. Feldman died tonight."

He let her be quiet for a time. Then:

"Who is Feldman?"

"My pilot." She was talking hollowly into her hands. "He's been dying for weeks. He's been on his nerve-ends. I don't think he had any blood left. He buzzed your GHQ and made for the landing strip. He came in with the motor dead, free rotors, giro. Smashed the landing gear. He was dead, too. He killed a man in Chicago so he could steal gas. The man didn't want the gas. There was a dead girl by the pump. He didn't want us to go near. I'm not going anywhere. I'm going to stay here. I'm tired."

At last she cried.

Pete left her alone, and walked out to the center of the parade ground, looking back at the faint huddled glimmer on the bleachers. His mind flickered over the show that evening, and the way she had sung before the merciless transmitter. "Hello, you." "If we must destroy, let us stop with destroying ourselves!"

The dimming spark of humankind . . . what could it mean to her? How could it mean so much?

"Thunder and roses." Twisted, sick, non-survival roses, killing themselves with their own thorns.

"And the world was a place of light!" Blue light, flickering in the contaminated air.

The enemy. The red-topped lever. Bonze. "They pray and starve and kill themselves and die in the fires."

What creatures were these, these corrupted, violent, murdering humans? What right had they to another chance? What was in them that was good?

Starr was good. Starr was crying. Only a human being could cry like that. Starr was a human being.

Had humanity anything of Starr Anthim in it?

Starr was a human being.

He looked down through the darkness for his hands. No planet, no universe, is greater to a man than his own ego, his own observing self. These hands were the hands of all history, and like the hands of all men, they could by their small acts make human history or end it. Whether this power of hands was that of a billion hands, or whether it came to a focus in these two—this was suddenly unimportant to the eternities which now enfolded him.

He put humanity's hands deep in his pockets and walked slowly back to the bleachers.

"Starr."

She responded with a sleepy-child, interrogative whimper.

"They'll get their chance, Starr. I won't touch the key."

She sat straight. She rose, and came to him, smiling. He could see her smile, because, very faintly in this air, her teeth fluoresced. She put her hands on his shoulders. "Pete."

He held her very close for a moment. Her knees buckled then, and he had to carry her.

There was no one in the Officers' Club, which was the nearest building. He stumbled in, moved clawing along the wall until he found a switch. The light hurt him. He carried her to a settee and put her down gently. She did not move. One side of her face was as pale as milk.

He stood looking stupidly at it, wiped it on the sides of his trousers, looking dully at Starr. There was blood on her shirt.

A doctor . . . but there was no doctor. Not since Anders had hanged himself. "Get somebody," he muttered. "*Do* something."

He dropped to his knees and gently unbuttoned her shirt. Between the sturdy, unfeminine GI bra and the top of her slacks, there was blood on her side. He whipped out a clean handkerchief and began to wipe it away. There was no wound, no puncture. But abruptly there was blood again. He blotted it carefully. And again there was blood.

It was like trying to dry a piece of ice with a towel.

He ran to the water cooler, wrung out the bloody handkerchief and ran back to her. He bathed her face carefully, the pale right side, the flushed left side. The handkerchief reddened again, this time with cosmetics, and then her face was pale all over, with great blue shadows under the eyes. While he watched, blood appeared on her left cheek.

"There must be somebody—" He fled to the door.

"Pete!"

Running, turning at the sound of her voice, he hit the doorpost stunningly, caromed off, flailed for his balance, and then was back at her side. "Starr! Hang on, now! I'll get a doctor as quick as—"

Her hand strayed over her left cheek. "You found out. Nobody else knew, but Feldman. It got hard to cover properly." Her hand went up to her hair.

"Starr, I'll get a—"

"Pete, darling, promise me something?"

"Why, sure; certainly, Starr."

"Don't disturb my hair. It isn't—all mine, you see." She sounded like a seven-year-old, playing a game. "It all came out on this side. I don't want you to see me that way."

He was on his knees beside her again. "What is it? What happened to you?" he asked hoarsely.

"Philadelphia," she murmured. "Right at the beginning. The mushroom went up a half-mile away. The studio caved in. I came to the next day. I didn't know I was burned, then. It didn't show. My left side. It doesn't matter, Pete. It doesn't hurt at all, now."

He sprang to his feet again. "I'm going for a doctor."

"Don't go away. Please don't go away and leave me. Please don't." There were tears in her eyes. "Wait just a little while. Not very long, Pete."

He sank to his knees again. She gathered both his hands in hers and held them tightly. She smiled happily. "You're good, Pete. You're so good."

(She couldn't hear the blood in his ears, the roar of the whirlpool of hate and fear and anguish that spun inside of him.)

She talked to him in a low voice, and then in whispers. Sometimes he hated himself because he couldn't quite follow her. She talked about school, and her first audition. "I was so scared that I got a vibrato in my voice. I'd never had one before. I always let myself get a little scared when I sing now. It's easy." There was something about a window-box when she was four years old. "Two real live tulips and a pitcher-plant. I used to be sorry for the flies."

There was a long period of silence after that, during which his muscles throbbed with cramp and stiffness, and gradually became numb. He must have dozed; he awoke with a violent start, feeling her fingers on his face. She was propped up on one elbow. She said clearly, "I just wanted to tell you, darling. Let me go first, and get everything ready for you. It's going to be wonderful. I'll fix you a special tossed salad. I'll make you a steamed chocolate pudding and keep it hot for you."

Too muddled to understand what she was saying, he smiled and pressed her back on the settee. She took his hands again.

The next time he awoke it was broad daylight, and she was dead.

Sonny Weisefreund was sitting on his cot when he got back to the barracks. He handed over the recording he had picked up from the parade-ground on the way back. "Dew on it. Dry it off. Good boy," he croaked, and fell face downward on the cot Bonze had used.

Sonny stared at him. "Pete! Where you been? What happened? Are you all right?"

Pete shifted a little and grunted. Sonny shrugged and took the audiovid disc out of its wet envelope. Moisture would not harm it particularly, though it could not be played while wet. It was made of a fine spiral of plastic, insulated between laminations. Electrostatic pickups above and below the turntable would fluctuate with changes in the dielectric constant which had been impressed by the recording, and these changes were amplified for the scanners. The audio was a conventional hill-and-dale needle. Sonny began to wipe it down carefully.

Pete fought upward out of a vast, green-lit place full of flickering cold fires. Starr was calling him. Something was punching him, too. He fought it weakly, trying to hear what she was saying. But someone else was jabbering too loud for him to hear.

He opened his eyes. Sonny was shaking him, his round face pink with excitement. The Audiovid was running. Starr was talking. Sonny got up impatiently and turned down the volume. "Pete! Pete! Wake up, will you? I got to tell you something. Listen to me! Wake up, will yuh?"

"Huh?"

"That's better. Now listen. I've just been listening to Starr Anthim—"

"She's dead," said Pete.

Sonny didn't hear. He went on, explosively, "I've figured it out. Starr was sent out here, and all over, to *beg* someone not to fire any more atom bombs. If the government was sure they wouldn't strike back, they wouldn't've taken the trouble. Somewhere, Pete, there's some way to launch bombs at those murdering cowards—and I've got a pret-ty shrewd idea of how to do it."

Pete strained groggily toward the faint sound of Starr's voice. Sonny talked on. "Now, s'posing there was a master radio key—an automatic code device something like the alarm signal they have on ships, that rings a bell on any ship within radio range when the operator sends four long dashes. Suppose there's an automatic code machine to launch bombs, with repeaters, maybe, buried all over the country. What would it be? Just a little lever to pull; that's all. How would the thing be hidden? In the middle of a lot of other equipment, that's where; in some place where you'd expect to find crazy-looking secret stuff. Like an experiment station. Like right here. You beginning to get the idea?"

"Shut up, I can't hear her."

"The hell with her! You can listen to her some other time. You didn't hear a thing I said!"

"She's dead."

"Yeah. Well, I figure I'll pull that handle. What can I lose? It'll give those murderin'—*what?*"

"She's dead."

"Dead? Starr Anthim?" His young face twisted, Sonny sank down to the cot. "You're half asleep. You don't know what you're saying."

"She's dead," Pete said hoarsely. "She got burned by one of the first bombs. I was with her when she—she— Shut up now and get out of here and let me listen!" he bellowed hoarsely.

Sonny stood up slowly. "They killed her, too. They killed her! That does it. That just fixes it up." His face was white. He went out.

Pete got up. His legs weren't working right. He almost fell. He brought up against the console with a crash, his outflung arm sending the pickup skittering across the record. He put it on again and turned up the volume, then lay down to listen.

His head was all mixed up. Sonny talked too much. Bomb launchers, automatic code machines—

"*You gave me your heart,*" sang Starr. "*You gave me your heart. You gave me your heart. You . . .*"

Pete heaved himself up again and moved the pickup arm. Anger, not at himself, but at Sonny for causing him to cut the disc that way, welled up.

Starr was talking, stupidly, her face going through the same expression over and over again. "*Struck from the east and from the struck from the east and from the . . .*"

He got up again wearily and moved the pickup.

"*You gave me your heart you gave me . . .*"

Pete made an agonized sound that was not a word at all, bent, lifted, and sent the console crashing over. In the bludgeoning silence he said, "I did, too."

Then, "Sonny." He waited.

"Sonny!"

His eyes went wide then, and he cursed and bolted for the corridor.

The panel was closed when he reached it. He kicked at it. It flew open, discovering darkness.

"Hey!" bellowed Sonny. "Shut it! You turned off the lights!"

Pete shut it behind them. The lights blazed.

"Pete! What's the matter?"

"Nothing's the matter, Son," croaked Pete.

"What are you looking at?" said Sonny uneasily.

"I'm sorry," said Pete as gently as he could. "I just wanted to find something out, is all. Did you tell anyone else about this?" He pointed to the lever.

"Why, no. I only just figured it out while you were sleeping, just now."

Pete looked around carefully, while Sonny shifted his weight. Pete moved toward a tool-rack. "Something you haven't noticed yet, Sonny," he said softly, and pointed. "Up there, on the wall behind you. High up. See?"

Sonny turned. In one fluid movement Pete plucked off a fourteen-inch box wrench and hit Sonny with it as hard as he could.

Afterward he went to work systematically on the power supplies. He pulled the plugs on the gas-engines and cracked their cylinders with a maul. He knocked off the tubing of the diesel starters—the tanks let go explosively—and he cut all the cables with bolt-cutters. Then he broke up the relay rack and its lever. When he was quite finished, he put away his tools and bent and stroked Sonny's tousled hair.

He went out and closed the partition carefully. It certainly was a wonderful piece of camouflage. He sat down heavily on a workbench nearby.

"You'll have your chance," he said into the far future. "And, by Heaven, you'd better make good."

After that he just waited.

First published: 1948

LATE NIGHT FINAL

by Eric Frank Russell

COMMANDER CRUIN WENT DOWN THE EXTENDING METAL LADDER, PAUSED a rung from the bottom, placed one important foot on the new territory, and then the other. That made him the first of his kind on an unknown world.

He posed there in the sunlight, a big bull of a man meticulously attired for the occasion. Not a spot marred his faultlessly cut uniform of gray-green on which jeweled orders of merit sparkled and flashed. His jack boots glistened as they had never done since the day of launching from the home planet. The golden bells of his rank tinkled on his heel-hooks as he shifted his feet slightly. In the deep shadow beneath the visor of his ornate helmet his hard eyes held a glow of self-satisfaction.

A microphone came swinging down to him from the air lock he'd just left. Taking it in a huge left hand, he looked straight ahead with the blank intentness of one who sees long visions of the past and longer visions of the future. Indeed, this was as visionary a moment as any there had been in his world's history.

"In the name of Huld and the people of Huld," he enunciated officiously, "I take this planet." Then he saluted swiftly, slickly, like an automaton.

Facing him, twenty-two long, black spaceships simultaneously thrust from their forward ports their glorypoles ringed with the red-black-gold colors of Huld. Inside the vessels twenty-two crews of seventy men apiece stood rigidly erect, saluted, broke into well-drilled song, "Oh, heavenly fatherland of Huld."

When they had finished, Commander Cruin saluted again. The crews repeated their salute. The glorypoles were drawn in. Cruin mounted the ladder, entered his flagship. All locks were closed. Along the valley the twenty-two invaders lay in military formation, spaced equidistantly, noses and tails dead in line.

On a low hill a mile to the east a fire sent up a column of thick smoke. It spat and blazed amid the remnants of what had been the twenty-third vessel—and the eighth successive loss since the fleet had set forth three years ago. Thirty then. Twenty-two now.

The price of empire.

Reaching his cabin, Commander Cruin lowered his bulk into the seat behind his desk, took off his heavy helmet, adjusted an order of merit which was hiding modestly behind its neighbor.

"Step four," he commented with satisfaction.

Second Commander Jusik nodded respectfully. He handed the other a book. Opening it, Cruin meditated aloud.

"Step one: Check planet's certain suitability for our form of life." He rubbed his big jowls. "We know it's suitable."

"Yes, sir. This is a great triumph for you."

"Thank you, Jusik." A craggy smile played momentarily on one side of Cruin's broad face. "Step two: Remain in planetary shadow at distance of not less than one diameter while scout boats survey world for evidence of superior life forms. Three: Select landing place far from largest sources of possible resistance but adjacent to a source small enough to be mastered. Four: Declare Huld's claim ceremoniously, as prescribed in manual on procedure and discipline." He worked his jowls again. "We've done all that."

The smile returned, and he glanced with satisfaction out of the small port near his chair. The port framed the smoke column on the hill. His expression changed to a scowl, and his jaw muscles lumped.

"Fully trained and completely qualified," he growled sardonically. "Yet he had to smash up. Another ship and crew lost in the very moment we reach our goal. The eighth such loss. There will be a purge in the astronautical training center when I return."

"Yes, sir," approved Jusik, dutifully. "There is no excuse for it."

"There are no excuses for anything," Cruin retorted.

"No, sir."

Snorting his contempt, Cruin looked at his book. "Step five: Make all protective preparations as detailed in defense manual." He glanced up into Jusik's lean, clearcut features. "Every captain has been issued with a defense manual. Are they carrying out its orders?"

"Yes, sir. They have started already."

"They better had! I shall arrange a demotion of the slowest." Wetting a large thumb, he flipped a page over. "Step six: If planet does hold life forms of suspected intelligence, obtain specimens." Lying back in his seat he mused a moment, then barked: "Well, for what are you waiting?"

"I beg your pardon, sir?"

"Get some examples," roared Cruin.

"Very well, sir." Without blinking, Jusik saluted, marched out.

The self-closer swung the door behind him. Cruin surveyed it with a jaundiced eye.

"Curse the training center," he rumbled. "It has deteriorated since I was there."

Putting his feet on the desk, he waggled his heels to make the bells tinkle while he waited for the examples.

Three specimens turned up of their own accord. They were seen standing wide-eyed in a row near the prow of number twenty-two, the endmost ship of the line. Captain Somir brought them along personally.

"Step six calls for specimens, sir," he explained to Commander Cruin. "I know that you require ones better than these, but I found these under our nose."

"Under your nose? You land and within short time other life forms are sightseeing around your vessel? What about your protective precautions?"

"They are not completed yet, sir. They take some time."

"What were your lookouts doing—sleeping?"

"No, sir," assured Somir desperately. "They did not think it necessary to sound a general alarm for such as these."

Reluctantly, Cruin granted the point. His gaze ran contemptuously over the trio. Three kids. One was a boy, knee-high, snubnosed, chewing at a chubby fist. The next, a skinny-legged, pigtailed girl obviously older than the boy. The third was another girl almost as tall as Somir, somewhat skinny, but with a hint of coming shapeliness hiding in her thin attire. All three were freckled, all had violently red hair.

The tall girl said to Cruin: "I'm Marva—Marva Meredith." She indicated her companions. "This is Sue and this is Sam. We live over there, in Williamsville." She smiled at him and suddenly he noticed that her eyes were a rich and startling green. "We were looking for blueberries when we saw you come down."

Cruin grunted, rested his hands on his paunch. The fact that this planet's life manifestly was of his own shape and form impressed him not at all. It had never occurred to him that it could have proved otherwise.

In Huldian thought, all superior life must be humanoid and no exploration had yet provided evidence to the contrary.

"I don't understand her alien gabble and she doesn't understand Huldian," he complained to Somir. "She must be dull-witted to waste her breath thus."

"Yes, sir," agreed Somir. "Do you wish me to hand them over to the tutors?"

"No. They're not worth it." He eyed the small boy's freckles with distaste, never having seen such a phenomenon before. "They are badly spotted and may be diseased. *Pfaugh!*" He grimaced with disgust. "Did they pass through the ray-sterilizing chamber as they came in?"

"Certainly, sir. I was most careful about that."

"Be equally careful about any more you may encounter." Slowly, his authoritative stare went from the boy to the pigtailed girl and finally to the tall one. He didn't want to look at her, yet knew that he was going to. Her cool green eyes held something that made him vaguely uncomfortable. Unwillingly he met those eyes. She smiled again, with little dimples. "Kick 'em out!" he rapped at Somir.

"As you order, sir."

Nudging them, Somir gestured toward the door. The three took hold of each other's hands, filed out.

"Bye!" chirped the boy, solemnly.

"Bye!" said pigtails, shyly.

The tall girl turned in the doorway. "Good-by!"

Gazing at her uncomprehendingly, Cruin fidgeted in his chair. She dimpled at him, then the door swung to.

"Good-by." He mouthed the strange word to himself. Considering the circumstances in which it had been uttered, evidently it meant farewell. Already he had picked up one word of their language.

"Step seven: Gain communication by tutoring specimens until they are proficient in Huldian."

Teach them. Do not let them teach you—teach *them*. The slaves must learn from the masters, not the masters from the slaves.

"Good-by." He repeated it with savage self-accusation. A minor matter, but still an infringement of the book of rules. There are no excuses for anything.

Teach them.

The slaves—

Rockets rumbled and blasted deafeningly as ships maneuvered themselves into the positions laid down in the manual of defense. Several hours of careful belly-edging were required for this. In the end, the line had reshaped itself into two groups of eleven-pointed stars, noses at the centers, tails outward. Ash of blast-destroyed grasses, shrubs and trees covered a wide area beyond the two menacing rings of main propulsion tubes which could incinerate anything within one mile.

This done, perspiring, dirt-coated crews lugged out their forward armaments, remounted them pointing outward in the spaces between the vessels' splayed tails. Rear armaments still aboard already were directed upward and outward. Armaments plus tubes now provided a formidable field of fire completely surrounding the double encampment. It was the Huldian master plan conceived by Huldian master planners. In other more alien estimation, it was the old covered-wagon technique, so incredibly ancient that it had been forgotten by all but most earnest students of the past. But none of the invaders knew that.

Around the perimeter they stacked the small, fast, well-armed scouts of which there were two per ship. Noses outward, tails inward, in readiness for quick take-off, they were paired just beyond the parent vessels, below the propulsion tubes, and out of line of the remounted batteries. There was a lot of moving around to get the scouts positioned at precisely the same distances apart and making precisely the same angles. The whole arrangement had that geometrical exactness beloved of the military mind.

Pacing the narrow catwalk running along the top surface of his flagship, Commander Cruin observed his toiling crews with satisfaction. Organization, discipline, energy, unquestioning obedience—those were the prime essentials of efficiency. On such had Huld grown great. On such would Huld grow greater.

Reaching the tail-end, he leaned on the stop-rail, gazed down upon the concentric rings of wide, stubby venturis. His own crew were checking the angles of their two scouts already positioned. Four guards, heavily armed, came marching through the ash with Jusik in the lead. They had six prisoners.

Seeing him, Jusik bowled: "Halt!" Guard and guarded stopped with a thud of boots and a rise of dust. Looking up, Jusik saluted.

"Six specimens, sir."

Cruin eyed them indifferently. Half a dozen middle-aged men in drab, sloppily fitting clothes. He would not have given a snap of the fingers for six thousand of them.

The biggest of the captives, the one second from the left, had red hair and was sucking something that gave off smoke. His shoulders were wider than Cruin's own though he didn't look half the weight. Idly, the commander wondered whether the fellow had green eyes; he couldn't tell that from where he was standing.

Calmly surveying Cruin, this prisoner took the smoke-thing from his mouth and said, tonelessly: "By hokey, a brasshat!" Then he shoved the thing back between his lips and dribbled blue vapor.

The others looked doubtful, as if either they did not comprehend or found it past belief.

"Jeepers, *no!*" said the one on the right, a gaunt individual with thin, saturnine features.

"I'm telling you," assured Redhead in the same flat voice.

"Shall I take them to the tutors, sir?" asked Jusik.

"Yes." Unleaning from the rail, Cruin carefully adjusted his white gloves. "Don't bother me with them again until they are certified as competent to talk." Answering the other's salute, he paraded back along the catwalk.

"See?" said Redhead, picking up his feet in time with the guard. He seemed to take an obscure pleasure in keeping in step with the guard. Winking at the nearest prisoner, he let a curl of aromatic smoke trickle from the side of his mouth.

Tutors Fane and Parth sought an interview the following evening. Jusik ushered them in, and Cruin looked up irritably from the report he was writing.

"Well?"

Fane said: "Sir, these prisoners suggest that we share their homes for a while and teach them to converse there."

"How did they suggest that?"

"Mostly by signs," explained Fane.

"And what made you think that so nonsensical a plan had sufficient merit to make it worthy of my attention?"

"There are aspects about which you should be consulted," Fane continued stubbornly. "The manual of procedure and discipline declares that such matters must be placed before the commanding officer whose decision is final."

"Quite right, quite right." He regarded Fane with a little more favor. "What are these matters?"

"Time is important to us, and the quicker these prisoners learn our language the better it will be. Here, their minds are occupied by their predicament. They think too much of their friends and families. In their own homes it would be different, and they could learn at great speed."

"A weak pretext," scoffed Cruin.

"That is not all. By nature they are naive and friendly. I feel that we have little to fear from them. Had they been hostile they would have attacked by now."

"Not necessarily. It is wise to be cautious. The manual of defense emphasizes that fact repeatedly. These creatures may wish first to gain the measure of us before they try to deal with us."

Fane was prompt to snatch the opportunity. "Your point, sir, is also my final one. Here, they are six pairs of eyes and six pairs of ears in the middle of us, and their absence is likely to give cause for alarm in their home town. Were they there, complacency would replace that alarm—and *we* would be the eyes and ears!"

"Well put," commented Jusik, momentarily forgetting himself.

"Be silent!" Cruin glared at him. "I do not recall any ruling in the manual pertaining to such a suggestion as this. Let me check up." Grabbing his books, he sought through them. He took a long time about it, gave up, and said: "The only pertinent rule appears to be that in circumstances not specified in the manual the decision is wholly mine, to be made in light of said circumstances providing that they do not conflict with the rulings of any other manual which may be applicable to the situation, and providing that my decision does not effectively countermand that or those of any senior ranking officer whose authority extends to the same area." He took a deep breath.

"Yes, sir," said Fane.

"Quite, sir," said Parth.

Cruin frowned heavily. "How far away are these prisoners' homes?"

"One hour's walk." Fane made a persuasive gesture. "If anything did happen to us—which I consider extremely unlikely—one scout could wipe out their little town before they'd time to realize what had happened. One scout, one bomb, one minute!" Dexterously, he added, "At your order, sir."

Cruin preened himself visibly. "I see no reason why we should not take advantage of their stupidity." His eyes asked Jusik what he thought, but that person failed to notice. "Since you two tutors have brought this plan to me, I hereby approve it, and I appoint you to carry it through." He consulted a list which he extracted from a drawer. "Take two psychologists with you—Kalma and Hefni."

"Very well, sir." Impassively, Fane saluted and went out, Parth following.

Staring absently at his half-written report, Cruin fiddled with his pen for a while, glanced up at Jusik, and spat: "At what are you smiling?"

Jusik wiped it from his face, looked solemn.

"Come on. Out with it!"

"I was thinking, sir," replied Jusik, slowly, "that three years in a ship is a very long time."

Slamming his pen on the desk, Cruin stood up. "Has it been any longer for others than for me?"

"For you," said Jusik, daringly but respectfully, "I think it has been longest of all."

"Get out!" shouted Cruin.

He watched the other go, watched the self-closer push the door, waited for its last click. He shifted his gaze to the port, stared hard-eyed into the gathering dusk. His heelbells were silent as he stood unmoving and saw the invisible sun sucking its last rays from the sky.

In short time, ten figures strolled through the twilight toward the distant, tree-topped hill. Four were uniformed; six in drab, shapeless clothes. They went by conversing with many gestures, and one of them laughed. He gnawed his bottom lip as his gaze followed them until they were gone.

The price of rank.

"Step eight: Repel initial attacks in accordance with techniques detailed in manual of defense." Cruin snorted, put up one hand, tidied his orders of merit.

"There have been no attacks," said Jusik.

"I am not unaware of the fact." The commander glowered at him. "I'd have preferred an onslaught. We are ready for them. The sooner they match their strength against ours the sooner they'll learn who's boss now!" He hooked big thumbs in his silver-braided belt. "And besides, it would give the men something to do. I cannot have them everlastingly repeating their drills of procedure. We've been here nine days and nothing has happened." His attention returned to the book. "Step nine: Follow defeat of initial attacks by taking aggressive action as detailed in manual of defense." He gave another snort. "How can one follow something that has not occurred?"

"It is impossible," Jusik ventured.

"Nothing is impossible," Cruin contradicted, harshly. "Step ten: In the unlikely event that intelligent life displays indifference or amity, remain in protective formation while specimens are being tutored, meanwhile employing scout vessels to survey surrounding area to the limit of their flight-duration, using no more than one-fifth of the numbers available at any time."

"That allows us eight or nine scouts on survey," observed Jusik, thoughtfully. "What is our authorized step if they fail to return?"

"Why d'you ask that?"

"Those eight scouts I sent out on your orders forty periods ago are overdue."

Viciously, Commander Cruin thrust away his book. His broad, heavy face was dark red.

"Second Commander Jusik, it was your duty to report this fact to me the moment those vessels became overdue."

"Which I have," said Jusik, imperturbably. "They have a flight-duration of forty periods, as you know. That, sir, made them due a short time ago. They are now late."

Cruin tramped twice across the room, medals clinking, heel-bells jangling. "The answer to nonappearance is immediately to obliterate the areas in which they are held. No half-measures. A salutary lesson."

"Which areas, sir?"

Stopping in mid-stride, Cruin bawled: "*You* ought to know that. Those scouts had properly formulated route orders, didn't they? It's a simple matter to—"

He ceased as a shrill whine passed overhead, lowered to a dull moan in the distance, curved back on a rising note again.

"Number one." Jusik looked at the little timemeter on the wall. "Late, but here. Maybe the others will turn up now."

"Somebody's going to get a sharp lesson if they don't!"

"I'll see what he has to report." Saluting, Jusik hurried through the doorway.

Gazing out of his port, Cruin observed the delinquent scout bellysliding up to the nearest formation. He chewed steadily at his bottom lip, a slow, persistent chew which showed his thoughts to be wandering around in labyrinths of their own.

Beyond the fringe of dank, dead ash were golden buttercups in the grasses, and a hum of bees, and the gentle rustle of leaves on trees. Four engine-room wranglers of ship number seventeen had found this sanctuary and sprawled flat on their backs in the shade of a big-leafed and blossom-ornamented growth. With eyes closed, their hands plucked idly at surrounding grasses while they maintained a lazy, desultory conversation through which they failed to hear the ring of Cruin's approaching bells.

Standing before them, his complexion florid, he roared: "Get up!"

Shooting to their feet, they stood stiffly shoulder to shoulder, faces expressionless, eyes level, hands at their sides.

"Your names?" He wrote them in his notebook while obediently they repeated them in precise, unemotional voices. "I'll deal with you later," he promised. "March!"

Together, they saluted, marched off with a rhythmic pounding of boots, one-two-three-hup! His angry stare followed them until they reached the shadow of their ship. Not until then did he turn and proceed. Mounting the hill, one cautious hand continually on the cold butt of his gun, he reached the crest, gazed down into the valley he'd just left. In neat, exact positioning, the two star-formations of the ships of Huld were silent and ominous.

His hard, authoritative eyes turned to the other side of the hill. There, the landscape was pastoral. A wooded slope ran down to a little river which meandered into the hazy distance, and on its farther side was a broad patchwork of cultivated fields in which three houses were visible.

Seating himself on a large rock, Cruin loosened his gun in its holster, took a wary look around, extracted a small wad of reports from his pocket and glanced over them for the twentieth time. A faint smell of herbs and resin came to his nostrils as he read.

"I circled this landing place at low altitude and recorded it photographically, taking care to include all the machines standing thereon. Two other machines which were in the air went on their way without attempting to interfere. It then occurred to me that the signals they were making from the ground might be an invitation to land, and I decided to utilize opportunism as recommended in the manual of procedure. Therefore I landed. They conducted my scout vessel to a dispersal point off the runway and made me welcome."

Something fluted liquidly in a nearby tree. Cruin looked up, his hand automatically seeking his holster. It was only a bird. Skipping parts of the report, he frowned over the concluding words.

". . . lack of common speech made it difficult for me to refuse, and after the sixth drink during my tour of the town I was suddenly afflicted with a strange paralysis in the legs and collapsed into the arms of my companions. Believing that they had poisoned me by guile, I prepared for death . . . tickled my throat while making jocular remarks . . . I was a little sick." Cruin rubbed his chin in puzzlement. "Not until they were satisfied about my recovery did they take me back to my vessel. They waved their hands at me as I took off. I apologize to my captain for overdue return and plead that it was because of factors beyond my control."

The fluter came down to Cruin's feet, piped at him plaintively. It cocked its head sidewise as it examined him with bright, beady eyes.

Shifting the sheet he'd been reading, he scanned the next one. It was neatly typewritten, and signed jointly by Parth, Fane, Kalma and Hefni.

"Do not appear fully to appreciate what has occurred . . . seem to view the arrival of a Huldian fleet as just another incident. They have a remarkable self-assurance which is incomprehensible inasmuch as we can find nothing to justify such an attitude. Mastery of them should be so easy that if our homing vessel does not leave too soon it should be possible for it to bear tidings of conquest as well as of mere discovery."

"Conquest," he murmured. It had a mighty imposing sound. A word like that would send a tremendous thrill of excitement throughout the entire world of Huld.

Five before him had sent back ships telling of discovery, but none had gone so far as he, none had traveled so long and wearily, none had been rewarded with a planet so big, lush, desirable—and none had reported the subjection of their finds. One cannot conquer a rocky waste. But this—

In peculiarly accented Huldian, a voice behind him said, brightly: "Good morning!"

He came up fast, his hand sliding to his side, his face hard with authority.

She was laughing at him with her clear green eyes. "Remember me—Marva Meredith?" Her flaming hair was windblown. "You see," she went on, in slow, awkward tones. "I know a little Huldian already. Just a few words."

"Who taught you?" he asked, bluntly.

"Fane and Parth."

"It is your house to which they have gone?"

"Oh, yes. Kalma and Hefni are guesting with Bill Gleeson; Fane and Parth with us. Father brought them to us. They share the welcome room."

"Welcome room?"

"Of course." Perching herself on his rock, she drew up her slender legs, rested her chin on her knees. He noticed that the legs, like her face, were freckled. "Of course. Everyone has a welcome room, haven't they?"

Cruin said nothing.

"Haven't you a welcome room in your home?"

"Home?" His eyes strayed away from hers, sought the fluting bird. It wasn't there. Somehow, his hand had left his holster without realizing it. He was holding his hands together, each nursing the other, clinging, finding company, soothing each other.

Her gaze was on his hands as she said, softly and hesitantly, "You have got a home . . . somewhere . . . haven't you?"

"No."

Lowering her legs, she stood up. "I'm so sorry."

"*You* are sorry for *me*?" His gaze switched back to her. It held incredulity, amazement, a mite of anger. His voice was harsh. "You must be singularly stupid."

"Am I?" she asked, humbly.

"No member of my expedition has a home," he went on. "Every man was carefully selected. Every man passed through a screen, suffered the most exacting tests. Intelligence and technical competence were not enough; each had also to be young, healthy, without ties of any sort. They were chosen for ability to concentrate on the task in hand without indulging morale-lowering sentimentalities about people left behind."

"I don't understand some of your long words," she complained. "And you are speaking far too fast."

He repeated it more slowly and with added emphasis, finishing, "Spaceships undertaking long absence from base cannot be handicapped by homesick crews. We picked men without homes because they can leave Huld and not care a hoot. They are pioneers!"

" 'Young, healthy, without ties,' " she quoted. "That makes them strong?"

"Definitely," he asserted.

"Men especially selected for space. Strong men." Her lashes hid her eyes as she looked down at her narrow feet. "But now they are not in space. They are here, on firm ground."

"What of it," he demanded.

"Nothing." Stretching her arms wide, she took a deep breath, then dimpled at him. "Nothing at all."

"You're only a child," he reminded, scornfully. "When you grow older—"

"You'll have more sense," she finished for him, chanting it in a high, sweet voice. "You'll have more sense, you'll have more sense. When you grow older you'll have more sense, tra-la-la-lala!"

Gnawing irritatedly at his lip, he walked past her, started down the hill toward the ships.

"Where are you going?"

"Back!" he snapped.

"Do you like it down there?" Her eyebrows arched in surprise.

Stopping ten paces away, he scowled at her. "Is it any of your business?"

"I didn't mean to be inquisitive," she apologized. "I asked because . . . because—"

"Because what?"

"I was wondering whether you would care to visit my house."

"Nonsense! Impossible!" He turned to continue downhill.

"Father suggested it. He thought you might like to share a meal. A fresh one. A change of diet. Something to break the monotony of your supplies." The wind lifted her crimson hair and played with it as she regarded him speculatively. "He consulted Fane and Parth. They said it was an excellent idea."

"They did, did they?" His features seemed molded in iron. "Tell Fane and Parth they are to report to me at sunset." He paused, added, "Without fail!"

Resuming her seat on the rock, she watched him stride heavily down the slope toward the double star-formation. Her hands were together in her lap, much as he had held his. But hers sought nothing of each other. In complete repose, they merely rested with the ineffable patience of hands as old as time.

Seeing at a glance that he was liverish, Jusik promptly postponed certain suggestions that he had in mind.

"Summon captains Drek and Belthan," Cruin ordered. When the other had gone, he flung his helmet onto the desk, surveyed himself in a mirror. He was still smoothing the tired lines on his face when approaching footsteps sent him officiously behind his desk.

Entering, the two captains saluted, remained rigidly at attention. Cruin studied them irefully while they preserved wooden expressions.

Eventually, he said: "I found four men lounging like undisciplined hoboes outside the safety zone." He stared at Drek. "They were from your vessel." The stare shifted to Belthan. "You are today's commander of the guard. Have either of you anything to say?"

"They were off-duty and free to leave the ship," exclaimed Drek. "They had been warned not to go beyond the perimeter of ash."

"I don't know how they slipped through," said Belthan, in official monotone. "Obviously the guards were lax. The fault is mine."

"It will count against you in your promotion records," Cruin promised. "Punish these four, and the responsible guards, as laid down in the manual of procedure and discipline." He leaned across the desk to survey them more closely. "A repetition will bring ceremonial demotion!"

"Yes, sir," they chorused.

Dismissing them, he glanced at Jusik. "When tutors Fane and Parth report here, send them in to me without delay."

"As you order, sir."

Cruin dropped the glance momentarily, brought it back. "What's the matter with you?"

"Me?" Jusik became self-conscious. "Nothing, sir."

"You lie! One has to live with a person to know him. I've lived on your neck for three years. I know you too well to be deceived. You have something on your mind."

"It's the men," admitted Jusik, resignedly.

"What of them?"

"They are restless."

"Are they? Well, I can devise a cure for that! What's making them restless?"

"Several things, sir."

Cruin waited while Jusik stayed dumb, then roared: "Do I have to prompt you?"

"No, sir," Jusik protested, unwillingly. "It's many things. Inactivity. The substitution of tedious routine. The constant waiting, waiting, waiting right on top of three years close incarceration. They wait—and nothing happens."

"What else?"

"The sight and knowledge of familiar life just beyond the ash. The realization that Fane and Parth and the others are enjoying it with your consent. The stories told by the scouts about their experiences on landing." His gaze was steady as he went on. "We've now sent out five squadrons of scouts, a total of forty vessels. Only six came back on time. All the rest were late on one plausible pretext or another. The pilots have talked, and shown the men various souvenir photographs and a few gifts. One of them is undergoing punishment for bringing back some bottles of paralysis-mixture. But the damage has been done. Their stories have unsettled the men."

"Anything more?"

"Begging your pardon, sir, there was also the sight of you taking a stroll to the top of the hill. They envied you even that!" He looked squarely at Cruin. "I envied you myself."

"I am the commander," said Cruin.

"Yes, sir." Jusik kept his gaze on him but added nothing more.

If the second commander expected a delayed outburst, he was disappointed. A complicated series of emotions chased each other across his superior's broad, beefy features. Laying back in his chair, Cruin's eyes looked absently through the port while his mind juggled with Jusik's words.

Suddenly, he rasped: "I have observed more, anticipated more and given matters more thought then perhaps you realize. I can see something which you may have failed to perceive. It has caused me some anxiety. Briefly, if we don't keep pace with the march of time we're going to find ourselves in a fix."

"Indeed, sir?"

"I don't wish you to mention this to anyone else: I suspect that we are trapped in a situation bearing no resemblance to any dealt with in the manuals."

"Really, sir?" Jusik licked his lips, felt that his own outspokenness was leading into unexpected paths.

"Consider our present circumstances," Cruin went on. "We are established here and in possession of power sufficient to enslave this planet. Any one of our supply of bombs could blast a portion of this earth stretching from horizon to horizon. But they're of no use unless we apply them effectively. We can't drop them anywhere, haphazardly. If parting with them in so improvident a manner proved unconvincing to our opponents, and failed to smash the hard core of their resistance, we would find ourselves unarmed in a hostile world. No more bombs. None nearer than six long years away, three there and three back. Therefore we must apply our power where it will do the most good." He began to massage his heavy chin. "We don't know where to apply it."

"No, sir," agreed Jusik, pointlessly.

"We've got to determine which cities are the key points of their civilization, which persons are this planet's acknowledged leaders, and where they're located. When we strike, it must be at the nerve-centers. That means we're impotent until we get the necessary information. In turn, that means we've got to establish communication with the aid of tutors." He started plucking at his jaw muscles. "And that takes time!"

"Quite, sir, but—"

"But while time crawls past the men's morale evaporates. This is our twelfth day and already the crews are restless. Tomorrow they'll be more so."

"I have a solution to that, sir, if you will forgive me for offering it," said Jusik, eagerly. "On Huld everyone gets one day's rest in five. They are free to do as they like, go where they like. Now if you promulgated an order permitting the men say one day's liberty in ten, it would mean that no more than ten percent of our strength would be lost on any one day. We could stand that reduction considering our power, especially if more of the others are on protective duty."

"So at last I get what was occupying your mind. It comes out in a swift flow of words." He smiled grimly as the other flushed. "I have thought of it. I am not quite so unimaginative as you may consider me."

"I don't look upon you that way, sir," Jusik protested.

"Never mind. We'll let that pass. To return to this subject of liberty—there lies the trap! There is the very quandary with which no manual deals, the situation for which I can find no officially prescribed formula." Putting a hand on his desk he tapped the polished surface impatiently. "If I refuse these men a little freedom, they will become increasingly restless—naturally. If I permit them the liberty they desire, they will experience contact with life more normal even though alien, and again become more restless—naturally!"

"Permit me to doubt the latter, sir. Our crews are loyal to Huld. Blackest space forbid that it should be otherwise!"

"They were loyal. Probably they are still loyal." Cruin's face quirked as his memory brought forward the words that followed. "They are young, healthy, without ties. In space, that means one thing. Here, another." He came slowly to his feet, big, bulky and imposing. "I *know!*"

Looking at him, Jusik felt that indeed he did know. "Yes, sir," he parroted, obediently.

"Therefore the onus of what to do for the best falls squarely upon me. I must use my initiative. As second commander it is for you to see that my orders are carried out to the letter."

"I know my duty, sir." Jusik's thinly-drawn features registered growing uneasiness.

"And it is my final decision that the men must be restrained from contact with our opponents, with no exceptions other than the four technicians operating under my orders. The crews are to be permitted no liberty, no freedom to go beyond the ash. Any form of resentment on their part must be countered immediately and ruthlessly. You will instruct the captains to watch for murmurers in their respective crews and take appropriate action to silence them as soon as found." His jowls lumped, and his eyes were cold as he regarded the other. "All scout-flights are canceled as from now, and all scout-vessels remain grounded. None moves without my personal instructions."

"That is going to deprive us of a lot of information," Jusik observed. "The last flight to the south reported discovery of ten cities completely deserted, and that's got some significance which we ought to—"

"I said the flights are canceled!" Cruin shouted. "If I say the scout-vessels are to be painted pale pink, they will be painted pale pink, thoroughly, completely, from end to end. I am the commander!"

"As you order, sir."

"Finally, you may instruct the captains that their vessels are to be prepared for my inspection at midday tomorrow. That will give the crews something to do."

"Very well, sir."

With a worried salute, Jusik opened the door, glanced out and said: "Here are Fane, Kalma, Parth and Hefni, sir."

"Show them in."

After Cruin had given forcible expression to his views, Fane said: "We appreciate the urgency, sir, and we are doing our best, but it is doubtful whether they will be fluent before another four weeks have passed. They are slow to learn."

"I don't want fluency," Cruin growled. "All they need are enough words to tell us the things we want to know, the things we *must* know before we can get anywhere."

"I said sufficient fluency," Fane reminded. "They communicate mostly by signs even now."

"That flame-headed girl didn't."

"She has been quick," admitted Fane. "Possibly she has an above-normal aptitude for languages. Unfortunately she knows the least in any military sense and therefore is of little use to us."

Cruin's gaze ran over him balefully. His voice became low and menacing. "You have lived with these people many days. I look upon your features and find them different. Why is that?"

"Different?" The four exchanged wondering looks.

"Your faces have lost their lines, their space-gauntness. Your cheeks have become plump, well-colored. Your eyes are no longer tired. They are bright. They hold the self-satisfied expression of a fat *skodar* wallowing in its trough. It is obvious that you have done well for yourselves." He bent forward, his mouth ugly. "Can it be that you are in no great hurry to complete your task?"

They were suitably shocked.

"We have eaten well and slept regularly," Fane said. "We feel better for it. Our physical improvement has enabled us to work so much the harder. In our view, the foe is supporting us unwittingly with his own hospitality, and since the manual of—"

"Hospitality?" Cruin cut in, sharply.

Fane went mentally off-balance as vainly he sought for a less complimentary synonym.

"I give you another week," the commander harshed. "No more. Not one day more. At this time, one week from today, you will report here with the six prisoners adequately tutored to understand my questions and answer them."

"It will be difficult, sir."

"Nothing is difficult. Nothing is impossible. There are no excuses for anything." He studied Fane from beneath forbidding brows. "You have my orders—obey them!"

"Yes, sir."

His hard stare shifted to Kalma and Hefni. "So much for the tutors; now *you*. What have you to tell me? How much have you discovered?"

Blinking nervously, Hefni said: "It is not a lot. The language trouble is—"

"May the Giant Sun burn up and perish the language trouble! How much have you learned while enjoyably larding your bellies?"

Glancing down at his uniform-belt as if suddenly and painfully conscious of its tightness, Hefni recited: "They are exceedingly strange in so far as they appear to be highly civilized in a purely domestic sense but quite primitive in all others. This Meredith family lives in a substantial, well-equipped house. They have every comfort, including a color-television receiver."

"You're dreaming! We are still seeking the secrets of plain television even on Huld. Color is unthinkable."

Kalma chipped in with: "Nevertheless, sir, they have it. We have seen it for ourselves."

"That is so," confirmed Fane.

"Shut up!" Cruin burned him with a glare. "I have finished with you. I am now dealing with these two." His attention returned to the quaking Hefni: "Carry on."

"There is something decidedly queer about them which we've not yet been able to understand. They have no medium of exchange. They barter goods for goods without any regard for the relative values of either. They work when they feel like it. If they don't feel like it, they don't work. Yet, in spite of this, they work most of the time."

"Why?" demanded Cruin, incredulously.

"We asked them. They said that one works to avoid boredom. We cannot comprehend that viewpoint." Hefni made a defeated gesture. "In many places they have small factories which, with their strange, perverted logic, they use as amusement centers. These plants operate only when people turn up to work."

"Eh?" Cruin looked baffled.

"For example, in Williamsville, a small town an hour's walk beyond the Meredith home, there is a shoe factory. It operates every day. Some days there may be only ten workers there, other days fifty or a hundred, but nobody can remember a time when the place stood idle for lack of one voluntary worker. Meredith's elder daughter, Marva, has worked there three days during our stay with them. We asked her the reason."

"What did she say?"

"For fun."

"Fun ... fun ... fun?" Cruin struggled with the concept. "What does that mean?"

"We don't know," Hefni confessed. "The barrier of speech—"

"Red flames lick up the barrier of speech!" Cruin bawled. "Was her attendance compulsory?"

"No, sir."

"You are certain of that?"

"We are positive. One works in a factory for no other reason than because one feels like it."

"For what reward?" topped Cruin, shrewdly.

"Anything or nothing." Hefni uttered it like one in a dream. "One day she brought back a pair of shoes for her mother. We asked if they were her reward for the work she had done. She said they were not, and that someone named George had made them and given them to her. Apparently the rest of the factory's output for that week was shipped to another town where shoes were required. This other town is going to send back a supply of leather, nobody knows how much—and nobody seems to care."

"Senseless," defined Cruin. "It is downright imbecility." He examined Hefni as if suspecting him of inventing confusing data. "It is impossible for even the most primitive of organizations to operate so haphazardly. Obviously you have seen only part of the picture; the rest has been concealed from you, or you have been too dull-witted to perceive it."

"I assure you, sir," began Hefni.

"Let it pass," Cruin cut in. "Why should I care how they function economically? In the end, they'll work the way *we* want them to!" He rested his heavy jaw in one hand. "There are other matters which interest me more. For instance, our scouts have brought in reports of many cities. Some are organized but grossly under-populated; others are completely deserted. The former have well-constructed landing places with air-machines making use of them. How is it that people so primitive have air-machines?"

"Some make shoes, some make air-machines, some play with television. They work according to their aptitudes as well as their inclinations."

"Has this Meredith got an air-machine?"

"No." The look of defeat was etched more deeply on Hefni's face. "If he wanted one he would have his desire inserted in the television supply-and-demand program."

"Then what?"

"Sooner or later, he'd get one, new or secondhand, either in exchange for something or as a gift."

"Just by asking for it?"

"Yes."

Getting up, Cruin strode to and fro across his office. The steel heel-plates on his boots clanked on the metal floor in rhythm with the bells. He was ireful, impatient, dissatisfied.

"In all this madness is nothing which tells us anything of their true character or their organization." Stopping his stride, he faced Hefni. "You boasted that *you* were to be the eyes and ears." He released a loud snort. "Blind eyes and deaf ears! Not one word about their numerical strength, not one—"

"Pardon me, sir," said Hefni, quickly, "there are twenty-seven millions of them."

"Ah!" Cruin registered sharp interest. "Only twenty-seven millions? Why, there's a hundred times that number on Huld which has no greater area of land surface." He mused a moment. "Greatly underpopulated. Many cities devoid of a living soul. They have air-machines and other items suggestive of a civilization greater than the one they now enjoy. They operate the remnants of an economic system. You realize what all this means?"

Hefni blinked, made no reply. Kalma looked thoughtful. Fane and Parth remained blank-faced and tight-lipped.

"It means two things," Cruin pursued. "War or disease. One or the other, or perhaps both—and on a large scale. I want information on that. I've got to learn what sort of weapons they employed in their war, how many of them remain available, and where. Or, alternatively, what disease ravished their numbers, its source, and its cure." He tapped Hefni's chest to emphasize his words. "I want to know what they've got hidden away, what they're trying to keep from your knowledge against the time when they can bring it out and use it against us. Above all, I want to know which people will issue orders for their general offensive and where they are located."

"I understand, sir," said Hefni, doubtfully.

"That's the sort of information I need from your six specimens. I want information, not invitations to meals!" His grin was ugly as he noted Hefni's wince. "If you can get it out of them before they're due here, I shall enter the fact on the credit side of your records. But if I, your commander, have to do your job by extracting it from them myself—" Ominously, he left the sentence unfinished.

Hefni opened his mouth, closed it, glanced nervously at Kalma who stood stiff and dumb at his side.

"You may go," Cruin snapped at the four of them. "You have one week. If you fail me, I shall deem it a front-line offense and deal with it in accordance with the active-service section of the manual of procedure and discipline."

They were pale as they saluted. He watched them file out, his lips curling contemptuously. Going to the port, he gazed into the gathering darkness, saw a pale star winking in the east. Low and far it was—but not so far as Huld.

In the mid-period of the sixteenth day, Commander Cruin strode forth polished and bemedaled, directed his bell-jangling feet toward the hill. A sour-faced guard saluted him at the edge of the ash and made a slovenly job of it.

"Is that the best you can do?" He glared into the other's surly eyes. "Repeat it!"

The guard saluted a fraction more swiftly.

"You're out of practice," Cruin informed. "Probably all the crews are out of practice. We'll find a remedy for that. We'll have a period of saluting drill every day." His glare went slowly up and down the guard's face. "Are you dumb?"

"No, sir."

"Shut up!" roared Cruin. He expanded his chest. "Continue with your patrol."

The guard's optics burned with resentment as he saluted for the third time, turned with the regulation heel-click and marched along the perimeter.

Mounting the hill, Cruin sat on the stone at the top. Alternately he viewed the ships lying in the valley and the opposite scene with its trees, fields and distant houses. The metal helmet with its ornamental wings was heavy upon his head but he did not remove it. In the shadow beneath the projecting visor, his cold eyes brooded over the landscape to one side and the other.

She came eventually. He had been sitting there for one and a half periods when she came as he had known she would—without knowing what weird instinct had made him certain of this. Certainly, he had no desire to see her—no desire at all.

Through the trees she tripped light-footed, with Sue and Sam and three other girls of her own age. The newcomers had large, dark, humorous eyes, their hair was dark, and they were leggy.

"Oh, hello!" She paused as she saw him.

"Hello!" echoed Sue, swinging her pigtails.

" 'Lo!" piped Sam, determined not to be left out.

Cruin frowned at them. There was a high gloss on his jack boots, and his helmet glittered in the sun.

"These are my friends," said Marva, in her alien-accented Huldian. "Becky, Rita and Joyce."

The three smiled at him.

"I brought them to see the ships."

Cruin said nothing.

"You don't mind them looking at the ships, do you?"

"No," he growled with reluctance.

Lankily but gracefully she seated herself on the grass. The others followed suit with the exception of Sam who stood with fat legs braced apart sucking his thumb, and solemnly studying Cruin's decorated jacket.

"Father was disappointed because you could not visit us."

Cruin made no reply.

"Mother was sorry, too. She's a wonderful cook. She loves a guest."

No reply.

"Would you care to come this evening?"

"No."

"Some other evening?"

"Young lady," he harshed, severely, "I do not pay visits. Nobody pays visits."

She translated this to the others. They laughed so heartily that Cruin reddened and stood up.

"What's funny about that?" he demanded.

"Nothing, nothing." Marva was embarrassed. "If I told you, I fear that you would not understand."

"I would not understand." His grim eyes became alert, calculating as they went over her three friends. "I do not think, somehow, that they were laughing at me. Therefore they were laughing at what I do not know. They were laughing at something I ought to know but which you do not wish to tell me." He bent over her, huge and muscular, while she looked up at him with her great green eyes. "And what remark of mine revealed my amusing ignorance?"

Her steady gaze remained on him while she made no answer. A faint but sweet scent exuded from her hair.

"I said that nobody pays visits," he repeated. "That was the amusing remark—nobody pays visits. And I am not a fool!" Straightening, he turned away. "So I am going to call the rolls!"

He could feel their eyes upon him as he started down the valley. They were silent except for Sam's high-pitched, childish, "Bye!" which he ignored.

Without once looking back, he gained his flagship, mounted its metal ladder, made his way to the office and summoned Jusik.

"Order the captains to call their rolls at once."

"Is something wrong, sir?" inquired Jusik, anxiously.

"Call the rolls!" Cruin bellowed, whipping off his helmet. "Then we'll know whether anything is wrong." Savagely, he flung the helmet onto a wall hook, sat down, mopped his forehead.

Jusik was gone for most of a period. In the end he returned, set-faced, grave.

"I regret to report that eighteen men are absent, sir."

"They laughed," said Cruin, bitterly. "They laughed—because they *knew!*" His knuckles were white as his hands gripped the arms of his chair.

"I beg your pardon, sir?" Jusik's eyebrows lifted.

"How long have they been absent?"

"Eleven of them were on duty this morning."

"That means the other seven have been missing since yesterday?"

"I'm afraid so, sir."

"But no one saw fit to inform me of this fact?"

Jusik fidgeted. "No, sir."

"Have you discovered anything else of which I have not been informed?"

The other fidgeted again, looked pained.

"Out with it, man!"

"It is not the absentees' first offense," Jusik said with difficulty. "Nor their second. Perhaps not their sixth."

"How long has this been going on?" Cruin waited a while, then bawled: "Come on! You are capable of speech!"

"About ten days, sir."

"How many captains were aware of this and failed to report it?"

"Nine, sir. Four of them await your bidding outside."

"And what of the other five?"

"They . . . they—" Jusik licked his lips.

Cruin arose, his expression dangerous. "You cannot conceal the truth by delaying it."

"They are among the absentees, sir."

"I see!" Cruin stamped to the door, stood by it. "We can take it for granted that others have absented themselves without permission, but were fortunate enough to be here when the rolls were called. That is their good luck. The real total of the disobedient cannot be discovered. They have sneaked away like nocturnal animals, and in the same manner they sneak back. All are guilty of desertion in the face of the enemy. There is one penalty for that."

"Surely, sir, considering the circ—"

"Considering nothing!" Cruin's voice shot up to an enraged shout. "Death! The penalty is death!" Striding to the table, he hammered the books lying upon it. "Summary execution as laid down in the manual of procedure and discipline. Desertion, mutinous conduct, defiance of a superior officer, conspiracy to thwart regulations and defy my orders—all punishable by death!" His voice lowered as swiftly as it had gone up. "Besides, my dear Jusik, if we fail through disintegration attributable to our own deliberate disregard of the manuals, what will be the penalty payable by *us*? What will it be, eh?"

"Death," admitted Jusik. He looked at Cruin. "On Huld, anyway."

"We are on Huld! *This* is Huld! I have claimed this planet in the name of Huld and therefore it is part of it."

"A mere claim, sir, if I may say—"

"Jusik, are *you* with these conspirators in opposing my authority?" Cruin's eyes glinted. His hand lay over his gun.

"Oh, no, sir!" The second commander's features mirrored the emotions conflicting within him. "But permit me to point out, sir, that we are a brotherly band who've been cooped together a long, long time and already have suffered losses getting here as we shall do getting back. One can hardly expect the men to—"

"I expect obedience!" Cruin's hand remained on the gun. "I expect iron discipline and immediate, willing, unquestionable obedience. With those, we conquer. Without them, we fail." He gestured to the door. "Are those captains properly prepared for examination as directed in the manuals?"

"Yes, sir. They are disarmed and under guard."

"Parade them in." Leaning on the edge of his desk, Cruin prepared to pass judgment on his fellows. The minute he waited for them was long, long as any minute he had ever known.

> There had been scent in her hair.
> And her eyes were cool and green.
> Iron discipline must be maintained.
> The price of power.

The manual provided an escape. Facing the four captains, he found himself taking advantage of the legal loophole to substitute demotion for the more drastic and final penalty.

Tramping the room before them while they stood in a row, pale-faced and rigid, their tunics unbuttoned, their ceremonial belts missing, the guards impassive on either side of them, he rampaged and swore and sprinkled them with verbal vitriol while his right fist hammered steadily into the palm of his left hand.

"But since you were present at the roll call, and therefore are not technically guilty of desertion, and since you surrendered yourself to my judgment immediately you were called upon to do so, I hereby sentence you to be demoted to the basic rank, the circumstances attending this sentence to be entered in your records." He dismissed them with a curt flourish of his white-gloved hand. "That is all."

They filed out silently.

He looked at Jusik. "Inform the respective lieutenant captains that they are promoted to full captains and now must enter recommendations for their vacated positions. These must be received by me before nightfall."

"As you order, sir."

"Also warn them to prepare to attend a commanding officer's court which will deal with the lower-ranking absentees as and when they reappear. Inform Captain Somir that he is appointed commander of the firing squad which will carry out the decisions of the court immediately they are pronounced."

"Yes, sir." Gaunt and hollow-eyed, Jusik turned with a click of heels and departed.

When the closer had shut the door, Cruin sat at his desk, placed his elbows on its surface, held his face in his hands. If the deserters did not return, they could not be punished. No power, no authority could vent its wrath upon an absent body. The law was impotent if its subjects lacked the essential feature of being present. All the laws of Huld could not put memories of lost men before a firing squad.

It was imperative that he make an example of the offenders. Their sly, furtive trips into the enemy's camp, he suspected, had been repeated often enough to have become a habit. Doubtless by now they were settled wherever they were visiting, sharing homes—welcome rooms—sharing food, company, laughter. Doubtless they had started to regain weight, to lose the space lines on their cheeks and foreheads, and the light in their eyes had begun to burn anew; and they had talked with signs and pictures, played games, tried to suck smoke things, and strolled with girls through the fields and the glades.

A pulse was beating steadily in the thickness of his neck as he stared through the port and waited for some sign that the tripled ring of guards had caught the first on his way in. Down, down, deep down inside him at a depth too great for him to admit that it was there, lay the disloyal hope that none would return.

One deserter would mean the slow, shuffling tread of the squad, the hoarse calls of "Aim!" and "Fire!" and the stepping forward of Somir, gun in hand, to administer the mercy shot.

Damn the manuals.

At the end of the first period after nightfall Jusik burst into the office, saluted, breathed heavily. The glare of the ceiling illumination deepened the lines on his thin features, magnified the bristles on his unshaven chin.

"Sir, I have to report that the men are getting out of control."

"What d'you mean?" Cruin's heavy brows came down as he stared fiercely at the other.

"They know of the recent demotions, of course. They know also that a court will assemble to deal with the absentees." He took another long-drawn breath. "And they also know the penalty these absentees must face."

"So?"

"So more of them have deserted—they've gone to warn the others not to return."

"Ah!" Cruin smiled lopsidedly. "The guards let them walk out, eh? Just like that?"

"Ten of the guards went with them," said Jusik.

"Ten?" Coming up fast, Cruin moved near to the other, studied him searchingly. "How many went altogether?"

"Ninety-seven."

Grabbing his helmet, Cruin slammed it on, pulled the metal chin strap over his jaw muscles. "More than one complete crew." He examined his gun, shoved it back, strapped on a second one. "At that rate they'll all be gone by morning." He eyed Jusik. "Don't you think so?"

"That's what I'm afraid of, sir."

Cruin patted his shoulder. "The answer, Jusik, is an easy one—we take off immediately."

"Take off?"

"Most certainly. The whole fleet. We'll strike a balanced orbit where it will be impossible for any man to leave. I will then give the situation more thought. Probably we'll make a new landing in some locality where none will be tempted to sneak away because there'll be nowhere to go. A scout can pick up Fane and his party in due course."

"I doubt whether they'll obey orders for departure, sir."

"We'll see, we'll see." He smiled again, hard and craggy. "As you would know if you'd studied the manuals properly, it is not difficult to smash incipient mutiny. All one has to do is remove the ringleaders. No mob is composed of men, as such. It is made up of a few ringleaders and a horde of stupid followers." He patted his guns. "You can always tell a ringleader—invariably he is the first to open his mouth!"

"Yes, sir," mouthed Jusik, with misgivings.

"Sound the call for general assembly."

The flagship's siren wailed dismally in the night. Lights flashed from ship to ship, and startled birds woke up and squawked in the trees beyond the ash.

Slowly, deliberately, impressively, Cruin came down the ladder, faced the audience whose features were a mass of white blobs in the glare of the ships' beams. The captains and lieutenant captains ranged themselves behind him and to either side. Each carried an extra gun.

"After three years of devoted service to Huld," he enunciated pompously, "some men have failed me. It seems that we have weaklings among us, weaklings unable to stand the strain of a few extra days before our triumph. Careless of their duty they disobey orders, fraternize with the enemy, consort with our opponents' females, and try to snatch a few creature comforts at the expense of the many." His hard, accusing eyes went over them. "In due time they will be punished with the utmost severity."

They stared back at him expressionlessly. He could shoot the ears off a running man at twenty-five yards, and he was waiting for his target to name itself. So were those at his side.

None spoke.

"Among you may be others equally guilty but not discovered. They need not congratulate themselves, for they are about to be deprived of further opportunities to exercise their disloyalty." His stare kept flickering over them while his hand remained ready at his side. "We are going to trim the ships and take off, seeking a balanced orbit. That means lost sleep and plenty of hard work for which you have your treacherous comrades to thank." He paused a moment, finished with: "Has anyone anything to say?"

One man holding a thousand.

Silence.

"Prepare for departure," he snapped, and turned his back upon them.

Captain Somir, now facing him, yelped: "Look out, commander!" and whipped up his gun to fire over Cruin's shoulder.

Cruin made to turn, conscious of a roar behind him, his guns coming out as he twisted around. He heard no crack from Somir's weapon, saw no more of his men as their roar cut off abruptly. There seemed to be an intolerable weight upon his skull, the grass came up to meet him, he let go his guns and put out his hands to save himself. Then the hazily dancing lights faded from his eyesight and all was black.

Deep in his sleep he heard vaguely and uneasily a prolonged stamping of feet, many dull, elusive sounds as of people shouting far, far away. This went on for a considerable time, and ended with a series of violent reports that shook the ground beneath his body.

Someone splashed water over his face.

Sitting up, he held his throbbing head, saw pale fingers of dawn feeling through the sky to one side. Blinking his aching eyes to clear them, he perceived Jusik, Somir and eight others. All were smothered in dirt, their faces bruised, their uniforms torn and bedraggled.

"They rushed us the moment you turned away from them," explained Jusik, morbidly. "A hundred of them in the front. They rushed us in one united frenzy, and the rest followed. There were too many for us." He regarded his superior with red-rimmed optics. "You have been flat all night."

Unsteadily, Cruin got to his feet, teetered to and fro. "How many were killed?"

"None. We fired over their heads. After that—it was too late."

"Over their heads?" Squaring his massive shoulders, Cruin felt a sharp pain in the middle of his back, ignored it. "What are guns for if not to kill?"

"It isn't easy," said Jusik, with the faintest touch of defiance. "Not when they're one's own comrades."

"Do you agree?" The commander's glare challenged the others.

They nodded miserably, and Somir said: "There was little time, sir, and if one hesitates, as we did, it becomes—"

"There are no excuses for anything. You had your orders; it was for you to obey them." His hot gaze burned one, then the other. "You are incompetent for your rank. You are both demoted!" His jaw came forward, ugly, aggressive, as he roared: "Get out of my sight!"

They mooched away. Savagely, he climbed the ladder, entered his ship, explored it from end to end. There was not a soul on board. His lips were tight as he reached the tail, found the cause of the earth-rocking detonations. The fuel tanks had been exploded, wrecking the engines and reducing the whole vessel to a useless mass of metal.

Leaving, he inspected the rest of his fleet. Every ship was the same, empty and wrecked beyond possibility of repair. At least the mutineers had been thorough and logical in their sabotage. Until a report-vessel arrived, the home world of Huld had no means of knowing where the expedition had landed. Despite even a systematic and wide-scale search it might well be a thousand years before Huldians found this particular planet again. Effectively the rebels had marooned themselves for the rest of their natural lives and placed themselves beyond reach of Huldian retribution.

Tasting to the full the bitterness of defeat, he squatted on the bottom rung of the twenty-second vessel's ladder, surveyed the double star-formations that represented his ruined armada. Futilely, their guns pointed over surrounding terrain. Twelve of the scouts, he noted, had gone. The others had been rendered as useless as their parent vessels.

Raising his gaze to the hill, he perceived silhouettes against the dawn where Jusik, Somir and the others were walking over the crest, walking away from him, making for the farther valley he had viewed so often. Four children joined them at the top, romped beside them as they proceeded. Slowly the whole group sank from sight under the rising sun.

Returning to the flagship, Cruin packed a patrol sack with personal possessions, strapped it on his shoulders. Without a final glance at the remains of his once-mighty command he set forth away from the sun, in the direction opposite to that taken by the last of his men.

His jack boots were dull, dirty. His orders of merit hung lopsidedly and had a gap where one had been torn off in the fracas. The bell was missing from his right boot; he endured the pad-*ding*, pad-*ding* of its fellow for twenty steps before he unscrewed it and slung it away.

The sack on his back was heavy, but not so heavy as the immense burden upon his mind. Grimly, stubbornly he plodded on, away from the ships, far, far into the morning mists—facing the new world alone.

Three and a half years had bitten deep into the ships of Huld. Still they lay in the valley, arranged with mathematical precision, noses in, tails out, as only authority could place them. But the rust had eaten a quarter of the way through the thickness of their tough shells, and their metal ladders were rotten and treacherous. The field mice and the voles had found refuge beneath them; the birds and spiders had sought sanctuary within them. A lush growth had sprung from encompassing ash, hiding the perimeter for all time.

The man who came by them in the midafternoon rested his pack and studied them silently, from a distance. He was big, burly, with a skin the color of old leather. His deep gray eyes were calm, thoughtful as they observed the thick ivy climbing over the flagship's tail.

Having looked at them for a musing half hour he hoisted his pack and went on, up the hill, over the crest and into the farther valley. Moving easily in his plain, loose-fitting clothes, his pace was deliberate, methodical.

Presently he struck a road, followed it to a stone-built cottage in the garden of which a lithe, dark-haired woman was cutting flowers. Leaning on the gate, he spoke to her. His speech was fluent but strangely accented. His tones were gruff but pleasant.

"Good afternoon."

She stood up, her arms full of gaudy blooms, looked at him with rich, black eyes. "Good afternoon." Her full lips parted with pleasure. "Are you touring? Would you care to guest with us? I am sure that Jusik—my husband—would be delighted to have you. Our welcome room has not been occupied for—"

"I am sorry," he chipped in. "I am seeking the Merediths. Could you direct me?"

"The next house up the lane." Deftly, she caught a falling bloom, held it to her breast. "If their welcome room has a guest, please remember us."

"I will remember," he promised. Eying her approvingly, his broad, muscular face lit up with a smile. "Thank you so much."

Shouldering his pack he marched on, conscious of her eyes following him. He reached the gate of the next place, a long, rambling, picturesque house fronted by a flowering garden. A boy was playing by the gate.

Glancing up as the other stopped near him, the boy said: "Are you touring, sir?"

"Sir?" echoed the man. "*Sir?*" His face quirked. "Yes, sonny, I am touring. I'm looking for the Merediths."

"Why, I'm Sam Meredith!" The boy's face flushed with sudden excitement. "You wish to guest with us?"

"If I may."

"Yow-ee!" He fled frantically along the garden path, shrieking at the top of his voice, "Mom, Pop, Marva, Sue—we've got a guest!"

A tall, red-headed man came to the door, pipe in mouth. Coolly, calmly, he surveyed the visitor.

After a little while, the man removed the pipe and said: "I'm Jake Meredith. Please come in." Standing aside, he let the other enter, then called, "Mary, Mary, can you get a meal for a guest?"

"Right away," assured a cheerful voice from the back.

"Come with me." Meredith led the other to the veranda, found him an easy-chair. "Might as well rest while you're waiting. Mary takes time. She isn't satisfied until the legs of the table are near to collapse—and woe betide you if you leave anything."

"It is good of you." Seating himself, the visitor drew a long breath, gazed over the pastoral scene before him.

Taking another chair, Meredith applied a light to his pipe. "Have you seen the mail ship?"

"Yes, it arrived early yesterday. I was lucky enough to view it as it passed overhead."

"You certainly were lucky considering that it comes only once in four years. I've seen it only twice, myself. It came right over this house. An imposing sight."

"Very!" indorsed the visitor, with unusual emphasis. "It looked to me about five miles long, a tremendous creation. Its mass must be many times greater than that of all those alien ships in the valley."

"Many times," agreed Meredith.

The other leaned forward, watching his host. "I often wonder whether those aliens attributed smallness of numbers to war or disease, not thinking of large-scale emigration, nor realizing what it means."

"I doubt whether they cared very much seeing that they burned their boats and settled among us." He pointed with the stem of his pipe. "One of them lives in that cottage down there. Jusik's his name. Nice fellow. He married a local girl eventually. They are very happy."

"I'm sure they are."

They were quiet a long time, then Meredith spoke absently, as if thinking aloud. "They brought with them weapons of considerable might, not knowing that we have a weapon truly invincible." Waving one hand, he indicated the world at large. "It took us thousands of years to learn about the sheer invincibility of an idea. That's what we've got—a way of life, an idea. Nothing can blast that to shreds. Nothing can defeat an idea—except a better one." He put the pipe back in his mouth. "So far, we have failed to find a better one.

"They came at the wrong time," Meredith went on. "Ten thousand years too late." He glanced sidewise at his listener. "Our history covers a long, long day. It was so lurid that it came out in a new edition every minute. But this one's the late night final."

"You philosophize, eh?"

Meredith smiled. "I often sit here to enjoy my silences. I sit here and think. Invariably I end up with the same conclusion."

"What may that be?"

"That if I, personally, were in complete possession of all the visible stars and their multitude of planets I would still be subject to one fundamental limitation"—bending, he tapped his pipe on his heel—"in this respect—that no man can eat more than his belly can hold." He stood up, tall, wide-chested. "Here comes my daughter, Marva. Would you like her to show you your room?"

Standing inside the welcome room, the visitor surveyed it appreciatively. The comfortable bed, the bright furnishings.

"Like it?" Marva asked.

"Yes, indeed." Facing her, his gray eyes examined her. She was tall, red-haired, green-eyed, and her figure was ripe with the beauty of young womanhood. Pulling slowly at his jaw muscles, he asked: "Do you think that I resemble Cruin?"

"Cruin?" Her finely curved brows crinkled in puzzlement.

"The commander of that alien expedition."

"Oh, him!" Her eyes laughed, and the dimples came into her cheeks. "How absurd! You don't look the least bit like him. He was old and severe. You are *young*—and far more handsome."

"It is kind of you to say so," he murmured. His hands moved aimlessly around in obvious embarrassment. He fidgeted a little under her frank, self-possessed gaze. Finally, he went to his pack, opened it. "It is conventional for the guest to bring his hosts a present." A tinge of pride crept into his voice. "So I have brought one. I made it myself. It took me a long time to learn . . . a long time . . . with these clumsy hands. About three years."

Marva looked at it, raced through the doorway, leaned over the balustrade and called excitedly down the stairs. "Pop, Mom, our guest has a wonderful present for us. A clock. A clock with a little metal bird that calls the time."

Beneath her, feet bustled along the passage and Mary's voice came up saying: "May I see it? Please let me see it." Eagerly, she mounted the stairs.

As he waited for them within the welcome room, his shoulders squared, body erect as if on parade, the clock whirred in Cruin's hands and its little bird solemnly fluted twice.

The hour of triumph.

First published: 1949

COLD WAR

by Kris Neville

THE GOVERNMENT NEEDS YOU!
if
you can qualify
YES!
Space Stations need men!
America's defense has an opening
for you!
Excellent pay!!
Generous Furloughs!

Applicants must be between the ages of 24 and 32, and must pass a rigid physical examination. For full particulars, and application blanks visit or write any government post office.

"The President is in conference," the third assistant secretary informed Leland Kreiger.

Leland Kreiger took out his calling card. It contained nothing more than his name and the initials, XSSC, in pica type, in the lower left-hand corner. "Will you hand him this, please," he said. "He is expecting me."

"I'm sorry, Mr. . . . uh . . . Kreiger, but I must know the nature of your business."

"On the contrary; you must *not*," Leland Kreiger said. "I assure you the President will be interested."

And ten minutes later, Leland Kreiger was seated before the President's desk.

The President was a tired man. His face showed it, his body showed it, his eyes showed it. His cheeks were hollow, his shoulders bent, and, under his eyes, there were large, black rings. He had been in office only two years.

"Mr. President. Failure."

It was a bleak statement. But the expression on his face never changed. The President took it calmly.

The President sighed. "I should have known. It was the last chance—" His voice trailed off. "You did the best you could. I don't blame you."

"I tried," Leland Kreiger said. There was nothing else to say.

"Did they believe you? Your credentials—?"

"Of course. They were certain I was your direct representative. No doubt about that."

"And they said?"

"That there are things more precious than life; that their people could never tolerate a foreign rule—" He hesitated for a moment, and then added, hastily, "And that we were bluffing."

"I expected it, of course. But I could hope. Now . . . Leland, is there no answer?"

The President asked the last much in the spirit of a man appealing to a doctor who has told him he has but three weeks to live.

"There is only one answer, sir. I was sent to tell them to submit all their armaments to us or we would destroy them. They said it was a bluff. The only thing to do is—to destroy them."

"Leland, you know I could never do that," said the President, looking down at his hands. "Perhaps the rulers, yes. But think of the innocent men, women, and children . . . the uncounted millions—"

He looked up. "It's strange, isn't it? If a state of war existed between us, then perhaps I would. But no such state exists. Ostensibly we are friendly nations. I might rouse our people to a point where they would support a war—but I could never justify it. The enemy will go just so far, and no further. They are careful not to give us an excuse."

He paused a moment. "How cruel it would sound: 'He could find no solution but slaughter!' If we used the weapon once, what would the world think? How could we ever *hope* for peace?"

"But, sir, the risk—"

"With one hundred million lives at stake, no risk is too great! What would history say? What would all Christian instinct tell us?"

"If we only had time."

"Time? How I hate that word. Yes, yes. If we had time— In twenty or thirty years we could discontinue the Space Stations. But not now."

The President looked up at the ceiling. And beyond it. He shuddered.

The President called in Senator Tyler of New York, leader of the opposition in Congress. The President did not like him personally. And, yet, this was not a question of personalities.

"Senator, please be seated," he said, after shaking the man's hand as warmly as possible.

The senator sat down, and, without asking, extracted a cigar. He lit it.

The President set his lips grimly. "I have asked you here on a matter of vital interest to this country. *Vital.* Anything that I tell you today is in the strictest confidence."

The senator leaned back. He did not commit himself.

The President ruffed some papers on his desk.

"I want to stress the importance of secrecy. The newspapers must never discover what I am about to tell you. It would . . . well, it would throw the world into a panic."

"That is very strong language, Mr. President."

The President looked him over carefully. He was a huge man. Fat. Heavy jowls. Tiny eyes. Eyes that glittered with shrewdness.

And the President wished it weren't necessary to tell him.

Outside, unknown to the senator, a secret service man was waiting for him to leave the office. From this day, the senator would be watched every hour of the day and night. His private mail would be opened—his telephones tapped—everything he said and did monitored by the secret service.

And if he started to reveal the secret, his life would be extinguished like a cupped candle.

The President stood up. "No, keep your seat," he said. "I assure you that it is not a strong statement." He walked across the room. "Let me ask you once again to call off this investigation. If you were to say the word—"

"Mr. President, that is impossible. The people have a *right* to know," he sucked on his cigar, "that every safeguard is being taken to insure that the Space Stations are manned by loyal American citizens."

If that were only the problem, the President thought.

"Why," the senator went on, "think of what would happen if an enemy spy managed to get control of a Station—he could wipe out half of the United States merely by flicking his wrist." Here the senator flicked ashes onto the carpet by way of emphasis.

Almost automatically the President thought, *Mrs. Thorne, the housekeeper, will be very angry.* He caught himself. Of late his mind had a tendency to rove, and to concern itself with the inconsequential.

The President said: "Let me assure you that every precaution is being taken. Each man is checked so thoroughly that we know him better than he knows himself. *Will you call off the investigation?*"

"NO! You're hiding something, and we are going to find out what! Don't forget that we have the right—"

"You win," the President said wearily. "I was afraid of it. It's not the loyalty check that you want to look into—you're after something else. Something's wrong, and you don't know quite what, but you intend to find out."

"Exactly," the senator said, smiling.

"If you go through with this investigation, it would result in publicity that we could not stand. There is a chance, because you gentlemen are so thorough, that you would discover what I am concealing. To prevent that, I am going to be frank with you. For, after all, one man is easier to bind to secrecy than fifteen. After you hear me out, I am sure that you will call off the investigation."

"I must reserve judgment," the senator told him.

"Very well. But, sir, remember that you have forced me. The responsibility, and the consequences, are yours, and yours alone."

"Naturally," the senator said. "I can look after myself."

The President walked to the wall chart. He unrolled it, and it rustled dryly.

"I am going to cover material with which you are completely familiar. You will forgive me, but it is necessary to stress a few points. But first, are you *sure*—?"

"Get on with it; I'm listening."

"These," the President said, pointing to circles in red on the map, "are our nine Space Stations. You will note that they are located so that, at every second, some station is in direct target line with every point on Earth. Due to physical considerations, the stations move very rapidly in their orbits. But this has been made to serve a military purpose. To destroy this defense network, it is necessary to destroy every station, because every station, in its orbit, comes within range of every point on Earth. One might be eliminated, or maybe even two, with our present technical knowledge, but not all nine. And each one, in the space of ninety seconds from a given signal, can blanket an area half the size of Asia with atomic destruction. Each space station *carries enough pure death to annihilate any nation on Earth!*"

He paused.

"It is a perfect defense against an atom bomb. But, at the same time, it is a negative defense. It cannot prevent this nation from being attacked. But an attacker would, at most, launch only a few dozen rockets before he was completely and utterly destroyed.

"And it is our only defense against aggression. It is all that we have. All of our atomic power is concentrated in those nine stations. If they were to be grounded tomorrow, we would be practically defenseless. Any one of several countries could conquer us within the space of weeks."

The President let the chart snap back on its roller.

"In effect, we rule the world. But, as you know, our 'rule' is of a negative sort. We rule by threat." He laughed dryly. "We have something hanging over their heads. They—the enemy, shall I say?—knows that we will never take positive action without strong justification—without what must amount to an open declaration of war upon us, or a definitely aggressive move against one of her weak neighbors. Therefore, the enemy has a wide range of free action. Their only consideration is this: 'Will America use the Space Stations to stop us?', and if the answer is 'no,' then they may proceed."

He looked down at the senator.

"The international situation has become pretty much of a touch and go affair. Bluff and counter bluff."

"I know all that," the senator replied.

"You will recall, also, the only time that we used a Space Station. The whole world shuddered."

"Of course. Who doesn't remember? Russia was bent on setting up a Space Station of her own. We warned her. But she thought it was a bluff. The day they were ready to launch it, we dropped a single bomb on it. After all, we couldn't permit another nation to have a Station. It would be intolerable."

"Yes," the President said, musingly, "one tiny bomb. Not an attack—but only one bomb. And yet the feeling ran high against us. Both here and abroad. The people of the world felt that surely some other means could have been found. Not involving death!"

The President sighed. "It postponed for ten years at least the day when we would no longer need Space Stations."

The President walked over and sat down.

"Russia, you will remember, protested to the U. N. She wanted the Stations placed under international control. We could not permit that, because, primarily, the Stations are not a method of enforcing peace, but of defending our own country against any and all aggressors. Russia could take no further action—for she existed only under our sufferance. She had merely gambled and lost."

"I, and any high school child," the senator said, "know that. Please come to the point."

The President ignored him. "The whole problem of Space Stations is to much for one man. I wish that I had never heard of them!"

The senator put out his cigar.

"Well, senator, let me review."

"You realize that Space Stations are our only defense?"

The senator grunted. "Yes."

"And that we cannot use them offensively against an enemy unless she gives us ample justification?"

"Yes."

"And do you know that if we discontinued them, we would be attacked tomorrow? By a nation who would absorb a calculated amount of destruction in order to dominate the world—by a ruthless enemy, an enemy who bears us not the slightest love?"

The senator snorted.

And the President smiled. "Of course," he said, "we could surrender to the enemy."

The senator jerked upright. It was an effort that made his face red. "Man, do you realize what you're saying!"

"Calm down," the President advised. "I know my oath of office as well as you do."

He hesitated a moment while the senator settled back somewhat uneasily.

"What I have done is merely mention various alternatives that would confront us if we decided to discontinue the Space Stations. Bloodshed or subjugation. The alternatives are all untenable."

"Naturally," the senator said.

"But I must discontinue the Space Stations," the President told him as mildly as if he were mentioning that eggs were on the White House breakfast menu for tomorrow.

"That will be impossible for many years," the senator said with equal mildness.

"Oh, but I don't have many years, senator. In fact I don't have any time at all."

The President got up again and walked over to the far wall and stood looking at a picture of President Lincoln. He put his hands behind his back and seemed to be talking, not to the senator, but to the picture. "Now you can begin to appreciate my position."

Adam Kregg had, for a long time, been covering the national picture, as it looked from Washington, in his daily column. Recently he had been writing on the seriousness of the military situation, and of repeated rumors "from high official sources" that the United States was planning to attack the enemy without warning. He deplored these reports, as a matter of course. He pointed out that, at present, we were in no danger; indeed, that we were able to keep peace, although an uneasy sort of peace, and that since affairs couldn't get worse, they were bound to get better. "It is possible," he wrote, "that within the next twenty years, if we continue on our present policy, differences between both nations may be resolved. At any rate, it is obvious that we can gain nothing by the use of force; it can only result in needless bloodshed. It is not justifiable. Eventually every nation will see, by our judicious use of the Space Stations, that we do not seek to rule, but that we do seek to live in Peace, unmolested by *any* aggressor."

Undoubtedly, Mr. Kregg had the welfare of man at heart. However, he was, first and foremost, a reporter. He had an unfailing nose for news. He could put 2 and 2 and 2 and 2 together every time and come up with the correct total. A hint here, a word there, an omission elsewhere, and Adam Kregg had a scoop.

Washington was honeycombed with his sources. And nothing was sacred. If it was startling, if it would set well in type, then Mr. Kregg put it in his column.

Several times he had roused the wrath of the government. They called him irresponsible. Others called him a brave and fearless reporter. And his motto was "All the News." Period. He would rather chop off his two hands than suppress a story.

To him nothing was confidential. Everything was grist for his mill.

Once the government sought to bring a criminal action against him. The nation's press took up the hue and cry: "If convicted, this will mean the end of a free press in America."

And Adam Kregg went happily on his way, reporting "all the news." That is, until he happened across the most closely guarded of government secrets.

Perhaps he deduced it. Perhaps someone told him. At any rate, he found out.

It was shocking. It even stunned him. He became frightened. And then he saw the story in headlines—the nation and the world thrown into the same state of terror that he was in. Naturally he decided to print it.

He was going to give it to the great American public. But if not in print, then by some other means. That was that. Arrest him, and it would come out at his trial. Any action the government chose to take, *still* the people were going to be told.

For, as Adam Kregg knew, he lived in a democracy. And the government tactics did not include—

He tucked the column into his coat pocket. He was going to take it to the syndicate personally. He was going to see it go out over the wires. And nobody was going to talk him out of it. It was the scoop of a lifetime. Maybe ten lifetimes. Better, even, than when the reporter had discovered, during the last war, that the Government had broken the Japanese code.

He got into his car and drove crosstown to the syndicate branch office. He got out and started across the sidewalk.

A huge, black car hurtled around the corner and flashed by him. Two shotgun blasts erupted from it.

He fell, his chest torn away. He squirmed once and died.

Almost immediately, a plainclothes agent was bending over him. The man removed the bloody sheaf of typed paper. He stood up and flashed his badge to the crowd.

"This man is dead," he said.

And a policeman came running up.

The FBI seized all of Adam Kregg's personal papers. They told the press that they were looking for clues.

And there were headlines:

FBI STARTS INVESTIGATION
OF ADAM KREGG'S DEATH!

But the assassin was never found.

Adam Kregg failed to realize that the secret was too big to protect by normal, democratic procedures.

"It's a neat legal question," the Chief Psychiatrist admitted. "But you know very well we can never bring the case into court!"

The President agreed. "You're right, of course." He looked off into space. "And I hate it! The way it forces us to abridge all human rights—"

The Chief Psychiatrist nodded grimly.

"Well?" the President demanded. "Can't you *do* something? Isn't there any test? Anything?"

"No." The Chief Psychiatrist looked away. "There is no way of telling who's susceptible and who isn't. Frankly, we're puzzled. The first case came up a little over a year ago. This is the fifth. Each case follows the same pattern . . . I . . . well, that's all we know."

"How is the man now?"

"Aside from the memory blank, completely normal."

"And what do you recommend?"

"We can't take the case to court. As it stands, of course, we can't release him. If for no other reason than security. It's obvious that he can't be held accountable—but, as I said, that's a neat legal question. And, we must remember, that the condition may return at any time."

"Well?"

"Wait and see. What else *can* we do?"

There was a momentary pause. "Mr. President, I'd like to have you see for yourself what you're up against. Come and look at the patient."

The President stood up. It was the last thing in the world that he wanted to do. But after all, this whole mess was his responsibility.

The patient was isolated in a cell block of the Federal Prison. He was sitting on his bed in the far cell.

The keys grated harshly as the jailer admitted the President and the Chief Psychiatrist.

The patient stood up. His face was pallid. Tight anguish lines laced it. But it was still a handsome face—young, strong, tanned. The eyes were red rimmed, as if the man had been crying. Blond hair spread in an unruly thatch.

The President walked slowly to his cell.

The patient looked at him for a moment without recognition. Then the red circled eyes seemed to light up.

"You're . . . you're the President!" he gasped.

"I am," the President said, gently.

"I . . . I," he began and then stopped with a choke. Suddenly a wild look came into his eyes. "Why have they got me here?" He grabbed the bars and shook them. "Why? Why? WHY?" He sobbed. "Why won't they let me see my wife and baby? Why won't they let me see anybody? You're the President," his voice began almost to whine, "surely *you* can tell me. What have I done?"

He banged his fists on the bars.

"Tell me! Tell me!"

"Here, here," the Chief Psychiatrist said. "Control yourself!"

"I'm . . . I'm sorry. But why won't somebody tell me anything? I . . . I want to see Doris." He turned his face to the President. "That's my wife, sir. And Jerry. That's my baby—cutest little kid. *Why won't they let me see them?*"

He began to cry.

The Chief Psychiatrist touched the President's arm. "Let's go," he whispered. "We can't do anything. It's shock."

They turned and started to leave.

"NO!" the blond youth cried. "Oh, no! Don't leave me. Don't leave me here alone." He began to sob. "I'm afraid . . . afraid . . . afraid—"

"Doesn't he remember?" the President asked when they were out of the cell block.

"Doesn't seem to. He must have established a subconscious block. There is no conscious memory for the whole period."

"How do you explain it?"

"I can't. And what makes it more horrible, it happened after that poor kid's first tour of duty. Now we know it isn't necessarily the time element. And that's about all we know.

"Our tests are as perfect as human science can make them. We may screen as many as ten thousand applicants before we have found one who is qualified, even, for the solitary test. I'll bet we've screened half of the available men in America. We have been so selective that, if we went one step further, we could qualify no one. And yet—there is the human element there, that eludes us.

"There still remains those men upon whom the Space Stations act as a drug. Like marijuana. They seem to tower above mortality!

"And all that responsibility, all that tension—so many lives at their fingertips. And the suspense—what with the way the newspapers are playing up the international situation—sitting there, waiting, waiting, waiting. Listening for that deadly signal. Waiting to punch the controls that will destroy one hundred million people. One-hundred-million! And the tension mounting as they swirl over enemy territory . . . the flood of relief over their own—" He paused.

"I can imagine what the poor devils must think. Life and death . . . *life* and death . . . life and *death*— Over and over, producing a hypnotic effect —like the individual death-wish. And the mind falls into that pattern— starts working like a pump."

He paused for a moment. "And then there is the second stage. 'Suppose I should push this button here, what would happen? would *happen*? would h-a-p-p-e-n? Or this button . . . or this— Life *and* death. And one-hundred-million people . . . living . . . loving—' " He stopped. "You see?"

"I—see," said the President.

"No wonder they break. All the world, all that living, there, at their fingertips—" He sighed.

"All five of the men waited until they were home on furlough before they snapped." He snapped his fingers. "Like that! And all followed a pattern—like that poor boy in there, taking a butcher knife to his wife and kid. Insane—criminally insane. Or the one before—"

"Don't!" the President ordered, closing his eyes. "Please. No more."

Then after a while, he opened his eyes again and looked upward.

The law of averages, he thought, is catching up with us. Five on furlough. And swirling in one of those nine orbits, up there, is a man who may, at any moment, become . . . just like the five . . . murderous . . . insane!

And in each of the Stations there is enough power to destroy half a continent.

First published: 1949

ETERNITY LOST

by Clifford D. Simak

Mr. Reeves: *The situation, as I see it, calls for well defined safeguards which would prevent continuation of life from falling under the patronage of political parties or other groups in power.*
Chairman Leonard: *You mean you are afraid it might become a political football?*
Mr. Reeves: *Not only that, sir, I am afraid that political parties might use it to continue beyond normal usefulness the lives of certain so-called elder statesmen who are needed by the party to maintain prestige and dignity in the public eye.*

> From the Records of a hearing before the science subcommittee of the public policy committee of the World House of Representatives.

Senator Homer Leonard's visitors had something on their minds. They fidgeted mentally as they sat in the senator's office and drank the senator's good whiskey. They talked, quite importantly, as was their wont, but they talked around the thing they had come to say. They circled it like a hound dog circling a coon, waiting for an opening, circling the subject to catch an opportunity that might make the message sound just a bit offhanded—as if they had just thought of it in passing and had not called purposely on the senator to say it.

It was queer, the senator told himself. For he had known these two for a good while now. And they had known him equally as long. There should be nothing they should hesitate to tell him. They had, in the past, been brutally frank about many things in his political career.

It might be, he thought, more bad news from North America, but he was as well acquainted with that bad news as they. After all, he told himself philosophically, a man cannot reasonably expect to stay in office forever. The voters, from sheer boredom if nothing else, would finally reach the day when they would vote against a man who had served them faithfully and well. And the senator was candid enough to admit, at least to himself, that there had been times when he had served the voters of North America neither faithfully nor well.

Even at that, he thought, he had not been beaten yet. It was still several months until election time and there was a trick or two that he had never tried, political dodges that even at this late date might save the senatorial hide. Given the proper time and the proper place and he would win out yet. Timing, he told himself—proper timing is the thing that counts.

He sat quietly in his chair, a great hulk of a man, and for a single instant he closed his eyes to shut out the room and the sunlight in the window. Timing, he thought. Yes, timing and a feeling for the public, a finger on the public pulse, the ability to know ahead of time what the voter eventually will come to think—those were the ingredients of good strategy. To know ahead of time, to be ahead in thinking, so that in a week or a month or year, the voters would say to one another: "You know, Bill, old Senator Leonard had it right. Remember what he said last week —or month or year—over there in Géneva. Yes, sir, he laid it on the line. There ain't much that gets past that old fox of a Leonard."

He opened his eyes a slit, keeping them still half closed so his visitors might think he'd only had them half closed all the time. For it was impolite and a political mistake to close one's eyes when one had visitors. They might get the idea one wasn't interested. Or they might seize the opportunity to cut one's throat.

It's because I'm getting old again, the senator told himself. Getting old and drowsy. But just as smart as ever. Yes, sir, said the senator, talking to himself, just as smart and slippery as I ever was.

He saw by the tight expressions on the faces of the two that they finally were set to tell him the thing they had come to tell. All their circling and sniffing had been of no avail. Now they had to come out with it, on the line, cold turkey.

"There has been a certain matter," said Alexander Gibbs, "which has been quite a problem for the party for a long time now. We had hoped that matters would so arrange themselves that we wouldn't need to call it to your attention, senator. But the executive committee held a meeting in New York the other night and it seemed to be the consensus that we communicate it to you."

It's bad, thought the senator, even worse than I thought it might be— for Gibbs is talking in his best double-crossing manner.

The senator gave them no help. He sat quietly in his chair and held the whiskey glass in a steady hand and did not ask what it was all about, acting as if he didn't really care.

Gibbs floundered slightly. "It's a rather personal matter, senator," he said.

"It's this life continuation business," blurted Andrew Scott.

They sat in shocked silence, all three of them, for Scott should not have said it in that way. In politics, one is not blunt and forthright, but devious and slick.

"I see," the senator said finally. "The party thinks the voters would like it better if I were a normal man who would die a normal death."

Gibbs smoothed his face of shocked surprise.

"The common people resent men living beyond their normal time," he said. "Especially—"

"Especially," said the senator, "those who have done nothing to deserve it."

"I wouldn't put it exactly that way," Gibbs protested.

"Perhaps not," said the senator. "But no matter how you say it, that is what you mean."

They sat uncomfortably in the office chairs, with the bright Geneva sunlight pouring through the windows.

"I presume," said the senator, "that the party, having found I am no longer an outstanding asset, will not renew my application for life continuation. I suppose that is what you were sent to tell me."

Might as well get it over with, he told himself grimly. Now that it's out in the open, there's no sense in beating around the bush.

"That's just about it, senator," said Scott.

"That's exactly it," said Gibbs.

The senator heaved his great body from the chair, picked up the whiskey bottle, filled their glasses and his own.

"You delivered the death sentence very deftly," he told them. "It deserves a drink."

He wondered what they had thought that he would do. Plead with them, perhaps. Or storm around the office. Or denounce the party.

Puppets, he thought. Errand boys. Poor, scared errand boys.

They drank, their eyes on him, and silent laughter shook inside him from knowing that the liquor tasted very bitter in their mouths.

Chairman Leonard: *You are agreed then, Mr. Chapman, with the other witnesses, that no person should be allowed to seek continuation of life for himself, that it should be granted only upon application by someone else, that—*

Mr. Chapman: *It should be a gift of society to those persons who are in the unique position of being able to materially benefit the human race.*

Chairman Leonard: *That is very aptly stated, sir.*

> From the Records of a hearing before the science subcommittee of the public policy committee of the World House of Representatives.

The senator settled himself carefully and comfortably into a chair in the reception room of the Life Continuation Institute and unfolded his copy of the *North American Tribune.*

Column one said that system trade was normal, according to a report by the World Secretary of Commerce. The story went on at length to quote the secretary's report. Column two was headed by an impish box that said a new life form may have been found on Mars, but since the discoverer was a spaceman who had been more than ordinarily drunk, the report was being viewed with some skepticism. Under the box was a story reporting a list of boy and girl health champions selected by the state of Finland to be entered later in the year in the world health contest. The story in column three gave the latest information on the unstable love life of the world's richest woman.

Column four asked a question:

WHAT HAPPENED TO DR. CARSON?
NO RECORD OF REPORTED DEATH

The story, the senator saw, was by-lined Anson Lee and the senator chuckled dryly. Lee was up to something. He was always up to something, always ferreting out some fact that eventually was sure to prove embarrassing to someone. Smart as a steel trap, that Lee, but a bad man to get into one's hair.

There had been, for example, that matter of the spaceship contract.

Anson Lee, said the senator underneath his breath, is a pest. Nothing but a pest.

But Dr. Carson? Who was Dr. Carson?

The senator played a little mental game with himself, trying to remember, trying to identify the name before he read the story.

Dr. Carson?

Why, said the senator, I remember now. Long time ago. A biochemist or something of the sort. A very brilliant man. Did something with colonies of soil bacteria, breeding the things for therapeutic work.

Yes, said the senator, a very brilliant man. I remember that I met him once. Didn't understand half the things he said. But that was long ago. A hundred years or more.

A hundred years ago—maybe more than that.

Why, bless me, said the senator, he must be one of us.

The senator nodded and the paper slipped from his hands and fell upon the floor. He jerked himself erect. There I go again, he told himself. Dozing. It's old age creeping up again.

He sat in his chair, very erect and quiet, like a small scared child that won't admit it's scared, and the old, old fear came tugging at his brain. Too long, he thought. I've already waited longer than I should. Waiting for the party to renew my application and now the party won't. They've thrown me overboard. They've deserted me just when I needed them the most.

Death sentence, he had said back in the office, and that was what it was—for he couldn't last much longer. He didn't have much time. It would take a while to engineer whatever must be done. One would have to move most carefully and never tip one's hand. For there was a penalty— a terrible penalty.

The girl said to him: "Dr. Smith will see you now."

"Eh?" said the senator.

"You asked to see Dr. Dana Smith," the girl reminded him. "He will see you now."

"Thank you, miss," said the senator. "I was sitting here half dozing." He lumbered to his feet.

"That door," said the girl.

"I know," the senator mumbled testily. "I know. I've been here many times before."

Dr. Smith was waiting.

"Have a chair, senator," he said. "Have a drink? Well, then, a cigar, maybe. What is on your mind?"

The senator took his time, getting himself adjusted to the chair. Grunting comfortably, he clipped the end off the cigar, rolled it in his mouth.

"Nothing particular on my mind," he said. "Just dropped around to pass the time of day. Have a great and abiding interest in your work here. Always have had. Associated with it from the very start."

The director nodded. "I know. You conducted the original hearings on life continuation."

The senator chuckled. "Seemed fairly simple then. There were problems, of course, and we recognized them and we tried the best we could to meet them."

"You did amazingly well," the director told him. "The code you drew up five hundred years ago has never been questioned for its fairness and the few modifications which have been necessary have dealt with minor points which no one could have anticipated."

"But it's taken too long," said the senator.

The director stiffened. "I don't understand," he said.

The senator lighted the cigar, applying his whole attention to it, flaming the end carefully so it caught even fire.

He settled himself more solidly in the chair. "It was like this," he said. "We recognized life continuation as a first step only, a rather blundering first step toward immortality. We devised the code as an interim instrument to take care of the period before immortality was available—not to a selected few, but to everyone. We viewed the few who could be given life continuation as stewards, persons who would help to advance the day when the race could be granted immortality."

"That still is the concept," Dr. Smith said, coldly.

"But the people grow impatient."

"That is just too bad," Smith told him. "The people will simply have to wait."

"As a race, they may be willing to," explained the senator. "As individuals, they're not."

"I fail to see your point, senator."

"There may not be a point," said the senator. "In late years I've often debated with myself the wisdom of the whole procedure. Life continuation is a keg of dynamite if it fails of immortality. It will breed system-wide revolt if the people wait too long."

"Have you a solution, senator?"

"No," confessed the senator. "No, I'm afraid I haven't. I've often thought that it might have been better if we had taken the people into our confidence, let them know all that was going on. Kept them up with all developments. An informed people are a rational people."

The director did not answer and the senator felt the cold weight of certainty seep into his brain.

He knows, he told himself. He knows the party has decided not to ask that I be continued. He knows that I'm a dead man. He knows I'm almost through and can't help him any more—and he's crossed me out. He won't tell me a thing. Not the thing I want to know.

But he did not allow his face to change. He knew his face would not betray him. His face was too well trained.

"I know there is an answer," said the senator. "There's always been an answer to any question about immortality. You can't have it until there's living space. Living space to throw away, more than we ever think we'll need, and a fair chance to find more of it if it's ever needed."

Dr. Smith nodded. "That's the answer, senator. The only answer I can give."

He sat silent for a moment, then he said: "Let me assure you on one point, senator. When Extrasolar Research finds the living space, we'll have the immortality."

The senator heaved himself out of the chair, stood planted solidly on his feet.

"It's good to hear you say that, doctor," he said. "It is very heartening. I thank you for the time you gave me."

Out on the street, the senator thought bitterly:

They have it now. They have immortality. All they're waiting for is the living space and another hundred years will find that. Another hundred years will simply have to find it.

Another hundred years, he told himself, just one more continuation, and I would be in for good and all.

Mr. Andrews: *We must be sure there is a divorcement of life continuation from economics. A man who has money must not be allowed to purchase additional life, either through the payment of money or the pressure of influence, while another man is doomed to die a natural death simply because he happens to be poor.*

Chairman Leonard: *I don't believe that situation has ever been in question.*

Mr. Andrews: *Nevertheless, it is a matter which must be emphasized again and again. Life continuation must not be a commodity to be sold across the counter at so many dollars for each added year of life.*

> From the Records of a hearing before the science subcommittee of the public policy committee of the World House of Representatives.

The senator sat before the chessboard and idly worked at the problem. Idly, since his mind was on other things than chess.

So they had immortality, had it and were waiting, holding it a secret until there was assurance of sufficient living space. Holding it a secret from the people and from the government and from the men and women who had spent many lifetimes working for the thing which already had been found.

For Smith had spoken, not as a man who was merely confident, but as a man who knew. When Extrasolar Research finds the living space, he'd said, we'll have immortality. Which meant they had it now. Immortality was not predictable. You would not know you'd have it; you would only know if and when you had it.

The senator moved a bishop and saw that he was wrong. He slowly pulled it back.

Living space was the key, and not living space alone, but economic living space, self-supporting in terms of food and other raw materials, but particularly in food. For if living space had been all that mattered, Man had it in Mars and Venus and the moons of Jupiter. But not one of those worlds was self-supporting. They did not solve the problem.

Living space was all they needed and in a hundred years they'd have that. Another hundred years was all that anyone would need to come into possession of the common human heritage of immortality.

Another continuation would give me that hundred years, said the senator, talking to himself. A hundred years and some to spare, for this time I'll be careful of myself. I'll lead a cleaner life. Eat sensibly and cut out liquor and tobacco and the woman-chasing.

There were ways and means, of course. There always were. And he would find them, for he knew all the dodges. After five hundred years in world government, you got to know them all. If you didn't know them, you simply didn't last.

Mentally he listed the possibilities as they occurred to him.

ONE: A person could engineer a continuation for someone else and then have that person assign the continuation to him. It would be costly, of course, but it might be done.

You'd have to find someone you could trust and maybe you couldn't find anyone you could trust that far—for life continuation was something hard to come by. Most people, once they got it, wouldn't give it back.

Although on second thought, it probably wouldn't work. For there'd be legal angles. A continuation was a gift of society to one specific person to be used by him alone. It would not be transferable. It would not be legal property. It would not be something that one owned. It could not be bought or sold, it could not be assigned.

If the person who had been granted a continuation died before he got to use it—died of natural causes, of course, of wholly natural causes that could be provable—why, maybe, then— But still it wouldn't work. Not being property, the continuation would not be part of one's estate. It could not be bequeathed. It most likely would revert to the issuing agency.

Cross that one off, the senator told himself.

TWO: He might travel to New York and talk to the party's executive secretary. After all, Gibbs and Scott were mere messengers. They had their orders to carry out the dictates of the party and that was all. Maybe if he saw someone in authority—

But, the senator scolded himself, that is wishful thinking. The party's through with me. They've pushed their continuation racket as far as they dare push it and they have wrangled about all they figure they can get. They don't dare ask for more and they need my continuation for someone else most likely—someone who's a comer; someone who has vote appeal.

And I, said the senator, am an old has-been.

Although I'm a tricky old rascal, and ornery if I have to be, and slippery as five hundred years of public life can make one.

After that long, said the senator, parenthetically, you have no more illusions, not even of yourself.

I couldn't stomach it, he decided. I couldn't live with myself if I went crawling to New York—and a thing has to be pretty bad to make me feel like that. I've never crawled before and I'm not crawling now, not even for an extra hundred years and a shot at immortality.

Cross that one off, too, said the senator.

THREE: Maybe someone could be bribed.

Of all the possibilities, that sounded the most reasonable. There always was someone who had a certain price and always someone else who could act as intermediary. Naturally, a world senator could not get mixed up directly in a deal of that sort.

It might come a little high, but what was money for? After all, he reconciled himself, he'd been a frugal man of sorts and had been able to lay away a wad against such a day as this.

The senator moved a rook and it seemed to be all right, so he left it there.

Of course, once he managed the continuation, he would have to disappear. He couldn't flaunt his triumph in the party's face. He couldn't take a chance of someone asking how he'd been continuated. He'd have to become one of the people, seek to be forgotten, live in some obscure place and keep out of the public eye.

Norton was the man to see. No matter what one wanted, Norton was the man to see. An appointment to be secured, someone to be killed, a concession on Venus or a spaceship contract—Norton did the job. All quietly and discreetly and no questions asked. That is, if you had the money. If you didn't have the money, there was no use of seeing Norton.

Otto came into the room on silent feet.

"A gentleman to see you, sir," he said.

The senator stiffened upright in his chair.

"What do you mean by sneaking up on me?" he shouted. "Always pussyfooting. Trying to startle me. After this you cough or fall over a chair or something so I'll know that you're around."

"Sorry, sir," said Otto. "There's a gentleman here. And there are those letters on the desk to read."

"I'll read the letters later," said the senator.

"Be sure you don't forget," Otto told him, stiffly.

"I never forget," said the senator. "You'd think I was getting senile, the way you keep reminding me."

"There's a gentleman to see you," Otto said patiently. "A Mr. Lee."

"Anson Lee, perhaps."

Otto sniffed. "I believe that was his name. A newspaper person, sir."

"Show him in," said the senator.

He sat stolidly in his chair and thought: Lee's found out about it. Somehow he's ferreted out the fact the party's thrown me over. And he's here to crucify me.

He may suspect, but he cannot know. He may have heard a rumor, but he can't be sure. The party would keep mum, must necessarily keep mum, since it can't openly admit its traffic in life continuation. So Lee, having heard a rumor, had come to blast it out of me, to catch me by surprise and trip me up with words.

I must not let him do it, for once the thing is known, the wolves will come in packs knee deep.

Lee was walking into the room and the senator rose and shook his hand.

"Sorry to disturb you, senator," Lee told him, "but I thought maybe you could help me."

"Anything at all," the senator said, affably. "Anything I can. Sit down, Mr. Lee."

"Perhaps you read my story in the morning paper," said Lee. "The one on Dr. Carson's disappearance."

"No," said the senator. "No, I'm afraid I—"

He rumbled to a stop, astounded.

He hadn't read the paper!

He had forgotten to read the paper!

He always read the paper. He never failed to read it. It was a solemn rite, starting at the front and reading straight through to the back, skipping only those sections which long ago he'd found not to be worth the reading.

He'd had the paper at the institute and he had been interrupted when the girl told him that Dr. Smith would see him. He had come out of the office and he'd left the paper in the reception room.

It was a terrible thing. Nothing, absolutely nothing, should so upset him that he forgot to read the paper.

"I'm afraid I didn't read the story," the senator said lamely. He simply couldn't force himself to admit that he hadn't read the paper.

"Dr. Carson," said Lee, "was a biochemist, a fairly famous one. He died ten years or so ago, according to an announcement from a little village in Spain, where he had gone to live. But I have reason to believe, senator, that he never died at all, that he may still be living."

"Hiding?" asked the senator.

"Perhaps," said Lee. "Although there seems no reason that he should. His record is entirely spotless."

"Why do you doubt he died, then?"

"Because there's no death certificate. And he's not the only one who died without benefit of certificate."

"Hm-m-m," said the senator.

"Galloway, the anthropologist, died five years ago. There's no certificate. Henderson, the agricultural expert, died six years ago. There's no certificate. There are a dozen more I know of and probably many that I don't."

"Anything in common?" asked the senator. "Any circumstances that might link these people?"

"Just one thing," said Lee. "They were all continuators."

"I see," said the senator. He clasped the arms of his chair with a fierce grip to keep his hands from shaking.

"Most interesting," he said. "Very interesting."

"I know you can't tell me anything officially," said Lee, "but I thought you might give me a fill-in, an off-the-record background. You wouldn't let me quote you, of course, but any clues you might give me, any hint at all—"

He waited hopefully.

"Because I've been close to the Life Continuation people?" asked the senator.

Lee nodded. "If there's anything to know, you know it, senator. You headed the committee that held the original hearings on life continuation. Since then you've held various other congressional posts in connection with it. Only this morning you saw Dr. Smith."

"I can't tell you anything," mumbled the senator. "I don't know anything. You see, it's a matter of policy—"

"I had hoped you would help me, senator."

"I can't," said the senator. "You'll never believe it, of course, but I really can't."

He sat silently for a moment and then he asked a question: "You say all these people you mention were continuators. You checked, of course, to see if their applications had been renewed?"

"I did," said Lee. "There are no renewals for any one of them—at least no records of renewals. Some of them were approaching death limit and they actually may be dead by now, although I doubt that any of them died at the time or place announced."

"Interesting," said the senator. "And quite a mystery, too."

Lee deliberately terminated the discussion. He gestured at the chessboard. "Are you an expert, senator?"

The senator shook his head. "The game appeals to me. I fool around with it. It's a game of logic and also a game of ethics. You are perforce a gentleman when you play it. You observe certain rules of correctness of behavior."

"Like life, senator?"

"Like life should be," said the senator. "When the odds are too terrific, you resign. You do not force your opponent to play out to the bitter end. That's ethics. When you see that you can't win, but that you have a fighting chance, you try for the next best thing—a draw. That's logic."

Lee laughed, a bit uncomfortably. "You've lived according to those rules, senator?"

"I've done my best," said the senator, trying to sound humble.

Lee rose. "I must be going, senator."

"Stay and have a drink."

Lee shook his head. "Thanks, but I have work to do."

"I owe you a drink," said the senator. "Remind me of it sometime."

For a long time after Lee left, Senator Homer Leonard sat unmoving in his chair.

Then he reached out a hand and picked up a knight to move it, but his fingers shook so that he dropped it and it clattered on the board.

Any person who gains the gift of life continuation by illegal or extra-legal means, without bona fide recommendation or proper authorization through recognized channels, shall be, in effect, excommunicated from the human race. The facts of that person's guilt, once proved, shall be published by every means at humanity's command throughout the Earth and to every corner of the Earth so that all persons may know and recognize him. To further insure such recognition and identification, said convicted person must wear at all times, conspicuously displayed upon his person, a certain badge which shall advertise his guilt. While he may not be denied the ordinary basic requirements of life, such as food, adequate clothing, a minimum of shelter and medical care, he shall not be allowed to partake of or participate in any of the other refinements of civilization. He will not be allowed to purchase any item in excess of the barest necessities for the preservation of life, health and decency; he shall be barred from all endeavors and normal associations of humankind; he shall not have access to nor benefit of any library, lecture hall, amusement place or other facility, either private or public, designed for instruction, recreation or entertainment. Nor may any person, under certain penalties hereinafter set forth, knowingly converse with him or establish any human relationship whatsoever with him. He will be suffered to live out his life within the framework of the human community, but to all intent and purpose he will be denied all the privileges and obligations of a human being. And the same provisions as are listed above shall apply in full and equal force to any person or persons who shall in any way knowingly aid such a person to obtain life continuation by other than legal means.

From the Code of Life Continuation.

"What you mean," said J. Barker Norton, "is that the party all these years has been engineering renewals of life continuation for you. Paying you off for services well rendered."

The senator nodded miserably.

"And now that you're on the verge of losing an election, they figure you aren't worth it any longer and have refused to ask for a renewal."

"In curbstone language," said the senator, "that sums it up quite neatly."

"And you come running to me," said Norton. "What in the world do you think I can do about it?"

The senator leaned forward. "Let's put it on a business basis, Norton. You and I have worked together before."

"That's right," said Norton. "Both of us cleaned up on that spaceship deal."

The senator said: "I want another hundred years and I'm willing to pay for it. I have no doubt you can arrange it for me."

"How?"

"I wouldn't know," said the senator. "I'm leaving that to you. I don't care how you do it."

Norton leaned back in his chair and made a tent out of his fingers.

"You figure I could bribe someone to recommend you. Or bribe some continuation technician to give you a renewal without authorization."

"Those are a pair of excellent ideas," agreed the senator.

"And face excommunication if I were found out," said Norton. "Thanks, senator, I'm having none of it."

The senator sat impassively, watching the face of the man across the desk.

"A hundred thousand," the senator said quietly.

Norton laughed at him.

"A half million, then."

"Remember that excommunication, senator. It's got to be worth my while to take a chance like that."

"A million," said the senator. "And that's absolutely final."

"A million now," said Norton. "Cold cash. No receipt. No record of the transaction. Another million when and if I can deliver."

The senator rose slowly to his feet, his face a mask to hide the excitement that was stirring in him. The excitement and the naked surge of exultation. He kept his voice level.

"I'll deliver that million before the week is over."

Norton said: "I'll start looking into things."

On the street outside, the senator's step took on a jauntiness it had not known in years. He walked along briskly, flipping his cane.

Those others, Carson and Galloway and Henderson, had disappeared, exactly as he would have to disappear once he got his extra hundred years. They had arranged to have their own deaths announced and then had dropped from sight, living against the day when immortality would be a thing to be had for the simple asking.

Somewhere, somehow, they had got a new continuation, an unauthorized continuation, since a renewal was not listed in the records. Someone had arranged it for them. More than likely Norton.

But they had bungled. They had tried to cover up their tracks and had done no more than call attention to their absence.

In a thing like this, a man could not afford to blunder. A wise man, a man who took the time to think things out, would not make a blunder.

The senator pursed his flabby lips and whistled a snatch of music.

Norton was a gouger, of course. Pretending that he couldn't make arrangements, pretending he was afraid of excommunication, jacking up the price.

The senator grinned wryly. It would take almost every dime he had, but it was worth the price.

He'd have to be careful, getting together that much money. Some from one bank, some from another, collecting it piecemeal by withdrawals and by cashing bonds, floating a few judicious loans so there'd not be too many questions asked.

He bought a paper at the corner and hailed a cab. Settling back in the seat, he creased the paper down its length and started in on column one. Another health contest. This time in Australia.

Health, thought the senator, they're crazy on this health business. Health centers. Health cults. Health clinics.

He skipped the story, moved on to column two.

The head said:

SIX SENATORS POOR BETS FOR RE-ELECTION

The senator snorted in disgust. One of the senators, of course, would be himself.

He wadded up the paper and jammed it in his pocket.

Why should he care? Why knock himself out to retain a senate seat he could never fill? He was going to grow young again, get another chance at life. He would move to some far part of the earth and be another man.

Another man. He thought about it and it was refreshing. Dropping all the old dead wood of past association, all the ancient accumulation of responsibilities.

Norton had taken on the job. Norton would deliver.

Mr. Miller: *What I want to know is this: Where do we stop? You give this life continuation to a man and he'll want his wife and kids to have it. And his wife will want her Aunt Minnie to have it and the kids will want the family dog to have it and the dog will want—*
Chairman Leonard: *You're facetious, Mr. Miller.*
Mr. Miller: *I don't know what that big word means, mister. You guys here in Geneva talk fancy with them six-bit words and you get the people all balled up. It's time the common people got in a word of common sense.*

From the Records of a hearing before the science subcommittee of the public policy committee of the World House of Representatives.

"Frankly," Norton told him, "it's the first time I ever ran across a thing I couldn't fix. Ask me anything else you want to, senator, and I'll rig it up for you."

The senator sat stricken. "You mean you couldn't— But, Norton, there was Dr. Carson and Galloway and Henderson. Someone took care of them."

Norton shook his head. "Not I. I never heard of them."

"But someone did," said the senator. "They disappeared—"

His voice trailed off and he slumped deeper in the chair and the truth suddenly was plain—the truth he had failed to see.

A blind spot, he told himself. A blind spot!

They had disappeared and that was all he knew. They had published their own deaths and had not died, but had disappeared.

He had assumed they had disappeared because they had got an illegal continuation. But that was sheer wishful thinking. There was no foundation for it, no fact that would support it.

There could be other reasons, he told himself, many other reasons why a man would disappear and seek to cover up his tracks with a death report.

But it had tied in so neatly!

They were continuators whose applications had not been renewed. Exactly as he was a continuator whose application would not be renewed.

They had dropped out of sight. Exactly as he would have to drop from sight once he gained another lease on life.

It had tied in so neatly—and it had been all wrong.

"I tried every way I knew," said Norton. "I canvassed every source that might advance your name for continuation and they laughed at me. It's been tried before, you see, and there's not a chance of getting it put through. Once your original sponsor drops you, you're automatically cancelled out.

"I tried to sound out technicians who might take a chance, but they're incorruptible. They get paid off in added years for loyalty and they're not taking any chance of trading years for dollars."

"I guess that settles it," the senator said wearily. "I should have known."

He heaved himself to his feet and faced Norton squarely. "You are telling me the truth," he pleaded. "You aren't just trying to jack up the price a bit."

Norton stared at him, almost unbelieving. "Jack up the price! Senator, if I had put this through, I'd have taken your last penny. Want to know how much you're worth? I can tell you within a thousand dollars."

He waved a hand at a row of filing cases ranged along the wall.

"It's all there, senator. You and all the other big shots. Complete files on every one of you. When a man comes to me with a deal like yours, I look in the files and strip him to the bone."

"I don't suppose there's any use of asking for some of my money back?"

Norton shook his head. "Not a ghost. You took your gamble, senator. You can't even prove you paid me. And, beside, you still have plenty left to last you the few years you have to live."

The senator took a step toward the door, then turned back.

"Look, Norton, I can't die! Not now. Just one more continuation and I'd be—"

The look on Norton's face stopped him in his tracks. The look he'd glimpsed on other faces at other times, but only glimpsed. Now he stared at it—at the naked hatred of a man whose life is short for the man whose life is long.

"Sure, you can die," said Norton. "You're going to. You can't live forever. Who do you think you are!"

The senator reached out a hand and clutched the desk.

"But you don't understand."

"You've already lived ten times as long as I have lived," said Norton, coldly, measuring each word, "and I hate your guts for it. Get out of here, you sniveling old fool, before I throw you out."

Dr. Barton: *You may think that you would confer a boon on humanity with life continuation, but I tell you, sir, that it would be a curse. Life would lose its value and its meaning if it went on forever, and if you have life continuation now, you eventually must stumble on immortality. And when that happens, sir, you will be compelled to set up boards of review to grant the boon of death. The people, tired of life, will storm your hearing rooms to plead for death.*

Chairman Leonard: *It would banish uncertainty and fear.*

Dr. Barton: *You are talking of the fear of death. The fear of death, sir, is infantile.*

Chairman Leonard: *But there are benefits—*

Dr. Barton: *Benefits, yes. The benefit of allowing a scientist the extra years he needs to complete a piece of research; a composer an additional lifetime to complete a symphony. Once the novelty wore off, men in general would accept added life only under protest, only as a duty.*

Chairman Leonard: *You're not very practical-minded, doctor.*

Dr. Barton: *But I am. Extremely practical and down to earth. Man must have newness. Man cannot be bored and live. How much do you think there would be left to look forward to after the millionth woman, the billionth piece of pumpkin pie?*

> From the Records of the hearing before the science subcommittee of the public policy committee of the World House of Representatives.

So Norton hated him.

As all people of normal lives must hate, deep within their souls, the lucky ones whose lives went on and on.

A hatred deep and buried, most of the time buried. But sometimes breaking out, as it had broken out of Norton.

Resentment, tolerated because of the gently, skillfully fostered hope that those whose lives went on might some day make it possible that the lives of all, barring violence or accident or incurable disease, might go on as long as one would wish.

I can understand it now, thought the senator, for I am one of them. I am one of those whose lives will not continue to go on, and I have even fewer years than the most of them.

He stood before the window in the deepening dusk and saw the lights come out and the day die above the unbelievably blue waters of the far-famed lake.

Beauty came to him as he stood there watching, beauty that had gone unnoticed through all the later years. A beauty and a softness and a feeling of being one with the city lights and the last faint gleam of day above the darkening waters.

Fear? The senator admitted it.

Bitterness? Of course.

Yet, despite the fear and bitterness, the window held him with the scene it framed.

Earth and sky and water, he thought. I am one with them. Death has made me one with them. For death brings one back to the elementals, to the soil and trees, to the clouds and sky and the sun dying in the welter of its blood in the crimson west.

This is the price we pay, he thought, that the race must pay, for its life eternal—that we may not be able to assess in their true value the things that should be dearest to us; for a thing that has no ending, a thing that goes on forever, must have decreasing value.

Rationalization, he accused himself. Of course, you're rationalizing. You want another hundred years as badly as you ever did. You want a chance at immortality. But you can't have it and you trade eternal life for a sunset seen across a lake and it is well you can. It is a blessing that you can.

The senator made a rasping sound within his throat.

Behind him the telephone came to sudden life and he swung around. It chirred at him again. Feet pattered down the hall and the senator called out: "I'll get it, Otto."

He lifted the receiver. "New York calling," said the operator. "Senator Leonard, please."

"This is Leonard."

Another voice broke in. "Senator, this is Gibbs."

"Yes," said the senator. "The executioner."

"I called you," said Gibbs, "to talk about the election."

"What election?"

"The one here in North America. The one you're running in. Remember?"

"I am an old man," said the senator, "and I'm about to die. I'm not interested in elections."

Gibbs practically chattered. "But you have to be. What's the matter with you, senator? You have to do something. Make some speeches, make a statement, come home and stump the country. The party can't do it all alone. You have to do some of it yourself."

"I will do something," declared the senator. "Yes, I think that finally I'll do something."

He hung up and walked to the writing desk, snapped on the light. He got paper out of a drawer and took a pen out of his pocket.

The telephone went insane and he paid it no attention. It rang on and on and finally Otto came and answered.

"New York calling, sir," he said.

The senator shook his head and he heard Otto talking softly and the phone did not ring again.

The senator wrote:

To Whom It May Concern:

Then crossed it out.

He wrote:

A Statement to the World:

And crossed it out.

He wrote:

A Statement by Senator Homer Leonard:

He crossed that out, too.

He wrote:

Five centuries ago the people of the world gave into the hands of a few trusted men and women the gift of continued life in the hope and belief that they would work to advance the day when longer life spans might be made possible for the entire population.

From time to time, life continuation has been granted additional men and women, always with the implied understanding that the gift was made under the same conditions—that the persons so favored should work against the day when each inhabitant of the entire world might enter upon a heritage of near-eternity.

Through the years some of us have carried that trust forward and have lived with it and cherished it and bent every effort toward its fulfillment.

Some of us have not.

Upon due consideration and searching examination of my own status in this regard, I have at length decided that I no longer can accept further extension of the gift.

Human dignity requires that I be able to meet my fellow man upon the street or in the byways of the world without flinching from him. This I could not do should I continue to accept a gift to which I have no claim and which is denied to other men.

The senator signed his name, neatly, carefully, without the usual flourish.

"There," he said, speaking aloud in the silence of the night-filled room, "that will hold them for a while."

Feet padded and he turned around.

"It's long past your usual bedtime, sir," said Otto.

The senator rose clumsily and his aching bones protested. Old, he thought. Growing old again. And it would be so easy to start over, to regain his youth and live another lifetime. Just the nod of someone's head, just a single pen stroke and he would be young again.

"This statement, Otto," he said. "Please give it to the press."

"Yes, sir," said Otto. He took the paper, held it gingerly.

"Tonight," said the senator.

"Tonight, sir? It is rather late."

"Nevertheless, I want to issue it tonight."

"It must be important, sir."

"It's my resignation," said the senator.

"Your resignation! From the senate, sir!"

"No," said the senator. "From life."

Mr. Michaelson: *As a churchman, I cannot think otherwise than that the proposal now before you gentlemen constitutes a perversion of God's law. It is not within the province of man to say a man may live beyond his allotted time.*

Chairman Leonard: *I might ask you this: How is one to know when a man's allotted time has come to an end? Medicine has prolonged the lives of many persons. Would you call a physician a perverter of God's law?*

Mr. Michaelson: *It has become apparent through the testimony given here that the eventual aim of continuing research is immortality. Surely you can see that physical immortality does not square with the Christian concept. I tell you this, sir: You can't fool God and get away with it.*

From the Records of a hearing before the science subcommittee of the public policy committee of the World House of Representatives.

Chess is a game of logic.

But likewise a game of ethics.

You do not shout and you do not whistle, nor bang the pieces on the board, nor twiddle your thumbs, nor move a piece then take it back again. When you're beaten, you admit it. You do not force your opponent to carry on the game to absurd lengths. You resign and start another game if there is time to play one. Otherwise, you just resign and you do it with all the good grace possible. You do not knock all the pieces to the floor in anger. You do not get up abruptly and stalk out of the room. You do not reach across the board and punch your opponent in the nose.

When you play chess you are, or you are supposed to be, a gentleman.

The senator lay wide-awake, staring at the ceiling.

You do not reach across the board and punch your opponent in the nose. You do not knock the pieces to the floor.

But this isn't chess, he told himself, arguing with himself. This isn't chess; this is life and death. A dying thing is not a gentleman. It does not curl up quietly and die of the hurt inflicted. It backs into a corner and it fights, it lashes back and does all the hurt it can.

And I am hurt. I am hurt to death.

And I have lashed back. I have lashed back, most horribly.

They'll not be able to walk down the street again, not ever again, those gentlemen who passed the sentence on me. For they have no more claim to continued life than I and the people now will know it. And the people will see to it that they do not get it.

I will die, but when I go down I'll pull the others with me. They'll know I pulled them down, down with me into the pit of death. That's the sweetest part of all—they'll know who pulled them down and they won't be able to say a word about it. They can't even contradict the noble things I said.

Someone in the corner said, some voice from some other time and place: *You're no gentleman, senator. You fight a dirty fight.*

Sure I do, said the senator. They fought dirty first. And politics always was a dirty game.

Remember all that fine talk you dished out to Lee the other day?

That was the other day, snapped the senator.

You'll never be able to look a chessman in the face again, said the voice in the corner.

I'll be able to look my fellow men in the face, however, said the senator.

Will you? asked the voice.

And that, of course, was the question. Would he?

I don't care, the senator cried desperately. I don't care what happens. They played a lousy trick on me. They can't get away with it. I'll fix their clocks for them. I'll—

Sure, you will, said the voice, mocking.

Go away, shrieked the senator. Go away and leave me. Let me be alone.

You are alone, said the thing in the corner. *You are more alone than any man has ever been before.*

Chairman Leonard: *You represent an insurance company, do you not, Mr. Markely? A big insurance company.*

Mr. Markely: *That is correct.*

Chairman Leonard: *And every time a person dies, it costs your company money?*

Mr. Markely: *Well, you might put it that way if you wished, although it is scarcely the case—*

Chairman Leonard: *You do have to pay out benefits on deaths, don't you?*

Mr. Markely: *Why, yes, of course we do.*

Chairman Leonard: *Then I can't understand your opposition to life continuation. If there were fewer deaths, you'd have to pay fewer benefits.*

Mr.Markely: *All very true, sir. But if people had reason to believe they would live virtually forever, they'd buy no life insurance.*

Chairman Leonard: *Oh, I see. So that's the way it is.*

> From the Records of a hearing before the science subcommittee of the public policy committee of the World House of Representatives.

The senator awoke. He had not been dreaming, but it was almost as if he had awakened from a bad dream—or awakened to a bad dream— and he struggled to go back to sleep again, to gain the Nirvana of unawareness, to shut out the harsh reality of existence, to dodge the shame of knowing who and what he was.

But there was someone stirring in the room, and someone spoke to him and he sat upright in bed, stung to wakefulness by the happiness and something else that was almost worship which the voice held.

"It's wonderful, sir," said Otto. "There have been phone calls all night long. And the telegrams and radiograms still are stacking up."

The senator rubbed his eyes with pudgy fists.

"Phone calls, Otto? People sore at me?"

"Some of them were, sir. Terribly angry, sir. But not too many of them. Most of them were happy and wanted to tell you what a great thing you'd done. But I told them you were tired and I could not waken you."

"Great thing?" said the senator. "What great thing have I done?"

"Why, sir, giving up life continuation. One man said to tell you it was the greatest example of moral courage the world had ever known. He said all the common people would bless you for it. Those were his very words. He was very solemn, sir."

The senator swung his feet to the floor, sat on the edge of the bed, scratching at his ribs.

It was strange, he told himself, how a thing would turn out sometimes. A heel at bedtime and a hero in the morning.

"Don't you see, sir," said Otto, "you have made yourself one of the common people, one of the short-lived people. No one has ever done a thing like that before."

"I was one of the common people," said the senator, "long before I wrote that statement. And I didn't make myself one of them. I was forced to become one of them, much against my will."

But Otto, in his excitement, didn't seem to hear.

He rattled on: "The newspapers are full of it, sir. It's the biggest news in years. The political writers are chuckling over it. They're calling it the smartest political move that was ever pulled. They say that before you made the announcement you didn't have a chance of being re-elected senator and now, they say, you can be elected president if you just say the word."

The senator sighed. "Otto," he said, "please hand me my pants. It is cold in here."

Otto handed him his trousers. "There's a newspaperman waiting in the study, sir. I held all the others off, but this one sneaked in the back way. You know him, sir, so I let him wait. He is Mr. Lee."

"I'll see him," said the senator.

So it was a smart political move, was it? Well, maybe so, but after a day or so, even the surprised political experts would begin to wonder about the logic of a man literally giving up his life to be re-elected to a senate seat.

Of course the common herd would love it, but he had not done it for applause. Although, so long as the people insisted upon thinking of him as great and noble, it was all right to let them go on thinking so.

The senator jerked his tie straight and buttoned his coat. He went into the study and Lee was waiting for him.

"I suppose you want an interview," said the senator. "Want to know why I did this thing."

Lee shook his head. "No, senator, I have something else. Something you should know about. Remember our talk last week? About the disappearances."

The senator nodded.

"Well, I have something else. You wouldn't tell me anything last week, but maybe now you will. I've checked, senator, and I've found this—the health winners are disappearing, too. More than eighty percent of those who participated in the finals of the last ten years have disappeared."

"I don't understand," said the senator.

"They're going somewhere," said Lee. "Something's happening to them. Something's happening to two classes of our people—the continuators and the healthiest youngsters."

"Wait a minute," gasped the senator. "Wait a minute, Mr. Lee."

He groped his way to the desk, grasped its edge and lowered himself into a chair.

"There is something wrong, senator?" asked Lee.

"Wrong?" mumbled the senator. "Yes, there must be something wrong."

"They've found living space," said Lee, triumphantly. "That's it, isn't it? They've found living space and they're sending out the pioneers."

The senator shook his head. "I don't know, Lee. I have not been informed. Check Extrasolar Research. They're the only ones who know—and they wouldn't tell you."

Lee grinned at him. "Good day, senator," he said. "Thanks so much for helping."

Dully, the senator watched him go.

Living space? Of course, that was it.

They had found living space and Extrasolar Research was sending out handpicked pioneers to prepare the way. It would take years of work and planning before the discovery could be announced. For once announced, world government must be ready to confer immortality on a mass production basis, must have ships available to carry out the hordes to the far, new worlds. A premature announcement would bring psychological and economic disruption that would make the government a shambles. So they would work very quietly, for they must work quietly.

His eyes found the little stack of letters on one corner of the desk and he remembered, with a shock of guilt, that he had meant to read them. He had promised Otto that he would and then he had forgotten.

I keep forgetting all the time, said the senator. I forget to read my paper and I forget to read my letters and I forget that some men are loyal and morally honest instead of slippery and slick. And I indulge in wishful thinking and that's the worst of all.

Continuators and health champions disappearing. Sure, they're disappearing. They're headed for new worlds and immortality.

And I . . . I . . . if only I had kept my big mouth shut—

The phone chirped and he picked it up.

"This is Sutton at Extrasolar Research," said an angry voice.

"Yes, Dr. Sutton," said the senator. "It's nice of you to call."

"I'm calling in regard to the invitation that we sent you last week," said Sutton. "In view of your statement last night, which we feel very keenly is an unjust criticism, we are withdrawing it."

"Invitation," said the senator. "Why, I didn't—"

"What I can't understand," said Sutton, "is why, with the invitation in your pocket, you should have acted as you did."

"But," said the senator, "but, doctor—"

"Good-by, senator," said Sutton.

Slowly the senator hung up. With a fumbling hand, he reached out and picked up the stack of letters.

It was the third one down. The return address was Extrasolar Research and it had been registered and sent special delivery and it was marked both PERSONAL and IMPORTANT.

The letter slipped out of the senator's trembling fingers and fluttered to the floor. He did not pick it up.

It was too late now, he knew, to do anything about it.

THE WITCHES OF KARRES

by James H. Schmitz

I.

IT WAS AROUND THE HUB OF THE EVENING ON THE PLANET OF PORLUMMA that Captain Pausert, commercial traveler from the Republic of Nikkeldepain, met the first of the witches of Karres.

It was just plain fate, so far as he could see.

He was feeling pretty good as he left a high-priced bar on a cobbly street near the spaceport, with the intention of returning straight to his ship. There hadn't been an argument, exactly. But someone grinned broadly, as usual, when the captain pronounced the name of his native system; and the captain had pointed out then, with considerable wit, how much more ridiculous it was to call a planet Porlumma, for instance, than to call it Nikkeldepain.

He proceeded to collect a gradually increasing number of pained stares by a detailed comparison of the varied, interesting and occasionally brilliant role Nikkeldepain had played in history with Porlumma's obviously dull and dumpy status as a sixth-rate Empire outpost.

In conclusion, he admitted frankly that he wouldn't care to be found dead on Porlumma.

Somebody muttered loudly in Imperial Universum that in that case it might be better if he didn't hang around Porlumma too long. But the captain only smiled politely, paid for his two drinks and left.

There was no point in getting into a rhubarb on one of these border planets. Their citizens still had an innocent notion that they ought to act like frontiersmen—but then the Law always showed up at once.

He felt pretty good. Up to the last four months of his young life, he had never looked on himself as being particularly patriotic. But compared to most of the Empire's worlds, Nikkeldepain was downright attractive in its stuffy way. Besides, he was returning there solvent—would they ever be surprised!

And awaiting him, fondly and eagerly, was Illyla, the Miss Onswud, fair daughter of the mighty Councilor Onswud, and the captain's secretly affianced for almost a year. She alone had believed in him!

The captain smiled and checked at a dark cross-street to get his bearings on the spaceport beacon. Less than half a mile away— He set off again. In about six hours, he'd be beyond the Empire's space borders and headed straight for Illyla.

Yes, she alone had believed! After the prompt collapse of the captain's first commercial venture—a miffel-fur farm, largely on capital borrowed from Councilor Onswud—the future had looked very black. It had even included a probable ten-year stretch of penal servitude for "willful and negligent abuse of intrusted monies." The laws of Nikkeldepain were rough on debtors.

"But you've always been looking for someone to take out the old *Venture* and get her back into trade!" Illyla reminded her father tearfully.

"Hm-m-m, yes! But it's in the blood, my dear! His great-uncle Threbus went the same way! It would be far better to let the law take its course," Councilor Onswud said, glaring at Pausert who remained sulkily silent. He had *tried* to explain that the mysterious epidemic which suddenly wiped out most of the stock of miffels wasn't his fault. In fact, he more than suspected the tricky hand of young Councilor Rapport who had been wagging futilely around Illyla for the last couple of years!

"The *Venture*, now—!" Councilor Onswud mused, stroking his long, craggy chin. "Pausert can handle a ship, at least," he admitted.

That was how it happened. Were they ever going to be surprised! For even the captain realized that Councilor Onswud was unloading all the dead fish that had gathered the dust of his warehouses for the past fifty years on him and the *Venture*, in a last, faint hope of getting *some* return on those half-forgotten investments. A value of eighty-two thousand maels was placed on the cargo; but if he'd brought even three-quarters of it back in cash, all would have been well.

Instead—well, it started with that lucky bet on a legal point with an Imperial Official at the Imperial capitol itself. Then came a six-hour race fairly won against a small, fast private yacht—the old *Venture* 7333 had been a pirate-chaser in the last century and could still produce twice as much speed as her looks suggested. From there on, the captain was socially accepted as a sporting man and was in on a long string of jovial parties and meets.

Jovial and profitable—the wealthier Imperials just couldn't resist a gamble; and the penalty he always insisted on was that they had to buy!

He got rid of the stuff right and left! Inside of twelve weeks, nothing remained of the original cargo except two score bundles of expensively-built but useless tinklewood fishing poles and one dozen gross bales of useful but unattractive allweather cloaks. Even on a bet, nobody would take them! But the captain had a strong hunch those items had been hopefully added to the cargo from his own stocks by Councilor Rapport; so his failure to sell them didn't break his heart.

He was a neat twenty percent net ahead, at that point—

And finally came this last-minute rush-delivery of medical supplies to Porlumma on the return route. That haul alone would have repaid the miffel-farm losses three times over!

The captain grinned broadly into the darkness. Yes, they'd be surprised—but just where was he now?

He checked again in the narrow street, searching for the port-beacon in the sky. There it was—off to his left and a little behind him. He'd got turned around somehow!

He set off carefully down an excessively dark little alley. It was one of those towns where everybody locked their front doors at night and retired to lit-up, inclosed courtyards at the backs of the houses. There were voices and the rattling of dishes nearby, and occasional whoops of laughter and singing all around him; but it was all beyond high walls which let little or no light into the alley.

It ended abruptly in a cross-alley and another wall. After a moment's debate, the captain turned to his left again. Light spilled out on his new route a few hundred yards ahead, where a courtyard was opened on the alley. From it, as he approached, came the sound of doors being violently slammed, and then a sudden, loud mingling of voices.

"Yeeee-eep!" shrilled a high, childish voice. It could have been mortal agony, terror, or even hysterical laughter. The captain broke into an apprehensive trot.

"Yes, I see you up there!" a man shouted excitedly in Universum. "I caught you now—you get down from those boxes! I'll skin you alive! Fifty-two customers sick of the stomachache—YOW!"

The last exclamation was accompanied by a sound as of a small, loosely-built wooden house collapsing, and was followed by a succession of squeals and an angry bellowing, in which the only distinguishable words were: ". . . . threw the boxes on me!" Then more sounds of splintering wood.

"Hey!" yelled the captain indignantly from the corner of the alley.

All action ceased. The narrow courtyard, brightly illuminated under its single overhead bulb, was half covered with a tumbled litter of what appeared to be empty wooden boxes. Standing with his foot temporarily caught in one of them was a very large, fat man dressed all in white and waving a stick. Momentarily cornered between the wall and two of the boxes, over one of which she was trying to climb, was a smallish, fair-haired girl dressed in a smock of some kind, which was also white. She might be about fourteen, the captain thought—a helpless kid, anyway.

"What *you* want?" grunted the fat man, pointing the stick with some dignity at the captain.

"Lay off the kid!" rumbled the captain, edging into the courtyard.

"Mind your own business!" shouted the fat man, waving his stick like a club. "I'll take care of her! She—"

"I never did!" squealed the girl. She burst into tears.

"Try it, Fat and Ugly!" the captain warned. "I'll ram the stick down your throat!"

He was very close now. With a sound of grunting exasperation, the fat man pulled his foot free of the box, wheeled suddenly and brought the end of the stick down on the top of the captain's cap. The captain hit him furiously in the middle of the stomach.

There was a short flurry of activity, somewhat hampered by shattering boxes everywhere. Then the captain stood up, scowling and breathing hard. The fat man remained sitting on the ground, gasping about ". . . the law!"

Somewhat to his surprise, the captain discovered the girl standing just behind him. She caught his eye and smiled.

"My name's Maleen," she offered. She pointed at the fat man. "Is he hurt bad?"

"Huh—no!" panted the captain. "But maybe we'd better—"

It was too late! A loud, self-assured voice became audible now at the opening to the alley:

"Here, here, here, here, here!" it said in the reproachful, situation-under-control tone that always seemed the same to the captain, on whatever world and in whichever language he heard it.

"What's all this about?" it inquired rhetorically.

"You'll all have to come along!" it replied.

Police Court on Porlumma appeared to be a business conducted on a very efficient, around-the-clock basis. They were the next case up.

Nikkeldepain was an odd name, wasn't it, the judge smiled. He then listened attentively to the various charges, countercharges, and denials.

Bruth the Baker was charged with having struck a citizen of a foreign government on the head with a potentially lethal instrument—produced in evidence. Said citizen had admittedly attempted to interfere as Bruth was attempting to punish his slave Maleen—also produced in evidence—whom he suspected of having added something to a batch of cakes she was working on that afternoon, resulting in illness and complaints from fifty-two of Bruth's customers.

Said foreign citizen had also used insulting language—the captain admitted under pressure to "Fat and Ugly."

Some provocation could be conceded for the action taken by Bruth, but not enough. Bruth paled.

Captain Pausert, of the Republic of Nikkeldepain—everybody but the prisoners smiled this time—was charged (a) with said attempted interference, (b) with said insult, (c) with having frequently and severely struck Bruth the Baker in the course of the subsequent dispute.

The blow on the head was conceded to have provided a provocation for charge (c)—but not enough

Nobody seemed to be charging the slave Maleen with anything. The judge only looked at her curiously, and shook his head.

"As the Court considers this regrettable incident," he remarked, "it looks like two years for you, Bruth; and about three for you, captain. Too bad!"

The captain had an awful sinking feeling. He had seen something and heard a lot of Imperial court methods in the fringe systems. He could probably get out of this three-year rap; but it would be expensive.

He realized that the judge was studying him reflectively.

"The Court wishes to acknowledge," the judge continued, "that the captain's chargeable actions were due largely to a natural feeling of human sympathy for the predicament of the slave Maleen. The Court, therefore, would suggest a settlement as follows—subsequent to which all charges could be dropped:

"That Bruth the Baker resell Maleen of Karres—with whose services he appears to be dissatisfied—for a reasonable sum to Captain Pausert of the Republic of Nikkeldepain."

Bruth the Baker heaved a gusty sigh of relief. But the captain hesitated. The buying of human slaves by private citizens was a very serious offense in Nikkeldepain! Still, he didn't have to make a record of it. If they weren't going to soak him too much—

At just the right moment, Maleen of Karres introduced a barely audible, forlorn, sniffling sound.

"How much are you asking for the kid?" the captain inquired, looking without friendliness at his recent antagonist. A day was coming when he would think less severely of Bruth; but it hadn't come yet.

Bruth scowled back but replied with a certain eagerness: "A hundred and fifty m—" A policeman standing behind him poked him sharply in the side. Bruth shut up.

"Seven hundred maels," the judge said smoothly. "There'll be Court charges, and a fee for recording the transaction—" He appeared to make a swift calculation. "Fifteen hundred and forty-two maels—" He turned to a clerk: "You've looked him up?"

The clerk nodded. "He's right!"

"And we'll take your check," the judge concluded. He gave the captain a friendly smile. "Next case."

The captain felt a little bewildered.

There was something peculiar about this! He was getting out of it much too cheaply. Since the Empire had quit its wars of expansion, young slaves in good health were a high-priced article. Furthermore, he was practically positive that Bruth the Baker had been willing to sell for a tenth of what the captain actually had to pay!

Well, he wouldn't complain. Rapidly, he signed, sealed and thumb-printed various papers shoved at him by a helpful clerk; and made out a check.

"I guess," he told Maleen of Karres, "we'd better get along to the ship."

And now what was he going to do with the kid, he pondered, padding along the unlighted streets with his slave trotting quietly behind him. If he showed up with a pretty girl-slave in Nikkeldepain, even a small one, various good friends there would toss him into ten years or so of penal servitude—immediately after Illyla had personally collected his scalp. They were a moral lot.

Karres—?

"How far off is Karres, Maleen?" he asked into the dark.

"It takes about two weeks," Maleen said tearfully.

Two weeks! The captain's heart sank again.

"What are you blubbering about?" he inquired uncomfortably.

Maleen choked, sniffed, and began sobbing openly.

"I have two little sisters!" she cried.

"Well, well," the captain said encouragingly. "That's nice—you'll be seeing them again soon. I'm taking you home, you know!"

Great Patham—now he'd said it! But after all—

But this piece of good news seemed to be having the wrong effect on his slave! Her sobbing grew much more violent.

"No, I won't," she wailed. "They're here!"

"Huh?" said the captain. He stopped short. "Where?"

"And the people they're with are mean to them, too!" wept Maleen.

The captain's heart dropped clean through his boots. Standing there in the dark, he helplessly watched it coming:

"You could buy them awfully cheap!" she said.

II.

In times of stress, the young life of Karres appeared to take to the heights. It might be a mountainous place.

The Leewit sat on the top shelf of the back wall of the crockery and antiques store, strategically flanked by two expensive-looking vases. She was a doll-sized edition of Maleen; but her eyes were cold and gray instead of blue and tearful. About five or six, the captain vaguely estimated. He wasn't very good at estimating them around that age.

"Good evening," he said, as he came in through the door. The Crockery and Antiques Shop had been easy to find. Like Bruth the Baker's, it was the one spot in the neighborhood that was all lit up.

"Good evening, sir!" said what was presumably the store owner, without looking around. He sat with his back to the door, in a chair approximately at the center of the store and facing the Leewit at a distance of about twenty feet.

". . . and there you can stay without food or drink till the Holy Man comes in the morning!" he continued immediately, in the taut voice of a man who has gone through hysteria and is sane again. The captain realized he was addressing the Leewit.

"Your other Holy Man didn't stay very long!" the diminutive creature piped, also ignoring the captain. Apparently, she had not yet discovered Maleen behind him.

"This is a stronger denomination—much stronger!" the store owner replied, in a shaking voice but with a sort of relish. "*He'll* exorcise you, all right, little demon—you'll whistle no buttons off him! Your time is up! Go on and whistle all you want! Bust every vase in the place—"

The Leewit blinked her gray eyes thoughtfully at him.

"Might!" she said.

"But if you try to climb down from there," the store owner went on, on a rising note, "I'll chop you into bits—into little, little bits!"

He raised his arm as he spoke and weakly brandished what the captain recognized with a start of horror as a highly ornamented but probably still useful antique battle-ax.

"Ha!" said the Leewit.

"Beg your pardon, sir!" the captain said, clearing his throat.

"Good evening, sir!" the store owner repeated, without looking around. "What can I do for you?"

"I came to inquire," the captain said hesitantly, "about that child."

The store owner shifted about in his chair and squinted at the captain with red-rimmed eyes.

"You're not a Holy Man!" he said.

"Hello, Maleen!" the Leewit said suddenly. "That him?"

"We've come to buy you," Maleen said. "Shut up!"

"Good!" said the Leewit.

"Buy it? Are you mocking me, sir?" the store owner inquired.

"Shut up, Moonell!" A thin, dark, determined-looking woman had appeared in the doorway that led through the back wall of the store. She moved out a step under the shelves; and the Leewit leaned down from the top shelf and hissed. The woman moved hurriedly back into the doorway.

"Maybe he means it," she said in a more subdued voice.

"I can't sell to a citizen of the Empire," the store owner said defeatedly.

"I'm not a citizen," the captain said shortly. This time, he wasn't going to name it.

"No, he's from Nikkel—" Maleen began.

"Shut up, Maleen!" the captain said helplessly in turn.

"I never heard of Nikkel," the store owner muttered doubtfully.

"Maleen!" the woman called shrilly. "That's the name of one of the others—Bruth the Baker got her. He means it, all right! He's buying them—"

"A hundred and fifty maels!" the captain said craftily, remembering Bruth the Baker. "In cash!"

The store owner looked dazed.

"Not enough, Moonell!" the woman called. "Look at all it's broken! Five hundred maels!"

There was a sound then, so thin the captain could hardly hear it. It pierced at his eardrums like two jabs of a delicate needle. To right and left of him, two highly glazed little jugs went "*Clink-clink!*", showed a sudden veining of cracks, and collapsed.

A brief silence settled on the store. And now that he looked around more closely, the captain could spot here and there other little piles of shattered crockery—and places where similar ruins apparently had been swept up, leaving only traces of colored dust.

The store owner laid the ax down carefully beside his chair, stood up, swaying a little, and came towards the captain.

"You offered me a hundred and fifty maels!" he said rapidly as he approached. "I accept it here, now, see—before witnesses!" He grabbed the captain's right hand in both of his and pumped it up and down vigorously. "Sold!" he yelled.

Then he wheeled around in a leap and pointed a shaking hand at the Leewit.

"And NOW," he howled, "break something! Break anything! You're his! I'll sue him for every mael he ever made and ever will!"

"Oh, do come help me down, Maleen!" the Leewit pleaded prettily.

For a change, the store of Wansing, the jeweler, was dimly lit and very quiet. It was a sleek, fashionable place in a fashionable shopping block near the spaceport. The front door was unlocked, and Wansing was in.

The three of them entered quietly, and the door sighed quietly shut behind them. Beyond a great crystal display-counter, Wansing was moving about among a number of opened shelves, talking softly to himself. Under the crystal of the counter, and in close-packed rows on the satin-covered shelves, reposed a many-colored gleaming and glittering and shining. Wansing was no piker.

"Good evening, sir!" the captain said across the counter.

"It's morning!" the Leewit remarked from the other side of Maleen.

"Maleen!" said the captain.

"We're keeping out of this," Maleen said to the Leewit.

"All right," said the Leewit.

Wansing had come around jerkily at the captain's greeting, but had made no other move. Like all the slave owners the captain had met on Porlumma so far, Wansing seemed unhappy. Otherwise, he was a large, dark, sleek-looking man with jewels in his ears and a smell of expensive oils and perfumes about him.

"This place is under constant visual guard, of course!" he told the captain gently. "Nothing could possibly happen to me here. Why am I so frightened?"

"Not of me, I'm sure!" the captain said with an uncomfortable attempt at geniality. "I'm glad your store's still open," he went on briskly. "I'm here on business—"

"Oh, yes, it's still open, of course," Wansing said. He gave the captain a slow smile and turned back to his shelves. "I'm making inventory, that's why! I've been making inventory since early yesterday morning. I've counted them all seven times—"

"You're very thorough," the captain said.

"Very, very thorough!" Wansing nodded to the shelves. "The last time I found I had made a million maels. But twice before that, I had lost approximately the same amount. I shall have to count them again, I suppose!" He closed a shelf softly. "I'm sure I counted those before. But they move about constantly. Constantly! It's horrible."

"You've got a slave here called Goth," the captain said, driving to the point.

"Yes, I have!" Wansing said, nodding. "And I'm sure she understands by now I meant no harm! I do, at any rate. It was perhaps a little—but I'm sure she understands now, or will soon!"

"Where is she?" the captain inquired, a trifle uneasily.

"In her room perhaps," Wansing suggested. "It's not so bad when she's there in her room with the door closed. But often she sits in the dark and looks at you as you go past—" He opened another drawer, and closed it quietly again. "Yes, they do move!" he whispered, as if confirming an earlier suspicion. "Constantly—"

"Look, Wansing," the captain said in a loud, firm voice. "I'm not a citizen of the Empire. I want to buy this Goth! I'll pay you a hundred and fifty maels, cash."

Wansing turned around completely again and looked at the captain. "Oh, you do?" he said. "You're not a citizen?" He walked a few steps to the side of the counter, sat down at a small desk and turned a light on over it. Then he put his face in his hands for a moment.

"I'm a wealthy man," he muttered. "An influential man! The name of Wansing counts for a great deal on Porlumma. When the Empire suggests you buy, you buy, of course—but it need not have been I who bought her! I thought she would be useful in the business—and then, even I could not sell her again within the Empire. She has been here for a week!"

He looked up at the captain and smiled. "One hundred and fifty maels!" he said. "Sold! There are records to be made out—" He reached into a drawer and took out some printed forms. He began to write rapidly. The captain produced identifications.

Maleen said suddenly: "Goth?"

"Right here," a voice murmured. Wansing's hand jerked sharply, but he did not look up. He kept on writing.

Something small and lean and bonelessly supple, dressed in a dark jacket and leggings, came across the thick carpets of Wansing's store and stood behind the captain. This one might be about nine or ten.

"I'll take your check, captain!" Wansing said politely. "You must be an honest man. Besides, I want to frame it."

"And now," the captain heard himself say in the remote voice of one who moves through a strange dream, "I suppose we could go to the ship."

The sky was gray and cloudy; and the streets were lightening. Goth, he noticed, didn't resemble her sisters. She had brown hair cut short a few inches below her ears, and brown eyes with long, black lashes. Her nose was short and her chin was pointed. She made him think of some thin, carnivorous creature, like a weasel.

She looked up at him briefly, grinned, and said: "Thanks!"

"What was wrong with *him?*" chirped the Leewit, walking backwards for a last view of Wansing's store.

"Tough crook," muttered Goth. The Leewit giggled.

"You premoted this just dandy, Maleen!" she stated next.

"Shut up," said Maleen.

"All right," said the Leewit. She glanced up at the captain's face. "You been fighting!" she said virtuously. "Did you win?"

"Of course, the captain won!" said Maleen.

"Good for you!" said the Leewit.

"What about the take-off?" Goth asked the captain. She seemed a little worried.

"Nothing to it!" the captain said stoutly, hardly bothering to wonder how she'd guessed the take-off was the one operation on which he and the old *Venture* consistently failed to co-operate.

"No," said Goth, "I meant when?"

"Right now," said the captain. "They've already cleared us. We'll get the sign any second."

"Good," said Goth. She walked off slowly down the hall towards the back of the ship.

The take-off was pretty bad, but the *Venture* made it again. Half an hour later, with Porlumma dwindling safely behind them, the captain switched to automatic and climbed out of his chair. After considerable experimentation, he got the electric butler adjusted to four breakfasts, hot, with coffee. It was accomplished with a great deal of advice and attempted assistance from the Leewit, rather less from Maleen, and no comments from Goth.

"Everything will be coming along in a few minutes now!" he announced. Afterwards, it struck him there had been a quality of grisly prophecy about the statement.

"If you'd listened to me," said the Leewit, "we'd have been done eating a quarter of an hour ago!" She was perspiring but triumphant—she had been right all along.

"Say, Maleen," she said suddenly, "you premoting again?"

Premoting? The captain looked at Maleen. She seemed pale and troubled.

"Spacesick?" he suggested. "I've got some pills—"

"No, she's premoting," the Leewit said scowling. "What's up, Maleen?"

"Shut up," said Goth.

"All right," said the Leewit. She was silent a moment, and then began to wriggle. "Maybe we'd better—"

"Shut up," said Maleen.

"It's all ready," said Goth.

"What's all ready?" asked the captain.

"All right," said the Leewit. She looked at the captain. "Nothing," she said.

He looked at them then, and they looked at him—one set each of gray eyes, and brown, and blue. They were all sitting around the control room floor in a circle, the fifth side of which was occupied by the electric butler.

What peculiar little waifs, the captain thought. He hadn't perhaps really realized until now just how *very* peculiar. They were still staring at him.

"Well, well!" he said heartily. "So Maleen 'premotes' and gives people stomach-aches."

Maleen smiled dimly and smoothed back her yellow hair.

"They just thought they were getting them," she murmured.

"Mass history," explained the Leewit, offhandedly.

"Hysteria," said Goth. "The Imperials get their hair up about us every so often."

"I noticed that," the captain nodded. "And little Leewit here—she whistles and busts things."

"It's *the* Leewit," the Leewit said, frowning.

"Oh, I see," said the captain. "Like *the* captain, eh?"

"That's right," said the Leewit. She smiled.

"And what does little Goth do?" the captain addressed the third witch. Little Goth appeared pained. Maleen answered for her.

"Goth teleports mostly," she said.

"Oh, she does?" said the captain. "I've heard about that trick, too," he added lamely.

"Just small stuff really!" Goth said abruptly. She reached into the top of her jacket and pulled out a cloth-wrapped bundle the size of the captain's two fists. The four ends of the cloth were knotted together. Goth undid the knot. "Like this," she said and poured out the contents on the rug between them. There was a sound like a big bagful of marbles being spilled.

"Great Patham!" the captain swore, staring down at what was a cool quarter-million in jewel stones, or he was still a miffel-farmer.

"Good gosh," said the Leewit, bouncing to her feet. "Maleen, we better get at it right away!"

The two blondes darted from the room. The captain hardly noticed their going. He was staring at Goth.

"Child," he said, "don't you realize they hang you without trial on places like Porlumma, if you're caught with stolen goods?"

"We're not on Porlumma," said Goth. She looked slightly annoyed. "They're for you. You spent money on us, didn't you?"

"Not that kind of money," said the captain. "If Wansing noticed— They're Wansing's, I suppose?"

"Sure!" said Goth. "Pulled them in just before take-off!"

"If he reported, there'll be police ships on our tail any—"

"Goth!" Maleen shrilled.

Goth's head came around and she rolled up on her feet in one motion. "Coming," she shouted. "Excuse me," she murmured to the captain. Then she, too, was out of the room.

But again, the captain scarcely noticed her departure. He had rushed to the control desk with a sudden awful certainty and switched on all screens.

There they were! Two sleek, black ships coming up fast from behind, and already almost in gun-range! They weren't regular police boats, the captain recognized, but auxiliary craft of the Empire's frontier fleets. He rammed the *Venture's* drives full on. Immediately, red-and-black fire blossoms began to sprout in space behind him—then a finger of flame stabbed briefly past, not a hundred yards to the right of the ship.

But the communicator stayed dead. Porlumma preferred risking the sacrifice of Wansing's jewels to giving them a chance to surrender! To do the captain justice, his horror was due much more to the fate awaiting his three misguided charges than to the fact that he was going to share it.

He was putting the *Venture* through a wildly erratic and, he hoped, aim-destroying series of sideways hops and forward lunges with one hand,

and trying to unlimber the turrets of the nova guns with the other, when suddenly—!

No, he decided at once, there was no use trying to understand it— There were just no more Empire ships around. The screens all blurred and darkened simultaneously; and, for a short while, a darkness went flowing and coiling lazily past the *Venture*. Light jumped out of it at him once, in a cold, ugly glare, and receded again in a twisting, unnatural fashion. The *Venture's* drives seemed dead.

Then, just as suddenly, the old ship jerked, shivered, roared aggrievedly, and was hurling herself along on her own power again!

But Porlumma's sun was no longer in evidence. Stars gleamed and shifted distantly against the blackness of deep space all about. The patterns seemed familiar, but he wasn't a good enough navigator to be sure.

The captain stood up stiffly, feeling a heavy cloud. And at that moment, with a wild, hilarious clacking like a metallic hen, the electric butler delivered four breakfasts, hot, one after the other, right onto the center of the control room floor.

The first voice said distinctly: "Shall we just leave it on?"

A second voice, considerably more muffled, replied: "Yes, let's! You never know when you need it—"

The third voice, tucked somewhere in between them, said simply: "*Whew!*"

Peering about the dark room in bewilderment, the captain realized suddenly that the voices had come from the speaker of an intership communicator, leading to what had once been the *Venture's* captain's cabin.

He listened; but only a dim murmuring came from it now, and then nothing at all. He started towards the hall, then returned and softly switched off the communicator. He went quietly down the hall until he came to the captain's cabin. Its door was closed.

He listened a moment, and opened it suddenly.

There was a trio of squeals:

"Oh, don't! You spoiled it!"

The captain stood motionless. Just one glimpse had been given him of what seemed to be a bundle of twisted black wires arranged loosely like the frame of a truncated cone on—or was it just above?—a table in the center of the cabin. Where the tip of the cone should have been burned a round, swirling, orange fire. About it, their faces reflecting its glow, stood the three witches.

Then the fire vanished; the wires collapsed. There was only ordinary light in the room. They were looking up at him variously—Maleen with smiling regret, the Leewit in frank annoyance, Goth with no expression at all.

"What out of Great Patham's Seventh Hell was that?" inquired the captain, his hair bristling slowly.

The Leewit looked at Goth; Goth looked at Maleen. Maleen said doubtfully: "We can just tell you its name—"

"That was the Sheewash Drive," said Goth.

"The what-drive?" asked the captain.

"Sheewash," repeated Maleen.

"The one you have to do it with yourself," the Leewit said helpfully.

"Shut up," said Maleen.

There was a long pause. The captain looked down at the handful of thin, black, twelve-inch wires scattered about the table top. He touched one of them. It was dead-cold.

"I see," he said. "I guess we're all going to have a long talk." Another pause. "Where are we now?"

"About three light-years down the way you were going," said Goth. "We only worked it thirty seconds."

"Twenty-eight!" corrected Maleen, with the authority of her years. "The Leewit was getting tired."

"I see," said Captain Pausert carefully. "Well, let's go have some breakfast."

III.

They ate with a silent voraciousness, dainty Maleen, the exquisite Leewit, supple Goth, all alike. The captain, long finished, watched them with amazement and—now at last—with something like awe.

"It's the Sheewash Drive," explained Maleen finally, catching his expression.

"Takes it out of you!" said Goth.

The Leewit grunted affirmatively and stuffed on.

"Can't do too much of it," said Maleen. "Or too often. It kills you sure!"

"What," said the captain, "*is* the Sheewash Drive?"

They became reticent. People did it on Karres, said Maleen, when they had to go somewhere else fast. Everybody knew how there.

"But of course," she added, "we're pretty young to do it right!"

"We did it pretty good!" the Leewit contradicted positively. She seemed to be finished at last.

"But how?" said the captain.

Reticence thickened almost visibly. If you couldn't do it, said Maleen, you couldn't understand it either.

He gave it up, for the time being.

"I guess I'll have to take you home next," he said; and they agreed.

Karres, it developed, was in the Iverdahl System. He couldn't find any planet of that designation listed in his maps of the area, but that meant nothing. The maps were old and often inaccurate, and local names changed a lot.

Barring the use of weird and deadly miracle-drives, that detour was going to cost him almost a month in time—and a good chunk of his profits in power used up. The jewels Goth had illegally teleported must, of course, be returned to their owner, he explained. He'd intended to look severely at the culprit at that point; but she'd meant well, after all! They were extremely peculiar children, but still children—they couldn't really understand.

He would stop off en route to Karres at an Empire planet with banking facilities to take care of that matter, the captain added. A planet far enough off so the police wouldn't be likely to take any particular interest in the *Venture*.

A dead silence greeted this schedule. It appeared that the representatives of Karres did not think much of his logic.

"Well," Maleen sighed at last, "we'll see you get your money back some other way then!"

The junior witches nodded coldly.

"How did you three happen to get into this fix?" the captain inquired, with the intention of changing the subject.

They'd left Karres together on a jaunt of their own, they explained. No, they hadn't run away—he got the impression that such trips were standard procedure for juveniles in that place. They were on another planet, a civilized one but beyond the borders and law of Empire, when the town they were in was raided by a small fleet of slavers. They were taken along with most of the local youngsters.

"It's a wonder," he said reflectively, "you didn't take over the ship."

"Oh, brother!" exclaimed the Leewit.

"Not that ship!" said Goth.

"That was an Imperial Slaver!" Maleen informed him. "You behave yourself every second on those crates."

Just the same, the captain thought as he settled himself to rest in the control room on a couch he had set up there, it was no longer surprising that the Empire wanted no young slaves from Karres to be transported into the interior! Oddest sort of children— But he ought to be able to get his expenses paid by their relatives. Something very profitable might even be made of this deal—

Have to watch the record-entries though! Nikkeldepain's laws were explicit about the penalties invoked by anything resembling the purchase and sale of slaves.

He'd thoughtfully left the intership communicator adjusted so he could listen in on their conversation in the captain's cabin. However, there had been nothing for some time beyond frequent bursts of childish giggling. Then came a succession of piercing shrieks from the Leewit. It appeared she was being forcibly washed behind the ears by Maleen and obliged to brush her teeth, in preparation for bedtime.

It had been agreed that he was not to enter the cabin, because—for reasons not given—they couldn't keep the Sheewash Drive on in his presence; and they wanted to have it ready, in case of an emergency. Piracy was rife beyond the Imperial borders, and the *Venture* would keep beyond the border for a good part of the trip, to avoid the more pressing danger of police pursuit instigated by Porlumma. The captain had explained the potentialities of the nova guns the *Venture* boasted, or tried to. Possibly, they hadn't understood. At any rate, they seemed unimpressed.

The Sheewash Drive! Boy, he thought in sudden excitement, if he could just get the principles of that. Maybe he would!

He raised his head suddenly. The Leewit's voice had lifted clearly over the communicator:

". . . . not such a bad old dope!" the childish treble remarked.

The captain blinked indignantly.

"He's not so old," Maleen's soft voice returned. "And he's certainly no dope!"

He smiled. Good kid, Maleen.

"Yeah, yeah!" squeaked the Leewit offensively. "Maleen's sweet onthu-ulp!"

A vague commotion continued for a while, indicating, he hoped, that someone he could mention was being smothered under a pillow.

He drifted off to sleep before it was settled.

If you didn't happen to be thinking of what they'd done, they seemed more or less like normal children. Right from the start, they displayed a flattering interest in the captain and his background; and he told them all about everything and everybody in Nikkeldepain. Finally, he even showed them his treasured pocket-sized picture of Illyla—the one with which he'd held many cozy conversations during the earlier part of his trip.

Almost at once, though, he realized that was a mistake. They studied it intently in silence, their heads crowded close together.

"Oh, brother!" the Leewit whispered then, with entirely the wrong kind of inflection.

"Just what did you mean by that?" the captain inquired coldly.

"Sweet!" murmured Goth. But it was the way she closed her eyes briefly, as though gripped by a light spasm of nausea.

"Shut up, Goth!" Maleen said sharply. "I think she's very swee . . . I mean, she looks very nice!" she told the captain.

The captain was disgruntled. Silently, he retrieved the maligned Illyla and returned her to his breast pocket. Silently, he went off and left them standing there.

But afterwards, in private, he took it out again and studied it worriedly. His Illyla! He shifted the picture back and forth under the light. It wasn't really a very good picture of her, he decided. It had been bungled! From certain angles, one might even say that Illyla did look the least bit insipid.

What was he thinking, he thought, shocked.

He unlimbered the nova gun turrets next and got in a little firing practice. They had been sealed when he took over the *Venture* and weren't supposed to be used, except in absolute emergencies. They were somewhat uncertain weapons, though very effective, and Nikkeldepain had turned to safer forms of armament many decades ago. But on the third day out from Nikkeldepain, the captain made a brief notation in his log:

"Attacked by two pirate craft. Unsealed nova guns. Destroyed one attacker; survivor fled—"

He was rather pleased by that crisp, hard-bitten description of desperate space-adventure, and enjoyed rereading it occasionally. It wasn't true, though. He had put in an interesting four hours at the time pursuing and annihilating large, craggy chunks of substance of a meteorite-cloud he found the *Venture* plowing through. Those nova guns were fascinating stuff! You'd sight the turrets on something; and so long as it didn't move after that, it was all right. If it did move, it got it—unless you relented and deflected the turrets first. They were just the thing for arresting a pirate in midspace.

The *Venture* dipped back into the Empire's borders four days later and headed for the capitol of the local province. Police ships challenged them twice on the way in; and the captain found considerable comfort in the awareness that his passengers foregathered silently in their cabin on these occasions. They didn't tell him they were set to use the Sheewash Drive— somehow it had never been mentioned since that first day; but he knew the queer orange fire was circling over its skimpy framework of twisted wires there and ready to act.

However, the space police waved him on, satisfied with routine identification. Apparently, the *Venture* had not become generally known as a criminal ship, to date.

Maleen accompanied him to the banking institution that was to return Wansing's property to Porlumma. Her sisters, at the captain's definite request, remained on the ship.

The transaction itself went off without a visible hitch. The jewels would reach their destination in Porlumma within a month. But he had to take out a staggering sum in insurance— "Piracy, thieves!" smiled the clerk. "Even summary capital punishment won't keep the rats down." And, of course, he had to register name, ship, home planet, and so on. But since they already had all that information in Porlumma, he gave it without hesitation.

On the way back to the spaceport, he sent off a sealed message by radio-relay to the bereaved jeweler, informing him of the action taken, and regretting the misunderstanding.

He felt a little better after that, though the insurance payment had been a severe blow! If he didn't manage to work out a decent profit on Karres somehow, the losses on the miffel farm would hardly be covered now.

Then he noticed that Maleen was getting uneasy.

"We'd better hurry!" was all she would say, however. Her face grew pale.

The captain understood. She was having another premonition! The hitch to this premoting business was, apparently, that when something was brewing you were informed of the bare fact but had to guess at most of the details. They grabbed an aircab and raced back to the spaceport.

They had just been cleared there when he spotted a small group of uniformed men coming along the dock on the double. They stopped short and then scattered, as the *Venture* lurched drunkenly sideways into the air. Everyone else in sight was scattering, too.

That was a very bad take-off—one of the captain's worst! Once afloat, however, he ran the ship promptly into the nightside of the planet and turned her nose towards the border. The old pirate-chaser had plenty of speed when you gave her the reins; and throughout the entire next sleep-period, he let her use it all.

The Sheewash Drive was not required that time.

Next day, he had a lengthy private talk with Goth on the Golden Rule and the Law, with particular reference to individual property rights. If Councilor Onswud had been monitoring the sentiments expressed by the captain, he could not have failed to rumble surprised approval. The delinquent herself listened impassively; but the captain fancied she showed distinct signs of being rather impressed by his earnestness.

It was two days after that—well beyond the borders again—when they were obliged to make an unscheduled stop at a mining moon. For the captain discovered he had already miscalculated the extent to which the prolonged run on overdrive after leaving the capitol was going to deplete the *Venture's* reserves. They would have to juice up—

A large, extremely handsome Sirian freighter lay beside them at the Moon station. It was half a battlecraft really, since it dealt regularly beyond the borders. They had to wait while it was being serviced; and it took a long time. The Sirians turned out to be as unpleasant as their ship was good-looking—a snooty, conceited, hairy lot who talked only their own dialect and pretended to be unfamiliar with Imperial Universum.

The captain found himself getting irked by their bad manners—particularly when he discovered they were laughing over his argument with the service superintendent about the cost of repowering the *Venture*.

"You're out in deep space, captain!" said the superintendent. "And you haven't juice enough left even to travel back to the Border. You can't expect Imperial prices here!"

"It's not what you charged *them*!" The captain angrily jerked his thumb at the Sirian.

"Regular customers!" the superintendent shrugged. "You start coming by here every three months like they do, and we can make an arrangement with you, too."

It was outrageous—it actually put the *Venture* back in the red! But there was no help for it.

Nor did it improve the captain's temper when he muffed the take-off once more—and then had to watch the Sirian floating into space, as sedately as a swan, a little behind him!

An hour later, as he sat glumly before the controls, debating the chance of recouping his losses before returning to Nikkeldepain, Maleen and the Leëwit hurriedly entered the room. They did something to a port screen.

"They sure are!" the Leewit exclaimed. She seemed childishly pleased.

"Are what?" the captain inquired absently.

"Following us," said Maleen. She did not sound pleased. "It's that Sirian ship, Captain Pausert—"

The captain stared bewilderedly at the screen. There *was* a ship in focus there. It was quite obviously the Sirian and, just as obviously, it was following them.

"What do they want?" he wondered. "They're stinkers but they're not pirates. Even if they were, they wouldn't spend an hour running after a crate like the *Venture*!"

Maleen said nothing. The Leewit observed: "Oh, brother! Got their bow-turrets out now—better get those nova guns ready!"

"But it's all nonsense!" the captain said, flushing angrily. He turned suddenly towards the communicators. "What's that Empire general beam-length?"

".0044," said Maleen.

A roaring, abusive voice flooded the control room immediately. The one word understandable to the captain was "*Venture*." It was repeated frequently, sometimes as if it were a question.

"Sirian!" said the captain. "Can you understand them?" he asked Maleen.

She shook her head. "The Leewit can—"

The Leewit nodded, her gray eyes glistening.

"What are they saying?"

"They says you're for stopping," the Leewit translated rapidly, but apparently retaining much of the original sentence-structure. "They says you're for skinning alive . . . ha! They says you're for stopping right now and for only hanging. They says—"

Maleen scuttled from the control room. The Leewit banged the communicator with one small fist.

"Beak-Wock!" she shrieked. It sounded like that, anyway. The loud voice paused a moment.

"Beak-Wock?" it returned in an aggrieved, demanding roar.

"Beak-Wock!" the Leewit affirmed with apparent delight. She rattled off a string of similar-sounding syllables. She paused.

A howl of inarticulate wrath responded.

The captain, in a whirl of outraged emotions, was yelling at the Leewit to shut up, at the Sirian to go to Great Patham's Second Hell—the worst—and wrestling with the nova gun adjustors at the same time. He'd had about enough! He'd—

SSS-whoosh!
It was the Sheewash Drive.

"And where are we now?" the captain inquired, in a voice of unnatural calm.

"Same place, just about," said the Leewit. "Ship's still on the screen. Way back though—take them an hour again to catch up." She seemed disappointed; then brightened. "You got lots of time to get the guns ready!"

The captain didn't answer. He was marching down the hall towards the rear of the *Venture*. He passed the captain's cabin and noted the door was shut. He went on without pausing. He was mad clean through—he knew what had happened!

After all he'd told her, Goth had teleported again.

It was all there, in the storage. Items of half a pound in weight seemed to be as much as she could handle. But amazing quantities of stuff had met that one requirement—bottles filled with what might be perfume or liquor or dope, expensive-looking garments and cloths in a shining variety of colors, small boxes, odds, ends and, of course, jewelry!

He spent half an hour getting it loaded into a steel space crate. He wheeled the crate into the rear lock, sealed the inside lock and pulled the switch that activated the automatic launching device.

The outside lock clicked shut. He stalked back to the control room. The Leewit was still in charge, fiddling with the communicators.

"I could try a whistle over them," she suggested, glancing up. She added: "But they'd bust somewheres, sure."

"Get them on again!" the captain said.

"Yes, sir," said the Leewit surprised.

The roaring voice came back faintly.

"SHUT UP!" the captain shouted in Imperial Universum.

The voice shut up.

"Tell them they can pick up their stuff—it's been dumped out in a crate!" the captain told the Leewit. "Tell them I'm proceeding on my course. Tell them if they follow me one light-minute beyond that crate, I'll come back for them, shoot their front end off, shoot their rear end off, and ram 'em in the middle."

"Yes, SIR!" the Leewit sparkled. They proceeded on their course. Nobody followed.

"Now I want to speak to Goth," the captain announced. He was still at a high boil. "Privately," he added. "Back in the storage—"

Goth followed him expressionlessly into the storage. He closed the door to the hall. He'd broken off a two-foot length from the tip of one of Councilor Rapport's overpriced tinklewood fishing poles. It made a fair switch.

But Goth looked terribly small just now! He cleared his throat. He wished for a moment he were back on Nikkeldepain.

"I warned you," he said.

Goth didn't move. Between one second and the next, however, she seemed to grow remarkably. Her brown eyes focused on the captain's Adam's apple; her lip lifted at one side. A slightly hungry look came into her face.

"Wouldn't try that!" she murmured.

Mad again, the captain reached out quickly and got a handful of leathery cloth. There was a blur of motion, and what felt like a small explosion against his left kneecap. He grunted with anguished surprise and fell back on a bale of Councilor Rapport's all-weather cloaks. But he had retained his grip—Goth fell half on top of him, and that was still a favorable position. Then her head snaked around, her neck seemed to extend itself; and her teeth snapped his wrist.

Weasels don't let go—

"Didn't think he'd have the nerve!" Goth's voice came over the communicator. There was a note of grudging admiration in it. It seemed that she was inspecting her bruises.

All tangled up in the job of bandaging his freely bleeding wrist, the captain hoped she'd find a good plenty to count. His knee felt the size of a sofa pillow and throbbed like a piston engine.

"The captain is a brave man," Maleen was saying reproachfully. "You should have known better—"

"He's not very *smart*, though!" the Leewit remarked suggestively.

There was a short silence.

"Is he? Goth? Eh?" the Leewit urged.

"Perhaps not very," said Goth.

"You two lay off him!" Maleen ordered. "Useless," she added meaningly, "you want to *swim* back to Karres—on the Egger Route!"

"Not me," the Leewit said briefly.

"You could still do it, I guess," said Goth. She seemed to be reflecting. "All right—we'll lay off him. It was a fair fight, anyway."

IV.

They raised Karres the sixteenth day after leaving Porlumma. There had been no more incidents; but then, neither had there been any more stops or other contacts with the defenseless Empire. Maleen had cooked up a poultice which did wonders for his knee. With the end of the trip in sight, all tensions had relaxed; and Maleen, at least, seemed to grow hourly more regretful at the prospect of parting.

After a brief study, Karres could be distinguished easily enough by the fact that it moved counterclockwise to all the other planets of the Iverdahl System.

Well, it would, the captain thought.

They came soaring into its atmosphere on the dayside without arousing any visible interest. No communicator signals reached them; and no other ships showed up to look them over. Karres, in fact, had all the appearance of a completely uninhabited world. There were a larger number of seas, too big to be called Lakes and to small to be oceans, scattered over its surface. There was one enormously towering ridge of mountains that ran from pole to pole, and any number of lesser chains. There were two good-sized ice caps; and the southern section of the planet was speckled with intermittent stretches of snow. Almost all of it seemed to be dense forest.

It was a handsome place, in a wild, somber way.

They went gliding over it, from noon through morning and into the dawn fringe—the captain at the controls, Goth and the Leewit flanking him at the screens, and Maleen behind him to do the directing. After a few initial squeals, the Leewit became oddly silent. Suddenly the captain realized she was blubbering.

Somehow, it startled him to discover that her homecoming had affected the Leewit to that extent. He felt Goth reach out behind him and put her hand on the Leewit's shoulder. The smallest witch sniffled happily.

" 'S beautiful!" she growled.

He felt a resurge of the wondering, protective friendliness they had aroused in him at first. They must have been having a rough time of it, at that. He sighed; it seemed a pity they hadn't got along a little better!

"Where's everyone hiding?" he inquired, to break up the mood. So far, there hadn't been a sign of human habitation.

"There aren't many people on Karres," Maleen said from behind his shoulder. "But we're going to The Town—you'll meet about half of them there!"

"What's that place down there?" the captain asked with sudden interest. Something like an enormous lime-white bowl seemed to have been set flush into the floor of the wide valley up which they were moving.

"That's the Theater where . . . *ouch!*" the Leewit said. She fell silent then but turned to give Maleen a resentful look.

"Something strangers shouldn't be told about, eh?" the captain said tolerantly. Goth glanced at him from the side.

"We've got rules," she said.

He let the ship down a little as they passed over "the Theater where—" It was a sort of large, circular arena, with numerous steep tiers of seats running up around it. But all was bare and deserted now.

On Maleen's direction, they took the next valley fork to the right and dropped lower still. He had his first look at Karres animal life then. A flock of large, creamy-white birds, remarkably Terrestrial in appearance, flapped by just below them, apparently unconcerned about the ship. The forest underneath had opened out into a long stretch of lush meadow land, with small creeks winding down into its center. Here a herd of several hundred head of beasts was grazing—beasts of mastodonic size and build, with hairless, shiny black hides. The mouths of their long, heavy heads were twisted up into sardonic, crocodilian grins as they blinked up at the passing *Venture*.

"Black Bollems," said Goth, apparently enjoying the captain's expression. "Lots of them around; they're tame. But the gray mountain ones are good hunting."

"Good eating, too!" the Leewit said. She licked her lips daintily. "Breakfast—!" she sighed, her thoughts diverted to a familiar track. "And we ought to be just in time!"

"There's the field!" Maleen cried, pointing. "Set her down there, captain!"

The "field" was simply a flat meadow of close-trimmed grass running smack against the mountainside to their left. One small vehicle, bright blue in color, was parked on it; and it was bordered on two sides by very tall, blue-black trees.

That was all.

The captain shook his head. Then he set her down.

The town of Karres was a surprise to him in a good many ways. For one thing, there was much more of it than you would have thought possible after flying over the area. It stretched for miles through the forest, up the flanks of the mountain and across the valley—little clusters of houses or individual ones, each group screened from all the rest and from the sky overhead by the trees.

They liked color on Karres; but then they hid it away! The houses were bright as flowers, red and white, apple-green, golden-brown—all spick and span, scrubbed and polished and aired with that brisk, green forest-smell. At various times of the day, there was also the smell of remarkably good things to eat. There were brooks and pools and a great number of shaded vegetable gardens to the town. There were risky-looking treetop playgrounds, and treetop platforms and galleries which seemed to have no particular purpose. On the ground was mainly an enormously confusing maze of paths—narrow trails of sandy soil snaking about among great brown tree roots and chunks of gray mountain rock, and half covered with fallen needle leaves. The first six times the captain set out unaccompanied, he'd lost his way hopelessly within minutes, and had to be guided back out of the forest.

But the most hidden of all were the people! About four thousand of them were supposed to live in the town, with as many more scattered about the planet. But you never got to see more than three or four at any one time—except when now and then a pack of children, who seemed to the captain to be uniformly of the Leewit's size, would burst suddenly out of the undergrowth across a path before you, and vanish again.

As for the others, you did hear someone singing occasionally; or there might be a whole muted concert going on all about, on a large variety of wooden musical instruments which they seemed to enjoy tootling with, gently.

But it wasn't a real town at all, the captain thought. They didn't live like people, these Witches of Karres—it was more like a flock of strange forest birds that happened to be nesting in the same general area. Another thing: they appeared to be busy enough—but what was their business?

He discovered he was reluctant to ask Toll too many questions about it. Toll was the mother of his three witches; but only Goth really resembled her. It was difficult to picture Goth becoming smoothly matured and pleasantly rounded; but that was Toll. She had the same murmuring voice, the same air of sideways observation and secret reflection. And she answered all the captain's questions with apparent frankness; but he never seemed to get much real information out of what she said.

It was odd, too! Because he was spending several hours a day in her company, or in one of the next rooms at any rate, while she went about her housework. Toll's daughters had taken him home when they landed; and he was installed in the room that belonged to their father—busy just now, the captain gathered, with some sort of research of a geological nature elsewhere on Karres. The arrangement worried him a little at first, particularly since Toll and he were mostly alone in the house. Maleen was going to some kind of school; she left early in the morning and came back late in the afternoon; and Goth and the Leewit were just plain running wild! They usually got in long after the captain had gone to bed and were off again before he turned out for breakfast.

It hardly seemed like the right way to raise them! One afternoon, he found the Leewit curled up and asleep in the chair he usually occupied on the porch before the house. She slept there for four solid hours, while the captain sat nearby and leafed gradually through a thick book with illuminated pictures called "Histories of Ancient Yarthe." Now and then, he sipped at a cool, green, faintly intoxicating drink Toll had placed quietly beside him some while before, or sucked an aromatic smoke from the enormous pipe with a floor rest, which he understood was a favorite of Toll's husband.

Then the Leewit woke up suddenly, uncoiled, gave him a look between a scowl and a friendly grin, slipped off the porch and vanished among the trees.

He couldn't quite figure that look! It might have meant nothing at all in particular, but—

The captain laid down his book then and worried a little more. It was true, of course, that nobody seemed in the least concerned about his presence. All of Karres appeared to know about him, and he'd met quite a number of people by now in a casual way. But nobody came around to interview him or so much as dropped in for a visit. However, Toll's husband presumably would be returning presently, and—

How long had he been here, anyway?

Great Patham, the captain thought, shocked. He'd lost count of the days!

Or was it weeks?

He went in to find Toll.

"It's been a wonderful visit," he said, "but I'll have to be leaving, I guess. Tomorrow morning, early—"

Toll put some fancy sewing she was working on back in a glass basket, laid her thin, strong witch's hands in her lap, and smiled up at him.

"We thought you'd be thinking that," she said, "and so we— You know, captain, it was quite difficult to find a way to reward you for bringing back the children?"

"It was?" said the captain, suddenly realizing he'd also clean forgotten he was broke! And now the wrath of Onswud lay close ahead.

"Gold and jewel stones would have been just right, of course!" she said, "but unfortunately, while there's no doubt a lot of it on Karres somewhere, we never got around to looking for it. And we haven't money—none that you could use, that is!"

"No, I don't suppose you do," the captain agreed sadly.

"However," said Toll, "we've all been talking about it in the town, and so we've loaded a lot of things aboard your ship that we think you can sell at a fine profit!"

"Well now," the captain said gratefully, "that's fine of—"

"There are furs," said Toll, "the very finest furs we could fix up—two thousand of them!"

"Oh!" said the captain, bravely keeping his smile. "Well, that's wonderful!"

"And essences of perfume!" said Toll. "Everyone brought one bottle of their own, so that's eight thousand three hundred and twenty-three bottles of perfume essences—all different!"

"Perfume!" said the captain. "Fine, fine—but you really shouldn't—"

"And the rest of it," Toll concluded happily, "is the green Lepti liquor you like so much, and the Wintenberry jellies!" She frowned. "I forgot just how many jugs and jars," she admitted, "but there were a lot. It's all loaded now. And do you think you'll be able to sell all that?" she smiled.

"I certainly can!" the captain said stoutly. "It's wonderful stuff, and there's nothing like it in the Empire."

Which was very true. They wouldn't have considered miffel-furs for lining on Karres. But if he'd been alone he would have felt like he wanted to burst into tears.

The witches couldn't have picked more completely unsalable items if they'd tried! Furs, cosmetics, food and liquor—he'd be shot on sight if he got caught trying to run that kind of merchandise into the Empire. For the same reason that they couldn't use it on Nikkeldepain—they were that scared of contamination by goods that came from uncleared worlds!

He breakfasted alone next morning. Toll had left a note beside his plate, which explained in a large, not too legible script that she had to run off and fetch the Leewit; and that if he was gone before she got back she was wishing him good-by and good luck.

He smeared two more buns with Wintenberry jelly, drank a large mug of cone-seed coffee, finished every scrap of the omelet of swan hawk eggs and then, in a state of pleasant repletion, toyed around with his slice of roasted Bollem liver. Boy, what food! He must have put on fifteen pounds since he landed on Karres.

He wondered how Toll kept that sleek figure.

Regretfully, he pushed himself away from the table, pocketed her note for a souvenir, and went out on the porch. There a tear-stained Maleen hurled herself into his arms.

"Oh, captain!" she sobbed. "You're leaving—"

"Now, now!" the captain murmured, touched and surprised by the lovely child's grief. He patted her shoulders soothingly. "I'll be back," he said rashly.

"Oh, yes, do come back!" cried Maleen. She hesitated and added: "I become marriageable two years from now. Karres time—"

"Well, well," said the captain, dazed. "Well, now—"

He set off down the path a few minutes later, with a strange melody tinkling in his head. Around the first curve, it changed abruptly to a shrill keening which seemed to originate from a spot some two hundred feet before him. Around the next curve, he entered a small, rocky clearing full of pale, misty, early-morning sunlight and what looked like a slow-motion fountain of gleaming rainbow globes. These turned out to be clusters of large, vari-hued soap bubbles which floated up steadily from a wooden tub full of hot water, soap and the Leewit. Toll was bent over the tub; and the Leewit was objecting to a morning bath, with only that minimum of interruptions required to keep her lungs pumped full of a fresh supply of air.

As the captain paused beside the little family group, her red, wrathful face came up over the rim of the tub and looked at him.

"Well, Ugly," she squealed, in a renewed outburst of rage, "who you staring at?" Then a sudden determination came into her eyes. She pursed her lips.

Toll up-ended her promptly and smacked the Leewit's bottom.

"She was going to make some sort of a whistle at you," she explained hurriedly. "Perhaps you'd better get out of range while I can keep her head under. And good luck, captain!"

Karres seemed even more deserted than usual this morning. Of course, it was quite early. Great banks of fog lay here and there among the huge dark trees and the small bright houses. A breeze sighed sadly far overhead. Faint, mournful bird-cries came from still higher up—it could have been swan hawks reproaching him for the omelet.

Somewhere in the distance, somebody tootled on a wood-instrument, very gently.

He had gone halfway up the path to the landing field, when something buzzed past him like an enormous wasp and went *CLUNK*! into the bole of a tree just before him.

It was a long, thin, wicked-looking arrow. On its shaft was a white card; and on the card was printed in red letters:

STOP, MAN OF NIKKELDEPAIN!

The captain stopped and looked around slowly and cautiously. There was no one in sight. What did it mean?

He had a sudden feeling as if all of Karres were rising up silently in one stupendous, cool, foggy trap about him. His skin began to crawl. What was going to happen?

"Ha-ha!" said Goth, suddenly visible on a rock twelve feet to his left and eight feet above him. "You did stop!"

The captain let his breath out slowly.

"What else did you think I'd do?" he inquired. He felt a little faint.

She slid down from the rock like a lizard and stood before him. "Wanted to say good-by!" she told him.

Thin and brown, in jacket, breeches, boots, and cap of gray-green rock-lichen color, Goth looked very much in her element. The brown eyes looked up at him steadily; the mouth smiled faintly; but there was no real expression on her face at all. There was a quiverful of those enormous arrows slung over her shoulder, and some arrow-shooting gadget—not a bow—in her left hand.

She followed his glance.

"Bollem hunting up the mountain," she explained. "The wild ones. They're better meat—"

The captain reflected a moment. That's right, he recalled; they kept the tame Bollem herds mostly for milk, butter, and cheese. He'd learned a lot of important things about Karres, all right!

"Well," he said, "good-by, Goth!"

They shook hands gravely. Goth was the real Witch of Karres, he decided—more so than her sisters, more so even than Toll. But he hadn't actually learned a single thing about any of them.

Peculiar people!

He walked on, rather glumly.

"Captain!" Goth called after him. He turned.

"Better watch those take-offs," Goth called, "or you'll kill yourself yet!"

The captain cussed softly all the way up to the *Venture*.

And the take-off was terrible! A few swan hawks were watching but, he hoped, no one else.

V.

There wasn't the remotest possibility, of course, of resuming direct trade in the Empire with the cargo they'd loaded for him. But the more he thought about it now, the less likely it seemed that Councilor Onswud was going to let a genuine fortune slip through his hands on a mere technicality of embargoes. Nikkeldepain knew all the tricks of interstellar merchandising; and the councilor himself was undoubtedly the slickest unskinned miffel in the Republic.

More hopefully, the captain began to wonder whether some sort of trade might not be made to develop eventually between Karres and Nikkeldepain. Now and then, he also thought of Maleen growing marriageable two years hence, Karres time. A handful of witch-notes went tinkling through his head whenever that idle reflection occurred.

The calendric chronometer informed him he'd spent three weeks there. He couldn't remember how their year compared with the standard one.

He found he was getting remarkably restless on this homeward run; and it struck him for the first time that space travel could also be nothing much more than a large hollow period of boredom. He made a few attempts to resume his sessions of small-talk with Illyla, via her picture; but the picture remained aloof.

The ship seemed unnaturally quiet now—that was the trouble! The captain's cabin, particularly, and the hall leading past it had become as dismal as a tomb.

But at long last, Nikkeldepain II swam up on the screen ahead. The captain put the *Venture* 7333 on orbit, and broadcast the ship's identification number. Half an hour later, Landing Control called him. He repeated the identification number, and added the ship's name, his name, owner's name, place of origin and nature of cargo.

The cargo had to be described in detail.

"Assume Landing Orbit 21,203 on your instruments," Landing Control instructed him. "A customs ship will come out to inspect."

He went on the assigned orbit and gazed moodily from the vision ports at the flat continents and oceans of Nikkeldepain II as they drifted by below. A sense of equally flat depression ovecame him unexpectedly. He shook it off and remembered Illyla.

Three hours later, a ship ran up next to him; and he shut off the orbital drive. The communicator began buzzing. He switched it on.

"Vision, please!" said an official-sounding voice. The captain frowned, located the vision-stud of the communicator screen and pushed it down. Four faces appeared in vague outline on the screen, looking at him.

"Illyla!" the captain said.

"At least," young Councilor Rapport said unpleasantly, "he's brought back the ship, Father Onswud!"

"Illyla!" said the captain.

Councilor Onswud said nothing. Neither did Illyla. They both seemed to be staring at him, but the screen wasn't good enough to permit the study of expression in detail.

The fourth face, an unfamiliar one above a uniform collar, was the one with the official-sounding voice.

"You are instructed to open the forward lock, Captain Pausert," it said, "for an official investigation."

It wasn't till he was releasing the outer lock to the control room that the captain realized it wasn't Customs who had sent a boat out to him, but the police of the Republic.

However, he hesitated for only a moment. Then the outer lock gaped wide.

He tried to explain. They wouldn't listen. They had come on board in contamination-proof repulsor suits, all four of them; and they discussed the captain as if he weren't there. Illyla looked pale and angry and beautiful, and avoided looking at him.

However, he didn't want to speak to her before the others anyway.

They strolled back to the storage and gave the Karres cargo a casual glance.

"Damaged his lifeboat, too!" Councilor Rapport remarked.

They brushed past him down the narrow hallway and went back to the control room. The policeman asked to see the log and commercial records. The captain produced them.

The three men studied them briefly. Illyla gazed stonily out at Nikkeldepain II.

"Not too carefully kept!" the policeman pointed out.

"Surprising he bothered to keep them at all!" said Councilor Rapport.

"But it's all clear enough!" said Councilor Onswud.

They straightened up then and faced him in a line. Councilor Onswud folded his arms and projected his craggy chin. Councilor Rapport stood at ease, smiling faintly. The policeman became officially rigid.

Illyla remained off to one side, looking at the three.

"Captain Pausert," the policeman said, "the following charges—substantiated in part by this preliminary investigation—are made against you—"

"Charges?" said the captain.

"Silence, please!" rumbled Councilor Onswud.

"First: material theft of a quarter-million value of maels of jewels and jeweled items from a citizen of the Imperial Planet of Porlumma—"

"They were returned!" the captain protested.

"Restitution, particularly when inspired by fear of retribution, does not affect the validity of the original charge," Councilor Rapport quoted, gazing at the ceiling.

"Second," continued the policeman. "Purchase of human slaves, permitted under Imperial law but prohibited by penalty of ten years to lifetime penal servitude by the laws of the Republic of Nikkeldepain—"

"I was just taking them back where they belonged!" said the captain.

"We shall get to that point presently," the policeman replied. "Third, material theft of sundry items in the value of one hundred and eighty thousand maels from a ship of the Imperial Planet of Lepper, accompanied by threats of violence to the ship's personnel—"

"I might add in explanation of the significance of this particular charge," added Councilor Rapport, looking at the floor, "that the Regency of Sirius, containing Lepper, is allied to the Republic of Nikkeldepain by commercial and military treaties of considerable value. The Regency has taken the trouble to point out that such hostile conduct by a citizen of the Republic against citizens of the Regency is likely to have an adverse effect on the duration of the treaties. The charge thereby becomes compounded by the additional charge of a treasonable act against the Republic—"

He glanced at the captain. "I believe we can forestall the accused's plea that these pilfered goods also were restored. They were, in the face of superior force!"

"Fourth," the policeman went on patiently, "depraved and licentious conduct while acting as commercial agent, to the detriment of your employer's business and reputation—"

"WHAT?" choked the captain.

"—involving three of the notorious Witches of the Prohibited Planet of Karres—"

"Just like his great-uncle Threbus!" nodded Councilor Onswud gloomily. "It's in the blood, I always say!"

"—and a justifiable suspicion of a prolonged stay on said Prohibited Planet of Karres—"

"I never heard of that place before this trip!" shouted the captain.

"Why don't you read your Instructions and Regulations then?" shouted Councilor Rapport. "It's all there!"

"Silence, please!" shouted Councilor Onswud.

"Fifth," said the policeman quietly, "general willful and negligent actions resulting in material damage and loss to your employer to the value of eighty-two thousand maels."

"I've still got fifty-five thousand. And the stuff in the storage," the captain said, also quietly, "is worth half a million, at least!"

"Contraband and hence legally valueless!" the policeman said. Councilor Onswud cleared his throat.

"It will be impounded, of course," he said. "Should a method of resale present itself, the profits, if any, will be applied to the cancellation of your just debts. To some extent, that might reduce your sentence." He paused. "There is another matter—"

"The sixth charge," the policeman said, "is the development *and* public demonstration of a new type of space drive, which should have been brought promptly and secretly to the attention of the Republic of Nikkeldepain!"

They all stared at him—alertly and quite greedily.

So *that* was it—the Sheewash Drive!

"Your sentence may be greatly reduced, Pausert," Councilor Onswud said wheedlingly, "if you decide to be reasonable now. What have you discovered?"

"Look out, father!" Illyla said sharply.

"Pausert," Councilor Onswud inquired in a fading voice, "what is that in your hand?"

"A Blythe gun," the captain said, boiling.

There was a frozen stillness for an instant. Then the policeman's right hand made a convulsive movement.

"Uh-uh!" said the captain warningly.

Councilor Rapport started a slow step backwards.

"Stay where you are!" said the captain.

"Pausert!" Councilor Onswud and Illyla cried out together.

"Shut up!" said the captain.

There was another stillness.

"If you'd looked," the captain said, in an almost normal voice, "you'd have seen I've got the nova gun turrets out. They're fixed on that boat of yours. The boat's lying still and keeping its little yap shut. You do the same—"

He pointed a finger at the policeman. "You got a repulsor suit on," he said. "Open the inner port lock and go squirt yourself back to your boat!"

The inner port lock groaned open. Warm air left the ship in a long, lazy wave, scattering the sheets of the *Venture's* log and commercial records over the floor. The thin, cold upper atmosphere of Nikkeldepain II came eddying in.

"You next, Onswud!" the captain said.

And a moment later: "Rapport, you just turn around—"

Young Councilor Rapport went through the port at a higher velocity than could be attributed reasonably to his repulsor units. The captain winced and rubbed his foot. But it had been worth it.

"Pausert," said Illyla in justifiable apprehension, "you are stark, staring mad!"

"Not at all, my dear," the captain said cheerfully. "You and I are now going to take off and embark on a life of crime together."

"But, Pausert—"

"You'll get used to it," the captain assured her, "just like I did. It's got Nikkeldepain beat every which way."

"Pausert," Illyla said, whitefaced, "we told them to bring up revolt ships!"

"We'll blow them out through the stratosphere," the captain said belligerently, reaching for the port-control switch. He added, "But they won't shoot anyway while I've got you on board!"

Illyla shook her head. "You just don't understand," she said desperately. "You can't make me stay!"

"Why not?" asked the captain.

"Pausert," said Illyla, "I am Madame Councilor Rapport."

"Oh!" said the captain. There was a silence. He added, crestfallen: "Since when?"

"Five months ago, yesterday," said Illyla.

"Great Patham!" cried the captain, with some indignation. "I'd hardly got off Nikkeldepain then! We were engaged!"

"Secretly . . . and I guess," said Illyla, with a return of spirit, "that I had a right to change my mind!"

There was another silence.

"Guess you had, at that," the captain agreed. "All right—the port's still open, and your husband's waiting in the boat. Beat it!"

He was alone. He let the ports slam shut and banged down the oxygen release switch. The air had become a little thin.

He cussed.

The communicator began rattling for attention. He turned it on.

"Pausert!" Councilor Onswud was calling in a friendly but shaking voice. "May we not depart, Pausert? Your nova guns are still fixed on this boat!"

"Oh, that—" said the captain. He deflected the turrets a trifle. "They won't go off now. Scram!"

The police boat vanished.

There was other company coming, though. Far below him but climbing steadily, a trio of revolt ships darted past on the screen, swung around and came back for the next turn of their spiral. They'd have to get a good deal closer before they started shooting; but they'd try to stay under him so as not to knock any stray chunks out of Nikkeldepain.

He sat a moment, reflecting. The revolt ships went by once more. The captain punched in the *Venture's* secondary drives, turned her nose towards the planet and let her go. There were some scattered white puffs around as he cut through the revolt ships' plane of flight. Then he was below them, and the *Venture* groaned as he took her out of the dive.

The revolt ships were already scattering and nosing over for a counter-maneuver. He picked the nearest one and swung the nova guns towards it.

"—and ram them in the middle!" he muttered between his teeth.

SSS-*whoosh!*

It was the Sheewash Drive—but, like a nightmare now, it kept on and on!

VI.

"Maleen!" the captain bawled, pounding at the locked door of the captain's cabin. "Maleen—shut it off! Cut it off! You'll kill yourself. Maleen!"

The *Venture* quivered suddenly throughout her length, then shuddered more violently, jumped and coughed; and commenced sailing along on her secondary drives again. He wondered how many light-years from everything they were by now. It didn't matter!

"Maleen!" he yelled. "Are you all right?"

There was a faint *thump-thump* inside the cabin, and silence. He lost almost a minute finding the right cutting tool in the storage. A few seconds later, a section of door panel sagged inwards; he caught it by one edge and came tumbling into the cabin with it.

He had the briefest glimpse of a ball of orange-colored fire swirling uncertainly over a cone of oddly bent wires. Then the fire vanished, and the wires collapsed with a loose rattling to the table top.

The crumpled small shape lay behind the table, which was why he didn't discover it at once. He sagged to the floor beside it, all the strength running out of his knees.

Brown eyes opened and blinked at him blearily.

"Sure takes it out of you!" Goth grunted. "Am I hungry!"

"I'll whale the holy, howling tar out of you again," the captain roared, "if you ever—"

"Quit your bawling!" snarled Goth. "I got to eat."

She ate for fifteen minutes straight, before she sank back in her chair, and sighed.

"Have some more Wintenberry jelly," the captain offered anxiously. She looked pretty pale.

Goth shook her head. "Couldn't—and that's about the first thing you've said since you fell through the door, howling for Maleen. Ha-ha! Maleen's *got* a boy friend!"

"Button your lip, child," the captain said. "I was thinking." He added, after a moment: "Has she really?"

"Picked him out last year," Goth nodded. "Nice boy from town—they get married as soon as she's marriageable. She just told you to come back because she was upset about you. Maleen had a premonition you were headed for awful trouble!"

"She was quite right, little chum," the captain said nastily.

"What were you thinking about?" Goth inquired.

"I was thinking," said the captain, "that as soon as we're sure you're going to be all right, I'm taking you straight back to Karres!"

"I'll be all right now," Goth said. "Except, likely, for a stomach-ache. But you can't take me back to Karres."

"Who will stop me, may I ask?" the captain asked.

"Karres is gone," Goth said.

"Gone?" the captain repeated blankly, with a sensation of not quite definable horror bubbling up in him.

"Not blown up or anything," Goth reassured him. "They just moved it! The Imperialists got their hair up about us again. But this time, they were sending a fleet with the big bombs and stuff, so everybody was called home. But they had to wait then till they found out where we were—me and Maleen and the Leewit. Then you brought us in; and they had to wait again, and decide about you. But right after you'd left . . . *we'd* left, I mean . . . they moved it."

"Where?"

"Great Patham!" Goth shrugged. "How'd I know? There's lots of places!"

There probably were, the captain admitted silently. A scene came suddenly before his eyes—that lime-white, arenalike bowl in the valley, with the steep tiers of seats around it, just before they'd reached the town of Karres—"the Theater where—"

But now there was unnatural night-darkness all over and about that world; and the eight thousand-some Witches of Karres sat in circles around the Theater, their heads bent towards one point in the center, where orange fire washed hugely about the peak of a cone of curiously twisted girders.

And a world went racing off at the speeds of the Sheewash Drive! There'd be lots of places, all right. What peculiar people!

"Anyway," he sighed, "if I've got to start raising you—don't say 'Great Patham' any more. That's a cuss word!"

"I learned it from you!" Goth pointed out.

"So you did, I guess," the captain acknowledged. "I won't say it either. Aren't they going to be worried about you?"

"Not very much," said Goth. "We don't get hurt often—especially when we're young. That's when we can do all that stuff like teleporting, and whistling, like the Leewit. We lose it mostly when we get older—they're working on that now so we won't. About all Maleen can do right now is premote!"

"She premotes just dandy, though," the captain said. "The Sheewash Drive—they can all do that, can't they?"

"Uh-huh!" Goth nodded. "But that's learned stuff. That's one of the things they already studied out." She added, a trace uncomfortably: "I can't tell you about that till you're one yourself."

"Till I'm what myself?" the captain asked, becoming puzzled again.

"A witch, like us," said Goth. "We got our rules. And that won't be for four years, Karres time."

"It won't, eh?" said the captain. "What happens then?"

"That's when I'm marriageable age," said Goth, frowning at the jar of Wintenberry jelly. She pulled it towards her and inspected it carefully. "I got it all fixed," she told the jelly firmly, "as soon as they started saying they ought to pick out a wife for you on Karres, so you could stay. I said it was me, right away; and everyone else said finally that was all right then—even Maleen, because she had this boy friend."

"You mean," said the captain, stunned, "this was all planned out on Karres?"

"Sure," said Goth. She pushed the jelly back where it had been standing, and glanced up at him again. "For three weeks, that's about all everyone talked about in the town! It set a perceedent—"

She paused doubtfully.

"That would explain it," the captain admitted.

"Uh-huh," Goth nodded relieved, settling back in her chair. "But it was my father who told us how to do it so you'd break up with the people on Nikkeldepain. He said it was in the blood."

"What was in the blood?" the captain said patiently.

"That you'd break up with them. That's Threbus, my father," Goth informed him. "You met him a couple of times in the town. Big man with a blond beard—Maleen and the Leewit take after him."

"You wouldn't mean my great-uncle Threbus?" the captain inquired. He was in a state of strange calm by now.

"That's right," said Goth. "He liked you a lot."

"It's a small Galaxy," said the captain philosophically. "So that's where Threbus wound up! I'd like to meet him again some day."

"We'll start after Karres four years from now, when you learn about those things," Goth said. "We'll catch up with them all right. That's still thirteen hundred and seventy-two Old Sidereal days," she added, "but there's a lot to do in between. You want to pay the money you owe back to those people, don't you? I got some ideas—"

"None of those teleporting tricks now!" the captain warned.

"Kid stuff!" Goth said scornfully. "I'm growing up. This'll be fair swapping. But we'll get rich."

"I wouldn't be surprised," the captain admitted. He thought a moment. "Seeing we've turned out to be distant relatives, I suppose it is all right, too, if I adopt you meanwhile—"

"Sure," said Goth. She stood up.

"Where you going?" the captain asked.

"Bed," said Goth. "I'm tired." She stopped at the hall door. "About all I can tell you about us till then," she said, "you can read in those Regulations, like the one man said—the one you kicked off the ship. There's a lot about us in there. Lots of lies, too, though!"

"And when did you find out about the communicator between here and the captain's cabin?" the captain inquired.

Goth grinned. "A while back," she admitted. "The others never noticed!"

"All right," the captain said. "Good night, witch—if you get a stomach-ache, yell and I'll bring the medicine."

"Good night," Goth yawned. "I will, I think."

"And wash behind your ears!" the captain added, trying to remember the bedtime instructions he'd overheard Maleen giving the junior witches.

"All right," said Goth sleepily. The hall door closed behind her—but half a minute later, it was briskly opened again. The captain looked up startled from the voluminous stack of "General Instructions and Space Regulations of the Republic of Nikkeldepain" he'd just discovered in one of the drawers of the control desk. Goth stood in the doorway, scowling and wide-awake.

"And you wash behind yours!" she said.

"Huh?" said the captain. He reflected a moment. "All right," he said. "We both will, then."

"Right," said Goth, satisfied.

The door closed once more.

The captain began to run his finger down the lengthy index of K's— or could it be under W?

First published: 1949

OVER THE TOP

by Lester del Rey

THE SKY WAS LOUSY WITH STARS—NASTY LITTLE PINPOINTS OF COLD HOS-tility that had neither the remoteness of space nor the friendly warmth of Earth. They didn't twinkle honestly, but tittered and snickered down. And there wasn't even one moon. Dave Mannen knew better, but his eyes looked for the low scudding forms of Deimos and Phobos because of all the romanticists who'd written of them. They were up there, all right, but only cold rocks, too small to see.

Rocks in the sky, and rocks in his head—not to mention the lump on the back of his skull. He ran tense fingers over his wiry black hair until he found the swelling, and winced. With better luck, he'd have had every inch of his three-foot body mashed to jelly, instead of that, though. Blast Mars!

He flipped the searchlight on and looked out, but the view hadn't im-proved any. It was nothing but a drab plain of tarnished reddish sand, chucked about in ridiculous potholes, running out beyond the light with-out change. The stringy ropes of plantlike stuff had decided to clump into balls during the night, but their bilious green still had a clabbered ap-pearance, like the result of a three days' binge. There was a thin rime of frost over them, catching the light in little wicked sparks. That was prob-ably significant data; it would prove that there was more water in the air than the scientists had figured, even with revised calculations from the twenty-four-inch lunar refractor.

But that was normal enough. The bright boys got together with their hundred-ton electronic slipsticks and brought forth all manner of results; after that, they had to send someone out to die here and there before they found why the sticks had slipped. Like Dave. Sure, the refractory tube linings were good for twenty-four hours of continual blast—tested under the most rigorous lab conditions, even tried on a couple of Moon hops.

So naturally, with Unitech's billionaire backer and new power han-

480

dling methods giving them the idea of beating the Services to Mars—no need to stop on the Moon even, they were that good—they didn't include spare linings. They'd have had to leave out some of their fancy radar junk and wait for results until the rocket returned.

Well, the tubes had been good. It was only after three hours of blasting, total, when he was braking down for Mars, that they began pitting. Then they'd held up after a fashion until there was only forty feet of free fall left—about the same as fifteen on Earth. The ship hadn't been damaged, had even landed on her tripod legs, and the radar stuff had come through fine. The only trouble was that Dave had no return ticket. There was food for six months, water for more by condensing and re-using; but the clicking of the air machine wouldn't let him forget his supply of breathing material was being emptied, a trickle at a time. And there was only enough there for three weeks, at the outside. After that, curtains.

Of course, if the bright boys' plans had worked, he could live on compressed air drawn from outside by the air lock pumps. Too bad the landing had sprung them just enough so they could barely hold their own and keep him from losing air if he decided to go outside. A lot of things were too bad.

But at least the radar was working fine. He couldn't breathe it or take off with it, but the crystal amplifiers would have taken even a free fall all the way from mid-space. He cut the power on, fiddling until he found the lunar broadcast from Earth. It had a squiggly sound, but most of the words came through on the megacycle band. There was something about a fool kid who'd sneaked into a plane and got off the ground somehow, leaving a hundred honest pilots trying to kill themselves in getting him down. People could kill each other by the millions, but they'd go all out to save one spectacular useless life, as usual.

Then it came: "No word from the United Technical Foundation rocket, now fourteen hours overdue in reporting. Foundation men have given up hope, and feel that Mannen must have died in space from unknown causes, leaving the rocket to coast past Mars unmanned. Any violent crash would have tripped automatic signalers, and there was no word of trouble from Mannen—"

There was more, though less than on the kid. One rocket had been tried two years before, and gone wide because the tubes blew before reversal; the world had heard the clicking of Morse code right to the end, then. This failure was only a secondhand novelty, without anything new to gush over. Well, let them wonder. If they wanted to know what had happened, let 'em come and find out. There'd be no pretty last words from him.

Dave listened a moment longer, as the announcer picked up the latest rift in the supposedly refurbished United Nations, then cut off in disgust. The Atlantic Nations were as determined as Russia, and both had bombs now. If they wanted to blast themselves out of existence, maybe it was a good thing. Mars was a stinking world, but at least it had died quietly, instead of raising all that fuss.

Why worry about them. They'd never done him any favors. He'd been gypped all along. With a Grade-A brain and a matinee idol's face, he'd been given a three-foot body and the brilliant future of a circus freak—the kind the crowd laughed at, rather than looked at with awe. His only chance had come when Unitech was building the ship, before they knew how much power they had, and figured on saving weight by designing it for a midget and a consequently smaller supply of air, water and food. Even then, after he'd seen the ad, he'd had to fight his way into position through days of grueling tests. They hadn't tossed anything in his lap.

It had looked like the big chance, then. Fame and statues they could keep, but the book and endorsement rights would have put him where he could look down and laugh at the six-footers. And the guys with the electronic brains had cheated him out of it.

Let them whistle for their radar signals. Let them blow themselves to bits playing soldier. It was none of his worry now.

He clumped down from the observatory tip into his tiny quarters, swallowed a couple of barbiturates, and crawled into his sleeping cushions. Three weeks to go, and not even a bottle of whiskey on the ship. He cursed in disgust, turned over, and let sleep creep up on him.

It was inevitable that he'd go outside, of course. Three days of nothing but sitting, standing up, and sleeping was too much. Dave let the pumps suck at the air in the lock, zipping down his helmet over the soft rubber seal, tested his equipment, and waited until the pressure stood about even, outside and in. Then he opened the outer lock, tossed down the plastic ramp, and stepped out. He'd got used to the low gravity while still aboard, and paid no attention to it.

The tripod had dug into the sand, but the platform feet had kept the tubes in the open, and Dave swore at them softly. They looked good—except where part of one lining hung out in shreds. And with lining replacements, they'd be good—the blast had been cut off before the tubes themselves were harmed. He turned his back on the ship finally and faced out to the shockingly near horizon.

This, according to the stories, was supposed to be man's high moment—the first living human to touch the soil outside his own world and its useless satellite. The lock opened, and out stepped the hero—dying in pride with man's triumph and conquest of space! Dave pushed the rubbery flap of his helmet back against his lips, opened the orifice, and spat on the ground. If this was an experience, so was last year's stale beer.

There wasn't even a "canal" within fifty miles of him. He regretted that, in a way, since finding out what made the streaks would have killed time. He'd seen them as he approached, and there was no illusion to them —as the lunar scope had proved before. But they definitely weren't water ditches, anyhow. There'd been no chance to pick his landing site, and he'd have to get along without them.

It didn't leave much to explore. The ropes of vegetation were stretched out now, holding up loops of green fuzz to the sun, but there seemed to be no variation of species to break up the pattern. Probably a grove of trees on Earth would look the same to a mythical Martian. Possibly they represented six million and seven varieties. But Dave couldn't see it. The only point of interest was the way they wiggled their fuzz back and forth, and that soon grew monotonous.

Then his foot squeaked up at him, winding up in a gurgle. He jumped a good six feet up in surprise, and the squeak came again in the middle of his leap, making him stumble as he landed. But his eyes focused finally on a dull brownish lump fastened to his boot. It looked something like a circular cluster of a dozen pine cones, with fuzz all over, but there were little leglike members coming out of it—a dozen of them that went into rapid motion as he looked.

"Queeklrle," the thing repeated, sending the sound up through the denser air in his suit. It scrambled up briskly, coming to a stop over his supply kit, and fumbling hurriedly. "Queeklrle!"

Oddly, there was no menace in it, probably because it was anything but a bug-eyed monster; there were no signs of any sensory organs. Dave blinked. It reminded him of a kitten he'd once had, somehow, before his usual luck found him and killed the little creature with some cat disease. He reacted automatically.

"Queekle yourself." His fingers slipped into the kit and came out with a chocolate square, unpeeling the cellophane quickly. "It'll probably make you sick or kill you—but if that's what you're after, take it."

Queekle was after it, obviously. The creature took the square in its pseudopods, tucked it under its body, and relaxed, making faint gobbling sounds. For a second, it was silent, but then it squeaked again, sharper this time. "Queeklrle!"

Dave fed it two more of the squares before the creature seemed satisfied, and began climbing back down, leaving the nuts in the chocolate neatly piled on the ground behind it. Then Queekle went scooting off into the vegetation. Dave grimaced; its gratitude was practically human.

"Nuts to you, too," he muttered, kicking the pile of peanuts aside. But it proved at least that men had never been there before—humans were almost as fond of exterminating other life as they were of killing off their own kind.

He shrugged, and swung off toward the horizon at random in a loose, loping stride. After the cramped quarters of the ship, running felt good. He went on without purpose for an hour or more, until his muscles began protesting. Then he dug out his water bottle, pushed the tube through the helmet orifice, and drank briefly. Everything around him was the same as it had been near the ship, except for a small cluster of the plants that had dull red fuzz instead of green; he'd noticed them before, but couldn't tell whether they were one stage of the same plant or a different species. He didn't really care.

In any event, going further was purposeless. He'd been looking for another Queekle casually, but had seen none. And on the return route, he studied the ground under the fuzz plants more carefully, but there was nothing to see. There wasn't even a wind to break up the monotony, and he clumped up to the ramp of the ship as bored as he had left it. Maybe it was just as well his air supply was low, if this was all Mars had to offer.

Dave pulled up the ramp and spun the outer lock closed, blinking in the gloom, until the lights snapped on as the lock sealed. He watched the pressure gauge rise to ten pounds, normal for the ship, and reached for the inner lock. Then he jerked back, staring at the floor.

Queekle was there, and had brought along part of Mars. Now its squeaks came out in a steady stream as the inner seal opened. And in front of it, fifteen or twenty of the plant things went into abrupt motion, moving aside to form a narrow lane through which the creature went rapidly, on into the ship. Dave followed, shaking his head. Apparently there was no way of being sure about anything here. Plants that stood rock steady on their roots outside could move about at will, it seemed— and to what was evidently a command.

The fool beast! Apparently the warmth of the ship had looked good to it, and it was all set to take up housekeeping—in an atmosphere that was at least a hundred times too dense for it. Dave started up the narrow steps to his quarters, hesitated, and cursed. It still reminded him of the kitten, moving around in exploratory circles. He came back down, and made a dive for it.

Queekle let out a series of squeals as Dave tossed it back into the air lock and closed the inner seal. Its squeaks died down as the pressure was pumped back and the outer seal opened, though, and were inaudible by the time he moved back up the ladder. He grumbled to himself half-heartedly. That's what came of feeding the thing—it decided to move in and own him.

But he felt better as he downed what passed for supper. The lift lasted for an hour or so afterwards—and then left him feeling more cramped and disgusted than ever as he sat staring at the walls of his tiny room. There wasn't even a book to read, aside from the typed manual for general care of the ship, and he'd read that often enough already.

Finally he gave up in disgust and went up to the observation tip and cut on the radar. Maybe his death notices would be more interesting tonight.

They weren't. They were carrying speculations about what had happened to him—none of which included any hint that the bright boys could have made an error. They'd even figured out whether Mars might have captured the ship as a satellite, and decided against it. But the news was losing interest, obviously, and he could tell where it had been padded out from the general broadcast to give the Lunar men more coverage—apparently on the theory that anyone as far out as the Moon would be more interested in the subject. They'd added one new touch, though:

"It seems obvious that further study of space conditions beyond the gravitic or magnetic field of Earth is needed. The Navy announced that its new rocket, designed to reach Mars next year, will be changed for use as a deep-space laboratory on tentative exploratory trips before going further. United Technical Foundation has abandoned all further plans for interplanetary research, at least for the moment."

And that was that. They turned the microphone over to international affairs then, and Dave frowned. Even to him, it was obvious that the amount of words used had no relation to the facts covered. Already they were beginning to clamp down the lid, and that meant things were heading toward a crisis again. The sudden outbreak of the new and violent plague in China four years before had brought an end to the former crisis, as all nations pitched in through altruism or sheer self-interest, and were forced to work together. But that hadn't lasted; they'd found a cure after nearly two million deaths, and there had been nothing to hold the suddenly created co-operation of the powers. Maybe if they had new channels for their energies, such as the planets—

But it wouldn't wash. The Atlantic Nations would have taken over

Mars on the strength of his landing and return, and they were in the lead if another ship should be sent. They'd gobble up the planets as they had taken the Moon, and the other powers would simply have more fuel to feed their resentment, and bring things to a head.

Dave frowned more deeply as the announcer went on. There were the usual planted hints from officials that everything was fine for the Atlantic Powers—but they weren't usual. They actually sounded super-confident—arrogantly so. And there was one brief mention of a conference in Washington, but it was the key. Two of the names were evidence in full. Someone had actually found a way to make the lithium bomb work, and—

Dave cut off the radar as it hit him. It was all the human race needed—a chance to use what could turn into a self-sustaining chain reaction. Man had finally discovered a way to blow up his planet.

He looked up toward the speck that was Earth, with the tiny spot showing the Moon beside it. Behind him, the air machine clicked busily, metering out oxygen. Two and a half weeks. Dave looked down at that, then. Well, it might be long enough, though it probably wouldn't. But he had that much time for certain. He wondered if the really bright boys expected as much for themselves. Or was it only because he wasn't in the thick of a complacent humanity, and had time for thinking that he could realize what was coming?

He slapped the air machine dully, and looked up at the Earth again. The fools! They'd asked for it; let them take their medicine now. They liked war better than eugenics, nuclear physics better than the science that could have found his trouble and set his glands straight to give him the body he should have had. Let them stew in their own juice.

He found the bottle of sleeping tablets, and shook it. But only specks of powder fell out. That was gone, too. They couldn't get anything right. No whiskey, no cigarettes that might use up the precious air, no more amytal. Earth was reaching out for him, denying him the distraction of a sedative, just as she was denying herself a safe and impersonal contest for her clash of wills.

He threw the bottle onto the floor and went down to the air lock. Queekle was there—the faint sounds of scratching proved that. And it came in as soon as the inner seal opened, squeaking contentedly, with its plants moving slowly behind it. They'd added a new feature—a mess of rubbish curled up in the tendrils of the vines, mixed sand and dead plant forms.

"Make yourself to home," Dave told the creature needlessly. "It's all yours, and when I run down to the gasping point, I'll leave the locks open and the power on for the fluorescents. Somebody might as well get some good out of the human race. And don't worry about using up my air—I'll be better off without it, probably."

"Queeklrle." It wasn't a very brilliant conversation, but it had to do.

Dave watched Queekle assemble the plants on top of the converter shield. The bright boys had done fine, there—they'd learned to chain radiation and neutrons with a thin wall of metal and an intangible linkage of forces. The result made an excellent field for the vines, and Queekle scooted about, making sure the loads of dirt were spread out and its charges arranged comfortably, to suit it. It looked intelligent—but so would the behavior of ants. If the pressure inside the ship bothered the creature, there was no sign of it.

"Queek-lrle," it announced finally, and turned toward Dave. He let it follow him up the steps, found some chocolate, and offered it to the pseudopods. But Queekle wasn't hungry. Nor would the thing accept water, beyond touching it and brushing a drop over its fuzzy surface.

It squatted on the floor until Dave flopped down on his cushions, then tried to climb up beside him. He reached down, surprised to feel the fuzz give way instantly to a hard surface underneath, and lifted it up beside him. Queekle was neither cold nor warm; probably all Martian life had developed excellent insulation, and perhaps the ability to suck water out of the almost dehydrated atmosphere and then retain it.

For a second, Dave remembered the old tales of vampire beasts, but he rejected them at once. When you come down to it, most of the animal life wasn't too bad—not nearly as bad as man had pictured it to justify his own superiority. And Queekle seemed content to lie there, making soft monotonous little squeaks, and letting it go at that.

Surprisingly, sleep came quickly.

Dave stayed away from the ship most of the next two days, moving aimlessly, but working his energy out in pure muscular exertion. It helped, enough to keep him away from the radar. He found tongs and stripped the lining from the tubes, and that helped more, because it occupied his mind as well as his muscles. But it was only a temporary expedient, and not good enough for even the two remaining weeks. He started out the next day, went a few miles, and came back. For a while then, he watched the plants that were thriving unbelievably on the converter shielding.

Queekle was busy among them, nipping off something here and there and pushing it underneath where its mouth was. Dave tasted one of the buds, gagged, and spat it out; the thing smelled almost like an Earth plant, but combined all the quintessence of sour and bitter with something that was outside his experience. Queekle, he'd found, didn't care for chocolate—only the sugar in it; the rest was ejected later in a hard lump.

And then there was nothing to do. Queekle finished its work and they squatted side by side, but with entirely different reactions; the Martian creature seemed satisfied.

Three hours later, Dave stood in the observatory again, listening to the radar. There was some music coming through at this hour—but the squiggly reception ruined that. And the news was exactly what he'd expected—a lot of detail about national things, a few quick words on some conference at the United Nations, and more on the celebration in Israel over the anniversary of becoming an independent nation. Dave's own memories of that were dim, but some came back as he listened. The old United Nations had done a lot of wrangling over that, but it had been good for them, in a way—neither side had felt the issue offered enough chance for any direct gain to threaten war, but it kept the professional diplomats from getting quite so deeply into more dangerous grounds.

But that, like the Chinese plague, wouldn't come up again.

He cut off the radar, finally, only vaguely conscious of the fact that the rocket hadn't been mentioned. He could no longer even work up a feeling of disgust. Nothing mattered beyond his own sheer boredom, and when the air machine—

Then it hit him. There were no clicks. There had been none while he was in the tip. He jerked to the controls, saw that the meter indicated the same as it had when he was last here, and threw open the cover. Everything looked fine. There was a spark from the switch, and the motor went on when he depressed the starting button. When he released it, it went off instantly. He tried switching manually to other tanks, but while the valves moved, the machine remained silent.

The air smelled fresh, though—fresher than it had since the first day out from Earth, though a trifle drier than he'd have liked.

"Queekle!" Dave looked at the creature, watched it move nearer at his voice, as it had been doing lately. Apparently it knew its name now, and answered with the usual squeak and gurgle.

It was the answer, of course. No wonder its plants had been thriving. They'd had all the carbon dioxide and water vapor they could use, for a change. No Earth plants could have kept the air fresh in such a limited amount of space, but Mars had taught her children efficiency through sheer necessity. And now he had six months, rather than two weeks.

Yeah, six months to do nothing but sit and wait and watch for the blowup that might come, to tell him he was the last of his kind. Six months with nothing but a squeaking burble for conversation, except for the radar news.

He flipped it on again with an impatient slap of his hand, then reached to cut it off. But words were already coming out:

". . . Foundation will dedicate a plaque today to young Dave Mannen, the little man with more courage than most big men can hold. Andrew Buller, backer of the ill-fated Mars Rocket, will be on hand to pay tribute—"

Dave kicked the slush off with his foot. They would bother with plaques at a time like this, when all he'd ever wanted was the right number of marks on United States currency. He snapped at the dials, twisting them, and grabbed for the automatic key as more circuits coupled in.

"Tell Andrew Buller and the whole Foundation to go—"

Nobody'd hear his Morse at this late stage, but at least it felt good. He tried it again, this time with some Anglo-Saxon adjectives thrown in. Queekle came over to investigate the new sounds, and squeaked doubtfully. Dave dropped the key.

"Just human nonsense, Queekle. We also kick chairs when we bump into—"

"Mannen!" The radar barked it out at him. "Thank God, you got your radar fixed. This is Buller—been waiting here a week and more now. Never did believe all that folderol about it being impossible for it to be the radar at fault. *Oof*, your message still coming in and I'm getting the typescript. Good thing there's no FCC out there. Know just how you feel, though. Darned fools here. Always said they should have another rocket ready. Look, if your set is bad, don't waste it, just tell me how long you can hold out, and by Harry, we'll get another ship built and up there. How are you, what—"

He went on, his words piling up on each other as Dave went through a mixture of reactions that shouldn't have fitted any human situation. But he knew better than to build up hope. Even six months wasn't long enough—took time to finish and test a rocket—more than he had. Air was fine, but men needed food, as well.

He hit the key again. "Two weeks' air in tanks. Staying with Martian farmer of doubtful intelligence, but his air too thin, pumps no good." The last he let fade out, ending with an abrupt cut-off of power. There was no sense in their sending out fools in half-built ships to try to rescue him. He wasn't a kid in an airplane, crying at the mess he was in, and he didn't intend to act like one. That farmer business would give them enough to chew on; they had their money's worth, and that was that.

He wasn't quite prepared for the news that came over the radar later—particularly for the things he'd been quoted as saying. For the first time it occurred to him that the other pilot, sailing off beyond Mars to die, might have said things a little different from the clicks of Morse they had broadcast. Dave tried to figure the original version of "Don't give up the ship" as a sailor might give it, and chuckled.

And at least the speculation over their official version of his Martian farmer helped to kill the boredom. In another week at the most, there'd be an end to that, too, and he'd be back out of the news. Then there'd be more long days and nights to fill somehow, before his time ran out. But for the moment, he could enjoy the antics of nearly three billion people who got more excited over one man in trouble on Mars than they would have out of half the population starving to death.

He set the radar back on the Foundation wave length, but there was nothing there; Buller had finally run down, and not yet got his breath back. Finally, he turned back to the general broadcast on the Lunar signal. It was remarkable how Man's progress had leaped ahead by decades, along with his pomposity, just because an insignificant midget was still alive on Mars. They couldn't have discovered a prettier set of half-truths about anybody than they had from the crumbs of facts he hadn't even known existed concerning his life.

Then he sobered. That was the man on the street's reaction. But the diplomats, like the tides, waited on no man. And his life made no difference to a lithium bomb. He was still going through a counter-reaction when Queekle insisted it was bedtime and persuaded him to leave the radar.

After all, not a single thing had been accomplished by his fool message.

But he snapped back to the messages as a new voice came on: "And here's a late flash from the United Nations headquarters. Russia has just volunteered the use of a completed rocketship for the rescue of David Mannen on Mars, and we've accepted the offer. The Russian delegation is still being cheered on the floor! Here are the details we now have. This will be a one-way trip, radar guided by a new bomb control method—no, here's more news! It will be guided by radar and an automatic searching head that will put it down within a mile of Mannen's ship. Unmanned, it can take tremendous acceleration, and reach Mannen before another week is out! United Technical Foundation is even now trying to contact Mannen through a hookup to the big government high-frequency labs where a new type of receiver—"

It was almost eight minutes before Buller's voice came in, evidently while the man was still getting Dave's hurried message off the tape. "Mannen, you're coming in fine. O.K., those refractories—they'll be on the way to Moscow in six hours, some new type the scientists here worked out after you left. We'll send two sets this time to be sure, but they test almost twenty times as good as the others. We're still in contact with Moscow, and some details are still being worked on, but we're equipping their ship with the same type of refractories. Most of the other supplies will come straight from them—"

Dave nodded. And there'd be a lot of things he'd need—he'd see to that. Things that would be supplied straight from them. Right now, everything was milk and honey, and all nations were being the fool pilots rescuing the kid in the plane, suddenly bowled over by interplanetary success. But they'd need plenty later on to keep their diplomats busy—something to wrangle over and blow off steam that would be vented on important things, otherwise.

Well, the planets wouldn't be important to any nation for a long time, but they were spectacular enough. And just how was a planet claimed, if the man who landed was taken off in a ship that was a mixture of the work of two countries?

Maybe his theories were all wet, but there was no harm in the gamble. And even if the worst happened, all this might hold off the trouble long enough for colonies. Mars was still a stinking world, but it could support life if it had to.

"Queekle," he said slowly, "you're going to be the first Martian ambassador to Earth. But first, how about a little side trip to Venus on the way back, instead of going direct? That ought to drive them crazy, and tangle up their interplanetary rights a little more. Well? On to Venus, or direct home to Earth?"

"Queeklrle," the Martian creature answered. It wasn't too clear, but it was obviously a lot more like a two-syllable word.

Dave nodded. "Right! Venus."

The sky was still filled with the nasty little stars he'd seen the first night on Mars, but he grinned now as he looked up, before reaching for the key again. He wouldn't have to laugh at big men, after all. He could look up at the sky and laugh at every star in it. It shouldn't be long before those snickering stars had a surprise coming to them.

First published: 1950

METEOR

by William T. Powers

TOBIAS HENDERSON, MASTER OF THE BRITISH FREIGHTER, BRONSON, was relaxing at tea. The Callisto-Mars run was long and dull, but Tobias knew how to be comfortable. In fact, getting comfortable was the one thing at which Tobias was better than average. He had to be. Free-flight and Martian sauces had combined their effects to make him the third largest item on the *Bronson*, and one might have debated the advantage held by the computer-detector.

For reasons other than jealousy, Tobias hated the computer. The main drive might flatten him somewhat on take-off and landing, but the computer had been known to snatch the *Bronson* from under its master's feet, causing him to misname countless safety-engineers, just to avoid some pebble. Today, as usual, Tobias squinted at the computer before he injected his cream into the tea bag. Promptly, a red light popped on.

"Coward!" Tobias muttered. "It won't come within a hundred miles!" The red light went out. Tobias creased his face in brief triumph, then pulled the stopper out of the tea bag and inserted a straw, an uncivilized process made necessary by free-flight. The red light popped on again. Hopefully, Tobias ignored it.

Something clicked rapidly in the bulkhead where the monster was hidden; Tobias sighed and braced himself for the recoil of the blasters. Unfortunately, a grip on the desk was not enough to save him. The *Bronson* shuddered sideways, skittering out of its orbit to let something too big to blast go by. Tobias, unable to express himself, oscillated to a stop in his triple harness and glared in black silence at the globules of tea quivering off the bulkheads. After a suitable pause, the computer went *ahem* and slid a card out where Tobias could see it.

The lettering was red.

The meteor was out of sight of the *Bronson* in a few seconds, plunging on toward the orbit of Mars, aimed a little above the Orion nebula. This

492

was a fast meteor from outside the system, nearly zero Kelvin, six miles across. One flat side might have been a plain at one time; the other surfaces were harsh and jagged, signs of a cataclysm. The sun lit an exposed stratum, picking out the fossil of an ancient tree.

Thirty miles a second the meteor traveled. In twenty-four hours, it would have gone the twenty-five hundred kilomiles separating it from the orbit of Mars. The intersection point was no more than a thousand miles from the place where Mars' advancing limb would be tomorrow.

Phil Brownyard dropped a penny in the You-Vu-It just in time to see a screenful of little bright spots fade to a shot of an announcer.

"There you have it, folks. Danvers came up from the sixth quad at well over three miles per second, just in time to avert a scoring play by Syverson and Phelps. His ship snagged the Mark into free territory, but he couldn't turn fast enough to keep in-bounds. That, of course, ended the period. Now a word from—"

Phil reached out for a switch, but the commercial droned on. Frustrated, he grumbled and pushed his dessert away. He had a grudge against the game of Ten-Mark that included its sponsors. The pilots who played had a rugged, exciting life, full of pretty girls, big money, and sudden death. Two years were all a man could stand of the screaming accelerations and close shaves, but those two years—! Phil shoved his chair back and headed for the elevators. Pushing his way to the expresses, he glimpsed Fred Holland from Computing coming around the corner; he stood in the doorway of the car until Fred caught up.

"Hi, Phil!" Fred grinned. "Have a cigar!"

"Boy?"

"Yep." Fred grabbed for the handrail as the car shot up the shaft. "Twenty minutes ago. Aggie just vised me and everything's all right."

"Tell Aggie Claire will be over tonight to help out."

"Thanks. She could use some help. Well . . . so long. Wait, your cigar!" Fred thrust a couple at Phil and hopped out the door. The car lifted swiftly and Phil pushed the buzzer.

"Six-forty." The operator snapped as the door whipped open. Phil stepped out, ducking a little as a monorail messenger-car rushed by overhead. He pushed through the door marked Safety, waving hello to Doris, and went into the office.

Run, run, run, he thought. *Am I glad I'm not in public relations!* The swivel chair was big and soft, so he relaxed and pulled out a cigar.

Behind him, monstrous New York City stretched. The six hundred fortieth story of the Government Building overlooked the city from half a mile above the top passenger levels; sixty miles from Phil's window the lights of the North Highway glowed steadily.

Ten thousand square miles, eighteen million people, a vast system of conveyors, highways, terminals; a billion dollars worth of trade every day. New York City, 2055.

The periphery was lined with homes that spewed hordes of commuters every eight hours. Past neat factories and a few local airports the subways sped, the crowded tunnels boring into the deepening pile of the city. Above them mounted in higher and higher tiers interlocking roadways, flat, sinuous conveyer-housings, office buildings and freight terminals climbing over each other. The hum of the city deepened to a growl, grew to a rumble, swelled into thunder; the sound drifted up past the levels, picking up the *zum* of tires and the crowd-babble. The sound filtered around steel and stone and hung among the upthrust skyscrapers, fading at last into the dark upper air.

On the tip of every spire were thick-limbed UHF arrays pouring out power to the stars. The million kilowatt beams swept steadily through the sky, balancing on the rotating earth, hurling their messages through the system of planets.

Back through the Heaviside Layer, feeble signals returned, to be gathered and sorted by the city's robot brains.

In a corner of the government computing room, a silent coder came to life. A card hopped into one of its racks, and the machine buzzed briefly. The card, punched and stamped, slid quickly into the works of the nearest idle router.

Plate voltage flashed briefly, and the monster decided to send the card to Safety. Along a hidden wall the card sped, up one floor and into another router that punched it twice and sent it to Spatial Debris.

At the first sign of life from the next stage, a signal was shot down five stories to Computing, where the termination of phase one was recorded on microfilm.

Phase two began. Electronic fingers probed the card and withdrew. A rudimentary brain thought a moment, and a little set of thumbs descended to press the card, embossing on it the co-ordinates of an orbit. The card jumped ahead ten inches and a metal stamp jolted it. A pneumatic tube flipped open and the last machine capsuled the card, which now bore one red edge and the admonition, "DANGER." The card whistled up five stories and thumped to a stop by Phil's left elbow.

Phil looked indecisively at the ash on his cigar, then flipped it off and ground out the stub. He reached for the capsule, tingled a bit when he saw the red edge.

A print-send writer stood to the left of the desk; Phil inserted the card and the machine began to clatter. A strip of tape inched out.

"Meteor. A-2 to B-5. 27-32 mps. det. 2994663.6033. Coord. 270.665 — 160332 x 10³ — 710.4 Dir.Cos. 0.000355,-0.554639. 29.358 mps."

The rough equation of an hyperbolic orbit followed. Phil went to the lucite plan-map of the minor planets and began to plot points. Four points fed into the Curvator sufficed; an arm descended over the chart and began to trace a heavy black line, jogging at equal-time intervals. The tip of the arm approached the orbit of Mars, intersecting it just as the red spot designating Mars moved into its path. The Curvator, having reached the limit of its accuracy, stopped and flashed an orange light that meant "possible collision."

That meant that the meteor would miss the planet by no more than eight thousand miles, if at all. Phil was by now totally alert. The probable mass of the meteor was twelve billion tons, its velocity thirty miles per second. Only the heaviest of equipment would be capable of breaking it up and diverting the pieces into the sun. Were it to strike Mars, it would pick up another three miles per second before it hit, then it would release the equivalent of five billion kilowatt-hours of energy in a fraction of a second. A large piece of Martian vicinity could be vaporized.

Another card called Phil back to his desk; he gave it a quick glance and filed it. Now there was work to be done; Mars had to be warned, although New Pitt undoubtedly had received the report.

A quick call to Computing set Fred Holland to work on the exact orbit, and Phil turned to the chart again. The markers on the orbit showed that about twenty-two hours remained—New Pitt, on Mars, would pick up the meteor in roughly an hour. Phil sent a copy of the orbit out to Doris, with instructions to get it on the emergency circuit to Mars.

The preliminaries over, Phil sat behind his desk and began to have his customary regrets. Whenever a big rock struck the space lanes, Phil wondered what he was doing here. Whenever the rock was really big, the chief of SD slashed the arteries of the Solar System with efficiency and finality. The advent of robot freighters had made the job easier, but still each day's ban cost somebody millions. Phil bit his lip and lit another cigar. The responsibility of his office was not to save millions, but to save lives.

The minute hand crept forward, timing the flight of his message. In just seventeen minutes from the time Phil gave Doris the message, acknowledgment arrived. Doris brought in the spacegram personally.

"Mr. Brownyard—" She hesitated at the door.

"Good, they didn't waste any time." Phil reached out and Doris came up to him with the message.

"Mr. Brownyard, can I ask something?"

Phil looked up blankly from the spacegram. "Huh? Oh, sure. What?"

"Well . . . my boy friend is on the *North America*. I wondered if you could tell me—" She stopped. It was strictly against the rules to give any advance information.

Phil hesitated. The spacegram said that the route outbound from Mars had been changed, and nothing more.

"I'd like to help," he said, "but I'm afraid we don't know the situation yet about the Earth-Mars route. Don't worry, though. We don't miss on these big ones."

Twenty-one hours later, he was staring at another spacegram, remembering his comforting words of the day before. The heading was EMERGENCY; the spacegram was direct from the Stag Head detector station.

METEOR 842M2055 OUT OF CONTACT. EAST STATION INOPERATIVE, STAG HEAD STATION HORIZONED. LAST ACCURATE ORBIT—

Phil dropped the spacegram and looked back at the chart on the desk. The red line of the meteor's orbit made a shallow curve that missed the planet by a scant eighty miles. Arcing outward from Mars, the line was dotted. From there on, it was guesswork. Atmospheric drag and the proximity of Deimos combined to make the uncertainty in the orbit dangerous.

Phil buzzed Fred Holland and reached for the standard route-cancellation form. Forcing all misgivings out of his mind, he printed carefully the necessary information and orders.

The Earth-Mars route had to be cut. From now until SD said all clear, no ship would run in these lanes, or anywhere within a spreading truncated cone that represented the danger volume. No ship would move between Earth and Mars except by the long expensive detour out of the ecliptic. Phil sent the form out to Doris, glad to get it out of sight. As an afterthought, he buzzed her.

"You don't need to worry about your boy friend. He's taking the long way around."

"Thanks a lot, Mr. Brownyard. I guess I won't get his wire for a couple of days, then." She let him break the connection.

Phil paid no attention to her last words for a moment; then the implication sank in. "A couple of days—?" That could mean the *North America* was nearing the danger volume. He began to check.

"Terran Lines? Spatial Debris calling. Message number, July 3357-563.

Get the *North America* off the route, but quick. Never mind, just get her at least eight hundred kilomiles above the ecliptic, or equivalent. This is official. Now get me her position."

A short verification of his authority followed, then the Terran operator relayed the request to the *North America*. The wait was almost fourteen minutes, by which time Phil was visualizing a ship, crushed and shattered, being swept through space by the massive meteor. The Terran man reappeared, looking pale.

"I'll send it over on the writer. We just got the flash from your office, and we're right smack in the middle. I hope you guys know what you're talking about."

"If I were you, I'd hope we didn't," Phil said, and cut off.

He looked in the writer and and got the message. *The* North America *would be making an emergency turn by now,* he thought. *Hope it doesn't take them into the wrong spot at the wrong time.*

Spatial Debris began to hum. Phil had made the first decision; now the rest of the office was busy. A flight on another passenger line was canceled fifteen minutes before take-off—too close! All the robot freight companies were checked and individually warned. On the master chart in Phil's office, little dots accumulated, making a dense stream along the space route. Eight hundred ships, a quarter of them carrying passengers, were diverted. No more than two hours passed before complaints began to roll in by spacegram and by viser.

"I'll lose a good prospect if I don't deliver—"

"Exactly where *is* this meteor—?"

"Why don't you jerks leave us alone? I've been in space thirty years—"

"How long—" (*How long,* Phil thought, *can seventy million miles be?*)

He stood it for half an hour, then had the public line disconnected and received only official and emergency calls. The next call he got was from Terran Lines. The *North America* had reported a brief sight on the meteor, but no data on it; the ship was in its emergency turn. Could she go back on course?

Phil told them to hang on a while. He gave the meteor an approximate position, estimating from the position of the Terran ship. The dot lay far above the danger volume.

"Permission refused. Not the same meteor." Phil switched to video and explained. "It's probably a small, close one, blastable. You can sit easy, though. Your ship's out of danger as long as you keep her north." The Terran agent thanked him, with reservations—canceled reservations, probably.

The meteor's path clung obstinately to the trade route; its progress was measured not in linear kilomiles, but in days, and the days looked to add up to several weeks. Government blasters took off from Mars trying to locate the rock, while Phil started losing sleep.

A week passed. The blasters had returned four times and had hurtled off again. Somewhere out there a six-mile mote was falling toward the Sun, and while electronic nets were spreading, the system was suffering.

"SD STILL SAYS NO!" said one headline; another gently hinted, "FORTY MILLION DOLLARS SO FAR!" The safety bureau took a beating from all sides. Daily, on the financial pages, a little box appeared giving the space-time coordinates of the meteor. As the weeks wore on, the blasters began taking off from bases on Luna, searching doggedly for a grain of sand in a flour bin. By now the danger volume was an impossible ten trillion cubic miles. The thinning stream of ships was flowing almost Ecliptic North from the Earth as Mars approached conjunction. No ship gleamed along the whole free-flight trade orbit. Well—one.

Planetoid 17321 belonged to Terry Carson by virtue of a claim filed in Big Bay, Mars. Terry's ship was resting lightly against the half-mile boulder while Terry was "underground" in his pneumatic hut, tight. 17321 was on the chart in Spatial Debris, and its orbit was known exactly. The fact that it was inside the danger volume was of incidental interest. The fact that there was a man in it would have attracted a good deal more attention; however, Terry's flight plan was crushed somewhere in the works of the crippled East Station.

The tunnel Terry had dug extended forty yards into 17321. The walls were plain rock thirty-six yards of the way, right up to the door of the pneumatic hut. From there on, the pick strokes had flaked off blue-gray chips in isolated spots, spots that came more frequently over the last yard. Terry was sitting inside his rubber-canvas hut, a bottle in one hand and a chunk of pure galena in the other.

"I'm rich," he murmured happily. "Hear that, Carson? You're rich. He's rich, they say. She's rich, it's rich." He let his head drift down on the sleeping bag and chuckled in his belly.

The vein was ninety feet thick, fifty yards across, pure lead sulphide. Terry had been looking for this rock from the time of the Tompkins strike, eighteen years ago. Eleven fragments of a larger planetoid had been found, each containing a segment of lead ore vein. A topologist friend of Terry's had pieced the rocks together on paper. He had found a gap in the vein, and 17321 was the missing piece. Soviet Atomic was currently paying two-fifty a pound for lead, correspondingly for ore. Terry did some figuring.

Terry tilted the bottle again. He whispered: "Maybe a million bucks!" He reached for his portable radio.

If Terry had kept up on current events, he would have known that Earth station KWK had switched off its beam for the duration of the emergency. But then, Terry didn't know there was any emergency. He batted the plastic box, but all that came out was the hiss of the distant stars. The gold leaf showed that the filaments were still active; it indicated that the batteries and electrets were good enough. Terry began to feel uneasy.

He scrambled into his suit, the effect of the alcohol wearing off. Back at the ship, he switched on the long-range radio and fiddled the dial back and forth while the power supply warmed up. Still no KWK. He spun the dial to WLW, and blew out his breath in relief. The familiar reliable time-ticks beeped away, and Terry relaxed and listened. He spun the dial to the MBC—their wide beam inclosed 17321—and he had music. The default of KWK passed quickly from his mind, and he flopped in his bunk and day-dreamed, his fingers twitching now and then as he peeled off a hundred-dollar bill.

At 0645 UT, the news came on. Terry paused in the midst of purchasing an Indo-Venusian palace, sat up gradually, and froze.

". . . The situation is rapidly becoming serious," the commentator was saying. "For the last three weeks, trade has been falling off at an increasing rate. Conjunction is only a month away, and passenger lines are straining at the leash. Nobody wants to travel. The Department of Safety remains obstinate—no direct flights until the meteor is gone. One wonders a little—the government has sent over sixty long-range blasters after the meteor, and there hasn't been one contact. At a time like this, yours truly would be inclined to say, 'Look before you leap.' Are you listening, Mr. B?"

At 0700 the co-ordinates of the meteor were broadcast. Terry was startled to hear how large the uncertainty was, and it was with reluctance that he punched the necessary figures into the computer.

"I'm in it!" he despaired. "They can't do this to me!" But he knew they could. They could send out a blaster after him, leave 17321 unguarded. They could—

If they were coming after him, Terry reasoned, they would have arrived long ago. So, he guessed more or less correctly, his flight plan must have been snarled up in red tape. He chortled, then swallowed his laughter. Sure, he could stay here—but if the meteor hit, by some long chance, he'd lose both his strike *and* his life. He chortled again, uncontrollably, and then giggled.

In an instant he was through the mid-section hatch fumbling with the air-generator. The increasing numbness of his fingers hindered him, and he had to concentrate to remember which way the valve turned. The oxygen-content meter was up to sixty percent. Deliberately, Terry slowed his breathing, and reluctantly bled the ship, running helium into the ship's atmosphere until the oxy meter was back to normal. With a start he noticed that the helium tank was nearly exhausted; then he noticed that the hiss of incoming oxygen was still sounding. Terry's heart wrenched as he stared at the oxygen gauge. He figured quickly—twenty minutes. Twenty minutes! A leak. All the time he had been digging, celebrating, the main air supply had been draining out a puncture. As he watched the gauge needle twitched and came to rest again a fraction of a division from the stop. Terry tapped the dial, watching the needle quiver toward zero. Red flag, air supply gone. He breathed deeply, waited two more minutes, then when he could get no more from his ship's vanishing atmosphere, donned his suit. Four hours of air remained in its tank and regenerator, maybe twelve hours in the hut. Sixteen hours left to breathe. So Terry did what any old hand would have done. He set the distress signal to WLW, beamed it at Earth, and went to sleep. The signal screamed its hundred-megacycle note down the empty space lane, and was lost.

Peter Hedrick, smuggler by trade, watched a cold Alaskan sky darken, and wrote in his log, "0700. Sky becoming overcast. Take-off in thirty minutes. Consignment, Poppy seed to Big Bay." He had a fine load, a big fast ship and a space lane all to himself—almost. One meteor was worth chancing. He snapped the log shut and strolled toward the camouflaged ship.

"My dear," Mrs. Ashton confided to the private telescreen, "I know just how you feel. Now don't worry a bit. After all, your John always did like to have his little flings, and everyone understands. He'll be back. And I wouldn't worry too much. Peter says he has it from a very good source that this whole thing is just another meteor scare."

The screen babbled back briefly.

"All right," Mrs. Ashton smiled. "I'll surely let you know. Bye-bye." She cut off the screen and let the smile become a smirk. Mrs. Phelps' superb husband was in his private yacht somewhere between here and Mars, and everyone but Mrs. Phelps knew he had company. For a few moments, Mrs. Ashton considered the dramatic possibilities in Mr. Phelps and his yacht being crushed by the meteor, but not beyond recognition.

Phil Brownyard was beginning to repress all optimism concerning the position of the meteor. The failure of the blasters to locate it gave pretty good odds that it was well out of the volume assigned to it, and that meant out of the shipping lanes. But there was always one chance. Phil merely shoved the other nine hundred ninety-nine out of his consciousness and clung to that one.

He got to the office early the twenty-eighth day after the alert. There was no sense in sitting at home in the dark, so he opened the office at 0725. The reports were still the same—no contact. The black line on the chart extended now from Mars to within two million miles of Earth. Half a day at the most before Luna would pick up whatever was there. Phil gave a nervous yawn.

The clock crept laboriously to 0730. Phil doodled on a pad, drawing daggers and ominous blots. 0731. He got up and looked out the window at the city, noting the beauty of the towers in the early morning light. 0732. Out in the corridor messenger cars whipped back and forth; all the building was alive except for Spatial Debris and a few others. Phil sat in his soundproofed office and bit the end off a cigar. Paper rustled as he propped his elbows on the desk.

At 0734, the telescreen shrieked. Phil jumped, dropping his cigar. Before the automatic dial could switch the call to his home, he flipped the toggle and leaned forward.

"Brownyard?" A switchboard operator stared sleepily at him.

"Yeah, who is it?"

"Mr. Cushing of Terran Lines, collect. Will you accept the call?"

"Go ahead."

Cushing's face blurred too close to the pickup lens. "Brownyard, we've found your meteor!" He roared. "It just hit the *North America*!" The screen blanked out.

Instantly it came to life again. An excited young man appeared and stammered, "North Station Luna calling. Meteor 842M2055 detected. Co-ordinates and orbit follow."

Phil acknowledged automatically, knowing it was too late. Switching to another band, he called the night Safety office. His stomach knotted, and hurt.

"What's this about the *North America*?" he asked Jim Shepard.

"Oh . . . you, Phil. Well, she's hit all right. Taking off for Stag Head. Collided at sixty-eight thousand miles; almost nothing left. The patrols are going after her now."

"O.K." Phil started to sign off, then tensed. "Hey . . . hey—!"

"Yeah?" Jim reappeared, his face sympathetic.

"What did you say her distance was?"

"Sixty-eight kilomiles. Why, do you think—?"

"You bet!" Phil stiffened his aching back and went to work. "That couldn't have been our baby. I just got a contact report from Luna, and I was still convinced that 842 had got the *North America*. Let's get busy—here are the co-ordinates." Phil dug into the writer and came up with the message card. He stuck it into the slot under the screen, received the acknowledgment, and cut off. His hands were shaking badly.

How many hours to work? Phil retrieved the card and scanned it, then went to the chart and plotted the point. Nine hundred and eighty kilometers. That left—nine hours. Only nine hours for the blasters to try to match velocities, nine hours to— Phil tightened inside as the curvator started forward to trace a new black line. It swept inside the orbit of the Moon, straight into the green disk that was Earth. The crimson light went on.

He had known it would end this way, for a long time. From the instant he had deciphered the first flash, he had had a funny feeling; he had known that the danger volume would sweep over Earth, but he had hoped for just a little more luck, one little favor from the laws of probability. The invisible fingers of Earth tugged, and the great rock obeyed.

Trembling with tension, Phil called Computing and got them to work. In half an hour the answer returned. The west coast of the European continent would be hit; it would take three hours to pinpoint the spot.

Phil frowned and rubbed his forehead. It was silly to feel this way, of course. He had carried out his duties as well as he could—a thousand ships had been warned, the space lanes had been held clear. But he felt a sense of responsibility that he could not shake.

At eleven fifteen Fred Holland walked in holding a card. "Here it is. We've got it down to a twenty-mile circle in southwestern France. Impact time is 1618." He dropped the card on the desk. "Look, Phil, there's nothing you can do that you haven't done."

"One more thing." Phil took the card without looking at it and sent it to the main Safety office. "Now I can resign."

"This is Jim, Phil. The *North America* was hit by an unscheduled ship that took off from Alaska somewhere. What's the dope on the meteor? I heard it's bad."

"Yeah. Southwestern France, somewhere." Phil wondered vaguely about the identity of the other ship. For some reason, the feeling of guilt grew stronger. "Any survivors?" he asked.

And his heart did not change its pace when Jim said, "No."

Thirteen hundred, and the hourly news. Phil listened dully as the reports came in from the reopened space lanes. A private yacht had been sighted cruising illegally in the lane. Some scandal or other impended. Planetoid 17321 left the lane and the gap caused by its presence closed. Collision near Mars in the rush to take advantage of approaching conjunction. Stag Head Station operative again. On and on.

The meteor was between Earth and the Moon, now, its pace quickening. In two more hours and some minutes it would rocket into Earth's atmosphere; incandescent and thundering it would smash into France with a towering splash of earth, rock and living things. Ten million refugees streamed along the roads leading out of that imaginary circle, quiet and terrified, peering into the luminous afternoon sky. Police were thick in the mobs, suppressing panic.

Phil quit listening to the news at 1500. He busied himself around the office, collecting papers accumulated over the past eight years.

Maybe I can afford to retire. That would be nice. Get away, at any rate. Maybe Claire would like Venus.

He came on the computations he had made, those about the mass of the meteor. A strange hope kindled, but the figures were right. He began to fill his briefcase. As he started to leave, he looked long at the clock. Twelve minutes. As the door shut, a card in its capsule bumped against the end of the pneumatic tube. The punchings on it indicated that a distress signal had been picked up from somewhere near the trade route.

Eight years ago, a meteor had got by the warning net—another big one. That one had smashed into a loaded passenger liner, and the disaster had broken Phil's predecessor. Now Phil had to watch an even worse disaster— had watched it from its first remote beginnings.

He sat in a subway train, holding a newspaper and looking at his watch. Not many people were in the car—most of them were sitting by television screens, watching France with morbid anticipation. The car whistled past a few deserted stops and began to brake. The minute hand on Phil's watch crept over the ten, past it, while Phil read the billboards.

Two minutes. The train started smoothly, went quickly to maximum velocity, then slowed for Phil's stop.

"Phil—is that you? Hey, Phil?"

He looked up blindly, then glanced out the window. The end of the line. Must have missed my stop. Claire will be worried—

"Hey, Phil—" Fred stopped by the hunched figure. "Come on, Phil, I'll take you home in my car."

It was pleasant to lie in bed and only half-think. The sun shone warmly in the window and the sky was blue. Phil smiled and stretched. Then his head swung to the window—the sun was too high! It must be noon! He started to get up, and felt an overpowering lassitude cloud his mind. He lay back and thought, *They'll call me if they need me.* The dusk swirled around him and he relaxed in it again.

The second time he woke he felt his mind gradually coming to life. Bit by bit, his senses returned. The covers were too warm—it was dark again—someone was in the room.

"Claire?" A sense of panic stirred him.

"Quiet, darling. How do you feel?"

"All right, I guess. What time is it?" He relaxed.

"Nineteen thirty. Are you—all right?" Her voice showed strain.

"Sure, honey. Turn on the video, will you?" Claire turned, tears of relief in her eyes.

"All right. Fred wants to see you." She stopped at the door and smiled at him. "We were worried about you, darling."

Phil got up as soon as she had left and went to her dressing table. In the mirror his face was puffed with sleep and lined by long fatigue. He heard Fred coming and got back into bed.

Fred came over to the bed and grinned down at Phil. "Boy, you look like hell."

Phil found himself grinning back, feeling better. "I sure blew myself to a tantrum."

"The doctor said human beings still have to sleep now and then."

"What about the meteor?"

Fred sat back and looked quizzically at Phil. "Still think it must have been your fault?"

"No . . . I guess not. No."

"Well, then, you'll blow your cork when you hear." Phil's heart started pounding violently.

"It came in, all right, right where we planted it," Fred said. "Only it burned up before it got through fifty miles of atmosphere. What a show!"

"Did they blast it?" Phil sat up in bed.

"Nope. Same meteor Luna spotted. Only those kids on Luna never thought to check on the mass. It weighed just a little over half a ton, and blew up halfway down."

"But where's 842? Are the lanes still cleared?"

"Eight forty-two? Nobody knows. T. V. McPherson says he found some big gouges out of Deimos that look recent. Your baby is probably way, way south by now, according to him."

Phil began to laugh.

"What's the matter?"

"Nothing. Just struck me funny. I've been losing sleep over a ghost of a meteor for a whole month. Nine hundred and ninety-nine chances, and I had to take the one left over. Look . . . I'll see you tomorrow . . . come over for dinner. Right now, I'm going back to sleep. Excuse me." He rolled onto his side and began to drift off. As Fred reached out to turn off the video, the announcer was saying something about a prospector; something about a prospector who might have been lost if a patrol craft hadn't chased a yacht into his failing distress beam. But before Phil could get it straight, he fell asleep.

First published: 1950

LAST ENEMY

by H. Beam Piper

ALONG THE U-SHAPED TABLE, THE SUBDUED CLATTER OF DINNERWARE AND the buzz of conversation was dying out; the soft music that drifted down from the overhead sound outlets seemed louder as the competing noises diminished. The feast was drawing to a close, and Dallona of Hadron fidgeted nervously with the stem of her wineglass as last-moment doubts assailed her.

The old man at whose right she sat noticed, and reached out to lay his hand on hers.

"My dear, you're worried," he said softly. "You, of all people, shouldn't be, you know."

"The theory isn't complete," she replied. "And I could wish for more positive verification. I'd hate to think I'd got you into this—"

Garnon of Roxor laughed. "No, no!" he assured her. "I'd decided upon this long before you announced the results of your experiments. Ask Girzon; he'll bear me out."

"That's true," the young man who sat at Garnon's left said, leaning forward. "Father has meant to take this step for a long time. He was waiting until after the election, and then he decided to do it now, to give you an opportunity to make experimental use of it."

The man on Dallona's right added his voice. Like the others at the table, he was of medium stature, brown-skinned and dark-eyed, with a wide mouth, prominent cheek-bones and a short, square jaw. Unlike the others, he was armed, with a knife and pistol on his belt, and on the breast of his black tunic he wore a scarlet oval patch on which a pair of black wings, with a tapering silver object between them had been superimposed.

"Yes, Lady Dallona; the Lord Garnon and I discussed this, oh, two years ago at the least. Really, I'm surprised that you seem to shrink from

506

it, now. Of course, you're Venus-born, and customs there may be different, but with your scientific knowledge—"

"That may be the trouble, Dirzed," Dallona told him. "A scientist gets in the way of doubting, and one doubts one's own theories most of all."

"That's the scientific attitude, I'm told," Dirzed replied, smiling. "But somehow, I cannot think of you as a scientist." His eyes traveled over her in a way that would have made most women, scientists or otherwise, blush. It gave Dallona of Hadron a feeling of pleasure. Men often looked at her that way, especially here at Darsh. Novelty had something to do with it—her skin was considerably lighter than usual, and there was a pleasing oddness about the structure of her face. Her alleged Venusian origin was probably accepted as the explanation of that, as of so many other things.

As she was about to reply, a man in dark gray, one of the upper-servants who were accepted as social equals by the Akor-Neb nobles, approached the table. He nodded respectfully to Garnon of Roxor.

"I hate to seem to hurry things, sir, but the boy's ready. He's in a trance-state now," he reported, pointing to the pair of visiplates at the end of the room.

Both of the ten-foot-square plates were activated. One was a solid luminous white; on the other was the image of a boy of twelve or fourteen, seated at a big writing machine. Even allowing for the fact that the boy was in a hypnotic trance, there was an expression of idiocy on his loose-lipped, slack-jawed face, a pervading dullness.

"One of our best sensitives," a man with a beard, several places down the table on Dallona's right, said. "You remember him, Dallona; he produced that communication from the discarnate Assassin, Sirzim. Normally, he's a low-grade imbecile, but in trance-state he's wonderful. And there can be no argument that the communications he produces originate in his own mind; he doesn't have mind enough, of his own, to operate that machine."

Garnon of Roxor rose to his feet, the others rising with him. He unfastened a jewel from the front of his tunic and handed it to Dallona.

"Here, my dear Lady Dallona; I want you to have this," he said. "It's been in the family of Roxor for six generations, but I know that you will appreciate and cherish it." He twisted a heavy ring from his left hand and gave it to his son. He unstrapped his wrist watch and passed it across the table to the gray-clad upper-servant. He gave a pocket case, containing writing tools, slide rule and magnifier, to the bearded man on the other side of Dallona. "Something you can use, Dr. Harnosh," he said. Then he took a belt, with a knife and holstered pistol, from a servant who had brought it to him, and gave it to the man with the red badge. "And something for you, Dirzed. The pistol's by Farnor of Yand, and the knife was forged and tempered on Luna."

The man with the winged-bullet badge took the weapons, exclaiming in appreciation. Then he removed his own belt and buckled on the gift.

"The pistol's fully loaded," Garnon told him.

Dirzed drew it and checked—a man of his craft took no statement about weapons without verification—then slipped it back into the holster.

"Shall I use it?" he asked.

"By all means; I'd had that in mind when I selected it for you."

Another man, to the left of Girzon, received a cigarette case and lighter. He and Garnon hooked fingers and clapped shoulders.

. "Our views haven't been the same, Garnon," he said, "but I've always valued your friendship. I'm sorry you're doing this, now; I believe you'll be disappointed."

Garnon chuckled. "Would you care to make a small wager on that, Nirzav?" he asked. "You know what I'm putting up. If I'm proven right, will you accept the Volitionalist theory as verified?"

Nirzav chewed his mustache for a moment. "Yes, Garnon, I will." He pointed toward the blankly white screen. "If we get anything conclusive on that, I'll have no other choice."

"All right, friends," Garnon said to those around him. "Will you walk with me to the end of the room?"

Servants removed a section from the table in front of him, to allow him and a few others to pass through; the rest of the guests remained standing at the table, facing toward the inside of the room. Garnon's son, Girzon, and the gray-mustached Nirzav of Shonna, walked on his left; Dallona of Hadron and Dr. Harnosh of Hosh on his right. The gray-clad upper-servant, and two or three ladies, and a nobleman with a small chin-beard, and several others, joined them; of those who had sat close to Garnon, only the man in the black tunic with the scarlet badge hung back. He stood still, by the break in the table, watching Garnon of Roxor walk away from him. Then Dirzed the Assassin drew the pistol he had lately received as a gift, hefted it in his hand, thumbed off the safety, and aimed at the back of Garnon's head.

They had nearly reached the end of the room when the pistol cracked. Dallona of Hadron started, almost as though the bullet had crashed into her own body, then caught herself and kept on walking. She closed her eyes and laid a hand on Dr. Harnosh's arm for guidance, concentrating her mind upon a single question. The others went on as though Garnon of Roxor were still walking among them.

"Look!" Harnosh of Hosh cried, pointing to the image in the visiplate ahead. "He's under control!"

They all stopped short, and Dirzed, holstering his pistol, hurried forward to join them. Behind, a couple of servants had approached with a stretcher and were gathering up the crumpled figure that had, a moment ago, been Garnon.

A change had come over the boy at the writing machine. His eyes were still glazed with the stupor of the hypnotic trance, but the slack jaw had stiffened, and the loose mouth was compressed in a purposeful line. As they watched, his hands went out to the keyboard in front of him and began to move over it, and as they did, letters appeared on the white screen on the left.

Garnon of Roxor, discarnate, communicating, they read. The machine stopped for a moment, then began again. *To Dallona of Hadron: The question you asked, after I discarnated, was: What was the last book I read, before the feast? While waiting for my valet to prepare my bath, I read the first ten verses of the Fourth Canto of "Splendor of Space," by Larnov of Horka, in my bedroom. When the bath was ready, I marked the page with a strip of message tape, containing a message from the bailiff of my estate on the Shevva River, concerning a break-down at the powerplant, and laid the book on the ivory-inlaid table beside the big red chair.*

Harnosh of Hosh looked at Dallona inquiringly; she nodded.

"I rejected the question I had in my mind, and substituted that one, after the shot," she said.

He turned quickly to the upper-servant. "Check on that, right away, Kirzon," he directed.

As the upper-servant hurried out, the writing machine started again.

And to my son, Girzon: I will not use your son, Garnon, as a reincarnation-vehicle; I will remain discarnate until he is grown and has a son of his own; if he has no male child, I will reincarnate in the first available male child of the family of Roxor, or of some family allied to us by marriage. In any case, I will communicate before reincarnating.

To Nirzav of Shonna: Ten days ago, when I dined at your home, I took a small knife and cut three notches, two close together and one a little apart from the others, on the under side of the table. As I remember, I sat two places down on the left. If you find them, you will know that I have won that wager that I spoke of a few minutes ago.

"I'll have my butler check on that, right away," Nirzav said. His eyes were wide with amazement, and he had begun to sweat; a man does not casually watch the beliefs of a lifetime invalidated in a few moments.

To Dirzed the Assassin: the machine continued. *You have served me faithfully, in the last ten years, never more so than with the last shot you fired in my service. After you fired, the thought was in your mind that you would like to take service with the Lady Dallona of Hadron, whom you believe will need the protection of a member of the Society of Assassins. I advise you to do so, and I advise her to accept your offer. Her work, since she has come to Darsh, has not made her popular in some quarters. No doubt Nirzav of Shonna can bear me out on that.*

"I won't betray things told me in confidence, or said at the Councils of the Statisticalists, but he's right," Nirzav said. "You need a good Assassin, and there are few better than Dirzed."

I see that this sensitive is growing weary, the letters on the screen spelled out. *His body is not strong enough for prolonged communication. I bid you all farewell, for the time; I will communicate again. Good evening, my friends, and I thank you for your presence at the feast.*

The boy, on the other screen, slumped back in his chair, his face relaxing into its customary expression of vacancy.

"Will you accept my offer of service, Lady Dallona?" Dirzed asked. "It's as Garnon said; you've made enemies."

Dallona smiled at him. "I've not been too deep in my work to know that. I'm glad to accept your offer, Dirzed."

Nirzav of Shonna had already turned away from the group and was hurrying from the room, to call his home for confirmation on the notches made on the underside of his dining table. As he went out the door, he almost collided with the upper-servant, who was rushing in with a book in his hand.

"Here it is," the latter exclaimed, holding up the book. "Larnov's 'Splendor of Space,' just where he said it would be. I had a couple of servants with me as witnesses; I can call them in now, if you wish." He handed the book to Harnosh of Hosh. "See, a strip of message tape in it, at the tenth verse of the Fourth Canto."

Nirzav of Shonna re-entered the room; he was chewing his mustache and muttering to himself. As he rejoined the group in front of the now dark visiplates, he raised his voice, addressing them all generally.

"My butler found the notches, just as the communication described," he said. "This settles it! Garnon, if you're where you can hear me, you've won. I can't believe in the Statisticalist doctrines after this, or in the political program based upon them. I'll announce my change of attitude at the next meeting of the Executive Council, and resign my seat. I was elected by Statisticalist votes, and I cannot hold office as a Volitionalist."

"You'll need a couple of Assassins, too," the nobleman with the chin-beard told him. "Your former colleagues and fellow-party-members are regrettably given to the forcible discarnation of those who differ with them."

"I've never employed personal Assassins before," Nirzav replied, "but I think you're right. As soon as I get home, I'll call Assassins' Hall and make the necessary arrangements."

"Better do it now," Girzon of Roxor told him, lowering his voice. "There are over a hundred guests here, and I can't vouch for all of them. The Statisticalists would be sure to have a spy planted among them. My father was one of their most dangerous opponents, when he was on the Council; they've always been afraid he'd come out of retirement and stand for re-election. They'd want to make sure he was really discarnate. And if that's the case, you can be sure your change of attitude is known to old Mirzark of Bashad by this time. He won't dare allow you to make a public renunciation of Statisticalism." He turned to the other nobleman. "Prince Jirzyn, why don't you call the Volitionalist headquarters and have a couple of our Assassins sent here to escort Lord Nirzav home?"

"I'll do that immediately," Jirzyn of Starpha said. "It's as Lord Girzon says; we can be pretty sure there was a spy among the guests, and now that you've come over to our way of thinking, we're responsible for your safety."

He left the room to make the necessary visiphone call. Dallona, accompanied by Dirzed, returned to her place at the table, where she was joined by Harnosh of Hosh and some of the others.

"There's no question about the results," Harnosh was exulting. "I'll grant that the boy might have picked up some of that stuff telepathically from the carnate minds present here; even from the mind of Garnon, before he was discarnated. But he could not have picked up enough data, in that way, to make a connected and coherent communication. It takes a sensitive with a powerful mind of his own to practice telesthesia, and that boy's almost an idiot." He turned to Dallona. "You asked a question, mentally, after Garnon was discarnate, and got an answer that could have been contained only in Garnon's mind. I think it's conclusive proof that the discarnate Garnon was fully conscious and communicating."

"Dirzed also asked a question, mentally, after the discarnation, and got an answer. Dr. Harnosh, we can state positively that the surviving individuality is fully conscious in the discarnate state, is telepathically sensitive, and is capable of telepathic communication with other minds,"

Dallona agreed. "And in view of our earlier work with memory-recalls, we're justified in stating positively that the individual is capable of exercising choice in reincarnation vehicles."

"My father had been considering voluntary discarnation for a long time," Girzon of Roxor said. "Ever since the discarnation of my mother. He deferred that step because he was unwilling to deprive the Volitionalist Party of his support. Now it would seem that he has done more to combat Statisticalism by discarnating than he ever did in his carnate existence."

"I don't know, Girzon," Jirzyn of Starpha said, as he joined the group. "The Statisticalists will denounce the whole thing as a prearranged fraud. And if they can discarnate the Lady Dallona before she can record her testimony under truth hypnosis or on a lie detector, we're no better off than we were before. Dirzed, you have a great responsibility in guarding the Lady Dallona; some extraordinary security precautions will be needed."

In his office, in the First Level city of Dhergabar, Tortha Karf, Chief of Paratime Police, leaned forward in his chair to hold his lighter for his special assistant, Verkan Vall, then lit his own cigarette. He was a man of middle age—his three hundredth birthday was only a decade or so off—and he had begun to acquire a double chin and a bulge at his waistline. His hair, once black, had turned a uniform iron-gray and was beginning to thin in front.

"What do you know about the Second Level Akor-Neb Sector, Vall?" he inquired. "Ever work in that paratime-area?"

Verkan Vall's handsome features became even more immobile than usual as he mentally pronounced the verbal trigger symbols which should bring hypnotically-acquired knowledge into his conscious mind. Then he shook his head.

"Must be a singularly well-behaved sector, sir," he said. "Or else we've been lucky, so far. I never was on an Akor-Neb operation; don't even have a hypno-mech for that sector. All I know is from general reading.

"Like all the Second Level, its time-lines descend from the probability of one or more shiploads of colonists having come to Terra from Mars about seventy-five to a hundred thousand years ago, and then having been cut off from the home planet and forced to develop a civilization of their own here. The Akor-Neb civilization is of a fairly high cultureorder, even for Second Level. An atomic-power, interplanetary culture; gravity-counteraction, direct conversion of nuclear energy to electrical power, that sort of thing. We buy fine synthetic plastics and fabrics from them." He fingered the material of his smartly-cut green police uniform. "I think this cloth is Akor-Neb. We sell a lot of Venusian *zerfa*-leaf; they smoke it, straight and mixed with tobacco. They have a single System-wide government, a single race, and a universal language. They're a dark-brown race, which evolved in its present form about fifty thousand years ago; the present civilization is about ten thousand years old, developed out of the wreckage of several earlier civilizations which decayed or fell through wars, exhaustion of resources, et cetera. They have legends, maybe historical records, of their extraterrestrial origin "

Tortha Karf nodded. "Pretty good, for consciously acquired knowledge," he commented. "Well, our luck's run out, on that sector; we have troubles there, now. I want you to go iron them out. I know, you've been going pretty hard, lately—that nightbound business, on the Fourth Level Europo-American Sector, wasn't any picnic. But the fact is that a lot of my ordinary and deputy assistants have a little too much regard for the alleged sanctity of human life, and this is something that may need some pretty drastic action."

"Some of our people getting out of line?" Verkan Vall asked.

"Well, the data isn't too complete, but one of our people has run into trouble on that sector, and needs rescuing—a psychic-science researcher, a young lady named Hadron Dalla. I believe you know her, don't you?" Tortha Karf asked innocently.

"Slightly," Verkan Vall dead-panned. "I enjoyed a brief but rather hectic companionate-marriage with her, about twenty years ago. What sort of a jam's little Dalla got herself into, now?"

"Well, frankly, we don't know. I hope she's still alive, but I'm not un-duly optimistic. It seems that about a year ago, Dr. Hadron transposed to the Second Level to study alleged proof of reincarnation which the Akor-Neb people were reported to possess. She went to Gindrabar, on Venus, and transposed to the Second Paratime Level, to a station maintained by Outtime Import & Export Trading Corporation—a *zerfa* plantation just east of the High Ridge country. There she assumed an identity as the daughter of a planter, and took the name of Dallona of Hadron. Paren-thetically, all Akor-Neb family-names are prepositional; family-names were originally place names. I believe that ancient Akor-Neb marital re-lations were too complicated to permit exact establishment of paternity. And all Akor-Neb men's personal names have -*irz*- or -*arn*- inserted in the middle, and women's names end in -*itra*- or -*ona*. You could call yourself Virzal of Verkan, for instance.

"Anyhow, she made the Second Level Venus-Terra trip on a regular passenger liner, and landed at the Akor-Neb city of Ghamma, on the upper Nile. There she established contact with the Outtime Trading Corporation representative, Zortan Brend, locally known as Brarnend of Zorda. He couldn't call himself Brarnend of Zortan—in the Akor-Neb language, zortan is a particularly nasty dirty-word. Hadron Dalla spent a few weeks at his residence, briefing herself on local conditions. Then she went to the capital city, Darsh, in eastern Europe, and enrolled as a student at something called the Independent Institute for Reincarnation Research, having secured a letter of introduction to its director, a Dr. Harnosh of Hosh.

"Almost at once, she began sending in reports to her home organization, the Rhogom Memorial Foundation of Psychic Science, here at Dhergabar, through Zortan Brend. The people there were wildly enthusiastic. I don't have more than the average intelligent—I hope—layman's knowledge of psychics, but Dr. Volzar Darv, the director of Rhogom Foundation, tells me that even in the present incomplete form, her reports have opened whole new horizons in the science. It seems that these Akor-Neb people have actually demonstrated, as a scientific fact, that the human individuality reincarnates after physical death—that your personality, and mine, have existed, as such, for ages, and will exist for ages to come. More, they have means of recovering, from almost anybody, memories of past reincarnations.

"Well, after about a month, the people at this Reincarnation Institute realized that this Dallona of Hadron wasn't any ordinary student. She probably had trouble keeping down to the local level of psychic knowledge. So, as soon as she'd learned their techniques, she was allowed to undertake experimental work of her own. I imagine she let herself out on that; as soon as she'd mastered the standard Akor-Neb methods of recovering memories of past reincarnations, she began refining and developing them more than the local yokels had been able to do in the past thousand years. I can't tell you just what she did, because I don't know the subject, but she must have lit things up properly. She got quite a lot of local publicity; not only scientific journals, but general newscasts.

"Then, four days ago, she disappeared, and her disappearance seems to have been coincident with an unsuccessful attempt on her life. We don't know as much about this as we should; all we have is Zortan Brend's account.

"It seems that on the evening of her disappearance, she had been attending the voluntary discarnation feast—suicide party—of a prominent nobleman named Garnon of Roxor. Evidently when the Akor-Neb people get tired of their current reincarnation they invite in their friends, throw a big party, and then do themselves in in an atmosphere of general conviviality. Frequently they take poison or inhale lethal gas; this fellow had his personal trigger man shoot him through the head. Dalla was one of the guests of honor, along with this Harnosh of Hosh. They'd made rather elaborate preparations, and after the shooting they got a detailed and apparently authentic spirit-communication from the late Garnon. The voluntary discarnation was just a routine social event, it seems, but the communication caused quite an uproar, and rated top place on the System-wide newscasts, and started a storm of controversy.

"After the shooting and the communication, Dalla took the officiating gun artist, one Dirzed, into her own service. This Dirzed was spoken of as a generally respected member of something called the Society of Assassins, and that'll give you an idea of what things are like on that sector, and why I don't want to send anybody who might develop trigger-finger cramp at the wrong moment. She and Dirzed left the home of the gentleman who had just had himself discarnated, presumably for Dalla's apartment, about a hundred miles away. That's the last that's been heard of either of them.

"This attempt on Dalla's life occurred while the pre-mortem revels were still going on. She lived in a six-room apartment, with three servants, on one of the upper floors of a three-thousand-foot tower—Akor-Neb cities are built vertically, with considerable interval between units—and while she was at this feast, a package was delivered at the apartment, ostensibly from the Reincarnation Institute and made up to look as though it contained record tapes. One of the servants accepted it from a service employee of the apartments. The next morning, a little before noon, Dr. Harnosh of Hosh called her on the visiphone and got no answer; he then called the apartment manager, who entered the apartment. He found all three of the servants dead, from a lethal-gas bomb which had exploded when one of them had opened this package. However, Hadron Dalla had never returned to the apartment, the night before."

Verkan Vall was sitting motionless, his face expressionless as he ran Tortha Karf's narrative through the intricate semantic and psychological processes of the First Level mentality. The fact that Hadron Dalla had been a former wife of his had been relegated to one corner of his consciousness and contained there; it was not a fact that would, at the moment, contribute to the problem or to his treatment of it.

"The package was delivered while she was at this suicide party," he considered. "It must, therefore, have been sent by somebody who either did not know she would be out of the apartment, or who did not expect it to function until after her return. On the other hand, if her disappearance was due to hostile action, it was the work of somebody who knew she was at the feast and did not want her to reach her apartment again. This would seem to exclude the sender of the package bomb."

Tortha Karf nodded. He had reached that conclusion, himself.

"Thus," Verkan Vall continued, "if her disappearance was the work of an enemy, she must have two enemies, each working in ignorance of the other's plans."

"What do you think she did to provoke such enmity?"

"Well, of course, it just might be that Dalla's normally complicated love-life had got a little more complicated than usual and short-circuited on her," Verkan Vall said, out of the fullness of personal knowledge, "but I doubt that, at the moment. I would think that this affair has political implications."

"So?" Tortha Karf had not thought of politics as an explanation. He waited for Verkan Vall to elaborate.

"Don't you see, chief?" the special assistant asked. "We find a belief in reincarnation on many time-lines, as a religious doctrine, but these people accept it as a scientific fact. Such acceptance would carry much more conviction; it would influence a people's entire thinking. We see it reflected in their disregard for death—suicide as a social function, this Society of Assassins, and the like. It would naturally color their political thinking, because politics is nothing but common action to secure more favorable living conditions, and to these people, the term 'living conditions' includes not only the present life, but also an indefinite number of future lives as well. I find this title, 'Independent' Institute, suggestive. Independent of what? Possibly of partisan affiliation."

"But wouldn't these people be grateful to her for her new discoveries, which would enable them to plan their future reincarnations more intelligently?" Tortha Karf asked.

"Oh, chief!" Verkan Vall reproached. "You know better than that! How many times have our people got in trouble on other time-lines because they divulged some useful scientific fact that conflicted with the locally revered nonsense? You show me ten men who cherish some religious doctrine or political ideology, and I'll show you nine men whose minds are utterly impervious to any factual evidence which contradicts their beliefs, and who regard the producer of such evidence as a criminal who ought to be suppressed. For instance, on the Fourth Level Europo-American Sector, where I was just working, there is a political sect, the Communists, who, in the territory under their control, forbid the teaching of certain well-established facts of genetics and heredity, because those facts do not fit the world-picture demanded by their political doctrines. And on the same sector, a religious sect recently tried, in some sections successfully, to outlaw the teaching of evolution by natural selection."

Tortha Karf nodded. "I remember some stories my grandfather told me, about his narrow escapes from an organization called the Holy Inquisition, when he was a paratime trader on the Fourth Level, about four hundred years ago. I believe that thing's still operating, on the Europo-American Sector, under the name of the NKVD. So you think Dalla may have proven something that conflicted with local reincarnation theories, and somebody who had a vested interest in maintaining those theories is trying to stop her?"

"You spoke of a controversy over the communication alleged to have originated with this voluntarily discarnated nobleman. That would suggest a difference of opinion on the manner of nature of reincarnation or the discarnate state. This difference may mark the dividing line between the different political parties. Now, to get to this Darsh place, do I have to go to Venus, as Dalla did?"

"No. The Outtime Trading Corporation has transposition facilities at Ravvanan, on the Nile, which is spatially co-existent with the city of Ghamma on the Akor-Neb Sector, where Zortan Brend is. You transpose through there, and Zortan Brend will furnish you transportation to Darsh. It'll take you about two days, here, getting your hypno-mech indoctrinations and having your skin pigmented, and your hair turned black. I'll notify Zortan Brend at once that you're coming through. Is there anything special you'll want?"

"Why, I'll want an abstract of the reports Dalla sent back to Rhogom Foundation. It's likely that there is some clue among them as to whom her discoveries may have antagonized. I'm going to be a Venusian *zerfa*-planter, a friend of her father's; I'll want full hypno-mech indoctrination to enable me to play that part. And I'll want to familiarize myself with Akor-Neb weapons and combat techniques. I think that will be all, chief."

The last of the tall city-units of Ghamma were sliding out of sight as the ship passed over them—shaft-like buildings that rose two or three thousand feet above the ground in clumps of three or four or six, one at each corner of the landing stages set in series between them. Each of these units stood in the middle of a wooded park some five miles square; no unit was much more or less than twenty miles from its nearest neighbor, and the land between was the uniform golden-brown of ripening grain, crisscrossed with the threads of irrigation canals and dotted here and there with studdy farm-village buildings and tall, stacklike granaries. There were a few other ships in the air at the fifty-thousand-foot level, and below, swarms of small airboats darted back and forth on different levels, depending upon speed and direction. Far ahead, to the northeast, was the shimmer of the Red Sea and the hazy bulk of Asia Minor beyond.

Verkan Vall—the Lord Virzal of Verkan, temporarily—stood at the glass front of the observation deck, looking down. He was a different Verkan Vall from the man who had talked with Tortha Karf in the latter's office, two days before. The First Level cosmeticists had worked miracles upon him with their art. His skin was a soft chocolate-brown, now; his hair was jet-black, and so were his eyes. And in his subconscious mind, instantly available to consciousness, was a vast body of knowledge about conditions on the Akor-Neb sector, as well as a complete command of the local language, all hypnotically acquired.

He knew that he was looking down upon one of the minor provincial cities of a very respectably advanced civilization. A civilization which built its cities vertically, since it had learned to counteract gravitation. A civilization which still depended upon natural cereals for food, but one which had learned to make the most efficient use of its soil. The network of dams and irrigation canals which he saw was as good as anything on his own paratime level. The wide dispersal of buildings, he knew, was a heritage of a series of disastrous atomic wars of several thousand years before; the Akor-Neb people had come to love the wide inter-vistas of open country and forest, and had continued to scatter their buildings, even after the necessity had passed. But the slim, towering buildings could only have been reared by a people who had banished nationalism and, with it, the threat of total war. He contrasted them with the ground-hugging dome cities of the Khiftan civilization, only a few thousand para-years distant.

Three men came out of the lounge behind him and joined him. One was, like himself, a disguised paratimer from the First Level—the Outtime Export and Import man, Zortan Brend, here known as Brarnend of Zorda. The other two were Akor-Neb people, and both wore the black tunics and the winged-bullet badges of the Society of Assassins. Unlike Verkan Vall and Zortan Brend, who wore shoulder holsters under their short tunics, the Assassins openly displayed pistols and knives on their belts.

"We heard that you were coming two days ago, Lord Virzal," Zortan Brend said. "We delayed the take-off of this ship, so that you could travel to Darsh as inconspicuously as possible. I also booked a suite for you at the Solar Hotel, at Darsh. And these are your Assassins—Olirzon, and Marnik."

Verkan Vall hooked fingers and clapped shoulders with them.

"Virzal of Verkan," he identified himself. "I am satisfied to intrust myself to you."

"We'll do our best for you, Lord Virzal," the older of the pair, Olirzon, said. He hesitated for a moment, then continued: "Understand, Lord Virzal, I only ask for information useful in serving and protecting you. But is this of the Lady Dallona a political matter?"

"Not from our side," Verkan Vall told him. "The Lady Dallona is a scientist, entirely nonpolitical. The Honorable Brarnend is a business man; he doesn't meddle with politics as long as the politicians leave him alone. And I'm a planter on Venus; I have enough troubles, with the natives, and the weather, and blue-rot in the *zerfa* plants, and poison roaches, and javelin bugs, without getting into politics. But psychic science is inextricably mixed with politics, and the Lady Dallona's work had evidently tended to discredit the theory of Statistical Reincarnation."

"Do you often make understatements like that, Lord Virzal?" Olirzon grinned. "In the last six months, she's knocked Statistical Reincarnation to splinters."

"Well, I'm not a psychic scientist, and as I said, I don't know much about Terran politics," Verkan Vall replied. "I know that the Statisticalists favor complete socialization and political control of the whole economy, because they want everybody to have the same opportunities in every reincarnation. And the Volitionalists believe that everybody reincarnates as he pleases, and so they favor continuance of the present system of private ownership of wealth and private profit under a system of free competition. And that's about all I do know. Naturally, as a landowner and the holder of a title of nobility, I'm a Volitionalist in politics, but the socialization issue isn't important on Venus. There is still too much unseated land there, and too many personal opportunities, to make socialism attractive to anybody."

"Well, that's about it," Zortan Brend told him. "I'm not enough of a psychicist to know what the Lady Dallona's been doing, but she's knocked the theoretical basis from under Statistical Reincarnation, and that's the basis, in turn, of Statistical Socialism. I think we'll find that the Statisticalist Party is responsible for whatever happened to her."

Marnik, the younger of the two Assassins, hesitated for a moment, then addressed Verkan Vall:

"Lord Virzal, I know none of the personalities involved in this matter, and I speak without wishing to give offense, but is it not possible that the Lady Dallona and the Assassin Dirzed may have gone somewhere together voluntarily? I have met Dirzed, and he has many qualities which women find attractive, and he is by no means indifferent to the opposite sex. You understand, Lord Virzal—"

"I understand all too perfectly, Marnik," Verkan Vall replied, out of the fullness of experience. "The Lady Dallona has had affairs with a number of men, myself among them. But under the circumstances, I find that explanation unthinkable."

Marnik looked at him in open skepticism. Evidently, in his book, where an attractive man and a beautiful woman were concerned, that explanation was never unthinkable.

"The Lady Dallona is a scientist," Verkan Vall elaborated. "She is not above diverting herself with love affairs, but that's all they are—a not too important form of diversion. And, if you recall, she had just participated in a most significant experiment; you can be sure that she had other things on her mind at the time than pleasure jaunts with good-looking Assassins."

The ship was passing around the Caucasus Mountains, with the Caspian Sea in sight ahead, when several of the crew appeared on the observation deck and began preparing the shielding to protect the deck from gunfire. Zortan Brend inquired of the petty officer in charge of the work as to the necessity.

"We've been getting reports of trouble at Darsh, sir," the man said. "Newscast bulletins every couple of minutes; rioting in different parts of the city. Started yesterday afternoon, when a couple of Statisticalist members of the Executive Council resigned and went over to the Volitionalists. Lord Nirzav of Shonna, the only nobleman of any importance in the Statisticalist Party, was one of them; he was shot immediately afterward, while leaving the Council Chambers, along with a couple of Assassins who were with him. Some people in an airboat sprayed them with a machine rifle as they came out onto the landing stage."

The two Assassins exclaimed in horrified anger over this.

"That wasn't the work of members of the Society of Assassins!" Olirzon declared. "Even after he'd resigned, the Lord Nirzav was still immune till he left the Government Building. There's too blasted much illegal assassination going on!"

"What happened next?" Verkan Vall wanted to know.

"About what you'd expect, sir. The Volitionalists weren't going to take that quietly. In the past eighteen hours, four prominent Statisticalists were forcibly discarnated, and there was even a fight in Mirzark of Bashad's house, when Volitionalist Assassins broke in; three of them and four of Mirzark's Assassins were discarnated."

"You know, something is going to have to be done about that, too," Olirzon said to Marnik. "It's getting to a point where these political faction fights are being carried on entirely between members of the Society. In Ghamma alone, last year, thirty or forty of our members were discarnated that way."

"Plug in a newscast visiplate, Karnil," Zortan Brend told the petty officer. "Let's see what's going on in Darsh now."

In Darsh, it seemed, an uneasy peace was being established. Verkan Vall watched heavily-armed airboats and light combat ships patrolling among the high towers of the city. He saw a couple of minor riots being broken up by the blue-uniformed Constabulary, with considerable shooting and a ruthless disregard for who might get shot. It wasn't exactly the sort of policing that would have been tolerated in the First Level Civil Order Section, but it seemed to suit Akor-Neb conditions. And he listened to a series of angry recriminations and contradictory statements by different politicians, all of whom blamed the disorders on their opponents. The Volitionalists spoke of the Statisticalists as "insane criminals" and "underminers of social stability," and the Statisticalists called the Volitionalists "reactionary criminals" and "enemies of social progress." Politicians, he had observed, differed little in their vocabularies from one time-line to another.

This kept up all the while the ship was passing over the Caspian Sea; as they were turning up the Volga valley, one of the ship's officers came down from the control deck, above.

"We're coming into Darsh, now," he said, and as Verkan Vall turned from the visiplate to the forward windows, he could see the white and pastel-tinted towers of the city rising above the hardwood forests that covered the whole Volga basin on this sector. "Your luggage has been put into the airboat, Lord Virzal and Honorable Assassins, and it's ready for launching whenever you are." The officer glanced at his watch. "We dock at Commercial Center in twenty minutes; we'll be passing the Solar Hotel in ten."

They all rose, and Verkan Vall hooked fingers and clapped shoulders with Zortan Brend.

"Good luck, Lord Virzal," the latter said. "I hope you find the Lady Dallona safe and carnate. If you need help, I'll be at Mercantile House for the next day or so; if you get back to Ghamma before I do, you know who to ask for there."

A number of assassins loitered in the hallways and offices of the Independent Institute of Reincarnation Research when Verkan Vall, accompanied by Marnik, called there that afternoon. Some of them carried submachine-guns or sleep-gas projectors, and they were stopping people and questioning them. Marnik needed only to give them a quick gesture and the words, "Assassins' Truce," and he and his client were allowed to pass. They entered a lifter tube and floated up to the office of Dr. Harnosh of Hosh, with whom Verkan Vall had made an appointment.

"I'm sorry, Lord Virzal," the director of the Institute told him, "but I have no idea what has befallen the Lady Dallona, or even if she is still carnate. I am quite worried; I admired her extremely, both as an individual and as a scientist. I do hope she hasn't been discarnated; that would be a serious blow to science. It is fortunate that she accomplished as much as she did, while she was with us."

"You think she is no longer carnate, then?"

"I'm afraid so. The political effects of her discoveries—" Harnosh of Hosh shrugged sadly. "She was devoted, to a rare degree, to her work. I am sure that nothing but her discarnation could have taken her away from us, at this time, with so many important experiments still uncompleted."

Marnik nodded to Verkan Vall, as much as to say: "You were right."

"Well, I intend acting upon the assumption that she is still carnate and in need of help, until I am positive to the contrary," Verkan Vall said. "And in the latter case, I intend finding out who discarnated her, and send him to apologize for it in person. People don't forcibly discarnate my friends with impunity."

"Sound attitude," Dr. Harnosh commented. "There's certainly no positive evidence that she isn't still carnate. I'll gladly give you all the assistance I can, if you'll only tell me what you want."

"Well, in the first place," Verkan Vall began, "just what sort of work was she doing?" He already knew the answer to that, from the reports she had sent back to the First Level, but he wanted to hear Dr. Harnosh's version. "And what, exactly, are the political effects you mentioned? Understand, Dr. Harnosh, I am really quite ignorant of any scientific subject unrelated to zerfa culture, and equally so of Terran politics. Politics, on Venus, is mainly a question of who gets how much graft out of what."

Dr. Harnosh smiled; evidently he had heard about Venusian politics.

"Ah, yes, of course. But you are familiar with the main differences between Statistical and Volitional reincarnation theories?"

"In a general way. The Volitionalists hold that the discarnate individuality is fully conscious, and is capable of something analogous to sense-perception, and is also capable of exercising choice in the matter of reincarnation vehicles, and can reincarnate or remain in the discarnate state as it chooses. They also believe that discarnate individualities can communicate with one another, and with at least some carnate individualities, by telepathy," he said. "The Statisticalists deny all this; their opinion is that the discarnate individuality is in a more or less somnambulistic state, that it is drawn by a process akin to tropism to the nearest available reincarnation vehicle, and that it must reincarnate in and only in that vehicle. They are labeled Statisticalists because they believe that the process of reincarnation is purely at random, or governed by unknown and uncontrollable causes, and is unpredictable except as to aggregates."

"That's a fairly good generalized summary," Dr. Harnosh of Hosh grudged, unwilling to give a mere layman too much credit. He dipped a spoon into a tobacco humidor, dusted the tobacco lightly with dried *zerfa*, and rammed it into his pipe. "You must understand that our modern Statisticalists are the intellectual heirs of those ancient materialistic thinkers who denied the possibility of any discarnate existence, or of any extraphysical mind, or even of extrasensory perception. Since all these things have been demonstrated to be facts, the materialistic dogma has been broadened to include them, but always strictly within the frame of materialism.

"We have proven, for instance, that the human individuality can exist in a discarnate state, and that it reincarnates into the body of an infant, shortly after birth. But the Statisticalists cannot accept the idea of discarnate consciousness, since they conceive of consciousness purely as a function of the physical brain. So they postulate an unconscious discarnate personality, or, as you put it, one in a somnambulistic state. They have to concede memory to this discarnate personality, since it was by recovery of memories of previous reincarnations that discarnate existence and reincarnation were proven to be facts. So they picture the discarnate individuality as a material object, or physical event, of negligible but actual mass, in which an indefinite number of memories can be stored as electronic charges. And they picture it as being drawn irresistibly to the body of the nearest non-incarnated infant. Curiously enough, the reincarnation vehicle chosen is almost always of the same sex as the vehicle of the previous reincarnation, the exceptions being cases of persons who had a previous history of psychological sex-inversion."

Dr. Harnosh remembered the unlighted pipe in his hand, thrust it into his mouth, and lit it. For a moment, he sat with it jutting out of his black beard, until it was drawing to his satisfaction. "This belief in immediate reincarnation leads the Statisticalists, when they fight duels or perform voluntary discarnation, to do so in the neighborhood of maternity hospitals," he added. "I know, personally, of one reincarnation memory-recall, in which the subject, a Statisticalist, voluntarily discarnated by lethal-gas inhaler in a private room at one of our local maternity hospitals, and reincarnated twenty years later in the city of Jeddul, three thousand miles away." The square black beard jiggled as the scientist laughed.

"Now, as to the political implications of these contradictory theories: Since the Statisticalists believe that they will reincarnate entirely at random, their aim is to create an utterly classless social and economic order, in which, theoretically, each individuality will reincarnate into a condition of equality with everybody else. Their political program, therefore, is one of complete socialization of all means of production and distribution, abolition of hereditary titles and inherited wealth—eventually, all private wealth—and total government control of all economic, social and cultural activities. Of course," Dr. Harnosh apologized, "politics isn't my subject; I wouldn't presume to judge how that would function in practice."

"I would," Verkan Vall said shortly, thinking of all the different time-lines on which he had seen systems like that in operation. "You wouldn't like it, doctor. And the Volitionalists?"

"Well, since they believe that they are able to choose the circumstances of their next reincarnations for themselves, they are the party of the *status quo*. Naturally, almost all the nobles, almost all the wealthy trading and manufacturing families, and almost all professional people, are Volitionalists; most of the workers and peasants are Statisticalists. Or, at least, they were, for the most part, before we began announcing the results of the Lady Dallona's experimental work."

"Ah; now we come to it," Verkan Vall said as the story clarified.

"Yes. In somewhat oversimplified form, the situation is rather like this," Dr. Harnosh of Hosh said. "The Lady Dallona introduced a number of refinements and some outright innovations into our technique of recovering memories of past reincarnations. Previously, it was necessary to keep the subject in an hypnotic trance, during which he or she would narrate what was remembered of past reincarnations, and this would be recorded. On emerging from the trance, the subject would remember nothing; the tape-recording would be all that would be left. But the Lady Dallona devised a technique by which these memories would remain in what might be called the fore part of the subject's subconscious mind, so that they could be brought to the level of consciousness at will. More, she was able to recover memories of past discarnate existences, something we had never been able to do heretofore." Dr. Harnosh shook his head. "And to think, when I first met her, I thought that she was just another sensation-seeking young lady of wealth, and was almost about to refuse her enrollment!"

He wasn't the only one whom little Dalla had surprised, Verkan Vall thought. At least, he had been pleasantly surprised.

"You see, this entirely disproves the Statistical Theory of Reincarnation. For example, we got a fine set of memory-recalls from one subject, for four previous reincarnations and four intercarnations. In the first of these, the subject had been a peasant on the estate of a wealthy noble. Unlike most of his fellows, who reincarnated into other peasant families almost immediately after discarnation, this man waited for fifty years in the discarnate state for an opportunity to reincarnate as the son of an over-servant. In his next reincarnation, he was the son of a technician, and received a technical education; he became a physics researcher. For his next reincarnation, he chose the son of a nobleman by a concubine as his vehicle; in his present reincarnation, he is a member of a wealthy manufacturing family, and married into a family of the nobility. In five reincarnations, he has climbed from the lowest to the next-to-highest rung of the social ladder. Few individuals of the class from whence he began this ascent possess so much persistence or determination. Then, of course, there was the case of Lord Garnon of Roxor."

He went on to describe the last experiment in which Hadron Dalla had participated.

"Well, that all sounds pretty conclusive," Verkan Vall commented. "I take it the leaders of the Volitionalist Party here are pleased with the result of the Lady Dallona's work?"

"Pleased? My dear Lord Virzal, they're fairly bursting with glee over it!" Harnosh of Hosh declared. "As I pointed out, the Statisticalist program of socialization is based entirely on the proposition that no one can choose the circumstances of his next reincarnation, and that's been demonstrated to be utter nonsense. Until the Lady Dallona's discoveries were announced, they were the dominant party, controlling a majority of the seats in Parliament and on the Executive Council. Only the Constitution kept them from enacting their entire socialization program long ago, and they were about to legislate constitutional changes which would remove that barrier. They had expected to be able to do so after the forthcoming general elections. But now, social inequality has become desirable; it gives people something to look forward to in the next reincarnation. Instead of wanting to abolish wealth and privilege and nobility, the proletariat want to reincarnate into them." Harnosh of Hosh laughed happily. "So you can see how furious the Statisticalist Party organization is!"

"There's a catch to this, somewhere," Marnik the Assassin, speaking for the first time, declared. "They can't all reincarnate as princes, there aren't enough vacancies to go 'round. And no noble is going to reincarnate as a tractor driver to make room for a tractor driver who wants to reincarnate as a noble."

"That's correct," Dr. Harnosh replied. "There is a catch to it; a catch most people would never admit, even to themselves. Very few individuals possess the will power, the intelligence or the capacity for mental effort displayed by the subject of the case I just quoted. The average man's interests are almost entirely on the physical side; he actually finds mental effort painful, and makes as little of it as possible. And that is the only sort of effort a discarnate individuality can exert. So, unable to endure the fifty or so years needed to make a really good reincarnation, he reincarnates in a year or so, out of pure boredom, into the first vehicle he can find, usually one nobody else wants." Dr. Harnosh dug out the heel of his pipe and blew through the stem. "But nobody will admit his own mental inferiority, even to himself. Now, every machine operator and field hand on the planet thinks he can reincarnate as a prince or a millionaire. Politics isn't my subject, but I'm willing to bet that since Statistical Reincarnation is an exploded psychic theory, Statisticalist Socialism has been caught in the blast area and destroyed along with it."

Olirzon was in the drawing room of the hotel suite when they returned, sitting on the middle of his spinal column in a reclining chair, smoking a pipe, dressing the edge of his knife with a pocket-hone, gazing lecherously at a young woman in the visiplate. She was an extremely well-designed young woman, in a rather fragmentary costume, and she was heaving her bosom at the invisible audience in anger, sorrow, scorn, entreaty, and numerous other emotions.

". . . this revolting crime," she was declaiming, in a husky contralto, as Verkan Vall and Marnik entered, "foul even for the criminal beasts who conceived and perpetrated it!" She pointed an accusing finger. "This murder of the beautiful Lady Dallona of Hadron!"

Verkan Vall stopped short, considering the possibility of something having been discovered lately of which he was ignorant. Olirzon must have guessed his thought; he grinned reassuringly.

"Think nothing of it, Lord Virzal," he said, waving his knife at the visiplate. "Just political propaganda; strictly for the sparrows. Nice propagandist, though."

"And now," the woman with the magnificent natural resources lowered her voice reverently, "we bring you the last image of the Lady Dallona, and of Dirzed, her faithful Assassin, taken just before they vanished, never to be seen again."

The plate darkened, and there were strains of slow, dirgelike music; then it lighted again, presenting a view of a broad hallway, thronged with men and women in bright vari-colored costumes. In the foreground, wearing a tight skirt of deep blue and a short red jacket, was Hadron Dalla, just as she had looked in the solidographs taken in Dhergabar after her alteration by the First Level cosmeticians to conform to the appearance of the Malayoid Akor-Neb people. She was holding the arm of a man who wore the black tunic and red badge of an Assassin, a handsome specimen of the Akor-Neb race. Trust little Dalla for that, Verkan Vall thought. The figures were moving with exaggerated slowness, as though a very fleeting picture were being stretched out as far as possible. Having already memorized his former wife's changed appearance, Verkan Vall concentrated on the man beside her until the picture faded.

"All right, Olirzon; what did you get?" he asked.

"Well, first of all, at Assassins' Hall," Olirzon said, rolling up his left sleeve, holding his bare forearm to the light, and shaving a few fine hairs from it to test the edge of his knife. "Of course, they never tell one Assassin anything about the client of another Assassin; that's standard practice. But I was in the Lodge Secretary's office, where nobody but Assassins are ever admitted. They have a big panel in there, with the names of all the Lodge members on it in light-letters; that's standard in all Lodges. If an Assassin is unattached and free to accept a client, his name's in white light. If he has a client, the light's changed to blue, and the name of the client goes up under his. If his whereabouts are unknown, the light's changed to amber. If he is discarnated, his name's removed entirely, unless the circumstances of his discarnation are such as to constitute an injury to the Society. In that case, the name's in red light until he's been properly avenged, or, as we say, till his blood's been mopped up. Well, the name of Dirzed is up in blue light, with the name of Dallona of Hadron under it. I found out that the light had been amber for two days after the disappearance, and then had been changed back to blue. Get it, Lord Virzal?"

Verkan Vall nodded. "I think so. I'd been considering that as a possibility from the first. Then what?"

"Then I was about and around for a couple of hours, buying drinks for people—unattached Assassins, Constabulary detectives, political workers, newscast people. You owe me fifteen System Monetary Units for that, Lord Virzal. What I got, when it's all sorted out—I taped it in detail, as soon as I got back—reduces to this: The Volitionalists are moving mountains to find out who was the spy at Garnon of Roxor's discarnation feast, but are doing nothing but nothing at all to find the Lady Dallona or Dirzed. The Statisticalists are making all sorts of secret efforts to find out what happened to her. The Constabulary blame the Statistos for the package-bomb; they're interested in that because of the discarnation of the three servants by an illegal weapon of indiscriminate effect. They claim that the disappearance of Dirzed and the Lady Dallona was a publicity hoax. The Volitionalists are preparing a line of publicity to deny this."

Verkan Vall nodded. "That ties in with what you learned at Assassins' Hall," he said. "They're hiding out somewhere. Is there any chance of reaching Dirzed through the Society of Assassins?"

Olirzon shook his head. "If you're right—and that's the way it looks to me, too—he's probably just called in and notified the Society that he's still carnate and so is the Lady Dallona, and called off any search the Society might be making for him."

"And I've got to find the Lady Dallona as soon as I can. Well, if I can't reach her, maybe I can get her to send word to me," Verkan Vall said. "That's going to take some doing, too."

"What did you find out, Lord Virzal?" Olirzon asked. He had a piece of soft leather, now, and was polishing his blade lovingly.

"The Reincarnation Research people don't know anything," Verkan Vall replied. "Dr. Harnosh of Hosh thinks she's discarnate. I did find out that the experimental work she's done, so far, has absolutely disproved the theory of Statistical Reincarnation. The Volitionalists' theory is solidly established."

"Yes, what do you think, Olirzon?" Marnik added. "They have a case on record of a man who worked up from field hand to millionaire in five reincarnations. Deliberately, that is." He went on to repeat what Harnosh of Hosh had said; he must have possessed an almost eidetic memory, for he gave the bearded psychicist's words verbatim, and threw in the gestures and voice-inflections.

Olirzon grinned. "You know, there's a chance for the easy-money boys," he considered. "'You, too, can Reincarnate as a millionaire! Let Dr. Nirzutz of Futzbutz Help You! Only 49.98 System Monetary Units for the Secret, Infallible, Autosuggestive Formula.' And would it sell!" He put away the hone and the bit of leather and slipped his knife back into its sheath. "If I weren't a respectable Assassin, I'd give it a try, myself."

Verkan Vall looked at his watch. "We'd better get something to eat," he said. "We'll go down to the main dining room; the Martian Room, I think they call it. I've got to think of some way to let the Lady Dallona know I'm looking for her."

The Martian Room, fifteen stories down, was a big place, occupying almost half of the floor space of one corner tower. It had been fitted to resemble one of the ruined buildings of the ancient and vanished race of Mars who were the ancestors of Terran humanity. One whole side of the room was a gigantic cine-solidograph screen, on which the gullied desolation of a Martian landscape was projected; in the course of about two hours, the scene changed from sunrise through daylight and night to sunrise again.

It was high noon when they entered and found a table; by the time they had finished their dinner, the night was ending and the first glow of dawn was tinting the distant hills. They sat for a while, watching the light grow stronger, then got up and left the table.

There were five men at a table near them; they had come in before the stars had grown dim, and the waiters were just bringing their first dishes. Two were Assassins, and the other three were of a breed Verkan Vall had learned to recognize on any time-line—the arrogant, cocksure, ambitious, leftist politician, who knows what is best for everybody better than anybody else does, and who is convinced that he is inescapably right and that whoever differs with him is not only an ignoramus but a venal scoundrel as well. One was a beefy man in a gold-laced cream-colored dress tunic; he had thick lips and a too-ready laugh. Another was a rather monkish-looking young man who spoke earnestly and rolled his eyes upward, as though at some celestial vision. The third had the faint powdering of gray in his black hair which was, among the Akor-Neb people, almost the only indication of advanced age.

"Of course it is; the whole thing is a fraud," the monkish young man was saying angrily. "But we can't prove it."

"Oh, Sirzob, here, can prove anything, if you give him time," the beefy one laughed. "The trouble is, there isn't too much time. We know that that communication was a fake, prearranged by the Volitionalists, with Dr. Harnosh and this Dallona of Hadron as their tools. They fed the whole thing to that idiot boy hypnotically, in advance, and then, on a signal, he began typing out this spurious communication. And then, of course, Dallona and this Assassin of hers ran off somewhere together, so that we'd be blamed with discarnating or abducting them, and so that they wouldn't be made to testify about the communication on a lie detector."

A sudden happy smile touched Verkan Vall's eyes. He caught each of his Assassins by an arm.

"Marnik, cover my back," he ordered. "Olirzon, cover everybody at the table. Come on!"

Then he stepped forward, halting between the chairs of the young man and the man with the gray hair and facing the beefy man in the light tunic.

"You!" he barked. "I mean YOU."

The beefy man stopped laughing and stared at him; then sprang to his feet. His hand, streaking toward his left armpit, stopped and dropped to his side as Olirzon aimed a pistol at him. The others sat motionless.

"You," Verkan Vall continued, "are a complete, deliberate, malicious, and unmitigated liar. The Lady Dallona of Hadron is a scientist of integrity, incapable of falsifying her experimental work. What's more, her father is one of my best friends; in his name, and in hers, I demand a full retraction of the slanderous statements you have just made."

"Do you know who I am?" the beefy one shouted.

"I know *what* you are," Verkan Vall shouted back. Like most ancient languages, the Akor-Neb speech included an elaborate, delicately-shaded, and utterly vile vocabulary of abuse; Verkan Vall culled from it judiciously and at length. "And if I don't make myself understood verbally, we'll go down to the object level," he added, snatching a bowl of soup from in front of the monkish-looking young man and throwing it across the table.

The soup was a dark brown, almost black. It contained bits of meat, and mushrooms, and slices of hard-boiled egg, and yellow Martian rock lichen. It produced, on the light tunic, a most spectacular effect.

For a moment, Verkan Vall was afraid the fellow would have an apoplectic stroke, or an epileptic fit. Mastering himself, however, he bowed jerkily.

"Marnark of Bashad," he identified himself. "When and where can my friends consult yours?"

"Lord Virzal of Verkan," the paratimer bowed back. "Your friends can negotiate with mine here and now. I am represented by these Gentlemen-Assassins."

"I won't submit my friends to the indignity of negotiating with them," Marnark retorted. "I insist that you be represented by persons of your own quality and mine."

"Oh, you do?" Olirzon broke in. "Well, is your objection personal to me, or to Assassins as a class? In the first case, I'll remember to make a private project of you, as soon as I'm through with my present employment; if it's the latter, I'll report your attitude to the Society. I'll see what Klarnood, our President-General, thinks of your views."

A crowd had begun to accumulate around the table. Some of them were persons in evening dress, some were Assassins on the hotel payroll, and some were unattached Assassins.

"Well, you won't have far to look for him," one of the latter said, pushing through the crowd to the table.

He was a man of middle age, inclined to stoutness; he made Verkan Vall think of a chocolate figure of Tortha Karf. The red badge on his breast was surrounded with gold lace, and, instead of black wings and a silver bullet, it bore silver wings and a golden dagger. He bowed contemptuously at Marnark of Bashad.

"Klarnood, President-General of the Society of Assassins," he announced. "Marnark of Bashad, did I hear you say that you considered members of the Society as unworthy to negotiate an affair of honor with your friends, on behalf of this nobleman who has been courteous enough to accept your challenge?" he demanded.

Marnark of Bashad's arrogance suffered considerable evaporation-loss. His tone became almost servile.

"Not at all, Honorable Assassin-President," he protested. "But as I was going to ask these gentlemen to represent me, I thought it would be more fitting for the other gentleman to be represented by personal friends, also. In that way—"

"Sorry, Marnark," the gray-haired man at the table said. "I can't second you; I have a quarrel with the Lord Virzal, too." He rose and bowed. "Sirzob of Abo. Inasmuch as the Honorable Marnark is a guest at my table, an affront to him is an affront to me. In my quality as his host, I must demand satisfaction from you, Lord Virzal."

"Why, gladly, Honorable Sirzob," Verkan Vall replied. This was getting better and better every moment. "Of course, your friend, the Honorable Marnark, enjoys priority of challenge; I'll take care of you as soon as I have, shall we say, satisfied, him."

The earnest and rather consecrated-looking young man rose also, bowing to Verkan Vall.

"Yirzol of Narva. I, too, have a quarrel with you, Lord Virzal; I cannot submit to the indignity of having my food snatched from in front of me, as you just did. I also demand satisfaction."

"And quite rightly, Honorable Yirzol," Verkan Vall approved. "It looks like such good soup, too," he sorrowed, inspecting the front of Marnark's tunic. "My seconds will negotiate with yours immediately; your satisfaction, of course, must come after that of Honorable Sirzob."

"If I may intrude," Klarnood put in smoothly, "may I suggest that as the Lord Virzal is represented by his Assassins, yours can represent all three of you at the same time. I will gladly offer my own good offices as impartial supervisor."

Verkan Vall turned and bowed as to royalty. "An honor, Assassin-President; I am sure no one could act in that capacity more satisfactorily."

"Well, when would it be most convenient to arrange the details?" Klarnood inquired. "I am completely at your disposal, gentlemen."

"Why, here and now, while we're all together," Verkan Vall replied.

"I object to that!" Marnark of Bashad vociferated. "We can't make arrangements here; why, all these hotel people, from the manager down, are nothing but tipsters for the newscast services!"

"Well, what's wrong with that?" Verkan Vall demanded. "You knew that when you slandered the Lady Dallona in their hearing."

"The Lord Virzal of Verkan is correct," Klarnood ruled. "And the offenses for which you have challenged him were also committed in public. By all means, let's discuss the arrangements now." He turned to Verkan Vall. "As the challenged party, you have the choice of weapons; your opponents, then, have the right to name the conditions under which they are to be used."

Marnark of Bashad raised another outcry over that. The assault upon him by the Lord Virzal of Verkan was deliberately provocative, and therefore tantamount to a challenge; he, himself, had the right to name the weapons. Klarnood upheld him.

"Do the other gentlemen make the same claim?" Verkan Vall wanted to know.

"If they do, I won't allow it," Klarnood replied. "You deliberately provoked Honorable Marnark, but the offenses of provoking him at

Honorable Sirzob's table, and of throwing Honorable Yirzol's soup at him, were not given with intent to provoke. These gentlemen have a right to challenge, but not to consider themselves provoked."

"Well, I choose knives, then," Marnark hastened to say.

Verkan Vall smiled thinly. He had learned knife-play among the greatest masters of that art in all paratime, the Third Level Khanga pirates of the Caribbean Islands.

"And we fight barefoot, stripped to the waist, and without any parrying weapon in the left hand," Verkan Vall stipulated.

The beefy Marnark fairly licked his chops in anticipation. He outweighed Verkan Vall by forty pounds; he saw an easy victory ahead. Verkan Vall's own confidence increased at these signs of his opponent's assurance.

"And as for Honorable Sirzob and Honorable Yirzol, I choose pistols," he added.

Sirzob and Yirzol held a hasty whispered conference.

"Speaking both for Honorable Yirzol and for myself," Sirzob announced, "we stipulate that the distance shall be twenty meters, that the pistols shall be fully loaded, and that fire shall be at will after the command."

"Twenty rounds, fire at will, at twenty meters!" Olirzon hooted. "You must think our principal's as bad a shot as you are!"

The four Assassins stepped aside and held a long discussion about something, with considerable argument and gesticulation. Klarnood, observing Verkan Vall's impatience, leaned close to him and whispered:

"This is highly irregular; we must pretend ignorance and be patient. They're laying bets on the outcome. You must do your best, Lord Virzal; you don't want your supporters to lose money."

He said it quite seriously, as though the outcome were otherwise a matter of indifference to Verkan Vall.

Marnark wanted to discuss time and place, and proposed that all three duels be fought at dawn, on the fourth landing stage of Darsh Central Hospital; that was closest to the maternity wards, and statistics showed that most births occurred just before that hour.

"Certainly not," Verkan Vall vetoed. "We'll fight here and now; I don't propose going a couple of hundred miles to meet you at any such unholy hour. We'll fight in the nearest hallway that provides twenty meters' shooting distance."

Marnark, Sirzob and Yirzol all clamored in protest. Verkan Vall shouted them down, drawing on his hypnotically acquired knowledge of

Akor-Neb duelling customs. "The code explicitly states that satisfaction shall be rendered as promptly as possible, and I insist on a literal interpretation. I'm not going to inconvenience myself and Assassin-President Klarnood and these four Gentlemen-Assassins just to humor Statisticalist superstitions."

The manager of the hotel, drawn to the Martian Room by the uproar, offered a hallway connecting the kitchens with the refrigerator rooms; it was fifty meters long by five in width, was well-lighted and sound-proof, and had a bay in which the seconds and others could stand during the firing.

They repaired thither in a body, Klarnood gathering up several hotel servants on the way through the kitchen. Verkan Vall stripped to the waist, pulled off his ankle boots, and examined Olirzon's knife. Its tapering eight-inch blade was double-edged at the point, and its handle was covered with black velvet to afford a good grip, and wound with gold wire. He nodded approvingly, gripped it with his index finger crooked around the cross-guard, and advanced to meet Marnark of Bashad.

As he had expected, the burly politician was depending upon his greater brawn to overpower his antagonist. He advanced with a sidling, spread-legged gait, his knife hand against his right hip and his left hand extended in front. Verkan Vall nodded with pleased satisfaction; a wrist-grabber. Then he blinked. Why, the fellow was actually holding his knife reversed, his little finger to the guard and his thumb on the pommel!

Verkan Vall went briskly to meet him, made a feint at his knife hand with his own left, and then side-stepped quickly to the right. As Marnark's left hand grabbed at his right wrist, his left hand brushed against it and closed into a fist, with Marnark's left thumb inside of it. He gave a quick downward twist with his wrist, pulling Marnark off balance.

Caught by surprise, Marnark stumbled, his knife flailing wildly away from Verkan Vall. As he stumbled forward, Verkan Vall pivoted on his left heel and drove the point of his knife into the back of Marnark's neck, twisting it as he jerked it free. At the same time, he released Marnark's thumb. The politician continued his stumble and fell forward on his face, blood spurting from his neck. He gave a twitch or so, and was still.

Verkan Vall stooped and wiped the knife on the dead man's clothes—another Khanga pirate gesture—and then returned it to Olirzon.

"Nice weapon, Olirzon," he said. "It fitted my hand as though I'd been born holding it."

"You used it as though you had, Lord Virzal," the Assassin replied. "Only eight seconds from the time you closed with him."

The function of the hotel servants whom Klarnood had gathered up now became apparent; they advanced, took the body of Marnark by the heels, and dragged it out of the way. The others watched this removal with mixed emotions. The two remaining principals were impassive and frozen-faced. Their two Assassins, who had probably bet heavily on Marnark, were chagrined. And Klarnood was looking at Verkan Vall with a considerable accretion of respect. Verkan Vall pulled on his boots and resumed his clothing.

There followed some argument about the pistols; it was finally decided that each combatant should use his own shoulder-holster weapon. All three were nearly enough alike—small weapons, rather heavier than they looked, firing a tiny ten-grain bullet at ten thousand foot-seconds. On impact, such a bullet would almost disintegrate; a man hit anywhere in the body with one would be killed instantly, his nervous system paralyzed and his heart stopped by internal pressure. Each of the pistols carried twenty rounds in the magazine.

Verkan Vall and Sirzob of Abo took their places, their pistols lowered at their sides, facing each other across a measured twenty meters.

"Are you ready, gentlemen?" Klarnood asked. "You will not raise your pistols until the command to fire; you may fire at will after it. Ready. *Fire!*"

Both pistols swung up to level. Verkan Vall found Sirzob's head in his sights and squeezed; the pistol kicked back in his hand, and he saw a lance of blue flame jump from the muzzle of Sirzob's. Both weapons barked together, and with the double report came the whip-cracking sound of Sirzob's bullet passing Verkan Vall's head. Then Sirzob's face altered its appearance unpleasantly, and he pitched forward. Verkan Vall thumbed on his safety and stood motionless, while the servants advanced, took Sirzob's body by the heels, and dragged it over beside Marnark's.

"All right; Honorable Yirzol, you're next," Verkan Vall called out.

"The Lord Virzal has fired one shot," one of the opposing seconds objected, "and Honorable Yirzol has a full magazine. The Lord Virzal should put in another magazine."

"I grant him the advantage; let's get on with it," Verkan Vall said.

Yirzol of Narva advanced to the firing point. He was not afraid of death—none of the Akor-Neb people were; their language contained no word to express the concept of total and final extinction—and discarnation by gunshot was almost entirely painless. But he was beginning to suspect that he had made a fool of himself by getting into this affair, he had work in his present reincarnation which he wanted to finish, and his political party would suffer loss, both of his services and of prestige.

"Are you ready, gentlemen?" Klarnood intoned ritualistically. "You will not raise your pistols until the command to fire; you may fire at will after it. Ready, *Fire!*"

Verkan Vall shot Yirzol of Narva through the head before the latter had his pistol half raised. Yirzol fell forward on the splash of blood Sirzob had made, and the servants came forward and dragged his body over with the others. It reminded Verkan Vall of some sort of industrial assembly-line operation. He replaced the two expended rounds in his magazine with fresh ones and slid the pistol back into its holster. The two Assassins whose principals had been so expeditiously massacred were beginning to count up their losses and pay off the winners.

Klarnood, the President-General of the Society of Assassins, came over, hooking fingers and clapping shoulders with Verkan Vall.

"Lord Virzal, I've seen quite a few duels, but nothing quite like that," he said. "You should have been an Assassin!"

That was a considerable compliment. Verkan Vall thanked him modestly.

"I'd like to talk to you privately," the Assassin-President continued. "I think it'll be worth your while if we have a few words together."

Verkan Vall nodded. "My suite is on the fifteenth floor above; will that be all right?" He waited until the losers had finished settling their bets, then motioned to his own pair of Assassins.

As they emerged into the Martian Room again, the manager was waiting; he looked as though he were about to demand that Verkan Vall vacate his suite. However, when he saw the arm of the President-General of the Society of Assassins draped amicably over his guest's shoulder, he came forward bowing and smiling.

"Larnorm, I want you to put five of your best Assassins to guarding the approaches to the Lord Virzal's suite," Klarnood told him. "I'll send five more from Assassins' Hall to replace them at their ordinary duties. And I'll hold you responsible with your carnate existence for the Lord Virzal's safety in this hotel. Understand?"

"Oh, yes, Honorable Assassin-President; you may trust me. The Lord Virzal will be perfectly safe."

In Verkan Vall's suite, above, Klarnood sat down and got out his pipe, filling it with tobacco lightly mixed with *zerfa*. To his surprise, he saw his host light a plain tobacco cigarette.

"Don't you use *zerfa*?" he asked.

"Very little," Verkan Vall replied. "I grow it. If you'd see the bums who hang around our drying sheds, on Venus, cadging rejected leaves and smoking themselves into a stupor, you'd be frugal in using it, too."

Klarnood nodded. "You know, most men would want a pipe of fifty percent, or a straight *zerfa* cigarette, after what you've been through," he said.

"I'd need something like that, to deaden my conscience, if I had one to deaden," Verkan Vall said. "As it is, I feel like a murderer of babes. That overgrown fool, Marnark, handled his knife like a cow-butcher. The young fellow couldn't handle a pistol at all. I suppose the old fellow, Sirzob, was a fair shot, but dropping him wasn't any great feat of arms, either."

Klarnood looked at him curiously for a moment. "You know," he said, at length, "I believe you actually mean that. Well, until he met you, Marnark of Bashad was rated as the best knife-fighter in Darsh. Sirzob had ten dueling victories to his credit, and young Yirzol four." He puffed slowly on his pipe. "I like you, Lord Virzal; a great Assassin was lost when you decided to reincarnate as a Venusian landowner. I'd hate to see you discarnated without proper warning. I take it you're ignorant of the intricacies of Terran politics?"

"To a large extent, yes."

"Well, do you know who those three men were?" When Verkan Vall shook his head, Klarnood continued: "Marnark was the son and right-hand associate of old Mirzark of Bashad, the Statisticalist Party leader. Sirzob of Abo was their propaganda director. And Yirzol of Narva was their leading socio-economic theorist, and their candidate for Executive Chairman. In six minutes, with one knife thrust and two shots, you did the Statisticalist Party an injury second only to that done them by the young lady in whose name you were fighting. In two weeks, there will be a planet-wide general election. As it stands, the Statisticalists have a majority of the seats in Parliament and on the Executive Council. As a result of your work and the Lady Dallona's, they'll lose that majority, and more, when the votes are tallied."

"Is that another reason why you like me?" Verkan Vall asked.

"Unofficially, yes. As President-General of the Society of Assassins, I must be nonpolitical. The Society is rigidly so; if we let ourselves become involved, as an organization, in politics, we could control the System

Government inside of five years, and we'd be wiped out of existence in fifty years by the very forces we sought to control," Klarnood said. "But personally, I would like to see the Statisticalist Party destroyed. If they succeed in their program of socialization, the Society would be finished. A socialist state is, in its final development, an absolute, total, state; no total state can tolerate extra-legal and para-governmental organizations. So we have adopted the policy of giving a little inconspicuous aid, here and there, to people who are dangerous to the Statisticalists. The Lady Dallona of Hadron, and Dr. Harnosh of Hosh, are such persons. You appear to be another. That's why I ordered that fellow, Larnorm, to make sure you were safe in his hotel."

"Where is the Lady Dallona?" Verkan Vall asked. "From your use of the present tense, I assume you believe her to be still carnate."

Klarnood looked at Verkan Vall keenly. "That's a pretty blunt question, Lord Virzal," he said. "I wish I knew a little more about you. When you and your Assassins started inquiring about the Lady Dallona, I tried to check up on you. I found out that you had come to Darsh from Ghamma on a ship of the family of Zorda, accompanied by Brarnend of Zorda himself. And that's all I could find out. You claim to be a Venusian planter, and you might be. Any Terran who can handle weapons as you can would have come to my notice long ago. But you have no more ascertainable history than if you'd stepped out of another dimension."

That was getting uncomfortably close to the truth. In fact, it *was* the truth. Verkan Vall laughed.

"Well, confidentially," he said, "I'm from the Arcturus System. I followed the Lady Dallona here from our home planet, and when I have rescued her from among you Solarians, I shall, according to our customs, receive her hand in marriage. As she is the daughter of the Emperor of Arcturus, that'll be quite a good thing for me."

Klarnood chuckled. "You know, you'd only have to tell me that about three or four times and I'd start believing it," he said. "And Dr. Harnosh of Hosh would believe it the first time; he's been talking to himself ever since the Lady of Dallona started her experimental work here. Lord Virzal, I'm going to take a chance on you. The Lady Dallona is still carnate, or was four days ago, and the same for Dirzed. They both went into hiding after the discarnation feast of Garnon of Roxor, to escape the enmity of the Statisticalists. Two days after they disappeared, Dirzed called Assassins' Hall and reported this, but told us nothing more. I suppose, in about three or four days, I could re-establish contact with him. We want the public to think that the Statisticalists made away with the Lady Dallona, at least until the election's over."

Verkan Vall nodded. "I was pretty sure that was the situation," he said. "It may be that they will get in touch with me; if they don't, I'll need your help in reaching them."

"Why do you think the Lady Dallona will try to reach you?"

"She needs all the help she can get. She knows she can get plenty from me. Why do you think I interrupted my search for her, and risked my carnate existence, to fight those people over a matter of verbalisms and political propaganda?" Verkan Vall went to the newscast visiplate and snapped it on. "We'll see if I'm getting results, yet."

The plate lighted, and a handsome young man in a gold-laced green suit was speaking out of it:

". . . where he is heavily guarded by Assassins. However, in an exclusive interview with representatives of this service, the Assassin Hirzif, one of the two who seconded the men the Lord Virzal fought, said that in his opinion all of the three were so outclassed as to have had no chance whatever, and that he had already refused an offer of ten thousand System Monetary Units to discarnate the Lord Virzal for the Statisticalist Party. 'When I want to discarnate,' Hirzif the Assassin said, 'I'll invite in my friends and do it properly; until I do, I wouldn't go up against the Lord Virzal of Verkan for ten million S.M.U.' "

Verkan Vall snapped off the visiplate. "See what I mean?" he asked. "I fought those politicians just for the advertising. If Dallona and Dirzed are anywhere near a visiplate, they'll know how to reach me."

"Hirzif shouldn't have talked about refusing that retainer," Klarnood frowned. "That isn't good Assassin ethics. Why, yes, Lord Virzal; that was cleverly planned. It ought to get results. But I wish you'd get the Lady Dallona out of Darsh, and preferably off Terra, as soon as you can. We've benefited by this, so far, but I shouldn't like to see things go much further. A real civil war could develop out of this situation, and I don't want that. Call on me for help; I'll give you a code word to use at Assassins' Hall."

A real civil war was developing even as Klarnood spoke; by mid-morning of the next day, the fighting that had been partially suppressed by the Constabulary had broken out anew. The Assassins employed by the Solar Hotel—heavily re-enforced during the night—had fought a pitched battle with Statisticalist partisans on the landing-stage above Verkan Vall's suite, and now several Constabulary airboats were patrolling around the building. The rule on Constabulary interference seemed to be that while individuals had an unquestionable right to shoot out their differences among themselves, any fighting likely to endanger non-participants was taboo.

Just how successful in enforcing this rule the Constabulary were was open to some doubt. Ever since arising, Verkan Vall had heard the crash of small arms and the hammering of automatic weapons in other parts of the towering city-unit. There hadn't been a civil war on the Akor-Neb Sector for over five centuries, he knew, but then, Hadron Dalla, Doctor of Psychic Science, and intertemporal trouble-carrier extraordinary, had only been on this sector for a little under a year. If anything, he was surprised that the explosion had taken so long to occur.

One of the servants furnished to him by the hotel management approached him in the drawing room, holding a four-inch-square wafer of white plastic.

"Lord Virzal, there is a masked Assassin in the hallway who brought this under Assassins' Truce," he said.

Verkan Vall took the wafer and pared off three of the four edges, which showed black where they had been fused. Unfolding it, he found, as he had expected, that the pyrographed message within was in the alphabet and language of the First Paratime Level:

Vall, darling:

Am I glad you got here; this time I really *am* in the middle, but good! The Assassin, Dirzed, who brings this, is in my service. You can trust him implicitly; he's about the only person in Darsh you can trust. He'll bring you to where I am.

Dalla

P.S. I hope you're not still angry about that musician. I told you, at the time, that he was just helping me with an experiment in telepathy.

D.

Verkan Vall grinned at the postscript. That had been twenty years ago, when he'd been eighty and she'd been seventy. He supposed she'd expect him to take up his old relationship with her again. It probably wouldn't last any longer than it had, the other time; he recalled a Fourth Level proverb about the leopard and his spots. It certainly wouldn't be boring, though.

"Tell the Assassin to come in," he directed. Then he tossed the message down on a table. Outside of himself, nobody in Darsh could read it but the woman who had sent it; if, as he thought highly probable, the Statisticalists had spies among the hotel staff, it might serve to reduce some cryptanalyst to gibbering insanity.

The Assassin entered, drawing off a cowllike mask. He was the man whose arm Dalla had been holding in the visiplate picture; Verkan Vall even recognized the extremely ornate pistol and knife on his belt.

"Dirzed the Assassin," he named himself. "If you wish, we can visi-phone Assassins' Hall for verification of my identity."

"Lord Virzal of Verkan. And my Assassins, Marnik and Olirzon." They all hooked fingers and clapped shoulders with the newcomer. "That won't be needed," Verkan Vall told Dirzed. "I know you from seeing you with the Lady Dallona, on the visiplate; you're 'Dirzed, her faithful Assassin.'"

Dirzed's face, normally the color of a good walnut gunstock, turned almost black. He used shockingly bad language.

"And that's why I have to wear this abomination," he finished, display-ing the mask. "The Lady Dallona and I can't show our faces anywhere; if we did, every Statisticalist and his six-year-old brat would know us, and we'd be fighting off an army of them in five minutes."

"Where's the Lady Dallona, now?"

"In hiding, Lord Virzal, at a private dwelling dome in the forest; she's most anxious to see you. I'm to take you to her, and I would strongly advise that you bring your Assassins along. There are other people at this dome, and they are not personally loyal to the Lady Dallona. I've no reason to suspect them of secret enmity, but their friendship is based entirely on political expediency."

"And political expediency is subject to change without notice," Verkan Vall finished for him. "Have you an airboat?"

"On the landing stage below. Shall we go now, Lord Virzal?"

"Yes." Verkan Vall made a two-handed gesture to his Assassins, as though gripping a submachine-gun; they nodded, went into another room, and returned carrying light automatic weapons in their hands and pouches of spare drums slung over their shoulders. "And may I suggest, Dirzed, that one of my Assassins drives the airboat? I want you on the back seat with me, to explain the situation as we go."

Dirzed's teeth flashed white against his brown skin as he gave Verkan Vall a quick smile.

"By all means, Lord Virzal; I would much rather be distrusted than to find that my client's friends were not discreet."

There were a couple of hotel Assassins guarding Dirzed's airboat, on the landing stage. Marnik climbed in under the controls, with Olirzon beside him; Verkan Vall and Dirzed entered the rear seat. Dirzed gave Marnik the co-ordinate reference for their destination.

"Now, what sort of a place is this, where we're going?" Verkan Vall asked. "And who's there whom we may or may not trust?"

"Well, it's a dome house belonging to the family of Starpha; they own a five-mile radius around it, oak and beech forest and underbrush, stocked with deer and boar. A hunting lodge. Prince Jirzyn of Starpha, Lord

Girzon of Roxor, and a few other top-level Volitionalists, know that the Lady Dallona's hiding there. They're keeping her out of sight till after the election, for propaganda purposes. We've been hiding there since immediately after the discarnation feast of the Lord Garnon of Roxor."

"What happened, after the feast?" Verkan Vall wanted to know.

"Well, you know how the Lady Dallona and Dr. Harnosh of Hosh had this telepathic-sensitive there, in a trance and drugged with a *zerfa*-derivative alkaloid the Lady Dallona had developed. I was Lord Garnon's Assassin; I discarnated him, myself. Why, I hadn't even put my pistol away before he was in control of this sensitive, in a room five stories above the banquet hall; he began communicating at once. We had visiplates to show us what was going on.

"Right away, Nirzav of Shonna, one of the Statisticalist leaders who was a personal friend of Lord Garnon's in spite of his politics, renounced Statisticalism and went over to the Volitionalists, on the strength of this communication. Prince Jirzyn, and Lord Girzon, the new family-head of Roxor, decided that there would be trouble in the next few days, so they advised the Lady Dallona to come to this hunting lodge for safety. She and I came here in her airboat, directly from the feast. A good thing we did, too; if we'd gone to her apartment, we'd have walked in before that lethal gas had time to clear.

"There are four Assassins of the family of Starpha, and six menservants, and an upper-servant named Tarnod, the gamekeeper. The Starpha Assassins and I have been keeping the rest under observation. I left one of the Starpha Assassins guarding the Lady Dallona when I came for you, under brotherly oath to protect her in my name till I returned."

The airboat was skimming rapidly above the treetops, toward the northern part of the city.

"What's known about that package bomb?" Verkan Vall asked. "Who sent it?"

Dirzed shrugged. "The Statisticalists, of course. The wrapper was stolen from the Reincarnation Research Institute; so was the case. The Constabulary are working on it." Dirzed shrugged again.

The dome, about a hundred and fifty feet in width and some fifty in height, stood among the trees ahead. It was almost invisible from any distance; the concrete dome was of mottled green and gray concrete, trees grew so close as to brush it with their branches, and the little pavilion on the flattened top was roofed with translucent green plastic. As the airboat came in, a couple of men in Assassins' garb emerged from the pavilion to meet them.

"Marnik, stay at the controls," Verkan Vall directed. "I'll send Olirzon up for you if I want you. If there's any trouble, take off for Assassins' Hall and give the code word, then come back with twice as many men as you think you'll need."

Dirzed raised his eyebrows over this. "I hadn't known the Assassin-President had given you a code word, Lord Virzal," he commented. "That doesn't happen very often."

"The Assassin-President has honored me with his friendship," Verkan Vall replied noncommittally, as he, Dirzed and Olirzon climbed out of the airboat. Marnik was holding it an unobtrusive inch or so above the flat top of the dome, away from the edge of the pavilion roof.

The two Assassins greeted him, and a man in upper-servants' garb and wearing a hunting knife and a long hunting pistol approached.

"Lord Virzal of Verkan? Welcome to Starpha Dome. The Lady Dallona awaits you below."

Verkan Vall had never been in an Akor-Neb dwelling dome, but a description of such structures had been included in his hypno-mech indoctrination. Originally, they had been the standard structure for all purposes; about two thousand elapsed years ago, when nationalism had still existed on the Akor-Neb Sector, the cities had been almost entirely underground, as protection from air attack. Even now, the design had been retained by those who wished to live apart from the towering city units, to preserve the natural appearance of the landscape. The Starpha hunting lodge was typical of such domes. Under it was a circular well, eighty feet in depth and fifty in width, with a fountain and a shallow circular pool at the bottom. The storerooms, kitchens and servants' quarters were at the top, the living quarters at the bottom, in segments of a wide circle around the well, back of balconies.

"Tarnod, the gamekeeper," Dirzed performed the introductions. "And Erarno and Kirzol, Assassins."

Verkan Vall hooked fingers and clapped shoulders with them. Tarnod accompanied them to the lifter tubes—two percent positive gravitation for descent and two percent negative for ascent—and they all floated down the former, like air-filled balloons, to the bottom level.

"The Lady Dallona is in the gun room," Tarnod informed Verkan Vall, making as though to guide him.

"Thanks, Tarnod; we know the way," Dirzed told him shortly, turning his back on the upper-servant and walking toward a closed door on the other side of the fountain. Verkan Vall and Olirzon followed; for a moment, Tarnod stood looking after them, then he followed the other two Assassins into the ascent tube.

"I don't relish that fellow," Dirzed explained. "The family of Starpha use him for work they couldn't hire an Assassin to do at any price. I've been here often, when I was with the Lord Garnon; I've always thought he had something on Prince Jirzyn."

He knocked sharply on the closed door with the butt of his pistol. In a moment, it slid open, and a young Assassin with a narrow mustache and a tuft of chin beard looked out.

"Ah, Dirzed." He stepped outside. "The Lady Dallona is within; I return her to your care."

Verkan Vall entered, followed by Dirzed and Olirzon. The big room was fitted with reclining chairs and couches and low tables; its walls were hung with the heads of deer and boar and wolves, and with racks holding rifles and hunting pistols and fowling pieces. It was filled with the soft glow of indirect cold light. At the far side of the room, a young woman was seated at a desk, speaking softly into a sound transcriber. As they entered, she snapped it off and rose.

Hadron Dalla wore the same costume Verkan Vall had seen on the visiplate; he recognized her instantly. It took her a second or two to perceive Verkan Vall under the brown skin and black hair of the Lord Virzal of Verkan. Then her face lighted with a happy smile.

"Why, Va-a-a-ll!" she whooped, running across the room and tossing herself into his not particularly reluctant arms. After all, it had been twenty years— "I didn't know you, at first!"

"You mean, in these clothes?" he asked, seeing that she had forgotten, for the moment, the presence of the two Assassins. She had even called him by his First Level name, but that was unimportant—the Akor-Neb affectionate diminutive was formed by omitting the *-irz-* or *-arn-*. "Well, they're not exactly what I generally wear on the plantation." He kissed her again, then turned to his companions. "Your pardon, Gentlemen-Assassins; it's been something over a year since we've seen each other."

Olirzon was smiling at the affectionate reunion; Dirzed wore a look of amused resignation, as though he might have expected something like this to happen. Verkan Vall and Dalla sat down on a couch near the desk.

"That was really sweet of you, Vall, fighting those men for talking about me," she began. "You took an awful chance, though. But if you hadn't, I'd never have known you were in Darsh— Oh-oh! That was why you did it, wasn't it?"

"Well, I had to do something. Everybody either didn't know or weren't saying where you were. I assumed, from the circumstances, that you were hiding somewhere. Tell me, Dalla; do you really have scientific proof of reincarnation? I mean, as an established fact?"

"Oh, yes; these people on this sector have had that for over ten centuries. They have hypnotic techniques for getting back into a part of the subconscious mind that we've never been able to reach. And after I found out how they did it, I was able to adapt some of our hypno-epistemological techniques to it, and—"

"All right; that's what I wanted to know," he cut her off. "We're getting out of here, right away."

"But where?"

"Ghamma, in an airboat I have outside, and then back to the First Level. Unless there's a paratime-transposition conveyor somewhere nearer."

"But why, Vall? I'm not ready to go back; I have a lot of work to do here, yet. They're getting ready to set up a series of control-experiments at the Institute, and then, I'm in the middle of an experiment, a two-hundred-subject memory-recall experiment. See, I distributed two hundred sets of equipment for my new technique—injection-ampoules of this *zerfa*-derivative drug, and sound records of the hypnotic suggestion formula, which can be played on an ordinary reproducer. It's just a crude variant of our hypno-mech process, except that instead of implanting information in the subconscious mind, to be brought at will to the level of consciousness, it works the other way, and draws into conscious knowledge information already in the subconscious mind. The way these people have always done has been to put the subject in an hypnotic trance and then record verbal statements made in the trance state; when the subject comes out of the trance, the record is all there is, because the memories of past reincarnations have never been in the conscious mind. But with my process, the subject can consciously remember everything about his last reincarnation, and as many reincarnations before that as he wishes to. I haven't heard from any of the people who received these auto-recall kits, and I really must—"

"Dalla, I don't want to have to pull Paratime Police authority on you, but, so help me, if you don't come back voluntarily with me, I will. Security of the secret of paratime-transposition."

"Oh, my eye!" Dalla exclaimed. "Don't give me that, Vall!"

"Look, Dalla. Suppose you get discarnated here," Verkan Vall said. "You say reincarnation is a scientific fact. Well, you'd reincarnate on this sector, and then you'd take a memory-recall, under hypnosis. And when you did, the paratime secret wouldn't be a secret any more."

"Oh!" Dalla's hand went to her mouth in consternation. Like every paratimer, she was conditioned to shrink with all her being from the mere thought of revealing to any out-time dweller the secret ability of her race to pass to other time-lines, or even the existence of alternate lines of probability. "And if I took one of the old-fashioned trance-recalls, I'd blat out everything; I wouldn't be able to keep a thing back. And I even know the principles of transposition!" She looked at him, aghast.

"When I get back, I'm going to put a recommendation through department channels that this whole sector be declared out of bounds for all paratime-transposition, until you people at Rhogom Foundation work out the problem of discarnate return to the First Level," he told her. "Now, have you any notes or anything you want to take back with you?"

She rose. "Yes; just what's on the desk. Find me something to put the tape spools and notebooks in, while I'm getting them in order."

He secured a large game bag from under a rack of fowling pieces, and held it while she sorted the material rapidly, stuffing spools of record tape and notebooks into it. They had barely begun when the door slid open and Olirzon, who had gone outside, sprang into the room, his pistol drawn, swearing vilely.

"They've double-crossed us!" he cried. "The servants of Starpha have turned on us." He holstered his pistol and snatched up his submachine-gun, taking cover behind the edge of the door and letting go with a burst in the direction of the lifter tubes. "Got that one!" he grunted.

"What happened, Olirzon?" Verkan Vall asked, dropping the game bag on the table and hurrying across the room.

"I went up to see how Marnik was making out. As I came out of the lifter tube, one of the obscenities took a shot at me with a hunting pistol. He missed me; I didn't miss him. Then a couple more of them were coming up, with fowling pieces; I shot one of them before they could fire, and jumped into the descent tube and came down heels over ears. I don't know what's happened to Marnik." He fired another burst, and swore. "Missed him!"

"Assassins' Truce! Assassins' Truce!" a voice howled out of the descent tube. "Hold your fire, we want to parley."

"Who is it?" Dirzed shouted, over Olirzon's shoulder. "You, Sarnax? Come on out; we won't shoot."

The young Assassin with the mustache and chin beard emerged from the descent tube, his weapons sheathed and his clasped hands extended in front of him in a peculiarly ecclesiastical-looking manner. Dirzed and

Olirzon stepped out of the gun room, followed by Verkan Vall and Had-ron Dalla. Olirzon had left his submachine-gun behind. They met the other Assassin by the rim of the fountain pool.

"Lady Dallona of Hadron," the Starpha Assassin began. "I and my col-leagues, in the employ of the family of Starpha, have received orders from our clients to withdraw our protection from you, and to discarnate you, and all with you who undertake to protect or support you." That much sounded like a recitation of some established formula; then his voice became more conversational. "I and my colleagues, Erarno and Kir-zol and Harnif, offer our apologies for the barbarity of the servants of the family of Starpha, in attacking without declaration of cessation of friend-ship. Was anybody hurt or discarnated?"

"None of us," Olirzon said. "How about Marnik?"

"He was warned before hostilities were begun against him," Sarnax replied. "We will allow five minutes until—"

Olirzon, who had been looking up the well, suddenly sprang at Dalla, knocking her flat, and at the same time jerking out his pistol. Before he could raise it, a shot banged from above and he fell on his face. Dirzed, Verkan Vall, and Sarnax, all drew their pistols, but whoever had fired the shot had vanished. There was an outburst of shouting above.

"Get to cover," Sarnax told the others. "We'll let you know when we're ready to attack; we'll have to deal with whoever fired that shot, first." He looked at the dead body on the floor, exclaimed angrily, and hurried to the ascent tube, springing upward.

Verkan Vall replaced the small pistol in his shoulder holster and took Olirzon's belt, with his knife and heavier pistol.

"Well, there you see," Dirzed said, as they went back to the gun room. "So much for political expediency."

"I think I understand why your picture and the Lady Dallona's were exhibited so widely," Verkan Vall said. "Now, anybody would recognize your bodies, and blame the Statisticalists for discarnating you."

"That thought had occurred to me, Lord Virzal," Dirzed said. "I sup-pose our bodies will be atrociously but not unidentifiably mutilated, to further enrage the public," he added placidly. "If I get out of this car-nate, I'm going to pay somebody off for it."

After a few minutes, there was more shouting of: "Assassins' Truce!" from the descent tube. The two Assassins, Erarno and Kirzol, emerged, dragging the gamekeeper, Tarnod, between them. The upper-servant's face was bloody, and his jaw seemed to be broken. Sarnax followed, carry-ing a long hunting pistol in his hand.

"Here he is!" he announced. "He fired during Assassins' Truce; he's subject to Assassins' Justice!"

He nodded to the others. They threw the gamekeeper forward on the floor, and Sarnax shot him through the head, then tossed the pistol down beside him. "Any more of these people who violate the decencies will be treated similarly," he promised.

"Thank you, Sarnax," Dirzed spoke up. "But we lost an Assassin; discarnating this lackey won't equalize that. We think you should retire one of your number."

"That at least, Dirzed; wait a moment."

The three Assassins conferred at some length. Then Sarnax hooked fingers and clapped shoulders with his companions.

"See you in the next reincarnation, brothers," he told them, walking toward the gun-room door, where Verkan Vall, Dalla and Dirzed stood. "I'm joining you people. You had two Assassins when the parley began, you'll have two when the shooting starts."

Verkan Vall looked at Dirzed in some surprise. Hadron Dalla's Assassin nodded.

"He's entitled to do that, Lord Virzal; the Assassins' code provides for such changes of allegiance."

"Welcome, Sarnax," Verkan Vall said, hooking fingers with him. "I hope we'll all be together when this is over."

"We will be," Sarnax assured him cheerfully. "Discarnate. We won't get out of this in the body, Lord Virzal."

A submachine-gun hammered from above, the bullets lashing the fountain pool; the water actually steamed, so great was their velocity.

"All right!" a voice called down. "Assassins' Truce is over!"

Another burst of automatic fire smashed out the lights at the bottom of the ascent tube. Dirzed and Dalla struggled across the room, pushing a heavy steel cabinet between them; Verkan Vall, who was holding Olirzon's submachine-gun, moved aside to allow them to drop it on edge in the open doorway, then wedged the door half-shut against it. Sarnax came over, bringing rifles, hunting pistols, and ammunition.

"What's the situation, up there?" Verkan Vall asked him. "What force have they, and why did they turn against us?"

"Lord Virzal!" Dirzed objected, scandalized. "You have no right to ask Sarnax to betray confidences!"

Sarnax spat against the door. "In the face of Jirzyn of Starpha!" he said. "And in the face of his *zortan* mother, and of his father, whoever he was!

Dirzed, do not talk foolishly; one does not speak of betraying betrayers."
He turned to Verkan Vall. "They have three menservants of the family
of Starpha; your Assassin, Olirzon, discarnated the other three. There
is one of Prince Jirzyn's poor relations, named Girzad. There are three
other men, Volitionalist precinct workers, who came with Girzad, and
four Assassins, the three who were here, and one who came with Girzad.
Eleven, against the three of us."

"The four of us, Sarnax," Dalla corrected. She had buckled on a hunting pistol, and had a light deer rifle under her arm.

Something moved at the bottom of the descent tube. Verkan Vall gave
it a short burst, though it was probably only a dummy, dropped to draw
fire.

"The four of us, Lady Dallona," Sarnax agreed. "As to your other
Assassin, the one who stayed in the airboat, I don't know how he fared.
You see, about twenty minutes ago, this Girzad arrived in an airboat, with
an Assassin and these three Volitionalist workers. Erarno and I were at
the top of the dome when he came in. He told us that he had orders from
Prince Jirzyn to discarnate the Lady Dallona and Dirzed at once. Tarnod,
the gamekeeper"—Sarnax spat ceremoniously against the door again—
"told him you were here, and that Marnik was one of your men. He was
going to shoot Marnik at once, but Erarno and I and his Assassin stopped
him. We warned Marnik about the change in the situation, according
to the code, expecting Marnik to go down here and join you. Instead,
he lifted the airboat, zoomed over Girzad's boat, and let go a rocket blast,
setting Girzad's boat on fire. Well, that was a hostile act, so we all fired
after him. We must have hit something, because the boat went down,
trailing smoke, about ten miles away. Girzad got another airboat out of
the hangar and he and his Assassin started after your man. About that
time, your Assassin, Olirzon—happy reincarnation to him—came up, and
the Starpha servants fired at him, and he fired back and discarnated two
of them, and then jumped down the descent tube. One of the servants
jumped after him; I found his body at the bottom when I came down to
warn you formally. You know what happened after that."

"But why did Prince Jirzyn order our discarnation?" Dalla wanted
to know. "Was it to blame the Statisticalists with it?"

Sarnax, about to answer, broke off suddenly and began firing at the
opening of the ascent tube with a hunting pistol.

"I got him," he said, in a pleased tone. "That was Erarno; he was always
playing tricks with the tubes, climbing down against negative gravity and
up against positive gravity. His body will float up to the top— Why, Lady

Dallona, that was only part of it. You didn't hear about the big scandal on the newscast, then?"

"We didn't have it on. What scandal?"

Sarnax laughed. "Oh, the very father and family-head of all scandals! You ought to know about it, because you started it; that's why Prince Jirzyn wants you out of the body— You devised a process by which people could give themselves memory-recalls of previous reincarnations, didn't you? And distributed apparatus to do it with? And gave one set to young Tarnov, the son of Lord Tirzov of Fastor?"

Dalla nodded. Sarnax continued:

"Well, last evening, Tarnov of Fastor used his recall outfit, and what do you think? It seems that thirty years ago, in his last reincarnation, he was Jirzid of Starpha, Jirzyn's older brother. Jirzid was betrothed to the Lady Annitra of Zabna. Well, his younger brother was carrying on a clandestine affair with the Lady Annitra, and he also wanted the title of Prince and family-head of Starpha. So he bribed this fellow Tarnod, whom I had the pleasure of discarnating, and who was an underservant here at the hunting lodge. Between them, they shot Jirzid during a boar hunt. An accident, of course. So Jirzyn married the Lady Annitra, and when old Prince Jarnid, his father, discarnated a year later, he succeeded to the title. And immediately, Tarnod was made head gamekeeper here."

"What did I tell you, Lord Virzal? I knew that son of a *zortan* had something on Jirzyn of Starpha!" Dirzed exclaimed. "A nice family, this of Starpha!"

"Well, that's not the end of it," Sarnax continued. "This morning, Tarnov of Fastor, late Jirzid of Starpha, went before the High Court of Estates and entered suit to change his name to Jirzid of Starpha and laid claim to the title of Starpha family-head. The case has just been entered, so there's been no hearing, but there's the blazes of an argument among all the nobles about it—some are claiming that the individuality doesn't change from one reincarnatus to the next, and others claiming that property and titles should pass along the line of physical descent, no matter what individuality has reincarnated into what body. They're the ones who want the Lady Dallona discarnated and her discoveries suppressed. And there's talk about revising the entire system of estate-ownership and estate-inheritance. Oh, it's an utter obscenity of a business!"

"This," Verkan Vall told Dalla, "is something we will not emphasize when we get home." That was as close as he dared come to it, but she caught his meaning. The working of major changes in outtime social structures was not viewed with approval by the Paratime Commission on the First Level. "*If* we get home," he added. Then an idea occurred to him.

"Dirzed, Sarnax; this place must have been used by the leaders of the Volitionalists for top-level conferences. Is there a secret passage anywhere?"

Sarnax shook his head. "Not from here. There is one, on the floor above, but they control it. And even if there were one down here, they would be guarding the outlet."

"That's what I was counting on. I'd hoped to simulate an escape that way, and then make a rush up the regular tubes." Verkan Vall shrugged. "I suppose Marnik's our only chance. I hope he got away safely."

"He was going for help? I was surprised that an Assassin would desert his client; I should have thought of that," Sarnax said. "Well, even if he got down carnate, and if Girzad didn't catch him, he'd still be afoot ten miles from the nearest city unit. That gives us a little chance—about one in a thousand."

"Is there any way they can get at us, except by those tubes?" Dalla asked.

"They could cut a hole in the floor, or burn one through," Sarnax replied. "They have plenty of thermite. They could detonate a charge of explosives over our heads, or clear out of the dome and drop one down the well. They could use lethal gas or radiodust, but their Assassins wouldn't permit such illegal methods. Or they could shoot sleep-gas down at us, and then come down and cut our throats at their leisure."

"We'll have to get out of this room, then," Verkan Vall decided. "They know we've barricaded ourselves in here; this is where they'll attack. So we'll patrol the perimeter of the well; we'll be out of danger from above if we keep close to the wall. And we'll inspect all the rooms on this floor for evidence of cutting through from above."

Sarnax nodded. "That's sense, Lord Virzal. How about the lifter tubes?"

"We'll have to barricade them. Sarnax, you and Dirzed know the layout of this place better than the Lady Dallona or I; suppose you two check the rooms, while we cover the tubes and the well," Verkan Vall directed. "Come on, now."

They pushed the door wide-open and went out past the cabinet. Hugging the wall, they began a slow circuit of the well, Verkan Vall in the lead with the submachine-gun, then Sarnax and Dirzed, the former with a heavy boar-rifle and the latter with a hunting pistol in each hand, and Hadron Dalla brought up the rear with her rifle. It was she who noticed a movement along the rim of the balcony above and snapped a shot at it; there was a crash above, and a shower of glass and plastic and metal fragments rattled on the pavement of the court. Somebody had been trying to lower a scanner or a visiplate-pickup, or something of the sort; the exact nature of the instrument was not evident from the wreckage Dalla's bullet had made of it.

The rooms Dirzed and Sarnax entered were all quiet; nobody seemed to be attempting to cut through the ceiling, fifteen feet above. They dragged furniture from a couple of rooms, blocking the openings of the lifter tubes, and continued around the well until they had reached the gun room again.

Dirzed suggested that they move some of the weapons and ammunition stored there to Prince Jirzyn's private apartment, halfway around to the lifter tubes, so that another place of refuge would be stocked with munitions in event of their being driven from the gun room.

Leaving him on guard outside, Verkan Vall, Dalla and Sarnax entered the gun room and began gathering weapons and boxes of ammunition. Dalla finished packing her game bag with the recorded data and notes of her experiments. Verkan Vall selected four more of the heavy hunting pistols, more accurate than his shoulder-holster weapon or the dead Olirzon's belt arm, and capable of either full- or semi-automatic fire. Sarnax chose a couple more boar rifles. Dalla slung her bag of recorded notes, and another bag of ammunition, and secured another deer rifle. They carried this accumulation of munitions to the private apartment of Prince Jirzyn, dumping everything in the middle of the drawing room, except the bag of notes, from which Dalla refused to separate herself.

"Maybe we'd better put some stuff over in one of the rooms on the other side of the well," Dirzed suggested. "They haven't really begun to come after us; when they do, we'll probably be attacked from two or three directions at once."

They returned to the gun room, casting anxious glances at the edge of the balcony above and at the barricade they had erected across the openings to the lifter tubes. Verkan Vall was not satisfied with this last; it looked to him as though they had provided a breastwork for somebody to fire on them from, more than anything else.

He was about to step around the cabinet which partially blocked the gun-room door when he glanced up, and saw a six-foot circle on the ceiling turning slowly brown. There was a smell of scorched plastic. He grabbed Sarnax by the arm and pointed.

"Thermite," the Assassin whispered. "The ceiling's got six inches of spaceship-insulation between it and the floor above; it'll take them a few minutes to burn through it." He stooped and pushed on the barricade, shoving it into the room. "Keep back; they'll probably drop a grenade or so through, first, before they jump down. If we're quick, we can get a couple of them."

Dirzed and Sarnax crouched, one at either side of the door, with weapons ready. Verkan Vall and Dalla had been ordered, rather peremptorily, to stay behind them; in a place of danger, an Assassin was obliged to shield his client. Verkan Vall, unable to see what was going on inside the room, kept his eyes and his gun muzzle on the barricade across the openings to the lifter tubes, the erection of which he was now regretting as a major tactical error.

Inside the gun room, there was a sudden crash, as the circle of thermite burned through and a section of ceiling dropped out and hit the floor. Instantly, Dirzed flung himself back against Verkan Vall, and there was a tremendous explosion inside, followed by another and another. A second or so passed, then Dirzed, leaning around the corner of the door, began firing rapidly into the room. From the other side of the door, Sarnax began blazing away with his rifle. Verkan Vall kept his position, covering the lifter tubes.

Suddenly, from behind the barricade, a blue-white gun flash leaped into being, and a pistol banged. He sprayed the opening between a couch and a section of bookcase from whence it had come, releasing his trigger as the gun rose with the recoil, squeezing and releasing and squeezing again. Then he jumped to his feet.

"Come on, the other place; hurry!" he ordered.

Sarnax swore in exasperation. "Help me with her, Dirzed!" he implored.

Verkan Vall turned his head, to see the two Assassins drag Dalla to her feet and hustle her away from the gun room; she was quite senseless, and they had to drag her between them. Verkan Vall gave a quick glance into the gun room; two of the Starpha servants and a man in rather flashy civil dress were lying on the floor, where they had been shot as they had jumped down from above. He saw a movement at the edge of the irregular, smoking hole in the ceiling, and gave it a short burst, then fired another at the exit from the descent tube. Then he took to his heels and followed the Assassins and Hadron Dalla into Prince Jirzyn's apartment.

As he ran through the open door, the Assassins were letting Dalla down into a chair; they instantly threw themselves into the work of barricading the doorway so as to provide cover and at the same time allow them to fire out into the central well.

For an instant, as he bent over her, he thought Dalla had been killed, an assumption justified by his knowledge of the deadliness of Akor-Neb bullets. Then he saw her eyelids flicker. A moment later, he had the explanation of her escape. The bullet had hit the game bag at her side; it was full of spools of metal tape, in metal cases, and notes in written form, pyrographed upon sheets of plastic ring-fastened into metal binders. Because of their extreme velocity, Akor-Neb bullets were sure killers when they struck animal tissue, but for the same reason, they had very poor penetration on hard objects. The alloy-steel tape, and the steel spools and spool cases, and the notebook binders, had been enough to shatter the little bullet into tiny splinters of magnesium-nickel alloy, and the stout leather back of the game bag had stopped all of these. But the impact, even distributed as it had been through the contents of the bag, had been enough to knock the girl unconscious.

He found a bottle of some sort of brandy and a glass on a serving table nearby and poured her a drink, holding it to her lips. She spluttered over the first mouthful, then took the glass from him and sipped the rest.

"What happened?" she asked. "I thought those bullets were sure death."

"Your notes. The bullet hit the bag. Are you all right, now?"

She finished the brandy. "I think so." She put a hand into the game bag and brought out a snarled and tangled mess of steel tape. "Oh, *blast!* That stuff was important; all the records on the preliminary auto-recall experiments." She shrugged. "Well, it wouldn't have been worth much more if I'd stopped that bullet, myself." She slipped the strap over her shoulder and started to rise.

As she did, a bedlam of firing broke out, both from the two Assassins at the door and from outside. They both hit the floor and crawled out of line of the partly-open door; Verkan Vall recovered his submachine-gun, which he had set down beside Dalla's chair. Sarnax was firing with his rifle at some target in the direction of the lifter tubes; Dirzed lay slumped over the barricade, and one glance at his crumpled figure was enough to tell Verkan Vall that he was dead.

"You fill magazines for us," he told Dalla, then crawled to Dirzed's place at the door. "What happened, Sarnax?"

"They shoved over the barricade at the lifter tubes and came out into the well. I got a couple, they got Dirzed, and now they're holed up in rooms all around the circle. They— Aah!" He fired three shots, quickly, around the edge of the door. "That stopped that." The Assassin crouched to insert a fresh magazine into his rifle.

Verkan Vall risked one eye around the corner of the doorway, and as he did, there was a red flash and a dull roar, unlike the blue flashes and sharp cracking reports of the pistols and rifles, from the doorway of the gun room. He wondered, for a split second, if it might be one of the fowling pieces he had seen there, and then something whizzed past his head and exploded with a soft *plop* behind him. Turning, he saw a pool of gray vapor beginning to spread in the middle of the room. Dalla must have got a breath of it, for she was slumped over the chair from which she had just risen.

Dropping the submachine-gun and gulping a lungful of fresh air from outside, Verkan Vall rushed to her, caught her by the heels, and dragged her into Prince Jirzyn's bedroom, beyond. Leaving her in the middle of the floor, he took another deep breath and returned to the drawing room, where Sarnax was already overcome by the sleep-gas.

He saw the serving table from which he had got the brandy, and dragged it over to the bedroom door, overturning it and laying it across the doorway, its legs in the air. Like most Akor-Neb serving tables, it had a gravity-counteraction unit under it; he set this for double minus-gravitation and snapped it on. As it was now above the inverted table, the table did not rise, but a tendril of sleep-gas, curling toward it, bent upward and drifted away from the doorway. Satisfied that he had made a temporary barrier against the sleep-gas, Verkan Vall secured Dalla's hunting pistol and spare magazines and lay down at the bedroom door.

For some time, there was silence outside. Then the besiegers evidently decided that the sleep-gas attack had been a success. An Assassin, wearing a gas mask and carrying a submachine-gun, appeared in the doorway, and behind him came a tall man in a tan tunic, similarly masked. They stepped into the room and looked around.

Knowing that he would be shooting over a two hundred percent negative gravitation-field, Verkan Vall aimed for the Assassin's belt-buckle and squeezed. The bullet caught him in the throat. Evidently the bullet had not only been lifted in the negative gravitation, but lifted point-first and deflected upward. He held his front sight just above the other man's knee, and hit him in the chest.

As he fired, he saw a wisp of gas come sliding around the edge of the inverted table. There was silence outside, and for an instant, he was tempted to abandon his post and go to the bathroom, back of the bedroom, for wet towels to improvise a mask. Then, when he tried to crawl backward, he could not. There was an impression of distant shouting which turned to a roaring sound in his head. He tried to lift his pistol, but it slipped from his fingers.

When consciousness returned, he was lying on his back, and something cold and rubbery was pressing into his face. He raised his arms to fight off whatever it was, and opened his eyes, to find that he was staring directly at the red oval and winged bullet of the Society of Assassins. A hand caught his wrist as he reached for the small pistol under his arm. The pressure on his face eased.

"It's all right, Lord Virzal," a voice came to him. "Assassins' Truce!"

He nodded stupidly and repeated the words. "Assassins' Truce; I won't shoot. What happened?"

Then he sat up and looked around. Prince Jirzyn's bedchamber was full of Assassins. Dalla, recovering from her touch of sleep-gas, was sitting groggily in a chair, while five or six of them fussed around her, getting in each other's way, handing her drinks, chafing her wrists, holding damp cloths on her brow. That was standard procedure, when any group of males thought Dalla needed any help. Another Assassin, beside the bed, was putting away an oxygen-mask outfit, and the Assassin who had prevented Verkan Vall from drawing his pistol was his own follower, Marnik. And Klarnood, the Assassin-President, was sitting on the foot of the bed, smoking one of Prince Jirzyn's monogrammed and crested cigarettes critically.

Verkan Vall looked at Marnik, and then at Klarnood, and back to Marnik.

"You got through," he said. "Good work, Marnik; I thought they'd downed you."

"They did; I had to crash-land in the woods. I went about a mile on foot, and then I found a man and woman and two children, hiding in one of these little log rain shelters. They had an airboat, a good one. It seemed that rioting had broken out in the city unit where they lived, and they'd taken to the woods till things quieted down again. I offered them Assassins' protection if they'd take me to Assassins' Hall, and they did."

"By luck, I was in when Marnik arrived," Klarnood took over. "We brought three boatloads of men, and came here at once. Just as we got here, two boatloads of Starpha dependents arrived; they tried to give us an argument, and we discarnated the lot of them. Then we came down here, crying Assassins' Truce. One of the Starpha Assassins, Kirzol, was still carnate; he told us what had been going on." The President-General's face became grim. "You know, I take a rather poor view of Prince Jirzyn's procedure in this matter, not to mention that of his underlings. I'll have to speak to him about this. Now, how about you and the Lady Dallona? What do you intend doing?"

"We're getting out of here," Verkan Vall said. "I'd like air transport and protection as far as Ghamma, to the establishment of the family of Zorda. Brarnend of Zorda has a private space yacht; he'll get us to Venus."

Klarnood gave a sigh of obvious relief. "I'll have you and the Lady Dallona airborne and off for Ghamma as soon as you wish," he promised. "I will, frankly, be delighted to see the last of both of you. The Lady Dallona has started a fire here at Darsh that won't burn out in a half-century, and who knows what it may consume." He was interrupted by a heaving shock that made the underground dome dwelling shake like a light airboat in turbulence. Even eighty feet under the ground, they could hear a continued crashing roar. It was an appreciable interval before the sound and the shock ceased.

For an instant, there was silence, and then an excited bedlam of shouting broke from the Assassins in the room. Klarnood's face was frozen in horror.

"That was a fission bomb!" he exclaimed. "The first one that has been exploded on this planet in hostility in a thousand years!" He turned to Verkan Vall. "If you feel well enough to walk, Lord Virzal, come with us. I must see what's happened."

They hurried from the room and went streaming up the ascent tube to the top of the dome. About forty miles away, to the south, Verkan Vall saw the sinister thing that he had seen on so many other time-lines, in so many other paratime sectors—a great pillar of varicolored fire-shot smoke, rising to a mushroom head fifty thousand feet above.

"Well, that's it," Klarnood said sadly. "That is civil war."

"May I make a suggestion, Assassin-President?" Verkan Vall asked. "I understand that Assassins' Truce is binding even upon non-Assassins; is that correct?"

"Well, not exactly; it's generally kept by such non-Assassins as want to remain in their present reincarnations, though."

"That's what I meant. Well, suppose you declare a general, planet-wide Assassins' Truce in this political war, and make the leaders of both parties responsible for keeping it. Publish lists of the top two or three thousand Statisticalists and Volitionalists, starting with Mirzark of Bashad and Prince Jirzyn of Starpha, and inform them that they will be assassinated, in order, if the fighting doesn't cease."

"Well!" A smile grew on Klarnood's face. "Lord Virzal, my thanks; a good suggestion. I'll try it. And furthermore, I'll withdraw all Assassin protection permanently from anybody involved in political activity, and forbid any Assassin to accept any retainer connected with political factionalism. It's about time our members stopped discarnating each other in these political squabbles." He pointed to the three airboats drawn up on the top of the dome; speedy black craft, bearing the red oval and winged bullet. "Take your choice, Lord Virzal. I'll lend you a couple of my men, and you'll be in Ghamma in three hours." He hooked fingers and clapped shoulders with Verkan Vall, bent over Dalla's hand. "I still like you, Lord Virzal, and I have seldom met a more charming lady than you, Lady Dallona. But I sincerely hope I never see either of you again."

The ship for Dhergabar was driving north and west; at seventy thousand feet, it was still daylight, but the world below was wrapping itself in darkness. In the big visiscreens, which served in lieu of the windows which could never have withstood the pressure and friction heat of the ship's speed, the sun was sliding out of sight over the horizon to port. Verkan Vall and Dalla sat together, watching the blazing western sky— the sky of their own First Level time-line.

"I blame myself terribly, Vall," Dalla was saying. "And I didn't mean any of them the least harm. All I was interested in was learning the facts. I know, that sounds like, 'I didn't know it was loaded,' but—"

"It sounds to me like those Fourth Level Europo-American Sector physicists who are giving themselves guilt-complexes because they designed an atomic bomb," Verkan Vall replied. "All you were interested in was learning the facts. Well, as a scientist, that's all you're supposed to be interested in. You don't have to worry about any social or political implications. People have to learn to live with newly-discovered facts; if they don't, they die of them."

"But, Vall; that sounds dreadfully irresponsible—"

"Does it? You're worrying about the results of your reincarnation memory-recall discoveries, the shootings and riotings and the bombing we saw." He touched the pommel of Olirzon's knife, which he still wore. "You're no more guilty of that than the man who forged this blade is guilty of the death of Marnark of Bashad; if he'd never lived, I'd have killed Marnark with some other knife somebody else made. And what's more, you can't know the results of your discoveries. All you can see is a thin film of events on the surface of an immediate situation, so you can't say whether the long-term results will be beneficial or calamitous.

"Take this Fourth Level Europo-American atomic bomb, for example. I choose that because we both know that sector, but I could think of a hundred other examples in other paratime areas. Those people, because of deforestation, bad agricultural methods and general mismanagement, are eroding away their arable soil at an alarming rate. At the same time, they are breeding like rabbits. In other words, each successive generation has less and less food to divide among more and more people, and, for inherited traditional and superstitious reasons, they refuse to adopt any rational program of birth-control and population-limitation.

"But, fortunately, they now have the atomic bomb, and they are developing radioactive poisons, weapons of mass-effect. And their racial, nationalistic and ideological conflicts are rapidly reaching the explosion point. A series of all-out atomic wars is just what that sector needs, to bring their population down to their world's carrying capacity; in a century or so, the inventors of the atomic bomb will be hailed as the saviors of their species."

"But how about my work on the Akor-Neb Sector?" Dalla asked. "It seems that my memory-recall technique is more explosive than any fission bomb. I've laid the train for a century-long reign of anarchy!"

"I doubt that; I think Klarnood will take hold, now that he has committed himself to it. You know, in spite of his sanguinary profession, he's the nearest thing to a real man of good will I've found on that sector. And here's something else you haven't considered. Our own First Level life expectancy is from four to five hundred years. That's the main reason why we've accomplished as much as we have. We have, individually, time to accomplish things. On the Akor-Neb Sector, a scientist or artist or scholar or statesman will grow senile and die before he's as old as either of us. But now, a young student of twenty or so can take one of your autorecall treatments and immediately have available all the knowledge and experience gained in four or five previous lives. He can start where he left off in his last reincarnation. In other words, you've made those people time-binders, individually as well as racially. Isn't that worth the temporary discarnation of a lot of ward-heelers and plug-uglies, or even a few decent types like Dirzed and Olirzon? If it isn't, I don't know what scale of values you're using."

"Vall!" Dalla's eyes glowed with enthusiasm. "I never thought of that! And you said, 'temporary discarnation.' That's just what it is. Dirzed and Olirzon and the others aren't dead; they're just waiting, discarnate, between physical lives. You know, in the sacred writings of one of the Fourth Level peoples it is stated: 'Death is the last enemy.' By proving that death is just a cyclic condition of continued individual existence, these people have conquered their last enemy."

"Last enemy but one," Verkan Vall corrected. "They still have one enemy to go, an enemy within themselves. Call it semantic confusion, or illogic, or incomprehension, or just plain stupidity. Like Klarnood, stymied by verbal objections to something labeled 'political intervention.' He'd never have consented to use the power of his Society if he hadn't been shocked out of his inhibitions by that nuclear bomb. Or the Statisticalists, trying to create a classless order of society through a political program which would only result in universal servitude to an omnipotent government. Or the Volitionalist nobles, trying to preserve their hereditary feudal privileges, and now they can't even agree on a definition of the term 'hereditary.' Might they not recover all the silly prejudices of their past lives, along with the knowledge and wisdom?"

"But . . . I thought you said—" Dalla was puzzled, a little hurt.

Verkan Vall's arm squeezed around her waist, and he laughed comfortingly.

"You see? Any sort of result is possible, good or bad. So don't blame yourself in advance for something you can't possibly estimate." An idea occurred to him, and he straightened in the seat. "Tell you what; if you people at Rhogom Foundation get the problem of discarnate paratime transposition licked by then, let's you and I go back to the Akor-Neb Sector in about a hundred years and see what sort of a mess those people have made of things."

"A hundred years; that would be Year Twenty-Two of the next millennium. It's a date, Vall; we'll do it."

They bent to light their cigarettes together at his lighter. When they raised their heads again and got the flame glare out of their eyes, the sky was purple-black, dusted with stars, and dead ahead, spilling up over the horizon, was a golden glow—the lights of Dhergabar and home.

First published: 1951

HISTORICAL NOTE

by Murray Leinster

PROFESSOR VLADIMIR ROJESTVENSKY, IT HAS SINCE BEEN LEARNED, remade the world at breakfast one morning while eating a bowl of rather watery red-cabbage soup, with black bread on the side. It is now a matter of history that the soup was not up to par that day, and the black bread in Omsk all that week was sub-marginal. But neither of these factors is considered to have contributed to the remaking of civilization.

The essential thing was that, while blowing on a spoonful of red-cabbage soup, Professor Rojestvensky happened to think of an interesting inference or deduction to be drawn from the Bramwell-Weems Equation expressing the distribution of energy among the nucleus-particles of the lighter atoms. The Bramwell-Weems Equation was known in Russia as the Gabrilovitch-Brekhov Formula because, obviously, Russians must have thought of it first. The symbols, however, were the same as in the capitalist world.

Professor Rojestvensky contemplated the inference with pleasure. It was very interesting indeed. He finished his breakfast, drank a glass of hot tea, wrapped himself up warmly, and set out for his classrooms in the University of Omsk. It was a long walk, because the streetcars were not running. It was a fruitful one, though. For as he walked, Professor Rojestvensky arranged his reasoning in excellent order. When he arrived at the University he found a directive from the Council of Soviet Representatives for Science and Culture. It notified him that from now on Soviet scientists must produce more and better and more Earth-shaking discoveries—or else. Therefore he would immediately report, in quadruplicate, what first-rank discoveries he was prepared to make in the science of physics. And they had better be good.

He was a modest man, was Professor Rojestvensky, but to fail to obey the directive meant losing his job. So he quakingly prepared a paper outlining his extension of the Bramwell-Weems Equation—but he was careful to call it the Gabrilovitch-Brekhov Formula—and persuaded one of his students to make four copies of it in exchange for a quarter of a pound of cheese. Then he sent off the four copies and slept badly for weeks afterward. He knew his work was good, but he didn't know whether it was good enough. It merely accounted for the mutual repulsion of the molecules of gases, it neatly explained the formation of comets' tails, and it could have led to the prediction of clouds of calcium vapor— already observed—in interstellar space. Professor Rojestvensky did not guess he had remade the world.

Weeks passed, and nothing happened. That was a bad month in Russian science. The staffs of Medical Research and Surgical Advancement had already reported everything they could dream up. Workers in Aerodynamic Design weren't sticking out their necks. The last man to design a new plane went to prison for eight years when a fuel line clogged on his plane's test flight. And Nuclear Fission workers stuck to their policy of demanding unobtainable equipment and supplies for the furtherance of their work. So Professor Rojestvensky's paper was absolutely the only contribution paddable to Earth-shaking size. His paper itself was published in the *Soviet Journal of Advanced Science.* Then it was quoted unintelligibly in *Pravda* and *Tass,* with ecstatic editorials pointing out how far Russian science was ahead of mere capitalist-imperialistic research. And that was that.

Possibly that would have been the end of it all, but that some two weeks later an American jet bomber flew twelve thousand miles, dropped fifteen tons of simulated bombs—actually condensed milk lowered to Earth by parachutes—and returned to base without refueling. This, of course, could not be allowed to go unchallenged. So a stern directive went to Aerodynamic Design. An outstanding achievement in aviation must be produced immediately. It must wipe the Americans' decadent, capitalistic eyes. Or—so the directive said explicitly—else.

The brain trust which was Aerodynamic Design went into sweating executive session, seeking a really air-tight procedure for passing the buck. They didn't want to lose their jobs, which were fairly fat ones, any more than Professor Rojestvensky had. They had to cook up something in a hurry, something really dramatic, with an out putting the blame squarely on somebody else if it didn't work. They couldn't blame Aviation Production, though. The head of that splendid organization had an in with the Politbureau. Something new and drastic and good was needed.

In the end a desperate junior official began to hunt through recent Soviet contributions to science. If he could find something impressive that could be twisted into an advance in aerodynamics, it could be designed and built, and any failure blamed on the scientist who had furnished false data as a form of alien-inspired sabotage. Scientists were always expendable in Russian politics. It was time to expend one. Largely because his name was on top of the pile, Professor Rojestvensky was picked.

This, in detail, is the process by which his extension of the Bramwell-Weems—or Gabrilovitch-Brekhov—Equation was selected for practical development. Our brave new world is the result. Aerodynamic Design borrowed a man from Nuclear Fission in a deal between two department heads, and the Nuclear Fission man agreed to work up something elaborate and impressive. He set to work on Professor Rojestvensky's figures. And presently he turned pale, and gulped very rapidly several times, and muttered, *"Gospody pomilov!"* That meant, "Lord have mercy on us!" and it was not a good Russian expression any longer, but it was the way he felt. In time, he showed his results to Aerodynamic Design and said, in effect, "But, it might really work!"

Aerodynamic Design sent him out to Omsk to get Professor Rojestvensky to check his calculations. It was a shrewd move. The Nuclear Fission man and Professor Rojestvensky got along splendidly. They ate red-cabbage soup together and the professor O.K.'d the whole project. That made him responsible for anything that went wrong and Aerodynamic Design, en masse, was much relieved. They sent in a preliminary report on their intentions and started to make one gadget themselves. The Nuclear Fission man was strangely willing to play along and see what happened. He supervised the construction of the thing.

It consisted of a set of straps very much like a parachute harness, hung from a little bar of brass with a plating of metallic sodium, under another plating of nickel, and the whole thing inclosed in a plastic tube. There was a small box with a couple of controls. That was all there was to it.

When it was finished, the Nuclear-Fission man tried it out himself. He climbed into the harness in the Wind Tunnel Building of Aerodynamic Design's plant, said the Russian equivalent of "Here goes nothing!" and flipped over one of the controls. In his shakiness, he pushed it too far. He left the ground, went straight up like a rocket, and cracked his head against the three-story-high ceiling and was knocked cold for two hours. They had to haul him down from the ceiling with an extension ladder, because the gadget he'd made tried insistently to push a hole through the roof to the wide blue yonder.

When he recovered consciousness, practically all of Aerodynamic Design surrounded him, wearing startled expressions. And they stayed around while he found out what the new device would do. Put briefly, it would do practically anything but make fondant. It was a personal flying device, not an airplane, which would lift up to two hundred twenty-five pounds. It would hover perfectly. It would, all by itself, travel in any direction at any speed a man could stand without a windshield.

True, the Rojestvensky Effect which made it fly was limited. No matter how big you made the metal bar, it wouldn't lift more than roughly a hundred kilos, nearly two-twenty-five pounds. But it worked by the fact that the layer of metallic sodium on the brass pushed violently away from all other sodium more than three meters away from it. Sodium within three meters wasn't affected. And there was sodium everywhere. Sodium chloride—common table salt—is present everywhere on Earth and the waters under the Earth, but it isn't present in the heavens above. So the thing would fly anywhere over land or sea, but it wouldn't go but so high. The top limit for the gadget's flight was about four thousand feet, with a hundred-and-fifty-pound man in the harness. A heavier man couldn't get up so high. And it was infinitely safe. A man could fly night, day, or blind drunk and nothing could happen to him. He couldn't run into a mountain because he'd bounce over it. The thing was marvelous!

Aerodynamic Design made a second triumphant report to the Politbureau. A new and appropriately revolutionary device—it was Russian—had been produced in obedience to orders. Russian science had come through! When better revolutionary discoveries were made, Russia would make them! And if the device was inherently limited to one-man use—ha-ha! It gave the Russian army flying infantry! It provided the perfect modern technique for revolutionary war! It offered the perfect defense for peaceful, democratic Russia against malevolent capitalistic imperialism! In short, it was hot stuff!

As a matter of fact, it was. Two months later there was a May Day celebration in Moscow at which the proof of Russia's superlative science was unveiled to the world. Planes flew over Red Square in magnificent massed formations. Tanks and guns rumbled through the streets leading to Lenin's tomb. But the infantry—where was the infantry? Where were the serried ranks of armed men, shaking the earth with their steady tread? Behind the tanks and guns there was only emptiness.

For a while only. There was silence after the guns had gone clanking by. Then a far-distant, tumultuous uproar of cheering. Something new, something strange and marvelous had roused the remotest quarter of the city to enthusiasm. Far, far away, the flying infantry appeared!

Some of the more naïve of the populace believed at first that the U.S.S.R. had made a nonaggression pact with God and that a detachment of angels was parading in compliment to the Soviet Union. It wasn't too implausible, as a first impression. Shoulder to shoulder, rank after rank, holding fast to lines like dog leashes that held them in formation, no less than twelve thousand Russian infantrymen floated into the Red Square some fifteen feet off the ground. They were a bit ragged as to elevation, and they tended to eddy a bit at street corners, but they swept out of the canyons which were streets at a magnificent twenty-five miles an hour, in such a display of air-borne strength as the world had never seen before.

The population cheered itself hoarse. The foreign attachés looked inscrutable. The members of the Politbureau looked on and happily began to form in their minds the demands they would make for pacts of peace and friendship—and military bases—with formerly recalcitrant European nations. These pacts of closest friendship were going to be honeys!

That same morning Professor Rojestvensky breakfasted on red-cabbage soup and black bread, wholly unaware that he had remade the world. But that great events were in the making was self-evident even to members of the United States Senate. Newsreel pictures of the flying infantry parade were shown everywhere. And the Communist parties of the Western nations were, of course, wholly independent organizations with no connection whatever with Moscow. But they could not restrain their enthusiasm over this evidence of Russian greatness. Cheering sections of Communists attended every showing of the newsreels in every theater and howled themselves hoarse. They took regular turns at it and were supplied with throat lozenges by ardent Party workers. Later newsreels showing the flying infantry returning to camp over the rooftops of Moscow evoked screams of admiration. When a Russian documentary film appeared in the Western world, skillfully faking the number of men equipped with individual flying units, the national, patriotic Communist party members began to mention brightly that everybody who did not say loudly, at regular intervals, that Russia was the greatest country in the world was having his name written down for future reference.

Inspired news-stories mentioned that the entire Russian army would be air-borne within three months. The magnificent feat of Russian industry in turning out three million flying devices per month brought forth screaming headlines in the *Daily Worker*. There were only two minor discords in the choral antiphony of national-Communist hosannas and capitalistic alarm.

One was an air-force general's meditative answer to the question: "What defense can there be against an army traveling through the air like a swarm of locusts?" The general said mildly: "Wel-l-l, we carried eighteen tons of condensed milk fourteen thousand miles last week, and we've done pretty good work for the Agriculture Department dusting grasshoppers."

The other was the bitter protest made by the Russian ambassador in Washington. He denounced the capitalist-economy-inspired prevention of the shipment to Russia of an order for brass rods plated with metallic sodium, then plated with nickel, and afterward inclosed in plastic tubes. State Department investigation showed that while an initial order of twelve thousand five hundred such rods had been shipped in April, there had been a number of fires in the factory since, and it had been closed down until fire-prevention methods could be devised. It was pointed out that metallic sodium is hot stuff. It catches fire when wetted or even out of pure cussedness it is fiercely inflammable.

This was a fact that Aviation Production in Russia had already found out. The head man was in trouble with his own friends in the Polit-bureau for failing to meet production quotas, and he'd ordered the tricky stuff—the rods had to be dipped in melted sodium in a helium atmosphere for quantity production—manufactured in the benighted and scientifically retarded United States.

There was another item that should be mentioned, too. Within a week after the issue of personal fliers to Russian infantrymen, no less than sixty-four desertions by air to Western nations took place. On the morn-ing after the first night maneuvers of the air-borne force, ninety-two Rus-sians were discovered in the Allied half of Germany alone, trying to swap their gadgets for suits of civilian clothes.

They were obliged, of course. Enterprising black marketeers joyfully purchased the personal fliers, shipped them to France, to Holland, to Bel-gium, Sweden, Norway, and Switzerland, and sold them at enormous profits. In a week it was notorious that any Russian deserter from the flying infantry could sell his flight-equipment for enough money to buy forty-nine wrist watches and still stay drunk for six months. It was typical private enterprise. It was unprincipled and unjust. But it got worse.

Private entrepreneurs stole the invention itself. At first the units were reproduced one by one in small shops for high prices. But the fire-hazard was great. Production-line methods were really necessary both for econ-omy and industrial safety reasons. So after a while the Bofors Company, of Sweden, rather apologetically turned out a sport model, in quantity, selling for *kronen* worth twelve dollars and fifty cents in American money. Then the refurbished I. G. Farben put out a German type which sold openly for a sum in occupation marks equal to only nine eighty American. A Belgian model priced—in francs—at five fifty had a wide sale, but was not considered quite equal to the Dutch model at guilders exchanging for six twenty-five or the French model with leather-trimmed straps at seven dollars worth of devaluated francs.

The United States capitalists started late. Two bicycle makers switched their factories to the production of personal fliers, yet by the middle of June American production was estimated at not over fifty thousand per month. But in July, one hundred eighty thousand were produced and in August the production—expected to be about three hundred thousand —suddenly went sky-high when both General Electric and Westinghouse entered the market. In September American production was over three million and it became evident that manufacturers would have to compete with each other on finish and luxury of design. The days when anything that would fly was salable at three fifty and up were over.

The personal flier became a part of American life, as, of course, it became a part of life everywhere. In the United States the inherent four-thousand-foot ceiling of personal fliers kept regular air traffic from having trouble except near airports, and flier-equipped airport police soon developed techniques for traffic control. A blimp patrol had to be set up off the Atlantic Coast to head back enthusiasts for foreign travel and Gulf Stream fishing, but it worked very well. There were three million, then five million, and by November twelve million personal-flier-equipped Americans aloft. And the total continued to rise. Surburban railways— especially after weather-proof garments became really good—joyfully abandoned their short-haul passenger traffic and all the railroads settled down contentedly to their real and profitable business of long-haul heavy-freight carriage. Even the air lines prospered incredibly. The speed-limitation on personal fliers still left the jet-driven plane the only way to travel long distances quickly, and passengers desiring intermediate stops simply stepped out of a plane door when near their desired destination. Rural residential developments sprang up like mushrooms. A marked trend toward country life multiplied, Florida and California became so crowded that everybody got disgusted and went home, and the millennium appeared to be just around the corner.

Then came the dawn. It was actually the dawn of the remade world, but it looked bad for a while. The Soviet government stormed at the conscienceless, degraded theft of its own State secret by decadent and imperialistic outsiders. Actual Russian production of personal fliers was somewhere around twenty-five hundred per month at a time when half the population of Europe and America had proved that flying was cheaper than walking. Sternly, the Soviet government—through the Cominform —suggested that now was the time for all good Communists to come to the aid of their Party. The Party needed personal fliers. Fast. So enthusiastic Communists all over Europe flew loyally to Russia to contribute to the safety of their ideals, and to prove the international solidarity of the proletariat. They landed by tens of thousands without passports, without ration cards, and often with insufficient Party credentials. They undoubtedly had spies among them, along with noble comrades. So the U.S.S.R. had to protect itself. Regretfully, Russian officials clapped the new arrivals into jail as they landed, took away their fliers, and sent them back to their national borders in box cars. But they did send indoctrination experts to travel with them and explain that this was hospitable treatment and that they were experiencing the welcome due to heroes.

But borders were not only crossed by friends. Smuggling became a sport. Customs barriers for anything but heavy goods simply ceased to exist. The French national monopoly on tobacco and matches evaporated, and many Frenchmen smoked real tobacco for the first time in their lives. Some of them did not like it. And there were even political consequences of the personal-flier development. In Spain, philosophical anarchists and *syndicalistos* organized political demonstrations. Sometimes hundreds of them flew all night long to rendezvous above the former royal palace in Madrid—now occupied by the Caudillo—and empty chamber-pots upon it at dawn. Totalitarianism in Spain collapsed.

The Russian rulers were made of sterner stuff. True, the Iron Curtain became a figment. Political refugees from Russia returned—sometimes thoughtfully carrying revolvers in case they met somebody they disliked— and disseminated capitalistic propaganda and cast doubts upon the superiority of the Russian standard of living. Often they had wrist watches and some of them even brought along personal fliers as gifts to personal friends. Obviously, this sort of thing was subversive. The purity of Soviet culture could not be maintained when foreigners could enter Russia at will and call the leaders of the Soviet Union liars. Still less could it survive when they proved it.

So the Soviet Union fought back. The Army set up radars to detect the carriers of anti-dialectic-materialism propaganda. The Ministry of Propaganda worked around the clock. People wearing wrist watches were shot if they could not prove they had stolen them from Germans, and smugglers and young men flying Sovietward to ply Russian girls with chocolate bars were intercepted. For almost a week it seemed that radar and flying infantry might yet save the Soviet way of life.

But then unprincipled capitalists dealt a new foul blow. They advertised that anybody intending to slip through the Iron Curtain should provide himself with Bouffon's Anti-Radar Tin Foil Strips, available in one-kilogram cartons at all corner shops. Tin foil strips had been distributed by Allied bombers to confuse German radar during the last war. Smugglers and romantic young men, meditatively dripping tin foil as they flew through the Russian night, made Russian radar useless.

Nothing was left but war. So a splendid, overwhelming blow was planned and carried out. In two nights the entire Soviet force of flying infantry was concentrated. On the third night four hundred thousand flying infantry went sweeping westward in an irresistible swarm. The technique had been worked out by the General Staff on orders from the Politbureau to devise immediately a new and unbeatable system of warfare—or else. The horde of flying warriors was to swoop down from the darkness on Western European cities, confiscate all personal fliers and ship them back to Russia for the use of reinforcements. There could be no resistance. Every part of an enemy nation was equally reachable and equally vulnerable. Russian troops could not be bombed, because they would be deliberately intermixed with the native population. There could be no fighting but street-fighting. This would be war on a new scale, invasion from a new dimension; it would be conquest which could not be fought.

The only trouble was that practically every square mile of European sky was inhabited by somebody enjoying the fruits of Russian science in the form of a personal flier. And secrecy simply couldn't be managed. All Europe knew just about as much about the Russian plan as the Russians did.

So when the clouds of flying infantry came pouring through the night, great droning bombers with riding-lights and landing-lights aglow came roaring out of the west to meet them. There were, to be sure, Soviet jet-fighters with the defending fleet. They tangled with the Russian escort and fought all over the sky, while the bombers focused their landing-lights on the infantry and roared at them. The sensation of being ahead of a bellowing plane rushing at one was exactly that of being on a railroad track with an express train on the loose. There was nothing to do but duck. The Russian soldiers ducked. Then the bombers began to shoot star shells, rockets, Roman candles and other pyrotechnics. The Russian troops dispersed. And an army that is dispersed simply isn't an army. When finally vast numbers of enthusiastic personal-flier addicts came swooping through the night with flashlights and Very pistols, the debacle was complete. The still-fighting planes overhead had nothing left to fight for. Those that were left went home.

When dawn came the Russian soldiers were individuals scattered over three separate nations. And Russian soldiers, in quantity, tend to fight or loot as opportunity offers. But a Russian soldier, as an individual, craves civilian clothes above all else. Russian soldiers landed and tried to make deals for their flying equipment according to the traditions of only a few months before. They were sadly disillusioned. The best bargain most of them could make was simply a promise that they wouldn't be sent back home—and they took that.

It was all rather anticlimactic, and it got worse. Russia was still legally at war with everybody, even after its flying infantry sat down and made friends. And Russia was still too big to invade. On the other hand, it had to keep its air force in hand to fight off attempts at invasion. Just to maintain that defensive frame of mind, Allied bombers occasionally smashed some Russian airfields, and some railroads, and—probably at the instigation of decadent capitalists—they did blow up the Aviation Production factories, even away off in the Urals. Those Ural raids, by the way, were made by the United States Air Force, flying over the North Pole to prove that it could deliver something besides condensed milk at long distances.

But the war never really amounted to much. The Allies had all the flying infantry they wanted to use, but they didn't want to use it. The Russians worked frantically, suborning treason and developing black marketeers and so on, to get personal fliers for defense, but Russian civilians would pay more than even the Soviet government for them, so the Army hardly got any at all. To correct this situation the Supreme Soviet declared private possession of a personal flier a capital offense, and shot several hundred citizens to prove it. Among the victims of this purge, by the way, was the Nuclear-Fission man who had worked out the personal flier from Professor Rojestvensky's figures. But people wanted personal fliers. When owning one became a reason for getting shot, almost half the Russian government's minor officials piled out of the nearest window and went somewhere else, and the bigger officials kept their personal fliers where they could grab them at any instant and take off. And the smuggling kept on. Before long practically everybody had private fliers but the army—and flier-equipped soldiers tended to disappear over the horizon if left alone after nightfall.

So the Soviet Union simply fell to pieces. The Supreme Soviet couldn't govern when anybody who disagreed with it could go up the nearest chimney and stay gone. It lost the enthusiastic support of the population as soon as it became unable to shoot the unenthusiastic. And when it was committed to the policy of shooting every Russian citizen who possessed proof of the supreme splendor of Russian science—a personal flier—why public discipline disappeared. Party discipline went with it. All discipline followed. And when there wasn't any discipline there simply wasn't any Soviet Union and therefore there wasn't any war, and everybody might as well stop fooling around and cook dinner. The world, in fact, was remade.

Undoubtedly the world is a good deal happier since Professor Rojestvensky thought of an interesting inference to be drawn from the Bramwell-Weems Equation while at his breakfast of red-cabbage soup and black bread. There are no longer any iron-bound national boundaries, and therefore no wars or rumors of wars. There are no longer any particular reasons for cities to be crowded, and a reasonably equitable social system has to exist or people will go fishing or down to the South Seas, or somewhere where they won't be bothered.

But in some ways the change has not been as great as one might have expected. About a year after the world was remade, an American engineer thought up a twist on Professor Rojestvensky's figures. He interested the American continental government and they got ready to build a spaceship. The idea was that if a variation of that brass-sodium-nickel bar was curled around a hundred-foot-long tube, and metallic sodium vapor was introduced into one end of the tube, it would be pushed out of the other end with some speed. Calculation proved, indeed, that with all the acceleration possible, the metallic vapor would emerge with a velocity of ninety-eight point seven percent of the speed of light. Using Einstein's formula for the relationship of mass to speed, that meant that the tube would propel a rocketship that could go to the Moon or Mars or anywhere else. The American government started to build the ship, and then thought it would be a good idea to have Professor Rojestvensky in on the job as a consultant. Besides, the world owed him something. So he was sent for, and Congress voted him more money than he had ever heard of before, and he looked over the figures and O.K.'d them. They were all right.

But he was typical of the people whose happiness has not been markedly increased by the remade world. He was a rich man, and he liked America, but after a month or so he didn't look happy. So the government put him in the most luxurious suite in the most luxurious hotel in America, and assigned people to wait on him and a translator to translate for him, and did its very best to honor the man who'd remade the world. But still he didn't seem content.

One day a committee of reporters asked him what he wanted. He would be in all the history books, and he had done the world a great favor, and the public would like him to be pleased. But Professor Rojestvensky shook his head sadly.

"It's only," he said gloomily, "that since I am rich and the world is peaceable and everybody is happy—well, I just can't seem to find anyone who knows how to make good red-cabbage soup."

First published: 1951

PROTECTED SPECIES

by H. B. Fyfe

THE YELLOW STAR, OF WHICH TORANG WAS THE SECOND PLANET, SHONE hotly down on the group of men viewing the half-built dam from the heights above. At a range of eighty million miles, the effect was quite Terran, the star being somewhat smaller than Sol.

For Jeff Otis, fresh from a hop through space from the extra-bright star that was the other component of the binary system, the heat was enervating. The shorts and light shirt supplied him by the planet co-ordinator were soaked with perspiration. He mopped his forehead and turned to his host.

"Very nice job, Finchley," he complimented. "It's easy to see you have things well in hand here."

Finchley grinned sparingly. He had a broad, hard, flat face with tight lips and mere slits of blue eyes. Otis had been trying ever since the previous morning to catch a revealing expression on it.

He was uneasily aware that his own features were too frank and open for an inspector of colonial installations. For one thing, he had too many lines and hollows in his face, a result of being chronically underweight from space-hopping among the sixteen planets of the binary system.

Otis noticed that Finchley's aides were eying him furtively.

"Yes, Finchley," he repeated to break the little silence, "you're doing very well on the hydroelectric end. When are you going to show me the capital city you're laying out?"

"We can fly over there now," answered Finchley. "We have tentative boundaries laid out below those pre-colony ruins we saw from the 'copter."

"Oh, yes. You know, I meant to remark as we flew over that they looked a good deal like similar remnants on some of the other planets."

He caught himself as Finchley's thin lips tightened a trifle more. The co-ordinator was obviously trying to be patient and polite to an official from whom he hoped to get a good report, but Otis could see he would much rather be going about his business of building up the colony.

He could hardly blame Finchley, he decided. It was the fifth planetary system Terrans had found in their expansion into space, and there would be bigger jobs ahead for a man with a record of successful accomplishments. Civilization was reaching out to the stars at last. Otis supposed that he, too, was some sort of pioneer, although he usually was too busy to feel like one.

"Well, I'll show you some photos later," he said. "Right now, we—Say, why all that jet-burning down there?"

In the gorge below, men had dropped their tools and seemed to be charging toward a common focal point. Excited yells carried thinly up the cliffs.

"Ape hunt, probably," guessed one of Finchley's engineers.

"Ape?" asked Otis, surprised.

"Not exactly," corrected Finchley patiently. "That's common slang for what we mention in reports as Torangs. They look a little like big, skinny, gray apes; but they're the only life large enough to name after the planet."

Otis stared down into the gorge. Most of the running men had given up and were straggling back to their work. Two or three, brandishing pistols, continued running and disappeared around a bend.

"Never catch him now," commented Finchley's pilot.

"Do you just let them go running off whenever they feel like it?" Otis inquired.

Finchley met his curious gaze stolidly.

"I'm in favor of anything that will break the monotony, Mr. Otis. We have a problem of morale, you know. This planet is a key colony, and I like to keep the work going smoothly."

"Yes, I suppose there isn't much for recreation yet."

"Exactly. I don't see the sport in it myself but I let them. We're up to schedule."

"Ahead, if anything," Otis placated him. "Well, now, about the city?"

Finchley led the way to the helicopter. The pilot and Otis waited while he had a final word with his engineers, then they all climbed in and were off.

Later, hovering over the network of crude roads being leveled by Finchley's bulldozers, Otis admitted aloud that the location was well-chosen. It lay along a long, narrow bay that thrust in from the distant ocean to gather the waters of the same river that was being dammed some miles upstream.

"Those cliffs over there," Finchley pointed out, "were raised up since the end of whatever civilization used to be here—so my geologist tells me. We can fly back that way, and you can see how the ancient city was once at the head of the bay."

The pilot climbed and headed over the cliffs. Otis saw that these formed the edge of a plateau. At one point, their continuity was marred by a deep gouge.

"Where the river ran thousands of years ago," Finchley explained.

They reached a point from which the outlines of the ruined city were easily discerned. From the air, Otis knew, they were undoubtedly plainer than if he had been among them.

"Must have been a pretty large place," he remarked. "Any idea what sort of beings built it or what happened to them?"

"Haven't had time for that yet," Finchley said. "Some boys from the exploration staff poke around in there every so often. Best current theory seems to be that it belonged to the Torangs."

"The *animals* they were hunting before?" asked Otis.

"Might be. Can't say for sure, but the diggers found signs the city took more of a punch than just an earthquake. Claim they found too much evidence of fires, exploded missiles, and warfare in general—other places as well as here. So . . . we've been guessing the Torangs are degenerated descendents of the survivors of some interplanetary brawl."

Otis considered that.

"Sounds plausible," he admitted, "but you ought to do something to make sure you are right."

"Why?"

"If it *is* the case, you'll have to stop your men from hunting them; degenerated or not, the Colonial Commission has regulations about contact with any local inhabitants."

Finchley turned his head to scowl at Otis, and controlled himself with an obvious effort.

"Those *apes?*" he demanded.

"Well, how can you tell? Ever try to contact them?"

"Yes! At first, that is; before we figured them for animals."

"And?"

"Couldn't get near one!" Finchley declared heatedly. "If they had any sort of half-intelligent culture, wouldn't they let us make *some* sort of contact?"

"Offhand," admitted Otis, "I should think so. How about setting down a few minutes? I'd like a look at the ruins."

Finchley glared at his wrist watch, but directed the pilot to land at a cleared spot. The young man brought them down neatly and the two officials alighted.

Otis, glancing around, saw where the archaeologists had been digging. They had left their implements stacked casually at the site—the air was dry up here and who was there to steal a shovel?

He left Finchley and strolled around a mound of dirt that had been cleared away from an entrance to one of the buildings. The latter had been built of stone, or at least faced with it. A peep into the dim excavation led him to believe there had been a steel framework, but the whole affair had been collapsed as if by an explosion.

He walked a little way further and reached a section of presumably taller buildings where the stone ruins thrust above the sandy surface. After he had wandered through one or two arched openings that seemed to have been windows, he understood why the explorers had chosen to dig for their information. If any covering or decoration had ever graced the walls, it had long since been weathered off. As for ceiling or roof, nothing remained.

"Must have been a highly developed civilization just the same," he muttered.

A movement at one of the shadowed openings to his right caught his eye. He did not remember noticing Finchley leave the helicopter to follow him, but he was glad of a guide.

"Don't you think so?" he added.

He turned his head, but Finchley was not there. In fact, now that Otis was aware of his surroundings, he could hear the voices of the other two mumbling distantly back by the aircraft.

"Seeing things!" he grumbled, and started through the ancient window. Some instinct stopped him half a foot outside.

Come on, Jeff, he told himself, *don't be silly! What could be there? Ghosts?*

On the other hand, he realized, there were times when it was just as well to rely upon instinct—at least until you figured out the origin of the strange feeling. Any spaceman would agree to that. The man who developed an animal sixth sense was the man who lived longest on alien planets.

He thought he must have paused a full minute or more, during which he had heard not the slightest sound except the mutter of voices to the rear. He peered into the chamber, which was about twenty feet square and well if not brightly lit by reflected light.

Nothing was to be seen, but when he found himself turning his head stealthily to peer over his shoulder, he decided that the queer sensation along the back of his neck meant something.

Wait, now, he thought swiftly. *I didn't see quite the whole room.*

The flooring was heaped with wind-bared rubble that would not show footprints. He felt much more comfortable to notice himself thinking in that vein.

At least, I'm not imagining ghosts, he thought.

Bending forward the necessary foot, he thrust his head through the opening and darted a quick look to left, then to the right along the wall. As he turned right, his glance was met directly by a pair of very wide-set black eyes which shifted inward slightly as they got his range.

The Torang about matched his own six-feet-two, mainly because of elongated, gibbonlike limbs and a similarly crouching stance. Arms and legs, covered with short, curly, gray fur, had the same general proportions as human limbs, but looked half again too long for a trunk that seemed to be ribbed all the way down. Shoulder and hip joints were compactly lean, rather as if the Torang had developed on a world of lesser gravity than that of the human.

It was the face that made Otis stare. The mouth was toothless and probably constructed more for sucking than for chewing. But the eyes! They projected like ends of a dumbbell from each side of the narrow skull where the ears should have been, and focused with obvious mobility. Peering closer, Otis saw tiny ears below the eyes, almost hidden in the curling fur of the neck.

He realized abruptly that his own eyes felt as if they were bulging out, although he could not remember having changed his expression of casual curiosity. His back was getting stiff also. He straightened up carefully.

"Uh . . . hello," he murmured, feeling unutterably silly but conscious of some impulse to compromise between a tone of greeting for another human being and one of pacification to an animal.

The Torang moved then, swiftly but unhurriedly. In fact, Otis later decided, deliberately. One of the long arms swept downward to the rubble-strewn ground.

The next instant, Otis jerked his head back out of the opening as a stone whizzed past in front of his nose.

"Hey!" he protested involuntarily.

There was a scrabbling sound from within, as of animal claws churning to a fast start among the pebbles. Recovering his balance, Otis charged recklessly through the entrance.

"I don't know why," he admitted to Finchley a few minutes later. "If I stopped to think how I might have had my skull bashed in coming through, I guess I'd have just backed off and yelled for you."

Finchley nodded, but his narrow gaze seemed faintly approving for the first time since they had met.

"He was gone, of course," Otis continued. "I barely caught a glimpse of his rump vanishing through another window."

"Yeah, they're pretty fast," put in Finchley's pilot. "In the time we've been here, the boys haven't taken more than half a dozen. Got a stuffed one over at headquarters though."

"Hm-m-m," murmured Otis thoughtfully.

From their other remarks, he learned that he had not noticed everything, even though face to face with the creature. Finchley's mentioning the three digits of the hands or feet, for instance, came as a surprise.

Otis was silent most of the flight back to headquarters. Once there, he disappeared with a perfunctory excuse toward the rooms assigned him.

That evening, at a dinner which Finchley had made as attractive as was possible in a comparatively raw and new colony, Otis was noticeably sociable. The co-ordinator was gratified.

"Looks as if they finally sent us a regular guy," he remarked behind his hand to one of his assistants. "Round up a couple of the prettier secretaries to keep him happy."

"I understand he nearly laid hands on a Torang up at the diggings," said the other.

"Yep, ran right at it bare-handed. Came as close to bagging it as anybody could, I suppose."

"Maybe it's just as well he didn't," commented the assistant. "They're big enough to mess up an unarmed man some."

Otis, meanwhile and for the rest of the evening, was assiduously busy making acquaintances. So engrossed was he in turning every new conversation to the Torangs and asking seemingly casual questions about the little known of their habits and possible past, that he hardly noticed receiving any special attentions. As a visiting inspector, he was used to attempts to entertain and distract him.

The next morning, he caught Finchley at his office in the sprawling one-story structure of concrete and glass that was colonial headquarters.

After accepting a chair across the desk from the co-ordinator, Otis told him his conclusions. Finchley's narrow eyes opened a trifle when he heard the details. His wide, hard-muscled face became slightly pink.

"Oh, for—! I mean, Otis, why must you make something big out of it? The men very seldom bag one anyway!"

"Perhaps because they're so rare," answered Otis calmly. "How do we know they're not intelligent life? Maybe if you were hanging on in the ruins of your ancestors' civilization, reduced to a primitive state, *you'd* be just as wary of a bunch of loud Terrans moving in!"

Finchley shrugged. He looked vaguely uncomfortable, as if debating whether Otis or some disgruntled sportsman from his husky construction crews would be easier to handle.

"Think of the overall picture a minute," Otis urged. "We're pushing out into space at last, after centuries of dreams and struggles. With all the misery we've seen in various colonial systems at home, we've tried to plan these ventures so as to avoid old mistakes."

Finchley nodded grudgingly. Otis could see that his mind was on the progress charts of his many projects.

"It stands to reason," the inspector went on, "that some day we'll find a planet with intelligent life. We're still new in space, but as we probe farther out, it's bound to happen. That's why the Commission drew up rules about native life forms. Or have you read that part of the code lately?"

Finchley shifted from side to side in his chair.

"Now, look!" he protested. "Don't go making *me* out a hardboiled vandal with nothing in mind but exterminating everything that moves on all Torang. *I* don't go out hunting the apes!"

"I know, I know," Otis soothed him. "But before the Colonial Commission will sanction any destruction of indigenous life, we'll have to show—*besides* that it's not intelligent—that it exists in sufficient numbers to avoid extinction."

"What do you expect me to do about it?"

Otis regarded him with some sympathy. Finchley was the hard-bitten type the Commission needed to oversee the first breaking-in of a colony on a strange planet, but he was not unreasonable. He merely wanted to be left alone to handle the tough job facing him.

"Announce a ban on hunting Torangs," Otis said. "There must be something else they can go after."

"Oh, yes," admitted Finchley. "There are swarms of little rabbit-things and other vermin running through the brush. But, I don't know—"

"It's standard practice," Otis reminded him. "We have many a protected species even back on Terra that would be extinct by now, only for the game laws."

In the end, they agreed that Finchley would do his honest best to enforce a ban provided Otis obtained a formal order from the headquarters of the system. The inspector went from the office straight to the communications center, where he filed a long report for the chief co-ordinator's office in the other part of the binary system.

It took some hours for the reply to reach Torang. When it came that afternoon, he went looking for Finchley.

He found the co-ordinator inspecting a newly finished canning factory on the coast, elated at the completion of one more link in making the colony self-sustaining.

"Here it is," said Otis, waving the message copy. "Signed by the chief himself. 'As of this date, the apelike beings known as Torangs, indigenous to planet number and so forth, are to be considered a rare and protected species under regulations and so forth et cetera.'"

"Good enough," answered Finchley with an amiable shrug. "Give it here, and I'll have it put on the public address system and the bulletin boards."

Otis returned satisfied to the helicopter that had brought him out from headquarters.

"Back, sir?" asked the pilot.

"Yes . . . no! Just for fun, take me out to the old city. I never did get a good look the other day, and I'd like to before I leave."

They flew over the plains between the sea and the upjutting cliffs. In the distance, Otis caught a glimpse of the rising dam he had been shown the day before. This colony would go well, he reflected, as long as he checked up on details like preserving native life forms.

Eventually, the pilot landed at the same spot he had been taken on his previous visit to the ancient ruins. Someone else was on the scene today. Otis saw a pair of men he took to be archaeologists.

"I'll just wander around a bit," he told the pilot.

He noticed the two men looking at him from where they stood by the shovels and other equipment, so he paused to say hello. As he thought, they had been digging in the ruins.

"Taking some measurements in fact," said the sunburned blond introduced as Hoffman. "Trying to get a line on what sort of things built the place."

"Oh?" said Otis, interested. "What's the latest theory?"

"Not so much different from us," Hoffman told the inspector while his partner left them to pick up another load of artifacts.

"Judging from the size of the rooms, height of doorways, and such stuff as stairways," he went on, "they were pretty much our size. So far, of course, it's only a rough estimate."

"Could be ancestors of the Torangs, eh?" asked Otis.

"Very possible, sir," answered Hoffman, with a promptness that suggested it was his own view. "But we haven't dug up enough to guess at the type of culture they had, or draw any conclusions as to their psychology or social customs."

Otis nodded, thinking that he ought to mention the young fellow's name to Finchley before he left Torang. He excused himself as the other man returned with a box of some sort of scraps the pair had unearthed, and strolled between the outlines of the untouched buildings.

In a few minutes, he came to the section of higher structures where he had encountered the Torang the previous day.

"Wonder if I should look in the same spot?" he muttered aloud. "No . . . that would be the *last* place the thing would return to . . . unless it had a lair thereabouts—"

He stopped to get his bearings, then shrugged and walked around a mound of rubble toward what he believed to be the proper building.

Pretty sure this was it, he mused. *Yes, shadows around that window arch look the same . . . same time of day—*

He halted, almost guiltily, and looked back to make sure no one was observing his futile return to the scene of his little adventure. After all, an inspector of colonial installations was not supposed to run around ghost-hunting like a small boy.

Finding himself alone, he stepped briskly through the crumbling arch —*and froze in his tracks.*

"I am honored to know you," said the Torang in a mild, rather buzzing voice. "We thought you possibly would return here."

Otis gaped. The black eyes projecting from the sides of the narrow head tracked him up and down, giving him the unpleasant sensation of being measured for an artillery salvo.

"I am known as Jal-Ganyr," said the Torang. "Unless I am given incorrect data, you are known as Jeff-Otis. That is so."

The last statement was made with almost no inflection, but some still-functioning corner of Otis' mind interpreted it as a question. He sucked in a deep breath, suddenly conscious of having forgotten to breathe for a moment.

"I didn't know . . . yes, that is so . . . I didn't know you Torangs could speak Terran. Or anything else. How—?"

He hesitated as a million questions boiled up in his mind to be asked. Jal-Ganyr absently stroked the gray fur of his chest with his three-fingered left hand, squatting patiently on a flat rock. Otis felt somehow that he had been allowed to waste time mumbling only by grace of disciplined politeness.

"I am not of the Torangs," said Jal-Ganyr in his wheezing voice. "I am of the Myrbs. You would possibly say Myrbii. I have not been informed."

"You mean that is your name for yourselves?" asked Otis.

Jal-Ganyr seemed to consider, his mobile eyes swiveling inward to scan the Terran's face.

"More than that," he said at last, when he had thought it over. "I mean I am of the race originating at Myrb, not of this planet."

"Before we go any further," insisted Otis, "tell me, at least, how you learned our language!"

Jal-Ganyr made a fleeting gesture. His "face" was unreadable to the Terran, but Otis had the impression he had received the equivalent of a smile and a shrug.

"As to that," said the Myrb, "I possibly learned it before you did. We have observed you a very long time. You would unbelieve how long."

"But then—" Otis paused. That must mean before the colonists had landed on this planet. He was half-afraid it might mean before they had reached this sun system. He put aside the thought and asked, "But then, why do you live like this among the ruins? Why wait till now? If you had communicated, you could have had our help rebuilding—"

He let his voice trail off, wondering what sounded wrong. Jal-Ganyr rolled his eyes about leisurely, as if disdaining the surrounding ruins. Again, he seemed to consider all the implications of Otis' questions.

"We picked up your message to your chief," he answered at last. "We decided time is to communicate with one of you.

"We have no interest in rebuilding," he added. "We have concealed quarters for ourselves."

Otis found that his lips were dry from his unconsciously having let his mouth hang open. He moistened them with the tip of his tongue, and relaxed enough to lean against the wall.

"You mean my getting the ruling to proclaim you a protected species?" he asked. "You have instruments to intercept such signals?"

"I do. We have," said Jal-Ganyr simply. "It has been decided that you have expanded far enough into space to make necessary we contact a few of the thoughtful among you. It will possibly make easier in the future for our observers."

Otis wondered how much of that was irony. He felt himself flushing at the memory of the "stuffed specimen" at headquarters, and was peculiarly relieved that he had not gone to see it.

I've had the luck, he told himself. *I'm the one to discover the first known intelligent beings beyond Sol!*

Aloud, he said, "We expected to meet someone like you eventually. But why have you chosen me?"

The question sounded vain, he realized, but it brought unexpected results.

"Your message. You made in a little way the same decision we made in a big way. We deduce that you are one to understand our regret and shame at what happened between our races . . . long ago."

"Between—?"

"Yes. For a long time, we thought you were all gone. We are pleased to see you returning to some of your old planets."

Otis stared blankly. Some instinct must have enabled the Myrb to interpret his bewildered expression. He apologized briefly.

"I possibly forgot to explain the ruins." Again, Jal-Ganyr's eyes swiveled slowly about.

"They are not ours," he said mildly. "They are yours."

A NOTE ABOUT THE EDITOR

John W. Campbell, Jr. has been perhaps the strongest single influence in the steady progress of modern science fiction from its "space opera" beginnings to its present maturity and ever-increasing acceptance by the general public.

In his thirteen years as editor of Astounding Science Fiction *magazine, Campbell has guided, encouraged, and shaped the development of a great number of the foremost writers in the field, including many of those represented in this selection of his personal favorites.*

Born in 1910 in Newark, New Jersey, Campbell was educated as a nuclear physicist at M.I.T. and Duke. Finding, during the Depression, "a great lack of employment for physicists," he turned to science fiction. Campbell has written several notable s-f stories, under his own name and as "Don Stuart," (the recent science fiction movie, The Thing, *was derived from his story,* Who Goes There?*) and is the author of* The Atomic Story, *non-fiction, published in 1947. He now lives in Mountainside, New Jersey, with his wife and four children.*